Tarzan of the Apes

Four Volumes in One

Edgar Rice Burroughs

EDGAR RICE BURROUGHS was born in Chicago in 1875. It was only after years of working at a variety of jobs, including gold mining, cow punching, and managing a Sears Roebuck store, that he found his true calling, at the age of thirty-seven, as a writer of adventure stories. His first novel, the scientific romance *Under the Moons of Mars,* was written under the pseudonym "Normal Bean" (to indicate the author was not a madman) and published in a popular fiction magazine in 1912. It was followed by the immensely popular *Tarzan of the Apes,* the story that set Burroughs on the road to becoming a publishing phenomenon.

Over the next thirty-eight years, Burroughs wrote more than one hundred stories and novels—as many as seven in one year—on a variety of subjects ranging from the western frontier to urban life to historical adventure. Though many were deserving of it, none were to achieve the fame of his Mars stories, which fill eleven books, or the Tarzan novels, twenty-four of which saw print in the author's lifetime. In 1931, Burroughs created his own publishing company, Edgar Rice Burroughs, Inc., in Tarzana, California, the town named for his most famous creation. During World War II, he worked as an accredited war correspondent in the Pacific theater for the *Los Angeles Times.*

When Burroughs died in 1950, his books had already sold in the millions. Today, he is credited with having given an enormous boost to the early fantasy, science fiction, and adventure genres, and a number of fan clubs devoted exclusively to his work are still active. Adaptations of his works for film, radio, and comic books, and translations of his books into foreign languages, have gained him worldwide renown.

TARZAN OF THE APES

Four Volumes in One

by Edgar Rice Burroughs

TARZAN OF THE APES
THE SON OF TARZAN
TARZAN AT THE EARTH'S CORE
TARZAN TRIUMPHANT

Illustrated by
J. Allen St. John, Studley Burroughs,
and Esteban Maroto

AVENEL BOOKS
NEW YORK

Publishers Note: Selections in this work contain racial references and language which the modern reader may find offensive. These references and language are part of the time period and environment written about, and do not reflect the attitudes of the editors or publisher of this current edition.

This 1988 edition is published by Avenel Books, distributed by Crown Publishers, Inc., 225 Park Avenue South, New York, New York 10003.

Printed and bound in the United States of America

Library of Congress Cataloging-in-Publication Data

Burroughs, Edgar Rice, 1875-1950.
  Tarzan of the apes.

  "Four volumes in one."
  Contents: Tarzan of the apes.—The son of Tarzan.—
Tarzan triumphant.—[etc.]
  1. Tarzan (Fictitious character)—Fiction. I. Title.
PS3503.U687A6 1988   813'.52   87-31920
ISBN 0-517-65957-3

Book design by Jean Krulis

h g f e d c b a

CONTENTS

Preface to This Illustrated Edition

> There is one man who has absorbed the spirit of the Tarzan stories and who visualizes the characters and scenes almost precisely as I visualize them.

Thus did Edgar Rice Burroughs describe J. Allen St. John, the illustrator of a number of Tarzan books, in a letter to a New York literary agent,* and he never found another artist that he felt had greater ability or imagination for the task. He certainly did, however, admire and champion the work of his nephew, Studley Burroughs, who also illustrated his fiction.

Both of these artists are well represented in this volume: J. Allen St. John's striking drawings for *The Son of Tarzan* and *Tarzan at the Earth's Core* capture the beauty and sinewy vitality of man, beast, and jungle; and illustrations by Studley Burroughs for *Tarzan Triumphant* are dramatic and action-filled.

To celebrate this special collection, the publishers have commissioned Esteban Maroto, a noted artist of fantasy and science fiction, to portray *Tarzan of the Apes* in powerful scenes that blend perfectly with the work of the earlier masters.

CLAIRE BOOSS
Editor

1988

---

* Letter to Paul Reynolds of June 9, 1919, quoted in *Edgar Rice Burroughs: The Man Who Created Tarzan* by Irwin Porges (Brigham Young University Press, 1975).

Introduction

EDGAR RICE BURROUGHS violated one of the first rules for beginning writers: he wrote on things he knew nothing about.

Some of the results were predictable: he put Asian tigers in Africa; he had a character who had never heard a word of spoken English learn to write a name that had been given to him by jungle animals; and he stretched some interpretations of heredity and evolution to the breaking point.

One thing, though, no one could have predicted: the story in which Burroughs committed these errors would become an immediate and perpetual hit with readers, one that would make its author one of the best-selling writers of modern times and give rise to a character, and series, of mythic stature. The story was *Tarzan of the Apes.*

Had Burroughs chosen to write on things he did know about, fate might have treated him less kindly. His own story was not the stuff of high adventure: a Chicagoan in his late thirties who had failed at being a cowboy, a railroad policeman, and a gold miner, and who was then reduced to working in his father's battery plant to support wife and family. In his spare hours, he had written a moderately successful first novel, *Under the Moons of Mars,* and the second time out, wrote a historical novel, *The Outlaw of Torn,* that took three years to be published. But in time, Burroughs had things he wished to say about the innate nobility of mankind and the good and bad effects wrought upon man's nature by civilization. So, in his third novel, *Tarzan of the Apes,* he took equal parts of the myths of Romulus and Remus, Kipling's *Jungle Book,* together with popular legends of the "noble savage," and distilled them into a single character. And he built a plot around this character by doing what he did best—telling a good yarn.

The story of Tarzan, the child of noble English blood who is raised to manhood by a family of apes, is so familiar that many people who have never read the book *Tarzan of the Apes* are unaware that it begins as just that, a good yarn:

I had this story from one who had no business to tell it to me, or to any other. I may credit the seductive influence of an old vintage upon the narrator for the beginning of it and my own skeptical incredulity during the days that followed for the balance of the strange tale.

With these two sentences, Burroughs created the perfect context for his fabulous story: on the one hand they are used to disavow any authorial responsibility for the story's truthfulness—the narrator is telling a tale got second-hand that becomes even more remote from its source when he gives Tarzan's family the pseudonym of Greystoke to protect their true identity. On the other hand, the two sentences also express concisely two complementary facets of human nature: the inescapable curiosity to listen to a story and the equally inescapable desire to tell one. Both inclinations meet head on in a moment of weakness that might be called a typical display of human nature. Questions about strengths and weaknesses of human nature, and how they set man apart from other creatures are what lie at the heart of *Tarzan of the Apes*.

Initially, it would seem that Burroughs equated savagery with strength and civility with weakness. As a child among the apes, Tarzan first perceives himself as a weakling because he does not have the brute characteristics of his ape brothers. He would like nothing more than to be an ape, not the scrawny white monkey he appears to be. Yet, as surely as the civilized moral virtues displayed by Tarzan's father, John Clayton, are what save him and his wife, Alice, during the savage mutiny at the story's beginning, so does Tarzan quickly learn to use virtues of civilization to master the savage jungle. They are, so to speak, in his blood.

To overcome his comparative physical weakness, Tarzan learns to use tools like the noose and the knife. He teaches himself the intricacies of the English language, and his ingenuity vaults him over the beasts. But it is his fundamental and ineradicable sense of right and wrong that ultimately lifts him above the level of King of the Apes to become a true "Lord" of the jungle. And when he finally meets with human beings in the second half of the book, we see that his rough primitive life has so sharpened his noble intellect and instincts that he is a human being superior to most of those whom he encounters.

The actions of "civilized" human beings are a constant source of bemusement to Tarzan, but also a source of pain, because at the same time Tarzan rightly rejects much of what he sees in other men, he realizes that unless he embraces it to some degree, he is destined to be forever alone, trapped somewhere between civilization and the jungle. The law of the jungle and the understanding that has helped man to rise above it are the two extremes which Tarzan must choose between, and, as the unexpected ending of the novel indicates, it is not an easy choice.

Regardless of the moral Burroughs instilled into his story, *Tarzan of the Apes* is first and foremost a tale of adventure. The book takes place in the jungle not only because it was the best setting for Burroughs to get across what he wished to say, but also because the jungle was wild and exotic, a source of unlimited imaginative potential for adventure writers in the early twentieth century. The jungle gave Burroughs the raw material to create his wonderful animal society, conceived along the same lines as human society. It also gave him a setting where a human could break free of the restraints of society, swing through trees like an ape, and even bellow a bloodcurdling cry after a kill.

This was the essence of the type of daydream Burroughs and other authors supplied to readers of the pulp magazines, and the best of them did it well enough that one could overlook their occasional lapses of accuracy. The text of *Tarzan of the Apes* reprinted here is from the original popular magazine edition, and the reader may follow the story to its conclusion without realizing that Sabor the Tiger, Tarzan's most formidable enemy, is rather far from her Asian homeland. When this was brought to Burroughs' attention, he corrected it for the later book publication, changing Sabor to a lionness. In subsequent Tarzan novels, the lion is named Numa.

Another element that pulp writers like Burroughs supplied to their fans were character types familiar to readers of the day. Such stereotypes could be identified with, laughed at, or held in contempt, but they always provided readers with a recognizable point of reference, no matter how far removed the adventure was from the everyday world. Though Burroughs has received criticism for unflattering ethnic and racial stereotypes, it should be noted that in *Tarzan of the Apes,* almost no one comes off looking completely unblemished except the title character. Burroughs distributed his scenes of savagery equally among the black cannibals and the white mutineers, and his comic views of human foibles among black domestics and no less eminent a man than Archimedes Q. Porter, Tarzan's somewhat egg-headed future father-in-law. If one considers the Tarzan stories as a single long saga, one finds that Burroughs created good guys and bad guys of every race, color, and creed. He saw conduct not as specific to a demographic category, but to a particular kind of personality.

Burroughs did not set out to write "literature." He wrote page-turners, and it does his work a disservice to single out from it caricatures that are found in much of the popular literature of the time, or to take an unflattering portrayal of a member of a minority or religious group out of its narrative context. It is more enriching and relevant to dwell on the thoughtful mind that could render the poignant scene in which Tarzan happens upon the remains of his true parents and doesn't realize it, or our final view of Tarzan as he demonstrates his humanity most fully by renouncing it altogether.

The ending of *Tarzan of the Apes* suggests that Burroughs did not intend to continue the saga, and yet acclaim was so overwhelming that he was compelled to continue for another twenty-three books. Having firmly established Tarzan's character and his hedged preference for the jungle over civilization in the first Tarzan story, Burroughs used the later novels to show how Tarzan's personality gave rise naturally to heroic adventures.

The Son of Tarzan, the second novel included here, is the fourth book in the series, written in 1915. It follows *The Return of Tarzan* (1913), in which Tarzan thwarts the sinister intentions of two Russians, Nikolas Rolkoff and Alexis Paulvitch, and finally marries Jane Porter. That leads, naturally, to the birth of the son of Tarzan, Jack Clayton, who is kidnapped by Rolkoff and Paulvitch in *The Beasts of Tarzan* (1914), but rescued by Tarzan with the help of Akut the ape. Jack Clayton had actually appeared even earlier in one of Burroughs's many non-Tarzan books, *The Eternal Lover.* (That book was also written in 1914; Burroughs was prolific, to say the least, writing a novel in two or three months and tallying several per year.) In that book, Burroughs made Tarzan a model of domesticity and had him fade into the background of someone else's adventure—a consequence of the civilized life, perhaps. This is the same portrait of Tarzan we see at the beginning of *Son of Tarzan,* and his seeming normalcy is the epitome of the kind of life Jack Clayton wishes to escape.

So in *The Son of Tarzan,* Burroughs wrote *Tarzan of the Apes* in reverse. He had the English schoolboy, Jack, meet up with the ape, Akut, whom he liberates from the clutches of Paulvitch. Next, Jack masters the primitive tongue and escapes into the African jungle. He sheds his clothing and his civilized veneer to learn how to become a wise savage in the jungle, and he is finally given a name in the ape tongue—Korak, the Killer. Can anyone doubt that Jack will, like his father before him, meet the woman of his dreams, and that the story will turn on noble human impulses overcoming baser instincts to save the day?

But Jack is not quite a carbon copy of his father. If anything, the childish petulance that got him into trouble with his teachers gets him into more than one scrape that even a younger Tarzan would have avoided. Jack's jungle experience helps him to grow out of his natural adolescent wildness and shows him the importance of being a responsible adult like his father. The final chapters of the book, in which Jack and Tarzan work together to thwart Ali ben Kadin and to rescue Jack's girlfriend, Meriem, reveal *The Son of Tarzan* to be a touching treatment of an idea that predates Burroughs—and all writers for that matter: that the boy who grows up wanting to be anything *but* like his father eventually realizes his father is someone worthy of admiration.

During the entire period that Burroughs was writing the Tarzan series he was also writing series of scientific romances set on Mars, the Moon, and Venus; realistic novels set in Hollywood and Chicago; and historical adventures. Much to the author's chagrin, these books never met with the same popularity among readers as the Tarzan stories, but that neither discouraged Burroughs from writing them nor from working Tarzan into them. A possible ancestor of Tarzan, named Greystoke, appeared long enough to be killed off in *The Outlaw of Torn,* the book immediately preceding *Tarzan of the Apes.* As mentioned earlier, Tarzan's son made his first appearance in *The Eternal Lover,* the story Burroughs wrote between the third and fourth Tarzan novels. In the thirteenth Tarzan novel, *Tarzan at the Earth's Core* (1929), Burroughs openly merged the Tarzan chronicles with one of his more popular non-Tarzan series, the science fiction tales of Pellucidar.

The hollow-Earth theory was a pseudoscientific conception that had been dismissed long before authors as diverse as Edgar Allan Poe, Jules Verne, and Arthur Conan Doyle wrote fantasies around it. Nevertheless, in *At the Earth's Core,* the first of what was to become a seven-book series, Burroughs took up the same thread and proposed that a land named Pellucidar exists at the center of our Earth. Its distinguishing trademark is a centrally located sun, suspended in midair. Because there is no horizon for that sun to fall beneath, the world is bathed in perpetual light, and because there are no darkness and dawn, the many races who live there have never learned to tell time. They rely on a system so primitive that men keep track of how many meals they've eaten in order to mark the sequence of events.

By accident, two explorer-inventors, David Innes and Abner Perry, tunnel down to this world and discover that it is the home of supposedly extinct dinosaurs, several near-human races, and a wondrous variety of flora and fauna not encountered on the surface of the Earth. They return to Pellucidar in subsequent novels, bringing with them the tools of civilization. In *Tanar of Pellucidar,* the third novel, Burroughs introduced the enormous canyon at the North Pole that is the opening connecting Pellucidar to the outside world and through which, centuries before, pirate ships fell. Their crews are the ancestors of the Korsar race, who have imprisoned David Innes at the beginning of the fourth Pellucidar book, *Tarzan at the Earth's Core.*

Jason Gridley, the man who contacts Tarzan to help him rescue Innes, is a character of some interest. A native of Tarzana, California (a real town that took its name from Burroughs's character and in which Burroughs lived for many years), who is intimately aware of the details of Pellucidar, Gridley is meant to represent Burroughs himself. To make this point obvious, Burroughs even gave Gridley's airship, the 0–220, the last four digits of his personal phone number. This was not the first that he wrote himself into one of his stories. Burroughs had also appeared by name in his first novel, *Under the Moons of Mars,* as the person to whom spacefarer John Carter tells his extraordinary story (although amusingly, Burroughs submitted the story under the pseudonym "Normal Bean," to imply the adventure was not the ravings of a madman). The author's willingness to poke fun at himself hints at how much he would have enjoyed being one of his own heroes.

These insider's jokes enhance the story of *Tarzan at the Earth's Core,* and indicate that Burroughs must have had a good time writing it. Indeed, some of its scenes stand out in such a way that it is easy to imagine that Burroughs must have been itching to write them: for instance, the scene in which Tarzan, the man who can find his way through a rain forest the way an American city dweller walks around his block, gets lost, because in Pellucidar there are no stars by which he can get his bearings; or Tarzan's first battle inside the Earth with what we recognize as sabor tooth tigers, to make up for the non-existent African tigers he fought in *Tarzan of the Apes.*

Having set up everything necessary for the plot of *Tarzan at the Earth's Core* in the earlier Pellucidar books, Burroughs was free to indulge in some inventive storytelling. Once his characters are inside Pellucidar, Burroughs split them up, put each at the center of his or her own subplot, and told the story as a gradual weaving together of those subplots. This allowed Burroughs to experiment with one of his more interesting narrative techniques, the use of overlapping points of view: the same event seen through Gridley's or Tarzan's eyes is witnessed and described by a Pellucidarian, whose conceptions of what is happening would obviously be different.

What primarily captures reader interest in *Tarzan at the Earth's Core,* though, is the imagination Burroughs displays in his portrayal of races as diverse as the Korsars, the Sagoths, and the Horib snake men. Burroughs crammed a large number of different species into the hothouse world of Pellucidar and made them sufficiently suspicious of one another to emphasize a point about the need for races to trust one another and to work together. And Pellucidar also stands as an example of how fancifully Burroughs could create an entire world out of whole cloth when not constrained by the realities of recognizable human civilization as he was in the other Tarzan books.

But as much as the Tarzan books were masterpieces of such escapism, it's an inescapable fact that they were written over a period of time marked by important historical events. Between the first magazine publication of *Tarzan of the Apes* and the last Tarzan novel, *Tarzan and the Castaways,* in 1947, the globe was rocked by two world wars and other social upheavals, the consequences of which are still very much with us today. Burroughs was not oblivious to what was happening in the real world. In his last years, he personally witnessed the bombing of Pearl Harbor and was an accredited correspondent during World War II, but he had been incorporating real history into his fiction long before that.

In the seventh Tarzan book, *Tarzan the Untamed* (1918), Jane is kidnapped by (and, of course, ultimately rescued from) German soldiers fighting in the East African campaign of World War I, and, in the sequel, *Tarzan the Terrible,* it is revealed that Jack, the son of Tarzan, fought at the battle of Argonne. (Not surprisingly, Burroughs' books were burned by the Nazis.) In *Tarzan and the Foreign Legion* (1944), Tarzan joins the Royal Air Force and battles the Japanese occupation troops in Sumatra. Between the two world wars, Burroughs wrote the fifteenth Tarzan book, *Tarzan the Triumphant* (1932), the last novel in this collection. Here we see two of the author's darkest villains, Leon Stabutch, a Stalinist cast in the mold of Rokoff and Paulvitch; and Dominic Capietro, a man so reviled that he was actually chased out of Mussolini's Italy by the Fascists.

It is not by accident that Stabutch and Capietro are lumped together on the same side of the fence as the Midianites, a culturally backward race of inbred religious zealots. Breeding and birth are dominant themes in the Tarzan books, from the early misunderstanding in *Tarzan of the Apes* that Tarzan may be the offspring of an ape and a man, through Jona's intention to kill herself in *Tarzan at the Earth's Core* if forced into a "miscegenated" match with a man from a race other than her own. In *Tarzan the Triumphant,* the Midianites stand as the terrifying opposite to the purity of Tarzan's own bloodline. Just as Tarzan stands for all that is strong and noble about man, the Midianites are the most weak and ignoble—superstitious and intolerant tyrants. In Burroughs's books, tyrants are tyrants, regardless of their race or creed, and tyrants like Stabutch and the slave raider Capietro, he seems to be saying, are little better than deformed monsters like the Midianites.

It would have been easy for Burroughs to adopt an attitude of racial superiority, but even here he holds out a chance for salvation in the character of Jezebel, a child of the Midianites who is both beautiful and innocent of their ways, and who stands as evidence that every race can produce good. This idea is reflected more comically, on a class level, in the pairing of the Runyonesque Chicago gangster Danny "Gunner" Patrick with another of Burroughs's amusing academics, Lafayette Smith. Both separately and together, this unlikely pair learn to overcome their worst inclinations and habits and draw on resources they never imagined they had. Although *Tarzan the Triumphant* is the story of how Tarzan helps rescue Jezebel, the Gunner, Smith, and the downed flyer, Lady Barbara Collis, these other characters nearly run away with the plot. And rightly so—it's not Tarzan who needs to be shown what he could be if he just showed a little more strength of character.

The four novels chosen for this book provide the reader with a balanced view of Tarzan as his creator saw him. The four different adventures give an idea of the kind of varied entertainment Burroughs was capable of producing even when the main character remained the same, and they refute the stereotype of Tarzan the inarticulate muscleman that has come down to us through comic strips and movies. After all, the reason Tarzan's popularity has endured for three-quarters of a century, since his first adventure was published, is that he fits no stereotype. Burroughs reinvented Tarzan's adventures to match the changing times he lived in, but he never had to change what was at the core of Tarzan's nature—that which was most admirable about the human species. Perhaps that is why Tarzan, who would be celebrating his 100th birthday in 1988, still seems ageless.

STEFAN R. DZIEMIANOWICZ

1988
New York

TARZAN OF THE APES

Illustrated by Esteban Maroto

Overleaf: *Tarzan of the apes placed his foot upon the neck of his lifelong enemy and voiced the wild cry of his people.*

CHAPTER 1

Out to Sea

I HAD THIS story from one who had no business to tell it to me, or to any other. I may credit the seductive influence of an old vintage upon the narrator for the beginning of it, and my own skeptical incredulity during the days that followed for the balance of the strange tale.

When my convivial host discovered that he had told me so much, and that I was prone to doubtfulness, his foolish pride assumed the task the old vintage had commenced, and so he unearthed written evidence in the form of musty manuscript, and dry official records of the British Colonial Office, to support many of the salient features of his remarkable narrative.

I do not say the story is true, for I did not witness the happenings which it portrays.

The fact, however, that in the telling of it to you I have taken fictitious names for the principal characters quite sufficiently evidences the sincerity of my own belief that it may be true.

The yellow, mildewed pages of the diary of a man long dead and the records of the Colonial Office dovetail perfectly with the narrative of my convivial host, and so I give you the story as I pieced it out from these several various agencies.

If you do not find it credible, you will at least be as one with me in acknowledging that it is unique, remarkable, and interesting.

From the records of the Colonial Office and from the dead man's diary we learn that a certain young English nobleman, whom we shall call John Clayton, Lord Greystoke, was commissioned to undertake a peculiarly delicate investigation of conditions in a British West Coast African colony from whose natives another European power was known to be recruiting soldiers for its army, which latter it used solely for the forcible collection of rubber and ivory from the savage tribes along the Congo and the Aruwimi.

The natives of the British colony complained that many of their young men were enticed away through the medium of fair and glowing promises, but that few, if any, ever returned to their families.

The Englishmen in Africa went even further, saying that these poor blacks were held in virtual slavery; for when their terms of enlistment expired, their ignorance was imposed upon by their white officers, and they were told that they had yet several years to serve.

So the Colonial Office appointed John Clayton to a new post in British West Africa, but his confidential instructions centered on a thorough investigation of the unfair treatment of black British subjects by the officers of a friendly European power.

Clayton was the type of Englishman that one likes best to associate with the noblest monuments of historic achievement upon a thousand victorious battle-fields—a strong, virile man— mentally, morally, and physically.

In stature he was above the average height; his eyes were gray, his features regular and strong; his carriage that of perfect, robust health influenced by his years of army training.

Political ambition had caused him to seek transference from the army to the Colonial Office, and so we find him, still young, entrusted with a delicate and important commission in the service of the queen.

When he received this appointment he was both elated and appalled. The preferment seemed to him in the nature of a well-merited reward for painstaking and intelligent service, and as a stepping-stone to posts of greater importance and responsibility; but, on the other hand, he had been married to the Hon. Alice Rutherford for scarce a three months, and it was the thought of taking this fair young girl into the dangers and isolation of tropical Africa that appalled him.

For her sake, he would have refused the appointment; but she would not have it so. Instead, she insisted that he accept, and take her with him.

There were mothers and brothers and sisters and aunts and

cousins to express various opinions on the subject, but as to what they severally advised history is silent.

We only know that on a bright May morning in 1888, John, Lord Greystoke, and Lady Alice sailed from Dover on their way to Africa.

A month later they arrived at Freetown, where they chartered a small sailing vessel, the Fuwalda, which was to bear them to their final destination.

And here John, Lord Greystoke, and Lady Alice, his wife, vanished from the eyes and from the knowledge of men.

Two months after they weighed anchor and cleared from the port of Freetown, a half-dozen British war-vessels were scouring the south Atlantic for trace of them or their little vessel, and it was almost immediately that the wreckage was found upon the shores of St. Helena which convinced the world that the Fuwalda had gone down with all on board, and thus the search was stopped ere it had scarce begun.

The Fuwulda, a barkantine of about one hundred tons, was a vessel of the type often seen in coastwise trade in the far southern Atlantic. Their crews composed of the offscourings of the sea— unhanged murderers and cutthroats of every race and every nation, and the Fuwalda was no exception to the rule.

Her officers were swarthy bullies, hating and hated by their crew.

The captain, while a competent seaman, was a brute in his treatment of his men. He knew, or at least he used, but two arguments in his dealings with them—a belaying-pin and a re- volver—nor is it likely that the motley aggregation he signed would have understood aught else.

From the second day out from Freetown, John Clayton and his young wife witnessed scenes upon the deck of the Fuwalda such as they had believed were never enacted outside the covers of printed stories of the sea.

It was on the morning of the second day that there was forged the first link in a chain of circumstances that ended in a life for one then unborn such as has probably never been paralleled in the history of man.

Two sailors were washing down the decks of the Fuwalda, the first mate was on duty, and the captain had stopped to speak with John Clayton and Lady Alice.

The men were working backward toward the little party, who

were turned away from the sailors. Closer and closer they came, until one of them was directly behind the captain. In another moment he would have passed by, and this strange narrative had never been recorded.

But just that instant the captain swung round to leave Lord and Lady Greystoke, and, as he did so, tripped against the sailor and sprawled headlong upon the deck, overturning the water-pail so that he was drenched in its dirty contents.

For an instant the scene was ludicrous; but only for an instant. With a volley of awful oaths, his face suffused with the scarlet of mortification and rage, the captain regained his feet, and with a terrific blow felled the sailor to the deck.

The man was small and rather old, so that the brutality of the act was thus accentuated.

The other seaman, however, was neither old nor small—a huge bear of a man, with fierce black mustache, and a great bull neck set between massive shoulders.

As he saw his mate go down he crouched, and, with a snarl, sprang upon the captain, crushing him to his knees with a single mighty blow.

From scarlet, the officer's face went white, for this was mutiny; and mutiny he had met and subdued before in his brutal career. Without waiting to rise, he whipped a revolver from his pocket and fired pointblank at the great mountain of muscle towering before him.

Quick as he was, John Clayton was almost as quick, so that the bullet which was intended for the sailor's heart lodged in the sailor's leg instead, for Lord Greystoke had struck down the captain's arm as he had seen the weapon flash in the sun.

Words passed between Clayton and the captain, and the former made it plain that he was disgusted with the brutality displayed toward the crew, nor would he countenance anything further of the kind while he and Lady Greystoke remained passengers.

The captain was on the point of making an angry reply, but, thinking better of it, turned on his heel and strode, black and scowling, forward.

He did not care to antagonize an English official, for the queen's mighty arm wielded a punitive instrument which he could appreciate, and which he feared—England's far-reaching navy.

The two sailors picked themselves up, the older man assisting his wounded comrade. The big fellow, who was known among his mates as Black Michael, tried his leg gingerly, and, finding that it bore his weight, turned to Clayton with a word of gruff thanks.

Though the fellow's tone was surly, his words were evidently well-meant. Ere he had scarce finished his little speech he had turned and was limping off toward the forecastle with the very apparent intention of forestalling any further conversation.

They did not see him again for several days, nor did the captain vouchsafe them more than the surliest of grunts when he was forced to speak to them.

They messed in his cabin, as they had before the unfortunate occurrence; but the captain was careful to see that his duties never permitted him to eat at the same time as they did.

The other officers were coarse, illiterate fellows, but little above the villainous crew they bullied, and were only too glad to avoid social intercourse with the polished English noble and his lady, so that the Claytons were left very much to themselves.

There was in the whole atmosphere of the craft that undefinable something which presages disaster. Outwardly, to the knowledge of the Claytons, all went on as before upon the little vessel, but that there was an undertow leading them toward some unknown danger both felt, though they did not speak of it to each other.

On the second day after the wounding of Black Michael, Clayton came on deck just in time to see the limp body of one of the crew being carried below by four of his fellows, while the first mate, a heavy belaying-pin in his hand, stood glowering at the little party of sullen sailors.

Clayton asked no questions—he did not need to—and the following day, as the great lines of a British battle-ship grew out of the distant horizon, he half determined to demand that he and Lady Alice be put aboard her, for his fears were steadily increasing that nothing but harm could result from remaining on the lowering, sullen Fuwalda.

Toward noon they were within speaking distance of the British vessel, but when Clayton had about decided to ask the captain to put them aboard her, the obvious ridiculousness of such a request became suddenly apparent. What reason could he give the officer commanding her majesty's ship for desiring to go back in the direction from which he had just come!

Faith, what if he told them that two insubordinate seamen had been roughly handled by their officers. They would but laugh in their sleeves and attribute his reason for wishing to leave the ship to but one thing—cowardice.

John Clayton, Lord Greystoke, did not ask to be transferred to the British man-of-war, and late in the afternoon he saw her upperworks fade below the far horizon, but not before he learned that which confirmed his greatest fears and caused him to curse the false pride which had restrained him from seeking safety for his young wife, when safety was within reach—a safety which was now gone forever.

It was mid-afternoon that brought the little old sailor, who had been felled by the captain a few days before, to where Clayton and his wife stood by the ship's side watching the ever-diminishing outlines of the great battle-ship. The old fellow was polishing brasses, and as he came close to Clayton he said, in a low tone:

" 'Ell's to pay, sir, on this 'ere craft, an' mark my word for it, sir. 'Ell's to pay."

"What do you mean, my good fellow?" asked Clayton.

"W'y, hasn't ye seen wat's goin' on? Hasn't ye 'eard that devil's spawn of a capting an' 'is mates knockin' the bloomin' lights outen 'arf the crew?

"Two busted 'eads yeste'day, an' three to-day. Black Michael's as good as new agin an' 'e's not the bully to stand for it, not 'e; an' mark my word for it, sir."

"You mean, my man, that the crew contemplates mutiny?" asked Clayton.

"Mutiny!" exclaimed the old fellow. "Mutiny! They means murder, sir, an' mark my word for it, sir."

"When?"

"Hit's comin', sir; hit's comin' but I'm not a sayin' w'en, an' I've said too much now, but ye was a good sort t'other day, an' I thought it no more'n right to warn ye. But keep a still tongue in yer 'ead, an' when ye hear shootin', git below an' stay there.

"That's all, only keep a still tongue in yer 'ead, or they'll put a pill between yer ribs, an' mark my word for it, sir."

The old fellow went on with his polishing, which carried him away from where the Claytons were standing.

"Deuced cheerful outlook, Alice," said Clayton.

"You should warn the captain at once, John. Possibly the trouble may be averted yet," she said.

"I suppose I should, but yet from purely selfish motives I am almost prompted 'to keep a still tongue in my 'ead.' Whatever they do now they will spare us in recognition of my stand for this fellow Black Michael, but should they find that I had betrayed them, there would be no mercy shown us, Alice."

"You have but one duty, John, and that lies in the interest of vested authority. If you do not warn the captain, you are as much a party to whatever follows as though you had helped to plot and carry it out with your own head and hands."

"You do not understand, dear," replied Clayton. "It is of you I am thinking—there lies my first duty. The captain has brought this condition upon himself, so why should I risk subjecting my wife to unthinkable horrors in a probably futile attempt to save him from his own brutal folly? You have no conception, dear, of what would follow were this pack of cutthroats to gain control of the Fuwalda."

"Duty is duty. No amount of sophistries may change it. I would be a poor wife for an English lord were I to be responsible for his shirking a plain duty."

"Have it as you will, then, Alice," he answered, smiling. "Maybe we are borrowing trouble.

"Mutiny on the high sea may have been common a hundred years ago, but in this good year 1888 it is the least likely of happenings.

"But there goes the captain to his cabin now. If I am going to warn him, I might as well get the beastly job over, for I have little stomach to talk with the brute at all."

So saying, he strolled carelessly in the direction of the companionway through which the captain had passed, and a moment later was knocking at his door.

"Come in," growled the deep tones of that surly officer.

And when Clayton had entered and closed the door behind him:

"Well?"

"I have come to report the gist of a conversation I heard to-day, because I feel that, while there may be nothing to it, it is as well that you be forearmed. In short, the men contemplate mutiny and murder."

"It's a lie!" roared the captain. "And if you have been interfering again with the discipline of this ship, or meddling in affairs that don't concern you, you can take the consequences on your own shoulders. I don't care whether you are an English lord or not. I'm captain of this here ship, and from now on you keep your meddling nose out of my business."

As he reached this peroration, the captain had worked himself up to such a frenzy of rage that he was fairly purple of face, and shrieked the last words at the top of his voice; emphasizing his remarks by a loud thumping of the table with one huge fist and shaking the other in Clayton's face.

Greystoke never turned a hair, but stood eying the excited man with level gaze.

"Captain Billings," he drawled finally, "if you will pardon my candor, I might remark that you are something of an ass."

Whereupon he turned and left the cabin with the same indifferent ease that was habitual with him, and which was more surely calculated to raise the ire of a man of Billings's class than a torrent of invective.

So, whereas the captain might easily have been brought to regret his hasty speech had Clayton attempted to conciliate him, his temper was now irrevocably set in the mold in which Clayton had left it, and the last chance of their working together for their common good was gone.

"If I had saved my breath," said Clayton, as he rejoined his wife, "I should likewise have saved myself a bit of a calling. The fellow proved ungrateful. Fairly jumped at me like a mad dog.

"He and his ship may go hang, for all I care; and until we are safe off the thing I shall spend my energies in looking after our own welfare. And I rather fancy the first step to that end should be to go to our cabin and look over my revolvers. I am sorry now that we packed the larger guns and the ammunition with the stuff below."

They found their quarters in a bad state of disorder. Clothing from their open boxes and bags strewed the little apartment, and even their beds had been torn to pieces.

"Evidently some one was more anxious about our belongings than we," said Clayton. "By Jove, I wonder what the bounder was after. Let's have a look, Alice, and see what's missing."

A thorough search revealed the fact that nothing had been taken but Clayton's two revolvers and the small supply of ammunition he had saved out for them.

"Those are the very things I most wish they had left us." said Clayton; "and the fact that they wished for them and them alone is the most sinister circumstance of all that have transpired since we set foot on this miserable hulk."

"What are we to do, John?" asked his wife. "I shall not urge you to go again to the captain, for I cannot see you affronted further by the ignorant fellow. Possibly our best chance for salvation lies in maintaining a neutral position.

"If the officers are able to prevent a mutiny, we have nothing to fear, while if the mutineers are victorious, our one slim hope lies in not having attempted to thwart or antagonize them."

"Right you are, Alice. We'll keep in the middle of the road."

As they fell to in an effort to straighten up their cabin, Clayton and his wife simultaneously noticed the corner of a piece of paper protruding from beneath the doorway of their quarters. As Clayton stooped to reach for it he was amazed to see it move further into the room, and then he realized that it was being pushed under the door by some one from without.

Quickly and silently he stepped toward the door, but, as he reached for the knob to throw it open, his wife's hand fell upon his wrist.

"No, John," she whispered. "They do not wish to be seen, and so we cannot afford to see them. Do not forget that we are keeping the middle of the road."

Clayton smiled and dropped his hand to his side. Thus they stood watching the little bit of white paper until it finally remained at rest upon the floor just inside the door.

Then Clayton stooped and picked it up. It was a bit of grimy, white paper, roughly folded into a ragged square. Opening it they found a crude message printed in uncouth letters, with many evidences of an accustomed task.

Translated, it was a warning to the Claytons to refrain from reporting the loss of the revolvers, or from repeating what the old sailor had told them—to refrain on pain of death.

"I rather imagine we'll be good," said Clayton with a rueful smile. "About all we can do is to sit tight and wait for whatever may come."

CHAPTER 2

The Savage Home

NOR DID THEY have long to wait, for the next morning, as Clayton was emerging on deck for his accustomed walk before breakfast, a shot rang out, and then another, and another.

The sight which met his eyes confirmed his worst fears. Facing the little knot of officers was the entire motley crew of the Fuwalda, and at their head stood Black Michael.

At the first volley from the officers the men ran for shelter, and from points of vantage behind masts, wheelhouse, and cabin they returned the fire of the five men who represented the hated authority of the ship.

Two of their number had gone down before the captain's revolver, and they lay where they had fallen between the combatants.

Presently the first mate lunged forward upon his face, and at a cry of command from Black Michael the bloodthirsty ruffians charged the remaining four. The crew had been able to muster but six firearms, so most of them were armed with boat-hooks, axes, hatchets, and crowbars.

The captain had emptied his revolver and was reloading as the charge was made. The second mate's gun had jammed, and so there were but two weapons opposed to them as they rapidly approached the officers, who now started to give back before the infuriated rush of their men.

Both sides were cursing and swearing in a frightful manner, which, together with the reports of the firearms and the screams and groans of the wounded, turned the deck of the Fuwalda to the likeness of a madhouse.

Before the officers had taken a dozen backward steps the men were upon them. An ax in the hands of a negro cleft the captain from forehead to chin, and an instant later the others were down, dead or wounded from dozens of blows and bullet wounds.

Short and grisly had been the work of the mutineers of the Fuwalda, and through it all John Clayton had stood leaning carelessly beside the companionway puffing meditatively upon his pipe as though he had been but watching an indifferent cricket match.

As the last officer went down he bethought him that it was time that he returned to his wife lest some member of the crew find her alone below.

Though outwardly calm and indifferent, Clayton was inwardly apprehensive and wrought up, for he feared for his wife's safety at the hands of these ignorant, half-brutes into whose hands fate had so remorselessly thrown them.

As he turned to descend the ladder he was surprised to see his wife standing at his elbow.

"How long have you been here, Alice?"

"Since the beginning," she replied. "What can we hope for at the hands of such as those?"

"Breakfast," he answered, smiling bravely in an attempt to alay her fears. "At least," he added, "I'm going to ask them. Come with me, Alice. We must not let them think we expect any but courteous treatment."

The men had by this time surrounded the dead and wounded officers, and without either partiality or compassion proceeded to throw both living and dead over the sides of the vessel. With equal heartlessness they disposed of their own wounded, and the bodies of the three sailors to whom a merciful Providence had vouchsafed instant death before the bullets of the officers.

Presently one of the crew spied the approaching Claytons, and with a cry of: "Here's two more for the fishes," rushed toward them with uplifted ax.

But Black Michael was even quicker, so that the fellow went down with a bullet in his back before he had taken a half-dozen steps.

With a loud roar, Black Michael attracted the attention of the others, and pointing to Lord and Lady Greystoke, cried:

"These here are my friends, and they are to be left alone. D'ye understand?

"I'm captain of this ship now, an' w'at I says goes," he added. Then to Clayton: "Keep to yourselves and nobody'll harm ye."

The Claytons heeded Black Michael's instructions so well that they saw but little of the crew and knew nothing of the plans the men were making.

Occasionally they heard faint echos of brawls and quarreling among the mutineers, and on two occasions the vicious bark of firearms rang out on the still air. But Black Michael was a fit leader for this heterogeneous band of cutthroats, and, withal, held them in fair subjection to his rule.

On the fifth day following the murder of the ship's officers, the lookout sighted land. Whether island or mainland, Black Michael did not know, but he announced to Clayton that if investigation showed that the place was habitable, he and Lady Greystoke were to be put ashore with their belongings.

"You'll be all right there for a few months," he explained, "and by that time we'll have been able to make an inhabited coast somewheres and scatter a bit. Then I'll see that yer gover'ment's notified where you be, an' they'll soon send a man-o'-war to fetch ye off.

"You may be all right, but it would be a hard matter to land you in civilization without a lot o' questions being asked, an' none o' us here has any very convincin' answers up our sleeves."

Clayton remonstrated against the inhumanity of landing them upon an unknown shore to be left to the mercies of savage beasts, and, possibly, still more savage men.

But his words were of no avail, and only tended to anger Black Michael, so Clayton was forced to desist and make the best of a bad situation.

About three o'clock in the afternoon they came about off a beautiful wooded shore opposite the mouth of what appeared to be a land-locked harbor.

Black Michael sent a small boat filled with men to sound the entrance in an effort to determine if the Fuwalda could be safely worked through the entrance.

In about an hour they returned and reported deep water through the passage as well as far into the little basin.

Before dark the Fuwalda lay peacefully at anchor upon the bosom of the still, mirrorlike surface of the harbor.

The surrounding shores were beautiful with semitropical verdure, while in the distance the country rose from the ocean in hill and tableland, almost uniformly clothed by primeval forest.

No signs of habitation were visible, but that the land might easily support human life was evidenced by the abundant bird and animal life of which the watchers on the Fuwalda's deck caught occasional glimpses, as well as by the shimmer of a little river which emptied into the harbor, insuring fresh water in plentitude.

As darkness settled upon the earth, Clayton and Lady Alice still stood by the ship's rail in silent contemplation of their future abode. From the dark shadows of the mighty forest came the wild calls of savage beasts—the deep roar of the lion, and, occasionally, the scream of a tiger.

The woman shrank closer to the man in terror-stricken anticipation of the horrors lying in wait for them in the awful blackness of the nights to come, when they two should be alone upon that wild and lonely shore.

Later in the evening Black Michael joined them long enough to instruct them to make their preparations for landing on the morrow. They tried to persuade him to take them to some more hospitable shore near enough to civilization, so that they might hope to fall into friendly hands. But no pleas, or threats, or promises of reward could move him.

"I am the only man aboard who would not rather see you both safely dead, and while I know that that's the sensible way to make sure of our own necks, yet I am not the man to forget a favor. You saved my life once, and in return I'm goin' to spare yours, but that's all I can do.

"The men won't stand for any more, and if we don't get you landed pretty quick, they may even change their minds about giving you that much show. I'll put all your stuff ashore with you, as well as cookin' utensils an' some old sails for tents, an' enough grub to last you until you can find fruit and game.

"So that with your guns for protection, you ought to be able to live here easy enough until help comes. When I get safely hid away, I'll see to it that the British gover'ment learns about where you be; for the life of me I couldn't tell 'em exactly where, for I don't know myself. But they'll find you all right."

After he had left them they went silently below, each wrapped in gloomy forebodings.

Clayton did not believe that Black Michael had the slightest intention of notifying the British government of their whereabouts, nor was he any too sure but that some treachery was contemplated for the following day when they should be on shore with the sailors who would have to accompany them with their belongings.

Once out of Black Michael's sight, any of the men might strike them down, and still leave Black Michael's conscience clear.

And even should they escape that fate, was it not but to be faced with far graver dangers? Alone, he might hope to survive for years; for he was a strong athletic man.

But what of Alice, and that other little life so soon to be

launched amid the hardships and grave dangers of a primeval world?

The man shuddered as he meditated upon the awful gravity, the fearful helplessness, of their situation. But it was a merciful Providence which prevented him from foreseeing the hideous reality which awaited them in the grim depths of that gloomy wood.

Early next morning their numerous chests and boxes were hoisted on deck and lowered to waiting small boats for transportation to shore.

There was a great quantity and variety of stuff, as the Claytons had expected a possible five to eight years' residence in their new home, so that, in addition to the many necessities they had brought, were also many luxuries.

Black Michael was determined that nothing belonging to the Claytons should be left on board. Whether out of compassion for them, or in furtherance of his own interests, it were difficult to say.

There is no question but that the presence of property of a missing British official upon a suspicious vessel would have been a difficult thing to explain in any civilized port in the world.

So zealous was he in his efforts to carry out his intentions that he insisted upon the return of Clayton's revolvers to him by the sailors in whose possession they were.

Into the small boats were also loaded salt meats and biscuit, with a small supply of potatoes and beans, matches and cooking vessels, a chest of tools, and the old sails which Black Michael had promised them.

As though himself fearing the very thing which Clayton had suspected, Black Michael accompanied them to shore, and was the last to leave them when the small boats, having filled the ship's casks with fresh water, were pushed out toward the waiting Fuwalda.

As the boats moved slowly over the smooth waters of the bay, Clayton and his wife stood silently watching their departure, in the breasts of both a feeling of impending disaster and utter hopelessness.

And behind them, over the edge of a low ridge, other eyes watched—close-set, wicked eyes, gleaming beneath shaggy brows.

As the Fuwalda passed through the narrow entrance to the harbor and out of sight behind a projecting point, Lady Alice threw her arms about Clayton's neck and burst into uncontrolled sobs.

Bravely had she faced the dangers of the mutiny; with heroic fortitude she had looked into the terrible future; but now that the horror of absolute solitude was upon them, her overwrought nerves gave way, and the reaction came.

He did not attempt to check her tears. It were better that nature have her way in relieving these long-pent emotions, and it was many minutes before the girl—little more than a child she was—could again gain mastery of herself.

"Oh, John," she cried at last, "the horror of it! What are we to do? What are we to do?"

"There is but one thing to do, Alice," and he spoke as quietly as though they were sitting in their snug living-room at home, "and that is work. Work must be our salvation. We must not give ourselves time to think, for in that direction lies madness.

"We must work and wait. I am sure that relief will come, and come quickly, when once it is apparent that the Fuwalda has been lost, even though Black Michael does not keep his word to us."

"But, John, if it were only you and I," she sobbed, "we could endure it, I know; but—"

"Yes, dear," he answered gently, "I have been thinking of that, also; but we must face it, as we must face whatever comes, bravely and with the utmost confidence in our ability to cope with circumstances whatever they may be. Hundreds of thousands of years ago our ancestors of the dim and distant past faced the same problems which we must face, possibly in these same primeval forests.

"That we are here to-day evidences their victory."

"Ah, John, I wish that I might be a man with a man's philosophy, but I am but a woman, seeing with my heart rather than my head, and all that I can see is too horrible, too unthinkable to put into words.

"I only hope you are right. I will do my best to be a brave primeval woman, a fit mate for the primeval man."

Clayton's first thought was to arrange a sleeping shelter for the night; something which might serve to protect them from prowling beasts of prey.

He opened the box containing his rifles and ammunition, that they might both be armed against possible attack while at work, and then together they sought a location for their first night's sleeping place.

A hundred yards from the beach was a little level spot, fairly free of trees, and here they decided eventually to build a permanent house, but, for the time being, they both thought it best to construct a little platform in the trees out of reach of the larger of the savage beasts.

To this end Clayton selected four trees which formed a rectangle about eight feet square, and cutting long branches from other trees, he constructed a framework around them, about ten feet from the ground, fastening the ends of the branches securely to the trees by means of rope, a quantity of which Black Michael had furnished him from the hold of the Fuwalda.

Across this framework Clayton placed other smaller branches quite close together. This platform he paved with the huge fronds of elephant's ear, which grew in profusion about them, and over the fronds he laid a great sail folded into several thicknesses.

Seven feet higher he constructed a similar, though lighter platform, to serve as roof, and from the sides of this he suspended the balance of his sail-cloth for walls.

When completed, he had a rather snug little nest, to which he carried their blankets and some of the lighter luggage.

It was now late in the afternoon, and the balance of the daylight hours were devoted to the building of a rude ladder by means of which Lady Alice could mount to her new home.

All during the day the forest about them had been filled with excited birds of brilliant plumage, and dancing, chattering monkeys, who watched these new arrivals and their wonderful nest-building operations with every mark of keenest interest and fascination.

Notwithstanding that both Clayton and his wife kept a sharp lookout, they saw nothing of larger animals, though on two occasions they had seen their little simian neighbors come screaming and chattering from the near-by ridge, casting affrighted glances back over their little shoulders, and evincing as plainly as though by speech that they were fleeing some terrible thing which lay concealed there.

Just before dusk Clayton finished his ladder, and, filling a great basin with water from the near-by stream, the two mounted to the comparative safety of their aerial chamber.

As it was quite warm, Clayton had left the side-curtains thrown back over the roof, and as they squatted, like Turks, upon their blankets, Lady Alice, straining her eyes into the darkening shadows of the wood, suddenly reached out and grasped Clayton's arm.

"John," she whispered, "look! What is it, a man?"

As Clayton turned his eyes in the direction she indicated, he saw silhouetted dimly against the shadows beyond, a great figure standing upright upon the ridge.

For a moment it stood as though listening, and then turned slowly, and melted into the shadows of the jungle.

"What is it, John?"

"I do not know, Alice," he answered gravely. "It is too dark to see so far, and it may have been but a shadow cast by the rising moon."

"No, John, if it was not a man it was some huge and grotesque mockery of man. Oh, I am afraid!"

He gathered her in his arms, whispering words of courage and love into her ears, for the greatest pain of their misfortunes, to Clayton, was the mental anguish of his young wife. Himself brave and fearless, he was yet able to appreciate the awful suffering which fear entails—a rare gift, though but one of many which had made the young Lord Greystoke respected and loved by all who knew him.

Soon after he lowered the curtain-walls, tying them securely to the trees so that, except for a little opening toward the beach, they were entirely enclosed.

As it was now pitch dark within their tiny eery, they lay down upon their blankets to try to wrest, through sleep, a brief respite of forgetfulness.

Clayton lay facing the opening at the front, a rifle and a brace of revolvers at his hand.

Scarcely had they closed their eyes than the terrifying cry of a tiger rang out from the jungle behind them.

Closer and closer it came until they could hear the great beast directly beneath them. For an hour or more they heard it sniffing and clawing at the trees which supported their platform, but at last it roamed away across the beach, where Clayton could see it clearly in the moonlight—a great, handsome beast, the largest he had ever seen.

During the long hours of darkness they caught but fitful snatches of sleep, for the night noises of a great jungle teeming with myriad animal life kept their overwrought nerves on edge. So that a hundred times they were startled to wakefulness by piercing screams, or the stealthy moving of great bodies beneath them.

CHAPTER 3

Life and Death

MORNING FOUND THEM but little, if at all refreshed, though it was with a feeling of intense relief that they saw the day dawn.

As soon as they had made their meager breakfast of salt pork, coffee, and biscuit, Clayton commenced work upon their house, for he realized that they could hope for no safety and no peace of mind at night until four strong walls effectually barred the jungle life from them.

The task was arduous and required the better part of a month, though he built but one small room. He constructed his cabin of small logs about six inches in diameter, stopping the chinks with clay which he found at the depth of a few feet beneath the surface soil.

At one end he built a fireplace of small stones from the beach. These also he set in clay, and when the house had been entirely completed he applied a coating of the clay to the entire outside surface to the thickness of four inches.

In the window opening he set small branches about an inch in diameter, both vertically and horizontally, and so woven that they formed a substantial grating that could withstand the strength of a powerful animal. Thus they obtained air and proper ventilation without fear of lessening the safety of their cabin.

The A-shaped roof was thatched with small branches laid close together, and over these long jungle grass, with a final coating of clay.

The door he built of pieces of the packing-boxes which had held their belongings; nailing one piece upon another, the grain of contiguous layers running transversely, until he had a solid body some three inches thick, and of such great strength that they were both forced to laugh as they gazed upon it.

Here the greatest difficulty confronted Clayton, for he had no means whereby to hang his massive door now that he had built it. After two days' work, however, he succeeded in fashioning two massive hard-wood hinges, and with these he hung the door so that it opened and closed easily.

The stuccoing and other final touches were added after they had moved into the house, which they had done as soon as the roof was on, piling their boxes before the door at night and thus having a comparatively safe and comfortable habitation.

The building of a bed, chairs, table, and shelves was a relatively easy matter, so that by the end of the second month they were well settled, and, but for the constant dread of attack by wild beasts and the ever-growing loneliness, they were not uncomfortable or unhappy.

At night great beasts snarled and roared about their tiny cabin, but so accustomed may one become to oft-repeated noises that soon they paid little attention to them, sleeping soundly the whole night through.

Thrice had they caught fleeting glimpses of the great manlike figures of the first night, but never at sufficiently close range to know positively whether they were man or brute.

The brilliant birds and the little monkeys had become accustomed to their new acquaintances. As they had evidently never seen human beings before, they presently, after their first fright had worn off, approached closer and closer, impelled by that strange curiosity which dominates wild creatures, so that within the first month several of the birds had gone so far as even to accept morsels of food from the hands of the Claytons.

One afternoon, while Clayton was working upon an addition to their cabin, for he contemplated building several more rooms, a number of their grotesque little friends came shrieking and scolding through the trees from the direction of the ridge.

Even as they fled, they cast fearful glances back at them, and, finally, they stopped near Clayton, jabbering excitedly to him as though to warn him of approaching danger.

At last he saw it, the thing the little monkeys so feared—the man-brute of which the Claytons had caught occasional fleeting glimpses.

It was approaching through the jungle in a semierect position, now and then placing the backs of its closed fists upon the ground—a great anthropoid ape, and, as it advanced, it emitted deep gutteral growls and an occasional low barking sound.

Clayton was at some distance from the cabin, having come to fell a particularly perfect tree for his building operations. Grown careless from months of continued safety, during which time they had seen no dangerous animals during the daylight hours, he had left his rifles and revolvers all within the little cabin, and now that he saw the great ape crashing through the underbrush directly toward him, and from a direction which practically cut him off from escape, he felt a vague little shiver play up and down his spine.

He knew that, armed only with an ax, his chances with this ferocious monster were small indeed, and Alice—oh, Heaven—he thought, what would become of Alice?

There was yet a slight chance of reaching the cabin, and he turned and ran toward it, shouting an alarm to his wife to run in and close the great door in case the ape cut off his retreat.

Lady Greystoke had been sitting a little way from the cabin, and when she heard his cry, she looked up to see the ape springing with almost incredible swiftness, in an effort to head off Clayton.

With a low cry she sprang toward the cabin, and, as she entered, gave a backward glance which filled her soul with terror, for the brute had intercepted her husband who now stood at bay, grasping his ax with both hands, ready to swing it upon the infuriated animal when he should make his final charge.

"Close and bolt the door, Alice," cried Clayton. "I can finish this fellow with my ax."

But he knew he lied, and so did she.

The ape was a huge bull, weighing probably three hundred pounds. His nasty, close-set eyes gleamed hatred from beneath his shaggy brows, while his great canine fangs were bared in a horrid snarl as he paused a moment before Clayton.

Over the brute's shoulder Clayton could see the doorway of his cabin, not twenty paces distant, and a great wave of horror and fear swept over him as he saw his young wife emerge, armed with one of his rifles.

She had always been afraid of firearms, and would never touch them, but now she rushed toward the ape with the fearlessness of a lioness protecting its young.

"Back, Alice!" shouted Clayton. "For Heaven's sake go back."

But she would not heed, and just then the ape charged so that Clayton could say no more.

The man swung his ax with all his mighty strength; but the powerful brute grasped it in those terrible hands, and, tearing it from Clayton's grasp, hurled it far to one side.

With a snarl he closed upon his defenseless victim; but ere his fangs had reached the throat they thirsted for there was a sharp report and a bullet entered the brute's back between his shoulders.

Throwing Clayton to the ground, the beast turned upon his new enemy. There before him stood the terrified girl, vainly trying to fire another bullet into the animal's body; but she did not understand the mechanism of the gun, and the hammer fell futilely upon an empty cartridge.

Screaming with rage and pain, the ape flew at the delicate woman, who went down beneath him to merciful unconsciousness.

Almost simultaneously Clayton regained his feet and, without thought of the utter hopelessness of it, he rushed forward to drag the ape from his wife's prostrate form.

With little or no effort he succeeded, and the great bulk rolled inertly upon the turf before him. The ape was dead. The bullet had done its work.

A hasty examination of his wife revealed no marks upon her, and Clayton decided that the huge brute had died the instant he had sprung toward Alice.

Gently he lifted his wife's still unconscious form and bore her to the little cabin, but it was fully two hours before she regained consciousness.

Her first words filled Clayton with vague apprehension. For some time after regaining her senses Alice gazed wonderingly about the interior of the little cabin, and then, with a satisfied little sigh, said:

"Oh, John, it is so good to be really home! I have had an awful dream, dear. I thought we were no longer in London, but in some horrible place where great beasts attacked us."

"There, there, Alice," he said, stroking her forehead. "Try to sleep again, and do not worry your little head about bad dreams."

That night a little son was born in the tiny cabin beside the primeval forest, while a great tiger screamed before the door and the deep notes of the lion's roar sounded from beyond the ridge.

Lady Greystoke never recovered from the shock of the great ape's attack, and, though she lived for a year after her baby was born, she was never again outside the cabin, nor did she ever fully realize that she was not in England.

Sometimes she would question Clayton as to the strange noises of the nights, the absence of servants and friends, and the strange rudeness of the furnishings within her room; but, though he made no effort to deceive her, never could she grasp the meaning of it all.

In other ways she was quite rational, and the joy and happiness she took in the possession of her little son and the constant attentions of her husband made that year a very happy one for her, the happiest of her life.

That it would have been beset by worries and apprehension had she been in full command of her mental faculties Clayton well knew; so that, while he suffered terribly to see her so, there were times when he was almost glad for her sake that she could not understand.

Long since had Clayton given up any hope of rescue, except through accident. With unremitting zeal he had worked to beautify the interior of the cabin.

Skins of lion and tiger covered the floor. Cupboards and book-cases lined the walls. Odd vases made by his own hands from the clay of the region held beautiful tropical flowers. Curtains of grass and bamboo covered the windows, and, most arduous task of all with his meager assortment of tools, he had fashioned lumber to neatly seal the walls and ceiling and lay a smooth floor within the cabin.

That he had been able to turn his hands at all to such unaccustomed labor was a source of mild wonder to him. He loved, however, the work because it was for her and the tiny life that had come to cheer them, though adding a hundredfold to his responsibilities and to the terribleness of their situation.

During the year that followed Clayton was several times attacked by the great apes which now seemed to infest the vicinity of the cabin; but, as he never ventured out except with both rifle and revolvers, he had little fear of the huge beasts.

He had strengthened the window protections and fitted a unique wooden lock to the cabin door, so that when he hunted for game and fruits he had no fear that any animal could break into the little home.

At first much of the game he shot from the cabin windows, but toward the end the animals learned to fear the strange lair whence issued the terrifying thunder of his rifle.

In his leisure Clayton read, often aloud to his wife, from the store of books he had brought for their new home. Among these were many for little children—picture-books, primers, readers— for they had known that their little child would be old enough for such before they had hoped to return to England.

At other times Clayton wrote in his diary, which he had always been accustomed to keep in French, and in which he recorded the details of their strange life. This book he kept locked in a little metal box.

A year from the day her little son was born Lady Alice passed quietly away in the night. So peaceful was her end that it was hours before Clayton could realize that his wife was dead.

The horror of the situation came to him very slowly, and it is doubtful that he ever fully realized the enormity of his sorrow and the fearful responsibility that had devolved upon him with the care of that wee thing, his son, still a nursing babe.

The last entry in his diary was made the morning following her death. In it he recites the sad details in a matter-of-fact way that adds to the pathos of it—for it breathes an apathy born of long sorrow and hopelessness, which even this cruel blow could scarcely awake to further suffering:

> My little son is crying for nourishment. Oh, Alice, Alice, what shall I do?

And as John Clayton wrote the last words his hand was ever destined to pen, he dropped his head wearily upon his outstretched arms where they rested upon the table he had built for her who lay still and cold in the bed beside him.

For a long time no sound broke the deathlike stillness of the jungle midday save the wailing of the tiny man-child.

CHAPTER 4

The Apes

IN THE FOREST of the tableland a mile back from the ocean old Kerchak, the ape, was on a rampage of rage among his people.

The younger and lighter members of his tribe scampered to the higher branches of the great trees to escape his wrath, risking their lives upon branches that scarce supported their weight rather than face old Kerchak in one of his fits of uncontrolled anger.

The other males scattered in all directions, but not before the infuriated brute had felt the vertebrae of one snap between his foaming jaws. A luckless young female slipped from an insecure hold upon a high branch and came crashing to the ground, almost at Kerchak's feet.

With a wild scream he was upon her, tearing a great piece from her side with his mighty teeth, and striking her viciously upon her head and shoulders with a broken tree-limb until her skull was crushed to a jelly.

Then he spied Kala, who, returning from a search for food with her young babe, was ignorant of the state of the mighty male's temper until the shrill warnings of her fellows caused her to scamper madly for safety.

But Kerchak was close upon her, so close that he had almost grasped her ankle had she not made a furious leap far into space from one tree to another—a perilous chance which apes seldom take, unless so closely pursued by danger that there is no other alternative.

She made the leap successfully, but as she grasped the limb of the further tree the sudden jar loosened the hold of the tiny babe where it clung frantically to her neck, and she saw the little thing hurled, turning and twisting, to the ground thirty feet below.

With a low cry of dismay Kala rushed headlong to its side, thoughtless now of the danger from Kerchak; but when she gathered the wee, mangled form to her bosom life had left it.

With low moans she sat cuddling the body to her, nor did Kerchak attempt to molest her. With the death of the babe his fit of demoniacal rage passed as suddenly as it had seized him.

Kerchak was a huge king ape, weighing perhaps three hundred and fifty pounds. His forehead was extremely low and receding, his eyes bloodshot, small and close set to his coarse, flat nose; his ears large and thin, but smaller than most of his kind.

His awful temper and his mighty strength made him supreme among the little tribe into which he had been born some twenty years before.

Now that he was in his prime, there was no simian in all the mighty forest through which he roved that dared contest his right to rule, nor did the other and larger animals molest him.

Old Tantor, the elephant, alone of all the wild, savage life, feared him not—and he alone did Kerchak fear. When Tantor trumpeted the great ape scurried with his fellows high among the trees of the second terrace.

The tribe of anthropoids, over which Kerchak ruled with an iron hand and bared fangs, numbered some six or eight families, each family consisting of an adult male with his wives and children—some sixty or seventy apes, all told.

Kala was the youngest wife of a male called Tublat, meaning "Broken-Nose," and the child she had seen dashed to death was her first, for she was but nine or ten years old.

Notwithstanding her youth, she was large and powerful—a splendid, clean-limbed animal, with a round, high forehead, which denoted more intelligence than most of her kind possessed. So, also, she had a greater capacity for mother love and mother sorrow.

But she was still an ape, a huge, fierce, terrible beast of a species closely allied to the gorilla, yet with more intelligence, which, with the strength of their cousins, made her kind the most fearsome of those awe-inspiring progenitors of man.

When the tribe saw that Kerchak's rage had ceased they came slowly down from their arboreal retreats and pursued again the various occupations which he had interrupted. The young played and frolicked about among the trees and bushes.

Some of the adults lay prone upon the soft mat of dead and decaying vegetation which covered the ground, while others turned over pieces of fallen branches and clods of earth in search of the small bugs and reptiles which formed a part of their food.

Others, again, searched the surrounding trees for fruit, nuts, small birds, and eggs.

They had passed an hour or so thus when Kerchak called them together, and, with a word of command to them to follow him, set off toward the sea.

They traveled for the most part upon the ground, where it was open, following the path of the great elephants whose comings and goings break the only roads through the tangled jungle mazes of bush, vine, creeper, and tree. When they walked it was a rolling, awkward motion, placing the knuckles of their closed hands upon the ground and swinging their ungainly bodies forward.

But when the way was through the lower trees they moved more swiftly, swinging from branch to branch with the agility of their smaller cousins, the monkeys. And all the way Kala carried her little dead baby hugged closely to her breast.

It was shortly after noon when they reached a ridge overlooking the beach, where, below them, lay the tiny cottage which was Kerchak's goal.

He had seen many of his kind go to their deaths before the loud noise made by the little black stick in the hands of the strange white ape who lived in that wonderful lair, and Kerchak had made up his brute mind to own that death-dealing contrivance and to explore the interior of the mysterious den.

He wanted to feel his teeth sink into the neck of the queer animal that he had learned to hate and fear, and, because of this, he came often with his tribe to reconnoiter, waiting for a time when the white ape should be off his guard.

Of late they had quit attacking, or even showing themselves; for every time they had done so in the past the little stick had roared out the terrible message of death to some member of the tribe.

To-day there was no sign of the man about, and from where they watched they could see that the cabin door was open. Slowly, cautiously, and noiselessly they crept through the jungle toward the little cabin.

There were no growls, no fierce screams of rage—the little black stick had taught them to come quietly, lest they awaken it.

On they came, until Kerchak himself slunk stealthily to the very door and peered within. Behind him were two males, and then Kala, closely straining the little dead form to her breast.

Inside the den they saw the strange white ape lying half across a table, his head buried in his arms; and on the bed lay a figure covered by a sail-cloth, while from a tiny rustic cradle came the plaintive wailing of a babe.

Noiselessly Kerchak entered crouching for the charge; and then John Clayton rose with a sudden start and faced them.

The sight that met his eyes must have frozen him with horror, for there, within the door, stood three great bull apes, while behind them crowded many more; how many he never knew, for his revolvers were hanging on the far wall beside his rifle, and Kerchak was charging.

When Kerchak released the limp form which had been John Clayton, Lord Greystoke, he turned his attention toward the little cradle; but Kala was there before him, and when he would have grasped the child she snatched it herself, and before he could intercept her she had bolted through the door and taken refuge in a high tree.

As she took up the little live baby of Alice Clayton she dropped the dead body of her own into the empty cradle.

The wail of the living had answered the call of universal motherhood within her wild breast which the dead could not still.

High up among the branches of a mighty tree she hugged the shrieking infant to her bosom, and soon the instinct that was as dominant in this fierce female as it had been in the breast of his tender and beautiful mother—the instinct of mother love—reached out to the tiny man-child's half-formed understanding, and he became quiet.

Then hunger closed the gap between them, and the son of an English lord and an English lady nursed at the breast of Kala, the great ape.

In the mean time the beasts within the cabin were warily examining the contents of this strange lair.

Once satisfied that Clayton was dead, Kerchak turned his attention to the thing which lay upon the bed, covered by a piece of sail-cloth.

Gingerly he lifted one corner of the shroud; but when he saw the body of the woman beneath he tore the cloth roughly from her form and seized the still, white throat in his huge, hairy hands.

A moment he let his fingers sink deep into the cold flesh, and then, realizing that she was already dead, he turned from her to examine the contents of the room; nor did he again molest the body of either Lady Alice or Sir John.

The rifle hanging upon the wall caught his first attention; it was for this strange, death-dealing thunder-stick that he had yearned for months; but, now that it was within his grasp, he scarcely had the temerity to seize it.

Cautiously he approached the thing, ready to flee precipitately should it speak in its roaring tones, as he had heard it speak before, the last words to those of his kind who, through ignorance or rashness, had attacked the wonderful white ape that had borne it.

Deep in the beast's intelligence was something which assured him that the thunder-stick was only dangerous when in the hands of one who could manipulate it; but yet it was several minutes ere he could bring himself to touch it.

Instead, he walked back and forth along the floor before it, turning his head so that never once did his eyes leave the object of his desire.

Using his long arms as a man uses crutches, and rolling his huge body from side to side with each stride, the great king ape paced to and fro, uttering deep growls, occasionally punctuated with that ear-piercing scream, than which there is no more terrifying noise in all the jungle.

Presently he halted before the rifle. Slowly he raised a huge hand until it almost touched the shining barrel, only to withdraw it once more and continue his hurried pacing.

It was as though the great brute, by this show of fearlessness, and through the medium of his wild voice, were endeavoring to bolster his courage to the point which would permit him to take the rifle in his hand.

Again he stopped, and this time succeeded in forcing his reluctant hand to the cold steel, only to snatch it away almost immediately and resume his restless beat.

Time after time this strange ceremony was repeated, but on each occasion with increased confidence, until, finally, the rifle was torn from its hook and lay in the grasp of the great brute.

Finding that it harmed him not, Kerchak began to examine it closely. He felt of it from end to end, peered down the black depths of the muzzle, fingered the sights, the breach, the stock, and finally the trigger.

During all these operations the apes who had entered sat huddled near the door watching their chief, while those outside strained and crowded to catch a glimpse of what transpired within.

Suddenly Kerchak's finger closed upon the trigger, there was a deafening roar in the little room, and the apes at and beyond the door fell over one another in their wild anxiety to escape.

Kerchak was equally frightened; so frightened, in fact, that he quite forgot to throw aside the author of that fearful noise, but bolted for the door with it tightly clutched in one hand.

As he passed through the opening, the front sight of the rifle caught upon the edge of the inswung door with sufficient force to close it tightly after the fleeing ape.

When Kerchak came to a halt a short distance from the cabin, and discovered that he still held the rifle, he dropped it as though it had burned him, nor did he again essay to recover it. The noise had been too much for his brute nerves; but he was now quite convinced that the terrible stick was quite harmless by itself if left alone.

It was an hour before the apes could again bring themselves to approach the cabin to continue their investigations; and when they finally did so, they found to their chagrin that the door was closed and so securely fastened that they could not force it.

The cleverly constructed latch which Clayton had made for the door had sprung as Kerchak passed out; nor could the apes find means of ingress through the heavily barred windows.

After roaming about the vicinity for a short time, they started back for the deeper forests and the higher land from whence they had come.

Kala had not once come to earth with her little adopted babe, but now Kerchak called to her to descend with the rest; and as there was no note of anger in his voice, she dropped lightly from branch to branch and joined the others on their homeward march.

Those of the apes who attempted to examine Kala's strange baby were repulsed with bared fangs and menacing growls, accompanied by words of warning from Kala.

When they assured her that they meant the child no harm she permitted them to come close, but would not allow them to touch her charge.

It was as though she knew that her baby was frail and delicate, and feared lest the rough hands of her fellows might injure the little thing.

Another thing she did, and which made traveling an onerous trial for her. Remembering the death of her own little one, she clung desperately to the new babe, with one hand, whenever they were upon the march.

The other young rode upon their mothers' backs, their little arms tightly clasping the hairy necks before them, while their legs were locked beneath their mothers' armpits.

Not so with Kala. She held the small form of the little Lord Greystoke tightly to her breast, where the dainty hands clutched the long black hair that covered her. She had seen one child fall from her back to terrible death, and she would take no further chances with this one.

CHAPTER 5

The White Ape

TENDERLY KALA NURSED her little waif, wondering silently why it did not gain strength and agility as did the little apes of other mothers. It was nearly a year from the time the little fellow came into her possession before he would walk alone; and as for climbing—my, but how stupid he was!

Kala sometimes talked with the older females about her young hopeful, but none of them could understand how a child could be so slow and backward in learning to care for itself. Why, it could not even find food alone, and more than twelve moons had passed since Kala had come upon it.

Had they known that the child had seen thirteen moons before it had come into Kala's possession, they would have considered its case as absolutely hopeless, for the little apes of their own tribe were as far advanced in two or three moons as was this little stranger after twenty-five.

Tublat, Kala's husband, was sorely vexed, and but for the female's careful watching would have put the child out of the way.

"He will never be a great ape," he argued. "Always will you have to carry him and protect him. What good will he be to the tribe? None; only a burden.

"Let us leave him quietly sleeping among the tall grasses, that you may bear other and stronger apes to guard us in our old age."

"Never, Broken-Nose," replied Kala. "If I must carry him forever, so be it."

Tublat went to Kerchak to urge him to use his authority with Kala, and force her to give up little Tarzan, which was the name they had given to the tiny Lord Greystoke, and which meant "White-Skin."

But when Kerchak spoke to her about it Kala threatened to run away from the tribe if they did not leave her in peace with the child; and as this is one of the unalienable rights of the junglefolk, if they be dissatisfied among their own people, they bothered her no more, for Kala was a fine clean-limbed young female, and they did not wish to lose her.

As Tarzan grew he made more rapid strides, so that by the time he was ten years old he was an excellent climber, and on the ground could do many wonderful things which were beyond the powers of his little brothers and sisters.

In many ways did he differ from them, and they often marveled at his superior cunning, but in strength and size he was deficient; for at ten the great anthropoids were fully grown, some of them towering over six feet in height, while little Tarzan was still but a half-grown boy.

Yet such a boy!

From early infancy he had used his hands to swing from branch to branch after the manner of his giant mother, and as he grew older he spent hour upon hour daily speeding through the tree-tops with his brothers and sisters.

He could spring twenty feet across space at the dizzy heights of the forest top, and grasp with unerring precision, and without apparent jar, a limb waving wildly in the path of an approaching tornado.

He could drop twenty feet at a stretch from limb to limb in rapid descent to the ground, or he could gain the utmost pinnacle of the loftiest tropical giant with the ease and swiftness of a squirrel. Though but ten years old he was fully as strong as the average man of thirty, and far more agile than the most practised athlete ever becomes. And day by day his strength was increasing.

His life among the fierce apes had been happy; for his recollection held no other life, nor did he know that there existed within the universe aught else than his little forest and the wild jungle animals with which he was familiar.

He was nearly ten before he commenced to realize that a great difference existed between himself and his fellows. His little body, burned almost black by exposure, suddenly caused him feelings of intense shame, for he realized that it was entirely hairless, like some low snake or reptile.

He attempted to obviate this by plastering himself from head to foot with mud, but this soon dried and fell off. Beside, it felt so uncomfortable that he quickly decided that he preferred the shame to the discomfort.

In the higher land which his tribe frequented was a little lake, and it was here that Tarzan first saw his face in the clear, still waters of its bosom.

It was on a sultry day of the dry season that he and one of his cousins had gone down to the bank to drink. As they leaned over, both little faces were mirrored on the placid pool; the fierce and terrible features of the ape beside those of the aristocratic scion of an old English house.

Tarzan was appalled. It had been bad enough to be hairless, but to own such a countenance! He wondered that the other apes could look at him at all.

That tiny slit of a mouth and those puny white teeth! How

they looked beside the mighty lips and powerful fangs of his more fortunate brothers!

And the little pinched nose of him; so thin was it that it looked half starved. He turned red as he compared it with the beautiful broad nostrils of his companion. Such a generous nose! Why, it spread half across his face! It certainly must be fine to be so handsome, thought poor little Tarzan.

But when he saw his own eyes—ah! that was the final blow— a brown spot, a gray circle, and then blank whiteness! Frightful! Not even the snakes had such hideous eyes as he.

So intent was he upon this personal appraisement of his features that he did not hear the parting of the tall grass behind him as a great body pushed itself stealthily through the jungle; nor did his companion, the ape, hear either, for he was drinking, and the noise of his sucking lips drowned the quiet approach of the intruder.

Not thirty paces behind the two he crouched—Sabor, the tiger— lashing his tail. Cautiously he moved a great padded paw forward, noiselessly placing it before he lifted the next. Thus he advanced; his belly low, almost touching the surface of the ground—a great cat preparing to spring upon its prey.

Now he was within ten feet of the two unsuspecting little play-fellows—carefully he drew his hind feet well up beneath his body, the great muscles rolling under the beautiful skin of black and yellow! So low he was crouching that he seemed flattened to the earth except for the upward bend of the glossy back as it gathered for the spring.

No longer the tail lashed—quiet and straight behind him it lay.

An instant he paused thus as though turned to stone, and then, with an awful scream, he sprang.

Sabor, the tiger, was a wise hunter. To one less wise the wild alarm of his fierce cry as he sprang would have seemed a foolish thing, for could he not more surely have fallen upon his victims had he but quietly leaped without that loud shriek?

But Sabor knew well the wondrous quickness of the junglefolk and their almost unbelievable powers of hearing. To them the sudden scraping of one blade of grass across another were as effectual a warning as his loudest cry, and Sabor knew that he could not make that leap without a little noise.

His wild scream was not a warning, but instead was meant to freeze his poor victims in a paralysis of terror for the tiny fraction of an instant, which would suffice for his mighty claws to sink into their soft flesh and hold them beyond peradventure of escape.

In so far as the ape was concerned Sabor reasoned correctly. The little fellow crouched trembling just an instant, but that instant was quite long enough to prove his undoing.

Not so, however, with Tarzan, the man-child. His life amidst the dangers of the jungle had taught him to meet emergencies with self-confidence, and his higher intelligence resulted in a quickness of mental action far beyond the powers of the apes.

So the scream of Sabor, the tiger, galvanized the brain and muscles of little Tarzan into instant action.

Before him lay the deep waters of the little lake, behind him certain death; a cruel death beneath tearing claws and rending fangs.

Tarzan had always hated water except as a medium for quenching his thirst. He hated it because he connected it with the chill and discomfort of the torrential rains, and he feared it for the thunder and lightning and wind which accompanied it.

The deep waters of the lake he had been taught by his wild mother to avoid, and further, had he not seen little Neeta sink beneath its quiet surface only a few short weeks before never to return to the tribe?

But of the two evils his quick mind chose the lesser, and before the great beast had covered half his leap Tarzan felt the chill waters close above his head.

He could not swim, and the water was very deep; but still he lost no particle of that self-confidence and resourcefulness which were the badges of his superior being.

Rapidly he moved his hands and feet in an attempt to scramble upward, and, possibly more by chance than design, he fell into the stroke that a dog uses when swimming, so that within a few seconds his nose was above water and he found that he could keep it there by continuing his strokes, and also make progress through the water.

He was much surprised and pleased with this new acquirement which had been so suddenly thrust upon him, but he had no time for thinking much upon it.

He was now swimming parallel to the bank, and there he saw the cruel beast that would have seized him crouching upon the still form of his playmate.

The tiger was intently watching Tarzan, evidently expecting him to return to shore; but this the boy had no intention of doing.

Instead he raised his voice in the call of distress common to his tribe, adding to it the warning which would prevent would-be rescuers from running into the clutches of Sabor.

Almost immediately there came an answer from the distance, and presently forty or fifty great apes swung rapidly and majestically through the trees toward the scenes of tragedy.

In the van was Kala, for she had recognized the tones of her best-beloved, and with her was the mother of the little ape who lay dead beneath cruel Sabor.

Though more powerful and better equipped for fighting than the apes, the tiger had no desire to meet these enraged adults, and with a snarl of hatred he sprang quickly into the brush and disappeared.

Tarzan now swam to shore and clambered quickly upon dry land. The feeling of freshness and exhilaration which the cool waters had imparted to him, filled his being with grateful surprise, and ever after he lost no opportunity to take a daily plunge in lake or stream or ocean when it was possible to do so.

For a long time Kala could not accustom herself to the sight; for though her people could swim when forced to it, they did not like to enter water; and never did so voluntarily.

The adventure with the tiger gave Tarzan food for pleasurable memories, for it was such affairs which broke the monotony of his daily life, which otherwise would have been but a dull round of searching for food, eating, and sleeping.

The tribe to which he belonged roamed a tract extending, roughly, twenty-five miles along the seacoast and some fifty miles inland. This they traversed almost continually, seldom remaining long in one locality; but as they moved through the trees with great speed they often covered the territory in a very few days. Again they would remain for months in the same locality.

Much depended upon food supply, climatic conditions, and the prevalence of animals of the more dangerous species; though Kerchak often led them on long marches for no other reason than that he had tired of remaining in the same place.

At night they slept where darkness overtook them, lying upon the ground, and sometimes covering their heads, and more seldom their bodies, with the great leaves of the elephant's ear. Two or three might lie cuddled in each other's arms for additional warmth if the night were chill, and thus Tarzan had slept in Kala's arms nightly for all these years.

That the huge fierce brute loved this child of another race is beyond question, and he, too, gave to the great, hairy beast all the affection that would have belonged to his fair young mother had she lived.

When he was disobedient she cuffed him, it is true, but she was never cruel to him, and was more often caressing than chastising him.

Tublat, her husband, always hated Tarzan, and on several occasions had come near ending his youthful career.

Tarzan on his part never lost an opportunity to show that he fully reciprocated his foster-father's sentiments, and whenever he could safely annoy him or make faces at him or hurl insults upon him from the safety of his mother's arms or the slender branches of the higher trees, he did so.

His superior intelligence and cunning permitted him to invent a thousand diabolical tricks to add to the burdens of Tublat's life.

Early in his boyhood he had learned to form ropes by twisting and tying long grasses together, and with these he was forever tripping Tublat or attempting to hang him from some overhanging branch.

By constant playing and experimenting with these he learned to tie rude knots, and make sliding nooses, and with these he and the younger apes amused themselves. What Tarzan did they tried to do also, but he alone originated and became proficient.

One day while playing thus Tarzan had thrown his rope at one of his fleeing companions, retaining the other end in his grasp. By accident the noose fell squarely about the running ape's neck, bringing him to a sudden and surprising halt.

Ah, here was a new game, a fine game, thought Tarzan, and immediately he attempted to repeat the trick. And thus, by painstaking and continued practise, he learned the art of roping.

Now, indeed, was the life of Tublat a living nightmare. In sleep, upon the march, night or day, he never knew when that quiet noose would slip about his neck and nearly choke the life out of him. Kala punished, Tublat swore dire vengeance, and old Kerchak took notice and warned and threatened; but all to no avail.

Tarzan defied them all, and the thin, strong noose continued to settle about Tublat's neck whenever he least expected it. The other apes derived unlimited amusement from Tublat's discomfiture, for Broken-Nose was a disagreeable old fellow, whom no one liked, anyway.

In Tarzan's clever little mind many thoughts revolved, and back of these was his divine power of reason.

If he could catch his fellow apes with his long arm of many grasses, why not Sabor, the tiger?

It was the germ of a thought, which, however, was destined to mull round in his conscious and subconscious minds until it resulted in magnificent achievement.

But that came in later years.

CHAPTER 6

Jungle Battles

THE WANDERINGS OF the tribe brought them often near the closed and silent cabin by the little landlocked harbor. To Tarzan this was always a source of never-ending mystery and pleasure.

He would peek into the curtained windows, or, climbing upon the roof, peer down the black depths of the chimney in vain endeavor to solve the unknown wonders that lay within those strong walls.

His little childish imagination pictured wonderful creatures within, and the very impossibility of forcing entrance added a thousandfold to his desire to do so.

He would clamber about the roof and windows for hours attempting to discover means of ingress, but to the door he paid little attention, for this was apparently as solid as the walls.

It was in the next visit to the vicinity following the adventure with old Sabor that, as he approached the cabin, Tarzan noticed that from a distance the door appeared as though an independent part of the wall in which it was set, and for the first time it occurred to him that this might prove the means of entrance which had so long eluded him.

He was alone, as was often the case when he visited the cabin. The apes had no love for it, the story of the thunder-stick, having lost nothing in the telling during these ten years, had quite surrounded the white man's deserted cabin with an atmosphere of weirdness and terror for the simians.

The story of his own connection with the cabin had never been told him, for the language of the apes has few words, and so they could talk but little of what they had seen in the cabin, for they had no words accurately to describe either the strange people or their belongings, and so, long before Tarzan was old enough to understand, the subject had been forgotten by the tribe.

Only in a dim, vague way had Kala explained to him that his father had been a strange white ape, but he did not know that Kala was not his own mother.

On this day, then, he went directly to the door and spent hours examining it and fussing with the hinges, the knob, and the latch. Finally he stumbled upon the right combination and the door swung creakingly open before his astonished eyes.

For some minutes he did not dare venture within, but finally, as his eyes became accustomed to the dim light of the interior he slowly and cautiously entered.

In the middle of the floor lay a skeleton, every vestige of flesh gone from the bones to which still clung the mildewed remnants of what had once been clothing; upon the bed lay a similar gruesome thing, but smaller, while in a tiny cradle near by was a third, a wee mite of a skeleton.

To none of these evidences of an old tragedy did little Tarzan give but passing heed. His wild jungle life had inured him to the sight of dead and dying animals, and had he known that he was looking upon the remains of his own father and mother he would have been no more greatly moved.

The furnishings and other contents of the room it was which riveted his attention. He examined many things minutely—strange tools and weapons, books, papers, clothing—what little had withstood the ravages of time in the humid atmosphere of the jungle coast.

He opened chests and cupboards, such as did not baffle his small experience, and in these he found the contents much better preserved.

Among other things he found a sharp hunting-knife, on the keen blade of which he immediately proceeded to cut his finger. Nothing daunted, he continued his experiments, finding that he could hack and hew splinters of wood from the table and chairs with this new toy.

For a long time this amused him, but finally tiring he continued his explorations. In a cupboard filled with books he came across one with brightly colored pictures—it was a child's illustrated alphabet—

A is for Archer
Who shoots with a bow.
B is for Boy.
His first name is Joe.

The pictures interested him greatly.

There were many apes with faces similar to his own, and farther over in the book he found, under "M," some little monkeys such as he saw daily flitting through the trees of his primeval forest. But nowhere was pictured any of his own people: in all the book was none that resembled Kerchak or Tublat or Kala.

At first he tried to pick the little figures from the paper, but he soon saw that they were not real, though he knew not what they might be, nor had he any words to describe them.

The boats and trains and cows and horses were quite meaningless to him, but not quite so baffling as the odd little figures which appeared beneath and between the colored pictures—some strange kind of bugs he thought they might be, for many of them had legs, though nowhere could he find one with eyes and a mouth. It was his first introduction to the letters of the alphabet, and he was over ten years old.

Of course he had never before seen print, or never had spoken with any living thing which had the remotest idea that such a thing as a written language existed, and never had he seen any one reading.

So what wonder that the little boy was quite at a loss to guess the meaning of these strange figures.

Near the back of the book he found his old enemy, Sabor, the tiger, and, just above him, coiled Histah, the snake.

Oh, it was most engrossing! Never before in all his ten years had he enjoyed anything so much. So absorbed was he that he did not note the approaching dusk, until it was quite upon him.

He put the book back in the cupboard and closed the door, for he did not wish any one else to find and destroy his treasure, and as he went out into the gathering darkness he closed the great door of the cabin behind him as it had been before he discovered the secret of its lock, but before he left he had noticed the hunting-knife lying where he had thrown it upon the floor, and this he picked up and took with him to show to his fellows.

He had taken scarce a dozen steps toward the jungle when a

great form rose up before him from the shadows of a low bush.

At first he thought it was one of his own people, but in another instant he realized that it was a huge gorilla.

So close was he that there was no chance for flight, and little Tarzan knew that he must stand and fight for his life; for these great beasts were the deadly enemies of his tribe, and neither one or the other ever asked or gave quarter.

Had Tarzan been a full-grown bull ape of the species of his tribe he would have been more than a match for the gorilla, but being only a little English boy, though enormously muscular for such, he stood no show against his cruel antagonist. In his veins, however, flowed the blood of the best of a race of mighty fighters, and back of this was the training of his short lifetime among the fierce brutes of the jungle.

He knew no fear, as we know it; his heart beat the faster, but from the excitement and exhilaration of adventure. Had the opportunity presented itself he would have escaped, but solely because his judgment told him he was no match for the great thing which confronted him. And as flight was out of the question, he faced the gorilla squarely and bravely without a tremor of a single muscle, or any sign of panic.

In fact, he met the brute midway in its charge, striking its huge body with his closed fists and as futilely as if he had been a fly attacking an elephant. But in one hand he still clutched the knife he had found, and as the brute, striking and biting, closed upon him, the boy accidentally turned the point toward the hairy beast.

As it sank deep into the body of him, the gorilla shrieked in pain and rage.

But the boy had learned in that brief second a use for his sharp and shining toy, so that, as the tearing, striking beast dragged him to earth he plunged the blade repeatedly into its breast.

The gorilla, fighting after the manner of its kind, struck terrific blows with its open hand, and tore the flesh at the boy's throat and chest with its mighty tusks.

For a moment they rolled upon the ground in the fierce frenzy of combat. More and more weakly the torn and bleeding arm struck home with the long sharp blade, then the little figure stiffened with a spasmodic jerk, and Tarzan, the young Lord Greystoke, rolled senseless upon the dead and decaying vegetation which carpeted his jungle home.

A mile back in the forest the tribe had heard the fierce challenge of the gorilla, and, as was his custom when any danger threatened, Kerchak called his people together, partly for mutual protection against a common enemy, since this gorilla might be but one of several, and also to see that all members of the tribe were accounted for.

It was soon discovered that Tarzan was missing, and Tublat was strongly opposed to sending assistance. Kerchak himself had no liking for the strange little waif, so he listened to Tublat, and finally, with a shrug of his shoulders, turned back to the pile of leaves on which he had made his bed.

But Kala was of a different mind. In fact, she had waited but to learn that Tarzan was absent ere she was fairly flying through the matted branches toward the point from which the cries of the gorilla were still plainly audible.

Darkness had fallen, and an early moon was sending its faint light to cast strange, grotesque shadows among the dense foliage of the forest.

Here and there the brilliant rays penetrated to earth, but for the most part they only served to accentuate the Stygian blackness of the jungle.

Like some huge fantom, Kala swung noiselessly from tree to tree, now running nimbly along a great branch, now swinging through space at the end of another, to grasp that of a further tree in her rapid progress toward the tragedy her knowledge of jungle life told her was being enacted.

The cries of the gorilla had told her plainly that it was in mortal combat with some other denizen of the fierce wood. Suddenly the cries ceased, and the silence of death reigned throughout the jungle.

Kala could not understand, for the voice of the gorilla had at the last been raised in the agony of suffering and death; but no sound had come to her by which she possibly could determine the nature of his antagonist.

That her little Tarzan could destroy a great bull gorilla she knew to be improbable; and, so, as she neared the spot from which the sounds of the struggle had come, she moved more warily. With extreme caution she traversed the lowest branches, peering eagerly into the moon-splashed blackness for a sign of the combatants.

Presently she came upon them, lying in an open space full under the brilliant moon—Tarzan's torn and bloody form, and beside it a great bull gorilla, stone dead. With a low cry Kala rushed to Tarzan's side, and, gathering the poor, blood-covered body to her breast, listened for a sign of life. Faintly she heard it—the weak beating of the little heart.

Tenderly she bore him back through the inky jungle to where the tribe lay, and for many days and nights she sat guard beside him, bringing him food and water, and brushing the flies and other insects from his cruel wounds.

Of medicine or surgery the poor thing knew nothing. She could but lick the wounds, and thus she kept them cleansed, that healing nature might the more quickly do her work.

At first Tarzan would eat nothing, but rolled and tossed in a wild delirium of fever. All he craved was water, and this she brought him in the only way she could, bearing it in her own mouth.

No human mother could have shown more unselfish and sacrificing devotion than did this poor wild brute for the little orphaned waif whom fate had thrown into her keeping.

At last the fever abated, and the boy commenced to mend. No complaint passed his tight-set lips, though the pain of his wounds was excruciating.

A portion of his chest was laid bare to the ribs, three of which had been broken by the mighty blows of the gorilla; one arm was nearly severed by the giant fangs, and a great piece had been torn from his neck, exposing his jugular vein, which the cruel jaws had missed but by a miracle.

With the stoicism of the brutes who had raised him, he endured his suffering quietly, preferring to crawl away from the others and lie huddled in some clump of tall grasses rather than to show his misery before their eyes.

Kala, alone, he was glad to have with him.

CHAPTER 7

The Light of Knowledge

AFTER WHAT SEEMED an eternity to the little sufferer he was once more able to walk, and from then on his recovery was rapid, so that in another month he was as strong and active as ever.

During his convalescence he had gone over in his mind many times the battle with the gorilla, and his first thought was to recover the wonderful little weapon which had transformed him from a hopelessly outclassed weakling to the superior of the mighty terror of the jungle.

Also, he was anxious to return to the cabin and continue his investigations of the wondrous contents.

So, early one morning, he set forth alone upon his quest. After a little search he located the clean-picked bones of his late adversary, and close by, partly buried beneath the fallen leaves, he found the knife, now red with rust from its exposure to the dampness of the ground and from the dried blood of the gorilla.

He did not like the change in its former bright and gleaming surface; but it was still a formidable weapon, and one which he meant to use to advantage whenever the opportunity presented itself. He had in mind that no more would he run from the wanton attacks of old Tublat.

In another moment he was at the cabin, and after a short time had again thrown the latch and entered. His first concern was to learn the mechanism of the lock, and this he did by examining it closely, while the door was open so that he could learn precisely what caused it to hold the door and by what means it released at his touch.

He found that he could close and lock the door from within, and this he did so that there would be no chance of his being molested while at his investigations.

He commenced a systematic search of the cabin; but his attention was soon riveted by the books which seemed to exert a strange and powerful influence over him, so that he could scarce attend to aught else for the lure of the wondrous puzzle which their purpose presented to him.

Among the other books were a primer, some child's readers, numerous picture-books, and a great dictionary. All of these he examined; but the pictures caught his fancy most, though the strange little bugs which covered the pages where there were no pictures excited his wonder and deepest thought.

Squatting upon his haunches on the table-top—his smooth, brown, naked body bent over the book which rested in his strong, slender hands, and his great shock of long, black hair falling about his well-shaped head and bright, intelligent eyes—Tarzan of the apes, little primitive man, presented a picture filled at once with pathos and with promise—an allegorical figure of the primordial groping through the black night of ignorance toward the light of learning.

His face was tense in study, for he had grasped in a hazy, nebulous way the rudiments of a thought which was destined to prove the key and the solution to the puzzling problem of the strange little bugs.

In his hands was a primer opened at a picture of a little ape similar to himself, but covered, except for hands and face, with strange, colored fur, for such he thought the jacket and trousers to be.

Beneath the picture were three little bugs:

BOY

And now he had discovered in the text upon the page that these three were repeated many times in the same sequence.

Another fact he learned, and that was that there were comparatively few individual bugs; but these were repeated many times, occasionally alone, but more often in company with others.

Slowly he turned the pages, scanning the pictures and the text for a repetition of the combination b-o-y; presently he found it beneath a picture of another little ape and a strange animal which went upon four legs like the jackal, and somewhat resembled him. Beneath this picture the bugs appeared as—

A BOY AND A DOG

There they were, the three little bugs which always accompanied the little ape.

And so he progressed very, very slowly, for it was a hard and laborious task which he had set himself without knowing it—a task which might seem to you or to me impossible—learning to read without having the slightest knowledge of letters or written language, or the faintest idea that such things existed.

He did not accomplish it in a day, or in a week, or in a month, or in a year; but slowly, very slowly, he learned.

By the time he was fifteen he knew the various combinations of letters which stood for every pictured figure in the little primer and in one or two of the picture-books.

Of the meaning and use of the articles and conjunctions, verbs, adverbs, and pronouns he had but the faintest and haziest conception.

One day when he was about twelve he found a number of lead-pencils in a hitherto undiscovered drawer beneath the table, and in scratching upon the table with one of them he was delighted to discover the black line it left behind it.

He worked so assiduously with this new toy that the table-top was soon a mass of scrawly loops and irregular lines and his pencil-point worn down to the wood. Then he took another pencil, but this time he had a definite object in view.

He would attempt to reproduce some of the little bugs that scrambled over the pages of his books.

It was a difficult task, for he held the pencil as one would grasp the hilt of a dagger, which does not add greatly to ease in writing nor to the legibility of the results.

But he persevered for months, at such times as he was able to come to the cabin, until at last by repeated experimenting he found a position in which to hold the pencil that best permitted him to guide and control it; so that at last he could roughly reproduce any of the little bugs.

Thus he made a beginning at writing.

Copying the bugs taught him another thing, their number; and, though he could not count as we understand it, yet he had an idea of quantity, the base of his calculations being the number of fingers upon one of his hands.

His search through the various books convinced him that he had discovered all the different kinds of bugs most often repeated in combination, and he arranged them in proper order with great ease because of the frequency with which he had perused the fascinating alphabet picture-book.

His education progressed—but his greatest finds were in the inexhaustable storehouse of the huge illustrated dictionary; for he learned more through the medium of pictures than text, even after he had grasped the significance of the bugs.

When he discovered the arrangement of words in alphabetical order he delighted in searching for and finding the combinations with which he was familiar, and the words which followed them, their definitions, led him still further into the mazes of erudition.

By the time he was seventeen he had learned to read the simple child's primer and had fully realized the true and wonderful purpose of the bugs.

No longer did he feel shame for his hairless body or his human features, for now his reason told him that he was of a different race from his wild and hairy companions. He was a "M-A-N," they were "A-P-E-S," and the little apes which scurried through the forest top were "M-O-N-K-E-Y-S." He knew, too, that old Sabor was a "T-I-G-E-R," and Histah a "S-N-A-K-E," and Tantor an "E-L-E-P-H-A-N-T."

From then on his progress was rapid. With the help of the great dictionary and the active intelligence of a healthy mind endowed by inheritance with more than ordinary reasoning powers he shrewdly guessed at much which he could not really understand, and more often than not his guesses were close to the mark of truth.

There were many breaks in his education, caused by the migratory habits of his tribe, but even when removed from recourse to his books his active brain continued to search out the mysteries of his fascinating avocation.

Pieces of bark and flat leaves, and even smooth stretches of flat earth provided him with copy-books whereon to scratch with the point of his hunting-knife the lessons he was learning.

Nor did he neglect the sterner duties of life while following the bent of his inclination toward the solving of the mystery of his library.

He practised with his rope and played with his sharp knife, which he had learned to keep keen by whetting upon flat stones.

The tribe had grown larger since Tarzan had come among them.

Under the leadership of Kerchak they had been able to frighten the other tribes from their part of the jungle so that they had plenty to eat and little or no loss from predatory incursions of neighbors.

The younger males as they became adult found it more comfortable to take wives from their own tribe, or, if they captured one of another tribe, to bring her back to Kerchak's band and live in amity rather than attempt to set up new establishments of their own or make war upon the redoubtable Kerchak.

Occasionally one more ferocious than his fellows would attempt this latter alternative, but none had come yet who could wrest the palm of victory from the fierce and brutal ape.

Tarzan held a peculiar position in the tribe.

They seemed to consider him one of them and yet in some way different. The older males either ignored him entirely or else hated him so vindictively that but for his wonderous agility and speed and the fierce protection of the huge Kala he would have been despatched at an early age.

Tublat was his most consistent enemy, but it was through Tublat that, when he was about thirteen, the persecution of his enemies suddenly ceased and he was left severely alone, except on the occasions when one of them ran amuck in the throes of one of those strange fits of insane rage which attack the males of many of the fiercer animals of the jungle. Then none was safe.

On the day that Tarzan established his right to respect, the tribe was gathered about a small natural amphitheater which the jungle had left free from its entangling vines and creepers.

The space was almost circular in shape. Upon every hand rose the mighty giants of the untouched forest, with the matted undergrowth banked so closely that the only opening into the arena was through the upper branches of the trees.

Here, safe from interruption, the tribe often gathered. In the center of the amphitheater was one of those strange earthen drums which the anthropoids build for the queer rites the sounds of which men have heard in the fastnesses of the jungle, but which none has ever witnessed.

Many travelers have seen the drums of the great apes, and some have heard the sounds of its beating and the noise of the weird revelry of these first lords of the jungle, but Tarzan, Lord Greystoke, is, doubtless, the only human being who ever joined in the fierce intoxication of the Dum-Dum.

From this primitive function has risen, unquestionably, all the forms and ceremonials of modern church and state. Down through the countless ages from beyond the uttermost ramparts of a dawning humanity our hand forebears danced the rites of the Dum-Dum to the sound of their earthen drums, beneath the bright light of a tropical moon in the depth of the mighty jungles.

On the day that Tarzan won his emancipation from the persecution that had followed him remorselessly for twelve of his thirteen years of life, the tribe, now a full hundred strong, trooped silently through the lower terrace of the jungle-trees and dropped noiselessly upon the floor of the amphitheater.

The rites of the Dum-Dum marked important events in the life of the tribe—a victory, the capture of a prisoner, the killing of some large, fierce denizen of the jungle, the death or accession of a king.

To-day it was the killing of a giant ape, a member of another tribe, and as the people of Kerchak entered the arena, two mighty bulls might have been seen bearing the body of the vanquished between them. They laid their burden before the earthen drum and then squatted beside it as guards, while the other members of the community curled themselves in grassy nooks to sleep until the rising moon should give the signal for the commencement of the orgy.

For hours absolute quiet reigned in the little clearing, except as it was broken by the discordant notes of parrots or the screeching and twittering of the thousand jungle birds flitting ceaselessly among the vivid orchids and flamboyant blossoms which festooned the moss-covered branches.

At length, as darkness settled upon the jungle, the apes commenced to bestir themselves, and soon they formed a great circle about the earthen drum.

The females and young squatted in a thin line at the outer periphery of the circle, while just in front of them ranged the adult males. Before the drum sat three old females, each armed with a knotted branch fifteen or eighteen inches in length.

Slowly and softly they began tapping upon the resounding surface of the drum as the first faint rays of the ascending moon silvered the tree-tops.

As the light increased the females augmented the frequency and force of their blows until presently a rhythmical din pervaded the jungle for miles in every direction. Huge brutes stopped in their hunting, with up-pricked ears and raised heads, to listen to the dull booming that betokened the Dum-Dum of the apes.

Occasionally one would raise his shrill scream or thunderous roar in answering challenge to the savage din of the anthropoids, but none came near to investigate or attack, for the great apes, assembled in all the power of their numbers, filled the breasts of their jungle neighbors with deep respect.

As the din of the drum rose to almost deafening volume Kerchak sprang into the open space between the squatting males and the drummers.

Standing erect he threw his head far back, and looking full into the eye of the rising moon, he beat upon his breast with his great hairy paws and emitted his fearful roaring shriek.

Once—twice—thrice that terrifying cry rang out across the teeming solitude of that unspeakably quick, yet unthinkably dead, world.

Then, crouching, Kerchak slunk noiselessly round the open circle, veering far away from the dead body lying before the altar-drum, but, as he passed, keeping his little, fierce, wicked, red eyes upon the corpse.

Another male then sprang into the arena, and, repeating the horrid cries of his king, followed stealthily in his wake. Another and another followed in quick succession until the jungle reverberated with the now almost ceaseless notes of their bloodthirsty screams.

It was the challenge and the hunt.

When all the adult males had joined in the thin line of circling dancers the attack commenced.

Kerchak, seizing a huge club from the pile which lay at hand for the purpose, rushed furiously upon the dead ape, dealing the corpse a terrific blow, at the same time emitting the growls and snarls of combat!

The din of the drum was now increased, as well as the frequency of the blows, and the warriors, as each approached the victim of the hunt and delivered his bludgeon blow, joined in the mad whirl of the death dance.

Tarzan was one of the wild, leaping horde. His brown, sweat-streaked, muscular body glistening in the moonlight, shone supple and graceful among the uncouth, awkward, hairy brutes about him.

None more craftily stealthy in the mimic hunt, none more ferocious than he in the fierceness of the attack, none leaped higher into the air in the dance of death.

As the noise and rapidity of the drum-beats increased, the dancers apparently became intoxicated with the rhythm and the savage yells. Their leaps and bounds increased, their bared fangs dripped, and their lips and breasts were flecked with foam.

For half an hour the weird dance went on, until, at a sign from Kerchak, the noise of the drums ceased, the female drummers scampering hurriedly through the line of dancers toward the outer rim of squatting spectators. Then, as one man, the males rushed headlong upon the thing which their terrific blows had reduced to a mass of hairy pulp.

Flesh seldom came to their jaws in satisfying quantities, so a fit finale to their wild revel was a taste of fresh-killed meat, and it was to the purpose of devouring their late enemy that they now turned their attention.

Tarzan, more than the apes, craved and needed flesh. Descended from a race of meat-eaters, never in his life, he thought, had he once satisfied his appetite for animal food, and so now his agile little body wormed its way far into the mass of struggling apes in an endeavor to obtain a share which his strength would have been unequal to the task of winning for him.

At his side hung the hunting-knife of his unknown father in a sheath self-fashioned in copy of one he had seen among the pictures of his treasure-books.

At last he reached the fast-disappearing feast and with his sharp knife slashed off a more generous portion than he had hoped for.

Then he wriggled out from beneath the struggling mass, clutching his prize close.

Among those circling futilely the outskirts of the banqueters was old Tublat. He had been among the first at the feast, but had retreated with a goodly share to eat in quiet, and was now forcing his way back for more.

So it was that he spied Tarzan emerging from the clawing throng.

Tublat's bloodshot pig eyes sent out wicked gleams of hate as they fell upon the object of his loathing. In them, too, was greed for the meat the boy carried.

But Tarzan saw his arch enemy as quickly, and, divining what the beast would do, leaped nimbly away toward the women and children, hoping to hide himself among them. Tublat, however, was close upon him, so that he had no opportunity to seek a place of concealment, but saw that he would be put to it to escape at all.

Swiftly he sped toward the trees, and with a bound gained a lower limb with one hand, and then, transferring his burden to his teeth, he climbed rapidly upward, closely followed by Tublat.

Up, up he went to the waving pinnacle of a lofty monarch of the forest where his heavy pursuer dare not follow him. Perched there he hurled taunts and insults at the raging beast fifty feet below him.

And then Tublat went mad.

With horrifying screams and roars he rushed to the ground, and among the females and young, sinking his great fangs into a dozen tiny necks and tearing great pieces from the backs and breasts of the females who fell into his clutches.

In the brilliant moonlight Tarzan witnessed the mad carnival of rage. He saw the females and the young scamper to the safety of the trees, and then the great bulls in the center of the arena felt the mighty fangs of their demented fellow, and with one accord melted into the black shadows of the overhanging forest.

There was but one in the amphitheater beside Tublat, a belated female rushing swiftly toward the tree where Tarzan perched, and close behind her came the awful Tublat.

It was Kala, and as quickly as Tarzan saw that Tublat was gaining on her he dropped with the rapidity of a falling stone from branch to branch toward his foster-mother.

Now she was beneath the overhanging limbs, and close above her crouched Tarzan, waiting the outcome of the race.

She leaped into the air, grasping a low-hanging branch, but almost over the head of Tublat, so nearly had he distanced her. She should have been safe now, but there was a rending, tearing sound, the branch broke and precipitated her full upon the head of Tublat, knocking him to the ground.

Both were up in an instant; but as quick as they had been, Tarzan had been quicker, so that the infuriated bull found himself facing the man-child who stood between him and Kala.

Nothing could have suited the fierce beast better, and with a roar of triumph he leaped upon the little Lord Greystoke. But his fangs never closed in that nut-brown flesh.

A muscular hand shot out and grasped the hairy throat, and another plunged a keen hunting-knife a dozen times into the broad breast. Like lightning the blows fell, and only ceased when Tarzan felt the limp form crumple beneath him.

As the body rolled to the ground Tarzan of the apes placed his foot upon the neck of his lifelong enemy and, raising his eyes to the full moon, threw back his fierce young head, and voiced the wild cry of his people.

One by one the tribe swung down from their arboreal retreats and formed a circle about Tarzan and his vanquished foe. When they had all come Tarzan turned toward them.

"I am Tarzan," he cried. "I am a great killer. Let all respect Tarzan of the apes and Kala, his mother. There be none among you as mighty as Tarzan. Let his enemies beware."

Looking full into the wicked red eyes of Kerchak, the young

Tarzan of the apes placed his foot upon the neck of his lifelong enemy and voiced the wild cry of his people.

Lord Greystoke beat upon his mighty breast and screamed out once more his shrill cry of defiance.

CHAPTER 8

The Tree-Top Hunter

THE MORNING AFTER the Dum-Dum the tribe started slowly back through the forest toward the coast.

The body of Tublat lay where it had fallen, for the people of Kerchak did not eat their own dead.

The march was but a leisurely search for food. Cabbage-palm and gray plum, pisang and scitamine, they found in abundance, with wild pineapple, and occasionally small mammals, birds, eggs, reptiles, and insects. The nuts they cracked between their powerful jaws, or, if too hard, broke by pounding between stones.

Once old Sabor, crossing their path, sent them scurrying to the safety of the higher branches; for if he respected their number and their sharp fangs, they, on their part, held his cruel and mighty ferocity in equal esteem.

Upon a low-hanging branch sat Tarzan, directly above the majestic, supple body as it forged silently through the thick jungle. He hurled a pineapple at the ancient enemy of his people. The great breast stopped and, turning, eyed the taunting figure above him.

With an angry lash of his tail he bared his yellow fangs, curling his great lips in a hideous snarl that wrinkled his bristling snout in serried ridges, and closed his wicked eyes to two narrow slits of rage and hatred.

With back-laid ears, he looked into the eyes of Tarzan of the apes and sounded his fierce, shrill challenge.

And from the safety of his overhanging limb the ape-child sent back the fearsome answer of his kind.

For a moment the two eyed each other in silence, and then the great cat turned into the jungle, which swallowed him as the ocean engulfs a tossed pebble.

But into the mind of Tarzan a great plan sprang. He had killed the fierce Tublat, so was he not therefore a mighty fighter? Now would he track down the crafty Sabor, and slay him likewise. He would be a mighty hunter, also.

At the bottom of his little English heart beat the great desire to cover his nakedness with clothes, for he had learned from his picture-books that all men were so covered, while monkeys and apes and every other living thing went naked.

Clothes, therefore, must be truly a badge of greatness, the insignia of the superiority of man over all other animals; for surely there could be no other reason for wearing the hideous things.

Many moons ago, when he had been much smaller, he had desired the skin of Sabor, the tiger, or Numa, the lion, or Sheeta, the leopard, to cover his hairless body that he might no longer resemble hideous Histah, the snake. Now he was proud of his sleek skin, for it betokened his descent from a mighty race, and the conflicting desires to go naked in prideful proof of his ancestry, or to conform to the customs of his own kind and wear uncomfortable apparel, found first one and then the other in the ascendency.

As the tribe continued their slow way through the forest after the passing of Sabor, the tiger, Tarzan's head was filled with his great scheme for slaying his enemy, and for many days thereafter he thought of little else.

On this day, however, he presently had other and more immediate interests to attract his attention.

Of a sudden it became as midnight; the noises of the jungle ceased; the trees stood motionless, as though in paralyzed expectancy of some great and imminent disaster. All nature waited.

Faintly, from a distance, came a low, sad moaning. Nearer and nearer it approached, mounting louder and louder in volume.

The great trees bent in unison as though pressed earthward by a mighty hand. Further and further toward the ground they inclined, and still there was no sound save the deep and awesome moaning of the wind.

Then, suddenly, the jungle giants whipped back, lashing their mighty tops in angry and deafening protest. A vivid and blinding light flashed from the whirling, inky clouds above. The cannonade of thunder belched forth its fearsome challenge. The deluge came— an inferno broke loose upon the jungle.

The tribe huddled, shivering from the cold rain, at the base of great trees. The lightning, darting and flashing through the blackness, showed wildly waving branches, whipping streamers, and bending trunks.

Now and again some patriarch of the woods, rent by a flashing bolt, would crash in a thousand pieces among the surrounding trees, carrying down numberless branches and smaller neighbors to add to the tangle of the jungle.

Branches, great and small, hurtled through the verdure, carrying death and destruction to countless unhappy denizens of the world below.

For hours the fury of the storm continued without surcease, and still the tribe huddled close in shivering fear. In constant danger from falling trunks and branches, and paralyzed by the lightning and the bellowing thunder, they crouched in pitiful misery until the storm passed.

The end was as sudden as the beginning. The wind ceased; the sun shone forth—nature smiled once more.

The dripping leaves and branches and the moist petals of gorgeous flowers glistened in the splendor of the returning day. And so—as Nature forgot, her children forgot also. Busy life went on as it had before the darkness and the fright.

But to Tarzan a dawning light had come to explain the mystery of clothes. How snug he would have been beneath the heavy coat of Sabor, the tiger! And so was added a further incentive to the adventure.

For several months the tribe hovered near the beach where stood Tarzan's cabin, and his studies took up the greater portion of his time, but always when journeying through the forest he kept his rope in readiness, and many were the smaller animals that fell into the snare of the quick-thrown noose.

Once it fell about the short neck of Horta, the boar, and his mad lunge for freedom toppled Tarzan from the overhanging limbs where he had lain in wait and from whence he had launched his sinuous coil.

The mighty tusker turned at the sound of his falling body, and, seeing only the easy prey of a young ape, he lowered his head and charged madly at the surprised youth.

Tarzan, happily, was uninjured by the fall, alighting catlike upon all-fours far outspread to take up the shock. He was on his feet in an instant, and had gained the safety of a low limb as Horta, the boar, rushed futilely beneath.

Thus it was that Tarzan learned by experience the limitations as well as the possibilities of his strange weapon.

He lost a long rope on this occasion, but he knew that had it been Sabor, the tiger, who had thus dragged him from his perch, the outcome might have been very different, for he would have lost his life, doubtless, into the bargain.

It took him many days to braid a new rope, but when, finally, it was done, he went forth purposely to hunt, and lie in wait among the dense foliage of a great branch right above a well-beaten trail that led to water.

Several small animals passed unharmed beneath him. He did not want such insignificant game. It would take a strong animal to test the efficacy of his new scheme.

At last came he whom Tarzan sought, with lithe sinews rolling beneath shimmering hide; fat and glossy came Sabor, the tiger.

His great padded feet fell soft and noiseless on the narrow trail. His head was high in ever alert attention; his long tail moved slowly in sinuous and graceful undulations.

Nearer and nearer he came to where Tarzan of the apes crouched upon his limb, the coils of his long rope ready in his hand.

Like a thing of bronze, motionless as death, sat Tarzan. Sabor, the tiger, passed beneath. One stride beyond he took—a second, a third, and then the silent coil shot out above him.

For an instant the spreading noose hung above his head like a great snake, and then, as he looked upward to detect the origin of the swishing sound of the rope, it settled about his neck. With a quick jerk Tarzan snapped the noose tight about the snowy throat, and then he dropped the rope and clung to his support with both hands.

Sabor, the tiger, was trapped.

With a bound the startled beast turned into the jungle, but Tarzan was not to lose another rope through the same cause as the first. He had learned from experience.

Sabor, the tiger, had taken but half his second bound when he felt the rope tighten about his neck. His body turned completely over in the air, and he fell with a heavy crash upon his back. Tarzan had fastened the end of the rope securely to the trunk of the great tree on which he sat.

Thus far his plan had worked to perfection, but when he grasped the rope, bracing himself behind a crotch of two mighty branches, he found that dragging the mighty, struggling, clawing, biting, screaming mass of iron-muscled fury up to the tree and hanging him was a very different proposition.

The weight of old Sabor was immense, and when he braced his

huge paws nothing less than Tantor, the elephant, himself, could have budged him.

The tiger was now back in the path where he could see the author of the indignity which had been placed upon him. Screaming with rage he suddenly charged, leaping high into the air, but when his huge body struck the limb on which Tarzan had been, the boy was no longer there.

Instead he perched lightly upon a smaller branch twenty feet above the raging captive. For a moment Sabor hung himself across the branch, while Tarzan mocked, and hurled twigs and branches at his unprotected face.

Presently the beast dropped to the earth again, and Tarzan came quickly to seize the rope, but Sabor had now found that it was only a slender cord that held him, and grasping it in his huge jaws, severed it before Tarzan could tighten the strangling noose a second time.

Tarzan was much hurt. His well-laid plan had come to naught. He sat there screaming at the roaring creature beneath him and making mocking grimaces.

Sabor paced back and forth beneath the tree for hours. Four times he crouched and sprang at the dancing sprite above him, but he might as well have clutched at the illusive wind that murmured through the tree-tops.

At last Tarzan tired of the sport, and with a parting roar of challenge and a well-aimed ripe fruit that spread soft and sticky over the snarling face of his enemy, he swung rapidly through the trees, a hundred feet above the ground, and in a short time was among the members of his tribe.

Here he recounted the details of his adventure, with swelling chest and such considerable swagger that he quite impressed even his bitterest enemies, while Kala fairly danced for joy and pride.

CHAPTER 9

Man and Man

TARZAN OF THE apes lived on in his wild, jungle existence with little change for several years, only that he grew stronger and wiser, and learned from his books more and more of the strange worlds which lay somewhere outside his primeval forest.

To him life was never monotonous or stale. There was always Pisah, the fish, to be caught in the streams and the lakes, and Sabor, the tiger, with his ferocious cousins to keep one ever on the alert and give zest to every instant that one spent upon the ground.

Often they hunted him, and more often he hunted them, but though they never quite reached him with their cruel claws, yet there were times when one could scarce have passed a thick leaf between their talons and his smooth hide.

Quick was Sabor, the tiger, and quick were Numa and Sheeta, his cousins, but Tarzan of the apes was lightning.

With Tantor, the elephant, he made friends. On many moonlight nights Tarzan and the elephant walked together, and where the way was clear Tarzan rode, perched high upon Tantor's mighty back.

All else of the jungle were his enemies, except his own tribe, among whom he now had many friends.

Many days during these years he spent in the cabin of his father, where still lay, untouched, the bones of his parents and the little skeleton of Kala's baby. At eighteen he read fluently and understood nearly all he read.

Also could he write, with printed letters, rapidly and plainly, but script he had not mastered, for, though there were several copy-books among his treasures, there was so little written English in the cabin that he saw no use for bothering with this other form of writing, though he could read it laboriously.

Thus, at eighteen, we find him, an English lordling, who could speak no English, yet who could read and write his native language. Never had he seen a human being other than himself, for the little area traversed by his tribe was watered by no great river to bring down the savage natives of the interior.

High hills shut it off on three sides, the ocean on the fourth. It was alive with lions, and tigers, and leopards, and poisonous snakes. Its untouched mazes of matted jungle had as yet invited no hardy pioneer from among the humans beyond its frontier.

But as Tarzan of the apes sat one day in the cabin of his father, delving into the mysteries of a new book, the ancient security of his jungle was broken forever.

At the far eastern confine a strange cavalcade strung, in single file, over the brow of a low hill.

In advance were fifty black warriors armed with slender wooden spears with ends hard baked over slow fires, and long bows and poisoned arrows. On their backs were oval shields, in their noses hung rings, while from the kinky wool of their heads protruded tufts of gay feathers.

Across their foreheads were tattooed three parallel lines of color, and on each breast three concentric circles. Their yellow teeth were filed to sharp points, and their great protruding lips added still further to the brutishness of their appearance.

Following them were several hundred women and children, the former bearing upon their heads great burdens of cooking-pots, household utensils, and ivory. In the rear were a hundred warriors, similar in all respects to the advance guard.

That they more greatly feared an attack from the rear than whatever unknown enemies might lurk ahead was evidenced by the formation of the column; and such was the fact, for they were fleeing from the white man's soldiers who had so harassed them for rubber and ivory that they had turned upon their conquerors one day and massacred a white officer and a small detachment of his black troops.

For many days they had gorged themselves on meat, but eventually a stronger body of troops had come and fallen upon their village by night to revenge the death of their comrades. That night the black soldiers of the white man had had meat a plenty, and this little remnant of a once powerful tribe had slunk off into the gloomy jungle toward the unknown and freedom.

But what meant freedom and the pursuit of happiness to these savage blacks meant consternation and death to many of the wild denizens of their new home.

For three days the little calvalcade marched slowly through the heart of this unknown and untracked forest, until finally, early in the fourth day, they came upon a little spot, near the banks of a small river, which seemed less thickly overgrown than any ground they had encountered before.

Here they set to work to build a new village, and in a month a great clearing had been made, huts and palisades erected, plantains, yams, and maize planted, and they had taken up their old life in their new home. Here there were no white men, no soldiers, nor any rubber or ivory to be gathered for thankless task-masters.

Several moons passed ere the blacks ventured far into the territory surrounding their new village. Several had already fallen prey to old Sabor, the tiger, and because the jungle was so infested with these fierce and bloodthirsty cats, and with lions and leopards,

*On many moonlit nights, Tarzan rode, perched high upon
Tantor's mighty back.*

the ebony warriors hesitated to trust themselves far from the safety of their palisades.

But one day Kulonga, a son of the old king, Mbonga, wandered far into the dense mazes to the west. Warily he stepped, his slender lance ever ready, his long oval shield grasped in his left hand close to his body.

At his back his bow, and in the quiver upon his shield many slim, straight arrows, well smeared with the thick, dark, tarry substance that rendered deadly their tiniest needle prick.

Night found Kulonga far from the palisades of his father's village, but still headed westward, and climbing into the fork of a great tree he fashioned a rude platform and curled himself for sleep.

Three miles west of him slept the tribe of Kerchak.

Early the next morning the apes were astir, moving through the jungle in search of food. Tarzan, as was his custom, prosecuted his search in the direction of the cabin, so that by leisurely hunting on the way his hunger was appeased by the time he reached the beach.

The apes scattered by ones, and twos, and threes in all directions, but always within sound of a signal of alarm.

Kala had moved slowly along an elephant track toward the east, and was busily engaged in turning over rotted limbs and logs in search of esculent bugs and fungi, when the faintest shadow of a strange noise brought her to startled attention.

For fifty yards before her the trail was straight, and down this leafy tunnel she looked straight at the stealthily advancing figure of a strange and fearful creature.

It was Kulonga.

Kala did not wait to see more; but, turning, moved rapidly back along the trail. She did not run; but, after the manner of her kind when not roused, sought rather to avoid than to escape.

Close after her came Kulonga. Here was meat. He could make a killing and feast well this day. On he hurried, his spear poised for the throw.

At a turning of the trail he came in sight of her again upon another straight stretch. His spear-hand went far back, the muscles rolled, lightning like, beneath the sleek hide. Out shot the arm, and the spear sped toward Kala.

A poor cast. It but grazed her side.

With a cry of rage and pain Kala turned upon her tormentor. In an instant the trees were crashing beneath the weight of hurrying apes, swinging rapidly toward the scene of trouble in answer to Kala's scream.

As Kala charged, Kulonga unslung his bow and fitted an arrow with almost unthinkable quickness. Drawing the shaft far back, he drove the poisoned missile straight into the heart of the great she-ape.

With a horrid scream Kala plunged forward upon her face before the astonished members of her tribe.

Roaring and shrieking, the apes dashed toward Kulonga; but that wary savage was fleeing down the trail like a frightened antelope. He knew something of the ferocity of these wild, hairy creatures, and his one desire was to put as many miles between himself and them as he possibly could.

They followed him, racing through the trees for a long distance; but finally one by one they abandoned the chase and returned to the scene of the tragedy.

None of them had ever seen a man before other than Tarzan, and so they wondered vaguely what strange manner of creature it might be that had invaded their jungle.

On the far beach by the little cabin Tarzan heard the faint echoes of the conflict, and, knowing that something was seriously amiss among the tribe, he hastened rapidly toward the direction of the sound.

When he arrived he found the entire tribe gathered jabbering about the dead body of his slain mother.

Tarzan's grief and anger were unbounded. He roared out his hideous challenge time and again. He beat upon his chest with his fists, and then he fell upon the body of Kala and sobbed out the pitiful sorrowing of his lonely heart.

To lose the only creature in all one's world who ever had manifested love and affection for one is a great bereavement indeed.

What though Kala was a fierce and hideous ape! To Tarzan she had been kind; she had been beautiful.

Upon her he had lavished, unknown to himself, all the reverence and respect and love that a normal English boy feels for his own mother. He had never known another; and so to Kala was given, though mutely, all that would have belonged to the fair and lovely Lady Alice had she lived.

After the first outburst of grief Tarzan controlled himself, and, questioning the members of the tribe who had witnessed the killing of Kala, he learned all that their meager vocabulary could vouchsafe him.

It was enough, however, for his needs. It told him of a strange, hairless, black ape with feathers growing upon its head, who launched death from a slender branch, and then ran with the fleetness of Bara, the deer, toward the rising sun.

Tarzan waited no longer; but, leaping into the branches of the trees, sped rapidly through the forest. He knew the windings of the elephant trail along which Kala's murderer had flown, and he cut straight through the jungle to intercept the black warrior, who was evidently following the tortuous detours of the trail.

At his side was the hunting-knife of his unknown sire, and across his shoulders the coils of his own long rope. In an hour he struck the trail again, and, coming to earth, examined the soil minutely.

In the soft mud on the bank of a tiny rivulet he found footprints such as he alone in all the jungle had ever made, but much larger than his. His heart beat fast. Could it be that he was trailing a man—one of his own race?

There were two sets of imprints pointing in opposite directions. So his quarry had already passed on his return along the trail. As he examined the newer spoor a tiny particle of earth toppled from the outer edge of one of the footprints to the bottom of its shallow depression—ah, the trail was very fresh, his prey must have but scarcely passed.

Tarzan swung himself to the trees once more, and with swift noiselessness sped along high above the trail.

He had covered barely a mile when he came upon the black warrior standing in a little open space. In his hand was his slender bow, to which he had fitted one of his death-dealing arrows.

Opposite him across the little clearing stood Horta, the boar, with lowered head and foam-flecked tusks, ready to charge.

Tarzan looked with wonder upon the strange creature beneath him—so like him in form, and yet so different in face and color. His books had portrayed a *negro;* but how different had been the dull, dead print to this sleek thing of ebony, pulsing with life.

As the man stood there with taut-drawn bow Tarzan recognized in him not so much the negro as the *"archer"* of his picture-book—

A stands for Archer

How wonderful! Tarzan almost betrayed his presence in the deep excitement of his discovery.

But things were commencing to happen below him. The sinewy black arm had drawn the shaft far back; Horta, the boar, was charging.

The black released the poisoned arrow, and Tarzan saw it fly with the quickness of thought and lodge in the bristling neck of the boar.

Scarcely had the shaft left his bow ere Kulonga had fitted another to it; but Horta, the boar, was upon him so quickly that he had no time to discharge it. With a bound the black leaped entirely over the rushing beast, and, turning with incredible swiftness, planted a second arrow in Horta's back.

Then Kulonga sprang into a near-by tree.

Horta wheeled to charge his enemy once more. A dozen steps he took, then he staggered and fell upon his side. For a moment his muscles stiffened and relaxed convulsively, then he lay still.

Kulonga came down from his tree.

With the knife that hung at his side he cut several large pieces from the boar's body, and in the center of the trail he built a fire, cooking and eating as much as he wanted. The rest he left where it had fallen.

Tarzan was an interested spectator. His desire to kill burned fiercely in his wild breast, but his desire to learn was even greater. He would follow this savage creature for a while and know from whence he came. He could kill him at his leisure later, when the bow and deadly arrows were laid aside.

When Kulonga had finished his repast and disappeared beyond a near turning of the path, Tarzan dropped quietly to the ground. With his knife he severed many strips of meat from Horta's carcass, but he did not cook them.

He had seen fire, but only when the lightning had destroyed some great tree. That any creature of the jungle could produce the red-and-yellow fangs which devoured wood and left nothing but fine dust surprised Tarzan greatly. Also, why the black warrior had ruined his delicious repast by plunging it into the blighting heat was quite beyond him. Possibly the fire was a friend with whom the archer was sharing his food.

Tarzan would not ruin good meat in any such foolish manner, so he gobbled down a great quantity of the raw flesh, burying the balance of the carcass beside the trail where he could find it upon his return.

And then Lord Greystoke wiped his greasy fingers upon his naked thighs and took up the trail of Kulonga, the son of Mbonga, the king; while in far-off London another Lord Greystoke, the younger brother of the real Lord Greystoke's father, sent back his chops to the club's chef because they were underdone, and when he had finished his repast he dipped his finger-ends into a silver bowl of scented water and dried them upon a piece of snowy damask.

All day Tarzan followed Kulonga, hovering above him in the trees like some malign spirit. Twice more he saw him hurl his arrows of destruction—once at Dango, the hyena, and again at Manu, the monkey. In each instance the animal died almost instantly, for Kulonga's poison was very fresh and very deadly.

Tarzan thought much on this wonderous method of slaying as he swung slowly along at a safe distance behind his quarry. He knew that alone the tiny prick of the arrow could not so quickly despatch these wild things of the jungle, who were often torn and scratched and gored in a frightful manner as they fought with their jungle neighbors, yet as often recovered as not.

No, there was something mysterious connected with these tiny slivers of wood which could bring death by a mere scratch. He must look into the matter.

That night Kulonga slept in the crotch of a mighty tree, and far above him crouched Tarzan of the apes.

When Kulonga awoke he found that his bow and arrows had disappeared. The black warrior was furious and frightened, but more frightened than furious. He searched the ground below the tree, and he searched the tree above the ground; but there was no sign of either bow or arrows or of the nocturnal marauder.

Kulonga was panic-stricken. His spear he had hurled at Kala, and had not recovered; and, now that his bow and arrows were gone, he was defenseless except for a single knife. His only hope lay in reaching the village of Mbonga as quickly as his legs would carry him.

That he was not far from home he was certain, so he took to the trail at a rapid trot. From a great mass of impenetrable foliage a few yards away emerged Tarzan of the apes to swing quietly in his wake.

Kulonga's bow and arrows were securely tied high in the top

of a giant tree, from which a patch of bark had been removed by a sharp knife near to the ground and a branch half cut through and left hanging about fifty feet higher up. Thus Tarzan blazed the forest trails and marked his caches.

As Kulonga continued his journey Tarzan closed up on him until he traveled almost over the black's head. His rope he now held coiled in his right hand; he was almost ready for the kill.

The moment was delayed only because Tarzan was anxious to ascertain the black warrior's destination, and presently he was rewarded, for they came suddenly in view of a great clearing, at one end of which lay many strange lairs.

Tarzan was directly over Kulonga as he made the discovery. The forest ended abruptly, and beyond lay two hundred yards of planted fields between the jungle and the village.

Tarzan must act quickly or his prey would be gone; but Tarzan's life training left so little space between decision and action when an emergency confronted him that there was not even room for the shadow of a thought between.

Thus, as Kulonga emerged from the shadow of the jungle, a slender coil of rope sped sinuously above him from the lowest branch of a mighty tree directly upon the edge of Mbonga's fields. Ere the king's son had taken a half-dozen steps into the clearing the quick noose tightened about his neck.

So rapidly did Tarzan of the apes drag back his prey that Kulonga's cry of alarm was throttled in his windpipe. Hand over hand Tarzan drew the struggling black until he had him hanging by his neck in mid air; then Tarzan, climbing to a larger branch, pulled the still thrashing victim well up into the sheltering verdure of the tree.

He fastened the rope securely to a stout branch, and then, descending, plunged his hunting-knife into Kulonga's heart. Kala was avenged.

Tarzan examined the black minutely; never had he seen any other human being. The knife with its sheath and belt caught his fancy; he appropriated them. A copper anklet also took his fancy, and this he put on his own leg.

He examined and admired the tattooing on the forehead and breast. He marveled at the sharp-filed teeth. He investigated and appropriated the feathered head-dress, and then he prepared to get down to business, for Tarzan of the apes was hungry, and here was meat; meat of the kill, which jungle ethics permitted him to eat.

How may we judge him, by what standards, this ape-man with the heart and head and body of an English gentleman, and the training of a wild beast?

Tublat, whom he had hated and who had hated him, he had killed in fair fight, and yet never had the thought of eating of Tublat's flesh entered his head. It would have been as revolting to him as is cannibalism to us.

But who was Kulonga, that he might not be eaten as fairly as Horta, the boar, or Bara, the deer? Was he not simply another of the countless wild things of the jungle who preyed upon one another to satisfy the cravings of hunger?

Of a sudden, a strange doubt stayed his hand. Had not his books taught him that he was a man? And was not "the archer" a man, also?

Did men eat men? Alas, he did not know. Why, then, this hesitancy? Once more he essayed the effort, but of a sudden a qualm of nausea overwhelmed him. He did not understand.

All he knew was that he could not eat the flesh of this black man, and thus a hereditary instinct, ages old, usurped the functions of his untaught mind and saved him from transgressing a world-wide law of whose very existence he was ignorant.

Quickly he lowered Kulonga's body to the ground, removed the noose, and took to the trees again.

CHAPTER 10

The Fear-Fantom

FROM A LOFTY perch Tarzan viewed the village of thatched huts across the intervening plantation.

He saw that at one point the forest touched the village, and to this spot he made his way, lured by a fever of curiosity to behold animals of his own kind, and to learn more of their ways and view the strange lairs in which they lived.

His life among the brutes of the jungle left no opening for any thought that these could be other than enemies. Similarity of form led him to no erroneous conception of the welcome that would be accorded him should he be discovered.

Tarzan of the apes was no sentimentalist. He knew nothing of the brotherhood of man. All things outside his own tribe were his deadly enemies, with the few exceptions of which Tantor, the elephant, was a marked example.

And he realized all this without malice or hatred. To kill was the law of the wild world he knew. Few were his primitive pleasures, but the greatest of these was to hunt and kill, and so he accorded to others the right to cherish the same desires as he, even though he himself might be the object of their hunt.

His strange life had left him neither morose nor bloodthirsty. That he joyed in killing, and that he killed with a laugh upon his handsome lips, betokened no innate cruelty. He killed for food most often, but, being a man, he sometimes killed for pleasure, a thing which no other animal does; for it has remained for man alone among all creatures to kill senselessly and wantonly for the mere pleasure of inflicting suffering and death.

And when he killed for revenge, or in defense, he did that also without hysteria, but it was a very businesslike proceeding which admitted of no levity.

So it was that now, as he cautiously approached the village of Mbonga he was quite prepared either to kill or be killed should he be discovered. He proceeded with unwonted stealth, for Kulonga had taught him great respect for the little sharp splinters of wood which dealt death so swiftly and unerringly.

At length he came to a great tree, heavy with thick foliage and loaded with pendant loops of giant creepers. From this almost impenetrable bower above the village he crouched, looking down upon the scene below him.

There were naked children running and playing in the street. There were women grinding dried plantain in crude stone mortars, while others were fashioning cakes from the powdered flour. Out in the fields he could see still other women hoeing, weeding, or gathering.

All wore strange protruding girdles of dried grass about their hips and many were loaded with brass and copper anklets, armlets, and bracelets. Round many a dusky neck hung curiously coiled strands of wire, while several were further ornamented by huge nose-rings.

Tarzan of the apes looked with growing wonder at these strange creatures. Dozing in the shade he saw several men, while at the extreme outskirts of the clearing he occasionally caught glimpses of armed warriors apparently on guard.

He noticed that the women alone worked. Nowhere was there evidence of a man tilling the fields or performing any of the homely duties of the village.

Finally his eyes rested upon a woman directly beneath him.

Before her was a small caldron standing over a low fire and in it bubbled a thick, reddish, tarry mass. On one side of her lay a quantity of wooden arrows which she dipped into the seething substance, and then laid them on a narrow rack of boughs which stood at her other side.

Tarzan of the apes was fascinated. Here was the secret of the destructiveness of "the archer's" tiny missiles. He noted the extreme care which the woman took that none of the matter should touch her hands, and once when a part spattered upon one of her fingers he saw her plunge the member into a vessel of water and quickly rub the tiny stain away with a handful of leaves.

Tarzan of the apes knew nothing of poison, but his shrewd reasoning told him that it was this deadly stuff that killed; not the little arrow, which was merely the messenger that carried it into the body of its victim.

How he should like to have more of those little death-dealing slivers. If the woman would only leave her work for an instant he could drop down, gather up a handful, and be back in the tree again before she drew three breaths.

As he was trying to think out some plan to distract her attention he heard a wild cry from across the clearing. He looked and saw a black warrior standing beneath the very tree in which he had killed the murderer of Kala an hour before.

The fellow was shouting and waving his spear above his head. Now and again he would point to something on the ground before him.

The village was in an uproar instantly. Armed men rushed from the interior of many a hut and raced madly across the clearing toward the excited sentry. After them trooped the old men, and the women and children until, in a moment, the village was deserted.

Tarzan of the apes knew that they had found the body of his victim, but that interested him far less than the fact that no one remained in the village to prevent his taking a supply of the arrows which lay below him.

He dropped to the ground beside the caldron of poison, and stood motionless, his quick eyes scanning the interior of the palisade.

No one was in sight. His eyes rested upon the open doorway of a near-by hut. He would take a look within, thought Tarzan, and so, cautiously, he approached the low thatched building.

For a moment he hesitated without, listening intently. There was no sound, and he glided into the semidarkness of the interior.

Weapons hung against the walls, long spears, strangely shaped knives, a couple of narrow shields. In the center of the room was a cooking-pot, and at the far end a litter of dry grasses covered by woven mats which evidently served the owners as beds and bedding. Several human skulls lay upon the floor.

Tarzan of the apes felt of each article, hefted the spears, smelled of them, for he "saw" largely through his sensitive and highly trained nostrils. He determined to own one of these long-pointed sticks, but he could not take one on this trip because of the arrows he meant to carry.

One by one, as he took each article from the walls, he placed them in a pile in the center of the room, and on top of all he placed the cooking-pot, inverted, and on top of this he laid one of the grinning skulls, upon which he fastened the head-dress of the dead Kulonga.

Then he stood back and surveyed his work, and grinned. Tarzan of the apes was a joker.

But now he heard, without, the sounds of many voices, and long mournful howls, and mighty wailing. He was startled. Had he remained too long?

Quickly he reached the doorway and peered down the village street toward the village gate.

The natives were not yet in sight, though he could plainly hear them approaching across the plantation. They must be very near.

Like a flash he sprang across the opening to the pile of arrows. Gathering up all he could carry under one arm, with a kick he overturned the seething caldron, and disappeared into the foliage, just as the first of the returning natives entered the gate at the far end of the village. He turned to watch the proceedings below, poised like some wild bird ready to take swift wing at the first sign of danger.

The natives filed up the street, four of them bearing the body of Kulonga. Behind trailed the women, uttering strange cries and weird lamentation. On they came to the portals of the very hut in which Tarzan had wrought his depredations.

Scarcely had half a dozen entered the building ere they came rushing out in wild, jabbering confusion. The others hastened to gather about. There was much excited gesticulating, pointing, and chattering. Several of the warriors approached and peered within.

Finally an old fellow with many ornaments of metal about his arms and legs, and a necklace of dried human hands depending upon his chest, entered the hut.

It was Mbonga, the king, father of Kulonga.

For a few moments all were silent. Then Mbonga emerged, a look of mingled wrath and fear writ upon his hideous countenance. He spoke a few words to the assembled warriors, and in an instant the men were flying through the little village searching minutely every hut and corner within the palisade.

Scarcely had the search commenced than the overturned caldron was discovered, and with it the theft of the poisoned arrows. Nothing more they found, and it was a thoroughly awed and frightened group of savages which huddled round their king a few moments later.

Mbonga could explain nothing of the strange events that had taken place. The finding of the still warm body of Kulonga—on the very verge of their fields, and within easy ear-shot of the village—knifed and stripped at the door of his father's home, was in itself sufficiently mysterious, but these last awesome discoveries within the village, within the dead Kulonga's own hut, filled their hearts with dismay, and conjured in their poor brains only the most frightful of superstitious explanations.

They stood in little groups, talking in low tones, and casting affrighted glances behind them from their great rolling eyes.

Tarzan of the apes watched them for a while from his lofty perch in the great tree. There was much in their demeanor which he could not understand, for he was ignorant of superstition, and of fear of any kind he had but a vague conception.

The sun was high in the heavens. Tarzan had not broken fast this day, and it was many miles to where lay the toothsome remains of Horta the boar.

So he turned his back upon the village of Mbonga and melted away into the leafy fastness of the forest.

CHAPTER 11

King of the Apes

IT WAS NOT yet dark when he reached the tribe, though he stopped to exhume and devour the remains of the wild boar he had cached the preceding day, and again to get Kulonga's bow and arrows from the tree-top in which he had hidden them.

It was a well-laden Tarzan who dropped from the branches into the midst of the tribe of Kerchak.

With swelling chest he narrated the glories of his adventure and exhibited the spoils of conquest.

Kerchak grunted and turned away, for he was jealous of this strange member of his band. In his little evil brain he sought for some excuse to wreak his hatred upon Tarzan.

The next day Tarzan was practising with his bow and arrows at the first gleam of dawn. At first he lost nearly every bolt he shot, but finally he learned to guide the little shafts with fair accuracy, and ere a month had passed he was no mean shot; but his proficiency had cost him nearly his entire supply of arrows.

The tribe continued to find the hunting good in the vicinity of the beach, and so Tarzan of the apes varied his archery practise with further investigation of his father's little store of books.

It was during this period that the young English lord found hidden in the back of one of the cupboards in the cabin a little metal box. The key was in the lock, and a few moments investigation and experimentation were rewarded with the successful opening of the receptacle.

In it he found a faded photograph of a smooth-faced young man, a golden locket studded with diamonds, linked to a small gold chain, a few letters and a small book.

Tarzan examined these all minutely.

The photograph he liked most of all, for the eyes were smiling, and the face was open and frank. It was his father.

The locket, too, took his fancy, and he placed the chain about his neck in imitation of the ornamentation he had seen to be so common among the black men he had visited. The brilliant stones gleamed strangely against his smooth, brown hide.

The letters he could scarcely decipher for he had learned little or nothing of script, so he put them back in the box with the photograph and turned his attention to the little book.

This was almost entirely filled with fine script, but while the little bugs were all familiar to him, their arrangement and the combinations in which they occurred were strange and entirely incomprehensible.

Tarzan had long since learned the use of the dictionary, but much to his sorrow and perplexity it proved of no avail to him in this emergency. Not a word of all that was writ in the little book could he find, and so he put it back in the little metal box, but with a determination to work out the mysteries of it later on.

Poor little ape-man! Had he but known it that baffling little mystery held between its seal covers the key to his origin, the answer to the strange riddle of his strange life.

It was the diary of John Clayton, Lord Greystoke—kept in French, as had always been his custom.

Tarzan replaced the box in the cupboard, but always thereafter he carried the features of the strong, smiling face of his father in his heart, and in his head a fixed determination to solve the mystery of the strange words in the little black book.

At present he had more important business in hand, for his supply of arrows was exhausted, and he must needs journey to the black men's village and renew it.

Early the following morning he set out, and, traveling rapidly, he came before midday to the little clearing. Once more he took up his position in the great tree, and, as before, he saw the women in the fields and the village street, and the little caldron of bubbling poison directly beneath him.

For hours he lay awaiting his opportunity to drop down unseen and gather up the arrows for which he had come, but nothing now occurred to call the villagers away from their homes. The day wore on, and still Tarzan of the apes crouched above the unsuspecting woman at the caldron.

Presently the workers in the fields returned. The hunting warriors emerged from the forest, and when all were within the palisade, the gates were closed and barred.

Many cooking-pots were now in evidence about the village. Before each hut a woman presided over a boiling stew, while little cakes of plantain and cassava puddings were on every hand.

Suddenly there came a hail from the edge of the clearing.

Tarzan looked.

It was a party of belated hunters returning from the north, and among them they half led, half carried a struggling animal.

As they approached the village the gates were thrown open to admit them, and then, as the people saw the victim of the chase, a savage cry rose to the heavens, for the quarry was a man.

As he was dragged, still resisting, into the village street, the women and children set upon him with sticks and stones, and Tarzan of the apes, young and savage beast of the jungle, wondered at the cruel brutality of his own kind.

Sabor, the tiger, alone of all the junglefolk, tortured his prey. The ethics of all the others meted a quick and merciful death to their victims.

Tarzan had learned from his books but scattered fragments of the ways of human beings.

When he had followed Kulonga through the forest he had expected to come to a city of strange houses on wheels, puffing clouds of black smoke from a huge tree stuck in the roof of one of them—or a sea covered with mighty floating buildings which he had learned were called, variously, ships and boats and steamers and craft.

He had been sorely disappointed with the poor little village of the blacks, hidden away in his own jungle, and with not a single house as large as his own cabin upon the distant beach.

Now, he saw that these people were more wicked than his own apes, and as savage and cruel as Sabor himself. Tarzan began to hold his own kind in but low esteem.

Now they had tied their victim to a post near the center of the village, directly before Mbonga's hut, and they formed a dancing, yelling circle about him, alive with flashing knives and menacing spears.

In a larger circle squatted the women, yelling and beating upon drums. It reminded Tarzan of the Dum-Dum, and so he knew what to expect. He wondered if they would spring upon their meat while it was still alive. The apes did not do such things as that.

The circle of warriors about the cringing captive drew closer to their prey, in savage abandon to the maddening music of the drums. Presently a spear reached out and pricked the victim. It was the signal for fifty others.

Eyes, ears, arms, and legs were pierced; every inch of the poor writhing body that did not cover a vital organ became the target of the cruel lancers.

The women and children shrieked their delight. The warriors licked their hideous lips in anticipation of the feast to come, and vied with one another in the savagery and loathsomeness of the cruel indignities with which they tortured the still conscious prisoner.

Then it was that Tarzan of the apes saw his chance. All eyes were fixed upon the thrilling spectacle at the stake. The light of day had given place to the darkness of a moonless night, and only the fires in the immediate vicinity of the orgy had been kept alight to cast a restless light upon the scene.

Gently the lithe boy dropped to the earth at the end of the village street. Quickly he gathered up the arrows—all of them this time, for he had brought a number of long fibers to bind them into a bundle.

Without haste he wrapped them securely, and then, ere he turned to leave, the devil of capriciousness entered his heart. He looked about for some hint of a wild prank to play upon these strange, grotesque creatures that they might be again aware of his presence among them.

Dropping his bundle of arrows at the foot of the tree, Tarzan crept among the shadows at the side of the street until he came to the same hut he had entered on the occasion of his first visit.

Inside all was darkness. His groping hands soon found the object for which he sought, and without further delay he turned again toward the door.

He had taken but a step, however, ere his quick ear caught the sound of approaching footsteps. In another instant the figure of a woman darkened the entrance of the hut.

Tarzan drew back silently to the far wall, and his hand sought his knife. The woman came quickly to the center of the hut, and there she paused for an instant, feeling about with her hands for the thing she sought. Evidently it was not in its accustomed place, for she explored ever nearer and nearer the wall where Tarzan stood.

So close was she now that the ape-man felt the animal warmth of her naked body. Up went the hunting-knife, and then the woman turned to one side, and soon a guttural "Ah!" proclaimed that her search had at last been successful.

Immediately she turned and left the hut, and as she passed through the doorway Tarzan saw that she carried a cooking pot in her hand.

He followed closely after her, and as he reconnoitered from the shadows of the doorway he saw that all the women of the village were hastening to and from the various huts with pots and kettles. These they were filling with water and placing over a number of fires near the stake where the dying victim now hung inert and bloody.

Choosing a moment when none seemed near, Tarzan hastened to his bundle of arrows beneath the great tree at the end of the village street. As on the former occasion, he overthrew the caldron before leaping, sinuous and catlike, into the lower branches of the forest giant.

Silently he climbed to a great height until he found a point where he could look through a leafy opening upon the scene beneath him.

The women were now preparing the prisoner for their cooking pots, while the men stood about resting after the fatigue of their mad revel. Comparative quiet reigned in the village.

Tarzan raised aloft the thing he had pilfered from the hut, and, with aim made true by years of fruit and coconut throwing, launched it toward the group of savages.

Squarely among them it fell, striking one of the warriors full upon the head and felling him to the ground, and then it rolled among the women and stopped beside the half-butchered thing they were preparing to feast upon.

All gazed in consternation at it for an instant, and then, with one accord, broke and ran for their huts.

It was a grinning human skull which looked up at them from the ground. The dropping of the thing out of the open sky was a miracle well aimed to work upon their superstitious fears.

Tarzan of the apes left them filled with terror at this new manifestation of the presence of some unseen and unearthly power which lurked in the forest about their village.

Later, when they discovered the overturned caldron, and that once more their arrows had been pilfered, it dawned upon them that they had offended some great god who ruled this part of the jungle. From then on an offering of food was daily placed below the great tree from whence the arrows had disappeared, in an effort to conciliate the mighty one.

But the seed of fear was deep sown, and had he but known it, Tarzan of the apes had laid the foundation for much future misery for himself and his tribe.

That night he slept in the forest not far from the village, and early the next morning set out slowly on his homeward march, hunting as he traveled. Only a few berries and an occasional grubworm rewarded his search, and he was half famished when, looking up from a log he had been rooting beneath, he saw Sabor, the tiger, standing in the center of the trail not twenty paces from him.

The great yellow eyes were fixed upon him with a wicked and baleful gleam, and the red tongue licked the longing lips as Sabor crouched, worming his stealthy way with belly flattened against the earth.

Tarzan did not attempt to escape. He welcomed the opportunity for which, in fact, he had been searching for days past.

Quickly he unslung his bow and fitted a well-daubed arrow, and as Sabor sprang, the tiny missile leaped to meet him in mid air. At the same instant Tarzan of the apes jumped to one side, and as the tiger struck the ground beyond another death-tipped arrow sank deep into his loin.

With a mighty roar the beast turned and charged once more, only to be met with a third arrow full in one eye; but this time he was too close upon the ape-man for the latter to side-step.

Tarzan of the apes went down beneath the body of his enemy, but with gleaming knife drawn and striking home. For a moment they lay there, and then Tarzan realized that the inert mass lying upon him was beyond power to injure.

With difficulty he wriggled from beneath the great weight, and as he stood erect and gazed down upon the trophy of his skill, a mighty wave of exultation swept over him.

With swelling breast, he placed a foot upon the body of his powerful enemy, and throwing back his fine young head, roared out the awful challenge of the victorious bull ape.

The forest echoed with the savage and triumphant pæan. Birds fell still, and the larger animals and beasts of prey slunk stealthily away, for few there were of all the jungle who sought for trouble with the great anthropoids.

And in London another Lord Greystoke was speaking to his kind in the House of Lords, but none trembled at the sound of his soft voice.

Sabor proved most unsavory eating even to Tarzan of the apes, but hunger served as a sauce, and ere long the well-fed ape-man was ready to sleep again. First, however, he must remove the hide, for it was as much for this as for any other purpose that he had desired to encompass the destruction of Sabor, the tiger.

Deftly he removed the great pelt, for he had practised often on smaller animals, and, when the task was finished, he carried his trophy to the fork of a high tree. There, curling himself securely in a crotch, he fell into deep slumber.

What with loss of sleep, arduous exercise, and a hearty meal, Tarzan of the apes slept the sun round, awakening about noon of the following day. He straightway repaired to the carcass of Sabor, but was angered to find the bones picked clean by other hungry denizens of the jungle.

Half an hour's leisurely progress through the forest brought to sight a young deer, and before ever the creature knew that an enemy was near a tiny arrow had lodged in its neck.

So quickly the virus worked that at the end of a dozen leaps the deer plunged headlong into the undergrowth, dead. Again did Tarzan feast well, but this time he did not sleep.

Instead, he hastened on toward the point where he had left the tribe, and when he had found them proudly exhibited the skin of Sabor, the tiger.

"Look!" he cried, "Apes of Kerchak. See what Tarzan, the killer, has done. Who else among you has ever killed one of Sabor's people? Tarzan is mightiest among you, for Tarzan is no ape; Tarzan is—" But here he stopped, for in the language of the anthropoids there was no word for man, and Tarzan could only write the word in English; he could not pronounce it.

The tribe had gathered about to look upon the proof of his wondrous prowess, and to listen to his words.

Only Kerchak hung back, nursing his hatred and his rage.

Suddenly something snapped in the brain of the anthropoid. With a frightful roar the great beast sprang among the assemblage.

Biting and striking with his huge hands, he killed and maimed a dozen ere the balance could escape to the upper terraces of the forest.

Frothing and shrieking in the insanity of his fury, Kerchak looked about for the object of his greatest hatred, and there, upon a near-by limb, he saw him sitting.

"Come down, Tarzan, great killer!" cried Kerchak, ready for

battle. "Come down and feel the fangs of a greater! Do mighty fighters fly to the trees at danger?"

And he emitted the volleying challenge of his kind.

Quietly Tarzan dropped to the ground. Breathlessly the tribe watched Kerchak, still roaring, charge the relatively puny figure.

Nearly seven feet stood Kerchak on his short legs. His enormous shoulders were bunched and rounded with huge muscles. The back of his short neck was as a single lump of iron sinew which bulged beyond the base of his skull, so that his head seemed like a small ball protruding from a huge mountain of flesh.

His back-drawn, snarling lips exposed his great fighting fangs, and his bloodshot eyes gleamed in horrid reflection of his madness.

Awaiting him stood Tarzan, himself a mighty muscled animal, but his six feet of height and his great rolling sinews seemed pitifully inadequate to the ordeal which awaited them in their struggle with Kerchak.

His bow and arrows lay some distance away, where he had dropped them while showing Sabor's hide to his fellow apes, and he confronted Kerchak with only his knife and his superior intellect to offset the ferocious strength of his enemy.

As his antagonist came roaring toward him, Lord Greystoke tore his long knife from its sheath, and with an answering challenge as horrid and blood-curdling as that of the beast he faced, rushed swiftly to meet the attack. He was too shrewd to allow those long hairy arms to encircle him, and just as their bodies were about to crash together, Tarzan of the apes grasped one of the huge wrists of his assailant, and, springing lightly to one side, drove his knife to the hilt into Kerchak's body, below the heart.

Before he could wrench the blade free again, Kerchak's quick lunge to grasp him in those awful arms had torn the hilt from Tarzan's hand.

Kerchak aimed a terrific blow at the ape-man's head with the flat of his hand, a blow which had it landed might easily have crushed in the side of Tarzan's skull.

The man was too quick, and, ducking the blow, himself delivered a mighty one with clenched fist in the pit of Kerchak's stomach.

The ape was staggered by the blow, and what with the mortal wound in his side had almost collapsed, when, with one mighty effort he rallied for an instant—just long enough to enable him to wrest his arm free from Tarzan's grasp and close in a terrific clinch with his wiry opponent.

Straining the ape-man close to him, his great jaws sought Tarzan's throat, but the young lord's sinewy fingers were at Kerchak's own before the cruel fangs could close on the sleek brown skin.

Thus they struggled, the one to crush out his opponent's life with those awful teeth, the other to close forever the windpipe beneath his strong grasp, the while he held the snarling mouth from him.

The greater strength of the ape was slowly prevailing, and the teeth of the straining beast were scarce an inch from Tarzan's throat when, with a shuddering tremor, the great body stiffened for an instant and then sank limply to the ground.

Kerchak was dead, and Tarzan of the apes the victor.

Withdrawing the knife that had so often rendered him master of far mightier muscles than his own, Tarzan of the apes placed his foot upon the neck of his vanquished enemy, and once again, loud through the forest rang the fierce, wild cry of the conqueror.

And thus came the young Lord Greystoke into the kingship of the apes.

CHAPTER 12

Man's Reason

THERE WAS ONE of the tribe of Tarzan who questioned his authority, and that was Terkoz, the son of Tublat, but he so feared the keen knife and the deathly arrows of his new lord that he confined the manifestation of his objections to petty disobediences and irritating mannerisms. Tarzan knew, however, that he but waited his opportunity to wrest the kingship from him by some sudden stroke of treachery, and so he was always on guard against surprise.

For months the life of the little band went on much as it had before, except that Tarzan's greater intelligence and his ability as a hunter were the means of providing for them more bountifully than ever before. Most of them, therefore, were more than content with the change in rulers.

Tarzan led them by night to the fields of the black men, and there, warned by their chief's superior wisdom, they ate only what they required, nor did they destroy what they could not eat, as is the way of Manu, the monkey, and of most apes. While the blacks were wroth at the continued pilfering of their fields, they were not discouraged in their efforts to cultivate the land as would have been the case had Tarzan permitted his people to lay wanton waste the plantation.

During this period Tarzan paid many nocturnal visits to the village, where he often renewed his supply of arrows. He soon noticed the food always standing at the foot of the tree, which was his avenue into the palisade, and, after a little, he commenced to eat whatever the blacks put there.

When the poor savages saw that the food disappeared overnight, they were filled with consternation and awe, for it was one thing to put food out to propitiate a god or a devil, but quite another thing to have the spirit really come into the village and eat it.

Nor was this all. The periodic disappearance of their arrows, and the strange pranks perpetrated by unseen hands, had wrought them to such a state that life became a burden in their new home. Mbonga and his head men began to talk of abandoning the village and seeking a site farther in the jungle.

Presently the black warriors began to strike farther and farther into the heart of the forest when they went to hunt, looking for a site for a new village.

More and more often was the tribe of Tarzan disturbed by these wandering huntsmen. The fierce solitude of the primeval forest was broken by new, strange cries. No longer was there safety for bird or beast. Man had come.

Other animals passed up and down the jungle by day and by night—fierce, cruel beasts—but their weaker neighbors only fled from their immediate vicinity to return again when the danger was past.

With man it is different. When he comes many of the larger animals instinctively leave the district entirely, seldom if ever to return; and it has always been thus with the great anthropoids. They flee man as man flees a pestilence.

For a short time the tribe of Tarzan lingered in the vicinity of the beach because their new chief hated the thought of leaving the treasured contents of the little cabin forever. But when one day a member of the tribe discovered the blacks in great numbers on the banks of a stream that had for generations been their watering-place, and in the act of clearing the jungle and erecting many huts, the apes would remain no longer, and so Tarzan led them away inland for many marches to a spot as yet undefiled by the foot of a human being.

Once every moon Tarzan would go swinging rapidly back through the swaying branches to have a day with his books, and to replenish his supply of arrows. This latter task was becoming more and more difficult, for the blacks had taken to hiding their supply at night in granaries and living-huts.

This necessitated watching by day to discover where the arrows were being concealed.

Twice he had entered huts at night while the inmates lay sleeping upon their mats, and stolen the arrows from the very sides of the warriors. But he realized this to be too fraught with danger, and so he commenced picking up solitary hunters with his long deadly noose, stripping them of weapons and ornaments and dropping their bodies from a high tree into the village street during the still watches of the night.

These various escapades again so terrorized the blacks that, had it not been for the monthly respite between Tarzan's visits, in which they had opportunity to renew hope that each fresh incursion would prove the last, they soon would have abandoned their new village.

The blacks had not as yet come upon Tarzan's cabin on the distant beach, but the ape-man lived in constant dread that, while he was away with the tribe, they would discover and despoil his treasure. So it came that he spent more and more time in the vicinity of his father's last home, and less and less with the tribe.

Presently the members of his little community began to suffer on account of his neglect, for disputes and quarrels constantly arose which only the king might settle peaceably.

At last some of the older apes spoke to Tarzan on the subject, and for a month thereafter he remained constantly with the tribe.

The duties of kingship among the anthropoids are not many or arduous.

In the afternoon comes Thaka, possibly, to complain that old Mungo has stolen his new wife. Then must Tarzan summon all before him, and if he finds that the wife prefers her new lord, he commands that matters remain as they are, or possibly that Mungo give Thaka one of his daughters in exchange.

Whatever his decision, the apes accept it as final, and return to their occupations satisfied.

Then comes Tana, shrieking and holding tight her side from

which blood is streaming. Gunto, her husband, has cruelly bitten her! And Gunto, summoned, says that Tana is lazy and will not bring him nuts and beetles or scratch his back for him.

So Tarzan scolds them both and threatens Gunto with a taste of the death-bearing slivers if he abuses Tana further. Tana, for her part, is compelled to promise better attention to her wifely duties.

And so it goes, little family differences for the most part, which, if left unsettled, would result finally in greater factional strife, and the eventual dismemberment of the tribe.

Tarzan tired of it as he found that kingship meant the curtailment of his liberty. He longed for the little cabin and the sun-kissed sea—for the cool interior of the well-built house, and for the never-ending wonders of the many books.

As he had grown older, he found that he had grown away from his people. Their interests and his were far removed. They had not kept pace with him, nor could they understand aught of the many strange and wonderful dreams that passed through the active brain of their human king.

So limited was their vocabulary that Tarzan could not even talk with them of the many new truths, and the fields of thought that his reading had opened up before his longing eyes.

Among the tribe he no longer had friends and cronies as of old. A little child may find companionship in many strange and simple creatures, but to a grown man there must be some semblance of equality in intellect as the basis for agreeable consociation.

Had Kala lived, Tarzan would have sacrificed all else to remain near her, but now that she was dead, and the playful friends of his childhood grown into surly brutes, he felt that he much preferred the peace and solitude of his cabin to the irksome duties of leadership among a horde of wild beasts.

The hatred and jealousy of Terkoz, son of Tublat, did much to counteract the effect of Tarzan's desire to renounce his kingship among the apes, for, stubborn young Englishman that he was, he could not bring himself to retreat in the face of so malignant an enemy.

That Terkoz would be chosen leader in his stead, he knew full well, for time and again the ferocious brute had established his claim to physical supremacy over the few bull apes who had dared resent his savage bullying.

Tarzan would have liked to subdue the beast without recourse to knife or arrows. So much had his great strength and agility increased in the period following his maturity that he had come to believe that he might master the redoubtable Terkoz in a hand-to-hand fight were it not for the terrible advantage the anthropoid's huge fighting fangs gave him over the poorly armed Tarzan.

The entire matter was taken out of Tarzan's hands one day by force of circumstances, and his future left open to him, so that he might go or stay without any stain upon his savage escutcheon.

It happened thus:

The tribe was feeding quietly, spread over a considerable area, when a great screaming rose some distance east of where Tarzan lay upon his belly beside a limpid brook, attempting to catch an elusive fish in his quick, brown hands.

With one accord the tribe swung rapidly toward the frightened cries, and there found Terkoz holding an old female by the hair and beating her unmercifully with his great hands.

As Tarzan approached, he raised his hand aloft for Terkoz to desist, for the female was not his, but belonged to a poor old ape whose fighting days were long over, and who, therefore, could not protect his family.

Terkoz knew that it was against the laws of his kind to strike the woman of another, but being a bully, he had taken advantage of the weakness of the female's husband to chastise her because she had refused to give up to him a tender young rodent she had captured.

When Terkoz saw Tarzan approaching without his arrows, he continued to belabor the poor woman in a studied effort to affront his hated chieftain.

Tarzan did not repeat his warning signal, but instead rushed bodily upon the waiting Terkoz.

Never had the ape-man fought so terrible a battle since that long-gone day when the great king gorilla had so horribly man-handled him ere the new-found knife had, by accident, pricked the savage heart.

Tarzan's knife on the present occasion but barely offset the gleaming fangs of Terkoz, and what little advantage the ape had over the man in brute strength was almost balanced by the latter's wonderful quickness and agility.

In the sum total of their points, however, the anthropoid had a shade the better of the battle, and had there been no other personal attribute to influence the final outcome, Tarzan of the apes, the young Lord Greystoke, would have died as he had lived—an unknown savage beast in equatorial Africa.

But there was that which had raised him far above his fellows of the jungle—that little spark which spells the vast difference between man and brute—Reason. This it was that saved him from death beneath the iron muscles and tearing fangs of Terkoz.

Scarcely had they fought a dozen seconds ere they were rolling upon the ground, striking, tearing and rending—two great savage beasts battling to the death.

Terkoz had a dozen knife-wounds on head and breast, and Tarzan was torn and bleeding—his scalp in one place half torn from his head, so that a great piece hung down over one eye, obstructing his vision.

But so far the young Englishman had been able to keep the horrible fangs from his jugular and, as they fought less fiercely for a moment to regain their breath, Tarzan formed a cunning plan. He would work his way to the other's back and, clinging there with tooth and nail, drive his knife home until Terkoz was no more.

The maneuver was accomplished more easily than he had hoped, for the stupid beast, not knowing what Tarzan was attempting, made no particular effort to prevent the accomplishment of the design.

But when, finally, he realized that his antagonist was fastened to him where his teeth and fists alike were useless against him, Terkoz hurled himself about upon the ground so violently that Tarzan could but cling desperately to the leaping, turning, twisting body, and ere he had struck a blow the knife was hurled from his hand by a heavy impact against the earth.

Tarzan found himself defenseless.

During the rollings and squirmings of the next few minutes, Tarzan's hold was loosened a dozen times until finally an accidental circumstance of those swift and ever-changing evolutions gave him a new hold with his right hand, which he soon realized was absolutely unassailable.

His arm was passed beneath Terkoz's arm from behind, and his hand and forearm encircled the back of Terkoz's neck. It was the half-Nelson of modern wrestling which the untaught ape-man had stumbled upon, but divine reason showed him in an instant the value of the thing he had discovered. It was the difference to him between life and death.

And so he struggled to encompass a similar hold with the left hand. In a few moments Terkoz's bull-neck was creaking beneath a full-Nelson.

There was no more lunging about now, the two lay perfectly still upon the ground. Tarzan upon Terkoz's back. Slowly the bullet-head of the ape was being forced lower and lower upon his chest.

Tarzan knew what the result would be. In an instant the neck would break. Then there came to Terkoz's rescue the same thing that had put him in these sore straights—a man's reasoning power.

"If I kill him," thought Tarzan, "what advantage will it be to me? Will it not but rob the tribe of a great fighter? And if Terkoz is dead, he will know nothing of my supremacy, while alive he will be an example to the other apes."

"*Ka-goda?*" hissed Tarzan in Terkoz's ear, which, in ape tongue, means, freely translated: "Do you surrender?"

For a moment there was no reply, and Tarzan added a few more ounces of pressure, which elicited a horrified shriek of pain from the great beast.

"*Ka-goda?*" repeated Tarzan.

"*Ka-goda!*" cried Terkoz.

"Listen," said Tarzan, easing up a trifle, but not releasing his hold. "I am Tarzan, King of the Apes, mighty hunter, mighty fighter. In all the jungle there is none so great.

"You have said: '*Ka-goda*' to me. All the tribe have heard. Quarrel no more with your king or your people, for next time I shall kill you. Do you understand?"

"*Huh,*" assented Terkoz.

"And you are satisfied?"

"*Huh,*" said the ape.

Tarzan let him up, and in a few minutes all were back at their vocations, as though naught had occurred to mar the tranquillity of their primeval forest haunts.

But deep in the minds of the apes was rooted the conviction that Tarzan was a mighty fighter and a strange creature. Strange because he had had it in his power to kill his enemy, but had allowed him to live—unharmed.

That afternoon as the tribe came together, as was their wont before darkness settled on the jungle, Tarzan, his wounds washed in the limpid waters of the little stream, called the old males about him.

"You have seen again to-day that Tarzan of the apes is the greatest among you," he said.

"Huh," they replied with one voice. "Tarzan is great."

"Tarzan," he continued, "is not an ape. He is not like his people. His ways are not their ways, and so Tarzan is going back to the lair of his own kind by the waters of the great lake which has no further shore. You must choose another to rule you. Tarzan will not return."

And thus young Lord Greystoke took the first step toward the goal which he had set himself—the finding of other white men like himself.

CHAPTER 13

His Own Kind

THE FOLLOWING MORNING Tarzan, lame and sore from the wounds of his battle with Terkoz, set out toward the west and the sea-coast.

He traveled very slowly, sleeping in the jungle at night, and reaching his cabin late the following morning.

For several days he moved about but little, only enough to gather what fruit and nuts he required to satisfy the demands of hunger.

In ten days he was quite sound again, except for a terrible, half-healed scar which, starting above his left eye, ran across the top of his head, ending at the right ear. It was the mark left by Terkoz when he had torn the scalp away.

During his convalescence Tarzan tried to fashion a mantle from the skin of Sabor, the tiger, which had lain all this time in the cabin. But he found the hide had dried as stiff as a board, and, as he knew naught of tanning, he was forced to abandon his cherished plan.

Then he determined to filch what few garments he could from one of the black men of Mbonga's village, for he had decided to mark his evolution from the lower orders in every possible manner, and nothing seemed to him a more distinguishing badge of man-hood than ornaments and clothing.

To this end, therefore, he collected the various arm and leg ornaments he had taken from the black warriors who had succumbed to his swift and silent noose, and donned them all.

About his neck hung the golden chain from which depended the diamond-encrusted locket of his mother, the Lady Alice. At his back was a quiver of arrows slung from a leathern shoulder-belt, another piece of loot from some vanquished black.

About his waist was a belt of tiny strips of rawhide fashioned by himself as a support for the home-made scabbard in which hung his father's hunting-knife. The long bow which had been Kulonga's hung over his left shoulder.

The young Lord Greystoke was indeed a strange and warlike figure, his mass of black hair falling to his shoulders behind and cut with his hunting knife to a rude bang upon his forehead, that it might not fall before his eyes.

His straight and perfect figure, muscled as the best of the ancient Roman gladiators must have been muscled, and yet with the soft and sinuous curves of a Greek god, told at a glance the wondrous combination of enormous strength with suppleness and speed.

A personification was Tarzan of the apes, of the primitive man, the hunter, the warrior.

With the noble poise of his handsome head upon those broad shoulders, and the fire of life and intelligence in those fine, clear eyes, he might readily have typified some demigod of a wild and warlike bygone people of his ancient forest.

But of these things Tarzan did not think.

He was worried because he had no clothing to indicate to all the jungle folks that he was a man and not an ape, and grave doubt often entered his mind as to whether he might not yet become an ape.

Was not hair commencing to grow upon his face? All the apes had hair upon theirs, but the black men were entirely hairless, with very few exceptions.

True, he had seen pictures in his books of men with great masses of hair upon lip and cheek and chin, but, nevertheless, Tarzan was afraid. Almost daily he whetted his keen knife and scraped and whittled at his young beard to eradicate this degrading emblem of apehood.

And so he learned to shave—rudely and painfully, it is true— but, nevertheless, effectively.

When he felt quite strong again, after his bloody battle with Terkoz, Tarzan set off one morning toward Mbonga's village. He was moving carelessly along a winding jungle trail, instead of making his progress through the trees, when suddenly he came face to face with a black warrior.

The look of surprise on the savage face was almost comical, and before Tarzan could unsling his bow the fellow had turned and fled down the path crying out in alarm as though to others before him.

Tarzan took to the trees in pursuit, and in a few moments came in view of the fleeing quarry.

There were three of them, and they were racing madly in single file through the dense undergrowth.

Tarzan easily distanced them, nor did they see his silent passage above their heads, nor note the crouching figure squatted upon a low branch ahead of them beneath which the trail led them.

Tarzan let the first two pass beneath him, but as the third came swiftly on the quiet noose dropped about the black throat. A quick jerk drew it taut.

There was an agonized scream from the victim, and his fellows turned to see his struggling body rise as by magic slowly into the dense foliage of the trees above.

With shrieks they wheeled once more and plunged on in their effort to escape.

Tarzan despatched his prisoner quickly and silently, removed the weapons and ornaments and—greatest joy of all—a handsome doeskin breechcloth, which he quickly transferred to his own person.

Now indeed was he dressed as a man should be. None there was who could doubt his high origin. How he should like to have returned to the tribe to parade before their envious gaze this wondrous finery.

Taking the body across his shoulder, he moved more slowly through the trees toward the little palisaded village, for he again needed arrows.

As he approached quite close to the enclosure he saw an excited group surrounding the two fugitives, who, trembling with fright and exhaustion, were scarce able to recount the uncanny details of their adventure.

Mirando, they said, who had been ahead of them a short distance, had suddenly come screaming toward them, crying that a terrible white and naked warrior was pursuing him. The three of them had made for the village as rapidly as their legs would carry them.

Again Mirando's cry of terror had caused them to look back, and there they had seen the most horrible sight—their companion's body flying upward into the trees, his arms and legs beating the air, and his tongue protruding from his open mouth. No other sound did he utter, nor was there any creature in sight about him.

The villagers were worked up into a state of panic, but wise Mbonga affected to feel considerable skepticism regarding the tale, and attributed the whole fabrication to their fright in the face of some real danger.

"You tell us this great story," he said, "because you do not dare to speak the truth. You do not dare admit that when the tiger sprang upon Mirando you ran away and left him. You are cowards."

Scarcely had Mbonga ceased speaking when a great crashing of branches in the trees above them caused the blacks to look up in renewed terror. The sight that met their eyes made even Mbonga shudder.

Turning and twisting in the air came the dead body of Mirando, to sprawl with a sickening limpness upon the ground at their feet.

With one accord the blacks took to their heels, nor did they stop until the last of them was lost in the shadows of the jungle.

Again Tarzan came down into the village and renewed his supply of arrows, and ate of the offering of food which the blacks had made to appease his wrath.

Before he left he carried the body of Mirando to the gate of the village, and propped it up against the palisade in such a way that the dead face seemed to be peering round the edge of the gate-post down the path which led to the jungle.

Then he returned, hunting, always hunting, to the cabin by the beach.

It took a dozen attempts on the part of the thoroughly frightened blacks to reenter the village, past the grinning face of their dead fellow, and when they found the food and arrows gone, they knew, what they only too well feared, that Mirando had seen the evil spirit of the jungle.

Only those who saw this terrible god of the jungle died; for was it not true that none left alive in the village had ever seen him? Therefore, those who had died at his hands must have seen him and paid the penalty with their lives.

As long as they supplied him with arrows and food, he would

not harm them unless they looked upon him, so it was ordered by Mbonga that in addition to the food offering there should also be laid out an offering of arrows for this Munango-Keewati, and this was done from then on.

When Tarzan came in sight of the beach where stood his cabin, a strange and unusual spectacle met his vision.

On the placid waters of the land-locked harbor floated a great ship, and on the beach a small boat was drawn up.

But, most wonderful of all, a number of white men like himself were moving about between the beach and his cabin.

Tarzan saw that in many ways they were like the men of his picture-books. He crept closer through the trees until he was almost above them.

There were ten men. Swarthy, sun-tanned, and villainous-looking fellows. Now they had congregated by the boat and were talking in loud, angry tones, with much gesticulating and shaking of fists.

Presently one of them, a dwarfed, mean-faced, black-bearded fellow with a countenance which reminded Tarzan of Pamba, the rat, laid his hand upon the shoulder of a giant who stood next him, and with whom all the others had been arguing and quarreling.

The little man pointed inland, so that the giant was forced to turn away from the others to look in the direction indicated. As he turned, the mean-faced man drew a revolver from his belt and shot the giant in the back.

The big fellow threw his hands above his head, his knees bent beneath him, and, without a sound, he tumbled forward upon the beach, dead.

Tarzan puckered his brows into a frown of deep thought. It was well, thought he, that he had not given way to his first impulse to rush forward and greet these white men as brothers.

They were evidently no different from the black men—no more civilized than the apes—no less cruel than Sabor, the tiger.

For a moment the others stood looking at the killer and the giant lying dead upon the beach.

Then one of them laughed and slapped the little man upon the back. There was much more talk and gesticulating, but less quarreling.

Presently they launched the boat and all jumped into it and rowed away toward the great ship, upon whose deck Tarzan could see other figures moving about.

When they had clambered aboard, Tarzan slipped to earth

behind a great tree and crept to his cabin, keeping it always between himself and the ship.

Creeping in at the door he found that everything had been ransacked. His books and pencils strewed the floor. His weapons and shields and other little store of treasures were littered about.

As he saw what had been done a wave of anger surged through him. The new scar upon his forehead stood suddenly out, a bar of inflamed crimson against his tawny hide.

Quickly he ran to the cupboard and searched in the far recess of the lower shelf. Ah! He breathed a sigh of relief as he drew out the little tin box, and, opening it, found his greatest treasures undisturbed.

The photograph of the smiling, strong-faced young man, and the little black puzzle book were safe.

What was that?

His quick ear had caught a faint but unfamiliar sound.

Running to the window he looked toward the harbor. Another boat was being lowered from the ship. Soon he saw many people clambering over the sides of the larger vessel and dropping into the boats. They were coming back in full force.

For a moment longer Tarzan watched while a number of boxes and bundles were lowered into the waiting boats, then, as they shoved off from the ship's side, the ape-man snatched up a piece of paper, and with a pencil printed on it several lines of strong, well-made, almost letter-perfect characters.

This notice he stuck upon the door with a small, sharp splinter of wood. Then gathering up his precious tin box, his arrows, and as many bows and spears as he could carry, he hastened out of doors and disappeared into the forest.

When the two boats were beached upon the silvery sand it was a strange assortment of humanity that clambered ashore.

Some twenty souls in all there were, if the fifteen rough and villainous appearing seamen could have been said to possess that immortal spark, since they were, forsooth, a most filthy and blood-thirsty-looking aggregation.

The others of the party were of different stamp.

One was an elderly man, with white hair and large rimmed spectacles. His slightly stooped shoulders were draped in an ill-fitting, though immaculate, frock-coat; a shiny silk hat added to the incongruity of his garb in an African jungle.

The second member of the party was a tall young man in white ducks. While directly behind came another elderly man with a very high forehead and a fussy, excitable manner.

After these came a huge negress clothed like Solomon as to colors. Her great eyes rolling in evident terror, first toward the jungle and then toward the cursing band of sailors who were removing the bales and boxes from the boats.

The last member of the party to disembark was a girl of about nineteen, and it was the young man who stood at the boat's bow to lift her high and dry upon land. She gave him a brave and pretty smile of thanks.

In silence the party advanced toward the cabin. It was evident that whatever their intentions, all had been decided upon before they left the ship.

They came to the door, the sailors carrying the boxes and bales, followed by the five who were of so different a class. Then the men put down their burdens, and then one caught sight of the notice which Tarzan had posted.

"Ho, mates!" he cried. "What's here? This sign was not posted an hour ago or I'll eat the cook."

The others gathered about, craning their necks over the shoulders of those before them, but as few of them could read at all, and then only after the most laborious fashion, one finally turned to the little old man of the top-hat and frock-coat.

"Hi, perfesser," he called, "step for'rd and read the bloomin' notice."

Thus addressed, the old man came slowly to where the sailors stood, followed by the other members of his party. Adjusting his spectacles, he looked for a moment at the placard, and then, turning away, strolled off, muttering to himself: "Most remarkable—most remarkable!"

"Hi, old fossil!" cried the man who had first called on him for assistance, "didje think we wanted of you to read the bloomin' notice to yourself? Come back here and read it out loud, you old barnacle."

The old man stopped and, turning back, said: "Oh, yes, my dear sir, a thousand pardons. It was thoughtless of me, yes—very thoughtless. Most remarkable—most remarkable!"

Again he faced the notice and read it through, and doubtless would have turned off again to ruminate had not the sailor grasped him roughly by the collar and howled into his ear:

"Read it out loud, you blithering idiot."

"Ah, yes, indeed," replied the professor softly, and, adjusting his spectacles once more, he read aloud:

THIS IS THE HOUSE OF TARZAN, THE KILLER OF
   BEASTS AND MANY BLACK MEN.
DO NOT HARM THE THINGS WHICH ARE TARZAN'S.
TARZAN WATCHES.
                        TARZAN OF THE APES.

"Who the devil is Tarzan?" cried the sailor who had before spoken.

"He evidently speaks English," said the young man.

"But what does 'Tarzan of the apes' mean?" cried the girl.

"I do not know, Miss Porter," replied the young man, "unless we have discovered a runaway simian from the London Zoo who has brought back a European education to his jungle home. What do you make of it, Professor Porter?" he added, turning to the old man.

Professor Archimedes Q. Porter adjusted his spectacles.

"Ah, yes, indeed; yes, indeed—most remarkable, most remarkable. I can add nothing further to what I have already remarked in elucidation of this truly momentous occurrence." The professor turned slowly in the direction of the jungle.

"But, papa," cried the girl. "you haven't said anything about it yet!"

"Tut-tut, child; tut-tut," responded Professor Porter, in a kindly and indulgent tone.

He wandered slowly off in still another direction, his eyes bent upon the ground at his feet, his hands clasped behind him beneath the flowing tails of his coat.

"I reckon the daffy old bounder don't know no more'n we do about it," growled the rat-faced sailor.

"Keep a civil tongue in your head," cried the young man, his face paling in anger at the insulting tone of the sailor. "You've murdered our officers and robbed us. We are absolutely in your power, but, so help me, you'll treat Professor Porter and Miss Porter with respect or I'll break that neck of yours with my bare hands—guns or no guns."

The young fellow stepped so close to the rat-faced sailor that the latter, though he bore two revolvers and a villainous-looking knife in his belt, slunk back abashed.

"You coward!" cried the young man. "You've never dared shoot a man until his back was turned. You don't dare shoot me even then."

He turned his back full upon the sailor and walked nonchalantly away.

The sailor's hand crept slyly to the butt of one of his revolvers; his wicked eyes glared vengefully at the retreating form of the young Englishman. The gaze of his fellows was upon him, but he hesitated. At heart he was even a greater coward than Mr. William Cecil Clayton had imagined.

What he would have done will never be known, for there was another factor abroad which none of the party had yet guessed would enter so largely into the problems of their life on this inhospitable African shore.

Two keen eyes had watched every move of the party from the foliage of a near-by tree. Tarzan had seen the surprise caused by his notice, and while he could understand nothing of the spoken language of these strange people their gestures and facial expressions told him much.

The act of the little rat-faced sailor in killing one of his comrades had aroused a strong dislike in Tarzan, and now that he saw him quarreling with the fine-looking young man his animosity was still further stirred.

Tarzan had never seen the effects of a firearm before, though his books had taught him something of them, but when he saw the rat-faced one fingering the butt of his revolver he thought of the scene he had witnessed so short a time before, and naturally expected to see the young man murdered as had been the huge sailor earlier in the day.

So Tarzan fitted a poisoned arrow to his bow and drew a bead upon the rat-faced sailor, but the foliage was so thick that he soon saw the arrow would be deflected by the leaves or some small branch, and instead he launched a heavy spear from his lofty perch.

Clayton had taken but a dozen steps, the rat-faced sailor had half drawn his revolver; the other sailors stood watching the scene intently.

Professor Porter had already disappeared into the jungle, whither he was being followed by the fussy Samuel T. Philander, his secretary and assistant.

Esmeralda, the negress, was busy sorting her mistress's baggage from the pile of bales and boxes beside the cabin, and Miss Porter had turned away to follow Clayton—when something caused her to turn again toward the sailor.

And then three things happened almost simultaneously—the sailor jerked out his weapon and leveled it at Clayton's back, Miss Porter screamed a warning, and a long, metal-shod spear shot like a bolt from above and passed entirely through the right shoulder of the rat-faced man.

The revolver exploded harmlessly in the air, and the seaman crumpled up with a scream of pain and terror.

Clayton turned and rushed back toward the scene. The sailors stood in a frightened group, with drawn weapons, peering into the jungle. The wounded man writhed and shrieked upon the ground.

Clayton, unseen by any, picked up the fallen revolver, and slipped it inside his shirt, then he joined the sailors.

"Who could it have been?" whispered Jane Porter, and the young man turned to see her standing wide-eyed beside him.

"I dare say Tarzan of the apes is watching us," he answered. "I wonder, now, who that spear was intended for. If for Snipes— then our ape friend is a friend indeed.

"By Jove, where are your father and Mr. Philander? There's some one or something in that jungle, and it's armed, whatever it is. Ho! Professor! Mr. Philander!" young Clayton shouted. There was no response.

"What's to be done, Miss Porter? I can't leave you here alone with these cutthroats. You certainly can't venture into the jungle with me; yet some one must go in search of your father. He is more than apt at wandering off aimlessly, regardless of danger or direction, and Mr. Philander is only a trifle less impractical."

"I quite agree with you," said the girl. "Dear old papa would sacrifice his life for me without an instant's hesitation, provided one could keep his mind on so frivolous a matter for an entire instant. There is only one way to keep him in safety, and that is to chain him to a tree. The poor dear is so impractical."

"I have it!" suddenly exclaimed Clayton. "You can use a revolver, can't you?"

"Yes—why?"

"I have one. With it you and Esmeralda will be comparatively safe in this cabin while I am searching for your father and Mr.

Philander. Come, call the woman and I will hurry on. They can't have gone far."

Jane Porter did as he suggested and, when he saw the door close safely behind them, Clayton turned toward the jungle.

Some of the sailors were drawing the spear from their wounded comrade and, as Clayton approached, he asked if he could borrow a revolver from one of them while he searched the jungle for the professor.

The rat-faced one, finding he was not dead, had regained his composure, and with a volley of oaths, refused.

This man, Snipes, had assumed the role of chief since he had killed their former leader, and so little time had elapsed that none of his companions had as yet questioned his authority.

Clayton's only response was a shrug of the shoulders, but as he left them he picked up the spear which had transfixed Snipes, and thus primitively armed—the son of the then Lord Greystoke strode into the dense jungle.

Every few moments he called aloud the names of the wanderers. The watchers in the cabin by the beach heard the sound of his voice growing ever fainter and fainter, until at last it was swallowed up by the myriad noises of the primeval wood.

When Professor Archimedes Q. Porter and his assistant, Samuel T. Philander, after much insistence on the part of the latter, had finally turned their steps toward camp, they were as completely lost in the wild and tangled labyrinth of the jungle as two human beings could be, though they did not know it.

It was by the merest caprice of fortune that they headed toward the west coast of Africa, instead of toward Zanzibar on the opposite side of the dark continent.

When in a short time they reached the beach, only to find no camp in sight, Philander was positive that they were north of their proper destination, while, as a matter of fact, they were about two hundred yards south of it.

It never occurred to either of these impractical theorists to call aloud on the chance of attracting their friends' attention. Instead, with all the assurance that deductive reasoning from a wrong premise induces in one, Mr. Samuel T. Philander grasped Professor Archimedes Q. Porter firmly by the arm and hurried the weakly protesting old gentleman off in the direction of Cape Town, fifteen hundred miles to the south.

When Jane Porter and Esmeralda found themselves safely behind the cabin door the negress's first thought was to barricade the portal from the inside. With this idea in view she turned to search for some means of putting it into execution—but her first view of the interior of the cabin brought a shriek of terror to her lips, and like a frightened child the huge black ran to bury her face in her mistress's shoulders.

Jane Porter, turning at the cry, saw the cause of it lying prone upon the floor before them—the whitened skeleton of a man. A further glance revealed a second skeleton upon the bed.

"What horrible place are we in?" murmured the awestricken girl. But there was no panic in her fright.

At last disengaging herself from the frantic clutch of the still shrieking Esmeralda, Jane Porter crossed the room to look into the little cradle, knowing what she should see there before ever the tiny skeleton disclosed itself in all its pitiful and pathetic frailty.

What an awful tragedy these mute bones proclaimed! The girl shuddered at thought of the possibilities that might lie before herself and her friends in this ill-fated cabin.

Quickly, with an impatient stamp of her foot, she endeavored to shake off the gloomy forebodings, and turning to Esmeralda bade her cease her wailing.

"Stop, Esmeralda; stop it this minute!" she cried. "You are only making it worse. I never saw such a big baby."

She ended lamely, a little quiver in her own voice as she thought of the three men, upon whom she depended for protection, wandering in the depth of that awful forest.

Soon the girl found that the door was equipped with a heavy wooden bar upon the inside. After several efforts the combined strength of the two enabled them to slip it into place—the first time in twenty years.

Then they sat down upon a bench, with their arms about one another, and waited.

CHAPTER 14

At the Mercy of the Jungle

AFTER CLAYTON HAD plunged into the jungle, the sailors—mutineers of the Arrow—fell into a discussion of their next step; but on one point all were agreed—that they should hasten to put off to the anchored Arrow, where they could at least be safe from the spears of their unseen foe. Thus, while Jane Porter and Esmeralda were barricading themselves within the cabin, the crew of cutthroats were pulling rapidly for their ship in the two boats that had brought them ashore.

So much had Tarzan seen that day that his head was in a whirl of wonder. But the most wonderful sight of all to him was the face of the beautiful white girl.

Here at last was one of his own kind; of that he was positive. And the young man and the two old men, they, too, were much as he had pictured his own people to be.

But doubtless they were as ferocious and cruel as other men he had seen. The fact that they of all the party were unarmed might account for the fact that they had killed no one. They might be very different if provided with weapons.

Tarzan had seen the young man pick up the fallen revolver of the wounded Snipes and hide it away in his breast; he had also seen him hand it cautiously to the girl as she entered the cabin door.

He did not understand anything of the motives behind all that he had seen; but, somehow, intuitively he liked the young man and the two old men, and for the girl he had a strange longing which he scarcely understood. As for the big black woman, she was evidently connected in some way to the girl, and so he liked her also.

For the sailors, however, and especially Snipes, he had developed a great hatred. He knew by their threatening gestures and by the expressions upon their evil faces that they were enemies of the others, and so he decided to watch them very closely.

Tarzan wondered why the men had gone into the jungle, nor did it ever occur to him that one could become lost in that maze of undergrowth which to him was as simple as the main street of your own home town.

When he saw the sailors row away toward the ship, and knew that the girl and her companion were safe in his cabin, he decided to follow the young man into the jungle and learn what his errand might be. He swung off rapidly in the direction taken by Clayton, and in a short time heard faintly in the distance the now only occasional calls of the Englishman to his friends.

Presently Tarzan came up with the white man, who, almost fagged, was leaning against a tree wiping the perspiration from his forehead. The ape-man, hiding safe behind a screen of foliage, sat watching this new specimen of his own race intently.

At intervals Clayton called aloud, and finally it came to Tarzan that he was searching for the old men.

Tarzan was on the point of going off to look for them himself, when he caught the yellow glint of a sleek hide moving cautiously through the jungle toward Clayton.

It was Sheeta, the leopard. He heard the soft bending of grasses, and wondered why the young white man was not warned. Could it be he had failed to note the loud warning? Never before had Tarzan known Sheeta to be so clumsy.

No, the white man did not hear. Sheeta was crouching for the spring, and then, shrill and horrible, there rose upon the stillness of the jungle the awful cry of the challenging ape, and Sheeta turned, crashing into the underbrush.

Clayton came to his feet with a start. His blood ran cold. Never had so fearful a sound smote upon his ears. He was no coward; but if ever man felt the icy fingers of fear upon his heart, Cecil Clayton, eldest son of Lord Greystoke of England, did that day in the fastness of the African jungle.

The noise of some great body crashing through the underbrush so close beside him, and the sound of that blood-curdling shriek from above, tested Clayton's courage to the limit; but he could not know that it was to that very voice he owed his life, nor that the creature who hurled it forth was his own cousin—the real Lord Greystoke.

The afternoon was drawing to a close, and Clayton, disheartened and discouraged, was in a terrible quandary as to the proper course to pursue, whether to keep on in search of Professor Porter, at the almost certain risk of his own death in the jungle by night, or to return to the cabin where he might at least serve to protect Jane Porter from the perils which confronted her on all sides.

He disliked to return to camp without her father; still more he shrank from the thought of leaving her alone and unprotected in the hands of the mutineers of the Arrow, or the hundred unknown dangers of the jungle.

Possibly too, he thought, before this the professor and Philander had returned to camp. Yes, that was more than likely. At least he would return and see, before he continued, what bade fare to be a most fruitless quest. He started, stumbling back through the thick and matted underbrush in the direction that he thought the cabin lay.

To Tarzan's surprise, the young man was heading further into the jungle in the general direction of Mbonga's village, and the shrewd young ape-man was convinced that he was lost.

To Tarzan this was incomprehensible; but his judgment told him that no man would venture toward the village of the cruel blacks armed only with a spear which, from the awkward way he carried it, was evidently an unfamiliar weapon to this white man. Nor was he following the trail of the old men, that they had crossed and long since left, though it had been fresh and plain before Tarzan's eyes.

Tarzan was perplexed. The fierce jungle would make easy prey of this unprotected stranger in a very short time if he were not guided quickly to the beach.

Yes, there was Numa, the lion, even now, stalking the white man a dozen paces to the right.

Clayton heard the great body paralleling his course, and now there rose upon the evening air the great beast's thunderous roar. The man stopped with upraised spear and faced the brush from which issued the awful sound. The shadows were deepening, darkness was coming on.

To die here alone, torn by the fangs of wild beasts; to feel the hot breath of the brute on his face as the great paw crushed down upon his breast!

For a moment all was still. Clayton stood rigid with raised spear. Presently a faint rustling of the bush behind him apprised him of the stealthy creeping of the thing. It was gathering for a spring, when at last he saw it, not twenty feet away—the long, lithe, muscular body and tawny head of a huge black-maned lion.

The beast was on its belly, moving forward very slowly. As its eyes met Clayton's it stopped and deliberately, cautiously gathered its hind quarters beneath it.

In agony the man watched, fearful to launch his spear, powerless to fly.

He heard a noise in the tree above him. Some new danger, he thought, but he dared not take his eyes from the yellow-green orbs before him. There was a sharp twang, like the sound of a broken banjo-string, and at the same instant an arrow appeared in the yellow hide of the crouching lion.

With a roar of pain and anger the beast sprang; but Clayton stumbled to one side, and as he turned again to face the infuriated king of beasts, he was appalled at the sight which confronted him.

Almost simultaneously with the lion's turning to renew the attack a naked giant had dropped from the tree above squarely on the brute's back.

With lightning speed an arm that was corded with layers of iron muscle encircled the huge neck, and the great beast was raised from behind, roaring and pawing the air—raised as easily as Clayton would have lifted a pet dog.

That scene he witnessed in the twilight depths of an African jungle was burned forever into the Englishman's brain.

The man before him was the embodiment of physical perfection and giant strength, yet it was not upon this he had depended in his battle with the great cat, for, mighty as were his muscles, they were as nothing by comparison with those possessed by Numa. To his agility, to his brain, and to his long, keen knife he owed his supremacy.

His right arm encircled the lion's neck, while the left hand plunged the knife time and time again into the unprotected side behind the left shoulder, while the infuriated beast, drawn upward and backward until he stood on his hind legs, struggled impotently in this unnatural position.

Had the battle continued a few seconds longer the outcome might have been different, but all was accomplished so quickly that the lion had scarce time to recover from its surprise before it sank lifeless to the ground.

Then the strange figure which had vanquished it stood erect upon the carcass, and, throwing back the wild, handsome head, gave the fearsome cry which a few moments earlier had so startled Clayton.

Before him he saw the figure of a young man, naked except for a loincloth and a few barbaric ornaments on arms and legs, and on the breast a priceless diamond locket gleaming against a smooth brown skin.

The hunting-knife had been returned to its homely sheath, and the man was gathering up his bow and quiver from where he had tossed them, when he leaped to attack the lion.

Clayton spoke to the man in English, thanking him for his brave rescue and complimenting him on his wondrous strength and dexterity.

The only answer was a steady stare and a faint shrug of the mighty shoulders, which may have betokened either disparagement of the service rendered or ignorance of the language.

The bow and quiver slung on his back, the wild man once more drew his knife and deftly carved a dozen large strips of meat from the lion's carcass. Then, squatting upon his haunches, he proceeded to eat, motioning Clayton to join him.

The strong white teeth sank into the raw and dripping flesh in apparent relish, but Clayton could not bring himself to share the uncooked meat with his strange host; instead he watched him, and presently there dawned upon him the conviction that this was Tarzan of the apes, whose notice he had seen posted upon the cabin door that morning.

If so, he must speak English.

Again Clayton essayed speech with the ape-man; but the replies were in a strange tongue, which resembled the chattering of monkeys mingled with the growling of some wild beast.

No, this could not be Tarzan of the apes, for it was very evident that he was an utter stranger to the English language.

When Tarzan had finished his repast he rose and, pointing in a very different direction from that which Clayton had been pursuing, started through the jungle toward the point he had indicated.

Clayton, bewildered and confused, hesitated to follow him, for he thought he was but being led more deeply into the mazes of the forest; but the ape-man returned, and, grasping him by the coat, dragged him along until he was convinced that Clayton understood what was required of him, and then left him to follow voluntarily.

The Englishman finally concluded that he was a prisoner, and saw no alternative but to accompany his captor, and thus they traveled slowly through the jungle while the sable mantle of the impenetrable night of the forest fell about them.

The stealthy footfalls of padded paws mingled with the breaking of twigs and the wild calls of the savage life, and Clayton felt all this closing in on him.

Suddenly Clayton heard the faint report of a firearm—a single shot, and then silence.

In the cabin by the beach two thoroughly terrified women clung to each other as they crouched upon the low bench in the gathering darkness.

The negress, sobbing hysterically, bemoaned the evil day that had witnessed her departure from her dear Maryland, while the white girl, dry-eyed and outwardly calm, was tortured by inward

The infuriated beast, drawn upward and backward, struggled impotently.

forebodings. She feared not more for herself than for the three men whom she knew to be wandering in the abysmal depths of the jungle, from which now issued the incessant shrieks and roars, barkings, and growlings of its terrifying and fearsome inmates.

Now came the sound of a heavy body brushing against the side of the cabin. She could hear the great padded paws upon the ground without. Then for an instant all was silence; even the bedlam of the forest died out to a faint murmur; then she distinctly heard the beast outside sniffing at the door, not two feet from where she crouched. Instinctively the girl shuddered and shrank closer to the black woman.

"Hush!" she whispered. "Hush, Esmeralda," for the woman's sobs and groans seemed to have attracted the thing that stalked there just beyond the thin wall.

A gentle scratching sound was heard on the door. The brute tried to force an entrance; but presently this ceased, and again she heard the great padded paws creep stealthily around the cabin. Again they stopped—beneath the window on which the terrified eyes of the girl now glued themselves.

"Heavens!" she murmured, for, silhouetted against the moonlit sky beyond, she saw framed in the tiny square of the latticed window the head of a huge tiger. The gleaming eyes were fixed upon her in tense ferocity.

"Look, Esmeralda!" she whispered. "What shall we do? Look! Quick! The window!"

Esmeralda cowered still closer to her mistress and glanced, affrighted, toward the little square of moonlight just as the tiger emitted a low, savage snarl.

The sight that met the poor black's eyes was too much for the already overstrung nerves.

"Oh, Gaberelle!" she shrieked and slid to the floor, an inert and senseless mass.

For what seemed an eternity the great brute stood with its forepaws upon the sill, glaring into the little room. Presently it tried the strength of the lattice with its great talons.

The girl had almost ceased to breathe, when to her relief the head disappeared and she heard the brute's footsteps leaving the window. But now they came to the door again, and once more the scratching commenced; but this time with increasing force until the great beast was tearing at the massive panels in a perfect frenzy of fury.

Could Jane Porter have known the immense strength of that door, builded piece by piece, she would have felt less fear of the tiger reaching her by this avenue. Little did John Clayton imagine when he fashioned that crude but mighty portal that one day, twenty years later, it would shield a fair American girl, then unborn, from the teeth and talons of the man-eater.

For fully twenty minutes the brute alternatively sniffed and tore at the door, occasionally giving voice to a cry of baffled rage. At length, however, he gave up the attempt, and Jane Porter heard him returning toward the window, beneath which he paused for an instant, and then launched his great weight against the time-worn lattice.

The girl heard the wooden rods groan beneath the impact; but they held, and the huge body dropped back to the ground below.

Again and again the tiger repeated these tactics, until finally the horrified prisoner within saw a portion of the lattice give way, and in an instant one great paw and the head of the animal were thrust within the room.

Slowly the powerful neck and shoulders were spreading the bars apart, and the lithe body came further and further into the room.

As in a trance, the girl rose, her hand upon her breast, wide eyes staring horror-stricken into the snarling face of the beast scarce ten feet from her. At her feet lay the prostrate form of the negress. If she could but arouse her, their combined efforts might possibly avail to beat back the blood-thirsty intruder.

Jane Porter stooped to grasp the black woman by the shoulder. Roughly she shook her.

"Esmeralda! Esmeralda!" she cried. "Help me, or we are lost!"

Esmeralda slowly opened her eyes. The first object they encountered was the dripping fangs of Sabor.

With a horrified scream the poor woman rose to her hands and knees, and in this position scurried across the room, shrieking, "Oh, Gaberelle! Oh, Gaberelle!" at the top of her lungs.

Esmeralda weighed some two hundred and eighty pounds, which added nothing to the grace of her carriage when walking erect, and her extreme haste, added to her extreme corpulency, produced a most amazing result when Esmeralda elected to travel on all-fours.

For a moment the tiger remained quiet with intense gaze directed upon the flitting Esmeralda, whose goal appeared to be the cupboard, into which she attempted to propel her huge bulk; but, as the shelves were but nine or ten inches apart, she only succeeded in getting her head in, whereupon, with a final screech, which paled the jungle noises into insignificance, she fainted once again.

With the subsidence of Esmeralda the tiger renewed his efforts to wriggle his huge bulk through the weakening lattice.

The girl, standing pale and rigid against the farther wall, sought with increasing terror for some loophole of escape. Suddenly her hand, tight-pressed against her bosom, felt the hard outlines of the revolver that Clayton had left with her earlier in the day.

Quickly she snatched it from its hiding-place, and, leveling it full at the tiger's face, pulled the trigger.

There was a flash of flame, the roar of the discharge, and an answering roar of pain and anger from the beast.

Jane Porter saw the great form disappear from the window, and then she, too, fainted.

But the tiger was not killed. The bullet had but inflicted a painful wound in one of the great shoulders. It was the surprise at the blinding flash and the deafening roar that had caused his hasty, though but temporary, retreat.

In another instant he was back at the lattice, and with renewed fury was clawing at the aperture, but with lessened effect, since the wounded member was almost useless.

He saw his prey—two women—lying senseless upon the floor; there was no longer any resistance to be overcome. Sabor had only to worm his way through the lattice to claim it.

Slowly he forced his great bulk, inch by inch, through the opening. Now his head was through, now one great foreleg and shoulder.

Carefully he drew up the wounded member to insinuate it gently beyond the tight-pressing bars.

A moment more and both shoulders through, the long, sinuous body and the narrow hips would glide quickly after.

It was on this sight that Jane Porter again opened her eyes.

CHAPTER 15

The Forest God

WHEN CLAYTON HEARD the report of the firearm he fell into an agony of fear and apprehension. He knew that it might be one of the sailors; but the fact that he had left the revolver with Jane Porter, together with the overwrought condition of his nerves, made him morbidly positive that she was threatened with some great danger; perhaps even now was attempting to defend herself against man or beast.

What were the thoughts of his strange captor or guide Clayton could only vaguely conjecture; but that he had heard the shot, and was in some manner affected by it, was quite evident, for he quickened his pace so appreciably that Clayton, stumbling blindly in his wake, was down a dozen times in as many minutes in a vain effort to keep pace with him, and soon was left hopelessly behind.

Fearing that he would again be irretrievably lost, he called aloud to the wild man ahead of him, and in a moment had the satisfaction of seeing him drop lightly to his side from the branches above.

For a moment Tarzan looked at the young man closely, as though undecided as to just what was best to do; then, stooping before Clayton, he motioned him to grasp him about the neck, and, with the white man upon his back, Tarzan took to the trees.

The next few minutes were such as the young Englishman never forgot. High into bending and swaying branches he was borne with what seemed to him incredible swiftness, while Tarzan chafed at the slowness of his progress.

From one lofty branch the agile creature swung with Clayton through a dizzy arc to a neighboring tree; then for a hundred yards maybe the sure feet threaded a maze of interwoven limbs, balancing like a tight-rope walker high above the black depths of verdure beneath.

From the first sensation of chilling fear Clayton passed to one of admiration and envy of those giant muscles and that wondrous instinct or knowledge which guided this forest god through the inky blackness of the night as easily and safely as Clayton could have strolled a London street at high noon.

Occasionally they would enter a spot where the foliage above was less dense, and the bright rays of the moon lit up before Clayton's wondering eyes the strange path they were traversing.

At such times the man fairly caught his breath at sight of the horrid depths below them, for Tarzan took the easiest way, which often led over a hundred feet above the earth.

With all his seeming speed, Tarzan was in reality feeling his way with comparative slowness, searching constantly for limbs of adequate strength for the maintenance of this double weight.

Presently they came to the clearing before the beach. Tarzan's quick ears had heard the strange sounds of Sabor's efforts to force his way through the lattice, and it seemed to Clayton that they dropped a straight hundred feet to earth, so quickly did Tarzan descend. Yet when they struck the ground it was with scarce a jar; and as Clayton released his hold on the ape-man he saw him dart like a squirrel for the opposite side of the cabin.

The Englishman sprang quickly after him just in time to see the hind-quarters of some huge animal about to disappear within the cabin.

As Jane Porter opened her eyes to a realization of the again imminent peril which threatened her, her brave heart gave up its final vestige of hope, and she turned to grope for the fallen weapon that she might mete to herself a merciful death before the cruel fangs tore at her flesh.

The tiger was almost through the window before she found the weapon, and she raised it quickly to her temple to shut out forever the hideous jaws gaping for their prey.

An instant she hesitated, to breathe a short and silent prayer to her Maker, and as she did so her eyes fell upon the poor Esmeralda lying inert, but alive, beside the cupboard.

How could she leave the poor, faithful thing to those merciless yellow fangs? No, she must use one cartridge on the senseless woman ere she turned the cold muzzle toward herself again.

She shrank from the ordeal. But it would have been cruelty a thousand times less justifiable to have left the loving black woman who had reared her from infancy, to regain consciousness beneath the rending claws of the tiger.

Quickly the girl sprang to her feet and ran to the side of the negress. She pressed the muzzle of the revolver tight against that devoted heart, closed her eyes, and—

The tiger emitted a frightful shriek.

Jane Porter, startled, pulled the trigger and turned to face the beast, and with the same movement raised the weapon against her own temple.

She did not fire a second time. Astounded, she saw the huge beast being slowly drawn back through the window, and in the moonlight beyond she saw the heads and shoulders of two men.

As Clayton rounded the corner of the cabin to behold the animal disappearing within, it was also to see the ape-man seize the long black-and-yellow tail in both hands, and, bracing himself with his feet against the side of the cabin, throw all his mighty strength into the effort to draw the beast out of the interior.

Clayton was quick to lend a hand, but the ape-man jabbered to him in a commanding and peremptory tone. Orders, Clayton knew, though he could not understand them.

At last, under their combined efforts, the great body commenced to appear farther and farther without the window, and then there came to Clayton's mind a dawning conception of the rash bravery of his companion's act.

For a naked man to drag a shrieking, clawing man-eater forth from a window by the tail to save a strange white girl, was indeed the last word in heroism.

In so far as Clayton was concerned it was a very different matter, since the girl was not only of his own kind, but was the woman whom he loved.

Though he knew that the tiger would make short work of both of them, he pulled with a will to keep it from Jane Porter. And then he recalled the battle between this man and the lion, which he had witnessed a short time before, and he commenced to feel more assurance.

Tarzan was still issuing orders which Clayton could not understand.

He was trying to tell the stupid white man to plunge his poisoned arrows into Sabor's back and sides, and to reach the savage heart with the long, thin hunting-knife that hung at Tarzan's hip; but the man would not understand, and Tarzan did not dare release his hold to do the things himself. He knew that the puny white man never could hold mighty Sabor alone for an instant.

Slowly the tiger was emerging from the window. At last his shoulders were out.

And then Clayton saw a thing done which not even the eternal heavens had ever seen before. Tarzan, racking his brains for some means to cope single-handed with the infuriated beast, had suddenly recalled his battle with Terkoz; and as the great shoulders came clear of the window, so that the tiger hung upon the sill only by his forepaws, Tarzan sudenly released his hold upon the brute.

With incredible quickness he launched himself full upon Sabor's back, his strong young arms seeking and gaining a full-Nelson upon the beast, as he had learned it that other day during his bloody victory over Terkoz.

With a shriek the tiger turned completely over upon his back, falling full upon his enemy. The black-haired giant only closed tighter his hold.

Pawing and tearing at earth and air, Sabor rolled and threw himself this way and that in an effort to dislodge his antagonist. Always tighter and tighter drew the iron bands that were forcing his head lower and lower upon his white breast.

Higher and higher crept the steel forearms of the ape-man about the back of Sabor's neck. Weaker and weaker became the tiger's efforts.

At last Clayton saw the immense muscles of Tarzan's shoulders and biceps leap into corded knots. There was a long-sustained and supreme effort on the ape-man's part—and the vertebræ of Sabor's neck parted with a sharp snap.

In an instant Tarzan was upon his feet, and for the second time that day Clayton heard the bull ape's savage roar of victory—and then he heard Jane Porter's agonized cry:

"Cecil!—Mr. Clayton! Oh, what is it? What is it?"

Running quickly to the cabin door, Clayton called out that all was right, and bade her open. As quickly as she could she raised the great bar and fairly dragged Clayton within.

"What was that awful noise?" she whispered, shrinking close to him.

"It was the cry of the kill from the throat of the man who has just saved your life, Miss Porter. Wait, I will fetch him that you may thank him."

The frightened girl would not be left alone, so she accompanied Clayton to the side of the cabin where lay the dead body of the tiger.

Tarzan of the apes was gone.

Clayton called several times, but there was no reply, and so the two returned to the greater safety of the interior.

"What a frightful sound!" cried Jane Porter. "Don't tell me that a human being made it!"

"But it did, Miss Porter," replied Clayton; "or at least if not a human throat, that of a forest god."

And he told her of his experiences with this creature—of how twice the wild man had saved his life—of his wondrous strength and agility and bravery—of the brown skin and the handsome face.

"I cannot make it out at all," he concluded. "At first I thought he might be Tarzan of the apes. But he neither speaks nor understands English, so that theory is untenable."

"Well, whatever he may be," cried the girl, "we owe him our lives. May Heaven bless him and keep him in safety in his jungle!"

"Amen," said Clayton fervently.

"Fo' de good Lawd's sake, ain' Ah daid?"

The two turned to see Esmeralda sitting upright upon the floor, her great eyes rolling from side to side, as though she could not believe their testimony as to her whereabouts.

The tiger's shriek, as Jane Porter had been about to put a bullet into poor Esmeralda, had saved the black's life, for the little start the girl gave had turned the muzzle of the revolver to one side, and the bullet had passed harmlessly into the floor.

And now, for Jane Porter, the reaction came, and she threw herself upon the bench, screaming with laughter.

CHAPTER 16

"Most Remarkable"

SEVERAL MILES SOUTH of the cabin, upon a strip of sandy beach, stood two old men, arguing.

Before them stretched the broad Atlantic; at their backs the Dark Continent; close around them loomed the impenetrable blackness of the jungle.

Savage beasts roared and growled; noises, hideous and weird, assailed their ears. They had wandered miles in search of their camp, but always in the wrong direction. They were as hopelessly lost as though they suddenly had been transported to another world.

At such a time indeed every fiber of their combined intellects should have been concentrated upon the vital question of the minute—the life-and-death question to them of retracing their steps to camp.

Samuel T. Philander was speaking.

"But, my dear professor," he was saying, "I still maintain that but for the victories of Ferdinand and Isabella over the fifteenth-century Moors in Spain the world would be to-day a thousand years in advance of where we now find ourselves.

"The Moors were essentially a tolerant, broad-minded, liberal race of agriculturists, artisans, and merchants—the very type of people that has made possible such civilization as we find to-day in America and Europe—while the Spaniards—"

"Tut-tut, Mr. Philander," interrupted Professor Porter, "their religion positively precluded the possibilities you suggest. Moslemism was, is, and always will be a blight on that scientific progress which has marked—"

"Bless me! Professor," interjected Mr. Philander, who had turned his gaze toward the jungle, "there seems to be some one approaching."

Professor Archimedes Q. Porter turned in the direction indicated by the near-sighted Mr. Philander.

"Tut-tut, Mr. Philander!" he chided. "How often must I urge you to seek after that absolute concentration of your mental faculties which alone may permit you to bring to bear the highest powers of intellectuality upon the momentous problems which naturally fall to the lot of great minds? And now I find you guilty of a most flagrant breach of courtesy in interrupting my discourse to call attention to a mere quadruped of the genus *Felis*. As I was saying, Mr.—"

"Heavens, professor, a lion?" cried Mr. Philander, straining his weak eyes toward the dim figure outlined against the dark tropical underbrush.

"Yes, yes, Mr. Philander, if you insist upon employing slang in your discourse, a 'lion.' But, as I was saying—"

"Bless me, professor," again interrupted Mr. Philander, "permit me to suggest that doubtless the Moors who were conquered in the fifteenth century will continue in that most regretable condition for the time being at least, even though we postpone discussion of that world calamity until we may attain the enchanting view of yon *Felis carnivora* which distance proverbially is credited with lending."

In the mean time the lion had approached with quiet dignity to within ten paces of the two men, where he stood curiously watching them.

The moonlight flooded the beach, and the strange group stood out in bold relief against the yellow sand.

"Most reprehensible, most reprehensible!" exclaimed Professor Porter, with a faint trace of irritation in his voice.

"Never, Mr. Philander, never before in my life have I known one of these animals to be permitted to roam at large from its cage. I shall most certainly report this most outrageous breach of ethics to the directors of the zoological garden."

"Quite right, professor," agreed Mr. Philander, "and the sooner it is done the better. Let us start now."

Seizing the professor by the arm, Mr. Philander set off in the direction that would put the greatest distance between themselves and the lion.

They had proceeded but a short distance when a backward glance revealed that the lion was following them. Mr. Philander tightened his grip upon the professor and increased his speed.

"As I was saying, Mr. Philander—" repeated Professor Porter.

Mr. Philander took another hasty glance rearward. The lion also had quickened his gait, and was doggedly maintaining an unvarying distance behind them.

"He is following us!" gasped Mr. Philander, breaking into a run.

"Tut-tut, Mr. Philander!" remonstrated the professor. "This unseemly haste is most unbecoming men of letters."

Mr. Philander stole another observation astern.

The lion was bounding along in easy leaps scarce five paces behind.

Mr. Philander dropped the professor's arm, and broke into a mad orgy of speed that would have done credit to any varsity track team.

"As I was saying, Mr. Philander—" screamed Professor Porter as, metaphorically speaking, he himself "threw her into high." He, too, had caught a fleeting backward glimpse of cruel yellow eyes and half-open mouth within startling proximity of his person.

With streaming coat-tails and shiny silk hat, Professor Archimedes Q. Porter fled through the moonlight close upon the heels of Mr. Samuel T. Philander.

Before them a point of the jungle ran out toward a narrow promontory, and it was for the haven of the trees he saw there that Mr. Samuel T. Philander directed his prodigious leaps and bounds; and from the shadows of this same spot peered two keen eyes in interested appreciation of the race.

It was Tarzan of the apes who watched, with face agrin, this odd game of follow-the-leader.

He knew the two men were safe enough from attack in so far as the lion was concerned. The very fact that Numa had foregone such easy prey at all convinced the wise forest craft of Tarzan that Numa had already dined.

The lion might stalk them until hungry again, but the chances were that if not angered he would soon tire of the sport and slink away to his jungle lair.

Really, the one great danger was that one of the men might stumble and fall, and then the yellow devil would be upon him in a moment and the joy of the kill would be too great a temptation to withstand.

So Tarzan swung quickly to a lower limb in line with the approaching fugitives; and as Mr. Samuel T. Philander came panting and blowing beneath him, already too spent to struggle up to the safety of the limb, Tarzan reached down and, grasping him by the collar of his coat, yanked him to the limb by his side.

Another moment brought the professor within the sphere of the friendly grip, and he, too, was drawn upward to safety just as the baffled Numa, with a roar, leaped to recover his vanishing quarry.

For a moment the two men clung, panting, to the great branch, while Tarzan squatted with his back to the stem of the tree, watching them with mingled curiosity and amusement.

It was the professor who first broke the silence.

"I am deeply pained, Mr. Philander, that you should have evinced such a paucity of manly courage in the presence of one of the lower orders, and by your crass timidity have caused me to exert myself to such an unaccustomed degree in order that I might resume my discourse. As I was saying, Mr. Philander, when you interrupted me, the Moors—"

"Professor Archimedes Q. Porter," broke in Mr. Philander in icy tones, "the time has arrived when patience becomes a crime and mayhem appears garbed in the mantle of virtue. You have accused me of cowardice. You have insinuated that you ran only to overtake me, not to escape the clutches of the lion."

"Have a care, Professor Archimedes Q. Porter; I am a desperate man. Goaded by long-suffering patience, the worm will turn."

"Tut-tut, Mr. Philander—tut-tut!" cautioned Professor Porter; "you forget yourself."

"I forget nothing as yet, Professor Archimedes Q. Porter; but, believe me, sir, I am tottering on the verge of forgetfulness as to your exalted position in the world of science and your gray hairs."

The professor sat in silence for a few minutes, and the darkness hid the grim smile that wreathed his wrinkled countenance. Presently he spoke.

"Look here, Skinny Philander," he said in belligerent tones, "if you are lookin' for a scrap, peel off your coat and come down on the ground, and I'll punch your head just as I did sixty years ago in the alley back of Porky Evans's barn."

"Ark!" gasped the astonished Mr. Philander. "Lordy, how good that sounds! When you're human, Ark, I love you. Somehow, it seems as though you had forgotten how to be human for the last twenty-years."

The professor reached out a thin, trembling old hand through the darkness until it found his old friend's shoulder.

"Forgive me, Skinny," he said softly. "It hasn't been quite twenty years, and Heaven alone knows how hard I have tried to be 'human' for Jane's sake, and yours, too, since my other Jane was taken away."

Another old hand stole up from Mr. Philander's side to clasp the one that lay upon his shoulder, and no other message could better have translated the one heart to the other.

They did not speak for some minutes. The lion below them paced nervously back and forth. The third figure in the tree was hidden by the dense shadows near the stem. He, too, was silent—motionless as a graven image.

"You certainly pulled me up into this tree just in time," said the professor at last. "I want to thank you. You saved my life."

"But I didn't pull you up here, professor," said Mr. Philander. "Bless me! The excitement of the moment quite caused me to forget that I myself was drawn up here by some outside agency. There must be some one or something in this tree with us."

"Eh?" ejaculated Professor Porter. "Are you quite positive, Mr. Philander?"

"Most positive, professor," replied Mr. Philander. "And," he added, "I think we should thank the party. He may be sitting right next to you now, professor."

"Eh? What's that? Tut-tut, Mr. Philander, tut-tut!" said Professor Porter, edging cautiously nearer to Mr. Philander.

Just then it occurred to Tarzan of the apes that Numa had loitered beneath the tree for a sufficient length of time, so he raised his young head toward the heavens, and there rang out upon the terrified ears of the two old men the awful warning challenge of the anthropoid.

The two friends, huddled trembling in their precarious position on the limb, saw the great lion halt in his restless pacing as the blood-curdling cry smote his ears, and then slink quickly into the jungle, to be instantly lost to view.

"Even the lion trembles in fear," whispered Mr. Philander.

"Most remarkable, most remarkable," murmured Professor Porter, clutching frantically at Mr. Philander to regain the balance which the sudden fright had so perilously endangered. Unfortunately for them both, Mr. Philander's center of equilibrium was at that very moment hanging upon the ragged edge of nothing, so that it needed but the gentle impetus supplied by the additional weight of Professor Porter's body to topple the devoted secretary from the limb.

For a moment they swayed uncertainly, and then, with mingled and most unscholarly shrieks, they pitched headlong from the tree, locked in frenzied embrace.

It was quite some moments ere either moved, for both were positive that any such attempt would reveal so many breaks and fractures as to make further progress impossible.

At length Professor Porter essayed an attempt to move one leg. To his surprise, it responded to his will as in days gone by. He now drew up its mate and stretched it forth again.

"Most remarkable," he murmured.

"Thank Heaven, professor" whispered Mr. Philander fervently. "You're not dead, then?"

"Tut-tut, Mr. Philander, tut-tut!" cautioned Professor Porter. "I do not know as yet."

With infinite solicitude Professor Porter wiggled his right arm— joy! It was intact. Breathlessly he waved his left arm above his prostrate body—it waved!

"Most remarkable, most remarkable," he said.

"To whom are you signaling professor?" asked Mr. Philander in an excited tone.

Professor Porter deigned to make no response to this puerile inquiry. Instead, he raised his head gently from the ground, nodding it back and forth a half-dozen times.

"Most remarkable," he breathed. "It remains intact."

Mr. Philander had not moved from where he had fallen; he had not dared the attempt. How, indeed, could one move when one's arms and legs and back were broken?

One eye was buried in the soft loam; the other, rolling sidewise, was fixed in awe upon the strange gyrations of Professor Porter.

"How sad!" exclaimed Mr. Philander, half aloud. "Concussion of the brain, superinducing total mental aberration. How very sad indeed!"

Professor Porter rolled over upon his stomach. Gingerly he bowed his back until he resembled a huge tomcat in proximity to a yelping dog. Then he sat up and felt of various portions of his anatomy.

"They are all here," he ejaculated.

Whereupon he rose, and, bending a scathing glance upon the still prostrate form of Mr. Samuel T. Philander, he said:

"Tut-tut, Mr. Philander; this is no time to indulge in slothful ease. We must be up and doing."

Mr. Philander lifted his other eye out of the mud and gazed in speechless rage at Professor Porter. Then he attempted to rise; nor could there have been any one more surprised than he when his efforts were immediately crowned with marked success.

He was still bursting with rage, however, at the cruel injustice of Professor Porter's insinuation, and was on the point of rendering a tart rejoinder when his eyes fell upon a strange figure standing a few paces away, scrutinizing them intently.

Professor Porter had recovered his shiny silk hat, which he had brushed carefully upon the sleeve of his coat and replaced upon his head. When he saw Mr. Philander pointing to something behind him, he turned to behold a giant, naked but for a loin-cloth and a few metal ornaments, standing motionless before him.

"Good evening, sir!" said the professor, lifting his hat.

For reply, the giant motioned them to follow him, and set off up the beach in the direction from which they had recently come.

"I think it the part of discretion to follow him," said Mr. Philander.

"Tut-tut, Mr. Philander," returned the professor. "A short time since you were advancing most logical argument in substantiation of your theory that camp lay directly south of us. I was skeptical, but you finally convinced me; so now I am positive that toward the south we must travel to reach our friends. Therefore, I shall continue south."

"But, Professor Porter, this man may know better than either of us. He seems to be indigenous to this part of the world. Let us at least follow him for a short distance."

"Tut-tut, Mr. Philander," repeated the professor. "I am a difficult man to convince, but when once convinced my decision is unalterable. I shall continue in the proper direction, if I have to circumambulate the continent of Africa to reach my destination."

Further argument was interrupted by Tarzan, who, seeing that these strange men were not following him, had returned to their side.

Again he motioned them to follow him; but still they stood in argument.

Presently the ape-man lost patience with their stupid ignorance. He grasped the frightened Mr. Philander by the shoulder, and before that worthy gentleman knew whether he was being killed or merely maimed for life, Tarzan had tied one end of his rope securely about Mr. Philander's neck.

"Tut-tut, Mr. Philander," remonstrated Professor Porter; "it is most unbeseeming in you to submit to such indignities."

But scarcely were the words out of his mouth ere he, too, had been seized and securely bound by the neck with the same rope. Then Tarzan set off toward the north, leading the now thoroughly frightened professor and his secretary.

In deathly silence they proceeded for what seemed hours to the two tired and hopeless old men; but presently, as they topped a little rise of ground, they were overjoyed to see the cabin lying before them, not a hundred yards distant.

Here Tarzan released them and, pointing toward the little building, vanished into the jungle beside them.

"Most remarkable, most remarkable!" gasped the professor. "But you see, Mr. Philander, that I was quite right, as usual; and but for your stubborn wilfulness we should have escaped a series of most humiliating, not to say dangerous, accidents. Pray allow yourself to be guided by a more mature and practical mind in future."

Mr. Samuel T. Philander was too much relieved at the happy outcome of their adventure to take umbrage at the professor's cruel fling. Instead, he grasped his friend's arm and hastened him forward in the direction of the cabin.

It was a much-relieved party of castaways that found itself once more united. Dawn discovered them still recounting their various adventures, and speculating upon the identity of the strange guardian and protector they had found on this savage shore.

Esmeralda was positive that it was none other than an angel sent down especially to watch over them.

"Had you seen him devour the raw meat of the lion, Esmeralda," laughed Clayton, "you would have thought him a very material angel."

"Ah doan know nuffin' 'bout dat, Marse Clayton," rejoined Esmeralda; "but Ah 'specs de Lawd clean fergot to gib him any matches, He sent him down in sech a hurry to look after we-all. An' he suttinly cain't cook nuffin' 'thout matches—no, sah."

"There was nothing heavenly about his voice," said Jane Porter, with a little shudder at recollection of the awful roar which had followed the killing of the tiger.

"Nor did it precisely comport with my preconceived ideas of the dignity of divine messengers," remarked Professor Porter, "when the—ah—gentlemen tied two highly respectable and erudite scholars neck to neck and dragged them through the jungle as though they had been cows."

CHAPTER 17

Burials

As it was now quite light, the party, none of whom had eaten or slept since the previous morning, began to bestir themselves to prepare food.

The mutineers of the Arrow had landed a small supply of dried meats, canned soups, and vegetables, crackers, flour, tea, and coffee for the five they had marooned, and these were hurriedly drawn upon to satisfy the cravings of long-famished appetites.

The next task was to make the cabin habitable, and to this end it was first decided to remove the gruesome relics of the tragedy which had taken place there on some bygone day.

Professor Porter and Mr. Philander were deeply interested in examining the skeletons. The two larger, they stated, to have belonged to a male and female of one of the higher white races.

The smallest skeleton was given but passing attention, as its location in the crib left no doubt as to its having been the infant offspring of this unhappy couple.

As they were preparing the skeleton of the man for burial, Clayton discovered a massive ring which had evidently encircled the man's finger at the time of his death, for one of the slender bones of the hand still lay within the golden bauble.

Picking it up to examine it, Clayton gave a cry of astonishment, for the ring bore the crest of the house of Greystoke.

At the same time, Jane Porter discovered the books in the cupboard, and on opening to the fly-leaf of one of them saw the name "John Clayton, London." In a second book which she hurriedly examined, was the single name "Greystoke."

"Why, Mr. Clayton," she cried, "what does this mean? Here are the names of some of your own people in these books."

"And here," he replied gravely, "is the great ring of the house of Greystoke which has been lost since my uncle, John Clayton, the former Lord Greystoke, disappeared, presumably lost at sea."

"But how do you account for these things being here in this savage African jungle?" exclaimed the girl.

"There is but one way to account for it, Miss Porter," said Clayton. "The late Lord Greystoke was not drowned. He died here in this cabin, and this poor thing upon the floor is all that is mortal of him."

"Then this must have been Lady Greystoke," said Jane Porter reverently, indicating the mass of bones upon the bed.

"The beautiful Lady Alice," replied Clayton, "of whose many virtues and charms I often have heard my mother and father speak."

With reverence and solemnity the bodies of the late Lord and Lady Greystoke were buried beside their little African cabin, and between them was placed the tiny skeleton of the baby of Kala, the ape.

As Mr. Philander was placing the frail bones of the infant in a bit of sail-cloth, he examined the skull minutely. Then he called Professor Porter to his side, and the two argued in low tones for several minutes.

"Most remarkable, most remarkable," said Professor Porter.

"Bless me," said Mr. Philander, "we must acquaint Mr. Clayton with our discovery at once."

"Tut-tut, Mr. Philander, tut-tut!" remonstrated Professor Archimedes Q. Porter. "Let the dead past bury its dead."

And so the white-haired old man repeated the burial service over this strange grave, while his four companions stood with bowed and uncovered heads about him.

From the trees Tarzan of the apes watched this strange ceremony; but, most of all, he watched the sweet face and graceful figure of Jane Porter.

In his savage, untutored breast new emotions were stirring. He could not fathom them. He wondered why he felt so great an interest in these people—why he had gone to such pains to save the three men. But he did not wonder why he had torn Sabor from the tender flesh of the strange girl.

Surely the men were stupid and ridiculous and cowardly. Even Manu, the monkey, was more intelligent than they. If these were creatures of his own kind, he was doubtful if his past pride in blood was warranted.

But the girl, ah!—that was a different matter. He did not reason here. He knew that she was created to be protected, and that he was created to protect her.

He wondered why they had dug a great hole in the ground merely to bury dry bones. Surely there was no sense in that; no one wanted to steal dry bones.

Had there been meat upon them he could have understood; for thus alone might one keep his meat from Dango, the hyena, and the other robbers of the jungle.

When the grave had been filled with earth the little party turned back toward the cabin, and Esmeralda, still weeping copiously for the two she had never heard of before, and who had been dead twenty years, chanced to glance toward the harbor. Instantly her tears ceased.

"Look at dem low down white trash out dere!" she shrilled, pointing toward the Arrow. "They-all's a desecratin' us, right yere on dis yere perverted islan'."

Surely enough the Arrow was being worked toward the open sea slowly through the harbor's entrance.

"They promised to leave us firearms and ammunition," said Clayton. "The merciless beasts!"

"It is the work of that fellow they call Snipes, I am sure," said Jane Porter. "King was a scoundrel, but he had a little sense of humanity. If they had not killed him I know that he would have seen that we were properly provided for before they left us to our fate."

"I regret that they did not visit us before sailing," said Professor Porter. "I had purposed requesting them to leave the treasure with us, as I shall be a ruined man if that is lost."

Jane looked at her father sadly.

"Never mind, dear," she said. "It wouldn't have done any good, because it is solely for the treasure that they killed their officers and landed us upon this awful shore."

"Tut-tut, child, tut-tut!" replied Professor Porter. "You are a good child, but inexperienced in practical matters."

Professor Porter turned and walked slowly away toward the jungle, his hands clasped beneath his long coat-tails and his eyes bent upon the ground.

His daughter watched him with a pathetic smile upon her lips, and then, turning to Mr. Philander, she whispered:

"Please don't let him wander off again as he did yesterday. We depend upon you, you know, to keep a close watch upon him."

"He becomes more difficult to handle each day," replied Mr. Philander, with a sigh and a shake of his head. "I presume he is now off to report to the directors of the Zoo that one of their lions was at large last night. Oh, Miss Jane, you don't know what I have to contend with."

"Yes, I do, Mr. Philander. But, while we all love him, you alone are best fitted to manage him; for, regardless of what he may say to you, he respects your learning, and, therefore, has immense confidence in your judgment. The poor dear cannot differentiate between erudition and wisdom."

Mr. Philander, with a mildly puzzled expression on his face, turned to pursue Professor Porter, and in his mind he was revolving the question of whether he should feel complimented or aggrieved at Miss Porter's rather back-handed compliment.

Tarzan had seen the consternation depicted upon the faces of the little group as they witnessed the departure of the Arrow; so, as the ship was a wonderful novelty to him in addition, he determined to hasten out to the point of land at the north of the harbor's mouth and obtain a nearer view of the great boat, as well as to learn, if possible, the direction of its flight.

Swinging through the trees with great speed, he reached the point but a moment after the ship had passed out of the harbor; so that he obtained an excellent view of the wonders of this strange floating house.

There were some twenty men running hither and thither about the deck, pulling and hauling on ropes.

A very light land breeze was blowing, and the ship had been worked through the harbor's mouth under flying jib, fore and main royals and mizzen spanker, but, now that they had cleared the point, every available shred of canvas was being spread that she might stand out to sea as handily as possible.

Tarzan watched the graceful movements of the ship in rapt admiration, and longed to be aboard her. Presently his keen eyes caught the faintest suspicion of smoke on the far northern horizon, and he wondered what the cause of it might be.

At about the same time the lookout on the Arrow must have discerned it, for in a few minutes Tarzan saw the sails being shifted. The ship came about, and presently he knew that she was coming back toward land.

A man at the bows was constantly heaving into the sea a rope, to the end of which a small object was fastened. Tarzan wondered what the purpose of this action might be.

At last the ship came up directly into the wind; the anchor was lowered; down came the sails. There was great scurrying about on deck.

A boat was lowered, and into the boat a great chest was placed. Then a dozen sailors bent to the oars and pulled rapidly toward the point where Tarzan crouched in the branches of a great tree.

In the stern of the boat, as it drew nearer, Tarzan saw the rat-faced man.

It was but a few minutes later that the boat touched the beach. The men jumped out and lifted the great chest to the sand. They were on the north side of the point so that their presence was concealed from those at the cabin.

The men argued angrily for a moment. Then the rat-faced one, with several companions, ascended the low bluff on which stood the tree that concealed Tarzan. They looked about for several minutes.

"Here is a good place," said the rat-faced sailor, indicating a spot beneath Tarzan's tree.

"It is as good as any," replied one of his companions. "If they catch us with the treasure aboard it will be confiscated anyway. We might as well bury it here on the chance that some of us will escape the gallows to enjoy it later."

The rat-faced one now called to the men who had remained at the boat, and they came slowly up the bank carrying picks and shovels.

"Hurry—you!" cried Snipes.

"Stow it!" retorted one of the men in a surly tone. "You're no admiral, you shrimp."

"I'm cap'n here, though, I'll have you to understand, you swab," shrieked Snipes with a volley of oaths.

"Steady, boys," cautioned one of the men who had not spoken before. "It ain't goin' to get us nothing by fightin' amongst ourselves."

"Right enough," replied the sailor who had resented Snipe's autocratic tones. "But by the same token it ain't a-goin' to get nobody nothin' to put on airs in this bloomin' company neither."

"You fellows dig here," said Snipes, indicating a spot beneath the tree. "And while you're diggin', Peter kin be a-makin' of a map of the location so's we kin find it again. You, Tom, and Bill, take a couple more down and fetch up the chest."

"Wot are you a-goin' to do?" asked he of the previous altercation. "Just boss?"

"Git busy there!" growled Snipes. "You didn't think your cap'n was a-goin' to dig with a shovel, did you?"

The men all looked up angrily. None of them liked Snipes, and his disagreeable show of authority since he had murdered King, the real head and ringleader of the mutineers, had only added fuel to the flames of their hatred.

"Do you mean to say that you don't intend to take a shovel and lend a hand with this work?" asked Tarrant, the sailor who had before spoken.

"No," replied Snipes simply, fingering the butt of his revolver.

"Then," shouted Tarrant, "if you won't take a shovel you'll take a pick-ax."

With the words he raised his pick above his head, and with a mighty blow buried the point in Snipe's brain.

For a moment the men stood silently looking at the result of their fellow's grim humor. Then one of them spoke.

"Served the rat jolly well right," he said.

One of the others commenced to ply his pick to the ground.

The soil was soft and he threw aside the pick and grasped a shovel; then the others joined him. There was no further comment on the killing, but the men worked in a better frame of mind than they had since Snipes had assumed command.

When they had a trench of ample size to bury the chest, Tarrant suggested that they enlarge it and inter Snipe's body on top of the chest.

"It might 'elp fool any as 'appened to be diggin' 'ereabouts," he explained.

The others saw the cunning of the suggestion, and so the trench was lengthened to accommodate the corpse, and in the center a deeper hole was excavated for the box, which was first wrapped in sail-cloth, and then lowered to its place, which brought its top about a foot below the bottom of the grave. Earth was shoveled in and tamped down about the chest until the bottom of the grave showed level and uniform.

Two of the men then rolled the rat-faced corpse unceremoniously into the grave, after first stripping it of its weapons and various other articles which the several members of the party coveted.

They then filled the grave with earth and tramped upon it until it would hold no more.

The balance of the loose earth was thrown far and wide, and a mass of dead undergrowth spread in as natural a manner as possible over the new-made grave to obliterate all signs of the ground having been disturbed.

Their work done, the sailors returned to the small boat, and pulled off rapidly toward the Arrow.

The breeze had increased considerably, and as the smoke upon the horizon was now plainly discernable in considerable volume, the mutineers lost no time in getting under full sail and bearing away toward the southwest.

Tarzan, an interested spectator of all that had taken place, sat speculating on the strange actions of these peculiar creatures.

Men were indeed more foolish and more cruel than the beasts of the jungle! How fortunate was he who lived in the peace and security of the great forest!

Tarzan wondered what the chest they had buried contained. If they did not wish it why did they not merely throw it into the water? That would have been much easier.

Ah, he thought, but they do wish it. They have hidden it here because they intend returning for it later.

He dropped to the ground and commenced to examine the earth about the excavation. He was looking to see if these creatures had dropped anything which he might like to own. Soon he discovered a spade hidden by the underbrush which they had laid upon the grave.

He seized it and attempted to use it as he had seen the sailors do. It was awkward work and hurt his bare feet, but he persevered until he had partially uncovered the body. This he dragged from the grave and laid to one side.

Then he continued digging until he had unearthed the chest. This also he dragged to the side of the corpse. Then, he filled in the smaller hole below the grave, replaced the body and the earth around and above it, covered it over with underbrush and returned to the chest.

Four sailors had sweated beneath the burden of its weight— Tarzan of the apes picked it up as though it had been empty, and with the spade slung to his back by a piece of rope, carried it off into the densest part of the jungle.

He could not well negotiate the trees with this awkward burden, but he kept to the trails, and so made fairly good time.

For several hours he traveled until he came to an impenetrable wall of matted and tangled vegetation. Then he took to the lower branches, and in another fifteen minutes he emerged into the amphitheater of the apes, where they met in council or to celebrate the rites of the Dum-Dum.

Near the center of the clearing, and not far from the drum, or altar, he commenced to dig. This was harder work than turning up the freshly excavated earth at the grave, but Tarzan of the apes was persevering, and so he kept at his labor until he was rewarded by seeing a hole sufficiently deep to receive the chest and effectually hide it from view. Why had he gone to all this labor without knowing the value of the contents of the chest?

Tarzan of the apes had a man's figure and a man's brain, but he was an ape by training and environment. His brain told him that the chest contained something valuable, or the men would not have hidden it; his training had taught him to imitate whatever was new and unusual, and now the natural curiosity, which is as common to men as to apes, prompted him to open the chest and examine its contents.

But the heavy lock and massive iron bands baffled both his cunning and his immense strength, so that he was compelled to bury the chest without having his curiosity satisfied.

By the time Tarzan had hunted his way back to the vicinity of the cabin, feeding as he went, it was quite dark.

Within the little building a light was burning, for Clayton had found an unopened tin of oil which had stood intact for twenty years. The lamps also were still usable, and thus the interior of the cabin appeared as bright as day to the astonished Tarzan.

He had often wondered at the exact purpose of the lamps. His reading and the pictures had told him what they were, but he had no idea of how they could be made to produce the wondrous sunlight that some of his pictures had portrayed them as diffusing upon all surrounding objects.

As he approached the window nearest the door he saw that the cabin had been divided into two rooms by a rough partition of boughs and sail-cloth.

In the front room were the three men; the two older deep in argument, while the younger, tilted back against the wall on an improvised stool, was deeply engrossed in reading one of Tarzan's books.

Tarzan was not particularly interested in the men, however, so he sought the other window. There was the girl. How beautiful her features! How delicate her snowy skin!

She was writing at Tarzan's own table beneath the window. Upon a pile of grasses at the far side of the room lay the negress, asleep.

For an hour Tarzan feasted his eyes upon her while she wrote. He longed to speak to her, but dared not attempt, for he was convinced that she would not understand him, and he feared, too, that he might frighten her away.

At length she arose, leaving her manuscript upon the table. She went to the bed upon which had been spread several layers of soft grasses. These she rearranged.

Then she loosened the soft mass of golden hair which crowned her head. Like a shimmering waterfall turned to burnished metal by a dying sun it fell about her oval face; in waving lines, below her waist, it tumbled.

Tarzan was spellbound. Then she extinguished the lamp and all within the cabin was wrapped in Cimmerian darkness.

Still Tarzan watched without. Creeping close beneath the window he waited, listening, for half an hour. At last he was rewarded by the sounds of the regular breathing within, which denotes sleep.

Cautiously he intruded his hand between the meshes of the lattice until his whole arm was within the cabin. Carefully he felt upon the desk. At last he grasped the paper upon which Jane Porter had been writing, and withdrew his hand, holding the precious treasure.

Tarzan folded the sheets into a small parcel, which he tucked into the quiver with his arrows. Then he sped away into the jungle as softly and as noiselessly as a shadow.

CHAPTER 18

The Jungle-Toll

EARLY THE FOLLOWING morning Tarzan awoke, and the first thought of the new day, as the last of yesterday, was of the wonderful writing which lay hidden in his quiver.

Hurriedly he brought it forth, hoping against hope that he could read what the beautiful white girl had written there the preceding evening.

At the first glance he suffered the bitterest disappointment of his whole life; never before had he so yearned for anything as now he did for the ability to interpret a message from the divinity who had come so suddenly and so unexpectedly into his life.

What if the message were not intended for him? It was an expression of her thoughts, and that was all sufficient for Tarzan of the apes.

And now to be baffled by strange, uncouth characters the like of which he had never seen before! Why, they even tipped in the opposite direction from all that he had ever examined either in printed books or the difficult script of the few letters he had found.

Even the little bugs of the black book were familiar friends, though their arrangement meant nothing to him; but these bugs were new and unheard of.

For twenty minutes he pored over them, when suddenly they commenced to take familiar though distorted shapes. Ah, they were his old friends, but badly crippled.

Then he began to make out a word here and a word there. His heart leaped for joy. He could read it, and he would.

In another half-hour he was progressing rapidly, and, but for an exceptional word now and again, he found it very plain sailing. Here is what he read:

West coast of Africa, about 10 degrees south latitude. (So Mr. Clayton says).

February 3(?), 1900.

DEAREST HAZEL:

It seems foolish to write you a letter that you may never see, but I simply must tell somebody of our awful experiences since we sailed from Europe on the ill-fated Arrow.

If we never return to civilization, as now seems only too likely, this will at least prove a brief record of the events which led up to our fate, whatever it may be.

As you know, we were supposed to have set out upon a scientific expedition to the Congo. Papa was presumed to entertain some wondrous theory of an unthinkable ancient civilization, the remains of which lay buried somewhere in the Congo valley. But after we were well under sail the truth came out.

It seems that an old bookworm who has a book and curio shop in Baltimore discovered between the leaves of a very old Spanish manuscript a letter written in 1750, detailing the adventures of a crew of mutineers of a Spanish galleon bound from Spain to South America with a vast treasure of "doubloons" and "pieces of eight," I suppose, for they certainly sound weird and piraty.

The writer had been one of the crew, and the letter was to his son, who was, at the time the letter was written, master of a Spanish merchantman.

Many years had elapsed since the events the letter narrated had transpired, and the old man had become a respected citizen of an obscure Spanish town, but the love of gold was still so strong upon him that he risked all to acquaint his son with the means of attaining fabulous wealth for them both.

The writer told how when but a week out from Spain the crew had mutinied and murdered every officer and man who opposed them. They defeated their own ends by this very act, for there was none left competent to navigate a ship at sea.

They were blown hither and thither for two months, until sick and dying of scurvy, starvation, and thirst, they had been wrecked on a small islet.

The galleon was washed high upon the beach, where she

went to pieces; but not before the survivors, who numbered but ten souls, had rescued one of the great chests of treasure.

This they buried well upon the island, and for three years they lived there in constant hope of being rescued.

One by one they sickened and died, until only one man was left, the writer of the letter.

The men had built a boat from the wreckage of the galleon, but having no idea where the island was located they had not dared to put to sea.

When all were dead except himself, however, the awful loneliness so weighed upon the mind of the sole survivor that he could endure it no longer, and choosing to risk death upon the open sea rather than madness on the lonely isle, he set sail in his little boat after nearly a year of solitude.

Fortunately he sailed due north, and within a week was in the track of the Spanish merchantmen plying between the West Indies and Spain, and was picked up by one of these vessels homeward bound.

The story he told was merely one of shipwreck in which all but a few had perished, the balance, except himself, dying after they reached the island. He did not mention the mutiny or the chest of buried treasure.

The master of the merchantman assured him that from the position at which they picked him up, and the prevailing winds for the past week, he could have been on no other island than one of the Cape Verde group, which lie off the west coast of Africa in about 16 degrees or 17 degrees north latitude.

His letter described the island minutely, as well as the location of the treasure, and was accompanied by the crudest, funniest little old map you ever saw; with trees and rocks all marked by scrawly "X's" to show the exact spot where the treasure had been buried.

When papa explained the real nature of the expedition, my heart sank, for I know so well how visionary and impractical the poor dear has always been that I feared that he had again been duped; especially when he told me that he had paid a thousand dollars for the letter and map.

To add to my distress I learned that he had borrowed ten thousand dollars more from Robert Canler, and had given his notes for the amount.

Mr. Canler had asked for no security, and you know, dearie, what that will mean for me if papa cannot meet them. Oh, how I detest that man!

We all tried to look on the bright side of things, but Mr. Philander, and Mr. Clayton—he joined us in London just for the adventure—both felt as skeptical as I.

To make a long story short, we found the island and the treasure—a great iron-bound oak chest, wrapped in many layers of oiled sail-cloth, and as strong and firm as when it had been buried nearly two hundred years ago.

It was *simply filled* with gold coin, and was so heavy that four men bent beneath its weight.

The horrid thing seems to bring nothing but murder and misfortune to those who have to do with it, for three days after we sailed from the Cape Verde Islands our own crew mutinied and killed every one of their officers.

It was the most terrifying experience one could imagine— I cannot even write of it.

They were going to kill us too, but one of them, the leader, a man named King, would not let them, and so they sailed south along the coast to a lonely spot where they found a good harbor, and here they have landed and left us.

They sailed away with the treasure to-day, but Mr. Clayton says they will meet with a fate similar to the mutineers of the ancient galleon, because King, the only man aboard who knew aught of navigation, was murdered on the beach by one of the men the day we landed.

I wish you could know Mr. Clayton, he is the dearest fellow imaginable, and unless I am mistaken, he has fallen very much in love with poor little me.

He is the only son of Lord Greystoke, and some day will inherit the title and estates. In addition he is wealthy in his own right. But the fact that he is going to be an English lord makes me very sad—you know what my sentiments have always been relative to American girls who married titled foreigners. Oh, if he were only a plain American gentleman!

But it isn't his fault, poor fellow, and in everything except birth he would do credit to my darling old country, and that is the greatest compliment I know how to pay any man.

We have had the most weird experiences since we were landed here. Papa and Mr. Philander lost in the jungle and chased by a real lion.

Mr. Clayton lost, and attacked twice by wild beasts. Esmeralda and I cornered in an old cabin by a perfectly awful man-eating tiger. Oh, it was simply "terrifical," as Esmeralda would say.

But the strangest part of it all is the wonderful creature who rescued us all. I have not seen him, but Mr. Clayton and papa and Mr. Philander have, and they say that he is a perfectly godlike white man tanned to a dusky brown, with the strength of a wild elephant, the agility of a monkey, and the bravery of a lion.

He speaks no English and vanishes as quickly and as mysteriously after he has performed some valorous deed, as though he were a disembodied spirit.

Then we have another weird neighbor, who printed a beautiful sign in English and tacked it on the door of his cabin, which we have preempted, warning us to destroy none of his belongings, and signing himself "Tarzan of the Apes."

We have never seen him, though we think he is about, for one of the sailors who was going to shoot Mr. Clayton in the back received a spear in his shoulder from some unseen hand in the jungle.

The sailors left us but a meager supply of food, so, as we have only a single revolver with but three cartridges left in it, we do not know how we can procure meat, though Mr. Philander says that we can exist indefinitely on the wild fruit and nuts which abound in the jungle.

I am very tired now, so I shall go to my funny bed of grasses which Mr. Clayton gathered for me, but will add to this from day to day as things happen.

Lovingly,

Jane Porter.

To Hazel Strong, Baltimore, Maryland.

Tarzan sat in a brown study for a long time after he finished reading the letter. It was filled with so many new and wonderful things that his brain was in a whirl as he attempted to digest them all.

So they did not know that he was Tarzan of the apes. He would tell them.

In his tree he had constructed a rude shelter of leaves and boughs, beneath which, protected from the rain, he had placed the few treasures brought from the cabin. Among these were some pencils.

He took one, and beneath Jane Porter's signature he wrote:

I am Tarzan of the apes.

He thought that would be sufficient. Later he would return the letter to the cabin.

In the matter of food, thought Tarzan, they had no need to worry—he would provide, and he did.

The next morning Jane Porter found her missing letter in the exact spot from which it had disappeared two nights before. She was mystified, but when she saw the printed words beneath her signature, she felt a chill run up her spine. She showed the letter, or rather the last sheet with the signature, to Clayton.

"To think," she said, "that uncanny thing was probably watching me all the time that I was writing—oo! It makes me shudder just to think of it."

"But he must be friendly," reassured Clayton, "for he has returned your letter, nor did he offer to harm you, and unless I am mistaken he left a very substantial memento of his friendship outside the cabin door last night, for I just found the carcass of a wild boar there as I came out."

From then on scarcely a day passed that did not bring its offering of game or other food. Sometimes it was a young deer, again a quantity of strange, cooked food, cassava cakes pilfered from the village of Mbonga, or a boar, or leopard, and once a lion.

Tarzan derived the greatest pleasure of his life in hunting meat for these strangers. It seemed to him that no pleasure on earth could compare with laboring for the welfare and protection of the beautiful white girl.

Some day he would venture into the camp in daylight and talk with these people through the medium of the little bugs which were familiar to them and to Tarzan.

But he found it difficult to overcome the timidity of the wild thing of the forest, and so day followed day without seeing a fulfilment of his good intentions.

The party in the camp, emboldened by familiarity, wandered further and further into the jungle in search of nuts and fruit.

Scarcely a day passed that did not find Professor Porter straying in his preoccupied indifference toward the jaws of death. Mr. Samuel T. Philander, never what one might call robust, was worn to the shadow of a shadow through the ceaseless worry and mental distraction resultant from his Herculean efforts to safeguard the professor.

A month passed. Tarzan had finally determined to visit the camp by daylight.

It was early afternoon. Clayton had wandered to the point at the harbor's mouth to look for passing vessels. Here he kept a great mass of wood, high piled, ready to be ignited as a signal should a steamer or a sail top the far horizon.

Professor Porter was wandering along the beach south of the camp with Mr. Philander at his elbow, urging him to turn his steps back before the two became again the sport of some savage beast.

The others gone, Jane Porter and Esmeralda had wandered into the jungle to gather fruit, and in their search were led further and further from the cabin.

Tarzan waited in silence before the door of the little house until they should return.

His thoughts were of the beautiful white girl. They were always of her now. He wondered if she would fear him, and the thought all but caused him to relinquish his plan.

He was rapidly becoming impatient for her return, that he might feast his eyes upon her and be near her, perhaps touch her. The ape-man knew no God, but he was as near to worshiping his divinity as mortal man ever comes to worshiping.

While he waited he passed the time printing a message to her; whether he intended giving it to her he himself could not have told, but he took infinite pleasure in seeing his thoughts expressed in print—in which he was not so uncivilized after all.

> I am Tarzan of the apes (he wrote). I am yours. You are mine. We will live here together always in my house. I will bring you the best fruits, the tenderest deer, the finest meats that roam the jungle.
>
> I will hunt for you. I am the greatest of the jungle hunters.
>
> I will fight for you. I am the mightiest of the jungle fighters.
>
> You are Jane Porter, I saw it in your letter. When you see this you will know that it is for you and that Tarzan of the apes loves you.

As he stood, straight as a young Indian by the door, waiting after he had finished the message, there came to his keen ears a familiar sound. It was the passing of a great ape through the lower branches of the forest.

For an instant he listened intently, and then from the jungle came the agonized scream of a woman, and Tarzan of the apes, dropping his first love-letter upon the ground, shot like a panther into the forest.

Clayton, also, heard the scream, and Professor Porter and Mr. Philander, and in a few minutes they came panting to the cabin, calling out to each other as they approached, a volley of excited questions. A glance within confirmed their worst fears.

Jane Porter and Esmeralda were not there.

Instantly Clayton, followed by the two old men, plunged into the jungle, calling the girl's name aloud. For half an hour they stumbled on, until Clayton, by merest chance, came upon the prostrate form of Esmeralda.

He stooped beside her, feeling for her pulse and then listening for her heart-beats. She lived. He shook her.

"Esmeralda!" he shrieked in her ear. "Esmeralda! Where is Miss Porter? What has happened? Esmeralda!"

Slowly the black opened her eyes. She saw Clayton. She saw the jungle about her.

"Oh, Gaberelle!" she screamed, and fainted again.

By this time Professor Porter and Mr. Philander had come up.

"What shall we do, Mr. Clayton?" asked the old professor. "Where shall we look? Heaven could not have been so cruel as to take my little girl away from me now."

"We must rouse Esmeralda first," replied Clayton. "She can tell us what has happened. Esmeralda!" he cried again, shaking the black woman roughly by the shoulder.

"Oh, Gaberelle, Ah wants to die!" cried the poor woman, but with eyes fast closed. "Lemme die, but doan lemme see dat awrful face again. Whafer de devil round after po' ole Esmeralda? She ain't done nuffin' to nobody."

"Come, Esmeralda!" cried Clayton. "Open your eyes!"

Esmeralda did as she was bade.

"Oh, Gaberelle! T'ank de Lawd," she said.

"Where's Miss Porter? What happened?" questioned Clayton.

"Ain' Miss Jane here?" cried Esmeralda, sitting up with wonderful celerity for one of her bulk. "Oh, Lawd, now Ah 'members! It done must have tooked her away." The negress commenced to sob and wail her lamentations.

"What took her away?" cried Professor Porter.

"A great big gi'nt all covered with hair."

"A gorilla, Esmeralda?" questioned Mr. Philander, and the three men scarcely breathed as he voiced the horrible thought.

"Ah done thought it was de devil; Ah guess it mus' 'a' been one of dem gorilephants. Oh, my po' baby, my po' li'l' honey!"

Clayton immediately began to look about for tracks, but he could find nothing save a confusion of trampled grasses in the close vicinity, and his woodcraft was too meager for the translation of what he did see.

All the balance of the day they sought through the jungle; but as night drew on they were forced to give up in despair and hopelessness, for they did not even know in what direction the thing had borne Jane Porter.

It was long after dark ere they reached the cabin, and a grief-stricken party it was that sat silently within the little structure.

Professor Porter finally broke the silence. His tones were no longer those of the erudite pedant theorizing upon the abstract and the unknowable, but those of the man of action—determined, but tinged by a note of indescribable hopelessness and grief which wrung an answering pang from Clayton's heart.

"I shall lie down now," said the old man, "and try to sleep. Early tomorrow, so soon as it is light, I shall take what food I can carry and continue the search until I have found Jane. I will not return without her."

His companions did not reply at once. Each was immersed in his own sorrowful thoughts, and each knew, as did the old professor, what the last words meant—Professor Porter would never return from the jungle.

At length Clayton rose and laid his hand gently upon Professor Porter's bent old shoulder.

"I shall go with you, of course," he said. "Do not tell me that I need even have said so."

"I knew that you would offer—that you would wish to go, Mr. Clayton; but you must not. Jane is beyond human assistance now. I simply go that I may face my Maker with her, and know, too, that what was once my dear girl does not lie all alone and friendless in the jungle.

"The same vines and leaves will cover us, the same rains beat upon us; and when the spirit of her mother is abroad, it will find us together in death, as it has always found us in life.

"No; it is I alone who may go, for she was my daughter—all that was left on earth for me to love."

"I shall go with you," said Clayton simply.

The old man looked up, regarding the strong, handsome face of William Cecil Clayton intently. Perhaps he read there the love that lay in the heart beneath—the love for his daughter.

He had been too preoccupied with his own scholarly thoughts in the past to consider the little occurrences, the chance words, which would have indicated to a more practical man that these young people were being drawn more and more closely to one another. Now they came back to him.

"As you wish," he said.

"You may count on me, also," said Mr. Philander.

"No, my dear old friend," said Professor Porter. "We may not all go. It would be cruelly wicked to leave poor Esmeralda here alone, and three of us would be no more successful than one.

"There are enough dead things in the cruel forest as it is. Come—let us try to sleep a little."

CHAPTER 19

The Call of the Primitive

FROM THE TIME Tarzan left the tribe of great anthropoids in which he had been raised, it was torn by continual strife and discord. Terkoz proved a cruel and capricious king, so that, one by one, many of the older and weaker apes, upon whom he was particularly prone to vent his brutish nature, took their families and sought the quiet and safety of the far interior.

But at last those who remained were driven to desperation by the continued truculence of Terkoz, and it so happened that one of them recalled the parting admonition of Tarzan.

"If you have a chief who is cruel, do not as the other apes do, and attempt, any one of you, to pit yourself against him alone. But, instead, let two or three or four of you attack him together. Then no chief will dare to be other than he should be, for four of you can kill any chief."

And the ape who recalled this wise counsel repeated it to several of his fellows, so that when Terkoz returned to the tribe that day he found a warm reception awaiting him.

There were no formalities. As Terkoz reached the group five

huge, hairy beasts sprang upon him.

At heart he was an arrant coward, which is the way with bullies among apes as well as among men; so he did not remain to fight and die, but tore himself away from them as quickly as he could and fled into the sheltering boughs of the forest.

Two more attempts he made to rejoin the tribe, but on each occasion he was set upon and driven away. At last he gave it up and turned, foaming with rage and hatred, into the jungle.

For several days he wandered aimlessly, nursing his spite and looking for some weak thing on which to vent his pent anger.

It was in this state of mind that the horrible manlike beast, swinging from tree to tree, came suddenly upon two women in the jungle.

He was right above them when he discovered them. The first intimation Jane Porter had of his presence was when the great hairy body dropped to the earth beside her, and she saw the awful face and the snarling, hideous mouth thrust within a foot of her.

One piercing scream escaped her lips as the brute's hand clutched her arm. Then she was dragged toward those awful fangs which yawned at her throat. But ere they touched that fair skin another mood claimed the anthropoid.

The tribe had kept his women. He must find others to replace them. This hairless white ape would be the first of his new household.

He threw her roughly across his broad shoulders and leaped back into the trees, bearing Jane Porter away toward a fate a thousand times worse than death.

Esmeralda's scream had mingled with that of Jane Porter; then, as was Esmeralda's manner under stress of emergency which required presence of mind, she swooned.

But Jane Porter did not once lose consciousness. It is true that that awful face, pressing close to hers, and the foul breath beating upon her nostrils, paralyzed her with terror; but her brain was clear, and she comprehended all that transpired.

With what seemed to her marvelous rapidity the brute bore her through the forest, but still she did not cry out or struggle. The sudden advent of the ape had confused her to such an extent that she thought now that he was bearing her toward the beach.

For this reason she conserved her energies and her voice until she could see that they had approached near enough to the camp to attract the succor she craved.

Poor child! Could she but have known it, she was being borne farther and farther into the impenetrable jungle.

The scream that had brought Clayton and the two older men stumbling through the undergrowth had led Tarzan of the apes straight to where Esmeralda lay, but it was not Esmeralda in whom his interest centered.

For a moment he scrutinized the ground below and the trees above, until the ape that was in him by virtue of training and environment, combined with the intelligence that was his by right of birth, told his woodcraft the whole story as plainly as though he had seen the thing happen with his own eyes.

Instantly he was gone again into the swaying trees, following the high-flung spoor which no other human eye could have detected, much less translated.

At boughs ends, where the anthropoid swings from one tree to another, there is most to mark the trail but least to point the direction of the quarry. The pressure is downward always, toward the small end of the branch, whether the ape be leaving or entering a tree; but nearer the center of the tree, where the signs of passage are fainter, the direction is plainly marked.

Here, on this branch, a caterpillar has been crushed by the fugitive's great foot, and Tarzan knows instinctively where that same foot would touch in the next stride. Here he looks to find a tiny particle of the demolished larva, ofttimes not more than a speck of moisture.

Again, a minute bit of bark has been upturned by the scraping hand, and the direction of the break indicates the direction of the passage. Or some great limb, or the stem of the tree itself, has been brushed by the hairy body, and a tiny shred of hair tells him by the direction from which it is wedged beneath the bark that he is on the right trail.

Nor does he need to check his speed to catch these seemingly faint records of the fleeing beast.

To Tarzan they stand out boldly against all the myriad other scars and bruises and signs upon the leafy way; but strongest of all is the scent, for Tarzan is pursuing up the wind, and his trained nostrils are as sensitive as a hound's.

Almost silently the ape-man sped on in the track of Terkoz and his prey, but the sound of his approach reached the ears of the fleeing beast and spurred it on to greater speed.

Three miles were covered before Tarzan overtook them, and

then Terkoz, seeing that further flight were futile, dropped to the ground in a small open glade, that he might turn and fight for his prize, or be free to escape unhampered if he saw that the pursuer was more than a match for him.

He still grasped Jane Porter in one great arm as Tarzan bounded like a leopard into the arena which nature had provided for this primeval-like battle.

When Terkoz saw that it was Tarzan who pursued him, he jumped to the conclusion that this was Tarzan's woman, since they were of the same kind—white and hairless—and so he rejoiced at this opportunity for double revenge upon his hated enemy.

To Jane Porter the apparition of this godlike man was as wine to sick nerves.

From the description which Clayton and her father and Mr. Philander had given her, she knew that it must be the same wonderful creature who had saved them, and she saw in him only a protector and a friend.

But as Terkoz pushed her roughly aside to meet Tarzan's charge, and she saw the great proportions of the ape and the mighty muscles and the fierce fangs, her heart quailed. How could any animal vanquish such a mighty antagonist?

Like two charging bulls they came together, and like two wolves sought each other's throat. Against the long canines of the ape was pitted the thin blade of the man's knife.

Jane Porter—her lithe form flattened against the trunk of a great tree, her hands tight pressed against her rising and falling bosom, and her eyes wide with mingled horror, fascination, fear, and admiration—watched the primordial ape battle with the primeval man for possession of a woman—for her.

As the great muscles of the man's back and shoulders knotted beneath the tension of his efforts, and the huge biceps and forearm held at bay those mighty tusks, the veil of centuries of civilization and culture was swept from the blurred vision of the Baltimore girl. When the thin knife drank deep a dozen times of Terkoz's heart's blood, and the great carcass rolled lifeless upon the ground, it was a primeval woman who sprang forward with outstretched arms toward the primeval man who had fought for her and won her.

And Tarzan?

He did what no red-blooded man needs lessons in doing. He

took his woman in his arms and smothered her upturned, panting lips with kisses.

For a moment Jane Porter lay there with half-closed eyes. For a moment—the first in her young life—she knew the meaning of love.

But as suddenly as the veil had been withdrawn it dropped again, and an outraged conscience suffused her face with its scarlet mantle, and a mortified woman thrust Tarzan of the apes from her and buried her face in her hands.

Tarzan had been surprised when he had found the girl he had learned to love after a vague and abstract manner a willing prisoner in his arms. Now he was surprised that she repulsed him.

He came close to her once more and took hold of her arm. She turned upon him like a tigress, striking his great breast with her tiny hands.

Tarzan could not understand it.

A moment ago and it had been his intention to hasten Jane Porter back to her people, but that moment was lost in the dim and distant past of things which were but can never be again, and with it the good intention had gone to join the impossible.

Since then Tarzan of the apes had felt the warm form close pressed to his. The hot, sweet breath against his cheek and mouth had fanned a new flame to life within his breast. The perfect lips had clung to his in burning kisses that had seared deep into his soul.

Again he laid his hand upon her arm. Again she repulsed him. And then Tarzan of the apes did just what his first ancestor would have done.

He took his woman in his arms and carried her into the jungle.

Early the following morning the four within the little cabin by the beach were awakened by the booming of a cannon. Clayton was the first to rush out, and there, beyond the harbor's mouth, he saw two vessels lying at anchor.

One was the Arrow and the other a small French cruiser. The sides of the latter were crowded with men gazing shoreward, and it was evident to Clayton, as to the others who had now joined him, that the gun which they had heard had been fired to attract their attention if they still remained at the cabin.

Both vessels lay at a considerable distance from shore, and it was doubtful if their glasses would locate the waving hats of the little party far in between the harbor's points.

Esmeralda had removed her red apron, and was waving it frantically above her head; but Clayton, still fearing that even this might not be seen, hurried off toward the northern point where lay his signal pyre ready for the match.

It seemed an age to him as to those who waited breathlessly behind ere he reached the great pile of dry branches and underbrush.

As he broke from the dense wood and came in sight of the vessels again, he was filled with consternation to see that the Arrow was making sail and that the cruiser was already under way.

Quickly lighting the pyre in a dozen places, he hurried on to the extreme point of the promontory, where he stripped off his shirt, and, tying it to a fallen branch, stood waving it back and forth above him.

But still the vessels continued to stand out; and he had given up all hope, when the great column of smoke rising above the forest in one dense, vertical shaft attracted the attention of a lookout aboard the cruiser, and instantly a dozen glasses were leveled on the beach.

Presently Clayton saw the two ships come about again; and while the Arrow lay drifting quietly on the ocean, the cruiser steamed slowly back toward shore. At some distance away she stopped, and a boat was lowered and despatched toward the beach.

As it was drawn up a young officer stepped out.

"M. Clayton, I presume?" he asked.

"Thank Heaven, you have come!" was Clayton's reply. "And it may be that it is not too late even now."

"What do you mean, *monsieur?*" asked the officer.

Clayton told of the abduction of Jane Porter and the need of armed men to aid in the search for her.

"Mon Dieu!" exclaimed the officer sadly. "Yesterday and it would not have been too late. To-day and it may be better that the poor lady were never found. It is horrible, *monsieur*. It is too horrible."

Other boats had now put off from the cruiser, and Clayton, having pointed out the harbor's entrance to the officer, entered the boat with him, and its nose was turned toward the little landlocked bay, into which the other craft followed.

Soon the entire party had landed where stood Professor Porter, Mr. Philander, and Esmeralda.

Among the officers in the last boats to put off from the cruiser

He took his woman in his arms.

was the commander of the vessel; and when he had heard the story of Jane Porter's abduction, he generously called for volunteers to accompany Professor Porter and Clayton in their search.

Not an officer or a man of those brave Frenchmen who did not quickly beg leave to be one of the expedition.

The commander selected twenty men and two officers, Lieutenant d'Arnot and Lieutenant Charpentier. A boat was despatched to the cruiser for provisions, ammunition, and carbines. The men were already armed with revolvers.

Then, to Clayton's inquiries as to how they had happened to anchor offshore and fire a signal-gun, the commander, Captain Dufranne, explained that a month before they had sighted the Arrow bearing southwest under considerable canvas, and that when they had signaled her to come about she had but crowded on more sail.

They had kept her hull-up until sunset, firing several shots after her, but the next morning she was nowhere to be seen. They had then continued to cruise up and down the coast for several weeks, and had about forgotten the incident of the recent chase when, early one morning a few days before, the lookout had descried a vessel laboring in the trough of a heavy sea and evidently entirely from under control.

As they steamed nearer to the derelict they were surprised to note that it was the same vessel that had run from them a few weeks earlier. Her forestaysail and mizzen-spanker were set as though an effort had been made to hold her nose up into the wind, but the sheets had parted and the sails were both tearing to ribbons in the wind.

In the high sea that was running it was a difficult and dangerous task to attempt to put a prize crew aboard her; and as no signs of life had been seen above deck, it was decided to stand by until the wind and sea abated; but just then a figure was seen clinging to the rail and feebly waving a mute signal of despair toward them.

Immediately a boat's crew was ordered out, and an attempt was successfully made to board the Arrow. The sight that met the Frenchmen's eyes as they clambered over the ship's side was appalling.

A dozen dead and dying men rolled hither and thither upon the pitching deck, the living intermingled with the dead. Two of the corpses appeared to have been partially devoured as though by wolves.

The prize crew soon had the vessel under proper sail once more and the living members of the ill-starred company carried below to their hammocks.

The dead were wrapped in tarpaulins and lashed on deck to be identified by their comrades before being consigned to the deep.

None of the living were conscious when the Frenchmen reached the Arrow's deck. Even the poor devil who had waved the single despairing signal of distress had lapsed into unconsciousness before he had learned whether it had availed or not.

It did not take the French officer long to learn what had caused the terrible condition aboard; for when water and brandy were sought to restore the men, it was found that not only was there none of either, but not a vestige of food of any description.

He immediately signaled to the cruiser to send water, medicine, and provisions, and another boat made the perilous trip to the Arrow.

When restoratives had been applied several of the men regained consciousness, and then the whole story was told. That part of it we know up to the sailing of the Arrow after the murder of Snipes and the burial of his body above the treasure-chest.

It seems that the pursuit by the cruiser had so terrorized the mutineers that they had continued out across the Atlantic for several days after losing her; but on discovering the meager supply of water and provisions aboard, they had turned back toward the east.

With no one on board who understood navigation, discussions soon rose as to their whereabouts; and as three days' sailing did not raise land, they bore off to the north, fearing that the high north winds that had prevailed had driven them south of the southern extremity of Africa.

They kept on a north-northeasterly course for two days, when they were overtaken by a calm which lasted for nearly a week. Their water was gone, and in another day they would be without food.

Conditions changed rapidly from bad to worse. One man went mad and leaped overboard. Soon another opened his veins and drank his own blood.

When he died they threw him overboard also, though there were those among them who wanted to keep the corpse on board.

Hunger was changing them from human beasts to wild beasts.

Two days before they had been picked up by the cruiser they had become too weak to handle the vessel, and that same day three men died. On the following morning it was seen that one of the corpses had been partially devoured.

All that day the men lay glaring at each other like beasts of prey, and the following morning two of the corpses lay almost entirely stripped of flesh.

The men were but little stronger for their ghoulish repast, for the want of water was by far the greatest agony with which they had to contend. And then the cruiser had come.

When those who could had recovered, the entire story had been told to the French commander, but the men were too ignorant to be able to tell him at just what point on the coast the professor and his party had been marooned, so the cruiser had steamed slowly along within sight of land, firing occasional signal-guns and scanning every inch of the beach with glasses.

They had anchored at night so as not to neglect a particle of the shore-line, and it had happened that the preceding night had brought them off the very beach where lay the little camp they sought.

The signal-guns of the afternoon before had not been heard by those on shore, it was presumed, because they had doubtless been in the thick of the jungle searching for Jane Porter, where the noise of their own crashing through the underbrush would have drowned the report of a far distant gun.

By the time the two parties had narrated their several adventures, the cruiser's boat had returned with supplies and arms for the expedition.

Within a few minutes the little body of sailors and two French officers, together with Professor Porter and Clayton, set off upon their quest into the untracked jungle.

CHAPTER 20

Heredity

WHEN JANE PORTER realized that she was being borne away a captive by the strange forest creature who had rescued her from the clutches of the ape she struggled desperately to escape, but the strong arms held her as easily as though she had been but a day-old babe.

Presently she gave up the futile effort and lay quietly, looking through half-closed lids at the face of the man who strode easily through the tangled undergrowth with her.

The face above her was one of extraordinary beauty.

A perfect type of the strongly masculine, unmarred by dissipation or degrading passions. For, though Tarzan of the apes was a killer of men and of beasts, he killed as the hunter kills, for pleasure, except on those rare occasions when he had killed for hate— though not the brooding, malevolent hate which marks the features of its own with hideous lines.

When Tarzan killed he more often smiled than scowled, and smiles are the foundation of beauty.

One thing the girl had noticed particularly when she had seen Tarzan rushing upon Terkoz—the vivid scarlet band upon his forehead, from above the left eye to the scalp; but now as she scanned his features she noticed that it was gone, and only a thin white line marked the spot where it had been.

As she lay more quietly in his arms Tarzan slightly relaxed his grip upon her.

Once he looked down into her eyes and smiled. The girl had to close her own to shut out the vision of that handsome, winning face.

Presently Tarzan took to the trees, and Jane Porter, wondering that she felt no fear, began to realize that in many respects she had never felt more secure in her whole life than now as she lay in the arms of this wild creature, being borne, Heaven knew where or to what fate, deeper and deeper into the untamed forest.

When with closed eyes she commenced to speculate upon the future, and terrifying fears were conjured by a vivid imagination, she had but to raise her lids and look upon that face so close to hers to dissipate the last remnant of apprehension.

No, he could never harm her; of that she was convinced when she translated the fine features and the frank, brave eyes above her into the chivalry which they proclaimed.

On and on they went through what seemed a solid mass of verdure, yet ever there appeared to open before this forest god a passage, as by magic, which closed behind them as they passed.

Scarce a branch scraped against her, yet above and below, before and behind, the view presented only a solid mass of interwoven branches and creepers.

As Tarzan moved steadily onward his mind was occupied with many strange and new thoughts. Here was a problem the like of which he had never encountered, and he felt rather than reasoned that he must meet it as a man and not as an ape.

The free movement through the middle terrace, which was the route he had followed for the most part, had helped to cool the ardor of the first fierce passion of his love.

Now he discovered himself speculating upon the fate which would have fallen to the girl had he not rescued her from Terkoz.

He knew why the ape had not killed her, and he commenced to compare his intentions with those of Terkoz.

True, it was the order of the jungle for the male to take his mate by force; but could Tarzan be guided by the laws of the beasts? Was not Tarzan a man? But how did men do? He was puzzled; he did not know.

He wished that he might ask the girl, and then it came to him that she had already answered him in the futile struggle she had made to escape and to repulse him.

But now they had come to their destination, and Tarzan of the apes, with Jane Porter in his strong arms, swung lightly to the turf of the arena where the great apes held their councils and danced the wild orgy of the Dum-Dum.

Though they had come many miles, it was still but midafternoon, and the amphitheater was bathed in the half light which filtered through the maze of encircling foliage.

The green turf looked cool and inviting. The myriad noises of the jungle seemed distant and hushed to a mere echo of blurred sounds, rising and falling like the surf upon a remote shore.

A feeling of dreamy peacefulness stole over Jane Porter as she sank down upon the grass where Tarzan had placed her. She looked up at his great figure towering above her, and there was added a strange sense of perfect security.

As she watched him, Tarzan crossed the clearing toward the trees upon the farther side. She noted the graceful majesty of his carriage, the symmetry of his figure, and the poise of his head upon his broad shoulders.

What a perfect creature! There could be naught of cruelty or baseness beneath the godlike exterior.

With a bound Tarzan sprang into the trees and disappeared. Jane Porter wondered where he had gone. Had he left her there to her fate in the lonely jungle?

She glanced nervously about. Every vine and bush seemed but the lurking-place of some huge and horrible beast waiting to bury gleaming fangs in her soft flesh. Every sound she magnified into the stealthy creeping of a sinuous and malignant body.

How different now that he had left her!

For a few minutes that seemed hours to the frightened girl she sat with tense nerves waiting for the spring of the crouching thing that was to end her misery of apprehension.

She almost prayed for the cruel teeth that would give her unconsciousness and surcease from the agony of fear.

She heard a sudden, slight sound behind her. With a shriek she sprang to her feet and turned to face her end.

There stood Tarzan, his arms filled with ripe and luscious fruit.

Jane Porter reeled and would have fallen, but Tarzan, dropping his burden, caught her in his arms. She did not lose consciousness, but clung to him, shuddering and trembling.

Tarzan of the apes stroked her soft hair, and tried to comfort and quiet her as Kala had him when, as a little ape, he had been frightened by Sabor, the tiger, or Histah, the snake.

Once he pressed his lips lightly upon her forehead, and she did not move, but closed her eyes and sighed.

She could not analyze her feelings, nor did she wish to attempt it. She was satisfied to feel the safety of those strong arms, and to leave her future to fate.

As she thought of the strangeness of it, there commenced to dawn upon her the realization that she had, possibly, learned something she had never known before—love. She wondered and then she smiled.

Still smiling, she pushed Tarzan gently away; and looking at him with a half-quizzical expression that made her face wholly entrancing, she pointed to the fruit upon the ground, and seated herself upon the edge of the earthen drum of the anthropoids.

Tarzan quickly gathered up the fruit and, bringing it, laid it at her feet; and then he, too, sat upon the drum beside her, and with his knife proceeded to open and prepare the various viands for her meal.

Together and in silence they ate, occasionally stealing sly glances at one another, until finally Jane Porter broke into a merry laugh in which Tarzan joined.

"I wish you spoke English," said the girl.

Tarzan shook his head and an expression of wistful and pathetic longing sobered his laughing eyes.

Then Jane Porter tried speaking to him in French, and then in German, but she had to laugh at her own blundering attempt at the latter tongue.

"Anyway," she said to him in English, "you understand my German as well as they did in Berlin."

Tarzan had long since reached a decision as to what his future procedure should be. He had had time to recollect all that he had read of the ways of men and women in the books at the cabin. He would act as he imagined the men in the books would have acted were they in his place.

Again he rose and went into the trees, but first he tried to explain by means of signs that he would return shortly, and he did so well that Jane Porter understood and was not afraid when he had gone.

Only a feeling of loneliness came over her and she watched the point where he had disappeared, with longing eyes, awaiting his return. As before she was apprised of his presence by a soft sound behind her, and turned to see him coming across the turf with a great armful of branches.

Then he went back again into the jungle and in a few minutes reappeared with a quantity of soft grasses and ferns. Two more trips he made until he had quite a pile of material at hand.

Then he spread the ferns and grasses upon the ground in a soft, flat bed, and above it he leaned many branches together so that they met a few feet over its center. Upon these he spread layers of huge leaves of the great elephant's-ear, and with more branches and more leaves he closed one end of the little shelter he had built.

Then they sat down together again upon the edge of the drum and tried to talk by signs.

The magnificent diamond locket which hung about Tarzan's neck had been a source of much wonderment to Jane Porter. She pointed to it now, and Tarzan removed it and handed it to her.

She saw that it was the work of a skilled artizan and that the diamonds were of great brilliancy and superbly set, but the cutting of them denoted that they were of a former day.

She noticed that the locket opened, and, pressing the hidden clasp, she saw the two halves spring apart to reveal in either section an ivory miniature.

One was of a beautiful woman and the other might have been the likeness of the man who sat beside her, except for a difference of expression that was scarcely definable.

She looked up at Tarzan to find him leaning toward her gazing on the miniatures with an expression of astonishment. He reached out his hand for the locket and took it away from her, examining the likenesses within with unmistakable signs of surprise and new interest.

His manner clearly denoted that he had never before seen them, nor imagined that the locket opened.

This fact caused Jane Porter to indulge in still more speculation, and it taxed her imagination to picture how this beautiful ornament came into the possession of a wild and savage creature of the unexplored jungles of Africa.

Still more wonderful, how did it contain the likeness of one who might be a brother, or, more likely, the father of this woodland demigod who was even ignorant of the fact that the locket opened.

Tarzan was still gazing with fixity at the two faces. Presently he removed the quiver from his shoulder, and emptying the arrows upon the ground reached into the bottom of the bag-like receptacle and drew forth a flat object wrapped in many soft leaves and tied with bits of long grass.

Carefully he unwrapped it, removing layer after layer of leaves until at length he held a photograph in his hand.

Pointing to the minature of the man within the locket he handed the photograph to Jane Porter, holding the open locket beside it.

The photograph only served to puzzle the girl still more, for it was evidently another likeness of the same man whose picture rested in the locket beside that of the beautiful young woman.

Tarzan was looking at her with an expression of puzzled bewilderment in his eyes as she glanced up at him. He seemed to be framing a question with his lips.

The girl pointed to the photograph and then to the miniature and then to him, as though to indicate that she thought the likenesses were of him, but he only shook his head, and then shrugging his great shoulders, he took the photograph from her and having carefully rewrapped it, placed it again in the bottom of his quiver.

For a few moments he sat in silence, his eyes bent upon the ground, while Jane Porter held the little locket in her hand, turning it over and over in an endeavor to find some further clue that might lead to the identity of its original owner.

At length a simple explanation occurred to her.

The locket had belonged to Lord Greystoke. The likenesses were those of he and Lady Alice. This wild creature had simply found it in the cabin by the beach. How stupid of her not to have thought of that solution before.

But to account for the strange likeness between Lord Greystoke and this forest god—that was quite beyond her, and it is not strange that she did not imagine that this naked savage was indeed an English nobleman.

At length Tarzan looked up to watch the girl as she examined the locket. He could not fathom the meaning of the faces within, but he could read the interest and fascination upon the face of the live young creature by his side.

She noticed that he was watching her and thinking that he wished his ornament again, she held it out to him. He took it from her and taking the chain in his two hands he placed it about her neck, smiling at her expression of surprise.

Jane Porter shook her head vehemently and would have removed the golden links from about her throat, but Tarzan would not let her. Taking her hands in his he held them tightly to prevent her.

At last she desisted and with a little laugh raised the locket to her lips, and, rising, dropped him a little curtsy.

Tarzan did not know precisely what she meant, but he guessed correctly that it was her way of acknowledging the gift, and so he rose, too, and taking the locket in his hand, stooped gravely like some courtier of old, and pressed his lips upon it where hers had rested.

It was a stately and gallant little compliment performed with the grace and dignity of utter unconsciousness of self. It was the hall-mark of his aristocratic birth, the natural outcropping of many generations of fine breeding. A hereditary instinct of graciousness which a lifetime of savage environment could not eradicate.

It was growing dark now, and so they ate again of the fruit which was both food and drink for them, and then Tarzan rose and leading Jane Porter to the little bower he had erected, motioned her to go within.

For the first time in hours a feeling of fear swept over her, and Tarzan felt her draw away as though shrinking from him.

Contact with this girl for half a day had left a very different Tarzan from he whom the morning's sun had risen upon.

Now, in every fiber of his being, heredity spoke louder than training.

He was not in one swift transition become a polished gentleman from a savage ape-man, but at last the instincts of the former predominated, and over all was the desire to please the woman he loved, to appear well in her eyes.

So Tarzan of the apes did the only thing he knew to assure Jane Porter of her safety. He removed his hunting knife from its sheath and handed it to her hilt first, again motioning her into the bower.

The girl understood, and taking the long knife she entered and lay down upon the soft grasses while Tarzan of the apes stretched himself upon the ground across the entrance.

And thus the rising sun found them in the morning.

When Jane Porter awoke, she did not at first recall the strange events of the preceding day, and so she wondered at her odd surroundings—the little leafy bower, the soft grasses of her bed, the unfamiliar prospect from the opening at her feet.

Slowly the circumstances of her position crept one by one into her mind. Then a great wonderment rose in her heart—a mighty wave of thankfulness and gratitude that though she had been in such terrible danger, yet she was unharmed.

She moved to the entrance of the shelter to look for Tarzan. He was gone; but this time no fear assailed her for she knew that he would return.

In the grass at the entrance to her bower she saw the imprint of his body, where he had lain all night to guard her. She knew that the fact that he had been there was all that had permitted her to sleep in such peaceful security.

With him near, who could entertain fear? She wondered if there was another man on earth with whom a girl could feel so safe in the heart of this savage African jungle. Why even the lions and tigers had no terrors for her now.

She looked up to see his lithe form drop softly from a near-by tree. As he caught her eyes upon him his face lighted with that frank and radiant smile that had won her confidence the day before.

As he approached her Jane Porter's heart beat faster and her eyes brightened as they had never done before at the approach of any man.

He had again been gathering fruit which he laid at the entrance of her bower. Once more they sat down together to eat.

Jane Porter commenced to wonder what his plans were. Would he take her back to the beach or would he keep her here? Suddenly she realized that the matter did not seem to give her much concern. Could it be that she did not care!

She began to comprehend, also, that she was contented sitting here by the side of this smiling giant, eating delicious fruit in a sylvan paradise far within the remote depths of an African jungle— that she was contented and happy.

She could not understand it. Her reason told her that she should be torn by wild anxieties, weighted by dread fears, cast down by gloomy forebodings. Instead, her heart was singing and she was smiling into the answering face of the man beside her.

When they had finished their breakfast Tarzan went to her bower and recovered his knife. The girl had entirely forgotten it. She realized that it was because she had forgotten the fear that prompted her to accept it.

Motioning her to follow, Tarzan walked toward the trees at the edge of the arena, and taking her in one strong arm swung to the branches above.

The girl knew that he was taking her back to her people, and she could not understand the sudden feeling of sorrow which crept over her.

For hours they swung slowly along.

Tarzan of the apes did not hurry. He tried to draw out the sweet pleasure of that journey with those dear arms about his neck as long as possible, and so he went far south of the direct route to the beach.

Several times they halted for brief rests, which Tarzan did not need, and at noon they stopped for an hour at a little brook where they quenched their thirst and ate.

It was nearly sunset when they came to the clearing, and Tarzan, dropping to the ground beside a great tree, parted the tall jungle-grass and pointed out the little cabin to her.

She took him by the hand to lead him to it, that she might tell her father that this man had saved her from worse than death; that he had watched over her as carefully as a mother.

But again the timidity of the wild thing in the face of human habitation swept over Tarzan of the apes. He drew back, shaking his head.

The girl came close to him, looking up with pleading eyes. Somehow she could not bear the thought of his going back into the jungle alone.

Still he shook his head, and finally he drew her to him very gently and stooped to kiss her, but first he looked into her eyes and waited to learn if she were pleased, or if she would repulse him.

Just an instant the girl hesitated, and then she realized the truth, and throwing her arms about his neck she drew his face to hers and kissed him—unashamed.

"I love you—I love you," she murmured.

From far in the distance came the faint sound of many guns. Tarzan and Jane Porter raised their heads.

From the cabin came Mr. Philander and Esmeralda. From where Tarzan and the girl stood they could not see the two vessels lying in the harbor.

Tarzan pointed toward the sounds, touched his breast and pointed again. She understood. He was going, and something told her that it was because he thought her people were in danger.

Again he kissed her.

"Come back to me," she whispered. "I shall wait for you—always."

He was gone—and Jane Porter turned to walk across the clearing to the cabin.

Mr. Philander was the first to see her. It was dusk and Mr. Philander was very near-sighted.

"Quickly, Esmeralda!" he cried. "Let us seek safety within. It is a tiger. Bless me!"

Esmeralda did not bother to verify Mr. Philander's vision. His tone was enough. She was within the cabin and had slammed and bolted the door before he had finished pronouncing her name.

The "Bless me" was started out of Mr. Philander by the discovery that Esmeralda, in the exuberance of her haste, had fastened him upon the same side of the door as was the tiger.

He beat ferociously upon the heavy portal.

"Esmeralda! Esmeralda!" he shrieked. "Let me in. I am being devoured by a lion."

Esmeralda thought that the noise upon the door was made by the tiger in his attempts to pursue her, so after her custom, she fainted.

Mr. Philander cast a frightened glance behind him.

Horrors! The thing was quite close now. He tried to scramble up the side of the cabin, and succeeded in catching a fleeting hold upon the thatched roof.

For a moment he hung there, clawing with his feet like a cat on a clothesline, but presently a piece of the thatch came away, and Mr. Philander, preceding it, was precipitated upon his back.

At the instant he fell a remarkable item of natural history leaped to his mind. If one feigns death lions and tigers are supposed to ignore one, according to Mr. Philander's faulty memory.

So Mr. Philander lay as he had fallen, frozen into the horrid semblance of death. As his arms and legs had been extended stiffly upward as he came to earth upon his back the attitude of death was anything but impressive.

Jane Porter had been watching his antics in mild-eyed surprise. Now she laughed—a little choking, gurgle of a laugh; but it was enough. Mr. Philander rolled over upon his side and peered about. At length he discovered her.

"Jane!" he cried. "Jane Porter. Bless me!"

He scrambled to his feet and rushed toward her. He could not believe that it was she, and alive.

"Bless me! Where did you come from? Where in the world have you been? How—"

"Mercy, Mr. Philander," interrupted the girl, "I never can remember so many questions."

"Well, well," said Mr. Philander. "Bless me! I am so filled with surprise and exuberant delight at seeing you safe and well again that I scarcely know what I am saying, really. But come, tell me all that has happened to you."

CHAPTER 21

The Village of Torture

AS THE LITTLE expedition of sailors toiled through the dense jungle searching for signs of Jane Porter, the futility of their venture became more and more apparent, but the grief of the old man and the hopeless eyes of the young Englishman prevented the kind-hearted D'Arnot from turning back.

He thought that there might be a bare possibility of finding her body, or the remains of it, for he was positive that she had been devoured by some beast of prey. He deployed his men into a skirmish line from the point where Esmeralda had been found, and in this extended formation they rushed their way, sweating and panting.

It was slow work. Noon found them but a few miles inland. They halted for a brief rest then, and after pushing on for a short distance further one of the men discovered a well-marked trail.

It was an old elephant track, and D'Arnot after consulting with Professor Porter and Clayton, decided to follow it.

The path wound through the jungle in a northeasterly direction, and along it the column moved in single file.

Lieutenant d'Arnot was in the lead and moving at a quick pace, for the trail was comparatively open. Immediately behind him came Professor Porter, but as he could not keep pace with the younger man D'Arnot was a hundred yards in advance when suddenly a half-dozen black warriors rose about him.

D'Arnot gave a warning shout to his column as the blacks closed on him, but before he could draw his revolver he had been pinioned and dragged into the jungle.

His cry had alarmed the sailors, and a dozen of them sprang forward past Professor Porter, running up the trail to their officer's aid.

They did not know the cause of his outcry, only that it was a warning of danger ahead.

They had rushed past the spot where D'Arnot had been seized when a spear hurled from the jungle transfixed one of the men, and then a volley of arrows fell among them.

Raising their carbines they fired into the underbrush in the direction from which the missiles had come.

By this time the balance of the party had come up, and volley after volley was fired toward the concealed foe. It was these shots that Tarzan and Jane Porter had heard.

Lieutenant Charpentier, who had been bringing up the rear of the column, now came running to the scene, and on hearing the details of the ambuscade ordered the men to follow him, and plunged into the tangled vegetation.

In an instant they were in a hand-to-hand fight with some fifty black warriors of Mbonga's village. Arrows and bullets flew thick and fast.

Queer African knives and French gun-butts mingled for a moment in savage and bloody duels, but soon the natives fled into the jungle, leaving the Frenchmen to count their losses.

Four of the twenty were dead, a dozen others were wounded and Lieutenant d'Arnot was missing. Night was falling rapidly, and their predicament was rendered doubly worse through the fact that they could not even find the elephant trail which they had been following.

There was but one thing to do, make camp where they were until daylight. Lieutenant Charpentier ordered a clearing made and an abatis of underbrush constructed in circular form about the camp.

This work was not completed until long after dark, the men building a huge fire in the center of the clearing to give them light to work by.

When all was as safe as could be made from the attack of wild beasts and savage men, Lieutenant Charpentier placed sentries about the little camp, and the tired and hungry men threw themselves upon the ground to sleep.

The groans of the wounded, mingled with the roaring and growling of the great beasts kept sleep except in its most fitful form from the tired eyes. It was a sad and hungry party that lay through the long night praying for dawn.

The blacks, who had seized D'Arnot, had not waited to participate in the fight which followed, but instead had dragged their prisoner a little way through the jungle and then struck the trail further on beyond the scene of the fighting.

They hurried him along, the sounds of battle growing fainter and fainter as they drew away from the contestants until there suddenly broke upon D'Arnot's vision a good-sized clearing at one end of which stood a thatched and palisaded village.

It was now dusk, but the watchers at the gate saw the approaching trio and distinguished one as a prisoner ere they reached the portals.

A cry went up within the palisade. A great throng of women and children rushed out to meet the party.

And then began for the French officer the most terrifying experience which man can encounter upon earth—the reception of a white prisoner into a village of African cannibals.

They fell upon D'Arnot tooth and nail, beating him with sticks and stones and tearing at him with clawlike hands. Every vestige of clothing was torn from him, and the merciless blows fell upon his bare and quivering flesh.

But not once did the Frenchman cry out in pain. A silent prayer rose that he be quickly delivered from his torture.

The death he prayed for was not to be so easily had. Soon the warriors beat the women away from their prisoner.

He was to be saved for nobler sport than this; and the first wave of their passion having subsided they contented themselves with crying out taunts and insults, and spitting upon him.

Presently they gained the center of the village. There D'Arnot was bound securely to the great post from which no live man had ever been released.

A number of the women scattered to their several huts to fetch pots and water, while others built a row of fires on which portions of the feast were to be boiled.

The festivities were delayed awaiting the return of the warriors who had remained to engage in the skirmish with the white men, so that it was quite late when all were in the village, and the dance of death commenced to circle round the doomed officer.

Half fainting from pain and exhaustion, D'Arnot watched what seemed but a vagary of delirium, or some horrid nightmare from which he must soon awake.

The bestial faces, daubed with color—the huge mouths and hanging lips—the yellow teeth, sharp filed—the rolling, demon eyes: the shining naked bodies—the cruel spears. Surely no such creatures really existed—he must indeed be dreaming.

The savage, whirling bodies circled nearer. Now a spear sprang forth and touched his arm. The sharp pain and the feel of hot, trickling blood assured him of the awful reality of his position. Another spear and then another touched him.

He closed his eyes and held his teeth firm, set—he would not cry out.

He was a soldier of France, and he would teach these beasts how an officer and a gentleman died.

Tarzan of the apes needed no interpreter to translate the story of those distant shots. With Jane Porter's kisses still warm upon his lips he was swinging with incredible rapidity through the forest trees straight toward the village of Mbonga.

He was not interested in the location of the encounter for he judged that that would soon be over. Those who were killed he could not aid, those who escaped would not need his assistance.

It was to those who had neither been killed or escaped that he hastened. And he knew that he would find them by the great post in the center of Mbonga's village.

Many times had Tarzan seen Mbonga's black raiding parties return from the northward with prisoners, and always were the same scenes enacted about that grim stake, beneath the flaring light of many fires.

He knew, too, that they seldom lost much time before consummating the fiendish purpose of their captures. He doubted that he would arrive in time to do more than avenge.

Tarzan had looked with complacency upon their former orgies, only occasionally interfering for the pleasure of baiting the blacks; but heretofore their victims had been men of their own color.

To-night it was different—white men, men of Tarzan's own race—might be even now suffering the agonies of torture.

On he sped. Night had fallen, and he traveled high along the upper terrace where the gorgeous tropic moon lighted his dizzy pathway.

Presently he caught the reflection of a distant blaze. It lay to the right of his path.

So sure was Tarzan of his jungle knowledge that he did not turn from his course, but passed the glare at a distance of a half mile. It was the campfire of the Frenchmen.

In a few minutes more Tarzan swung into the trees above Mbonga's village. Ah, he was not quite too late! Or, was he? He could not tell. The figure at the stake was very still, yet the black warriors were not pricking it.

Tarzan knew their customs. The death blow had not been struck. He could tell almost to a minute how far the dance had gone.

In another instant Mbonga's knife would sever one of the victim's ears—that would mark the beginning of the end, for very shortly after only a writhing mass of mutilated flesh would remain.

There would still be life in it, but death then would be the only charity it craved.

The stake stood forty feet from the nearest tree. Tarzan coiled his rope. Then there rose suddenly above the fiendish cries of the dancing demons the awful challenge of the ape-man.

The dancers halted as though turned to stone. The rope sped with a singing whir high above the heads of the blacks. It was quite invisible in the flaring lights of the camp-fires.

D'Arnot opened his eyes.

A huge black, standing directly before him, lunged backward as though felled by an invisible hand.

Struggling and shrieking, his body rolling from side to side, moved quickly toward the shadows beneath the trees. The blacks, their eyes protruding in horror, watched spellbound.

Once beneath the trees the body rose straight into the air, and as it disappeared into the foliage above, the terrified negroes, screaming with fright, broke into a mad race for the village gate.

D'Arnot was left alone.

He was a brave man, but he had felt the short hairs bristle upon the nape of his neck when that uncanny cry rose upon the air.

As the writhing body of the black soared, as though by unearthly power, into the foliage of the forest, D'Arnot felt an icy shiver run along his spine, as though death had risen from a dank grave and laid a clammy finger on his flesh.

As D'Arnot watched the spot where the body had entered the tree he heard the sounds of movement there.

The branches swayed as though under the weight of a man's body—there was a crash and the black came sprawling to earth again—to lie very quietly where he had fallen.

Immediately after him came a white body, but this one alighted erect.

D'Arnot saw a clean-limbed young giant emerge from the shadows into the firelight and come quickly toward him.

What could it mean? Who could it be? Some new creature of torture and destruction, doubtless.

D'Arnot waited. His eyes never left the face of the advancing man. The frank, clear eyes did not waver beneath his fixed gaze.

D'Arnot was reassured, but still without much hope, though he felt that that face could not mask a cruel heart.

Without a word Tarzan of the apes cut the bonds which held the Frenchman. Weak from suffering and loss of blood, he would have fallen but for the strong arm that caught him.

He felt himself lifted from the ground.

There was a sensation as of flying, and then he lost consciousness.

CHAPTER 22

The Search Party

WHEN DAWN BROKE upon the little camp of Frenchmen in the heart of the jungle it found a sad and disheartened group.

As soon as it was light enough to see their surroundings, Lieutenant Charpentier sent men in groups of three in several directions to locate the trail, and in ten minutes it was found and the expedition was hurrying back toward the beach.

It was slow work, for they bore the bodies of six dead men, two more having succumbed during the night, and several of those who were wounded required support to move even very slowly.

Charpentier had decided to return to camp for reenforcements, and then make an attempt to track down the natives and rescue D'Arnot.

It was late in the afternoon when the exhausted men reached the clearing by the beach, but for two of them the return brought so great a happiness that all their suffering and heart-breaking grief was forgotten on the instant.

As the little party emerged from the jungle the first person that Professor Porter and Cecil Clayton saw was Jane Porter, standing by the cabin door.

With a little cry of joy and relief she ran forward to greet them, throwing her arms about her father's neck and bursting into tears for the first time since they had been cast upon this hideous and adventurous shore.

Professor Porter strove manfully to suppress his own emotions, but the strain upon his nerves and weakened vitality were too much for him. At length, burying his old face in the girl's shoulder, he sobbed like a tired child.

Jane Porter led him toward the cabin, and the Frenchmen

turned toward the beach from which several of their fellows were advancing to meet them.

Clayton, wishing to leave father and daughter alone, joined the sailors and remained talking with the officers until their boat pulled away toward the cruiser whither Lieutenant Charpentier was bound to report the unhappy outcome of his adventure.

Then Clayton turned back slowly toward the cabin. His heart was filled with happiness. The woman he loved was safe.

He wondered by what manner of miracle she had been spared. It seemed almost unbelievable.

As he approached the cabin he saw her coming out. When she saw him she hurried forward to meet him.

"Jane!" he cried, "Heaven has been good to us, indeed. Tell me how you escaped—what form Providence took to save you for—us."

He had never before called her by her given name. Forty-eight hours before it would have suffused Jane Porter with a soft glow of pleasure to have heard that name from Clayton's lips—now it frightened her.

"Mr. Clayton," she said quietly, extending her hand, "first let me thank you for your loyalty to my father. He has told me how noble and self-sacrificing you have been. How can we ever repay you!"

Clayton noticed that she did not return his familiar salutation, but he felt no misgivings on that score. She had been through so much. This was no time to force his love upon her, he quickly realized.

"I am already repaid," he laughed. "Just to see you and Professor Porter both safe, well, and together again."

The girl bowed her head. There was a question she wanted to ask, but it seemed almost sacrilegious in the face of the love of these two men, and the terrible suffering they had endured while she sat laughing and happy beside a godlike creature of the forest, eating delicious fruits and looking with eyes of love into answering eyes.

But love is a strange master, and human nature is still stranger, so she asked her question, though she was not coward enough to attempt to justify herself to her own conscience. She felt self-hate, but she asked her question nevertheless.

"Where is the forest man who went to rescue you? Why did he not return?"

"I do not understand," said Clayton. "Whom do you mean?"

"He who has saved each of us—who saved me from the gorilla."

"Oh," cried Clayton in surprise. "It was he who rescued you? You have not told me anything of your adventure, don't you know; tell me, do."

"But the woodman," she urged. "Have you not seen him? When we heard the shots in the jungle, very faint and far away, he left me. We had just reached the clearing, and he hurried off in the direction of the fighting. I know he went to aid you."

Her tone was almost pleading—her manner tense with suppressed emotion. Clayton could not but notice it, and he wondered, vaguely, why she was so deeply moved—so anxious to know the whereabouts of this strange creature. He did not suspect the truth, for how could he?

Yet a feeling of apprehension of some impending sorrow haunted him, and in his breast, unknown to himself, was implanted the first germ of jealousy and suspicion of the ape-man to whom he owed his life.

"We did not see him," he replied quietly. "He did not join us." And then after a moment of thoughtful pause: "Possibly he joined his own tribe—the men who attacked us."

He did not know why he had said it, for he did not believe it; but love is a strange master.

The girl looked at him wide-eyed for a moment.

"No!" she exclaimed vehemently, much too vehemently, he thought. "It could not be. They were negroes—he is a white man—and a gentleman."

Clayton looked puzzled. The little green-eyed devil taunted him.

"He is a strange, half-savage creature of the jungle, Miss Porter. We know nothing of him. He neither speaks nor understands any European tongue—and his ornaments and weapons are those of the west coast savages."

Clayton was speaking rapidly.

"There are no other human beings than savages within hundreds of miles, Miss Porter, he must belong to the tribe which attacked us, or to some other equally savage. He may even be a cannibal."

Jane Porter blanched.

"I will not believe it," she half-whispered. "It is not true. You shall see," she said, addressing Clayton, "that he will come back and that he will prove you are wrong. You do not know him as I do. I tell you that he is a gentleman."

Clayton was a generous and chivalrous man, but something in the girl's defense of the forest man stirred him to unreasoning jealousy, so that for the instant he forgot all that they owed to this wild demigod, and he answered her with a half-sneer upon his lip.

"Possibly you are right, Miss Porter," he said, "but I do not think that any of us need worry about our carrion-eating acquaintance. The chances are that he is some half-demented castaway who will forget us more quickly, but no more surely, than we shall forget him. He is only a beast of the jungle, Miss Porter."

The girl did not answer, but she felt her heart shrivel within her. Anger and hate against one we love steels our hearts, but contempt or pity leaves us silent and ashamed.

She knew that Clayton spoke merely what he thought, and for the first time she began to analyze the structure which supported her new found love, and to subject its object to a critical examination.

Slowly she turned and walked back to the cabin. She tried to imagine her wood-god by her side in the saloon of an ocean liner. She saw him eating with his hands, tearing his food like a beast of prey, and wiping his greasy fingers upon his thighs. She shuddered.

She saw him as she introduced him to her friends—uncouth, illiterate—a boor; and she winced.

She had reached her room now, and as she sat upon the edge of her bed of ferns and grasses, with one hand resting upon her rising and falling bosom, she felt the hard outlines of the man's locket beneath her waist.

She drew it out, holding it in the palm of her hand for a moment with tear-blurred eyes bent upon it. Then she raised it to her lips, and crushing it there buried her face in the soft ferns, sobbing.

"Beast?" she murmured. "Then Heaven make me a beast; for, man or beast, I am yours."

She did not see Clayton again that day. Esmeralda brought her supper to her, and she sent word to her father that she was suffering from the reaction following her adventure.

The next morning Clayton left early with the relief expedition in search of Lieutenant d'Arnot. There were two hundred armed men this time, with ten officers and two surgeons, and provisions for a week.

They carried bedding and hammocks, the latter for transporting their sick and wounded.

It was a determined and angry company—a punitive expedition as well as one of relief. They reached the sight of the skirmish of the previous expedition shortly after noon, for they were now traveling a known trail and no time was lost in exploring.

From there on the elephant-trail led straight to Mbonga's village. It was but two o'clock when the head of the column halted upon the edge of the clearing.

Lieutenant Charpentier, who was in command, immediately sent a portion of his force through the jungle to the opposite side of the village. Another detachment was despatched to a point before the village gate, while he remained with the balance upon the south side of the clearing.

It was arranged that the party which was to take position to the north, and which would be the last to gain its station, should commence the assault, and that their opening volley should be the signal for a concerted rush from all sides in an attempt to carry the village by storm at the first charge.

For half an hour the men with Lieutenant Charpentier crouched in the dense foliage of the jungle, waiting the signal. To them it seemed like hours. They could see natives in the fields, and others moving in and out of the village gate.

At length the signal came—a sharp rattle of musketry, and, like one man, an answering volley tore from the jungle to the west and to the south.

The natives of the field dropped their implements and broke madly for the palisade. The French bullets mowed them down, and the French sailors bounded over their prostrate bodies straight for the village gate.

So sudden and unexpected the assault had been that the whites reached the gates before the frightened natives could bar them, and in another minute the village street was filled with armed men fighting hand-to-hand in an inextricable tangle.

For a few moments the blacks held their ground within the entrance to the street, but the revolvers, carbines, and cutlases of the Frenchmen crumpled the native spearmen and struck down the black archers with their bolts half-drawn.

Soon the battle turned to a wild rout, and then to grim massacre; for the French sailors had seen bits of D'Arnot's uniform upon several of the black warriors who opposed them.

They spared the children and those of the women whom they

were not forced to kill in self-defense, but when at length they stopped, panting, blood-covered, and sweating, it was because there lived to oppose them no single warrior of all the savage village of Mbonga.

Carefully they ransacked every hut and corner of the village, but no sign of D'Arnot could they find. They questioned the prisoners by signs, and finally one of the sailors who had served in the French Congo found that he could make them understand the hybrid tongue that passes for language between the whites and the more degraded tribes of the coast, but even then they could learn nothing of the fate of D'Arnot.

Only excited gestures and expressions of fear could they obtain in response to their inquiries concerning their fellows, and at last they became convinced that these were but evidences of the guilt of these demons who had slaughtered and eaten their comrade two nights before.

At length all hope left them, and they prepared to camp for the night within the village.

The prisoners were herded into three huts where they were heavily guarded.

Sentries were posted at the barred gates, and finally the village was wrapped in the silence of slumber, except for the wailing of the native women for their dead.

The next morning they set out upon the return march. Their original intention had been to burn the village, but this idea was abandoned and the prisoners were left behind, weeping and moaning, but with roofs to cover them and a palisade for refuge from the beasts of the jungle.

Slowly the expedition retraced its steps of the preceding day. Ten loaded hammocks retarded its pace. In eight of them lay the more seriously wounded, while two swung beneath the weight of the dead.

Clayton and Lieutenant Charpentier brought up the rear of the column, the Englishman silent in respect for the other's grief, for D'Arnot and Charpentier had been inseparable since boyhood.

Clayton could not but realize that the Frenchman felt his grief the more keenly because D'Arnot's sacrifice had been so futile, since Jane Porter had been rescued before D'Arnot had fallen into the hands of the savages, and again because the service in which he had lost his life had been outside his duty and for strangers.

When he spoke of it to Lieutenant Charpentier, the latter shook his head.

"No, *monsieur,*" he said, "D'Arnot would have chosen to die thus. I only grieve that I could not have died for him, or at least with him. I wish that you could have known him better, *monsieur.* He was indeed an officer and a gentleman—a title conferred on many, but deserved by so few.

"He did not die futilely, for his death in the cause of a strange American girl will make us, his comrades, face our ends the more bravely, however they may come to us."

Clayton did not reply, but within him there arose a new respect for Frenchmen which remained undimmed ever after.

It was quite late when they reached the cabin by the beach. A single shot before they emerged from the jungle had announced to those in camp as well as on the ship that the expedition had been too late—for it had been prearranged that when they came within a mile or two of camp one shot was to be fired to denote failure, or three for success, while two would have indicated that they had found no sign of either D'Arnot or the blacks.

So it was a solemn party that awaited their coming, and few words were spoken as the dead and wounded men were tenderly placed in boats and rowed silently toward the cruiser.

Clayton, exhausted from his five days of laborious marching through the jungle and from the effects of his two battles with the blacks, turned toward the cabin to seek a mouthful of food and then the comparative ease of his bed of grasses, after two nights in the jungle.

By the cabin door stood Jane Porter.

"The poor lieutenant?" she asked. "Did you find no trace of him?"

"We were too late, Miss Porter," he replied sadly.

"Tell me. What had happened?" she asked.

"I cannot, Miss Porter. It is too horrible."

"You do not mean that they had tortured him?" she whispered.

"We do not know what they did to him before they killed him," he answered, his face drawn with fatigue and the sorrow he felt for poor D'Arnot—and he emphasized the word before.

"Before they killed him! What do you mean? They are not— they are not—"

She was thinking of what Clayton had said of the forest man's probable relationship to this tribe, and she could not frame the awful word.

"Yes, Miss Porter, they were—cannibals," he said, almost bitterly.

To him, too, had suddenly come the thought of the forest man. The strange jealousy he had felt two days before swept over him once more.

In sudden brutality that was unlike him, he blurted out:

"When your forest god left you he was doubtless hurrying to the feast."

He was sorry ere the words were spoken, though he did not know how cruelly they had cut the girl. His regret was for his baseless disloyalty to one who had saved the lives of every member of his party, nor ever offered harm to one.

The girl's head went high.

"There could be but one suitable reply to your assertion," she said icily, "and I regret that I am not a man, that I might make it."

She turned quickly and entered the cabin.

Clayton was an Englishman, so the girl had passed quite out of sight before he deduced what reply a man would have made.

"Upon my word," he said ruefully, "she called me a liar. And I fancy I deserved it. I'd better go to bed."

But before he did so he called gently to Jane Porter upon the opposite side of the sail-cloth partition, for he wished to apologize, but he might as well have addressed the Sphinx. Then he wrote upon a piece of paper and shoved it beneath the partition.

Jane Porter saw the little note and ignored it, for she was very angry and hurt and mortified, but—she was a woman, and so eventually she picked it up and read it. It said:

MY DEAR MISS PORTER: I had no reason to insinuate what I did. My only excuse is that my nerves must be unstrung— which is no excuse at all.

Please try and think that I did not say it, I am very sorry. I would not have hurt you, above all others in the world. Say that you forgive me.

WM. CECIL CLAYTON.

"He did think it or he never would have said it," reasoned the girl. "But it cannot be true—I know it is not true!"

One sentence in the letter frightened her: "I would not have hurt you above all others in the world."

A week ago that sentence would have filled her with delight, now it depressed her.

She wished she had never met Clayton. She was sorry that she had ever seen the forest god—no, she was glad. And there was that other note she had found in the grass before the cabin the day after her return from the jungle, the love-note signed by Tarzan of the apes.

Who could be this new suitor? If he were another of the wild denizens of this terrible forest, what might he not do to claim her?

"Esmeralda! Wake up," she cried. "You make me so irritable, sleeping there peacefully when you know perfectly well that the world is filled with sorrow."

"Gaberelle!" screamed Esmeralda, sitting up. "What is it now? A hipponocerous?"

"Nonsense, Esmeralda, there is nothing. Go back to sleep. You are bad enough asleep, but you are infinitely worse awake."

"Yas, honey, but what's de matter wif you, precious? You acks sorter kinder disgranulated dis ebenin'."

"Oh, Esmeralda, I'm just plain ugly to-night," said the girl. "Don't pay any attention to me—that's a dear."

"Yas, honey; now you go right to sleep. Yo' nerves am all on aidge. What wif all dese ripotamuses an' man-eatin' geniuses dat Marse Philander been a tellin' about—Lawd, it ain't no wonder we all get nervous prosecution."

Jane Porter crossed the little room laughing, and, kissing the faithful old black cheek, bade her good night.

CHAPTER 23

Brother Men

WHEN D'ARNOT REGAINED consciousness, he found himself lying upon a bed of soft ferns and grasses beneath a little A-shaped shelter of boughs.

At his feet an opening looked out upon a greensward, and at a little distance beyond was the dense wall of jungle and forest.

He was very lame and sore and weak, and as full consciousness returned he felt the sharp torture of many cruel wounds, and the dull aching of every bone and muscle in his body as a result of the hideous beating he had received.

Even the turning of his head caused him such agony that he lay still with closed eyes for a long time.

He tried to piece out the details of his adventures prior to the time he lost consciousness. He wondered if he were among friends or foes.

At length he recollected the hideous scene at the stake, and finally recalled the strange white figure in whose arms he had sunk into oblivion.

D'Arnot wondered what fate lay in store for him now. He could neither see nor hear any signs of life about him.

The incessant hum of the jungle—the rustling of millions of leaves—the buzz of insects—the voices of the birds and monkeys seemed blended into a strangely soothing purr, as though he lay apart, far from the myriad life that surrounded him and whose sounds came to him only faintly.

At length he fell into slumber, nor did he awake again until afternoon.

Once more he experienced the strange sense of bewilderment that had marked his earlier awakening, but soon he recalled the recent past, and looking through the opening at his feet he saw the figure of a man squatting on his haunches.

The broad, muscular back was turned toward him, but, tanned though it was, D'Arnot saw that it was the back of a white man, and he thanked Heaven.

The Frenchman called faintly. The man turned, and, rising, came toward the shelter. His face was very handsome—the handsomest, thought D'Arnot, that he had ever seen.

Stooping, he crawled into the shelter beside the wounded officer, and placed a cool hand upon his forehead.

D'Arnot spoke to him in French, but the man only shook his head—sadly, it seemed to the Frenchman.

Then D'Arnot tried English, but still the man shook his head. Italian, Spanish, and German brought similar discouragement.

D'Arnot knew a few words of Norwegian, Russian, Greek, and also had a smattering of the language of one of the west coast negro tribes—the man denied them all.

After examining D'Arnot's wounds, the man left the shelter and disappeared. In half an hour he was back with fruit and a hollow gourdlike vegetable filled with water.

D'Arnot drank and ate a little. He was surprised that he had no fever. Again he tried to converse with his strange nurse, but the attempt was useless.

Suddenly the man hastened from the shelter only to return a few minutes later with several pieces of bark and—wonder of wonders—a lead-pencil.

Squatting beside D'Arnot, he wrote for a minute on the smooth inner surface of the bark; then he handed it to the Frenchman.

D'Arnot was astonished to see, in plain printlike characters, a message in English.

> I am Tarzan of the apes. Who are you? Can you read this language?

D'Arnot eagerly seized the pencil then he stopped. This strange man wrote English—evidently he was an Englishman.

"Yes," said D'Arnot, "I read English. I speak it also. Now we may talk. First let me thank you for all that you have done for me."

The man only shook his head and pointed to the pencil and the bark.

"Mon Dieu!" cried D'Arnot. "If you are English, why is it then that you cannot speak English?"

And then in a flash it came to him—the man was a mute, possibly a deaf mute.

So D'Arnot wrote a message on the bark, in English.

> I am Paul d'Arnot, lieutenant in the navy of France. I thank you for what you have done for me. You have saved my life, and all that I have is yours. May I ask how it is that one who writes English does not speak it?

Tarzan's reply filled D'Arnot with still greater wonder.

> I speak only the language of my tribe—the great apes who were Kerchak's; and a little of the languages of Tantor, the elephant, and Numa, the lion, and of the other folks of the jungle I understand. With a human being I have never spoken, except once with Jane Porter, by signs. This is the first time I have spoken with another of my kind through written words.

D'Arnot was mystified. It seemed incredible that there lived upon the earth a full-grown man who had never spoken with a fellow man, and still more preposterous that such a one could read and write.

He looked again at Tarzan's message—"except once, with Jane Porter." That was the American girl who had been carried into the jungle by a gorilla.

A sudden light commenced to dawn on D'Arnot—this, then, was the "gorilla." He seized the pencil and wrote.

Where is Jane Porter?

And Tarzan replied, below:

Back with her people in the cabin of Tarzan of the apes.

She is not dead, then? Where was she? What happened to her?

She is not dead. She was taken by Terkoz to be his wife. Tarzan of the apes took her away from Terkoz and killed him before he could harm her. None in all the jungle may face Tarzan of the apes in battle, and live. I am Tarzan of the apes—mighty fighter.

D'Arnot wrote:

I am glad she is safe. It pains me to write. I will rest a while.

And then Tarzan:

Yes, rest. When you are well I shall take you back to your people.

For many days D'Arnot lay upon his bed of soft ferns. The second day a fever had come, and D'Arnot thought that it meant infection and he knew that he would die.

An idea came to him. He wondered why he had not thought of it before.

He called Tarzan and indicated by signs that he would write, and when Tarzan had fetched the bark and pencil, D'Arnot wrote:

Can you go to my people and lead them here? I will write
a message that you may take to them, and they will follow
you.

Tarzan shook his head and taking the bark wrote:

I thought of that—the first day. I dared not. The great
apes come often to this spot. If they found you here, wounded
and alone, they would kill you.

D'Arnot turned on his side and closed his eyes. He did not
wish to die; but he felt that he was going, for the fever was
mounting higher and higher. That night he lost consciousness.

For three days he was in delirium, and Tarzan sat beside him
and bathed his head and hands and washed his wounds.

On the fourth day the fever broke as suddenly as it had come,
but it left D'Arnot a shadow of his former self, and very weak.
Tarzan had to lift him that he might drink from the gourd.

The fever had not been the result of infection, as D'Arnot had
thought, but one of those that commonly attack whites in the
jungles of Africa, and either kill or leave them as suddenly as
D'Arnot's had left him.

Two days after, D'Arnot was tottering about the amphitheater,
Tarzan's strong arm about him to keep him from falling.

They sat beneath the shade of a great tree, and Tarzan found
some smooth bark that they might converse.

D'Arnot wrote:

What can I do to repay you for all that you have done
for me?

Teach me to speak the language of men,

wrote Tarzan in reply.

And so D'Arnot commenced at once, pointing out familiar
objects and repeating their names in French, for he thought that
it would be easier to teach this man his own language, since he
understood it himself best of all.

It meant nothing to Tarzan, of course, for he could not tell
one language from another, so when he pointed to the word
"man" which he had printed upon a piece of bark he learned
from D'Arnot that it was pronounced *"homme,"* and in the same

way he was taught to pronounce ape, *"singe,"* and tree, *"arbre."*

He was a most eager student and in two more days had mastered so much French that he could speak little sentences such as: "That is a tree." "This is grass." "I am hungry," and the like, but D'Arnot found that it was difficult to teach him the French construction upon a foundation of English.

The Frenchman wrote little lessons for him in English and had Tarzan repeat them in French, but as a literal translation was usually very poor French, Tarzan was often confused.

D'Arnot realized now that he had made a mistake, but it seemed too late to go back and do it all over again and force Tarzan to unlearn all that he had learned, especially as they were rapidly approaching a point where they would be able to converse.

On the third day after the fever broke, Tarzan wrote a message asking D'Arnot if he felt strong enough to be carried back to the cabin. Tarzan was as anxious to go as D'Arnot, for he longed to see Jane Porter again.

It had been hard for him to remain with the Frenchman all these days. That he had done so spoke more glowingly for his nobility of character than even did his rescuing of the French officer from Mbonga's clutches.

D'Arnot was only too willing to attempt the journey.

> But you cannot carry me all the distance through this tangled forest,

he wrote.

Tarzan laughed.

"Mais oui," he said, and D'Arnot laughed aloud to hear the phrase that he used so often glide from Tarzan's tongue.

So they set out, D'Arnot marveling as had Clayton and Jane Porter at the wondrous strength and agility of the ape-man.

Mid-afternoon brought them to the clearing, and as Tarzan dropped to earth from the branches of the last tree his heart leaped and bounded against his ribs in anticipation of seeing Jane Porter so soon again.

No one was in sight without the cabin. D'Arnot was perplexed to note that neither the cruiser nor the Arrow was at anchor in the bay.

An atmosphere of loneliness pervaded the spot, which caught suddenly at both men as they strode toward the cabin.

Neither spoke, yet both knew before they opened the closed door what they would find beyond.

Tarzan lifted the latch and pushed the great door in upon its wooden hinges. It was as they had feared. The cabin was deserted.

The men turned and looked at one another. D'Arnot knew that his people thought him dead; but Tarzan thought only of the woman who had kissed him in love and now had fled from him while he was serving one of her people.

A great bitterness rose in his heart. He would go away, far into the jungle and join his tribe. Never would he see one of his own kind again; nor could he bear the thought of returning to the cabin. He would leave that forever behind him with the great hopes he had nursed there of finding his own race and becoming a man among men.

And the Frenchman? D'Arnot? What of him? He could get along as Tarzan had. Tarzan did not want to see him more. He wanted to get away from everything that might remind him of Jane Porter.

As Tarzan stood upon the threshold, brooding, D'Arnot had entered the cabin. Many comforts he saw that had been left behind.

He recognized numerous articles from the cruiser—a camp oven, some kitchen utensils, a carbine and many rounds of ammunition, canned foods, blankets, two chairs, and a cot—and several books and periodicals, mostly American. "They must intend returning," thought D'Arnot.

He walked over to the table that John Clayton had built so many years before to serve as a desk, and on it he saw two notes addressed to Tarzan of the apes.

One was in a strong masculine hand and was unsealed. The other, in a woman's hand, was sealed.

"Here are two messages for you, Tarzan of the apes," cried D'Arnot, turning toward the door, but his companion was not there.

D'Arnot walked to the door and looked out. Tarzan was nowhere in sight. He called aloud but there was no response.

"Mon Dieu!" exclaimed D'Arnot. "He has left me. I feel it. He has gone back to his jungle and left me here alone."

And then he remembered the look on Tarzan's face when they had discovered that the cabin was empty—such a look as the hunter sees in the eyes of the deer he has brought down. The man had been hard hit—D'Arnot realized it now—but why? He could not understand.

The Frenchman looked about him. The loneliness and the horror of the place commenced to get on his nerves—already weakened by the ordeal of suffering and sickness he had passed through.

To be left here alone beside this awful jungle—never to hear a human voice or see a human face—in constant dread of savage beasts and more terribly savage men—a prey to solitude and hopelessness. It was awful.

And far to the east Tarzan of the apes was speeding through the middle terrace back to his tribe. Never had he traveled with such reckless speed.

He felt that he was running away from himself—that by hurtling through the forest like a frightened squirrel he was escaping from his own thoughts. But no matter how fast he went he found them always with him.

He passed above the sinuous, striped body of Sabor, the tiger, going in the opposite direction; toward the cabin, thought Tarzan.

What could D'Arnot do against Sabor—or if Bolgani, the gorilla, should come upon him—or Numa, the lion, or cruel Sheeta.

Tarzan paused in his flight.

"What are you, Tarzan?" he asked aloud. "An ape or a man?

"If you are an ape you will do as the apes would do—leave one of your kind to die in the jungle, if it suited your whim to go elsewhere.

"If you are a man, you will return to protect your kind. You will not run away from one of your own people, because one of them has run away from you."

D'Arnot closed the cabin door. He was very nervous. Even brave men, and D'Arnot was a brave man, are sometimes frightened by solitude.

He loaded one of the carbines and placed it within easy reach. Then he went to the desk and took up the unsealed letter addressed to Tarzan.

Possibly it contained word that his people had but left the beach temporarily. He felt that it would be no breach of ethics to read this letter, so he took the enclosure from the envelope and read:

To Tarzan of the Apes:
We thank you for the use of your cabin, and are sorry

that you did not permit us the pleasure of seeing and thanking you in person.

We have harmed nothing, but have left many things for you which may add to your comfort and safety here in your lonely home.

If you know the strange white man who saved our lives so many times, and brought us food, and if you can converse with him, thank him also for his kindness.

We sail within the hour, never to return, but we wish you and that other jungle friend to know that we shall always thank you for what you did for strangers on your shore, and that we should have done infinitely more to reward you both had you given us the opportunity.

Very respectfully,
WM. CECIL CLAYTON.

" 'Never to return,' " muttered D'Arnot, and threw himself face downward upon the cot.

An hour later he started up, listening.

Something was at the door trying to enter.

D'Arnot reached for the loaded carbine and placed it to his shoulder, ready for any emergency that might arise.

Dusk was falling, and the interior of the cabin was very dark; but the man could see the latch rising from its seat.

He felt his hair rising upon his scalp.

Gently the door opened until a thin crack showed something standing just without.

D'Arnot sighted along the blue barrel at the crack of the door— and then he pulled the trigger.

CHAPTER 24

Lost Treasure

WHEN THE EXPEDITION returned, following their fruitless endeavor to succor D'Arnot, Captain Dufranne was anxious to steam away as quickly as possible, and all save Jane Porter had acquiesced.

"No," she said determinedly, "I shall not go, nor should you, for there are two friends in that jungle who will come out of it some day, expecting to find us awaiting them.

"Your officer, Captain Dufranne, is one of them, and the forest man who has saved the lives of every member of my father's party is the other.

"He left me at the edge of the jungle two days ago to hasten to the aid of my father and Clayton, as he thought, and he has stayed to rescue Lieutenant d'Arnot; of that you may be sure.

"Had he been too late to be of service to the lieutenant he would have been back before now—the fact that he is not back is sufficient proof to me that he is delayed because Lieutenant d'Arnot is wounded, or he has had to follow his captors farther than the village which your sailors attacked."

"But poor D'Arnot's uniform and all his belongings were found in that village, Miss Porter," argued the captain. "The natives showed great excitement when questioned as to the white man's fate."

"But they did not admit that he was dead. As for his clothes and accouterments being in their possession—more civilized peoples than these poor savage negroes strip their prisoners of every article of value whether they intend killing them or not."

"Possibly your forest man was captured or killed by the savages," suggested Captain Dufranne.

The girl laughed.

"You do not know him," she replied, a little thrill of pride setting her nerves a tingle at the thought that she spoke of her own.

"I admit that he would be worth waiting for, this superman of yours," laughed the captain. "I most certainly should like to see him."

"Then wait for him, my dear captain," urged the girl, "for I intend doing so."

The Frenchman would have been a very much surprised man could he have interpreted the true meaning of the girl's words.

They had been walking from the beach toward the cabin as they talked, and now they joined a little group sitting on camp-stools in the shade of a great tree beside the cabin.

Professor Porter was there, and Mr. Philander and Clayton, with Lieutenant Charpentier and two of his brother officers, while Esmeralda hovered in the background, ever and anon venturing opinions and comments with the freedom of an old and much-indulged family servant.

The officers rose and saluted as their superior approached, and

Clayton surrendered his camp-stool to Jane Porter.

"We were just discussing poor Paul's fate," said Captain Dufranne. "Miss Porter insists that we have no proof of his death—nor have we.

"On the other hand, she maintains that the continued absence of your omnipotent jungle friend indicates that D'Arnot is still in need of his services, either because he is wounded, or still is a prisoner in a more distant native village."

"It has been suggested," ventured Lieutenant Charpentier, "that the wild man may have been a member of the tribe of blacks who attacked our party—that he was hastening to aid them—his own people."

Jane Porter shot a quick glance at Clayton.

"It seems vastly more reasonable," said Professor Porter.

"I do not agree with you," objected Mr. Philander. "He had ample opportunity to harm us himself, or to lead his people against us. Instead, during all our residence here, he has been uniformly consistent in his role of protector and provider."

"That is true," interjected Clayton, "yet we must not overlook the fact that except for himself the only human beings within hundreds of miles are savage cannibals.

"He was armed precisely as are they, which indicates that he has maintained relations of some nature with them, and the fact that he is but one against possibly thousands suggests that these relations could scarcely have been other than friendly."

"It seems improbable, then, that he is not connected with them," remarked the captain, "possibly a member of this tribe."

"Or," added another of the officers, "that he could even have lived a sufficient length of time among the savage denizens of the jungle, brute and human, to have become proficient in woodcraft, or in the use of African weapons."

"You are judging him according to your own standards, gentlemen," said Jane Porter. "An ordinary white man such as any of you—pardon me, I did not mean just that—rather, a white man above the ordinary in physique and intelligence could never, I grant you, have lived a year alone and naked in this tropical jungle.

"But this man not only surpasses the average white man in strength and agility, but as far transcends our trained athletes and 'strong men' as they surpass a day-old baby; and his courage and ferocity in battle is that of the wild beast."

"He has certainly won a loyal champion, Miss Porter," said Captain Dufranne, laughing. "I am sure that there be none of us here but would willingly face death in its most terrifying forms to deserve the tributes of one even half so loyal—or so beautiful."

"You would not wonder that I defend him," said the girl, "could you have seen him as I saw him, battling in my behalf with that huge, hairy brute.

"Could you have seen him charge the monster as a bull might charge a grizzly—absolutely without sign of fear or hesitation—you would have believed him more than human.

"Could you have seen those mighty muscles knotting under the brown skin—could you have seen them force back those awful fangs—you, too, would have thought him invincible.

"And could you have seen the chivalrous treatment which he accorded a strange girl of a strange race, you would feel the same absolute confidence in him that I feel."

"You have won your suit," cried the captain. "The cruiser shall wait a few days longer."

"Fo' de Lawd's sake, honey," cried Esmeralda. "You doan' mean to tell me dat youse a goin' to stay right yere in dis yere lan' of carnivable animals when you all done got de oppahtunity to escapade on dat crosier? Doan' tell me dat, honey."

"Why, Esmeralda! You should be ashamed of yourself," cried Jane Porter. "Is this any way to show your gratitude to the man who saved your life twice?"

"Well, Miss Jane, das all jes' as yo' say; but dat dere fores' lawd never did save us to stay yere. He done save us so we all could get away from yere. Ah expec' he be mighty peevish when he fin' we ain't got no mo' sense'n to stay right yere after he done give us de chanct to get away.

"Ah hoped Ah'd never have to sleep in dis yere geological garden another night and listen to all dem lonesome noises dat come out of dat jumble after dark."

"I don't blame you a bit, Esmeralda," said Clayton.

"You and Esmeralda had better go and live on the cruiser," said Jane Porter, in fine scorn. "What would you think if you had to live all of your life in that jungle as our forest man has done?"

"Tut, tut, child," said Professor Porter. "Captain Dufranne is willing to remain, and for my part I am perfectly willing, perfectly willing—as I always have been to humor your childish whims."

"We can utilize the morrow in recovering the chest, professor," suggested Mr. Philander.

"Quite so, quite so, Mr. Philander. I had almost forgotten the treasure," exclaimed Professor Porter. "Possibly we can borrow some men to assist us, and some of the prisoners to point out the location of the chest."

"Most assuredly, my dear professor, we are all yours to command," said the captain.

It was arranged that on the next day Lieutenant Charpentier was to take a detail of ten men, and one of the mutineers of the Arrow as a guide, and unearth the treasure; also that the cruiser would remain for a full week in the little harbor. At the end of that time it was to be assumed that D'Arnot was truly dead, and that the forest man would not return while they remained. Then the two vessels were to leave with all the party.

Professor Porter did not accompany the treasure-seekers on the following day, but when he saw them returning empty-handed toward noon, he hastened forward to meet them—his usual preoccupied indifference entirely vanished, and in its place a nervous and excited manner.

"Where is the treasure?" he cried to Clayton, while yet a hundred feet separated them.

Clayton shook his head.

"Gone," he said, as he neared the professor.

"Gone! It cannot be. Who could have taken it?" cried Professor Porter.

"Heaven only knows, professor," replied Clayton. "We might have thought the fellow who guided us was lying about the location, but his surprise and consternation on finding no chest beneath the body of Snipes were too real to be feigned.

"And then our spades showed us that something had been buried beneath the corpse, for a hole had been there and it had been filled with loose earth."

"But who could have taken it?" repeated Professor Porter.

"Suspicion might naturally fall on the men of the cruiser," said Lieutenant Charpentier, "but for the fact that Sub-lieutenant Janviers here assures me that no men have had shore leave—that none has been on shore since we anchored here except under command of an officer.

"I do not know that you would suspect our men, but I am

glad that there is now no chance for suspicion to fall on them," he concluded.

"It would never have occurred to me to suspect the men to whom we owe so much," replied Professor Porter. "I would as soon suspect my dear Clayton here, or Mr. Philander."

The Frenchmen smiled, both officers and sailors. It was plain to see that a burden had been lifted from their minds.

"The treasure has been gone some time," continued Clayton. "In fact the body fell apart as we lifted it, which indicates that whoever removed the treasure did so while the corpse was still fresh, for it was intact when we first uncovered it."

"There must have been several in the party," said Jane Porter, who had joined them. "You remember that it took four men to carry it."

"By jove!" cried Clayton. "That's right. It must have been done by a party of blacks. Probably one of them saw the men bury the chest and then returned immediately after with a party of his friends, and carried it off."

"Speculation is futile," said Professor Porter sadly. "The chest is gone. We shall never see it more, nor the treasure that was in it."

Only Jane Porter knew what the loss meant to her father, and none there knew what it meant to her.

Six days later Captain Dufranne announced that they would sail early on the morrow.

Jane Porter would have begged for a further reprieve, had it not been that she, too, had begun to believe that her forest lover would return no more.

In spite of herself she began to entertain doubts and fears. The reasonableness of the arguments of these disinterested French officers commenced to convince her against her will.

That he was a cannibal she would not believe but that he was an adopted member of some savage tribe at length seemed possible to her.

She would not admit that he could be dead. It was impossible to believe that that perfect body, so filled with triumphant life, could ever cease to harbor the vital spark—as soon believe that immortality were dust.

As Jane Porter permitted herself to harbor these thoughts, others equally unwelcome forced themselves upon her.

If he belonged to some savage tribe he had a savage wife—a

dozen of them perhaps—and wild, half-caste children. The girl shuddered, and when they told her that the cruiser would sail on the morrow she was almost glad.

It was she, though, who suggested that arms, ammunition, supplies and comforts be left behind in the cabin, ostensibly for that intangible personality who had signed himself Tarzan of the apes, and for D'Arnot, should he still be living, but really, she hoped, for her forest god—even though his feet should prove of clay.

And at the last minute she left a message for him, to be transmitted by Tarzan of the apes.

Jane Porter was the last to leave the cabin, returning on some trivial pretext, after the others had started for the boat.

She kneeled down beside the bed in which she had spent so many nights, and offered up a prayer for the safety of her primeval man, and crushing his locket to her lips she murmured:

"I love you, and because I love you, I believe in you. But if I did not believe, still should I love. May Heaven have pity on my soul that I should acknowledge it. Had you come back for me, and there had been no other way, I would have gone into the jungle with you—forever."

CHAPTER 25

The Outpost of the World

WITH THE REPORT of his gun D'Arnot saw the door fly open and the figure of a man pitch headlong within onto the cabin floor.

The Frenchman in his panic raised his gun to fire again into the prostrate form, but suddenly in the half dusk of the open door he saw that the man was white and in another instant realized that he had shot his friend and protector, Tarzan of the apes.

With a cry of anguish D'Arnot sprang to the ape-man's side, and kneeling, lifted the black head in his arms—calling Tarzan's name aloud.

There was no response, and then D'Arnot placed his ear above the man's heart. To his joy he heard its steady beating beneath.

Carefully he lifted Tarzan to the cot, and then, after closing and bolting the door, he lighted one of the lamps and examined the wound.

The bullet had struck a glancing blow upon the skull, there was an ugly flesh wound, but no signs of a fracture of the skull beneath.

D'Arnot breathed a sigh of relief, and went about bathing the blood from Tarzan's face.

Soon the cool water revived him, and presently he opened his eyes to look in questioning surprise at D'Arnot.

The latter had bound the wound with pieces of cloth, and as he saw that Tarzan had regained consciousness he rose and going to the table wrote a message, which he handed to the ape-man, explaining the terrible mistake he had made and how thankful he was that the wound was not more serious.

Tarzan, after reading the message, sat on the edge of the couch and laughed.

"It is nothing," he said in French, and then, his vocabulary failing him, he wrote:

> You should have seen what Bolgani did to me, and Kerchak, and Terkoz, before I killed them—then you would laugh at a little scratch.

D'Arnot handed Tarzan the two messages that had been left for him.

Tarzan read the first one through with a look of sorrow on his face. The second one he turned over and over, searching for an opening—he had never seen a sealed envelope before. At length he handed it to D'Arnot.

The Frenchman had been watching him, and knew that Tarzan was puzzled over the envelope. How strange it seemed that to a full-grown white man an envelope was a mystery. D'Arnot opened it and handed the letter back to Tarzan.

Sitting on a camp-stool, the ape-man spread the written sheet before him and read:

> To Tarzan of the Apes:—
> Before I leave let me add my thanks to those of Mr. Clayton for the kindness you have shown in permitting us the use of your cabin.
> That you never came to make friends with us has been a great regret to us. We should have liked so much to have

seen and thanked our host.

There is another I should like to thank also, but he did not come back, though I cannot believe that he is dead.

I do not know his name. He is the great white giant who wore the diamond locket upon his breast.

If you know him and can speak his language, carry my thanks to him, and tell him that I waited seven days for him to return.

Tell him, also, that in my home in America, in the city of Baltimore, there will always be a welcome for him if he cares to come.

I found a note you wrote me lying among the leaves beneath a tree near the cabin. I do not know how you learned to love me, who have never spoken to me, and I am very sorry if it is true, for I have already given my heart to another.

But I know that I am always your friend.

JANE PORTER.

Tarzan sat with gaze upon the floor for nearly an hour. It was evident to him from the notes that they did not know that he and Tarzan of the apes were one and the same.

"I have given my heart to another," he repeated over and over again to himself.

Then she did not love him! How could she have pretended love and raised him to such a pinnacle of hope only to cast him down to such utter depths of despair!

Maybe her kisses were only signs of friendship. How did he know, who knew nothing of the customs of human beings?

Suddenly he rose, and, bidding D'Arnot good night as he had learned to do, threw himself upon the couch of ferns that had been Jane Porter's.

D'Arnot extinguished the lamp, and lay down upon the cot.

For a week they did little but rest, meanwhile D'Arnot coached Tarzan in French. At the end of that time the two men could converse quite easily.

One night, as they were sitting within the cabin before retiring, Tarzan turned to D'Arnot.

"Where is America?" he said.

D'Arnot pointed toward the northwest.

"Many thousands of miles across the ocean," he replied. "Why?"

"I am going there."

D'Arnot shook his head.

"It is impossible, my friend," he said.

Tarzan rose and, going to one of the cupboards, returned with a well-thumbed geography.

Turning to a map of the world, he said:

"I have never quite understood all this; explain it to me, please."

When D'Arnot had done so, showing him that the blue represented all the water on the earth, and the bits of other colors the continents and islands, Tarzan asked him to point out the spot where they now were.

D'Arnot did so.

"Now point out America," said Tarzan.

And as D'Arnot placed his finger upon North America, Tarzan smiled and placed his palm upon the page, spanning the great ocean that lay between the two continents.

"You see, it is not so very far," he said. "Scarce the width of my hand."

D'Arnot laughed. How could he make the man understand?

Then he took a pencil and made a tiny point upon the shore of Africa.

"This little mark," he said, "is many times larger upon this map than your cabin is upon the earth. Do you see now how very far it is?"

Tarzan thought for a long time.

"Do any white men live in Africa?" he asked.

"Yes."

"Where are the nearest?"

D'Arnot pointed out a spot on the shore just north of them.

"So close?" asked Tarzan in surprise.

"Yes," said D'Arnot. "But it is not close."

"Have they big boats to cross the ocean?"

"Yes."

"We shall go there to-morrow," announced Tarzan.

Again D'Arnot smiled and shook his head.

"It is too far. We should die long before we reached them."

"Do you wish to stay here then forever?" asked Tarzan.

"No," said D'Arnot.

"Then we shall start to-morrow. I do not like it here longer. I should rather die than remain here."

"Well," answered D'Arnot with a shrug, "I do not know, my friend, but that I also would rather die than remain here. If you go, I shall go with you."

"It is settled then," said Tarzan. "I shall start for America to-morrow."

"How will you get to America without money?" asked D'Arnot.

"What is money?" inquired Tarzan.

It took a long time to make him understand.

"How do men get money?" he asked at last.

"They work for it."

"Very well. I will work for it."

"No, my friend," returned D'Arnot, "you need not worry about money, nor need you work for it. I have enough for two—enough for twenty. Much more than is good for one man, and you shall have all you need if ever we reach civilization."

So on the following day they started north along the shore. Each man carried a carbine and ammunition, beside bedding and some food and cooking utensils.

The latter seemed to Tarzan a most useless encumbrance, so he threw his away.

"But you must learn to eat cooked food, my friend," remonstrated D'Arnot. "No civilized men eat raw flesh."

"There will be time enough when I reach civilization," said Tarzan. "I do not like the things, and they only spoil the taste of good meat."

For days they traveled north, sometimes finding food in plenty, and again going hungry for days.

They saw no signs of natives, nor were they molested by wild beasts. Their journey was a miracle of ease.

Tarzan asked questions and learned rapidly. D'Arnot taught him many of the refinements of civilization—even to the use of knife and fork; but sometimes Tarzan would drop them in disgust and grasp his food in his strong brown hands, tearing it with his molars like a wild beast.

Then D'Arnot would expostulate with him, saying:

"You must not eat like a brute, Tarzan, while I am trying to make a gentleman of you. *Mon Dieu!* Gentlemen do not thus—it is terrible."

Tarzan would grin sheepishly and pick up his knife and fork again, but at heart he hated them.

On the journey he told D'Arnot about the great chest he had seen the sailors bury, and how he had dug it up and carried it to the gathering-place of the apes and buried it there.

"It must be the treasure-chest of Professor Porter," said D'Arnot. "It is too bad, but of course you did not know."

Then Tarzan recalled the letter written by Jane Porter to her friend—the one he had stolen when they first came to his cabin, and now he knew what was in the chest and what it meant to Jane Porter.

"To-morrow we shall go back after it," he announced to D'Arnot.

"Go back?" exclaimed D'Arnot. "But, my dear fellow, we have now been three weeks upon the march. It would require three more to return to the treasure, and then, with that enormous weight which required, you say, four sailors to carry, it would be months before we had again reached this spot."

"It must be done, my friend," insisted Tarzan. "You may go on toward civilization, and I will return for the treasure. I can go very much faster alone."

"I have a better plan, Tarzan," exclaimed D'Arnot. "We shall go on together to the nearest settlement, and there we will charter a boat and sail back down the coast for the treasure.

"That will be safer and quicker, and also not require us to be separated. What do you think of that plan?"

"Very well," said Tarzan. "The treasure will be there whenever we go for it; and while I could fetch it now, and catch up with you in a moon or two, I shall feel safer for you to know that you are not alone on the trail.

"When I see how helpless you are, D'Arnot, I often wonder how the human race has escaped annihilation all these ages which you tell me about. Why, Sabor, single-handed, could exterminate a thousand of you."

D'Arnot laughed.

"You will think more highly of your genus when you have seen its armies and navies, its great cities, and its mighty engineering works. Then you will realize that it is mind, and not muscle, that makes the human animal greater than the mighty beasts of your jungle.

"Alone and unarmed, a single man is no match for any of the larger beasts; but if ten men were together, they would combine their wits and their muscles against their savage enemies, while the beasts, being unable to reason, would never think of combining against the men.

"Otherwise, Tarzan of the apes, how long would you have lasted in the savage wilderness?"

"You are right, D'Arnot," replied Tarzan. "For if Kerchak had come to Tublat's aid that night at the Dum-Dum, there would have been an end of me. But Kerchak could never think far enough ahead to take advantage of any such opportunity."

"Even Kala, my mother, could never plan ahead. She simply ate what she needed when she needed it, and if the supply was very scarce, even though she found plenty for several meals, she would never gather any ahead.

"I remember that she used to think it very silly of me to burden myself with extra food upon the march, though she was quite glad to eat it with me, if the way chanced to be barren of sustenance."

"Then you knew your mother, Tarzan?" asked D'Arnot, in surprise.

"Yes. She was a great, fine ape, larger than I, and weighing twice as much."

"And you also knew your father?" asked D'Arnot.

"I did not know him. Kala told me he was a white ape, and hairless like myself. I know now that he must have been a white man."

D'Arnot looked long and earnestly at his companion.

"Tarzan," he said at length, "it is impossible that the ape, Kala, was your mother. If such a thing can be, which I doubt, you would have inherited some of the characteristics of the ape, but you have not. You are pure man, and, I should say, the offspring of highly bred and intelligent parents.

"Have you not the slightest clue to your past?"

"Not the slightest," replied Tarzan.

"No writing in the cabin that might have told something of the lives of its original inmates?"

"I have read everything that was in the cabin with the exception of one book, which I know now to be written in a language other than English. Possibly you can read it."

Tarzan fished the little black diary from the bottom of his quiver and handed it to his companion.

D'Arnot glanced at the title-page.

"It is the diary of John Clayton, Lord Greystoke, an English nobleman, and it is written in French," he said.

Then D'Arnot proceeded to read the diary that had been written over twenty years before, and which recorded the details of the story which we already know—the story of adventure, hardships, and sorrow of John Clayton and his wife Alice, from the day they left England until an hour before he was struck down by Kerchak.

D'Arnot read aloud. Occasionally his voice broke, and he was forced to stop reading for the hopelessness that spoke between the lines.

Often he glanced at Tarzan; but the ape-man sat upon his haunches, like a carven image, his eyes fixed upon the ground.

Only when the little babe was mentioned did the tone of the diary alter from the habitual note of despair which had crept into it by degrees after the first two months upon the shore.

Then the passages were tinged with a subdued happiness that was even sadder than the rest.

One entry showed an almost hopeful spirit.

> To-day our little boy is six months old. He is sitting in Alice's lap beside the table where I am writing—a happy, healthy, perfect child.
>
> Somehow, even against all reason, I seem to see him a grown man, taking his father's place in the world—the second John Clayton—and bringing added honors to the house of Greystoke.
>
> There—as though to give my prophecy the weight of his endorsement—he has grabbed my pen in his chubby fist and with his ink-begrimed little fingers has placed the seal of his tiny fingerprints upon the page.

Upon the margin of the page were the partially blurred imprints of four wee fingers and the outer half of the thumb.

When D'Arnot had finished the diary the two men sat in silence for some minutes.

"Well! Tarzan of the apes, what think you?" asked D'Arnot. "Does not this little book clear up the mystery of your parentage? You are Lord Greystoke."

Tarzan shook his head.

"The book speaks of but one child," he replied. "Its skeleton lay in the crib, where it died crying for nourishment, from the first time I entered the cabin until Professor Porter's party buried it, with its father and mother, beside the cabin.

"No, that was the babe the book speaks of—and the mystery of my origin is deeper than before, for I have thought much of late of the possibility of that cabin having been my birthplace.

"I am afraid that Kala spoke the truth," he concluded sadly.

D'Arnot shook his head. He was unconvinced, and in his mind had sprung the determination to prove the correctness of his theory, for he had discovered the key which alone could unlock the mystery.

A week later the two men came suddenly upon a clearing in the forest.

In the distance were several buildings surrounded by a strong palisade. Between them and the enclosure stretched a cultivated field in which a number of negroes were working.

The two halted at the edge of the jungle.

Tarzan fitted his bow with a poisoned arrow, but D'Arnot placed a hand upon his arm.

"What would you do, Tarzan?" he asked.

"They will try to kill us, if they see us," replied Tarzan. "I prefer to be the killer."

"Maybe they are friends," suggested D'Arnot.

"They are black," was Tarzan's only reply.

Again he drew back his shaft.

"You must not, Tarzan!" cried D'Arnot. "White men do not kill wantonly. *Mon Dieu!* but you have much to learn.

"I pity the ruffler who crosses you, my wild man, when I take you to Paris. I will have my hands full keeping your neck from beneath the guillotine."

Tarzan lowered his bow and smiled.

"I do not know why I should kill the blacks back there in my jungle, yet not kill them here. Suppose Numa, the lion, should spring out upon us, I should say then, I presume: 'Good morning, M. Numa, how is Mme. Numa?' Eh?"

"Wait until the blacks spring upon you," replied D'Arnot, "then you may kill them. Do not assume that men are your enemies until they prove it."

"Come," said Tarzan, "let us go and present ourselves to be killed."

He started straight across the field, his head high held and the tropical sun beating upon his smooth, brown skin.

Behind him came D'Arnot, clothed in some garments which had been discarded at the cabin by Clayton when the officers of the French cruiser had fitted him out in more presentable fashion.

Presently one of the blacks looked up, and beholding Tarzan

striding toward him, turned, shrieking, and made for the palisade.

In an instant the air was filled with cries of terror from the fleeing gardeners, but before any had reached the palisade a white man emerged from the enclosure, rifle in hand, to discover the cause of the commotion.

What he saw brought his rifle to his shoulder, and Tarzan of the apes would have felt cold lead once again had not D'Arnot cried loudly to the man with the leveled gun:

"Do not fire! We are friends!"

"Halt, then!" was the reply.

"Stop, Tarzan!" cried D'Arnot, halting the ape-man in his tracks. "He thinks we are enemies."

Tarzan dropped into a walk, and, together, he and D'Arnot advanced toward the white man by the gate.

The latter eyed them in puzzled bewilderment.

"What manner of men are you?" he asked in French.

"White men," replied D'Arnot. "We have been lost in the jungle for a long time."

The man had lowered his rifle and now advanced toward them with out-stretched hand.

"I am Father Constantin, of the French mission here," he said. "I am glad to welcome you."

"This is M. Tarzan, Father Constantin," replied D'Arnot, indicating the ape-man; and as the priest extended his hand to Tarzan, D'Arnot added: "And I am Paul d'Arnot, of the French navy."

Father Constantin took the hand which Tarzan extended in imitation of the priest's act, while the latter took in the superb physique and handsome face in one quick, keen glance.

Thus came Tarzan of the apes to the first outpost of civilization.

For a week they remained there, and the ape-man, keenly observant, learned much of the ways of men, while black women sewed upon white duck garments for himself and D'Arnot that they might continue their journey properly clothed.

CHAPTER 26

The Light of Civilization

ANOTHER MONTH BROUGHT them to a little group of buildings at the mouth of a wide river, and there Tarzan saw many boats, and was filled with the old timidity by the sight of many men.

Gradually he became accustomed to the strange noises and the odd ways of civilization, so that presently none might know that two short months before, this handsome Frenchman in immaculate white ducks, who laughed and chatted with the gayest of them, had been swinging naked through primeval forests to pounce upon some unwary victim, which, raw, was to appease his savage appetite.

The knife and fork, so contemptuously flung aside a month before, Tarzan now manipulated as exquisitely as did the polished D'Arnot.

So apt a pupil had he been that the young Frenchman had labored assiduously to make of Tarzan a polished gentleman in so far as nicety of manners and speech were concerned.

"Heaven made you a gentleman at heart, my friend," D'Arnot had said; "but we want its work to show upon the exterior also."

As soon as they had reached the little port D'Arnot had cabled his government of his safety, and requested a three-months' leave, which had been granted.

He had also cabled his bankers for funds, and the enforced wait of a month, under which both chafed, was due to their inability to charter a vessel for the return to Tarzan's jungle after the treasure.

During their stay at the coast town "M. Tarzan" became the wonder of both whites and blacks because of several occurrences which to Tarzan seemed the merest of nothings.

Once a huge black, crazed by drink, had run amuck and terrorized the town, until his evil star had led him to where the black-haired French giant lolled upon the veranda of the hotel.

Mounting the broad steps with brandishing knife the negro made straight for a party of four men sitting at a table.

Shouting in alarm, the four took to their heels, and then the black spied Tarzan.

With a roar he charged the ape-man, while half a hundred heads peered from sheltering windows and doorways to witness the butchering of the poor Frenchman by the giant black.

Tarzan met the rush with the fighting smile that the joy of battle always brought to his lips.

As the negro closed, steel muscles gripped the black wrist of the uplifted knife-hand, and a single swift wrench left the hand dangling below a broken bone.

With the pain and surprise, the madness left the black man, and as Tarzan dropped back into his chair the fellow turned, crying with agony, and dashed wildly toward the native village.

On another occasion, as Tarzan and D'Arnot sat at dinner with a number of other whites, the talk fell upon lions and lion-hunting.

Opinion was divided as to the bravery of the king of beasts, some maintaining that he was an arrant coward, but all asserting that it was with a feeling of greater security that they gripped their express rifles when the monarch of the jungle roared about a camp at night.

D'Arnot and Tarzan had agreed that his past be kept secret, and so none other than the French officer knew of the ape-man's familiarity with the beasts of the jungle.

"M. Tarzan has not expressed himself," said one of the party. "A man of his prowess who has spent some time in Africa, as I understand M. Tarzan has, must have had experiences with lions— yes?"

"Some," replied Tarzan dryly. "Enough to know that each of you are right in your judgment of the characteristics of the lions— you have met. But one might as well judge all blacks by the fellow who ran amuck last week, or decide that all whites are cowards because one has met a cowardly white.

"There is as much individuality among the lower orders, gentlemen, as there is among ourselves.

"To-day we may go out and stumble upon a lion which is overtimid—he runs away from us. To-morrow we may meet his uncle or his twin brother, and our friends wonder why we do not return from the jungle.

"For myself, I always assume that a lion is ferocious, and so I am never caught off my guard."

"There would be little pleasure in hunting," retorted the first speaker, "if one is afraid of the thing he hunts."

D'Arnot smiled. Tarzan afraid!

"I do not exactly understand what you mean by fear," said Tarzan. "Like lions, fear is a different thing in different men, but to me the only pleasure of the hunt is the knowledge that the hunted thing has power to harm me as much as I have to harm him.

"If I went out with a couple of rifles and a gun-bearer and twenty or thirty beaters to hunt a lion, I should not feel that the lion had much chance, and so the pleasure of the hunt would be lessened in proportion to the increased safety which I felt."

"Then I am to take it that M. Tarzan would prefer to go naked into the jungle, armed only with a jack-knife, to kill the king of beasts," laughed the other good-naturedly, but with the merest touch of sarcasm in his tone.

"And a piece of rope," added Tarzan.

Just then the deep roar of a lion sounded from the distant jungle, as though to challenge whoever dared enter the lists with him.

"There is your opportunity, M. Tarzan," bantered the Frenchman good-naturedly.

"I am not hungry," said Tarzan simply.

The men laughed, all but D'Arnot. He alone knew that a savage beast had spoken its simple reason through the lips of the ape-man.

"But you are afraid, just as any of us would be, to go out there naked, armed only with a knife and a piece of rope," said the banterer. "Is it not so, M. Tarzan?"

"No," replied Tarzan. "Only a fool performs any act without reason."

"Five thousand francs is a reason," said the other. "I wager you that amount you cannot bring back a lion from the jungle under the conditions we have named—naked and armed only with a knife and a piece of rope."

Tarzan glanced toward D'Arnot and nodded his head.

"Make it ten thousand," said D'Arnot.

"Done," replied the other.

Tarzan rose.

"I shall have to leave my clothes at the edge of the settlement, so that if I do not return before daylight I shall have something to wear through the streets."

"You are not going now," exclaimed the wagerer—"at night?"

"Why not?" asked Tarzan. "Numa walks abroad at night. It

will be easier to find him."

"No," said the other, "I do not want your blood upon my hands. It will be foolhardy enough if you go forth by day."

"I shall go now," replied Tarzan, and went to his room for his knife and rope.

The men accompanied him to the edge of the jungle, where he left his clothes in a small storehouse.

But when he would have entered the blackness of the undergrowth they tried to dissuade him; and the wagerer was most insistent of all that he abandon his foolhardy venture.

"I will accede that you have won," he said. "The ten thousand francs are yours, if you will but give up this foolish attempt, which can only end in your death."

Tarzan laughed. In another moment the jungle had swallowed him.

The men stood silent for some moments and then slowly turned and walked back to the hotel veranda.

Tarzan had no sooner entered the jungle than he took to the trees, and it was with a feeling of exultant freedom that he swung once more through the forest branches.

This was life! Ah, how he loved it! Civilization held nothing like this in its narrow and circumscribed sphere, hemmed in by restrictions and conventionalities. Even clothes were a hindrance and a nuisance.

At last he was free. He had not realized what a prisoner he had been.

How easy it would be to circle back to the coast, and then make toward the south and his own jungle and cabin.

Now he caught the scent of Numa, for he was traveling up the wind. Presently his quick ears detected the familiar sound of padded feet and the brushing of a huge, fur-clad body through the undergrowth.

Tarzan came quietly above the unsuspecting beast and silently stalked him until he came into a little patch of moonlight.

Then the quick noose settled and tightened about the tawny throat and, as he had done it a hundred times in the past, Tarzan made fast the end to a strong branch and, while the beast fought and clawed for freedom, dropped to the ground behind him, and, leaping upon the great back, plunged his long, thin blade a dozen times into the fierce heart.

Then with his foot upon the carcass of Numa he raised his

voice in the awesome victory cry of his savage tribe.

For a moment Tarzan stood irresolute, swayed by conflicting emotions of loyalty to D'Arnot and a mighty lust for the freedom of his own jungle. At last the vision of a beautiful face, and the memory of warm lips crushed to his dissolved the fascinating picture he had been drawing of his old life.

The ape-man threw the warm carcass of Numa across his shoulders and took to the trees once more.

The men upon the veranda had sat for an hour, almost in silence.

They had tried ineffectually to converse on various subjects, and always the thing uppermost in the mind of each had caused the conversation to lapse.

"*Mon Dieu,*" said the wagerer at length, "I can endure it no longer! I am going into the jungle with my express and bring back that madman."

"I will go with you," said one.

"And I—and I—and I," chorused the others.

So they hastened to their various quarters, and presently they were headed toward the jungle, each man heavily armed.

"What was that?" suddenly cried one of the party, an Englishman, as Tarzan's savage cry came faintly to their ears.

"I heard the same thing once before," said a Belgian, "when I was in the gorilla country. My carriers said it was the cry of a great bull-ape who has made a kill."

D'Arnot remembered Clayton's description of the awful roar with which Tarzan had announced his kills, and he half smiled in spite of the horror which filled him to think that the uncanny sound could have issued from a human throat—from the lips of his friend.

As the party stood finally near the edge of the jungle, debating as to the best distribution of their forces, they were startled by a low laugh near them, and turning, beheld advancing toward them a giant figure bearing a dead lion upon its broad shoulders.

Even D'Arnot was thunderstruck, for it seemed impossible that the man could have so quickly despatched a lion with the pitiful weapons he had taken, or that alone he could have borne the huge carcass through the tangled jungle.

The men crowded about Tarzan with many questions, but his only answer was a laughing depreciation of his feat.

To Tarzan it was as though one should eulogize a butcher for his heroism in killing a cow, for Tarzan had killed so often for food and for self-preservation that the act seemed anything but remarkable to him. But he was indeed a hero in the eyes of these men, accustomed to hunting big game.

Incidentally he had won ten thousand francs, for D'Arnot insisted that he keep it all.

This was a very important item to Tarzan, who was just commencing to realize the power which lay behind the little pieces of metal and paper which always changed hands when human beings rode, or ate, or slept, or clothed themselves, or drank, or worked, or played, or sheltered themselves from the rain, or cold, or sun.

It had become evident to Tarzan that without money one must die. D'Arnot had told him not to worry, since he had more than enough for both, but the ape-man was learning many things, and one of them was that people looked down upon one who accepted money from another without giving something of equal value in exchange.

Shortly after the episode of the lion hunt, D'Arnot succeeded in chartering an ancient tub for the coastwise trip to Tarzan's land-locked harbor.

It was a happy morning for them both when the little vessel weighed anchor and made for the open sea.

The trip to the beach was uneventful, and the morning after they dropped anchor before the cabin, Tarzan, garbed once more in his jungle regalia, and carrying a spade, set out alone for the amphitheater of the apes where lay the treasure.

Late the next day he returned, bearing the great chest upon his shoulders, and at sunrise the little vessel was worked through the harbor's mouth and took up her northward journey.

Three weeks later Tarzan and D'Arnot were passengers on board a French steamer bound for Lyons, and after a few days in that city D'Arnot took Tarzan to Paris.

The ape-man was anxious to proceed to America, but D'Arnot insisted that he must accompany him to Paris first, nor would he divulge the nature of the urgent necessity upon which he based his demand.

One of the first things which D'Arnot accomplished after their arrival was to arrange to visit a high official of the police department, an old friend of D'Arnot's. He took Tarzan with him.

Adroitly D'Arnot led the conversation from point to point until the policeman had explained to the interested Tarzan many of the methods in vogue for apprehending and identifying criminals.

Not the least interesting to Tarzan was the part played by finger-prints in this fascinating science.

"But of what value are these imprints," asked Tarzan, "when after a few years the lines upon the fingers are entirely changed by the wearing out of the old tissue and the growth of new?"

"The lines never change," replied the official. "From infancy to senility the finger-prints of an individual change only in size, except as injuries alter the loops and whorls. If imprints have been taken of the thumb and four fingers of both hands one must needs lose all entirely to escape identification."

"It is marvelous," exclaimed D'Arnot. "I wonder what the lines upon my fingers resemble."

"We can soon see," replied the police officer, and ringing a bell he summoned an assistant to whom he issued a few directions.

The man left the room to return presently with a little hardwood box, which he placed on his superior's desk.

"Now," said the officer, "you shall have your finger-prints in a second."

He drew from the little case a square of plate-glass, a little tube of thick ink, a rubber roller, and a few snowy white cards.

Squeezing a drop of ink on to the glass, he spread it back and forth with the rubber roller until the entire surface of the glass was covered with a very thin and uniform layer of ink.

"Place the four fingers of your right hand upon the glass, thus," he said to D'Arnot. "Now the thumb. That's right. Now place them in just the same position upon this card here. No—a little to the right. We must leave room for the thumb and the fingers of the left hand. There, that's it. Now the same with the left."

"Come, Tarzan," cried D'Arnot. "Let's see what your whorls look like."

Tarzan complied readily, asking many questions of the officer during the operation.

"Do finger-prints show racial characteristics?" he asked. "Could you determine, for example, solely from finger-prints, whether the subject was negro or Caucasion?"

"I think not," replied the officer. "Though some claim that those of the negro are less complex."

"Could the finger-prints of an ape be detected from those of a man?"

"Probably, because the ape's would be far simpler than those of the higher organism."

"But a cross between an ape and a man might show the characteristics of either progenitor?" continued Tarzan.

"I should think likely," responded the official. "But the science has not progressed sufficiently to render it exact enough in such matters. I should hate to trust its findings further than to differentiate between individuals.

"There it is, absolutely definite. No two people born into the world probably have ever had identical lines upon all their digits. And it is very doubtful if any single finger-print will ever be exactly duplicated by any finger other than the one which originally made it."

"Does the comparison require much time or labor?" asked D'Arnot.

"Ordinarily but a few moments, if the impressions are distinct."

D'Arnot drew a little black book from his pocket and commenced turning the pages.

Tarzan looked at the book in surprise. How did D'Arnot come to have his book?

Presently D'Arnot stopped at a page on which were five tiny little smudges.

He handed the open book to the policeman.

"Are these imprints similar to mine or M. Tarzan's. Can you say that they are identical with either?"

The officer drew a powerful glass from his desk and examined all three specimens carefully, making notations meanwhile upon a pad of paper.

Tarzan realized now what was the meaning of their visit to the police officer.

The answer to his life's riddle lay in these tiny marks.

With tense nerves he sat leaning forward in his chair, but suddenly he relaxed and dropped back, smiling.

D'Arnot looked at him in surprise.

"You forget that for twenty years the dead body of the child who made those finger-prints lay in the cabin of his father, and that all my life I have seen it lying there," said Tarzan bitterly.

The policeman looked up in astonishment.

"Go ahead, captain, with your examination," said D'Arnot. "We will tell you the story later—provided M. Tarzan is agreeable."

Tarzan nodded his head.

"But you are mad, my dear D'Arnot," he insisted. "Those little fingers are buried on the west coast of Africa."

"I do not know as to that, Tarzan," replied D'Arnot. "It is possible, but if you are not the son of John Clayton, then how in Heaven's name did you come into that jungle where no white man other than John Clayton had ever set foot?"

"You forget—Kala," said Tarzan.

"I do not even consider her," replied D'Arnot.

The friends had walked to the broad window overlooking the boulevard as they talked. For some time they stood there gazing out upon the busy throng beneath, each wrapped in his own thoughts.

"It takes some time to compare finger-prints," thought D'Arnot, turning to look at the police officer.

To his astonishment he saw the official leaning back in his chair hastily scanning the contents of the little black diary.

D'Arnot coughed. The policeman looked up, and catching his eye, raised his finger to admonish silence.

D'Arnot turned back to the window, and presently the police officer spoke.

"Gentlemen," he said.

Both turned toward him.

"There is evidently a great deal at stake which must hinge to a greater or lesser extent upon the absolute correctness of this comparison. I therefore ask that you leave the entire matter in my hands until our expert returns."

"I had hoped to know at once," said D'Arnot. "M. Tarzan sails for America to-morrow."

"I will promise that you can cable him a report within two weeks," replied the officer. "What it will be I dare not say. There are resemblances, yet—well, we had better leave it for M. Leblanc to solve."

CHAPTER 27

The Giant Again

A TAXICAB DREW up before an old-fashioned residence upon the outskirts of Baltimore.

A man of about forty, well-built and with strong, regular features, stepped out, and paying the chauffeur, dismissed him.

A moment later the passenger was entering the library of the old home.

"Ah, Mr. Canler!" exclaimed an old man, rising to greet him.

"Good evening, my dear professor," cried the man, extending a cordial hand.

"Who admitted you?" asked the professor.

"Esmeralda."

"Then she will acquaint Jane with the fact that you are here," said the old man.

"No, professor," replied Canler, "for I came primarily to see you."

"Ah, I am honored," said Professor Porter.

"Professor," continued Robert Canler with great deliberation, as though carefully weighing his words, "I have come this evening to speak with you about Jane.

"You know my aspirations, and you have been generous enough to approve my suit."

Professor Archimedes Q. Porter fidgeted in his armchair. The subject always made him uncomfortable. He could not understand why. Canler was a splended match.

"But Jane," continued Canler, "I cannot understand her. She puts me off first on one ground and then another. I always have the feeling that she breathes a sigh of relief every time I bid her good-by."

"Tut-tut," said Professor Porter. "Tut-tut, Mr. Canler. Jane is a most obedient daughter. She will do precisely as I tell her."

"Then I can still count on your support?" asked Canler, a tone of relief marking his voice.

"Certainly, sir, certainly," exclaimed Professor Porter. "How could you doubt it?"

"There is young Clayton, you know," suggested Canler. "He has been hanging about for months.

"I don't know that Jane cares for him. But besides his title they say he has inherited a very considerable estate from his father. It might not be strange, if he finally won her, unless—"

Canler paused.

"Tut-tut, Mr. Canler. Unless—what?"

"Unless, you see fit to request that Jane and I be married at once," said Canler slowly and distinctly.

"I have already suggested to Jane that it would be desirable," said Professor Porter sadly, "for we can no longer afford to keep up this house, and live as her associations demand."

"What was her reply?"

"She said she was not ready to marry any one yet," replied Professor Porter. "That we could go and live upon the farm in northern Wisconsin which her mother left her.

"It is a little more than self-supporting. The tenants have always made a living from it, and been able to send Jane a trifle each year.

"She is planning our going up there the first of the week. Philander and Mr. Clayton have already gone to get things in readiness for us."

"Clayton has gone there!" exclaimed Canler, visibly chagrined. "Why was not I told? I would gladly have gone and seen that every comfort was provided."

"Jane feels that we are already too much in your debt, Mr. Canler," said Professor Porter.

Canler was about to reply when the sound of footsteps came from the hall without, and Jane Porter entered the room.

"Oh, I beg your pardon!" she exclaimed, pausing on the threshold. "I thought you were alone, papa."

"It is only I, Jane," said Canler, who had risen. "Won't you come in and join the group? We were just speaking of you."

"Thank you," said Jane, entering and taking the chair Canler placed for her. "I only wanted to tell papa that Tobey is coming down from the college to-morrow to pack his books. I want you to be sure, papa, to indicate all that you can do without until fall. Please don't carry this entire library to Wisconsin, as you would have carried it to Africa, if I had not put my foot down."

"Was Tobey here?" asked Professor Porter.

"Yes, I just left him. He and Esmeralda are exchanging religious experiences on the back porch now."

"Tut-tut, I must see him at once!" cried the professor. "Excuse me just a moment."

And the old man hastened from the room.

As soon as he was out of ear-shot Canler turned to Jane Porter.

"See here, Jane," he said bluntly. "How long is this thing to go on like this? You haven't refused to marry me, but you haven't promised either.

"I want to get the license to-morrow, so that we can be married quietly before you leave for Wisconsin. I don't care for any fuss or feathers, and I'm sure you don't either."

The girl turned cold, but she held her head bravely.

"Your father wishes it, you know," added Canler.

"Yes, I know."

She spoke scarcely above a whisper.

"Do you realize that you are buying me, Mr. Canler?" she asked finally, and in a cold, level voice. "Buying me for a few paltry dollars? Of course you do. And the hope of just such a contingency was in your mind when you loaned papa the money for that hare-brained escapade, which but for a most mysterious circumstance would have been successful.

"But you, Mr. Canler, would have been the most surprised. You had no idea that the venture would succeed. You are too good a business man for that. And you are too good a business man to loan money for buried treasure seeking, or to loan money without security—unless you had some special object in view.

"You knew that without security you had a greater hold on the honor of the Porters than with it. You knew the one best way to force me to marry you, without seeming to force me.

"You have never mentioned the loan. In any other man I should have thought that the prompting of a magnanimous and noble character. But you are deep.   ·

"I know you better than you think I know you. I shall certainly marry you if there is no other way, but let us understand each other once and for all."

While she spoke, Canler had alternately flushed and paled, and when she ceased he rose, and with a cynical smile upon his strong face, said:

"You surprise me, Jane. I thought you had more self-control—more pride. Of course you are right. I am buying you, and I knew that you knew it. But I thought you would prefer to pretend that it was otherwise. I should have thought your self-respect and your Porter pride would have shrunk from admitting, even to yourself, that you were a bought woman.

"But have it your own way," he added lightly. "I am going to have you, and that is all that interests me."

Without a word the girl turned and left the room.

Jane Porter was not married before she left with her father and Esmeralda for her little Wisconsin farm, and as she coldly bade Robert Canler good-by while the train pulled out, he called to her that he would join them in a week or two.

At their destination they were met by Clayton and Mr. Philander in a huge touring-car belonging to the former, and quickly whirled away through the dense northern woods toward the little farm which the girl had not visited before since childhood.

The farmhouse, which stood on a little elevation some hundred yards from the tenant's house, had undergone a complete transformation during the three weeks that Clayton and Mr. Philander had been there.

The former had imported a small army of carpenters and plasterers, plumbers and painters from a distant city, and what had been but a dilapidated shell was now a cozy little two-story house, filled with every modern convenience procurable in so short a time.

"Why, Mr. Clayton, what have you done?" cried Jane, her heart sinking within her as she realized the probable size of the expenditure that had been made.

"S-sh," cautioned Clayton. "Don't let your father guess. If you don't tell him, he will never notice. I simply couldn't think of him living in the terrible squalor and sordidness which Mr. Philander and I found. It was so little when I would do so much, Jane. For his sake, please never mention it."

"But you know that we can't repay you," cried the girl. "Why do you want to put me under such terrible obligations?"

"Don't, Jane," said Clayton sadly. "If it had been just now, believe me, I wouldn't have done it, for I knew from the start that it would only hurt me in your eyes. But I couldn't think of that dear old man living in the hole we found here.

"Won't you please believe that I did it just for him and give me that little crumb of pleasure at least."

"I do believe you," said the girl, "because I know you are big enough to have done it just for him—and, oh, Cecil, I wish I might repay you as you deserve—as you would wish."

"Why can't you, Jane?"

"Because I love some one else."

"Canler?"

"No."

"But you are going to marry him. He told me as much before I left Baltimore."

The girl winced.

"I do not love him," she said almost proudly.

"Is it because of the money, Jane?"

She nodded.

"Then am I so much less desirable than Canler? I have money

enough," he said bitterly.

"I don't love you, Cecil," she said, "but I respect you. If I must disgrace myself by such a bargain with any man, I prefer that it be one I already despise. I should loathe the man to whom I sold myself without love, whomsoever he might be.

"You will be happier," she concluded, "alone—with my respect and friendship, than with me and my contempt."

He did not press the matter further, but if ever a man had murder in his heart it was William Cecil Clayton, Lord Greystoke, when, a week later, Robert Canler drew up before the farmhouse in his purring six cylinder.

A week passed—a tense though uneventful week for all.

Canler was insistent that Jane marry him at once.

At length she gave in from sheer loathing of the continued and hateful importuning.

It was agreed that on the morrow Canler was to drive to town and bring back the license and a clergyman.

Clayton had wanted to leave as soon as the plan was announced, but the girl's tired, hopeless look kept him. He could not desert her.

Something might happen yet, he tried to console himself by thinking. In his heart, he knew that it would require but a tiny spark to turn his hatred for Canler into the bloodlust of the killer.

Early the next morning Canler set out for town.

In the east smoke could be seen lying low over the forest, for a fire had been raging for a week not far from them, but the wind still lay in the west and no danger threatened them.

About noon Jane Porter started off for a walk. She would not let Clayton accompany her. She wanted to be alone, she said, and he respected her wishes.

In the house Professor Porter and Mr. Philander were immersed in an absorbing discussion of some weighty scientific problem. Esmeralda dozed in the kitchen, and Clayton, heavy-eyed after a sleepless night, threw himself down upon the couch in the living-room and soon dropped into a fitful slumber.

To the east the black smoke clouds rose higher into the heavens, suddenly they eddied, and then commenced to drift rapidly toward the west.

On and on they came. The inmates of the tenant-house were gone, for it was market day, and none there was to see the rapid approach of the fire.

Soon the flames had spanned the road to the south and cut off Canler's return. A little fluctuation of the wind now carried the path of the forest fire to the north a little, then blew back and the flames nearly stood still as though held in leash by some master hand.

Suddenly, out of the northeast, a great black car came careening down the road.

With a jolt it stopped before the cottage and a black-haired giant leaped out and ran up onto the porch. Without a pause he rushed into the house. On the couch lay Clayton. The man started in surprise, but with a bound was at the side of the sleeping man.

Shaking him roughly by the shoulder, he cried:

"Are you all mad here? Don't you know you are nearly surrounded by fire? Where is Miss Porter?"

Clayton sprang to his feet. He did not recognize the man, but he understood the words, and was upon the veranda in a bound.

He cried out in consternation, then, dashing back into the house, called: "Jane! Jane! Where are you!?"

In an instant Esmeralda, Professor Porter, and Mr. Philander had joined the two men.

"Where is Miss Jane?" demanded Clayton, seizing Esmeralda by the shoulders and shaking her roughly.

"Oh, Gaberelle, Marse Clayton, she done gone for a walk."

"Hasn't she come back yet?"

And, without waiting for a reply, Clayton dashed out into the yard, followed by the others.

"Which way did she go?" cried the black-haired giant of Esmeralda.

"Down dat road," cried the frightened black, pointing toward the south where a mighty wall of roaring flames shut out the view.

"Put these people in the other car," shouted the stranger to Clayton. "I saw one as I drove up. Get them out of here by the north road.

"Leave my car here. If I find Miss Porter, we shall need it. If I don't, no one will need it. Do as I say," as Clayton hesitated.

They saw the lithe figure bound away across the clearing toward the northwest, where the forest still stood, untouched by flame.

In each rose the unaccountable feeling that a great responsibility had been raised from their shoulders—a kind of implicit confidence in the power of the stranger to save the girl if she could be saved.

"Who was that?" asked Professor Porter.

"I don't know," replied Clayton. "He called me by name and he knew Jane, for he asked for her. And he called Esmeralda by name."

"There was something most startlingly familiar about him," exclaimed Mr. Philander. "Yet, bless me, I know I never saw him before."

"Tut-tut," cried Professor Porter. "Most remarkable. Who could it have been, and why do I feel that Jane is safe, now that he has set out in search of her?"

"I can't tell you, professor," said Clayton soberly, "but I know I have the same uncanny feeling."

"But come," he cried, "we must get out of here ourselves, or we shall be shut off." And the party hastened toward Clayton's machine.

When Jane Porter turned to retrace her steps homeward, she was alarmed to note how near the smoke of the forest fire seemed, and, as she hastened onward, her alarm became almost a panic when she perceived that the rushing flames were rapidly forcing their way between herself and the cottage.

At length she was compelled to turn into the dense thicket and attempt to force her way to the west in an effort to circle around the flames and regain her home.

In a short time the futility of her attempt became apparent, and then her one hope lay in retracing her steps to the road and flying for her life to the south toward the town.

The twenty minutes that it took her to regain the road was all that had been needed to cut off her retreat as effectually as her advance had been cut off before.

A short run down the road brought her to a horrified stand, for there before her was another wall of flame. An arm of the parent conflagration had shot out a half-mile south to embrace this tiny strip of road in its clutches.

Jane Porter knew that it was useless to attempt to force her way again through the undergrowth.

She had tried it once and failed. Now she realized that it would be but a matter of minutes ere the whole space between the enemy on the north and the enemy on the south would be a seething mass of flames.

Calmly the girl kneeled down in the dust of the roadway and prayed for strength to meet her fate bravely, and to deliver her father and her friends from death. She did not think to pray for deliverance for herself; she knew there was no hope.

Suddenly she heard her name being called aloud through the forest:

"Jane! Jane Porter!" it rang strong and clear, but in a strange voice.

"Here!" she called in reply. "Here! In the roadway!"

Then through the branches of the trees she saw a figure swinging.

A veering of the wind blew a cloud of smoke about them and she could no longer see the man who was speeding toward her, but suddenly she felt a great arm about her. Then she was lifted up, and she felt the rushing of the wind and the occasional brush of a branch as she was borne along.

She opened her eyes.

Far below her lay the undergrowth and the hard earth.

About her was the waving foliage of the forest.

From tree to tree swung the giant figure which bore her, and it seemed to Jane Porter that she was living over in a dream the experience that had been hers in that far African jungle.

She stole a sudden glance at the face close to hers, and then she gave a little frightened gasp—it was he!

"My man!" she murmured. "No, it is the delirium which precedes death."

She must have spoken aloud, for the eyes that bent occasionally to hers lighted with a smile.

"Yes, your man, Jane Porter. Your savage, primeval man come out of the jungle to claim his mate—the woman who ran away from him," he added almost fiercely.

"I did not run away," she whispered. "I would only consent to leave when they had waited a week for you to return."

They had come to a point beyond the fire now, and he had turned back to the clearing.

Side by side they were walking toward the cottage. The wind had changed once more and the fire was burning back upon itself—another hour like that and it would be burned out.

"Why did you not return?" she asked.

"I was nursing D'Arnot. He was badly wounded."

"Ah, I knew it!" she exclaimed.

"They said you had gone to join the blacks—that they were your people."

He laughed.

"But you did not believe them?"

"No—what shall I call you?" she asked. "What is your name?"

"I was Tarzan of the apes when you first knew me," he said.

"Tarzan of the apes!" she cried. "And that was your note I answered when I left?"

"Yes; whose did you think it was?"

"I did not know. Only that it could not be yours, for Tarzan of the apes had written in English, and you could not understand a word of any language."

Again he laughed.

"It is a long story, but it was I who wrote what I could not speak. And now D'Arnot has made matters worse by teaching me to speak French instead of English.

"Come," he added, "jump into my car; we must overtake your father. They are only a little way ahead."

As they drove along, he said:

"Then when you said in your note to Tarzan of the apes that you loved another—you might have meant me?"

"I might have," she said simply.

"But in Baltimore—oh, how I have searched for you—they told me you would possibly be married by now. That a man named Canler had come up here to wed you. Is that true?"

"Yes."

"Do you love him?"

"No."

"Do you love me?"

She buried her face in her hands.

"I am promised to another. I cannot answer you, Tarzan of the apes," she cried.

"You have answered. Now, tell me why you would marry one you do not love."

"My father owes him money."

Suddenly there came back to Tarzan the memory of the letter he had read—and the name of Robert Canler and the hinted trouble which he had been unable to understand then.

He smiled.

"If your father had not lost the treasure you would not feel forced to keep your promise to this man Canler?"

"I could ask him to release me."

"And if he refused?"

"I have given my promise."

He was silent for a moment. The car was plunging along the uneven road at a reckless pace, for the fire showed threateningly at their right, and another change of the wind might sweep it on with raging fury across this one avenue of escape.

Finally they passed the danger-point, and Tarzan reduced their speed.

"Suppose I should ask him?" ventured Tarzan.

"He would scarcely accede to the demand of a stranger," said the girl. "Especially one who wanted me himself."

"Terkoz did," said Tarzan grimly.

Jane Porter shuddered and looked fearfully up at the giant figure beside her, for she knew he meant the great anthropoid he had killed in her defense.

"This is not an African jungle," she said. "You are no longer a savage beast. You are a gentleman, and gentlemen do not kill in cold blood."

"I am still a wild beast at heart," he said in a low voice, as though to himself.

Again they were silent for a time.

"Jane Porter," said the man at length, "if you were free, would you marry me?"

She did not reply at once, but he waited patiently.

The girl was trying to collect her thoughts.

What did she know of this strange creature at her side? What did he know of himself? Who was he? Who were his parents?

Why his very name echoed his mysterious origin and his savage life.

He had no name. Could she be happy with this jungle waif? Could she find anything in common with a husband whose life had been spent in the tree-tops of an African wilderness, frolicking and fighting with fierce anthropoids; tearing his food from the quivering flanks of fresh-killed prey, sinking his strong teeth into the raw flesh, and tearing away his portion, while his mates growled and fought about him for their share?

Could he ever rise to her social sphere? Could she bear to think of sinking to his? Would either of them be happy?

"You do not answer," he said. "Do you shrink from wounding me?"

"I do not know what answer to make," said Jane Porter sadly. "I do not know my own mind."

"You do not love me, then?" he asked in a level tone.

"Do not ask me. You will be happier without me. You were never meant for the restrictions and conventionalities of civilization. It would become irksome to you. In a little while you would long for the freedom of your old life—to which I am as totally unfitted as you to mine."

"I think I understand you," he replied quietly. "I shall not urge you, for I would rather see you happy than to be happy myself. And I see now that you could not be happy with—an ape."

There was the faintest tinge of bitterness in his voice.

"Don't," she remonstrated. "Don't say that. You don't understand."

But ere she could go on, a sudden turn in the road brought them into the midst of a little hamlet.

Before them stood Clayton's car surrounded by the party he had brought from the cottage.

CHAPTER 28

Lord Ape-Man

AT THE SIGHT of Jane, cries of relief and delight broke from every lip, and, as Tarzan's car stopped beside the other, Professor Porter caught his daughter in his arms.

For a moment no one noticed Tarzan sitting silently in his seat.

Clayton was the first to remember, and, turning held out his hand.

"How can we ever thank you?" he exclaimed. "You have saved us all. You called me by name at the cottage, but I do not seem to recall yours, though there is something very familiar about you.

"It is as though I had known you well under very different conditions a long time ago."

Tarzan smiled as he took the proffered hand.

"You are quite right, M. Clayton," he said in French. "You will pardon me if I do not speak to you in English. I am just learning it, and while I understand it fairly well, I speak it very poorly."

"But who are you?" insisted Clayton, speaking in French this time himself.

"Tarzan of the apes."

Clayton started back in surprise.

"By Jove!" he exclaimed. "It is true."

Professor Porter and Mr. Philander pressed forward to add their thanks to Clayton's, and to voice their surprise and pleasure at seeing this jungle-friend so far from his savage home.

The party now entered the modest little hostelry, where Clayton soon made arrangements for their entertainment.

They were sitting in the little, stuffy parlor when the distant chugging of an approaching automobile caught their attention.

Mr. Philander, who was sitting near the window, looked out as the machine drew in sight, finally stopping beside the other cars.

"Bless me!" said Mr. Philander, a shade of annoyance in his tone. "It is Mr. Canler. I had hoped—er—I had thought or—er—how very happy we should be that he was not caught in the fire," he ended lamely.

"Tut-tut, Mr. Philander," said Professor Porter, "Tut-tut. I have often admonished my pupils to count ten before speaking. Were I you, Mr. Philander, I should count at least a thousand, and then maintain a discreet silence."

"Bless me, yes!" acquiesced Mr. Philander. "But who is the clerical-appearing gentleman with him?"

Jane Porter blanched.

Clayton moved uneasily in his chair.

Professor Porter removed his spectacles nervously, and breathed upon them, but replaced them on his nose without wiping.

The ubiquitous Esmeralda grunted.

Only Tarzan did not comprehend.

Presently Robert Canler burst into the room.

"Thank Heaven!" he cried. "I feared the worst until I saw your car, Clayton. I was cut off on the south road and had to go away back to town, and then strike east to this road. I thought we'd never reach the cottage."

No one seemed very enthusiastic. Tarzan eyed Robert Canler as Sabor eyed his prey.

Jane Porter glanced at him and coughed nervously.

"Mr. Canler," she said, "this is M. Tarzan, an old friend."

Canler turned and extended his hand. Tarzan rose and bowed as only D'Arnot could have taught a gentleman to do it, but he did not seem to see Canler's hand.

Nor did Canler appear to notice the oversight.

"This is the Rev. Mr. Tousley, Jane," said Canler turning to the clerical party behind him. "Mr. Tousley, Miss Porter."

Mr. Tousley bowed and beamed.

Canler introduced him to the others.

"We can have the ceremony at once, Jane," said Canler. "Then you and I can catch the midnight train in town."

Tarzan understood the plan instantly. He glanced out of half-closed eyes at Jane Porter, but he did not move.

The girl hesitated. The room was tense with the silence of taut nerves.

All eyes turned toward Jane Porter, awaiting her reply.

"Can't we wait a few days?" she asked. "I am all unstrung. I have been through so much to-day."

Canler felt the hostility that emanated from each member of the party. It made him angry.

"We have waited as long as I intend to wait," he said roughly. "You have promised to marry me. I shall be played with no longer. I have the license and here is the clergyman.

"Come, Mr. Tousley; come Jane. There are witnesses aplenty— more than enough," he added with a disagreeable inflection, and taking Jane by the arm, he started to lead her toward the waiting minister.

But scarcely had he taken a single step ere a heavy hand closed upon his arm with a grip of steel.

Another hand shot to his throat, and in a moment he was being shaken high above the floor, as a cat might shake a mouse.

Jane Porter turned in horrified surprise toward Tarzan.

And, as she looked into his face, she saw the crimson band upon his forehead that she had seen that other day in far distant Africa, when Tarzan of the apes had closed in mortal combat with the great anthropoid—Terkoz.

She knew that murder lay in that savage heart, and with a little cry of horror she sprang forward to plead with the ape-man. But her fears were more for Tarzan than for Canler. She realized the stern retribution which justice metes to the murderer.

Before she could reach them, though, Clayton had jumped to Tarzan's side and attempted to drag Canler from his grasp.

With a single sweep of one mighty arm the Englishman was hurled across the room, and then Jane Porter laid a firm white hand upon Tarzan's wrist and looked up into his eyes.

"For my sake," she said.

The grasp upon Canler's throat relaxed.

Tarzan looked into the face before him.

"Do you wish this to live?" he asked in surprise.

"I do not wish him to die at your hands, my friend," she replied. "I do not wish you to become a murderer."

Tarzan removed his hand from Canler's throat.

"Do you release her from her promise?" he asked. "It is the price of your life."

Canler, gasping for breath, nodded.

"Will you go away and never molest her further?"

Again the man nodded his head, his face distorted by fear of the death that had been so close.

Tarzan released him, and Canler staggered toward the door. In another moment he was gone, and the terror-stricken preacher with him.

Tarzan turned toward Jane Porter.

"May I speak with you for a moment alone?" he asked.

The girl nodded and started toward the door leading to the narrow veranda of the little hotel. She passed out to await Tarzan, and so did not hear the conversation which followed.

"Wait!" cried Professor Porter, as Tarzan was about to follow.

The professor had been stricken dumb with surprise by the rapid developments of the past few minutes.

"Before we go further, sir, I should like an explanation of the events which have just transpired.

"By what right, sir, did you interfere between my daughter and Mr. Canler? I had promised him her hand, sir, and regardless of our personal likes or dislikes, sir, that promise must be kept."

"I interfered, Professor Porter," replied Tarzan, "because your daughter does not love Mr. Canler. She does not wish to marry him. That is enough for me to know."

"You do not know what you have done," said Professor Porter. "Now he will doubtless refuse to marry her."

"He most certainly will," said Tarzan emphatically.

"And further," added Tarzan, "you need not fear that your pride will suffer, Professor Porter, for you will be able to pay Canler what you owe him the moment you reach home."

"Tut-tut, sir!" exclaimed Professor Porter. "What do you mean?"

"Your treasure has been found," said Tarzan.

"What—what is that you are saying?" cried the professor. "You are mad. It cannot be."

"It is, though. It was I who stole it, not knowing either its value or to whom it belonged. I saw the sailors bury it, and apelike, I had to dig it up and bury it again elsewhere.

"When D'Arnot told me what it was and what it meant to you, I returned to the jungle and recovered it. It had caused so much crime and suffering and sorrow that D'Arnot thought it best not to attempt to bring the treasure itself on here, as had been my intention, so I have brought a letter of credit instead.

"Here it is, Professor Porter." Tarzan drew an envelope from his pocket and handed it to the astonished professor. "Two hundred and forty-one thousand dollars.

"The treasure was most carefully appraised by experts, but lest there should be any question in your mind, D'Arnot himself bought it and is holding it for you, should you prefer the treasure to the credit."

"To the already great burden of the obligations we owe you, sir," said Professor Porter, with trembling voice, "is now added this greatest of all services. You have given me the means to save my honor."

Clayton, who had left the room after Canler, now returned.

"Pardon me," he said. "I think we had better try to reach town before dark and take the first train out of this forest. A native just rode by from the north, who reports that the fire is moving slowly in this direction."

This announcement broke up further conversation, and the entire party went out to the waiting machines.

Clayton, with Jane Porter, the professor, and Esmeralda, occupied Clayton's car, while Tarzan took Mr. Philander in with him.

"Bless me!" exclaimed Mr. Philander, as the car moved off after Clayton's machine. "Who would ever have thought it possible? The last time I saw you you were a veritable wild-man, skipping about among the branches of a tropical African forest, and now you are driving me along a Wisconsin road in a French automobile. Bless me! But it is most remarkable."

"Yes," assented Tarzan, and then, after a pause: "Mr. Philander, do you recall the details of the finding and burying of three skeletons found in my cabin beside that African jungle?"

"Very distinctly, sir; very distinctly," replied Mr. Philander.

"Was there anything peculiar about any of those skeletons?"

Mr. Philander eyed Tarzan narrowly.

"Why do you ask?"

"It means a great deal to me to know," replied Tarzan. "Your answer may clear up a mystery. It can do no worse, at any rate, than to leave it still a mystery.

"I have been entertaining a theory concerning those skeletons for the past two months, and I want you to answer my question to the best of your knowledge—were the three skeletons you buried all human skeletons?"

"No," said Mr. Philander, "the smallest one, the one found in the crib, was the skeleton of an anthropoid ape."

"Thank you," said Tarzan.

In the car ahead, Jane Porter was thinking fast and furiously. She had felt the purpose for which Tarzan had asked a few words with her, and she knew that she must be prepared to give him an answer in the very near future.

He was not the sort of person one could put off, and somehow that very thought made her wonder if she did not really fear him.

Could she love where she feared?

She realized the spell that had been upon her in the depths of that far-off jungle, but there was no spell of enchantment now in prosaic Wisconsin.

Nor did the immaculate young Frenchman appeal to the primal woman in her, as had the stalwart forest-god.

Did she love him? She did not know—now.

She glanced at Clayton out of the corner of her eye. Was not here a man trained in the same school of environment in which she had been trained—with position and culture such as she had been taught to consider as the essentials to congenial association?

Did not her best judgment point to this young English nobleman whose love she knew to be of the sort a civilized woman should crave as the logical mate for such as she?

Could she love Clayton? She could see no reason why she could not. She was not calculating by nature, but training, environment, and heredity had all combined to teach her to reason even in matters of the heart.

That she had been carried off her feet by the strength of the young giant when his great arms were about her in the distant African forest, and again to-day, in the Wisconsin woods, seemed to her only attributable to a temporary mental reversion to type on her part—to the appeal of the primeval man to the primeval woman in her nature.

If he should never touch her again, she reasoned, she would

never feel attracted toward him. She had not loved him, then. It had been nothing more than a hallucination, induced by excitement and by personal contact.

Excitement would not always mark their future relations, should she marry him, and the power of personal contact would be dulled by familiarity.

Again she glanced at Clayton. He was very handsome and every inch a gentleman. She should be very proud of such a husband.

And then he spoke—a minute sooner or a minute later might have made all the difference in the world to three lives. But chance stepped in and pointed out to Clayton the psychological moment.

"You are free now, Jane," he said. "Won't you say 'yes'? I will devote my life to making you very happy."

"Yes," she whispered.

That evening, in the little waiting room at the station, Tarzan caught Jane Porter alone for a moment.

"You are free now, Jane," he said; "and I have come across the ages out of the past from the lair of the primeval man to claim you—for your sake I have become civilized—for your sake I have crossed oceans and continents—for your sake I will be whatever you will me to be. I can make you happy, Jane, in the life you know and love best. Will you marry me?"

For the first time she realized the depths of the man's love—all that he had accomplished in so short a time solely for love of her.

Turning her head, she buried her face in her arms.

What had she done? Because she had been afraid she might succumb to the pleas of this giant, she had burned her bridges behind her—in her groundless apprehension that she might make a terrible mistake, she had made a worse one.

And then she told him the truth, word by word, without attempting to shield herself or condone her error.

"What can we do?" he asked. "You have admitted that you love me. You know that I love you; but I do not know the ethics of society by which you are governed. I shall leave the decision to you, for you know best what will be for your eventual welfare."

"I cannot tell him, Tarzan," she said. "He, too, loves me, and he is a good man. I could never face you nor any other honest person if I repudiated my promise.

"I shall have to keep it. And you must help me bear the burden, though we may not see each other again after to-night."

The others were entering the room, and Tarzan turned toward the little window.

But he saw nothing without, though within he saw a patch of greensward surrounded by a matted mass of gorgeous tropical plants and flowers, and, above, the waving foliage of mighty trees, and, over all, the blue of an equatorial sky.

In the center of the greensward a young woman sat upon a little mound of earth, and beside her sat a young giant. And they ate pleasant fruit and looked into each other's eyes and smiled. They were very happy, and they were all alone.

His thoughts were broken in upon by the station-agent, who entered asking if there was a gentleman by the name of Tarzan in the party.

"I am Tarzan," said the ape-man.

"Here is a message for you, forwarded from Baltimore. It is a cablegram from Paris."

Tarzan took the envelope and tore it open. The message was from D'Arnot. It read:

Finger-prints prove you Greystoke. Congratulations.
D'ARNOT.

As Tarzan finished reading, Clayton entered, and came toward him with extended hand.

Here was the man who had Tarzan's title and Tarzan's estates, and was going to marry the woman whom Tarzan loved—the woman who loved Tarzan.

A single word would make a great difference in this man's life.

It would take away his title and his lands and his castles, and—it would take them away from Jane Porter also.

"I say, old man," cried Clayton, "I haven't had a chance to thank you for all you've done for us. It seems as though you had your hands full saving our lives in Africa and here.

"I'm awfully glad you came on. We must get better acquainted. I often thought about you, you know, and the remarkable circumstances of your environment.

"If it's any of my business, how the deuce did you ever get into that bally jungle?"

"I don't know," said Tarzan quietly. "I was born there. My mother was an ape, and, of course, she couldn't tell me anything about it. I never knew who my father was."

THE SON
OF TARZAN

Illustrated by J. Allen St. John

Overleaf: *The girl saw the spear and snatched it up, while Korak's fingers sought another hold upon the shaggy throat.*

CHAPTER 1

THE LONG BOAT of the *Marjorie W.* was floating down the broad Ugambi with ebb tide and current. Her crew were lazily enjoying this respite from the arduous labor of rowing up stream. Three miles below them lay the *Marjorie W.* herself, quite ready to sail so soon as they should have clambered aboard and swung the long boat to its davits. Presently the attention of every man was drawn from his dreaming or his gossiping to the northern bank of the river. There, screaming at them in a cracked falsetto and with skinny arms outstretched, stood a strange apparition of a man.

"Wot 'ell?" ejaculated one of the crew.

"A white man!" muttered the mate, and then: "Man the oars, boys, and we'll just pull over an' see what he wants."

When they came close to the shore they saw an emaciated creature with scant white locks tangled and matted. The thin, bent body was naked but for a loin cloth. Tears were rolling down the sunken pock-marked cheeks. The man jabbered at them in a strange tongue.

"Rooshun," hazarded the mate. "Savvy English?" he called to the man.

He did, and in that tongue, brokenly and haltingly, as though it had been many years since he had used it, he begged them to take him with them away from this awful country. Once on board the *Marjorie W.* the stranger told his rescuers a pitiful tale of privation, hardships, and torture, extending over a period of ten years. How he happened to have come to Africa he did not tell them, leaving them to assume that he had forgotten the incidents of his life prior to the frightful ordeals that had wrecked him mentally and physically. He did not even tell them his true name, and so they knew him only as Michael Sabrov, nor was there any resemblance between this sorry wreck and the virile, though un-principled, Alexis Paulvitch of old.

It had been ten years since the Russian had escaped the fate of his friend, the arch-fiend Rokoff, and not once, but many times during those ten years had Paulvitch cursed the fate that had given to Nicholas Rokoff death and immunity from suffering while it had meted to him the hideous terrors of an existence infinitely worse than the death that persistently refused to claim him.

Paulvitch had taken to the jungle when he had seen the beasts of Tarzan and their savage lord swarm the deck of the *Kincaid*, and in his terror lest Tarzan pursue and capture him he had stumbled on deep into the jungle, only to fall at last into the hands of one of the savage cannibal tribes that had felt the weight of Rokoff's evil temper and cruel brutality. Some strange whim of the chief of this tribe saved Paulvitch from death only to plunge him into a life of misery and torture. For ten years he had been the butt of the village, beaten and stoned by the women and children, cut and slashed and disfigured by the warriors; a victim of often recurring fevers of the most malignant variety. Yet he did not die. Smallpox laid its hideous clutches upon him, leaving him unspeakably branded with its repulsive marks. Between it and the attentions of the tribe the countenance of Alexis Paulvitch was so altered that his own mother could not have recognized in the pitiful mask he called his face a single familiar feature. A few scraggly, yellow-white locks had supplanted the thick, dark hair that had covered his head. His limbs were bent and twisted, he walked with a shuffling, unsteady gait, his body doubled forward. His teeth were gone—knocked out by his savage masters. Even his mentality was but a sorry mockery of what it once had been.

They took him aboard the *Marjorie W.,* and there they fed and nursed him. He gained a little in strength; but his appearance never altered for the better—a human derelict, battered and wrecked, they had found him; a human derelict, battered and wrecked, he would remain until death claimed him. Though still in his thirties, Alexis Paulvitch could easily have passed for eighty. Inscrutable Nature had demanded of the accomplice a greater penalty than his principal had paid.

In the mind of Alexis Paulvitch there lingered no thoughts of revenge—only a dull hatred of the man whom he and Rokoff had tried to break, and failed. There was hatred, too, of the memory of Rokoff, for Rokoff had led him into the horrors he had undergone. There was hatred of the police of a score of cities from which he had had to flee. There was hatred of law, hatred of order, hatred of everything. Every moment of the man's waking life was filled with morbid thought of hatred—he had become mentally as he was physically in outward appearance, the personification of the blighting emotion of Hate. He had little or nothing to do with the men who had rescued him. He was too weak to work and too morose for company, and so they quickly left him alone to his own devices.

The *Marjorie W.* had been chartered by a syndicate of wealthy manufacturers, equipped with a laboratory and a staff of scientists, and sent out to search for some natural product which the manufacturers who footed the bills had been importing from South America at an enormous cost. What the product was none on board the *Marjorie W.* knew except the scientists, nor is it of any moment to us, other than that it led the ship to a certain island off the coast of Africa after Alexis Paulvitch had been taken aboard.

The ship lay at anchor off the coast for several weeks. The monotony of life aboard her became trying for the crew. They went often ashore, and finally Paulvitch asked to accompany them—he too was tiring of the blighting sameness of existence upon the ship.

The island was heavily timbered. Dense jungle ran down almost to the beach. The scientists were far inland, prosecuting their search for the valuable commodity that native rumor upon the mainland had led them to believe might be found here in marketable quantity. The ship's company fished, hunted, and explored. Paulvitch shuffled up and down the beach, or lay in the shade of the great trees that skirted it. One day, as the men were gathered at a little distance inspecting the body of a panther that had fallen to the gun of one of them who had been hunting inland, Paulvitch lay sleeping beneath his tree. He was awakened by the touch of a hand upon his shoulder. With a start he sat up to see a huge, anthropoid ape squatting at his side, inspecting him intently. The Russian was thoroughly frightened. He glanced toward the sailors— they were a couple of hundred yards away. Again the ape plucked at his shoulder, jabbering plaintively. Paulvitch saw no menace in the inquiring gaze, or in the attitude of the beast. He got slowly to his feet. The ape rose at his side.

Half doubled, the man shuffled cautiously away toward the sailors. The ape moved with him, taking one of his arms. They had come almost to the little knot of men before they were seen, and by this time Paulvitch had become assured that the beast meant no harm. The animal evidently was accustomed to the association of human beings. It occurred to the Russian that the ape represented a certain considerable money value, and before they reached the sailors he had decided he should be the one to profit by it.

When the men looked up and saw the oddly paired couple shuffling toward them they were filled with amazement, and started on a run toward the two. The ape showed no sign of fear. Instead he grasped each sailor by the shoulder and peered long and earnestly into his face. Having inspected them all he returned to Paulvitch's side, disappointment written strongly upon his countenance and in his carriage.

The men were delighted with him. They gathered about, asking Paulvitch many questions, and examining his companion. The Russian told them that the ape was his—nothing further would he offer—but kept harping continually upon the same theme. "The ape is mine. The ape is mine." Tiring of Paulvitch, one of the men essayed a pleasantry. Circling about behind the ape he prodded the anthropoid in the back with a pin. Like a flash the beast wheeled upon its tormentor, and, in the brief instant of turning, the placid, friendly animal was metamorphosed to a frenzied demon of rage. The broad grin that had sat upon the sailor's face as he perpetrated his little joke froze to an expression of terror. He attempted to dodge the long arms that reached for him; but, failing, drew a long knife that hung at his belt. With a single wrench the ape tore the weapon from the man's grasp and flung it to one side, then his yellow fangs were buried in the sailor's shoulder.

With sticks and knives the man's companions fell upon the beast, while Paulvitch danced around the cursing, snarling pack mumbling and screaming pleas and threats. He saw his visions of wealth rapidly dissipating before the weapons of the sailors.

The ape, however, proved no easy victim to the superior numbers

Like a flash, the beast wheeled upon its tormentor.

that seemed fated to overwhelm him. Rising from the sailor who had precipitated the battle he shook his giant shoulders freeing himself from two of the men that were clinging to his back, and with mighty blows of his open palms felled one after another of his attackers, leaping hither and thither with the agility of a small monkey.

The fight had been witnessed by the captain and mate who were just landing from the *Marjorie W.,* and Paulvitch saw these two now running forward with drawn revolvers while the two sailors who had brought them ashore trailed at their heels. The ape stood looking about him at the havoc he had wrought, but whether he was awaiting a renewal of the attack or was deliberating which of his foes he should exterminate first Paulvitch could not guess. What he could guess, however, was that the moment the two officers came within firing distance of the beast they would put an end to him in short order unless something were done and done quickly to prevent. The ape had made no move to attack the Russian but even so the man was none too sure of what might happen were he to interfere with the savage beast, now thoroughly aroused to bestial rage, and with the smell of new spilled blood fresh in its nostrils. For an instant he hesitated, and then again there rose before him the dreams of affluence which this great anthropoid would doubtless turn to realities once Paulvitch had landed him safely in some great metropolis like London.

The captain was shouting to him now to stand aside that he might have a shot at the animal; but instead Paulvitch shuffled to the ape's side, and though the man's hair quivered at its roots he mastered his fear and laid hold of the ape's arm.

"Come!" he commanded, and tugged to pull the beast from among the sailors, many of whom were now sitting up in wide eyed fright or crawling away from their conqueror upon hands and knees.

Slowly the ape permitted itself to be led to one side, nor did it show the slightest indication of a desire to harm the Russian. The captain came to a halt a few paces from the odd pair.

"Get aside, Sabrov!" he commanded. "I'll put that brute where he won't chew up any more able seamen."

"It wasn't his fault, captain," pleaded Paulvitch. "Please don't shoot him. The men started it—they attacked him first. You see, he's perfectly gentle—and he's mine—he's mine—he's mine! I won't let you kill him," he concluded, as his half-wrecked mentality pictured anew the pleasure that money would buy in London—money that he could not hope to possess without some such windfall as the ape represented.

The captain lowered his weapon. "The men started it, did they?" he repeated. "How about that?" and he turned toward the sailors who had by this time picked themselves from the ground, none of them much the worse for his experience except the fellow who had been the cause of it, and who would doubtless nurse a sore shoulder for a week or so.

"Simpson done it," said one of the men. "He stuck a pin into the monk from behind, and the monk got him—which served him bloomin' well right—an' he got the rest of us, too, for which I can't blame him, since we all jumped him to once."

The captain looked at Simpson, who sheepishly admitted the truth of the allegation, then he stepped over to the ape as though to discover for himself the sort of temper the beast possessed, but it was noticeable that he kept his revolver cocked and leveled as he did so. However, he spoke soothingly to the animal who squatted at the Russian's side looking first at one and then another of the sailors. As the captain approached him the ape half rose and waddled forward to meet him. Upon his countenance was the same strange, searching expression that had marked his scrutiny of each of the sailors he had first encountered. He came quite close to the officer and laid a paw upon one of the man's shoulders, studying his face intently for a long moment, then came the expression of disappointment accompanied by what was almost a human sigh, as he turned away to peer in the same curious fashion into the faces of the mate and the two sailors who had arrived with the officers. In each instance he sighed and passed on, returning at length to Paulvitch's side, where he squatted down once more; thereafter evincing little or no interest in any of the other men, and apparently forgetful of his recent battle with them.

When the party returned aboard the *Marjorie W.*, Paulvitch was accompanied by the ape, who seemed anxious to follow him. The captain interposed no obstacles to the arrangement, and so the great anthropoid was tacitly admitted to membership in the ship's company. Once aboard he examined each new face minutely, evincing the same disappointment in each instance that had marked his scrutiny of the others. The officers and scientists aboard often discussed the beast, but they were unable to account satisfactorily for the strange ceremony with which he greeted each new face. Had he been discovered upon the mainland, or any other place than the almost unknown island that had been his home, they would have concluded that he had formerly been a pet of man; but that theory was not tenable in the face of the isolation of his uninhabited island. He seemed continually to be searching for someone, and during the first days of the return voyage from the island he was often discovered nosing about in various parts of the ship; but after he had seen and examined each face of the ship's company, and explored every corner of the vessel he lapsed into utter indifference of all about him. Even the Russian elicited only casual interest when he brought him food. At other times the ape appeared merely to tolerate him. He never showed affection for him, or for anyone else upon the *Marjorie W.*, nor did he at any time evince any indication of the savage temper that had marked his resentment of the attack of the sailors upon him at the time that he had come among them.

Most of his time was spent in the eye of the ship scanning the horizon ahead, as though he were endowed with sufficient reason to know that the vessel was bound for some port where there would be other human beings to undergo his searching scrutiny. All in all, Ajax, as he had been dubbed, was considered the most remarkable and intelligent ape that any one aboard the *Marjorie W.* had ever seen. Nor was his intelligence the only remarkable attribute he owned. His stature and physique were, for an ape, awe inspiring. That he was old was quite evident, but if his age had impaired his physical or mental powers in the slightest it was not apparent.

And so at length the *Marjorie W.* came to England, and there the officers and the scientists, filled with compassion for the pitiful wreck of a man they had rescued from the jungles, furnished Paulvitch with funds and bid him and his Ajax Godspeed.

Upon the dock and all through the journey to London the Russian had his hands full with Ajax. Each new face of the thousands that came within the anthropoid's ken must be carefully scrutinized, much to the horror of many of his victims; but at last, failing, apparently, to discover whom he sought, the great ape relapsed into morbid indifference, only occasionally evincing interest in a passing face.

In London, Paulvitch went directly with his prize to a certain famous animal trainer. This man was much impressed with Ajax with the result that he agreed to train him for a lion's share of the profits of exhibiting him, and in the mean time to provide for the keep of both the ape and his owner.

And so came Ajax to London, and there was forged another link in the chain of strange circumstances that were to affect the lives of many people.

CHAPTER 2

MR. HAROLD MOORE was a bilious-countenanced, studious young man. He took himself very seriously, and life, and his work, which latter was the tutoring of the young son of a British nobleman. He felt that his charge was not making the progress that his parents had a right to expect, and he was now conscientiously explaining this fact to the boy's mother.

"It's not that he isn't bright," he was saying; "if that were true I should have hopes of succeeding, for then I might bring to bear all my energies in overcoming his obtuseness; but the trouble is that he is exceptionally intelligent, and learns so quickly that I can find no fault in the matter of the preparation of his lessons. What concerns me, however, is the fact that he evidently takes no interest whatever in the subjects we are studying. He merely accomplishes each lesson as a task to be rid of as quickly as possible and I am sure that no lesson ever again enters his mind until the hours of study and recitation once more arrive. His sole interests seem to be feats of physical prowess and the reading of every thing that he can get hold of relative to savage beasts and the lives and customs of uncivilized peoples; but particularly do stories of animals appeal to him. He will sit for hours together poring over the work of some African explorer, and upon two occasions I have found him setting up in bed at night reading Carl Hagenbeck's book on men and beasts."

The boy's mother tapped her foot nervously upon the hearth rug.

"You discourage this, of course?" she ventured.

Mr. Moore shuffled embarrassedly.

"I—ah—essayed to take the book from him," he replied, a slight flush mounting his sallow cheek; "but—ah—your son is quite muscular for one so young."

"He wouldn't let you take it?" asked the mother.

"He would not," confessed the tutor. "He was perfectly good natured about it; but he insisted upon pretending that he was a gorilla and that I was a chimpanzee attempting to steal food from him. He leaped upon me with the most savage growls I ever heard, lifted me completely above his head, hurled me upon his bed, and after going through a pantomime indicative of choking me to death he stood upon my prostrate form and gave voice to a most fearsome shriek, which he explained was the victory cry of a bull ape. Then he carried me to the door, shoved me out into the hall and locked me from his room."

For several minutes neither spoke again. It was the boy's mother who finally broke the silence.

"It is very necessary, Mr. Moore," she said, "that you do everything in your power to discourage this tendency in Jack, he—"; but she got no further. A loud "Whoop!" from the direction of the window brought them both to their feet. The room was upon the second floor of the house, and opposite the window to which their attention had been attracted was a large tree, a branch of which spread to within a few feet of the sill. Upon this branch now they both discovered the subject of their recent conversation, a tall, well-built boy, balancing with ease upon the bending limb and uttering loud shouts of glee as he noted the terrified expressions upon the faces of his audience.

The mother and tutor both rushed toward the window but before they had crossed half the room the boy had leaped nimbly to the sill and entered the apartment with them.

" 'The wild man from Borneo has just come to town,' " he sang, dancing a species of war dance about his terrified mother and scandalized tutor, and ending by throwing his arms about the former's neck and kissing her upon either cheek.

"Oh, mother," he cried, "there's a wonderful, educated ape being shown at one of the music halls. Willie Grimsby saw it last night. He says it can do everything but talk. It rides a bicycle, eats with knife and fork, counts up to ten, and ever so many other wonderful things, and can I go and see it too? Oh, please, mother—please let me."

Patting the boy's cheek affectionately the mother shook her head negatively. "No, Jack," she said; "you know I do not approve of such exhibitions."

"I don't see why not, Mother," replied the boy. "All the other fellows go, and they go to the Zoo, too, and you'll never let me do even that. Anybody'd think I was a girl, or—or a mollycoddle. Oh, father," he exclaimed, as the door opened to admit a tall gray eyed man. "Oh, father, can't I go?"

"Go where, my son?" asked the newcomer.

"He wants to go to a music hall to see a trained ape," said the mother, looking warningly at her husband.

"Who, Ajax?" questioned the man.

The boy nodded.

"Well I don't know that I blame you, my son," said the father, "I wouldn't mind seeing him myself. They say he is very wonderful, and that for an anthropoid he is unusually large. Let's all go, Jane—what do you say?" And he turned toward his wife, but that lady only shook her head in a most positive manner, and turning to Mr. Moore asked him if it was not time that he and Jack were in the study for their morning recitations. When the two had left she turned toward her husband.

"John," she said, "something must be done to discourage Jack's tendency toward anything that may excite the craving for the savage life which I fear he has inherited from you. You know from your own experience how strong is the call of the wild at times. You know that often it has necessitated a stern struggle on your part to resist the almost insane desire which occasionally overwhelms you to plunge once again into the jungle life that claimed you for so many years, and at the same time you know, better than any other, how frightful a fate it would be for Jack, were the trail to the savage jungle made either alluring or easy to him."

"I doubt if there is any danger of his inheriting a taste for jungle life from me," replied the man, "for I cannot conceive that such a thing may be transmitted from father to son. And sometimes, Jane, I think that in your solicitude for his future you go a bit too far in your restrictive measures. His love for animals—his desire, for example, to see this trained ape—is only natural in a healthy, normal boy of his age. Just because he wants to see Ajax is no indication that he would wish to marry an ape, and even should he, far be it from you Jane to have the right to cry 'shame!' " and John Clayton, Lord Greystoke, put an arm about his wife, laughing good-naturedly down into her upturned face before he bent his head and kissed her. Then, more seriously, he continued: "You have never told Jack anything concerning my early life, nor have you permitted me to, and in this I think that you have made a mistake. Had I been able to tell him of the experiences of Tarzan of the Apes I could doubtless have taken much of the glamour and romance from jungle life that naturally surrounds it in the minds of those who have had no experience of it. He might then have profited by my experience, but now, should the jungle lust ever claim him, he will have nothing to guide him but his own impulses, and I know how powerful these may be in the wrong direction at times."

But Lady Greystoke only shook her head as she had a hundred other times when the subject had claimed their attention in the past.

"No, John," she insisted, "I shall never give my consent to the implanting in Jack's mind of any suggestion of the savage life which we both wish to preserve him from."

It was evening before the subject was again referred to and then it was raised by Jack himself. He had been sitting, curled in a large chair, reading, when he suddenly looked up and addressed his father.

"Why," he asked, coming directly to the point, "can't I go and see Ajax?"

"Your mother does not approve," replied his father.

"Do you?"

"That is not the question," evaded Lord Greystoke. "It is enough that your mother objects."

"I am going to see him," announced the boy, after a few moments of thoughtful silence. "I am not different from Willie Grimsby, or any other of the fellows who have been to see him. It did not harm them and it will not harm me. I could go without telling you; but I would not do that. So I tell you now, beforehand, that I am going to see Ajax."

There was nothing disrespectful or defiant in the boy's tone or manner. His was merely a dispassionate statement of facts. His father could scarce repress either a smile or a show of the admiration he felt for the manly course his son had pursued.

"I admire your candor, Jack," he said. "Permit me to be candid, as well. If you go to see Ajax without permission I shall punish you. I have never inflicted corporal punishment upon you, but I warn you that should you disobey your mother's wishes in this instance, I shall."

"Yes, sir," replied the boy; and then: "I shall tell you, sir, when

I have been to see Ajax."

Mr. Moore's room was next to that of his youthful charge, and it was the tutor's custom to have a look into the boy's each evening as the former was about to retire. This evening he was particularly careful not to neglect this duty, for he had just come from a conference with the boy's father and mother in which it had been impressed upon him that he must exercise the greatest care to prevent Jack visiting the music hall where Ajax was being shown. So, when he opened the boy's door at about half after nine, he was greatly excited, though not entirely surprised to find the future Lord Greystoke fully dressed for the street and about to crawl from his open bedroom window.

Mr. Moore made a rapid sprint across the apartment; but the waste of energy was unnecessary, for when the boy heard him within the chamber and realized that he had been discovered he turned back as though to relinquish his planned adventure.

"Where were you going?" panted the excited Mr. Moore.

"I am going to see Ajax," replied the boy, quietly.

"I am astonished," cried Mr. Moore; but a moment later he was infinitely more astonished, for the boy, approaching close to him, suddenly seized him about the waist, lifted him from his feet and threw him face downward upon the bed, shoving his face deep into a soft pillow.

"Be quiet," admonished the victor, "or I'll choke you."

Mr. Moore struggled; but his efforts were vain. Whatever else Tarzan of the Apes may or may not have handed down to his son he had at least bequeathed him almost as marvelous a physique as he himself had possessed at the same age. The tutor was as putty in the boy's hands. Kneeling upon him, Jack tore strips from a sheet and bound the man's hands behind his back. Then he rolled him over and stuffed a gag of the same material between his teeth, securing it with a strip wound about the back of his victim's head. All the while he talked in a low, conversational tone.

"I am Waja, chief of the Waji," he explained, "and you are Mohammed Dubn, the Arab sheik, who would murder my people and steel my ivory," and he dexterously trussed Mr. Moore's hobbled ankles up behind to meet his hobbled wrists. "Ah—ha! Villain! I have you in me power at last. I go; but I shall return!" And the son of Tarzan skipped across the room, slipped through the open window, and slid to liberty by way of the down spout from an eaves trough.

Mr. Moore wriggled and struggled about the bed. He was sure that he should suffocate unless aid came quickly. In his frenzy of terror he managed to roll off the bed. The pain and shock of the fall jolted him back to something like sane consideration of his plight. Where before he had been unable to think intelligently because of the hysterical fear that had claimed him he now lay quietly searching for some means of escape from his dilemma. It finally occurred to him that the room in which Lord and Lady Greystoke had been sitting when he left them was directly beneath that in which he lay upon the floor. He knew that some time had elapsed since he had come up stairs and that they might be gone by this time, for it seemed to him that he had struggled about the bed, in his efforts to free himself, for an eternity. But the best that he could do was to attempt to attract attention from below, and so, after many failures, he managed to work himself into a position in which he could tap the toe of his boot against the floor. This he proceeded to do at short intervals, until, after what seemed a very long time, he was rewarded by hearing footsteps ascending the stairs, and presently a knock upon the door. Mr. Moore tapped vigorously with his toe—he could not reply in any other way. The knock was repeated after a moment's silence. Again Mr. Moore tapped. Would they never open the door! Laboriously he rolled in the direction of succor. If he could get his back against the door he could then tap upon its base, when surely he must be heard. The knocking was repeated a little louder, and finally a voice called: "Mr. Jack!"

It was one of the house men—Mr. Moore recognized the fellow's voice. He came near to bursting a blood vessel in an endeavor to scream "come in" through the stifling gag. After a moment the man knocked again, quite loudly and again called the boy's name. Receiving no reply he turned the knob, and at the same instant a sudden recollection filled the tutor anew with numbing terror—he had, himself, locked the door behind him when he had entered the room.

He heard the servant try the door several times and then depart. Upon which Mr. Moore swooned.

In the meantime Jack was enjoying to the full the stolen pleasures of the music hall. He had reached that temple of mirth just as Ajax's act was commencing, and having purchased a box seat was now leaning breathlessly over the rail watching every move of the great ape, his eyes wide in wonder. The trainer was not slow to note the boy's handsome, eager face, and as one of Ajax's biggest hits consisted in an entry to one or more boxes during his performance, ostensibly in search of a long-lost relative, as the trainer explained, the man realized the effectiveness of sending him into the box with the handsome boy, who, doubtless, would be terror stricken by proximity to the shaggy, powerful beast.

When the time came, therefore, for the ape to return from the wings in reply to an encore the trainer directed its attention to the boy who chanced to be the sole occupant of the box in which he sat. With a spring the huge anthropoid leaped from the stage to the boy's side; but if the trainer had looked for a laughable scene of fright he was mistaken. A broad smile lighted the boy's features as he laid his hand upon the shaggy arm of his visitor. The ape, grasping the boy by either shoulder, peered long and earnestly into his face, while the latter stroked his head and talked to him in a low voice.

Never had Ajax devoted so long a time to an examination of another as he did in this instance. He seemed troubled and not a little excited, jabbering and mumbling to the boy, and now caressing him, as the trainer had never seen him caress a human being before. Presently he clambered over into the box with him and snuggled down close to the boy's side. The audience was delighted; but they were still more delighted when the trainer, the period of his act having elapsed, attempted to persuade Ajax to leave the box. The ape would not budge. The manager, becoming excited at the delay, urged the trainer to greater haste, but when the latter entered the box to drag away the reluctant Ajax he was met by bared fangs and menacing growls.

The audience was delirious with joy. They cheered the ape. They cheered the boy, and they hooted and jeered at the trainer and the manager, which luckless individual had inadvertently shown himself and attempted to assist the trainer.

Finally, reduced to desperation and realizing that this show of mutiny upon the part of his valuable possession might render the animal worthless for exhibition purposes in the future if not immediately subdued, the trainer had hastened to his dressing room and procured a heavy whip. With this he now returned to the box; but when he had threatened Ajax with it but once he found himself facing two infuriated enemies instead of one, for the boy had leaped to his feet, and seizing a chair was standing ready at the ape's side to defend his new found friend. There was no longer a smile upon his handsome face. In his gray eyes was an expression which gave the trainer pause, and beside him stood the giant anthropoid growling and ready.

What might have happened, but for a timely interruption, may only be surmised; but that the trainer would have received a severe mauling, if nothing more, was clearly indicated by the attitudes of the two who faced him.

It was a pale-faced house man who rushed into the Greystoke library to announce that he had found Jack's door locked and had been able to obtain no response to his repeated knocking and calling other than a strange tapping and the sound of what might have been a body moving about upon the floor.

Four steps at a time John Clayton took the stairs that led to the floor above. His wife and the servant hurried after him. Once he called his son's name in a loud voice; but receiving no reply he launched his great weight, backed by all the undiminished power of his giant muscles, against the heavy door. With a snapping of iron butts and a splintering of wood the obstacle burst inward.

At its foot lay the body of the unconscious Mr. Moore, across whom it fell with a resounding thud. Through the opening leaped Tarzan, and a moment later the room was flooded with light from a half dozen electric bulbs.

It was several minutes before the tutor was discovered, so completely had the door covered him; but finally he was dragged forth, his gag and bonds cut away, and a liberal application of cold water had hastened returning consciousness.

"Where is Jack?" was John Clayton's first question, and then; "Who did this?" as the memory of Rokoff and the fear of a second abduction seized him.

Slowly Mr. Moore staggered to his feet. His gaze wandered about the room. Gradually he collected his scattered wits. The details of his recent harrowing experience returned to him.

"I tender my resignation, sir, to take effect at once," were his first words. "You do not need a tutor for your son—what he needs is a wild animal trainer."

"But where is he?" cried Lady Greystoke.

"He has gone to see Ajax."

It was with difficulty that Tarzan restrained a smile, and after satisfying himself that the tutor was more scared than injured, he

The audience was delighted.

ordered his closed car around and departed in the direction of a certain well-known music hall.

CHAPTER 3

As THE TRAINER, with raised lash, hesitated an instant at the entrance to the box where the boy and the ape confronted him, a tall broad-shouldered man pushed past him and entered. As his eyes fell upon the newcomer a slight flush mounted the boy's cheeks.

"Father!" he exclaimed.

The ape gave one look at the English lord, and then leaped toward him, calling out in excited jabbering. The man, his eyes going wide in astonishment, stopped as though turned to stone.

"Akut!" he cried.

The boy looked, bewildered, from the ape to his father, and from his father to the ape. The trainer's jaw dropped as he listened to what followed, for from the lips of the Englishman flowed the gutturals of an ape that were answered in kind by the huge anthropoid that now clung to him.

And from the wings a hideously bent and disfigured old man watched the tableau in the box, his pock-marked features working spasmodically in varying expressions that might have marked every sensation in the gamut from pleasure to terror.

"Long have I looked for you, Tarzan," said Akut. "Now that I have found you I shall come to your jungle and live there always."

The man stroked the beast's head. Through his mind there was running rapidly a train of recollection that carried him far into the depths of the primeval African forest where this huge, man-like beast had fought shoulder to shoulder with him years before. He saw the black Mugambi wielding his deadly knob-stick, and beside them, with bared fangs and bristling whiskers, Sheeta the terrible; and pressing close behind savage and the savage panther, the hideous apes of Akut. The man sighed. Strong within him surged the jungle lust that he had thought dead. Ah! if he could go back even for a brief month of it, to feel again the brush of leafy branches against his naked hide; to smell the musty rot of dead vegetation—frankincense and myrrh to the jungle born; to sense the noiseless coming of the great carnivora upon his trail; to hunt and to be hunted; to kill! The picture was alluring. And then came another picture—a sweet-faced woman, still young and beautiful; friends; a home; a son. He shrugged his giant shoulders.

"It cannot be, Akut," he said; "but if you would return, I shall see that it is done. You could not be happy here—I may not be happy there."

The trainer stepped forward. The ape bared his fangs, growling.

"Go with him, Akut," said Tarzan of the Apes. "I will come and see you tomorrow."

The beast moved sullenly to the trainer's side. The latter, at John Clayton's request, told where they might be found. Tarzan turned toward his son.

"Come!" he said, and the two left the theater. Neither spoke for several minutes after they had entered the limousine. It was the boy who broke the silence.

"The ape knew you," he said, "and you spoke together in the ape's tongue. How did the ape know you, and how did you learn his language?"

And then, briefly and for the first time, Tarzan of the Apes told his son of his early life—of his birth in the jungle, of the death of his parents, and of how Kala, the great she ape had suckled and raised him from infancy almost to manhood. He told him, too, of the dangers and the horrors of the jungle; of the great beasts that stalked one by day and by night; of the periods of drought, and of the cataclysmic rains; of hunger; of cold; of intense heat; of nakedness and fear and suffering. He told him of all those things that seem most horrible to the creature of civilization in the hope that the knowledge of them might expunge from the lad's mind any inherent desire for the jungle. Yet they were the very things that made the memory of the jungle what it was to Tarzan—that made up the composite jungle life he loved. And in the telling he forgot one thing—the principal thing—that the boy at his side, listening with eager ears, was the son of Tarzan of the Apes.

After the boy had been tucked away in bed—and without the threatened punishment—John Clayton told his wife of the events of the evening, and that he had at last acquainted the boy with the facts of his jungle life. The mother, who had long foreseen that her son must some time know of those frightful years during which his father had roamed the jungle, a naked, savage beast of prey, only shook her head, hoping against hope that the lure she knew was still strong in the father's breast had not been transmitted to his son.

Tarzan visited Akut the following day, but though Jack begged to be allowed to accompany him he was refused. This time Tarzan saw the pock-marked old owner of the ape, whom he did not recognize as the wily Paulvitch of former days. Tarzan, influenced by Akut's pleadings, broached the question of the ape's purchase; but Paulvitch would not name any price, saying that he would consider the matter.

When Tarzan returned home Jack was all excitement to hear the details of his visit, and finally suggested that his father buy the ape and bring it home. Lady Greystoke was horrified at the suggestion. The boy was insistent. Tarzan explained that he had wished to purchase Akut and return him to his jungle home, and to this the mother assented. Jack asked to be allowed to visit the ape, but again he was met with flat refusal. He had the address, however, which the trainer had given his father, and two days later he found the opportunity to elude his new tutor—who had replaced the terrified Mr. Moore—and after a considerable search through a section of London which he had never before visited he found the smelly little quarters of the pock-marked old man. The old fellow himself replied to his knocking, and when he stated that he had come to see Ajax opened the door and admitted him to the little room which he and the great ape occupied. In former years Paulvitch had been a fastidious scoundrel; but ten years of hideous life among the cannibals of Africa had eradicated the last vestige of niceness from his habits. His apparel was wrinkled and soiled. His hands were unwashed, his few straggling locks uncombed. His room was a jumble of filthy disorder. As the boy entered he saw the great ape squatting upon the bed, the coverlets of which were a tangled wad of filthy blankets and ill-smelling quilts. At sight of the youth the ape leaped to the floor and shuffled forward. The man, not recognizing his visitor and fearing that the ape meant mischief, stepped between them, ordering the ape back to the bed.

"He will not hurt me," cried the boy. "We are friends, and before, he was my father's friend. They knew one another in the jungle. My father is Lord Greystoke. He does not know that I have come here. My mother forbid my coming; but I wished to see Ajax, and I will pay you if you will let me come here often and see him."

At the mention of the boy's identity Paulvitch's eyes narrowed. Since he had first seen Tarzan again from the wings of the theater there had been forming in his deadened brain the beginnings of a desire for revenge. It is a characteristic of the weak and criminal to attribute to others the misfortunes that are the result of their own wickedness, and so now it was that Alexis Paulvitch was slowly recalling the events of his past life and as he did so laying at the door of the man whom he and Rokoff had so assiduously attempted to ruin and murder all the misfortunes that had befallen him in the failure of their various schemes against their intended victim.

He saw at first no way in which he could, with safety to himself, wreak vengeance upon Tarzan through the medium of Tarzan's son; but that great possibilities for revenge lay in the boy was apparent to him, and so he determined to cultivate the lad in the hope that fate would play into his hands in some way in the future. He told the boy all that he knew of his father's past life in the jungle and when he found that the boy had been kept in ignorance of all these things for so many years, and that he had been forbidden visiting the zoological gardens; that he had had to bind and gag his tutor to find an opportunity to come to the music hall and see Ajax, he guessed immediately the nature of the great fear that lay in the hearts of the boy's parents—that he might crave the jungle as his father had craved it.

And so Paulvitch encouraged the boy to come and see him often, and always he played upon the lad's craving for tales of the savage world with which Paulvitch was all too familiar. He left him alone with Akut much, and it was not long until he was surprised to learn that the boy could make the great beast understand him—that he had actually learned many of the words of the primitive language of the anthropoids.

During this period Tarzan came several times to visit Paulvitch. He seemed anxious to purchase Ajax, and at last he told the man frankly that he was prompted not only by a desire upon his part to return the beast to the liberty of his native jungle; but also because his wife feared that in some way her son might learn the whereabouts of the ape and through his attachment for the beast become imbued with the roving instinct which, as Tarzan explained to Paulvitch, had so influenced his own life.

The Russian could scarce repress a smile as he listened to Lord Greystoke's words, since scarce a half hour had passed since the future Lord Greystoke had been sitting upon the disordered bed jabbering away to Ajax with all the fluency of a born ape.

It was during this interview that a plan occurred to Paulvitch, and as a result of it he agreed to accept a certain fabulous sum for the ape, and upon receipt of the money to deliver the beast to a vessel that was sailing south from Dover for Africa two days later. He had a double purpose in accepting Clayton's offer. Primarily, the money consideration influenced him strongly, as the ape was no longer a source of revenue to him, having consistently refused to perform upon the stage after having discovered Tarzan. It was as though the beast had suffered himself to be brought from his jungle home and exhibited before thousands of curious spectators for the sole purpose of searching out his long lost friend and master, and, having found him, considered further mingling with the common herd of humans unnecessary. However that may be, the fact remained that no amount of persuasion could influence him even to show himself upon the music hall stage, and upon the single occasion that the trainer attempted force the results were such that the unfortunate man considered himself lucky to have escaped with his life. All that saved him was the accidental presence of Jack Clayton, who had been permitted to visit the animal in the dressing room reserved for him at the music hall, and had immediately interfered when he saw that the savage beast meant serious mischief.

And after the money consideration, strong in the heart of the Russian was the desire for revenge, which had been growing with constant brooding over the failures and miseries of his life, which he attributed to Tarzan; the latest, and by no means the least, of which was Ajax's refusal to longer earn money for him. The ape's refusal he traced directly to Tarzan, finally convincing himself that the ape man had instructed the great anthropoid to refuse to go upon the stage.

Paulvitch's naturally malign disposition was aggravated by the weakening and warping of his mental and physical faculties through torture and privation. From cold, calculating, highly intelligent perversity it had deteriorated into the indiscriminating, dangerous menace of the mentally defective. His plan, however, was sufficiently cunning to at least cast a doubt upon the assertion that his mentality was waning. It assured him first of the competence which Lord Greystoke had promised to pay him for the deportation of the ape, and then of revenge upon his benefactor through the son he idolized. That part of his scheme was crude and brutal—it lacked the refinement of torture that had marked the master strokes of the Paulvitch of old, when he had worked with that virtuoso of villainy, Nickolas Rokoff—but it at least assured Paulvitch of immunity from responsibility, placing that upon the ape, who would thus also be punished for his refusal longer to support the Russian.

Everything played with fiendish unanimity into Paulvitch's hands. As chance would have it, Tarzan's son overheard his father relating to the boy's mother the steps he was taking to return Akut safely to his jungle home, and having overheard he begged them to bring the ape home that he might have him for a play-fellow. Tarzan would not have been averse to this plan; but Lady Greystoke was horrified at the very thought of it. Jack pleaded with his mother; but all unavailingly. She was obdurate, and at last the lad appeared to acquiesce in his mother's decision that the ape must be returned to Africa and the boy to school, from which he had been absent on vacation.

He did not attempt to visit Paulvitch's room again that day, but instead busied himself in other ways. He had always been well supplied with money, so that when necessity demanded he had no difficulty in collecting several hundred pounds. Some of this money he invested in various strange purchases which he managed to smuggle into the house, undetected, when he returned late in the afternoon.

The next morning, after giving his father time to precede him and conclude his business with Paulvitch, the lad hastened to the Russian's room. Knowing nothing of the man's true character the boy dared not take him fully into his confidence for fear that the old fellow would not only refuse him aid, but would report the whole affair to his father. Instead, he simply asked permission to take Ajax to Dover. He explained that it would relieve the old man of a tiresome journey, as well as placing a number of pounds in his pocket, for the lad purposed paying the Russian well.

"You see," he went on, "there will be no danger of detection since I am supposed to be leaving on an afternoon train for school. Instead I will come here after they have left me on board the train. Then I can take Ajax to Dover, you see, and arrive at school only a day late. No one will be the wiser, no harm will be done, and I shall have had an extra day with Ajax before I lose him forever."

The plan fitted perfectly with that which Paulvitch had in mind. Had he known what further the boy contemplated he would doubtless have entirely abandoned his own scheme of revenge and aided the boy whole heartedly in the consummation of the lad's, which would have been better for Paulvitch, could he have but read the future but a few short hours ahead.

That afternoon Lord and Lady Greystoke bid their son good-bye and saw him safely settled in a first-class compartment of the railway carriage that would set him down at school in a few hours. No sooner had they left him, however, than he gathered his bags together, descended from the compartment and sought a cab stand outside the station. Here he engaged a cabby to take him to the Russian's address. It was dusk when he arrived. He found Paulvitch awaiting him. The man was pacing the floor nervously. The ape was tied with a stout cord to the bed. It was the first time that Jack had ever seen Ajax thus secured. He looked questioningly at Paulvitch. The man, mumblingly, explained that he believed the animal had guessed that he was to be sent away and that he feared he would attempt to escape.

Paulvitch carried another piece of cord in his hand. There was a noose in one end of it which he was continually playing with. He walked back and forth, up and down the room. His pock-marked features were working horribly as he talked silently to himself. The boy had never seen him thus—it made him uneasy. At last Paulvitch stopped on the opposite side of the room, far from the ape.

"Come here," he said to the lad. "I will show you how to secure the ape should he show signs of rebellion during the trip."

The lad laughed. "It will not be necessary," he replied. "Ajax will do whatever I tell him to do."

The old man stamped his foot angrily. "Come here, as I tell you," he repeated. "If you do not do as I say you shall not accompany the ape to Dover—I will take no chances upon his escaping."

Still smiling, the lad crossed the room and stood before the Russ.

"Turn around, with your back toward me," directed the latter, "that I may show you how to bind him quickly."

The boy did as he was bid, placing his hands behind him when

Paulvitch told him to do so. Instantly the old man slipped the running noose over one of the lad's wrists, took a couple of half hitches about his other wrist, and knotted the cord.

The moment that the boy was secured the attitude of the man changed. With an angry oath he wheeled his prisoner about, tripped him and hurled him violently to the floor, leaping upon his breast as he fell. From the bed the ape growled and struggled with his bonds. The boy did not cry out—a trait inherited from his savage sire whom long years in the jungle following the death of his foster mother, Kala the great ape, had taught that there was none to come to the succor of the fallen.

Paulvitch's fingers sought the lad's throat. He grinned down horribly into the face of his victim.

"Your father ruined me," he mumbled. "This will pay him. He will think that the ape did it. I will tell him that the ape did it. That I left him alone for a few minutes, and that you sneaked in and the ape killed you. I will throw your body upon the bed after I have choked the life from you, and when I bring your father he will see the ape squatting over it," and the twisted fiend cackled in gloating laughter. His fingers closed upon the boy's throat.

Behind them the growling of the maddened beast reverberated against the walls of the little room. The boy paled, but no other sign of fear or panic showed upon his countenance. He was the son of Tarzan. The fingers tightened their grip upon his throat. It was with difficulty that he breathed, gaspingly. The ape lunged against the stout cord that held him. Turning, he wrapped the cord about his hands, as a man might have done, and surged heavily backward. The great muscles stood out beneath his shaggy hide. There was a rending as of splintered wood—the cord held, but a portion of the footboard of the bed came away.

At the sound Paulvitch looked up. His hideous face went white in terror—the ape was free.

With a single bound the creature was upon him. The man shrieked. The brute wrenched him from the body of the boy. Great fingers sunk into the man's flesh. Yellow fangs gaped close to his throat—he struggled, futilely—and when they closed, the soul of Alexis Paulvitch passed into the keeping of the demons who had long been awaiting it.

The boy struggled to his feet, assisted by Akut. For two hours under the instructions of the former the ape worked upon the knots that secured his friend's wrists. Finally they gave up their secret, and the boy was free. He cut the cord that still dangled from the ape's body. Then he opened one of his bags and drew forth some garments. His plans had been well made. He did not consult the beast, which did all that he directed. Together they slunk from the house, but no casual observer might have noted that one of them was an ape.

CHAPTER 4

THE KILLING OF the friendless old Russian, Michael Sabrov, by his great trained ape, was a matter for newspaper comment for a few days. Lord Greystoke read of it, and while taking special precautions not to permit his name to become connected with the affair, kept himself well posted as to the police search for the anthropoid.

As was true of the general public, his chief interest in the matter centered about the mysterious disappearance of the slayer. Or at least this was true until he learned, several days subsequent to the tragedy, that his son Jack had not reported at the public school en route for which they had seen him safely ensconced in a railway carriage. Even then the father did not connect the disappearance of his son with the mystery surrounding the whereabouts of the ape. Nor was it until a month later that careful investigation revealed the fact that the boy had left the train before it pulled out of the station at London, and the cab driver had been found who had driven him to the address of the old Russian, that Tarzan of the Apes realized that Akut had in someway been connected with the disappearance of the boy.

Beyond the moment that the cab driver had deposited his fare beside the curb in front of the house in which the Russian had been quartered there was no clue. No one had seen either the boy or the ape from that instant—at least no one who still lived. The proprietor of the house identified the picture of the lad as that of one who had been a frequent visitor in the room of the old man. Aside from this he knew nothing. And there, at the door of a grimy, old building in the slums of London, the searchers came to a blank wall—baffled.

The day following the death of Alexis Paulvitch a youth, accompanying his invalid grandmother, boarded a steamer at Dover. The old lady was heavily veiled, and so weakened by age and sickness that she had to be wheeled aboard the vessel in an invalid chair.

The boy would permit none but himself to wheel her, and with his own hands assisted her from the chair to the interior of their stateroom—and that was the last that was seen of the old lady by the ship's company until the pair disembarked. The boy even insisted upon doing the work of their cabin steward, since, as he explained, his grandmother was suffering from a nervous indisposition that made the presence of strangers extremely distasteful to her.

Outside the cabin—and none there was aboard who knew what he did in the cabin—the lad was just as any other healthy, normal English boy might have been. He mingled with his fellow passengers, became a prime favorite with the officers, and struck up numerous friendships among the common sailors. He was generous and unaffected, yet carried an air of dignity and strength of character that inspired his many new friends with admiration as well as affection for him.

Among the passengers there was an American named Condon, a noted blackleg and crook who was "wanted" in a half dozen of the larger cities of the United States. He had paid little attention to the boy until on one occasion he had seen him accidentally display a roll of bank notes. From then on Condon cultivated the youthful Briton. He learned, easily, that the boy was traveling alone with his invalid grandmother, and that their destination was a small port on the west coast of Africa, a little below the equator; that their name was Billings, and that they had no friends in the little settlement for which they were bound. Upon the point of their purpose in visiting the place Condon found the boy reticent, and so he did not push the matter—he had learned all that he cared to know as it was.

Several times Condon attempted to draw the lad into a card game; but his victim was not interested, and the black looks of several of the other men passengers decided the American to find other means of transferring the boy's bank roll to his own pocket.

At last came the day that the steamer dropped anchor in the lee of a wooded promontory where a score or more of sheet-iron shacks making an unsightly blot upon the fair face of nature proclaimed the fact that civilization had set its heel. Straggling upon the outskirts were the thatched huts of natives, picturesque in their primeval savagery, harmonizing with the background of tropical jungle and accentuating the squalid hideousness of the white man's pioneer architecture.

The boy, leaning over the rail, was looking far beyond the man-made town deep into the God-made jungle. A little shiver of anticipation tingled his spine, and then, quite without volition, he found himself gazing into the loving eyes of his mother and the strong face of the father which mirrored, beneath its masculine strength, a love no less than the mother's eyes proclaimed. He felt himself weakening in his resolve. Nearby one of the ship's officers was shouting orders to a flotilla of native boats that was approaching to lighter the consignment of the steamer's cargo destined for this tiny post.

"When does the next steamer for England touch here?" the boy asked.

"The *Emanuel* ought to be along most any time now," replied the officer. "I figgered we'd find her here," and he went on with his bellowing remarks to the dusky horde drawing close to the steamer's side.

The task of lowering the boy's grandmother over the side to a waiting canoe was rather difficult. The lad insisted on being always at her side, and when at last she was safely ensconced in the bottom of the craft that was to bear them shoreward her grandson dropped catlike after her. So interested was he in seeing her comfortably disposed that he failed to notice the little package that had worked from his pocket as he assisted in lowering the sling that contained the old woman over the steamer's side, nor did he notice it even as it slipped out entirely and dropped into the sea.

Scarcely had the boat containing the boy and the old woman started for the shore than Condon hailed a canoe upon the other side of the ship, and after bargaining with its owner finally lowered his baggage and himself aboard. Once ashore he kept out of sight of the two-story atrocity that bore the legend "Hotel" to lure unsuspecting wayfarers to its multitudinous discomforts. It was quite dark before he ventured to enter and arrange for accommodations.

In a back room upon the second floor the lad was explaining, not without considerable difficulty, to his grandmother that he had decided to return to England upon the next steamer. He was endeavoring to make it plain to the old lady that she might remain in Africa if she wished but that for his part his conscience demanded that he return to his father and mother, who doubtless were even now suffering untold sorrow because of his absence; from which it may be assumed that his parents had not been acquainted with the plans that he and the old lady had made for their adventure into African wilds.

Having come to a decision the lad felt a sense of relief from the worry that had haunted him for many sleepless nights. When he closed his eyes in sleep it was to dream of a happy reunion with those at home. And as he dreamed, Fate, cruel and inexorable, crept stealthily upon him through the dark corridor of the squalid building in which he slept—Fate in the form of the American crook, Condon.

Cautiously the man approached the door of the lad's room. There he crouched listening until assured by the regular breathing of those within that both slept. Quietly he inserted a slim, skeleton key in the lock of the door. With deft fingers, long accustomed to the silent manipulation of the bars and bolts that guarded other men's property, Condon turned the key and the knob simultaneously. Gentle pressure upon the door swung it slowly inward upon its hinges. The man entered the room, closing the door behind him. The moon was temporarily overcast by heavy clouds. The interior of the apartment was shrouded in gloom. Condon groped his way toward the bed. In the far corner of the room something moved—moved with a silent stealthiness which transcended even the trained silence of the burglar. Condon heard nothing. His attention was riveted upon the bed in which he thought to find a young boy and his helpless, invalid grandmother.

The American sought only the bank roll. If he could possess himself of this without detection, well and good; but were he to meet resistance he was prepared for that too. The lad's clothes lay across a chair beside the bed. The American's fingers felt swiftly through them—the pockets contained no roll of crisp, new notes. Doubtless they were beneath the pillows of the bed. He stepped closer toward the sleeper; his hand was already half way beneath the pillow when the thick cloud that had obscured the moon rolled aside and the room was flooded with light. At the same instant the boy opened his eyes and looked straight into those of Condon. The man was suddenly conscious that the boy was alone in the bed. Then he clutched for his victim's throat. As the lad rose to meet him Condon heard a low growl at his back, then he felt his wrists seized by the boy, and realized that beneath those tapering, white fingers played muscles of steel.

He felt other hands at his throat, rough hairy hands that reached over his shoulders from behind. He cast a terrified glance backward, and the hairs of his head stiffened at the sight his eyes revealed, for grasping him from the rear was a huge, man-like ape. The bared fighting fangs of the anthropoid were close to his throat. The lad pinioned his wrists. Neither uttered a sound. Where was the grandmother? Condon's eyes swept the room in a single all-inclusive glance. His eyes bulged in horror at the realization of the truth which that glance revealed. In the power of what creatures of hideous mystery had he placed himself! Frantically he fought to beat off the lad that he might turn upon the fearsome thing at his back. Freeing one hand he struck a savage blow at the lad's face. His act seemed to unlose a thousand devils in the hairy creature clinging to his throat. Condon heard a low and savage snarl. It was the last thing that the American ever heard in his life. Then he was dragged backward upon the floor, a heavy body fell upon him, powerful teeth fastened themselves in his jugular, his head whirled in the sudden blackness which rims eternity—a moment later the ape rose from his prostrate form; but Condon did not know—he was quite dead.

The lad, horrified, sprang from the bed to lean over the body of the man. He knew that Akut had killed in his defense, as he had killed Michael Sabrov; but here, in savage Africa, far from home and friends what would they do to him and his faithful ape? The lad knew that the penalty of murder was death. He even knew that an accomplice might suffer the death penalty with the principal. Who was there here who would plead for them? All would be against them. It was little more than a half-civilized community, and the chances were that they would drag Akut and him forth in the morning and hang them both to the nearest tree—he had read of such things being done in America, and Africa was worse even and wilder than the great West of his mother's native land. Yes, they would both be hanged in the morning!

Was there no escape? He thought in silence for a few moments, and then, with an exclamation of relief, he struck his palms together and turned toward his clothing upon the chair. Money would do anything! Money would save him and Akut! He felt for the bank roll in the pocket in which he had been accustomed to carry it. It was not there! Slowly at first and at last frantically he searched through the remaining pockets of his clothing. Then he dropped upon his hands and knees and examined the floor. Lighting the lamp he moved the bed to one side and, inch by inch, felt over the entire floor. Beside the body of Condon he hesitated, but at last he nerved himself to touch it. Rolling it over he sought beneath it for the money. Nor was it there. He guessed that Condon had entered their room to rob; but he did not believe that the man had had time to possess himself of the money; however, as it was nowhere else, it must be upon the body of the dead man. Jack searched the American's clothes—futilely. Again and again he went over the room, only to return each time to the corpse; but no where could he find the money.

He was half-frantic with despair. What were they to do? In the morning they would be discovered and killed. For all his inherited size and strength he was, after all, only a little boy—a frightened, homesick little boy—reasoning faultily from the meager experience of childhood. He could think of but a single glaring fact—they had killed a fellow man, and they were among savage strangers, thirsting for the blood of the first victim whom fate cast into their clutches. This much he had gleaned from penny-dreadfuls.

And they must have money!

Again he approached the corpse. This time resolutely. The ape squatted in a corner watching his young companion. The youth commenced to remove the American's clothing piece by piece, and, piece by piece, he examined each garment minutely. Even to the shoes he searched with painstaking care, and when the last article had been removed and scrutinized he dropped back upon the bed with dilated eyes that saw nothing in the present—only a grim tableau of the future in which two forms swung silently from the limb of a great tree.

How long he sat thus he did not know; but finally he was aroused by a noise coming from the floor below. Springing quickly to his feet he blew out the lamp, and crossing the floor silently locked the door. Then he turned toward the ape, his mind made up.

Last evening he had been determined to start for home at the first opportunity, to beg the forgiveness of his parents for this mad adventure. Now he knew that he might never return to them. The blood of a fellow man was upon his hands—in his morbid reflections he had long since ceased to attribute the death of Condon to the ape. The hysteria of panic had fastened the guilt upon himself. With money he might have bought justice; but penniless!—ah, what hope could there be for strangers without money here?

But what had become of the money? He tried to recall when last he had seen it. He could not, nor, could he, would he have been able to account for its disappearance, for he had been entirely unconscious of the falling of the little package from his pocket into the sea as he clambered over the ship's side into the waiting canoe that bore him to shore.

Now he turned toward Akut. "Come!" he said, in the language of the great apes. Forgetful of the fact that he wore only a thin pajama suit he led the way to the open window. Thrusting his head out he listened attentively. A single tree grew a few feet from the window. Nimbly the lad sprang to its bole, clinging cat-like for an instant before he clambered quietly to the ground below. Close behind him came the great ape. Two hundred yards away a spur of the jungle ran close to the straggling town. Toward this the lad led the way. None saw them, and a moment later the jungle swallowed them, and John Clayton, future Lord Greystoke passed from the eyes and the knowledge of men.

It was late the following morning that a native house-man knocked upon the door of the room that had been assigned to Mrs. Billings and her grandson. Receiving no response he inserted his pass key in the lock, only to discover that another key was already there, but from the inside. He reported the fact to Herr Skopf, the proprietor, who at once made his way to the second floor where he, too, pounded vigorously upon the door. Receiving no reply he bent to the key hole in an attempt to look through into the room beyond. In so doing, being portly, he lost his balance, which necessitated putting a palm to the floor to maintain his equilibrium. As he did so he felt something soft and thick and wet beneath his fingers. He raised his open palm before his eyes in the dim light of the corridor and peered at it. Then he gave a little shudder, for even in the semi-darkness he saw a dark red stain upon his hand. Leaping to his feet he hurled his shoulder against the door. Herr Skopf is a heavy man—or at least he was then—I have not seen him for several years. The frail door collapsed beneath his weight, and Herr Skopf stumbled precipitately into the room beyond.

Before him lay the greatest mystery of his life. Upon the floor at his feet was the dead body of a strange man. The neck was broken and the jugular severed as by the fangs of a wild beast. The body was entirely naked, the clothing being strewn about the corpse. The old lady and her grandson were gone. The window was open. They must have disappeared through the window for the door had been locked from the inside.

But how could the boy have carried his invalid grandmother from a second story window to the ground? It was preposterous. Again Herr Skopf searched the small room. He noticed that the bed was pulled well away from the wall—why? He looked beneath it again for the third or fourth time. The two were gone, and yet his judgment told him that the old lady could not have gone without porters to carry her down as they had carried her up the previous day.

Further search deepened the mystery. All the clothing of the two was still in the room—if they had gone then they must have gone naked or in their night clothes. Herr Skopf shook his head; then he scratched it. He was baffled. He had never heard of Sherlock Holmes or he would have lost no time in invoking the aid of that celebrated sleuth, for here was a real mystery: An old woman—an invalid who had to be carried from the ship to her room in the hotel—and a handsome lad, her grandson, had entered a room on the second floor of his hostelry the day before. They had had their evening meal served in their room—that was the last that had been seen of them. At nine the following morning the corpse of a strange man had been the sole occupant of that room. No boat had left the harbor in the meantime—there was not a railroad within hundreds of miles—there was no other white settlement that the two could reach under several days of arduous marching accompanied by a well-equipped *safari*. They had simply vanished into thin air, for the native he had sent to inspect the ground beneath the open window had just returned to report that there was no sign of a footstep there, and what sort of creatures were they who could have dropped that distance to the soft turf without leaving spoor? Herr Skopf shuddered. Yes, it was a great mystery—there was something uncanny about the whole thing— he hated to think about it, and he dreaded the coming of night.

It was a great mystery to Herr Skopf—and, doubtless, still is.

CHAPTER 5

CAPTAIN ARMAND JACOT of the Foreign Legion sat upon an outspread saddle blanket at the foot of a stunted palm tree. His broad shoulders and his close-cropped head rested in luxurious ease against the rough bole of the palm. His long legs were stretched straight before him overlapping the meager blanket, his spurs buried in the sandy soil of the little desert oasis. The captain was taking his ease after a long day of weary riding across the shifting sands of the desert.

Lazily he puffed upon his cigarette and watched his orderly who was preparing his evening meal. Captain Armand Jacot was well satisfied with himself and the world. A little to his right rose the noisy activity of his troop of sun-tanned veterans, released for the time from the irksome trammels of discipline, relaxing tired muscles, laughing, joking, and smoking as they, too, prepared to eat after a twelve hour fast. Among them, silent and taciturn, squatted five white-robed Arabs, securely bound and under heavy guard.

It was the sight of these that filled Captain Armand Jacot with the pleasurable satisfaction of a duty well-performed. For a long, hot, gaunt month he and his little troop had scoured the waste places of the desert waste in search of a band of marauders to the sin-stained account of which were charged innumerable thefts of camels, horses, and goats, as well as murders enough to have sent the whole unsavory gang to the guillotine several times over.

A week before he had come upon them. In the ensuing battle he had lost two of his own men, but the punishment inflicted upon the marauders had been severe almost to extinction. A half dozen, perhaps, had escaped; but the balance, with the exception of the five prisoners, had expiated their crimes before the nickel jacketed bullets of the legionaires. And, best of all, the ring leader, Achmet ben Houdin, was among the prisoners.

From the prisoners Captain Jacot permitted his mind to traverse the remaining miles of sand to the little garrison post where, upon the morrow, he should find awaiting him with eager welcome his wife and little daughter. His eyes softened to the memory of them, as they always did. Even now he could see the beauty of the mother reflected in the childish lines of little Jeanne's face, and both those faces would be smiling up into his as he swung from his tired mount late the following afternoon. Already he could feel a soft cheek pressed close to each of his—velvet against leather.

His reverie was broken in upon by the voice of a sentry summoning a non-commissioned officer. Captain Jacot raised his eyes. The sun had not yet set; but the shadows of the few trees huddled about the water hole and of his men and their horses stretched far away into the east across the now golden sand. The sentry was pointing in this direction, and the corporal, through narrowed lids, was searching the distance. Captain Jacot rose to his feet. He was not a man content to see through the eyes of others. He must see for himself. Usually he saw things long before others were aware that there was anything to see—a trait that had won for him the sobriquet of Hawk. Now he saw, just beyond the long shadows, a dozen specks rising and falling among the sands. They disappeared and reappeared, but always they grew larger. Jacot recognized them immediately. They were horsemen—horsemen of the desert. Already a sergeant was running toward him. The entire camp was straining its eyes into the distance. Jacot gave a few terse orders to the sergeant who saluted, turned upon his heel and returned to the men. Here he gathered a dozen who saddled their horses, mounted and rode out to meet the strangers. The remaining men disposed themselves in readiness for instant action. It was not entirely beyond the range of possibilities that the horsemen riding thus swiftly toward the camp might be friends of the prisoners bent upon the release of their kinsmen by a sudden attack. Jacot doubted this, however, since the strangers were evidently making no attempt to conceal their presence. They were galloping rapidly toward the camp in plain view of all. There might be treachery lurking beneath their fair appearance; but none who knew The Hawk would be so gullible as to hope to trap him thus.

The sergeant with his detail met the Arabs two hundred yards from the camp. Jacot could see him in conversation with a tall, white-robed figure—evidently the leader of the band. Presently the sergeant and this Arab rode side by side toward camp. Jacot awaited them. The two reined in and dismounted before him.

"Sheik Amor ben Khatour," announced the sergeant by way of introduction.

Captain Jacot eyed the newcomer. He was acquainted with nearly every principal Arab within a radius of several hundred miles. This man he never had seen. He was a tall, weather beaten, sour looking man of sixty or more. His eyes were narrow and evil. Captain Jacot did not relish his appearance.

"Well?" he asked, tentatively.

The Arab came directly to the point.

"Achmet ben Houdin is my sister's son," he said. "If you will give him into my keeping I will see that he sins no more against the laws of the French."

Jacot shook his head. "That cannot be," he replied. "I must take him back with me. He will be properly and fairly tried by a civil court. If he is innocent he will be released."

"And if he is not innocent?" asked the Arab.

"He is charged with many murders. For any one of these, if he is proved guilty, he will have to die."

The Arab's left hand was hidden beneath his burnous. Now he withdrew it disclosing a large goatskin purse, bulging and heavy with coins. He opened the mouth of the purse and let a handful of the contents trickle into the palm of his right hand—all were pieces of good French gold. From the size of the purse and its bulging proportions Captain Jacot concluded that it must contain a small fortune. Sheik Amor ben Khatour dropped the spilled gold pieces one by one back into the purse. He drew the tie-strings tight. All the time he was silent. Jacot was eyeing him narrowly. They were alone. The sergeant, having introduced the visitor, had withdrawn to some little distance—his back was toward them. Now the sheik, having returned all the gold pieces, held the bulging purse outward upon his open palm toward Captain Jacot.

"Achmet ben Houdin, my sister's son, *might* escape tonight," he said. "Eh?"

Captain Armand Jacot flushed to the roots of his close-cropped hair. Then he went very white and took a half-step toward the Arab. His fists were clenched. Suddenly he thought better of whatever impulse was moving him.

"Sergeant!" he called. The non-commissioned officer hurried toward him, saluting as his heels clicked together before his superior.

"Take this black dog back to his people," he ordered. "See that they leave at once. Shoot the first man who comes within range of camp tonight."

Sheik Amor ben Khatour drew himself up to his full height. His evil eyes narrowed. He raised the bag of gold level with the eyes of the French officer.

"You will pay more than this for the life of Achmet ben Houdin, my sister's son," he said. "And as much again for the name that you have called me, and a hundred fold in sorrow into the bargain."

"Get out of here!" growled Captain Armand Jacot, "before I kick you out."

All of this happened some three years before the opening of this tale. The trial of Achmet ben Houdin and his accomplices is a matter of record—you may verify it if you care to. He met the death he deserved, and he met it with the stoicism of the Arab.

A month later little Jeanne Jacot, the seven year old daughter of Captain Armand Jacot, mysteriously disappeared. Neither the wealth of her father and mother, or all the powerful resources of the great republic were able to wrest the secret of her whereabouts from the inscrutable desert that had swallowed her and her abductor.

A reward of such enormous proportions was offered that many adventurers were attracted to the hunt. This was no case for the modern detective of civilization, yet several of these threw themselves into the search—the bones of some are already bleaching beneath the African sun upon the silent sands of the Sahara.

Two Swedes, Carl Jenssen and Sven Malbihn, after three years of following false leads at last gave up the search far to the south of the Sahara to turn their attention to the more profitable business of ivory poaching. In a great district they were already known for their relentless cruelty and their greed for ivory. The natives feared and hated them. The European governments in whose possessions they worked had long sought them; but, working their way slowly out of the north they had learned many things in the no-man's-land south of the Sahara which gave them immunity from capture through easy avenues of escape that were unknown to those who pursued them. Their raids were sudden and swift. They seized ivory and retreated into the trackless wastes of the north before the guardians of the territory they raped could be made aware of their presence. Relentlessly they slaughtered elephants themselves as well as stealing ivory from the natives. Their following consisted of a hundred or more renegade Arabs and negro slaves—a fierce, relentless band of cut-throats. Remember them—Carl Jenssen and Sven Malbihn, yellow-bearded, Swedish giants—for you will meet them later.

* * *

In the heart of the jungle, hidden away upon the banks of a small unexplored tributary of a large river that empties into the Atlantic not so far from the equator, lay a small, heavily palisaded village. Twenty palm-thatched, beehive huts sheltered its black population, while a half-dozen goat skin tents in the center of the clearing housed the score of Arabs who found shelter here while, by trading and raiding, they collected the cargoes which their ships of the desert bore northward twice each year to the market at Timbuktu.

Playing before one of the Arab tents was a little girl of ten— a black-haired, black-eyed little girl who, with her nut-brown skin and graceful carriage looked every inch a daughter of the desert. Her little fingers were busily engaged in fashioning a skirt of grasses for a much-disheveled doll which a kindly disposed slave had made for her a year or two before. The head of the doll was rudely chipped from ivory, while the body was a rat skin stuffed with grass. The arms and legs were bits of wood, perforated at one end and sewn to the rat skin torso. The doll was quite hideous and altogether disreputable and soiled, but Meriem thought it the most beautiful and adorable thing in the whole world, which is not so strange in view of the fact that it was the only object within that world upon which she might bestow her confidence and her love.

Everyone else with whom Meriem came in contact was, almost without exception, either indifferent to her or cruel. There was, for example, the old black hag who looked after her, Mabunu— toothless, filthy and ill tempered. She lost no opportunity to cuff the little girl, or even inflict minor tortures upon her, such as pinching, or, as she had twice done, searing the tender flesh with hot coals. And there was The Sheik, her father. She feared him more than she did Mabunu. He often scolded her for nothing, quite habitually terminating his tirades by cruelly beating her, until her little body was black and blue.

But when she was alone she was happy, playing with Geeka, or decking her hair with wild flowers, or making ropes of grasses. She was always busy and always singing—when they left her alone. No amount of cruelty appeared sufficient to crush the innate happiness and sweetness from her full little heart. Only when The Sheik was near was she quiet and subdued. Him she feared with a fear that was at times almost hysterical terror. She feared the gloomy jungle too—the cruel jungle that surrounded the little village with chattering monkeys and screaming birds by day and the roaring and coughing and moaning of the carnivora by night. Yes, she feared the jungle; but so much more did she fear The Sheik that many times it was in her childish head to run away, out into the terrible jungle forever rather than longer to face the ever present terror of her father.

As she sat there this day before The Sheik's goatskin tent, fashioning a skirt of grasses for Geeka, The Sheik appeared suddenly approaching. Instantly the look of happiness faded from the child's face. She shrunk aside in an attempt to scramble from the path of the leathern-faced old Arab; but she was not quick enough. With a brutal kick the man sent her sprawling upon her face, where she lay quite still, tearless but trembling. Then, with an oath at her, the man passed into the tent. The old, black hag shook with appreciative laughter, disclosing an occasional and lonesome yellow fang.

When she was sure The Sheik had gone, the little girl crawled to the shady side of the tent, where she lay quite still, hugging Geeka close to her breast, her little form racked at long intervals by choking sobs. She dared not cry aloud, since that would have brought The Sheik upon her again. The anguish in her little heart was not alone the anguish of physical pain; but that infinitely more pathetic anguish—of love denied a childish heart that yearns for love.

Little Meriem could scarce recall any other existence than that of the stern cruelty of The Sheik and Mabunu. Dimly, in the back of her childish memory there lurked a blurred recollection of a gentle mother; but Meriem was not sure but that even this was but a dream picture induced by her own desire for the caresses she never received, but which she lavished upon the much loved Geeka. Never was such a spoiled child as Geeka. Its little mother, far from fashioning her own conduct after the example set her by her father and nurse, went to the extreme of indulgence. Geeka was kissed a thousand times a day. There was play in which Geeka was naughty; but the little mother never punished. Instead, she caressed and fondled; her attitude influenced solely by her own pathetic desire for love.

Now, as she pressed Geeka close to her, her sobs lessened gradually, until she was able to control her voice, and pour out her misery into the ivory ear of her only confidante.

"Geeka loves Meriem," she whispered. "Why does The Sheik,

my father, not love me, too? Am I so naughty? I try to be good; but I never know why he strikes me, so I cannot tell what I have done which displeases him. Just now he kicked me and hurt me so, Geeka; but I was only sitting before the tent making a skirt for you. That must be wicked, or he would not have kicked me for it. But why is it wicked, Geeka? Oh dear! I do not know, I do not know. I wish, Geeka, that I were dead. Yesterday the hunters brought in the body of *el adrea. El adrea* was quite dead. No more will he slink silently upon his unsuspecting prey. No more will his great head and his maned shoulders strike terror to the hearts of the grass eaters at the drinking ford by night. No more will his thundering roar shake the ground. *El adrea* is dead. They beat his body terribly when it was brought into the village; but *el adrea* did not mind. He did not feel the blows, for he was dead. When I am dead, Geeka, neither shall I feel the blows of Mabunu, or the kicks of The Sheik, my father. Then shall I be happy. Oh, Geeka, how I wish that I were dead!"

If Geeka contemplated a remonstrance it was cut short by sounds of altercation beyond the village gates. Meriem listened. With the curiosity of childhood she would have liked to have run down there and learn what it was that caused the men to talk so loudly. Others of the villagers were already trooping in the direction of the noise. But Meriem did not dare. The Sheik would be there, doubtless, and if he saw her it would be but another opportunity to abuse her, so Meriem lay still and listened.

Presently she heard the crowd moving up the street toward The Sheik's tent. Cautiously she stuck her little head around the edge of the tent. She could not resist the temptation, for the sameness of the village life was monotonous, and she craved diversion. What she saw was two strangers—white men. They were alone, but as they approached she learned from the talk of the natives that surrounded them that they possessed a considerable following that was camped outside the village. They were coming to palaver with The Sheik.

The old Arab met them at the entrance to his tent. His eyes narrowed wickedly when they had appraised the newcomers. They stopped before him, exchanging greetings. They had come to trade for ivory they said. The Sheik grunted. He had no ivory. Meriem gasped. She knew that in a near-by hut the great tusks were piled almost to the roof. She poked her little head further forward to get a better view of the strangers. How white their skins! How yellow their great beards!

Suddenly one of them turned his eyes in her direction. She tried to dodge back out of sight, for she feared all men; but he saw her. Meriem noticed the look of almost shocked surprise that crossed his face. The Sheik saw it too, and guessed the cause of it.

"I have no ivory," he repeated. "I do not wish to trade. Go away. Go now."

He stepped from his tent and almost pushed the strangers about in the direction of the gates. They demurred, and then The Sheik threatened. It would have been suicide to have disobeyed, so the two men turned and left the village, making their way immediately to their own camp.

The Sheik returned to his tent; but he did not enter it. Instead he walked to the side where little Meriem lay close to the goat skin wall, very frightened. The Sheik stooped and clutched her by the arm. Viciously he jerked her to her feet, dragged her to the entrance of the tent, and shoved her viciously within. Following her he again seized her, beating her ruthlessly.

"Stay within!" he growled. "Never let the strangers see thy face. Next time you show yourself to strangers I shall kill you!"

With a final vicious cuff he knocked the child into a far corner of the tent, where she lay stifling her moans, while The Sheik paced to and fro muttering to himself. At the entrance sat Mabunu, muttering and chuckling.

In the camp of the strangers one was speaking rapidly to the other.

"There is no doubt of it, Malbihn," he was saying. "Not the slightest; but why the old scoundrel hasn't claimed the reward long since is what puzzles me."

"There are some things dearer to an Arab, Jenssen, than money," returned the first speaker—"revenge is one of them."

"Anyhow it will not harm to try the power of gold," replied Jenssen.

Malbihn shrugged.

"Not on The Sheik," he said. "We might try it on one of his people; but The Sheik will not part with his revenge for gold. To offer it to him would only confirm his suspicions that we must have awakened when we were talking to him before his tent. If we got away with our lives, then, we should be fortunate."

"Well, try bribery, then," assented Jenssen.

But bribery failed—grewsomely. The tool they selected after a stay of several days in their camp outside the village, was a tall, old headman of The Sheik's native contingent. He fell to the lure of the shining metal, for he had lived upon the coast and knew the power of gold. He promised to bring them what they craved, late that night.

Immediately after dark the two white men commenced to make arrangements to break camp. By midnight all was prepared. The porters lay beside their loads, ready to swing them aloft at a moment's notice. The armed *askaris* loitered between the balance of the *safari* and the Arab village, ready to form a rear guard for the retreat that was to begin the moment that the head man brought that which the white masters awaited.

Presently there came the sound of footsteps along the path from the village. Instantly the *askaris* and the whites were on the alert. More than a single man was approaching. Jenssen stepped forward and challenged the newcomers in a low whisper.

"Who comes?" he queried.

"Mbeeda," came the reply.

Mbeeda was the name of the traitorous head man. Jenssen was satisfied, though he wondered why Mbeeda had brought others with him. Presently he understood. The thing they fetched lay upon a litter borne by two men. Jenssen cursed beneath his breath. Could the fool be bringing them a corpse? They had paid for a living prize!

The bearers came to a halt before the white men.

"This has your gold purchased," said one of the two. They sat the litter down, turned and vanished into the darkness toward the village. Malbihn looked at Jenssen, a crooked smile twisting his lips. The thing upon the litter was covered with a piece of cloth.

"Well?" queried the latter. "Raise the covering and see what you have bought. Much money shall we realize on a corpse—especially after the six months beneath the burning sun that will be consumed in carrying it to its destination!"

"The fool should have known that we desired her alive," grumbled Malbihn, grasping a corner of the cloth and jerking the cover from the thing that lay upon the litter.

At sight of what lay beneath both men stepped back—involuntary oaths upon their lips—for there before them lay the dead body of Mbeeda, the faithless head man.

Five minutes later the *safari* of Jenssen and Malbihn was forcing its way rapidly toward the west, nervous *askaris* guarding the rear from the attack they momentarily expected.

CHAPTER 6

HIS FIRST NIGHT in the jungle was one which the son of Tarzan held longest in his memory. No savage carnivora menaced him. There was never a sign of hideous barbarian. Or, if there were, the boy's troubled mind took no cognizance of them. His conscience was harassed by the thought of his mother's suffering. Self-blame plunged him into the depths of misery. The killing of the American caused him little or no remorse. The fellow had earned his fate. Jack's regret on this score was due mainly to the effect which the death of Condon had had upon his own plans. Now he could not return directly to his parents as he had planned. Fear of the primitive, borderland law, of which he had read highly colored, imaginary tales, had thrust him into the jungle a fugitive. He dared not return to the coast at this point—not that he was so greatly influenced through personal fear as from a desire to shield his father and mother from further sorrow and from the shame of having their honored name dragged through the sordid degradation of a murder trial.

With returning day the boy's spirits rose. With the rising sun rose new hope within his breast. He would return to civilization by another way. None would guess that he had been connected with the killing of the stranger in the little out-of-the-way trading post upon a remote shore.

Crouched close to the great ape in the crotch of a tree the boy had shivered through an almost sleepless night. His light pajamas had been but little protection from the chill dampness of the jungle, and only that side of him which was pressed against the warm body of his shaggy companion approximated to comfort. And so he welcomed the rising sun with its promise of warmth as well as light—the blessed sun, dispeller of physical and mental ills.

He shook Akut into wakefulness.

"Come," he said. "I am cold and hungry. We will search for food, out there in the sunlight," and he pointed to an open plain, dotted with stunted trees and strewn with jagged rock.

The boy slid to the ground as he spoke, but the ape first looked carefully about, sniffing the morning air. Then, satisfied that no danger lurked near, he descended slowly to the ground beside the boy.

"Numa, and Sabor his mate, feast upon those who descend first and look afterward, while those who look first and descend afterward live to feast themselves." Thus the old ape imparted to the son of Tarzan the boy's first lesson in jungle lore. Side by side they set off across the rough plain, for the boy wished first to be warm. The ape showed him the best places to dig for rodents and worms; but the lad only gagged at the thought of devouring the repulsive things. Some eggs they found, and these he sucked raw, as also he ate roots and tubers which Akut unearthed. Beyond the plain and across a low bluff they came upon water—brackish, ill-smelling stuff in a shallow water hole, the sides and bottom of which were trampled by the feet of many beasts. A herd of zebra galloped away as they approached.

The lad was too thirsty by now to cavil at anything even remotely resembling water, so he drank his fill while Akut stood with raised head, alert for any danger. Before the ape drank he cautioned the boy to be watchful; but as he drank he raised his head from time to time to cast a quick glance toward a clump of bushes a hundred yards away upon the opposite side of the water hole. When he had done he rose and spoke to the boy, in the language that was their common heritage—the tongue of the great apes.

"There is no danger near?" he asked.

"None," replied the boy. "I saw nothing move while you drank."

"Your eyes will help you but little in the jungle," said the ape.

"Here, if you would live, you must depend upon your ears and your nose but most upon your nose. When we came down to drink and I saw the zebras as they caught our scent I knew that no danger lurked near upon this side of the water hole, for else the zebras would have discovered it and fled before we came; but upon the other side toward which the wind blows danger might lie concealed. We could not smell it for its scent is being blown in the other direction, and so I bent my ears and eyes down wind where my nose cannot travel."

"And you found—nothing?" asked the lad, with a laugh.

"I found Numa crouching in that clump of bushes where the tall grasses grow," and Akut pointed.

"A lion?" exclaimed the boy. "How do you know? I can see nothing."

"Numa is there, though," replied the great ape. "First I heard him sigh. To you the sigh of Numa may sound no different from the other noises which the wind makes among the grasses and the trees; but later you must learn to know the sigh of Numa. Then I watched and at last I saw the tall grasses moving at one point to a force other than the force of the wind. See, they are spread there upon either side of Numa's great body, and as he breathes—you see? You see the little motion at either side that is not caused by the wind—the motion that none of the other grasses have?"

The boy strained his eyes—better eyes than the ordinary boy inherits—and at last he gave a little exclamation of discovery.

"Yes," he said, "I see. He lies there," and he pointed. "His head is toward us. Is he watching us?"

"Numa is watching us," replied Akut, "but we are in little danger, unless we approach too close, for he is lying upon his kill. His belly is almost full, or we should hear him crunching the bones. He is watching us in silence merely from curiosity. Presently he will resume his feeding or he will rise and come down to the water hole for a drink. As he neither fears or desires us he will not try to hide his presence from us; but now is an excellent time to learn to know Numa, for you must learn to know him well if you would live long in the jungle. Where the great apes are many Numa leaves us alone. Our fangs are long and strong, and we can fight; but when we are alone and he is hungry we are no match for him. Come, we will circle him and catch his scent. The sooner you learn to know it the better; but keep close to the trees as we go around him, for Numa often does that which he is least expected to do. And keep your ears and your eyes and your nose open. Remember always that there may be an enemy behind every bush, in every tree and amongst every clump of jungle grass. While you are avoiding Numa do not run into the jaws of Sabor, his mate. Follow me," and Akut set off in a wide circle about the water hole and the crouching lion.

The boy followed close upon his heels, his every sense upon the alert, his nerves keyed to the highest pitch of excitement. This was life! For the instant he forgot his resolutions of a few minutes past to hasten to the coast at some other point than that at which he had landed and make his way immediately back to London. He thought now only of the savage joy of living, and of pitting one's wits and prowess against the wiles and might of the savage jungle brood which haunted the broad plains and the gloomy forest aisles of the great, untamed continent. He knew no fear. His father had had none to transmit to him; but honor and conscience he did have and these were to trouble him many times as they battled with his inherent love of freedom for possession of his soul.

They had passed but a short distance to the rear of Numa when the boy caught the unpleasant odor of the carnivore. His face lighted with a smile. Something told him that he would have known that scent among a myriad of others even if Akut had not told him that a lion lay near. There was a strange familiarity—a weird familiarity in it that made the short hairs rise at the nape of his neck, and brought his upper lip into an involuntary snarl that bared his fighting fangs. There was a sense of stretching of the skin about his ears, for all the world as though those members were flattening back against his skull in preparation for deadly combat. His skin tingled. He was aglow with a pleasurable sensation that he never before had known. He was, upon the instant, another creature—wary, alert, ready. Thus did the scent of Numa, the lion, transform the boy into a beast.

He had never seen a lion—his mother had gone to too great pains to prevent it. But he had devoured countless pictures of them, and now he was ravenous to feast his eyes upon the king of beasts in the flesh. As he trailed Akut he kept an eye cocked over one shoulder, rearward, in the hope that Numa might rise from his kill and reveal himself. Thus it happened that he dropped some little way behind Akut, and the next he knew he was recalled suddenly to the contemplation of other matters than the hidden Numa by a shrill scream of warning from the Ape. Turning his eyes quickly in the direction of his companion, the boy saw that standing in the path directly before him which sent tremors of excitement racing along every nerve of his body. With body half-merging from a clump of bushes in which she must have lain hidden stood a sleek and beautiful lioness. Her yellow-green eyes were round and staring, boring straight into the eyes of the boy. Not ten paces separated them. Twenty paces behind the lioness stood the great ape, bellowing instructions to the boy and hurling taunts at the lioness in an evident effort to attract her attention from the lad while he gained the shelter of a near-by tree.

But Sabor was not to be diverted. She had her eyes upon the lad. He stood between her and her mate, between her and the kill. It was suspicious. Probably he had ulterior designs upon her lord and master or upon the fruits of their hunting. A lioness is short tempered. Akut's bellowing annoyed her. She uttered a little rumbling growl, taking a step toward the boy.

"The tree!" screamed Akut.

The boy turned and fled, and at the same instant the lioness charged. The tree was but a few paces away. A limb hung ten feet from the ground, and as the boy leaped for it the lioness leaped for him. Like a monkey he pulled himself up and to one side. A great forepaw caught him a glancing blow at the hips— just grazing him. One curved talon hooked itself into the waist band of his pajama trousers, ripping them from him as the lioness sped by. Half-naked the lad drew himself to safety as the beast turned and leaped for him once more.

Akut, from a near-by tree, jabbered and scolded, calling the lioness all manner of foul names. The boy, patterning his conduct after that of his preceptor, unstoppered the vials of his invective upon the head of the enemy, until in realization of the futility of words as weapons he bethought himself of something heavier to hurl. There was nothing but dead twigs and branches at hand, but these he flung at the upturned, snarling face of Sabor just as his father had before him twenty years ago, when as a boy he too had taunted and tantalized the great cats of the jungle.

The lioness fretted about the bole of the tree for a short time; but finally, either realizing the uselessness of her vigil, or prompted by the pangs of hunger, she stalked majestically away and disappeared in the brush that hid her lord, who had not once shown himself during the altercation.

Freed from their retreats Akut and the boy came to the ground, to take up their interrupted journey once more. The old ape scolded the lad for his carelessness.

"Had you not been so intent upon the lion behind you you might have discovered the lioness much sooner than you did," he said.

"But you passed right by her without seeing her," retorted the boy.

Akut was chagrined.

"It is thus," he said, "that jungle folk die. We go cautiously for a lifetime, and then, just for an instant, we forget, and—" he ground his teeth in mimicry of the crunching of great jaws in flesh. "It is a lesson," he resumed. "You have learned that you may not for too long keep your eyes and your ears and your nose all bent in the same direction."

That night the son of Tarzan was colder than he ever had been in all his life. The pajama trousers had not been heavy; but they had been much heavier than nothing. And the next day he roasted in the hot sun, for again their way led much across wide and treeless plains.

It was still in the boy's mind to travel to the south, and circle back to the coast in search of another outpost of civilization. He had said nothing of this plan to Akut, for he knew that the old ape would look with displeasure upon any suggestion that savored of separation.

For a month the two wandered on, the boy learning rapidly the laws of the jungle; his muscles adapting themselves to the new mode of life that had been thrust upon them. The thews of the sire had been transmitted to the son—it needed only the hardening of use to develop them. The lad found that it came quite naturally to him to swing through the trees. Even at great heights he never felt the slightest dizziness, and when he had caught the knack of the swing and the release he could hurl himself through space from branch to branch with even greater agility than the heavier Akut.

And with exposure came a toughening and hardening of his smooth, white skin, browning now beneath the sun and wind. He had removed his pajama jacket one day to bathe in a little stream that was too small to harbor crocodiles, and while he and Akut had been disporting themselves in the cool waters a monkey had dropped down from the over hanging trees, snatched up the boy's single remaining article of civilized garmenture, and scampered away with it.

For a time Jack was angry; but when he had been without the jacket for a short while he began to realize that being half-clothed is infinitely more uncomfortable than being entirely naked. Soon he did not miss his clothing in the least, and from that he came to revel in the freedom of his unhampered state. Occasionally a smile would cross his face as he tried to imagine the surprise of his schoolmates could they but see him now. They would envy him. Yes, how they would envy him. He felt sorry for them at such times, and again as he thought of them amid the luxuries and comforts of their English homes, happy with their fathers and mothers, a most uncomfortable lump would arise into the boy's throat, and he would see a vision of his mother's face through a blur of mist that came unbidden to his eyes. Then it was that he urged Akut onward, for now they were headed westward toward the coast. The old ape thought that they were searching for a tribe of his own kind, nor did the boy disabuse his mind of this belief. It would do to tell Akut of his real plans when they had come within sight of civilization.

One day as they were moving slowly along beside a river they came unexpectedly upon a native village. Some children were playing beside the water. The boy's heart leaped within his breast at sight of them—for over a month he had seen no human being. What if these were naked savages? What if their skins were black? Were they not creatures fashioned in the mold of their Maker, as was he? They were his brothers and sisters! He started toward them. With a low warning Akut laid a hand upon his arm to hold him back. The boy shook himself free, and with a shout of greeting ran forward toward the ebon players.

The sound of his voice brought every head erect. Wide eyes viewed him for an instant, and then, with screams of terror, the children turned and fled toward the village. At their heels ran their mothers, and from the village gate, in response to the alarm, came a score of warriors, hastily snatched spears and shields ready in their hands.

At sight of the consternation he had wrought the boy halted. The glad smile faded from his face as with wild shouts and menacing gestures the warriors ran toward him. Akut was calling to him from behind to turn and flee, telling him that the blacks would kill him. For a moment he stood watching them coming, then he raised his hand with the palm toward them in signal for them to halt, calling out at the same time that he came as a friend—that he had only wanted to play with their children. Of course they did not understand a word that he addressed to them, and their answer was what any naked creature who had run suddenly out of the jungle upon their women and children might have expected—a shower of spears. The missiles struck all about the boy, but none touched him. Again his spine tingled and the short hairs lifted at the nape of his neck and along the top of his scalp. His eyes narrowed. Sudden hatred flared in them to wither the expression of glad friendliness that had lighted them but an instant before. With a low snarl, quite similar to that of a baffled beast, he turned and ran into the jungle. There was Akut awaiting him in a tree. The ape urged him to hasten in flight, for the wise old anthropoid knew that they two, naked and unarmed, were no match for the sinewy black warriors who would doubtless make some sort of search for them through the jungle.

But a new power moved the son of Tarzan. He had come with a boy's glad and open heart to offer his friendship to these people who were human beings like himself. He had been met with suspicion and spears. They had not even listened to him. Rage and hatred consumed him. When Akut urged speed he held back. He wanted to fight, yet his reason made it all too plain that it would be but a foolish sacrifice of his life to meet these armed men with his naked hands and his teeth—already the boy thought of his teeth, of his fighting fangs, when possibility of combat loomed close.

Moving slowly through the trees he kept his eyes over his shoulder, though he no longer neglected the possibilities of other dangers which might lurk on either hand or ahead—his experience with the lioness did not need a repetition to insure the permanency of the lesson it had taught. Behind he could hear the savages advancing with shouts and cries. He lagged further behind until the pursuers were in sight. They did not see him, for they were not looking among the branches of the trees for human quarry. The lad kept just ahead of them. For a mile perhaps they continued the search, and then they turned back toward the village. Here was the boy's opportunity, that for which he had been waiting, while the hot blood of revenge coursed through his veins until he saw his pursuers through a scarlet haze.

When they turned back he turned and followed them. Akut was no longer in sight. Thinking that the boy followed he had gone on further ahead. He had no wish to tempt fate within range of those deadly spears. Slinking silently from tree to tree the boy dogged the footsteps of the returning warriors. At last one dropped behind his fellows as they followed a narrow path toward the village. A grim smile lit the lad's face. Swiftly he hurried forward until he moved almost above the unconscious black—stalking him as Sheeta, the panther, stalked his prey, as the boy had seen Sheeta do on many occasions.

Suddenly and silently he leaped forward and downward upon

the broad shoulders of his prey. In the instant of contact his fingers sought and found the man's throat. The weight of the boy's body hurled the black heavily to the ground, the knees in his back knocking the breath from him as he struck. Then a set of strong, white teeth fastened themselves in his neck, and muscular fingers closed tighter upon his wind-pipe. For a time the warrior struggled frantically, throwing himself about in an effort to dislodge his antagonist; but all the while he was weakening and all the while the grim and silent thing he could not see clung tenaciously to him, and dragged him slowly into the bush to one side of the trail.

Hidden there at last, safe from the prying eyes of searchers, should they miss their fellow and return for him, the lad choked the life from the body of his victim. At last he knew by the sudden struggle, followed by limp relaxation that the warrior was dead. Then a strange desire seized him. His whole being quivered and thrilled. Involuntarily he leaped to his feet and placed one foot upon the body of his kill. His chest expanded. He raised his face toward the heavens and opened his mouth to voice a strange, weird cry that seemed screaming within him for outward expression, but no sound passed his lips—he just stood there for a full minute, his face turned toward the sky, his breast heaving to the pent emotion, like an animate statue of vengeance.

The silence which marked the first great kill of the son of Tarzan was to typify all his future kills, just as the hideous victory cry of the bull ape had marked the kills of his mighty sire.

CHAPTER 7

AKUT, DISCOVERING THAT the boy was not close behind him, turned back to search for him. He had gone but a short distance in return when he was brought to a sudden and startled halt by sight of a strange figure moving through the trees toward him. It was the boy, yet could it be? In his hand was a long spear, down his back hung an oblong shield such as the black warriors who had attacked them had worn, and upon ankle and arm were bands of iron and brass, while a loin cloth was twisted about the youth's middle. A knife was thrust through its folds.

When the boy saw the ape he hastened forward to exhibit his

trophies. Proudly he called attention to each of his newly won possessions. Boastfully he recounted the details of his exploit.

"With my bare hands and my teeth I killed him," he said. "I would have made friends with them but they chose to be my enemies. And now that I have a spear I shall show Numa, too, what it means to have me for a foe. Only the white men and the great apes, Akut, are our friends. Them we shall seek, all others must we avoid or kill. This have I learned of the jungle."

They made a detour about the hostile village, and resumed their journey toward the coast. The boy took much pride in his new weapons and ornaments. He practiced continually with the spear, throwing it at some object ahead hour by hour as they traveled their loitering way, until he gained a proficiency such as only youthful muscles may attain to speedily. All the while his training went on under the guidance of Akut. No longer was there a single jungle spoor but was an open book to the keen eyes of the lad, and those other indefinable spoor that elude the senses of civilized man and are only partially appreciable to his savage cousin came to be familiar friends of the eager boy. He could differentiate the innumerable species of the herbivora by scent, and he could tell, too, whether an animal was approaching or departing merely by the waxing or waning strength of its effluvium. Nor did he need the evidence of his eyes to tell him whether there were two lions or four up wind,—a hundred yards away or half a mile.

Much of this had Akut taught him, but far more was instinctive knowledge—a species of strange intuition inherited from his father. He had come to love the jungle life. The constant battle of wits and senses against the many deadly foes that lurked by day and by night along the pathway of the wary and the unwary appealed to the spirit of adventure which breathes strong in the heart of every red-blooded son of primordial Adam. Yet, though he loved it, he had not let his selfish desires outweigh the sense of duty that had brought him to a realization of the moral wrong which lay beneath the adventurous escapade that had brought him to Africa. His love of father and mother was strong within him, too strong to permit unalloyed happiness which was undoubtedly causing them days of sorrow. And so he held tight to his determination to find a port upon the coast where he might communicate with them and receive funds for his return to London. There he felt sure that he could now persuade his parents to let him spend at least a portion of his time upon those African estates

which from little careless remarks dropped at home he knew his
father possessed. That would be something, better at least than a
lifetime of the cramped and cloying restrictions of civilization.

And so he was rather contented than otherwise as he made his
way in the direction of the coast, for while he enjoyed the liberty
and the savage pleasures of the wild his conscience was at the
same time clear, for he knew that he was doing all that lay in
his power to return to his parents. He rather looked forward, too,
to meeting white men again—creatures of his own kind—for there
had been many occasions upon which he had longed for other
companionship than that of the old ape. The affair with the blacks
still rankled in his heart. He had approached them in such innocent
good fellowship and with such childlike assurance of a hospitable
welcome that the reception which had been accorded him had
proved a shock to his boyish ideals. He no longer looked upon
the black man as his brother; but rather as only another of the
innumerable foes of the bloodthirsty jungle—a beast of prey which
walked upon two feet instead of four.

But if the blacks were his enemies there were those in the world
who were not. There were those who always would welcome him
with open arms; who would accept him as a friend and brother,
and with whom he might find sanctuary from every enemy. Yes,
there were always white men. Somewhere along the coast or even
in the depths of the jungle itself there were white men. To them
he would be a welcome visitor. They would befriend him. And
there were also the great apes—the friends of his father and of
Akut. How glad they would be to receive the son of Tarzan of
the Apes! He hoped that he would come upon them before he
found a trading post upon the coast. He wanted to be able to tell
his father that he had known his old friends of the jungle, that
he had hunted with them, that he had joined with them in their
savage life, and their fierce, primeval ceremonies—the strange
ceremonies of which Akut had tried to tell him. It cheered him
immensely to dwell upon these happy meetings. Often he rehearsed
the long speech which he would make to the apes, in which he
would tell them of the life of their former king since he had left
them.

At other times he would play at meeting with white men. Then
he would enjoy their consternation at sight of a naked white boy
trapped in the war togs of a black warrior and roaming the jungle
with only a great ape as his companion.

And so the days passed, and with the traveling and the hunting and the climbing the boy's muscles developed and his agility increased until even phlegmatic Akut marvelled at the prowess of his pupil. And the boy, realizing his great strength and revelling in it, became careless. He strode through the jungle, his proud head erect, defying danger. Where Akut took to the trees at the first scent of Numa, the lad laughed in the face of the king of beasts and walked boldly past him. Good fortune was with him for a long time. The lions he met were well-fed, perhaps, or the very boldness of the strange creature which invaded their domain so filled them with surprise that thoughts of attack were banished from their minds as they stood, round-eyed, watching his approach and his departure. Whatever the cause, however, the fact remains that on many occasions the boy passed within a few paces of some great lion without arousing more than a warning growl.

But no two lions are necessarily alike in character or temper. They differ as greatly as do individuals of the human family. Because ten lions act similarly under similar conditions one cannot say that the eleventh lion will do likewise—the chances are that he will not. The lion is a creature of high nervous development. He thinks, therefore he reasons. Having a nervous system and brains he is the possessor of temperament, which is affected variously by extraneous causes. One day the boy met the eleventh lion. The former was walking across a small plain upon which grew little clumps of bushes. Akut was a few yards to the left of the lad who was the first to discover the presence of Numa.

"Run, Akut," called the boy, laughing. "Numa lies hid in the bushes to my right. Take to the trees, Akut! I, the son of Tarzan, will protect you," and the boy, laughing, kept straight along his way which led close beside the brush in which Numa lay concealed.

The ape shouted to him to come away, but the lad only flourished his spear and executed an improvised war dance to show his contempt for the king of beasts. Closer and closer to the dread destroyer he came, until, with a sudden, angry growl, the lion rose from his bed not ten paces from the youth. A huge fellow he was, this lord of the jungle and the desert. A shaggy mane clothed his shoulders. Cruel fangs armed his great jaws. His yellow-green eyes blazed with hatred and challenge.

The boy, with his pitifully inadequate spear ready in his hand, realized quickly that this lion was different from the others he had met; but he had gone too far now to retreat. The nearest tree lay several yards to his left—the lion could be upon him before he had covered half the distance, and that the beast intended to charge none could doubt who looked upon him now. Beyond the lion was a thorn tree—only a few feet beyond him. It was the nearest sanctuary but Numa stood between it and his prey.

The feel of the long spear shaft in his hand and the sight of the tree beyond the lion gave the lad an idea—a preposterous idea—a ridiculous, forlorn hope of an idea; but there was no time now to weigh chances—there was but a single chance, and that was the thorn tree. If the lion charged it would be too late—the lad must charge first, and to the astonishment of Akut and none the less of Numa the boy leaped swiftly toward the beast. Just for a second was the lion motionless with surprise and in that second Jack Clayton put to the crucial test an accomplishment which he had practiced at school.

Straight for the savage brute he ran, his spear held butt foremost across his body. Akut shrieked in terror and amazement. The lion stood with wide, round eyes awaiting the attack, ready to rear upon his hind feet and receive this rash creature with blows that could crush the skull of a buffalo.

Just in front of the lion the boy placed the butt of his spear upon the ground, gave a mighty spring, and, before the bewildered beast could guess the trick that had been played upon him, sailed over the lion's head into the rending embrace of the thorn tree—safe but lacerated.

Akut had never before seen a pole-vault. Now he leaped up and down within the safety of his own tree, screaming taunts and boasts at the discomfited Numa, while the boy, torn and bleeding, sought some position in his thorny retreat in which he might find the least agony. He had saved his life; but at considerable cost in suffering. It seemed to him that the lion would never leave, and it was a full hour before the angry brute gave up his vigil and strode majestically away across the plain. When he was at a safe distance the boy extricated himself from the thorn tree; but not without inflicting new wounds upon his already tortured flesh.

It was many days before the outward evidence of the lesson he had learned had left him; while the impression upon his mind was one that was to remain with him for life. Never again did he uselessly tempt fate.

He took long chances often in his after life; but only when the taking of chances might further the attainment of some cherished end—and, always thereafter, he practiced pole-vaulting.

For several days the boy and the ape lay up while the former recovered from the painful wounds inflicted by the sharp thorns. The great anthropoid licked the wounds of his human friend, nor, aside from this, did they receive other treatment, but they soon healed, for healthy flesh quickly replaces itself.

When the lad felt fit again the two continued their journey toward the coast, and once more the boy's mind was filled with pleasurable anticipation.

And at last the much-dreamed of moment came. They were passing through a tangled forest when the boy's sharp eyes discovered from the lower branches through which he was traveling an old but well-marked spoor—a spoor that set his heart to leaping—the spoor of man, of white men, for among the prints of naked feet were the well defined outlines of European made boots. The trail, which marked the passage of a good-sized company, pointed north at right angles to the course the boy and the ape were taking toward the coast.

Doubtless these white men knew the nearest coast settlement. They might even be headed for it now. At any rate it would be worth while overtaking them if even only for the pleasure of meeting again creatures of his own kind. The lad was all excitement; palpitant with eagerness to be off in pursuit. Akut demurred. He wanted nothing of men. To him the lad was a fellow ape, for he was the son of the king of apes. He tried to dissuade the boy, telling him that soon they should come upon a tribe of their own folk where some day when he was older the boy should be king as his father had before him. But Jack was obdurate. He insisted that he wanted to see white men again. He wanted to send a message to his parents. Akut listened and as he listened the intuition of the beast suggested the truth to him—the boy was planning to return to his own kind.

The thought filled the old ape with sorrow. He loved the boy as he had loved the father, with the loyalty and faithfulness of a hound for its master. In his ape brain and his ape heart he had nursed the hope that he and the lad would never be separated. He saw all his fondly cherished plans fading away, and yet he remained loyal to the lad and to his wishes. Though disconsolate he gave in to the boy's determination to pursue the *safari* of the white men, accompanying him upon what he believed would be their last journey together.

The boy sailed over the lion's head.

The spoor was but a couple of days old when the two discovered it, which meant that the slow-moving caravan was but a few hours distant from them whose trained and agile muscles could carry their bodies swiftly through the branches above the tangled undergrowth which had impeded the progress of the laden carriers of the white men.

The boy was in the lead, excitement and anticipation carrying him ahead of his companion to whom the attainment of their goal meant only sorrow. And it was the boy who first saw the rear guard of the caravan and the white men he had been so anxious to overtake.

Stumbling along the tangled trail of those ahead a dozen heavily laden blacks who, from fatigue or sickness, had dropped behind were being prodded by the black soldiers of the rear guard, kicked when they fell, and then roughly jerked to their feet and hustled onward. On either side walked a giant white man, heavy blonde beards almost obliterating their countenances. The boy's lips formed a glad cry of salutation as his eyes first discovered the whites—a cry that was never uttered, for almost immediately he witnessed that which turned his happiness to anger as he saw that both the white men were wielding heavy whips brutally upon the naked backs of the poor devils staggering along beneath loads that would have overtaxed the strength and endurance of strong men at the beginning of a new day.

Every now and then the rear guard and the white men cast apprehensive glances rearward as though momentarily expecting the materialization of some long expected danger from that quarter. The boy had paused after his first sight of the caravan, and now was following slowly in the wake of the sordid, brutal spectacle. Presently Akut came up with him. To the beast there was less of horror in the sight than to the lad, yet even the great ape growled beneath his breath at useless torture being inflicted upon the helpless slaves. He looked at the boy. Now that he had caught up with the creatures of his own kind why was it that he did not rush forward and greet them. He put the question to his companion.

"They are fiends," muttered the boy. "I would not travel with such as they, for if I did I should set upon them and kill them the first time they beat their people as they are beating them now; but," he added, after a moment's thought, "I can ask them the whereabouts of the nearest port, and then, Akut, we can leave them."

The ape made no reply, and the boy swung to the ground and started at a brisk walk toward the *safari*. He was a hundred yards away, perhaps, when one of the whites caught sight of him. The man gave a shout of alarm, instantly levelling his rifle upon the boy and firing. The bullet struck just in front of its mark, scattering turf and fallen leaves against the lad's legs. A second later the other white and the black soldiers of the rear guard were firing hysterically at the boy.

Jack leaped behind a tree, unhit. Days of panic ridden flight through the jungle had filled Carl Jenssen and Sven Malbihn with jangling nerves and their native boys with unreasoning terror. Every new note from behind sounded to their frightened ears the coming of The Sheik and his bloodthirsty entourage. They were in a blue funk, and the sight of the naked white warrior stepping silently out of the jungle through which they had just passed had been sufficient shock to let loose in action all the pent nerve energy of Malbihn, who had been the first to see the strange apparition. And Malbihn's shout and shot had set the others going.

When their nervous energy had spent itself and they came to take stock of what they had been fighting it developed that Malbihn alone had seen anything clearly. Several of the blacks averred that they too had obtained a good view of the creature but their descriptions of it varied so greatly that Jenssen, who had seen nothing himself, was inclined to be a trifle skeptical. One of the blacks insisted that the thing had been eleven feet tall, with a man's body and the head of an elephant. Another had seen *three* immense Arabs with huge, black beards; but when, after conquering their nervousness, the rear guard advanced upon the enemy's position to investigate they found nothing, for Akut and the boy had retreated out of range of the unfriendly guns.

Jack was disheartened and sad. He had not entirely recovered from the depressing effect of the unfriendly reception he had received at the hands of the blacks, and now he had found an even more hostile one accorded him by men of his own color.

"The lesser beasts flee from me in terror," he murmured, half to himself, "the greater beasts are ready to tear me to pieces at sight. Black men would kill me with their spears or arrows. And now white men, men of my own kind, have fired upon me and driven me away. Are all the creatures of the world my enemies?

Has the son of Tarzan no friend other than Akut?"

The old ape drew closer to the boy.

"There are the great apes," he said. "They only will be the friends of Akut's friend. Only the great apes will welcome the son of Tarzan. You have seen that men want nothing of you. Let us go now and continue our search for the great apes—our people."

The language of the great apes is a combination of monosyllabic gutturals, amplified by gestures and signs. It may not be literally translated into human speech; but as near as may be this is what Akut said to the boy.

The two proceeded in silence for some time after Akut had spoken. The boy was immersed in deep thought—bitter thoughts in which hatred and revenge predominated. Finally he spoke: "Very well, Akut," he said, "we will find our friends, the great apes."

The anthropoid was overjoyed; but he gave no outward demonstration of his pleasure. A low grunt was his only response, and a moment later he had limped nimbly upon a small and unwary rodent that had been surprised at a fatal distance from its burrow. Tearing the unhappy creature in two Akut handed the lion's share to the lad.

CHAPTER 8

A YEAR HAD passed since the two Swedes had been driven in terror from the savage country where The Sheik held sway. Little Meriem still played with Geeka, lavishing all her childish love upon the now almost hopeless ruin of what had never, even in its palmiest days, possessed even a slight degree of loveliness. But to Meriem, Geeka was all that was sweet and adorable. She carried to the deaf ears of the battered ivory head all her sorrows all her hopes all her ambitions, for even in the face of hopelessness, in the clutches of the dread authority from which there was no escape, little Meriem yet cherished hopes and ambitions. It is true that her ambitions were rather nebulous in form, consisting chiefly of a desire to escape with Geeka to some remote and unknown spot where there were no Sheiks, no Mabunus—where *el adrea* could find no entrance, and where she might play all day surrounded only by flowers and birds and the harmless little monkeys playing in the tree tops.

The Sheik had been away for a long time, conducting a caravan of ivory, skins, and rubber far into the north. The interim had been one of great peace for Meriem. It is true that Mabunu had still been with her, to pinch or beat her as the mood seized the villianous old hag; but Mabunu was only one. When The Sheik was there also there were two of them, and The Sheik was stronger and more brutal even than Mabunu. Little Meriem often wondered why the grim old man hated her so. It is true that he was cruel and unjust to all with whom he came in contact; but to Meriem he reserved his greatest cruelties, his most studied injustices.

Today Meriem was squatting at the foot of a large tree which grew inside the palisade close to the edge of the village. She was fashioning a tent of leaves for Geeka. Before the tent were some pieces of wood and small leaves and a few stones. These were the household utensils. Geeka was cooking dinner. As the little girl played she prattled continuously to her companion, propped in a sitting position with a couple of twigs. She was totally absorbed in the domestic duties of Geeka—so much so that she did not note the gentle swaying of the branches of the tree above her as they bent to the body of the creature that had entered them stealthily from the jungle.

In happy ignorance the little girl played on, while from above two steady eyes looked down upon her—unblinking, unwavering. There was none other than the little girl in this part of the village, which had been almost deserted since The Sheik had left long months before upon his journey toward the north.

And out in the jungle, an hour's march from the village, The Sheik was leading his returning caravan homeward.

A year had passed since the white men had fired upon the lad and driven him back into the jungle to take up his search for the only remaining creatures to whom he might look for companionship—the great apes. For months the two had wandered eastward, deeper and deeper into the jungle. The year had done much for the boy—turning his already mighty muscles to thews of steel, developing his woodcraft to a point where it verged upon the uncanny, perfecting his arboreal instincts, and training him in the use of both natural and artificial weapons.

He had become at last a creature of marvelous physical powers and mental cunning. He was still but a boy, yet so great was his strength that the powerful anthropoid with which he often engaged in mimic battle was no match for him. Akut had taught him to fight as the bull ape fights, nor ever was there a teacher better fitted to instruct in the savage warfare of primordial man, or a pupil better equipped to profit by the lessons of a master.

As the two searched for a band of the almost extinct species of ape to which Akut belonged they lived upon the best the jungle afforded. Antelope and zebra fell to the boy's spear, or were dragged down by the two powerful beasts of prey who leaped upon them from some overhanging limb or from the ambush of the under-growth beside the trail to the water hole or the ford.

The pelt of a leopard covered the nakedness of the youth; but the wearing of it had not been dictated by any promptings of modesty. With the rifle shots of the white men showering about him he had reverted to the savagery of the beast that is inherent in each of us, but that flamed more strongly in this boy whose father had been raised a beast of prey. He wore his leopard skin at first in response to a desire to parade a trophy of his prowess, for he had slain the leopard with his knife in a hand-to-hand combat. He saw that the skin was beautiful, which appealed to his barbaric sense of ornamentation, and when it stiffened and later commenced to decompose because of his having no knowl-edge of how to cure or tan it it was with sorrow and regret that he discarded it. Later, when he chanced upon a lone, black warrior wearing the counterpart of it, soft and clinging and beautiful from proper curing, it required but an instant to leap from above upon the shoulders of the unsuspecting black, sink a keen blade into his heart and possess the rightly preserved hide.

There were no after-qualms of conscience. In the jungle might is right, nor does it take long to inculcate this axiom in the mind of a jungle dweller, regardless of what his past training may have been. That the black would have killed him had he had the chance the boy knew full well. Neither he nor the black were any more sacred than the lion, or the buffalo, the zebra or the deer, or any other of the countless creatures who roamed, or slunk, or flew, or wriggled through the dark mazes of the forest. Each had but a single life, which was sought by many. The greater number of enemies slain the better chance to prolong that life. So the boy smiled and donned the finery of the vanquished, and went his way with Akut, searching, always searching for the elusive an-thropoids who were to welcome them with open arms. And at last they found them. Deep in the jungle, buried far from sight of man, they came upon such another little natural arena as had witnessed the wild ceremony of the Dum-Dum in which the boy's father had taken part long years before.

First, at a great distance, they heard the beating of the drum of the great apes. They were sleeping in the safety of a huge tree when the booming sound smote upon their ears. Both awoke at once. Akut was the first to interpret the strange cadence.

"The great apes!" he growled. "They dance the Dum-Dum. Come, Korak, son of Tarzan, let us go to our people."

Months before Akut had given the boy a name of his own choosing, since he could not master the man-given name of Jack. Korak is as near as it may be interpreted into human speech. In the language of the apes it means Killer. Now the Killer rose upon the branch of the great tree where he had been sleeping with his back braced against the stem. He stretched his lithe young muscles, the moonlight filtering through the foliage from above dappling his brown skin with little patches of light.

The ape, too, stood up, half squatting after the manner of his kind. Low growls rumbled from the bottom of his deep chest— growls of excited anticipation. The boy growled in harmony with the ape. Then the anthropoid slid softly to the ground. Close by, in the direction of the booming drum, lay a clearing which they must cross. The moon flooded it with silvery light. Half-erect, the great ape shuffled into the full glare of the moon. At his side, swinging gracefully along in marked contrast to the awkwardness of his companion, strode the boy, the dark, shaggy coat of the one brushing against the smooth, clear hide of the other. The lad was humming now, a music hall air that had found its way to the forms of the great English public school that was to see him no more. He was happy and expectant. The moment he had looked forward to for so long was about to be realized. He was coming into his own. He was coming home. As the months had dragged or flown along, retarded or spurred on as privation or adventure predominated, thoughts of his own home, while oft recurring, had become less vivid. The old life had grown to seem more like a dream than a reality, and the balking of his determination to reach the coast and return to London had finally thrown the hope of realization so remotely into the future that it too now seemed little more than a pleasant but hopeless dream.

Now all thoughts of London and civilization were crowded so

far into the background of his brain that they might as well have been non-existent. Except for form and mental development he was as much an ape as the great, fierce creature at his side.

In the exuberance of his joy he slapped his companion roughly on the side of the head. Half in anger, half in play the anthropoid turned upon him, his fangs bared and glistening. Long, hairy arms reached out to seize him, and, as they had done a thousand times before, the two clinched in mimic battle, rolling upon the sward, striking, growling and biting, though never closing their teeth in more than a rough pinch. It was wondrous practice for them both. The boy brought into play wrestling tricks that he had learned at school, and many of these Akut learned to use and to foil. And from the ape the boy learned the methods that had been handed down to Akut from some common ancestor of them both, who had roamed the teeming earth when ferns were trees and crocodiles were birds.

But there was one art the boy possessed which Akut could not master, though he did achieve fair proficiency in it for an ape— boxing. To have his bull-like charges stopped and crumpled with a suddenly planted fist upon the end of his snout, or a painful jolt in the short ribs, always surprised Akut. It angered him too, and at such times his mighty jaws came nearer to closing in the soft flesh of his friend than at any other, for he was still an ape, with an ape's short temper and brutal instincts; but the difficulty was in catching his tormentor while his rage lasted, for when he lost his head and rushed madly into close quarters with the boy he discovered that the stinging hail of blows released upon him always found their mark and effectually stopped him—effectually and painfully. Then he would withdraw growling viciously, backing away with grinning jaws distended, to sulk for an hour or so.

Tonight they did not box. Just for a moment or two they wrestled playfully, until the scent of Sheeta, the panther, brought them to their feet, alert and wary. The great cat was passing through the jungle in front of them. For a moment it paused, listening. The boy and the ape growled menacingly in chorus and the carnivore moved on.

Then the two took up their journey toward the sound of the Dum-Dum. Louder and louder came the beating of the drum. Now, at last, they could hear the growling of the dancing apes, and strong to their nostrils came the scent of their kind. The lad trembled with excitement. The hair down Akut's spine stiffened—

the symptoms of happiness and anger are often similar.

Silently they crept through the jungle as they neared the meeting place of the apes. Now they were in the trees, worming their way forward, alert for sentinels. Presently through a break in the foliage the scene burst upon the eager eyes of the boy. To Akut it was a familiar one; but to Korak it was all new. His nerves tingled at the savage sight. The great bulls were dancing in the moonlight, leaping in an irregular circle about the flat-topped earthen drum about which three old females sat beating its resounding top with sticks worn smooth by long years of use.

Akut, knowing the temper and customs of his kind, was too wise to make their presence known until the frenzy of the dance had passed. After the drum was quiet and the bellies of the tribe well-filled he would hail them. Then would come a parley, after which he and Korak would be accepted into membership by the community. There might be those who would object; but such could be overcome by brute force, of which he and the lad had an ample surplus. For weeks, possibly months, their presence might cause ever decreasing suspicion among others of the tribe; but eventually they would become as born brothers to these strange apes.

He hoped that they had been among those who had known Tarzan, for that would help in the introduction of the lad and in the consummation of Akut's dearest wish, that Korak should become king of the apes. It was with difficulty, however, that Akut kept the boy from rushing into the midst of the dancing anthropoids—an act that would have meant the instant extermination of them both, since the hysterical frenzy into which the great apes work themselves during the performance of their strange rites is of such a nature that even the most ferocious of the carnivora give them a wide berth at such times.

As the moon declined slowly toward the lofty, foliaged horizon of the amphitheater the booming of the drum decreased and lessened were the exertions of the dancers, until, at last, the final note was struck and the huge beasts turned to fall upon the feast they had dragged hither for the orgy.

From what he had seen and heard Akut was able to explain to Korak that the rites proclaimed the choosing of a new king, and he pointed out to the boy the massive figure of the shaggy monarch, come into his kingship, no doubt, as many human rulers have come into theirs—by the murder of his predecessor.

When the apes had filled their bellies and many of them had sought the bases of the trees to curl up in sleep Akut plucked Korak by the arm.

"Come," he whispered. "Come slowly. Follow me. Do as Akut does."

Then he advanced slowly through the trees until he stood upon a bough overhanging one side of the amphitheater. Here he stood in silence for a moment. Then he uttered a low growl. Instantly a score of apes leaped to their feet. Their savage little eyes sped quickly around the periphery of the clearing. The king ape was the first to see the two figures upon the branch. He gave voice to an ominous growl. Then he took a few lumbering steps in the direction of the intruders. His hair was bristling. His legs were stiff, imparting a halting, jerky motion to his gait. Behind him pressed a number of bulls.

He stopped just a little before he came beneath the two—just far enough to be beyond their spring. Wary king! Here he stood rocking himself to and fro upon his short legs, baring his fangs in hideous grinnings, rumbling out an ever increasing volume of growls, which were slowly but steadily increasing to the proportions of roars. Akut knew that he was working himself up to a proper pitch of rage to warrant an attack upon them. The old ape did not wish to fight. He had come with the boy to cast his lot with the tribe.

"I am Akut," he said. "This is Korak. Korak is the son of Tarzan who was king of the apes. I, too, was king of the apes who dwelt in the midst of the great waters. We have come to hunt with you, to fight with you. We are great hunters. We are mighty fighters. Let us come in peace."

The king ceased his rocking. He eyed the pair from beneath his beetling brows. His bloodshot eyes were savage and crafty. His kingship was very new and he was jealous of it. He feared the encroachments of two strange apes. The sleek, brown, hairless body of the lad spelled "man," and man he feared and hated.

"Go away!" he growled. "Go away, or I will kill you."

The eager lad, standing behind the great Akut, had been pulsing with anticipation and happiness. He wanted to leap down among these hairy monsters and show them that he was their friend, that he was one of them. He had expected that they would receive him with open arms, and now the words of the king ape filled him with indignation and sorrow. The blacks had set upon him

and driven him away. Then he had turned to the white men—
to those of his own kind—only to hear the ping of bullets where
he had expected words of cordial welcome. The great apes had
remained his final hope. To them he looked for the companionship
man had denied him. Suddenly rage overwhelmed him.

The king ape was almost directly beneath him. The others were
formed in a half circle several yards behind the king. They were
watching events interestedly. Before Akut could guess his intention,
or prevent, the boy leaped to the ground directly in the path of
the king, who had now succeeded in stimulating himself to a
frenzy of fury.

"I am Korak!" shouted the boy. "I am the Killer. I came to
live among you as a friend. You want to drive me away. Very
well, then, I shall go; but before I go I shall show you that the
son of Tarzan is your master, as his father was before him—that
he is not afraid of your king or you."

For an instant the king ape had stood motionless with surprise.
He had expected no such rash action upon the part of either of
the intruders. Akut was equally surprised. Now he shouted excitedly
for Korak to come back, for he knew that in the sacred arena
the other bulls might be expected to come to the assistance of
their king against an outsider, though there was small likelihood
that the king would need assistance. Once those mighty jaws closed
upon the boy's soft neck the end would come quickly. To leap
to his rescue would mean death for Akut, too; but the brave old
ape never hesitated. Bristling and growling, he dropped to the
sward just as the king ape charged.

The beast's hands clutched for their hold as the animal sprang
upon the lad. The fierce jaws were wide distended to bury the
yellow fangs deeply in the brown hide. Korak, too, leaped forward
to meet the attack; but leaped crouching, beneath the outstretched
arms. At the instant of contact the lad pivoted on one foot, and
with all the weight of his body and the strength of his trained
muscles drove a clenched fist into the bull's stomach. With a
gasping shriek the king ape collapsed, clutching futilely for the
agile, naked creature nimbly sidestepping from his grasp.

Howls of rage and dismay broke from the bull apes behind the
fallen king, as with murder in their savage little hearts they rushed
forward upon Korak and Akut; but the old ape was too wise to
court any such unequal encounter. To have counseled the boy to
retreat now would have been futile, and Akut knew it. To delay

even a second in argument would have sealed the death warrants of them both. There was but a single hope and Akut seized it. Grasping the lad around the waist he lifted him bodily from the ground, and turning ran swiftly toward another tree which swung low branches above the arena. Close upon their heels swarmed the hideous mob; but Akut, old though he was and burdened by the weight of the struggling Korak, was still fleeter than his pursuers.

With a bound he grasped a low limb, and with the agility of a little monkey swung himself and the boy to temporary safety. Nor did he hesitate even here; but raced on through the jungle night, bearing his burden to safety. For a time the bulls pursued; but presently, as the swifter outdistanced the slower and found themselves separated from their fellows they abandoned the chase, standing roaring and screaming until the jungle reverberated to their hideous noises. Then they turned and retraced their way to the amphitheater.

When Akut felt assured that they were no longer pursued he stopped and released Korak. The boy was furious.

"Why did you drag me away?" he cried. "I would have taught them! I would have taught them all! Now they will think that I am afraid of them."

"What they think cannot harm you," said Akut. "You are alive. If I had not brought you away you would be dead now and so would I. Do you not know that even Numa slinks from the path of the great apes when there are many of them and they are mad?"

CHAPTER 9

IT WAS AN unhappy Korak who wandered aimlessly through the jungle the day following his inhospitable reception by the great apes. His heart was heavy from disappointment. Unsatisfied vengeance smouldered in his breast. He looked with hatred upon the denizens of his jungle world, baring his fighting fangs and growling at those that came within radius of his senses. The mark of his father's early life was strong upon him and enhanced by months of association with beasts, from whom the imitative faculty of youth had absorbed a countless number of little mannerisms of the predatory creatures of the wild.

He bared his fangs now as naturally and upon as slight provocation as Sheeta, the panther, bared his. He growled as ferociously
as Akut himself. When he came suddenly upon another beast his
quick crouch bore a strange resemblance to the arching of a cat's
back. Korak, the killer, was looking for trouble. In his heart of
hearts he hoped to meet the king ape who had driven him from
the amphitheater. To this end he insisted upon remaining in the
vicinity; but the exigencies of the perpetual search for food led
them several miles further away during day.

They were moving slowly down wind, and warily because the
advantage was with whatever beast might chance to be hunting
ahead of them, where their scent-spoor was being borne by the
light breeze. Suddenly the two halted simultaneously. Two heads
were cocked upon one side. Like creatures hewn from solid rock
they stood immovable, listening. Not a muscle quivered. For several
seconds they remained thus, then Korak advanced cautiously a
few yards and leaped nimbly into a tree. Akut followed close upon
his heels. Neither had made a noise that would have been appreciable to human ears at a dozen paces.

Stopping often to listen they crept forward through the trees.
That both were greatly puzzled was apparent from the questioning
looks they cast at one another from time to time. Finally the lad
caught a glimpse of a palisade a hundred yards ahead, and beyond
it the tops of some goatskin tents and a number of thatched huts.
His lip upcurled in a savage snarl. Blacks! How he hated them.
He signed Akut to remain where he was while he advanced to
reconnoiter.

Woe betide the unfortunate villager whom The Killer came
upon now. Slinking through the lower branches of the trees, leaping
lightly from one jungle giant to its neighbor where the distance
was not too great, or swinging from one hand hold to another
Korak came silently toward the village. He heard a voice beyond
the palisade and toward that he made his way. A great tree
overhung the enclosure at the very point from which the voice
came. Into this Korak crept. His spear was ready in his hand.
His ears told him of the proximity of a human being. All that
his eyes required was a single glance to show him his target. Then,
lightning like, the missile would fly to its goal. With raised spear
he crept among the branches of the tree glaring narrowly downward
in search of the owner of the voice which rose to him from below.

At last he saw a human back. The spear hand flew to the limit of the throwing position to gather the force that would send the iron shod missile completely through the body of the unconscious victim. And then The Killer paused. He leaned forward a little to get a better view of the target. Was it to insure more perfect aim, or had there been that in the graceful lines and the childish curves of the little body below him that had held in check the spirit of murder running riot in his veins?

He lowered his spear cautiously that it might make no noise by scraping against foliage or branches. Quietly he crouched in a comfortable position along a great limb and there he lay with wide eyes looking down in wonder upon the creature he had crept upon to kill—looking down upon a little girl, a little nut brown maiden. The snarl had gone from his lip. His only expression was one of interested attention—he was trying to discover what the girl was doing. Suddenly a broad grin overspread his face, for a turn of the girl's body had revealed Geeka of the ivory head and the rat skin torso—Geeka of the splinter limbs and the disreputable appearance. The little girl raised the marred face to hers and rocking herself backward and forward crooned a plaintive Arab lullaby to the doll. A softer light entered the eyes of The Killer. For a long hour that passed very quickly to him Korak lay with gaze riveted upon the playing child. Not once had he had a view of the girl's full face. For the most part he saw only a mass of wavy, black hair, one brown little shoulder exposed upon the side where her single robe was caught beneath her arm, and a shapely knee protruding from beneath her garment as she sat cross legged upon the ground. A tilt of the head as she emphasized some maternal admonition to the passive Geeka revealed occasionally a rounded cheek or a piquant little chin. Now she was shaking a slim finger at Geeka, reprovingly, and again she crushed to her heart this only object upon which she might lavish the untold wealth of her childish affections.

Korak, momentarily forgetful of his bloody mission, permitted the fingers of his spear hand to relax a little their grasp upon the shaft of his formidable weapon. It slipped, almost falling; but the occurrence recalled The Killer to himself. It reminded him of his purpose in slinking stealthily upon the owner of the voice that had attracted his vengeful attention. He glanced at the spear, with its well-worn grip and cruel, barbed head. Then he let his eyes wander again to the dainty form below him. In imagination he saw the heavy weapon shooting downward. He saw it pierce the tender flesh, driving its way deep into the yielding body. He saw the ridiculous doll drop from its owner's arms to lie sprawled and pathetic beside the quivering body of the little girl. The Killer shuddered, scowling at the inanimate iron and wood of the spear as though they constituted a sentient being endowed with a malignant mind.

Korak wondered what the girl would do were he to drop suddenly from the tree to her side. Most likely she would scream and run away. Then would come the men of the village with spears and guns and set upon him. They would either kill him or drive him away. A lump rose in the boy's throat. He craved the companionship of his own kind, though he scarce realized how greatly. He would have liked to slip down beside the little girl and talk with her, though he knew from the words he had overheard that she spoke a language with which he was unfamiliar. They could have talked by signs a little. That would have been better than nothing. Too, he would have been glad to see her face. What he had glimpsed assured him that she was pretty; but her strongest appeal to him lay in the affectionate nature revealed by her gentle mothering of the grotesque doll.

At last he hit upon a plan. He would attract her attention, and reassure her by a smiling greeting from a greater distance. Silently he wormed his way back into the tree. It was his intention to hail her from beyond the palisade, giving her the feeling of security which he imagined the stout barricade would afford.

He had scarcely left his position in the tree when his attention was attracted by a considerable noise upon the opposite side of the village. By moving a little he could see the gate at the far end of the main street. A number of men, women and children were running toward it. It swung open, revealing the head of a caravan upon the opposite side. In trooped the motley organization—black slaves and dark hued Arabs of the northern deserts; cursing camel drivers urging on their vicious charges; overburdened donkeys, waving sadly pendulous ears while they endured with stoic patience the brutalities of their masters; goats, sheep and horses. Into the village they all trooped behind a tall, sour, old man, who rode without greetings to those who shrunk from his path directly to a large goatskin tent in the center of the village. Here he spoke to a wrinkled hag.

Korak, from his vantage spot, could see it all. He saw the old man asking questions of the black woman, and then he saw the latter point toward a secluded corner of the village which was hidden from the main street by the tents of the Arabs and the huts of the natives in the direction of the tree beneath which the little girl played. This was doubtless her father, thought Korak. He had been away and his first thought upon returning was of his little daughter. How glad she would be to see him! How she would run and throw herself into his arms, to be crushed to his breast and covered with his kisses. Korak sighed. He thought of his own father and mother far away in London.

He returned to his place in the tree above the girl. If he couldn't have happiness of this sort himself he wanted to enjoy the happiness of others. Possibly if he made himself known to the old man he might be permitted to come to the village occasionally as a friend. It would be worth trying. He would wait until the old Arab had greeted his daughter, then he would make his presence known with signs of peace.

The Arab was striding softly toward the girl. In a moment he would be beside her, and then how surprised and delighted she would be! Korak's eyes sparkled in anticipation—and now the old man stood behind the little girl. His stern old face was still unrelaxed. The child was yet unconscious of his presence. She prattled on to the unresponsive Geeka. Then the old man coughed. With a start the child glanced quickly up over her shoulder. Korak could see her full face now. It was very beautiful in its sweet and innocent childishness—all soft and lovely curves. He could see her great, dark eyes. He looked for the happy love light that would follow recognition; but it did not come. Instead terror, stark, paralyzing terror, was mirrored in her eyes, in the expression of her mouth, in the tense, cowering attitude of her body. A grim smile curved the thin, cruel lip of the Arab. The child essayed to crawl away; but before she could get out of his reach the old man kicked her brutally, sending her sprawling upon the grass. Then he followed her up to seize and strike her as was his custom.

Above them, in the tree, a beast crouched where a moment before had been a boy—a beast with dilating nostrils and bared fangs—a beast that trembled with rage.

The Sheik was stooping to reach for the girl when The Killer dropped to the ground at his side. His spear was still in his left hand but he had forgotten it. Instead his right fist was clenched and as The Sheik took a backward step, astonished by the sudden materialization of this strange apparition apparently out of clear air, the heavy fist landed full upon his mouth backed by the weight of the young giant and the terrific power of his more than human muscles.

Bleeding and senseless The Sheik sank to earth. Korak turned toward the child. She had regained her feet and stood wide-eyed and frightened looking first into his face and then, horror struck, at the recumbent figure of The Sheik. In an involuntary gesture of protection The Killer threw an arm about the girl's shoulders and stood waiting for the Arab to regain consciousness. For a moment they remained thus, when the girl spoke.

"When he regains his senses he will kill me," she said, in Arabic.

Korak could not understand her. He shook his head, speaking to her first in English and then in the language of the great apes; but neither of these was intelligible to her. She leaned forward and touched the hilt of the long knife that the Arab wore. Then she raised her clasped hand above her head and drove an imaginary blade into her breast above her heart. Korak understood. The old man would kill her. The girl came to his side again and stood there trembling. She did not fear him. Why should she? He had saved her from a terrible beating at the hands of The Sheik. Never, in her memory, had another so befriended her. She looked up into his face. It was a boyish, handsome face, nut-brown like her own. She admired the spotted leopard skin that circled his lithe body from one shoulder to his knees. The metal anklets and armlets adorning him aroused her envy. Always had she coveted something of the kind; but never had The Sheik permitted her more than the single cotton garment that barely sufficed to cover her nakedness. No furs or silks or jewelry had there ever been for little Meriem.

And Korak looked at the girl. He had always held girls in a species of contempt. Boys who associated with them were, in his estimation, mollycoddles. He wondered what he should do. Could he leave her here to be abused, possibly murdered, by the villainous old Arab? No! But, on the other hand, could he take her into the jungle with him? What could he accomplish burdened by a weak and frightened girl? She would scream at her own shadow when the moon came out upon the jungle night and the great beasts roamed, moaning and roaring, through the darkness.

He stood for several minutes buried in thought. The girl watched his face, wondering what was passing in his mind. She, too, was thinking of the future. She feared to remain and suffer the vengeance of The Sheik. There was no one in all the world to whom she might turn, other than this half-naked stranger who had dropped miraculously from the clouds to save her from one of The Sheik's accustomed beatings. Would her new friend leave her now? Wistfully she gazed at his intent face. She moved a little closer to him, laying a slim, brown hand upon his arm. The contact awakened the lad from his absorption. He looked down at her, and then his arm went about her shoulder once more, for he saw tears upon her lashes.

"Come," he said. "The jungle is kinder than man. You shall live in the jungle and Korak and Akut will protect you."

She did not understand his words, but the pressure of his arm drawing her away from the prostrate Arab and the tents was quite intelligible. One little arm crept about his waist and together they walked toward the palisade. Beneath the great tree that had harbored Korak while he watched the girl at play he lifted her in his arms and throwing her lightly across his shoulder leaped nimbly into the lower branches. Her arms were about his neck and from one little hand Geeka dangled down his straight young back.

And so Meriem entered the jungle with Korak, trusting, in her childish innocence, the stranger who had befriended her, and perhaps influenced in her belief in him by that strange intuitive power possessed by woman. She had no conception of what the future might hold. She did not know, nor could she have guessed the manner of life led by her protector. Possibly she pictured a distant village similar to that of The Sheik in which lived other white men like the stranger. That she was to be taken into the savage, primeval life of a jungle beast could not have occurred to her. Had it, her little heart would have palpitated with fear. Often had she wished to run away from the cruelties of The Sheik and Mabunu; but the dangers of the jungle always had deterred her.

The two had gone but a short distance from the village when the girl spied the huge proportions of the great Akut. With a half-stifled scream she clung more closely to Korak, and pointed fearfully toward the ape.

Akut, thinking that The Killer was returning with a prisoner came growling toward them—a little girl aroused no more sympathy in the beast's heart than would a full-grown bull ape. She was a stranger and therefore to be killed. He bared his yellow fangs as he approached, and to his surprise The Killer bared his likewise, but he bared them at Akut, and snarled menacingly.

"Ah," thought Akut, "The Killer has taken a mate," and so, obedient to the tribal laws of his kind, he left them alone, becoming suddenly absorbed in a fuzzy caterpillar of peculiarly succulent appearance. The larva disposed of, he glanced from the corner of an eye at Korak. The youth had deposited his burden upon a large limb, where she clung desperately to keep from falling.

"She will accompany us," said Korak to Akut, jerking a thumb in the direction of the girl. "Do not harm her. We will protect her."

Akut shrugged. To be burdened by the young of man was in no way to his liking. He could see from her evident fright at her position on the branch, and from the terrified glances she cast in his direction that she was hopelessly unfit. By all the ethics of Akut's training and inheritance the unfit should be eliminated; but if The Killer wished this she there was nothing to be done about it but to tolerate her. Akut certainly didn't want her—of that he was quite positive. Her skin was too smooth and hairless. Quite snakelike, in fact, and her face was most unattractive. Not at all like that of a certain lovely she he had particularly noticed among the apes in the amphitheater the previous night. Ah, there was true feminine beauty for one!—a great, generous mouth; lovely, yellow fangs, and the cutest, softest side whiskers! Akut sighed. Then he rose, expanded his great chest and strutted back and forth along a substantial branch, for even a puny thing like this she of Korak's might admire his fine coat and his graceful carriage.

But poor little Meriem only shrank closer to Korak and almost wished that she were back in the village of The Sheik where the terrors of existence were of human origin, and so more or less familiar. The hideous ape frightened her. He was so large and so ferocious in appearance. His actions she could only interpret as a menace, for how could she guess that he was parading to excite admiration? Nor could she know of the bond of fellowship which existed between this great brute and the godlike youth who had rescued her from The Sheik.

Meriem spent an evening and a night of unmitigated terror. Korak and Akut led her along dizzy ways as they searched for food. Once they hid her in the branches of a tree while they stalked a near-by buck. Even her natural terror of being left alone in the awful jungle was submerged in a greater horror as she saw the man and the beast spring simultaneously upon their prey and drag it down, as she saw the handsome face of her preserver contorted in a bestial snarl; as she saw his strong, white teeth buried in the soft flesh of the kill.

When he came back to her blood smeared his face and hands and breast and she shrank from him as he offered her a huge hunk of hot, raw meat. He was evidently much disturbed by her refusal to eat, and when, a moment later, he scampered away into the forest to return with fruit for her she was once more forced to alter her estimation of him. This time she did not shrink, but acknowledged his gift with a smile that, had she known it, was more than ample payment to the affection starved boy.

The sleeping problem vexed Korak. He knew that the girl could not balance herself in safety in a tree crotch while she slept, nor would it be safe to permit her to sleep upon the ground open to the attacks of prowling beasts of prey. There was but a single solution that presented itself—he must hold her in his arms all night. And that he did, with Akut braced upon one side of her and he upon the other, so that she was warmed by the bodies of them both.

She did not sleep much until the night was half spent; but at last Nature overcame her terrors of the black abyss beneath and the hairy body of the wild beast at her side, and she fell into a deep slumber which outlasted the darkness. When she opened her eyes the sun was well up. At first she could not believe in the reality of her position. Her head had rolled from Korak's shoulder so that her eyes were directed upon the hairy back of the ape. At sight of it she shrank away. Then she realized that someone was holding her, and turning her head she saw the smiling eyes of the youth regarding her. When he smiled she could not fear him, and now she shrank closer against him in natural revulsion toward the rough coat of the brute upon her other side.

Korak spoke to her in the language of the apes; but she shook her head, and spoke to him in the language of the Arab, which was as unintelligible to him as was ape speech to her. Akut sat up and looked at them. He could understand what Korak said but the girl made only foolish noises that were entirely unintelligible and ridiculous. Akut could not understand what Korak saw in her to attract him. He looked at her long and steadily, appraising her carefully, then he scratched his head, rose and shook himself.

His movement gave the girl a little start—she had forgotten Akut for the moment. Again she shrank from him. The beast saw that she feared him, and being a brute enjoyed the evidence of the terror his brutishness inspired. Crouching, he extended his huge hand stealthily toward her, as though to seize her. She shrank still further away. Akut's eyes were busy drinking in the humor of the situation—he did not see the narrowing eyes of the boy upon him, nor the shortening neck as the broad shoulders rose in a characteristic attitude of preparation for attack. As the ape's fingers were about to close upon the girl's arm the youth rose suddenly with a short, vicious growl. A clenched fist flew before Meriem's eyes to land full upon the snout of the astonished Akut. With an explosive bellow the anthropoid reeled backward and tumbled from the tree.

Korak stood glaring down upon him when a sudden swish in the bushes close by attracted his attention. The girl too was looking down; but she saw nothing but the angry ape scrambling to his feet. Then, like a bolt from a cross bow, a mass of spotted, yellow fur shot into view straight for Akut's back. It was Sheeta, the leopard.

CHAPTER 10

As the leopard leaped for the great ape Meriem gasped in surprise and horror—not for the impending fate of the anthropoid, but at the act of the youth who but an instant before had angrily struck his strange companion; for scarce had the carnivore burst into view than with drawn knife the youth had leaped far out above him, so that as Sheeta was almost in the act of sinking fangs and talons in Akut's broad back The Killer landed full upon the leopard's shoulders.

The cat halted in mid air, missed the ape by but a hair's breadth, and with horrid snarlings rolled over upon its back, clutching and clawing in an effort to reach and dislodge the antagonist biting at its neck and knifing it in the side.

Akut, startled by the sudden rush from his rear, and following hoary instinct was in the tree beside the girl with an agility little short of marvelous in so heavy a beast. But the moment that he turned to see what was going on below him brought him as quickly to the ground again. Personal differences were quickly forgotten in the danger which menaced his human companion, nor was he a whit less eager to jeopardize his own safety in the service of his friend than Korak had been to succor him.

The result was that Sheeta presently found two ferocious creatures tearing him to ribbons. Shrieking, snarling and growling, the three rolled hither and thither among the underbrush, while with staring eyes the sole spectator of the battle royal crouched trembling in the tree above them hugging Geeka frantically to her breast.

It was the boy's knife which eventually decided the battle, and as the fierce feline shuddered convulsively and rolled over upon its side the youth and the ape rose and faced one another across the prostrate carcass. Korak jerked his head in the direction of the little girl in the tree.

"Leave her alone," he said; "she is mine."

Akut grunted, blinked his blood-shot eyes, and turned toward the body of Sheeta. Standing erect upon it he threw out his great chest, raised his face toward the heavens and gave voice to so horrid a scream that once again the little girl shuddered and shrank. It was the victory cry of the bull ape that has made a kill. The boy only looked on for a moment in silence; then he leaped into the tree again to the girl's side. Akut presently rejoined them. For a few minutes he busied himself licking his wounds, then he wandered off to hunt his breakfast.

For many months the strange life of the three went on unmarked by any unusual occurrences. At least without any occurrences that seemed unusual to the youth or the ape; but to the little girl it was a constant nightmare of horrors for days and weeks, until she too became accustomed to gazing into the eyeless sockets of death and to the feel of the icy wind of his shroudlike mantle. Slowly she learned the rudiments of the only common medium of thought exchange which her companions possessed—the language of the great apes. More quickly she perfected herself in jungle craft, so that the time soon came when she was an important factor in the chase, watching while the others slept, or helping them to trace the spoor of whatever prey they might be stalking. Akut accepted her on a footing which bordered upon equality when it was necessary for them to come into close contact; but for the most part he avoided her. The youth always was kind to her, and if there were many occasions upon which he felt the burden of her presence he hid it from her. Finding that the night damp and chill caused her discomfort and even suffering, Korak constructed a tight little shelter high among the swaying branches of a giant tree. Here little Meriem slept in comparative warmth

The victory cry of the bull ape.

and safety, while The Killer and the ape perched upon near-by branches, the former always before the entrance to the lofty domicile, where he best could guard its inmate from the dangers of arboreal enemies. They were too high to feel much fear of Sheeta; but there was always Histah, the snake, to strike terror to one's soul, and the great baboons who lived near-by, and who, while never attacking always bared their fangs and barked at any of the trio when they passed near them.

After the construction of the shelter the activities of the three became localized. They ranged less widely, for there was always the necessity of returning to their own tree at nightfall. A river flowed near by. Game and fruit were plentiful, as were fish also. Existence had settled down to the daily hum-drum of the wild—the search for food and the sleeping upon full bellies. They looked no further ahead than today. If the youth thought of his past and of those who longed for him in the distant metropolis it was in a detached and impersonal sort of way as though that other life belonged to another creature than himself. He had given up hope of returning to civilization, for since his various rebuffs at the hands of those to whom he had looked for friendship he had wandered so far inland as to realize that he was completely lost in the mazes of the jungle.

Then, too, since the coming of Meriem he had found in her that one thing which he had most missed before in his savage, jungle life—human companionship. In his friendship for her there was appreciable no trace of sex influence of which he was cognizant. They were friends—companions—that was all. Both might have been boys, except for the half tender and always masterful manifestation of the protective instinct which was apparent in Korak's attitude.

The little girl idolized him as she might have idolized an indulgent brother had she had one. Love was a thing unknown to either; but as the youth neared manhood it was inevitable that it should come to him as it did to every other savage, jungle male.

As Meriem became proficient in their common language the pleasures of their companionship grew correspondingly, for now they could converse and aided by the mental powers of their human heritage they amplified the restricted vocabulary of the apes until talking was transformed from a task into an enjoyable pastime. When Korak hunted, Meriem usually accompanied him, for she had learned the fine art of silence, when silence was desirable. She could pass through the branches of the great trees now with all the agility and stealth of The Killer himself. Great heights no longer appalled her. She swung from limb to limb, or she raced through the mighty branches, surefooted, lithe, and fearless. Korak was very proud of her, and even old Akut grunted in approval where before he had growled in contempt.

A distant village of blacks had furnished her with a mantle of fur and feathers, with copper ornaments, and weapons, for Korak would not permit her to go unarmed, or unversed in the use of the weapons he stole for her. A leather thong over one shoulder supported the ever present Geeka who was still the recipient of her most sacred confidences. A light spear and a long knife were her weapons of offense or defense. Her body, rounding into the fulness of an early maturity, followed the lines of a Greek goddess; but there the similarity ceased, for her face was beautiful.

As she grew more accustomed to the jungle and the ways of its wild denizens fear left her. As time wore on she even hunted alone when Korak and Akut were prowling at a great distance, as they were sometimes forced to do when game was scarce in their immediate vicinity. Upon these occasions she usually confined her endeavors to the smaller animals though sometimes she brought down a deer, and once even Horta, the boar—a great tusker that even Sheeta might have thought twice before attacking.

In their stamping grounds in the jungle the three were familiar figures. The little monkeys knew them well, often coming close to chatter and frolic about them. When Akut was by, the small folk kept their distance, but with Korak they were less shy and when both the males were gone they would come close to Meriem, tugging at her ornaments or playing with Geeka, who was a never ending source of amusement to them. The girl played with them and fed them, and when she was alone they helped her to pass the long hours until Korak's return.

Nor were they worthless as friends. In the hunt they helped her locate her quarry. Often they would come racing through the trees to her side to announce the near presence of antelope or giraffe, or with excited warnings of the proximity of Sheeta or Numa. Luscious, sun-kissed fruits which hung far out upon the frail bough of the jungle's waving crest were brought to her by these tiny, nimble allies. Sometimes they played tricks upon her; but she was always kind and gentle with them and in their wild, half-human way they were kind to her and affectionate. Their language being

similar to that of the great apes Meriem could converse with them
though the poverty of their vocabulary rendered these exchanges
anything but feasts of reason. For familiar objects they had names,
as well as for those conditions which induced pain or pleasure,
joy, sorrow, or rage. These root words were so similar to those
in use among the great anthropoids as to suggest that the language
of the Manus was the mother tongue. At best it lent itself to but
material and sordid exchange. Dreams, aspirations, hopes, the past,
the future held no place in the conversation of Manu, the monkey.
All was of the present—particularly of filling his belly and catching
lice.

Poor food was this to nourish the mental appetite of a girl just
upon the brink of womanhood. And so, finding Manu only amusing as an occasional playfellow or pet, Meriem poured out her
sweetest soul thoughts into the deaf ears of Geeka's ivory head.
To Geeka she spoke in Arabic, knowing that Geeka, being but a
doll, could not understand the language of Korak and Akut, and
that the language of Korak and Akut being that of male apes
contained nothing of interest to an Arab doll.

Geeka had undergone a transformation since her little mother
had left the village of The Sheik. Her garmenture now reflected
in miniature that of Meriem. A tiny bit of leopard skin covered
her ratskin torso from shoulder to splinter knee. A band of braided
grasses about her brow held in place a few gaudy feathers from
the parrakeet, while other bits of grass were fashioned into imi-
tations of arm and leg ornaments of metal. Geeka was a perfect
little savage; but at heart she was unchanged, being the same
omnivorous listener as of yore. An excellent trait in Geeka was
that she never interrupted in order to talk about herself. Today
was no exception. She had been listening attentively to Meriem
for an hour, propped against the bole of a tree while her lithe,
young mistress stretched catlike and luxurious along a swaying
branch before her.

"Little Geeka," said Meriem, "our Korak has been gone for a
long time today. We miss him, little Geeka, do we not? It is dull
and lonesome in the great jungle when our Korak is away. What
will he bring us this time, eh? Another shining band of metal for
Meriem's ankle? Or a soft, doeskin loin cloth from the body of
a black she? He tells me that it is harder to get the possessions
of the shes, for he will not kill them as he does the males, and
they fight savagely when he leaps upon them to wrest their or-

naments from them. Then come the males with spears and arrows and Korak takes to the trees. Sometimes he takes the she with him and high among the branches divests her of the things he wishes to bring home to Meriem. He says that the blacks fear him now, and at the first sight of him the women and children run shrieking to their huts; but he follows them within, and it is not often that he returns without arrows for himself and a present for Meriem. Korak is mighty among the jungle people—our Korak, Geeka—no, *my* Korak!"

Meriem's conversation was interrupted by the sudden plunge of an excited little monkey that landed upon her shoulders in a flying leap from a neighboring tree.

"Climb!" he cried. "Climb! The Mangani are coming."

Meriem glanced lazily over her shoulder at the excited disturber of her peace.

"Climb, yourself, little Manu," she said. "The only Mangani in our jungle are Korak and Akut. It is they you have seen returning from the hunt. Some day you will see your own shadow, little Manu, and then you will be frightened to death."

But the monkey only screamed his warning more lustily before he raced upward toward the safety of the high terrace where Mangani, the great ape, could not follow. Presently Meriem heard the sound of approaching bodies swinging through the trees. She listened attentively. There were two and they were great apes— Korak and Akut. To her Korak was an ape—a Mangani, for as such the three always described themselves. Man was an enemy, so they did not think of themselves as belonging longer to the same genus. Tarmangani, or great white ape, which described the white man in their language did not fit them all. Gomagani— great black ape, or negro—described none of them so they called themselves plain Mangani.

Meriem decided that she would feign slumber and play a joke on Korak. So she lay very still with eyes tightly closed. She heard the two approaching closer and closer. They were in the adjoining tree now and must have discovered her, for they had halted. Why were they so quiet? Why did not Korak call out his customary greeting? The quietness was ominous. It was followed presently by a very stealthy sound—one of them was creeping upon her. Was Korak planning a joke upon his own account? Well, she would fool him. Cautiously she opened her eyes the tiniest bit, and as she did so her heart stood still. Creeping silently toward her was a huge bull ape that she never before had seen. Behind him was another like him.

With the agility of a squirrel Meriem was upon her feet and at the same instant the great bull lunged for her. Leaping from limb to limb the girl fled through the jungle while close behind her came the two great apes. Above them raced a bevy of screaming, chattering monkeys, hurling taunts and insults at the Mangani, and encouragement and advice to the girl.

From tree to tree swung Meriem working ever upward toward the smaller branches which would not bear the weight of her pursuers. Faster and faster came the bull apes after her. The clutching fingers of the foremost were almost upon her again and again, but she eluded them by sudden bursts of speed or reckless chances as she threw herself across dizzy spaces.

Slowly she was gaining her way to the greater heights where safety lay, when, after a particularly daring leap, the swaying branch she grasped bent low beneath her weight, nor whipped upward again as it should have done. Even before the rending sound which followed Meriem knew that she had misjudged the strength of the limb. It gave slowly at first. Then there was a ripping as it parted from the trunk. Releasing her hold Meriem dropped among the foliage beneath, clutching for a new support. She found it a dozen feet below the broken limb. She had fallen thus many times before, so that she had no particular terror of a fall—it was the delay which appalled her most, and rightly, for scarce had she scrambled to a place of safety than the body of the huge ape dropped at her side and a great, hairy arm went about her waist.

Almost at once the other ape reached his companion's side. He made a lunge at Meriem; but her captor swung her to one side, bared his fighting fangs and growled ominously. Meriem struggled to escape. She struck at the hairy breast and bearded cheek. She fastened her strong, white teeth in one shaggy forearm. The ape cuffed her viciously across the face, then he had to turn his attention to his fellow who quite evidently desired the prize for his own.

The captor could not fight to advantage upon the swaying bough burdened as he was by a squirming, struggling captive, so he dropped quickly to the ground beneath. The other followed him, and here they fought, occasionally abandoning their duel to pursue and recapture the girl who took every advantage of her captors' preoccupation in battle to break away in attempted escape; but always they overtook her, and first one and then the other possessed her as they struggled to tear one another to pieces for the prize.

Often the girl came in for many blows that were intended for a hairy foe, and once she was felled, lying unconscious while the apes, relieved of the distraction of detaining her by force, tore into one another in fierce and terrible combat.

Above them screamed the little monkeys, racing hither and thither in a frenzy of hysterical excitement. Back and forth over the battle field flew countless birds of gorgeous plumage, squawking their hoarse cries of rage and defiance. In the distance a lion roared.

The larger bull was slowly tearing his antagonist to pieces. They rolled upon the ground biting and striking. Again, erect upon their hind legs they pulled and tugged like human wrestlers; but always the giant fangs found their bloody part to play until both combatants and the ground about them were red with gore.

Meriem, through it all, lay still and unconscious upon the ground. At last one found a permanent hold upon the jugular of the other and thus they went down for the last time. For several minutes they lay with scarce a struggle. It was the larger bull who arose alone from that last embrace. He shook himself. A deep growl rumbled from his hairy throat. He waddled back and forth between the body of the girl and that of his vanquished foe. Then he stood upon the latter and gave tongue to his hideous challenge. The little monkeys broke, screaming, in all directions as the terrifying noise broke upon their ears. The gorgeous birds took wing and fled. Once again the lion roared, this time at a greater distance.

The great ape waddled once more to the girl's side. He turned her over upon her back, and stooping commenced to sniff and listen about her face and breast. She lived. The monkeys were returning. They came in swarms, and from above hurled down insults upon the victor.

The ape showed his displeasure by baring his teeth and growling up at them. Then he stooped and lifting the girl to his shoulder waddled off through the jungle. In his wake followed the angry mob.

CHAPTER 11

KORAK, RETURNING FROM the hunt, heard the jabbering of the excited monkeys. He knew that something was seriously amiss. Histah, the snake, had doubtless coiled his slimy folds about some careless Manu. The youth hastened ahead. The monkeys were Meriem's friends. He would help them if he could. He traveled rapidly along the middle terrace. In the tree by Meriem's shelter he deposited his trophies of the hunt and called aloud to her. There was no answer. He dropped quickly to a lower level. She might be hiding from him.

Upon a great branch where Meriem often swung at indolent ease he saw Geeka propped against the tree's great bole. What could it mean? Meriem had never left Geeka thus alone before. Korak picked up the doll and tucked it in his belt. He called again, more loudly; but no Meriem answered his summons. In the distance the jabbering of the excited Manus was growing less distinct.

Could their excitement be in any way connected with Meriem's disappearance? The bare thought was enough. Without waiting for Akut who was coming slowly along some distance in his rear, Korak swung rapidly in the direction of the chattering mob. But a few minutes sufficed to overtake the rearmost. At sight of him they fell to screaming and pointing downward ahead of them, and a moment later Korak came within sight of the cause of their rage.

The youth's heart stood still in terror as he saw the limp body of the girl across the hairy shoulders of a great ape. That she was dead he did not doubt, and in that instant there arose within him a something which he did not try to interpret nor could have had he tried; but all at once the whole world seemed centered in that tender, graceful body, that frail little body, hanging so pitifully limp and helpless across the bulging shoulders of the brute.

He knew then that little Meriem was his world—his sun, his moon, his stars—with her going had gone all light and warmth and happiness. A groan escaped his lips, and after that a series of hideous roars, more bestial than the beasts', as he dropped plummet-like in mad descent toward the perpetrator of this hideous crime.

The bull ape turned at the first note of this new and menacing voice, and as he turned a new flame was added to the rage and hatred of The Killer, for he saw that the creature before him was none other than the king ape which had driven him away from the great anthropoids to whom he had looked for friendship and asylum.

Dropping the body of the girl to the ground the bull turned to battle anew for possession of his expensive prize; but this time he looked for an easy conquest. He too recognized Korak. Had he not chased him away from the amphitheater without even having to lay a fang or paw upon him? With lowered head and bulging shoulders he rushed headlong for the smooth-skinned creature who was daring to question his right to his prey.

They met head on like two charging bulls, to go down together tearing and striking. Korak forgot his knife. Rage and bloodlust such as his could be satisfied only by the feel of hot flesh between rending fangs, by the gush of new life blood against his bare skin, for, though he did not realize it, Korak, The Killer, was fighting for something more compelling than hate or revenge—he was a great male fighting another male for a she of his own kind.

So impetuous was the attack of the man-ape that he found his hold before the anthropoid could prevent him—a savage hold, with strong jaws closed upon a pulsing jugular, and there he clung, with closed eyes, while his fingers sought another hold upon the shaggy throat.

It was then that Meriem opened her eyes. At the sight before her they went wide.

"Korak!" she cried. "Korak! My Korak! I knew that you would come. Kill him, Korak! Kill him!" And with flashing eyes and heaving bosom the girl, coming to her feet, ran to Korak's side to encourage him. Nearby lay The Killer's spear, where he had flung it as he charged the ape. The girl saw it and snatched it up. No faintness overcame her in the face of this battle primeval at her feet. For her there was no hysterical reaction from the nerve strain of her own personal encounter with the bull. She was excited; but cool and entirely unafraid. Her Korak was battling with another Mangani that would have stolen her; but she did not seek the safety of an overhanging bough there to watch the battle from afar, as would a she Mangani. Instead she placed the point of Korak's spear against the bull ape's side and plunged the sharp point deep into the savage heart. Korak had not needed her aid, for the great bull had been already as good as dead, with the blood gushing from his torn jugular; but Korak rose smiling with a word of approbation for his helper.

How tall and fine she was! Had she changed suddenly within the few hours of his absence, or had his battle with the ape affected his vision? He might have been looking at Meriem through new eyes for the many startling and wonderful surprises his gaze revealed. How long it had been since he had found her in her father's village, a little Arab girl, he did not know, for time is of no import in the jungle and so he had kept no track of the passing days. But he realized, as he looked upon her now, that she was no longer such a little girl as he had first seen playing with Geeka beneath the great tree just within the palisade. The change must have been very gradual to have eluded his notice until now. And what was it that had caused him to realize it so suddenly? His gaze wandered from the girl to the body of the dead bull. For the first time there flashed to his understanding the explanation of the reason for the girl's attempted abduction. Korak's eyes went wide and then they closed to narrow slits of rage as he stood glaring down upon the abysmal brute at his feet. When next his glance rose to Meriem's face a slow flush suffused his own. Now, indeed, was he looking upon her through new eyes—the eyes of a man looking upon a maid.

Akut had come up just as Meriem had speared Korak's antagonist. The exultation of the old ape was keen. He strutted, stiff-legged and truculent about the body of the fallen enemy. He growled and upcurved his long, flexible lip. His hair bristled. He was paying no attention to Meriem and Korak. Back in the uttermost recesses of his little brain something was stirring—something which the sight and smell of this great bull had aroused. The outward manifestation of the germinating idea was one of bestial rage; but the inner sensations were pleasurable in the extreme. The scent of the great bull and the sight of his huge and hairy figure had wakened in the heart of Akut a longing for the companionship of his own kind. So Korak was not alone undergoing a change.

And Meriem? She was a woman. It is woman's divine right to love. Always she had loved Korak. He was her big brother. Meriem alone underwent no change. She was still happy in the companionship of her Korak. She still loved him—as a sister loves an indulgent brother—and she was very, very proud of him. In all the jungle there was no other creature so strong, so handsome, or so brave.

Korak came close to her. There was a new light in his eyes as she looked up into them; but she did not understand it. She did not realize how close they were to maturity, nor aught of all the difference in their lives the look in Korak's eyes might mean.

"Meriem," he whispered and his voice was husky as he laid a brown hand upon her bare shoulder. "Meriem!" Suddenly he crushed her to him. She looked up into his face, laughing, and then he bent and kissed her full upon the mouth. Even then she did not understand. She did not recall ever having been kissed before. It was very nice. Meriem liked it. She thought it was Korak's way of showing how glad he was that the great ape had not succeeded in running away with her. She was glad too, so she put her arms about The Killer's neck and kissed him again and again. Then, discovering the doll in his belt she transferred it to her own possession, kissing it as she had kissed Korak.

Korak wanted to say something. He wanted to tell her how he loved her; but the emotion of his love choked him and the vocabulary of the Mangani was limited.

There came a sudden interruption. It was from Akut—a sudden, low growl, no louder than those he had been giving vent to the while he pranced about the dead bull, nor half so loud in fact; but of a timbre that bore straight to the perceptive faculties of the jungle beast ingrained in Korak. It was a warning. Korak looked quickly up from the glorious vision of the sweet face so close to his. Now his other faculties awoke. His ears, his nostrils were on the alert. Something was coming!

The Killer moved to Akut's side. Meriem was just behind them. The three stood like carved statues gazing into the leafy tangle of the jungle. The noise that had attracted their attention increased, and presently a great ape broke through the underbrush a few paces from where they stood. The beast halted at sight of them. He gave a warning grunt back over his shoulder, and a moment later coming cautiously another bull appeared. He was followed by others—both bulls and females with young, until two score hairy monsters stood glaring at the three. It was the tribe of the dead king ape. Akut was the first to speak. He pointed to the body of the dead bull.

"Korak, mighty fighter, has killed your king," he grunted. "There is none greater in all the jungle than Korak, son of Tarzan. Now

Korak is king. What bull is greater than Korak?" It was a challenge to any bull who might care to question Korak's right to the kingship. The apes jabbered and chattered and growled among themselves for a time. At last a young bull came slowly forward rocking upon his short legs, bristling, growling, terrible.

The beast was enormous, and in the full prime of his strength. He belonged to that almost extinct species for which white men have long sought upon the information of the natives of the more inaccessible jungles. Even the natives seldom see these great, hairy, primordial men.

Korak advanced to meet the monster. He, too, was growling. In his mind a plan was revolving. To close with this powerful, untired brute after having just passed through a terrific battle with another of his kind would have been to tempt defeat. He must find an easier way to victory. Crouching, he prepared to meet the charge which he knew would soon come, nor did he have long to wait. His antagonist paused only for sufficient time to permit him to recount for the edification of the audience and the con- founding of Korak a brief rèsumè of his former victories, of his prowess, and of what he was about to do to this puny Tarmangani. Then he charged.

With clutching fingers and wide opened jaws he came down upon the waiting Korak with the speed of an express train. Korak did not move until the great arms swung to embrace him, then he dropped low beneath them, swung a terrific right to the side of the beast's jaw as he side-stepped his rushing body, and swinging quickly about stood ready over the fallen ape where he sprawled upon the ground.

It was a surprised anthropoid that attempted to scramble to its feet. Froth flecked its hideous lips. Red were the little eyes. Blood curdling roars tumbled from the deep chest. But it did not reach its feet. The Killer stood waiting above it, and the moment that the hairy chin came upon the proper level another blow that would have felled an ox sent the ape over backward.

Again and again the beast struggled to arise, but each time the mighty Tarmangani stood waiting with ready fist and pile driver blow to bowl him over. Weaker and weaker became the efforts of the bull. Blood smeared his face and breast. A red stream trickled from nose and mouth. The crowd that had cheered him on at first with savage yells, now jeered him—their approbation was for the Tarmangani.

"Kagoda?" inquired Korak, as he sent the bull down once more.

Again the stubborn bull essayed to scramble to his feet. Again The Killer struck him a terrific blow. Again he put the question, *kagoda*—have you had enough?

For a moment the bull lay motionless. Then from between battered lips came the single word: *"Kagoda!"*

"Then rise and go back among your people," said Korak. "I do not wish to be king among people who once drove me from them. Keep your own ways, and we will keep ours. When we meet we may be friends, but we shall not live together."

An old bull came slowly toward The Killer.

"You have killed our king," he said. "You have defeated him who would have been king. You could have killed him had you wished. What shall we do for a king?"

Korak turned toward Akut.

"There is your king," he said. But Akut did not want to be separated from Korak, although he was anxious enough to remain with his own kind. He wanted Korak to remain, too. He said as much.

The youth was thinking of Meriem—of what would be best and safest for her. If Akut went away with the apes there would be but one to watch over and protect her. On the other hand were they to join the tribe he would never feel safe to leave Meriem behind when he went out to hunt, for the passions of the ape-folk are not over well controlled. Even a female might develop an insane hatred for the slender white girl and kill her during Korak's absence.

"We will live near you," he said, at last. "When you change your hunting ground we will change ours, Meriem and I, and so remain near you; but we shall not dwell among you."

Akut raised objections to this plan. He did not wish to be separated from Korak. At first he refused to leave his human friend for the companionship of his own kind; but when he saw the last of the tribe wandering off into the jungle again and his glance rested upon the lithe figure of the dead king's young mate as she cast admiring glances at her lord's successor the call of blood would not be denied. With a farewell glance toward his beloved Korak he turned and followed the she ape into the labyrinthine mazes of the wood.

* * *

After Korak had left the village of the blacks following his last thieving expedition, the screams of his victim and those of the other women and children had brought the warriors in from the forest and the river. Great was the excitement and hot was the rage of the men when they learned that the white devil had again entered their homes, frightened their women and stolen arrows and ornaments and food.

Even their superstitious fear of this weird creature who hunted with a huge bull ape was overcome in their desire to wreak vengeance upon him and rid themselves for good and all of the menace of his presence in the jungle.

And so it was that a score of the fleetest and most doughty warriors of the tribe set out in pursuit of Korak and Akut but a few minutes after they had left the scene of The Killer's many depredations.

The youth and the ape had traveled slowly and with no precautions against a successful pursuit. Nor was their attitude of careless indifference to the blacks at all remarkable. So many similar raids had gone unpunished that the two had come to look upon the negroes with contempt. The return journey led them straight up wind. The result being that the scent of their pursuers was borne away from them, so they proceeded upon their way in total ignorance of the fact that tireless trackers but little less expert in the mysteries of woodcraft than themselves were dogging their trail with savage insistence.

The little party of warriors was led by Kovudoo, the chief; a middle-aged savage of exceptional cunning and bravery. It was he who first came within sight of the quarry which they had followed for hours by the mysterious methods of their almost uncanny powers of observation, intuition, and even scent.

Kovudoo and his men came upon Korak, Akut and Meriem after the killing of the king ape, the noise of the combat having led them at last straight to their quarry. The sight of the slender white girl had amazed the savage chief and held him gazing at the trio for a moment before ordering his warriors to rush out upon their prey. In that moment it was that the great apes came and again the blacks remained awestruck witnesses to the palaver, and the battle between Korak and the young bull.

But now the apes had gone, and the white youth and the white maid stood alone in the jungle. One of Kovudoo's men leaned close to the ear of his chief. "Look!" he whispered, and pointed to something that dangled at the girl's side. "When my brother and I were slaves in the village of The Sheik my brother made that thing for The Sheik's little daughter—she played with it always and called it after my brother, whose name is Geeka. Just before we escaped some one came and struck down The Sheik, stealing his daughter away. If this is she The Sheik will pay you well for her return."

Korak's arm had again gone around the shoulders of Meriem. Love raced hot through his young veins. Civilization was but a half-remembered state—London as remote as ancient Rome. In all the world there were but they two—Korak, The Killer, and Meriem, his mate. Again he drew her close to him and covered her willing lips with his hot kisses. And then from behind him broke a hideous bedlam of savage war cries and a score of shrieking blacks were upon them.

Korak turned to give battle. Meriem with her own light spear stood by his side. An avalanche of barbed missiles flew about them. One pierced Korak's shoulder, another his leg, and he went down.

Meriem was unscathed for the blacks had intentionally spared her. Now they rushed forward to finish Korak and make good the girl's capture; but as they came there came also from another point in the jungle the great Akut and at his heels the huge bulls of his new kingdom.

Snarling and roaring they rushed upon the black warriors when they saw the mischief they had already wrought. Kovudoo, realizing the danger of coming to close quarters with these mighty ape-men, seized Meriem and called upon his warriors to retreat. For a time the apes followed them, and several of the blacks were badly mauled and one killed before they succeeded in escaping. Nor would they have gotten off this easily had Akut not been more concerned with the condition of the wounded Korak than with the fate of the girl upon whom he had always looked as more or less of an interloper and an unquestioned burden.

Korak lay bleeding and unconscious when Akut reached his side. The great ape tore the heavy spears from his flesh, licked the wounds and then carried his friend to the lofty shelter that Korak had constructed for Meriem. Further than this the brute could do nothing. Nature must accomplish the rest unaided or Korak must die.

He did not die, however. For days he lay helpless with fever, while Akut and the apes hunted close by that they might protect him from such birds and beasts as might reach his lofty retreat. Occasionally Akut brought him juicy fruits which helped to slake his thirst and allay his fever, and little by little his powerful constitution overcame the effects of the spear thrusts. The wounds healed and his strength returned. All during his rational moments as he had lain upon the soft furs which lined Meriem's nest he had suffered more acutely from fears for Meriem than from the pain of his own wounds. For her he must live. For her he must regain his strength that he might set out in search of her. What had the blacks done to her? Did she still live, or had they sacrificed her to their lust for torture and human flesh? Korak almost trembled with terror as the more hideous possibilities of the girl's fate suggested themselves to him out of his knowledge of the customs of Kovudoo's tribe.

The days dragged their weary lengths along, but at last he had sufficiently regained his strength to crawl from the shelter and make his way unaided to the ground. Now he lived more upon raw meat, for which he was entirely dependent on Akut's skill and generosity. With the meat diet his strength returned more rapidly, and at last he felt that he was fit to undertake the journey to the village of the blacks.

CHAPTER 12

TWO TALL, BEARDED white men moved cautiously through the jungle from their camp beside a wide river. They were Carl Jenssen and Sven Malbihn, but little altered in appearance since the day, years before, that they and their *safari* had been so badly frightened by Korak and Akut as the former sought haven with them.

Every year had they come into the jungle to trade with the natives, or to rob them; to hunt and trap; or to guide other white men in the land they knew so well. Always since their experience with The Sheik had they operated at a safe distance from his territory.

Now they were closer to his village than they had been for years, yet safe enough from discovery owing to the uninhabited nature of the intervening jungle and the fear and enmity of Kovudoo's people for The Sheik, who, in time past, had raided

The capture of Meriem.

and all but exterminated the tribe.

This year they had come to trap live specimens for a European zoological garden, and today they were approaching a trap which they had set in the hope of capturing a specimen of the large baboons that frequented the neighborhood. As they approached the trap they became aware from the noises emanating from its vicinity that their efforts had been crowned with success. The barking and screaming of hundreds of baboons could mean naught else than that one or more of their number had fallen a victim to the allurements of the bait.

The extreme caution of the two men was prompted by former experiences with the intelligent and dog-like creatures with which they had to deal. More than one trapper has lost his life in battle with enraged baboons who will hesitate to attack nothing upon one occasion, while upon another a single gun shot will disperse hundreds of them.

Heretofore the Swedes had always watched near-by their trap, for as a rule only the stronger bulls are thus caught, since in their greediness they prevent the weaker from approaching the coveted bait, and when once within the ordinary rude trap woven on the spot of interlaced branches they are able, with the aid of their friends upon the outside, to demolish their prison and escape. But in this instance the trappers had utilized a special steel cage which could withstand all the strength and cunning of a baboon. It was only necessary, therefore, to drive away the herd which they knew were surrounding the prison and wait for their boys who were even now following them to the trap.

As they came within sight of the spot they found conditions precisely as they had expected. A large male was battering frantically against the steel wires of the cage that held him captive. Upon the outside several hundred other baboons were tearing and tugging in his aid, and all were roaring and jabbering and barking at the top of their lungs.

But what neither the Swedes nor the baboons saw was the half-naked figure of a youth hidden in the foliage of a near-by tree. He had come upon the scene at almost the same instant as Jenssen and Malbihn, and was watching the activities of the baboons with every mark of interest.

Korak's relations with the baboons had never been over friendly. A species of armed toleration had marked their occasional meetings. The baboons and Akut had walked stiff legged and growling past one another, while Korak had maintained a bared fang neutrality. So now he was not greatly disturbed by the predicament of their king. Curiosity prompted him to tarry a moment, and in that moment his quick eyes caught the unfamiliar coloration of the clothing of the two Swedes behind a bush not far from him. Now he was all alertness. Who were these interlopers? What was their business in the jungle of the Mangani? Korak slunk noiselessly around them to a point where he might get their scent as well as a better view of them, and scarce had he done so when he recognized them—they were the men who had fired upon him years before. His eyes blazed. He could feel the hairs upon his scalp stiffen at the roots. He watched them with the intentness of a panther about to spring upon its prey.

He saw them rise and, shouting, attempt to frighten away the baboons as they approached the cage. Then one of them raised his rifle and fired into the midst of the surprised an angry herd. For an instant Korak thought that the baboons were about to charge, but two more shots from the rifles of the white men sent them scampering into the trees. Then the two Europeans advanced upon the cage. Korak thought that they were going to kill the king. He cared nothing for the king but he cared less for the two white men. The king had never attempted to kill him—the white men had. The king was a denizen of his own beloved jungle— the white men were aliens. His loyalty therefore was to the baboon against the human. He could speak the language of the baboon— it was identical to that of the great apes. Across the clearing he saw the jabbering horde watching.

Raising his voice he shouted to them. The white men turned at the sound of this new factor behind them. They thought it was another baboon that had circled them; but though they searched the trees with their eyes they saw nothing of the now silent figure hidden by the foliage. Again Korak shouted.

"I am The Killer," he cried. "These men are my enemies and yours. I will help you free your king. Run out upon the strangers when you see me do so, and together we will drive them away and free your king."

And from the baboons came a great chorus: "We will do what you say, Korak."

Dropping from his tree Korak ran toward the two Swedes, and at the same instant three hundred baboons followed his example. At sight of the strange apparition of the half-naked white warrior rushing upon them with uplifted spear Jenssen and Malbihn raised their rifles and fired at Korak; but in the excitement both missed and a moment later the baboons were upon them. Now their only hope of safety lay in escape, and dodging here and there, fighting off the great beasts that leaped upon their backs, they ran into the jungle. Even then they would have died but for the coming of their men whom they met a couple of hundred yards from the cage.

Once the white men had turned in flight Korak gave them no further attention, turning instead to the imprisoned baboon. The fastenings of the door that had eluded the mental powers of the baboons, yielded their secret immediately to the human intelligence of The Killer, and a moment later the king baboon stepped forth to liberty. He wasted no breath in thanks to Korak, nor did the young man expect thanks. He knew that none of the baboons would ever forget his service, though as a matter of fact he did not care if they did. What he had done had been prompted by a desire to be revenged upon the two white men. The baboons could never be of service to him. Now they were racing in the direction of the battle that was being waged between their fellows and the followers of the two Swedes, and as the din of battle subsided in the distance, Korak turned and resumed his journey toward the village of Kovudoo.

On the way he came upon a herd of elephants standing in an open forest glade. Here the trees were too far apart to permit Korak to travel through the branches—a trail he much preferred not only because of its freedom from dense underbrush and the wider field of vision it gave him but from pride in his arboreal ability. It was exhilarating to swing from tree to tree; to test the prowess of his mighty muscles; to reap the pleasurable fruits of his hard won agility. Korak joyed in the thrills of the high-flung upper terraces of the great forest, where, unhampered and unhindered, he might laugh down upon the great brutes who must keep forever to the darkness and the gloom of the musty soil.

But here, in this open glade where Tantor flapped his giant ears and swayed his huge bulk from side to side, the ape-man must pass along the surface of the ground—a pygmy amongst giants. A great bull raised his trunk to rattle a low warning as he sensed the coming of an intruder. His weak eyes roved hither and thither but it was his keen scent and acute hearing which first located the ape-man. The herd moved restlessly, prepared for flight, for the old bull had caught the scent of man.

"Peace, Tantor," called The Killer. "It is I, Korak, Tarmangani."

The bull lowered his trunk and the herd resumed their interrupted meditations. Korak passed within a foot of the great bull. A sinuous trunk undulated toward him, touching his brown hide in a half caress. Korak slapped the great shoulder affectionately as he went by. For years he had been upon good terms with Tantor and his people. Of all the jungle folk he loved best the mighty pachyderm—the most peaceful and at the same time the most terrible of them all. The gentle gazelle feared him not, yet Numa, lord of the jungle, gave him a wide berth. Among the younger bulls, the cows and the calves Korak wound his way. Now and then another trunk would run out to touch him, and once a playful calf grasped his legs and upset him.

The afternoon was almost spent when Korak arrived at the village of Kovudoo. There were many natives lolling in shady spots beside the conical huts or beneath the branches of the several trees which had been left standing within the enclosure. Warriors were in evidence upon every hand. It was not a good time for a lone enemy to prosecute a search through the village. Korak determined to await the coming of darkness. He was a match for many warriors; but he could not, unaided, overcome an entire tribe—not even for his beloved Meriem. While he waited among the branches and foliage of a near-by tree he searched the village constantly with his keen eyes, and twice he circled it, sniffing the vagrant breezes which puffed erratically from first one point of the compass and then another. Among the various stenches peculiar to a native village the ape-man's sensitive nostrils were finally rewarded by cognizance of the delicate aroma which marked the presence of her he sought. Meriem was there—in one of those huts! But which one he could not know without closer investigation, and so he waited, with the dogged patience of a beast of prey, until night had fallen.

The camp fires of the blacks dotted the gloom with little points of light, casting their feeble rays in tiny circles of luminosity that brought into glistening relief the naked bodies of those who lay or squatted about them. It was then that Korak slid silently from the tree that had hidden him and dropped lightly to the ground within the enclosure.

Keeping well in the shadows of the huts he commenced a systematic search of the village—ears, eyes and nose constantly upon the alert for the first intimation of the near presence of Meriem. His progress must of necessity be slow since not even the keen-eared curs of the savages must guess the presence of a stranger within the gates. How close he came to detection on several occasions The Killer well knew from the restless whining of several of them.

It was not until he reached the back of a hut at the head of the wide village street that Korak caught again, plainly, the scent of Meriem. With nose close to the thatched wall Korak sniffed eagerly about the structure—tense and palpitant as a hunting hound. Toward the front and the door he made his way when once his nose had assured him that Meriem lay within; but as he rounded the side and came within view of the entrance he saw a burly negro armed with a long spear squatting at the portal of the girl's prison. The fellow's back was toward him, his figure outlined against the glow of cooking fires further down the street. He was alone. The nearest of his fellows were beside a fire sixty or seventy feet beyond. To enter the hut Korak must either silence the sentry or pass him unnoticed. The danger in the accomplishment of the former alternative lay in the practical certainty of alarming the warriors near by and bringing them and the balance of the village down upon him. To achieve the latter appeared practically impossible. To you or me it would have been impossible; but Korak, The Killer, was not as you or I.

There was a good twelve inches of space between the broad back of the black and the frame of the doorway. Could Korak pass through behind the savage warrior without detection? The light that fell upon the glistening ebony of the sentry's black skin fell also upon the light brown of Korak's. Should one of the many further down the street chance to look long in this direction they must surely note the tall, light-colored, moving figure; but Korak depended upon their interest in their own gossip to hold their attention fast where it already lay, and upon the firelight near them to prevent them seeing too plainly at a distance into the darkness at the village end where his work lay.

Flattened against the side of the hut, yet not arousing a single warning rustle from its dried thatching, The Killer came closer and closer to the watcher. Now he was at his shoulder. Now he had wormed his sinuous way behind him. He could feel the heat of the naked body against his knees. He could hear the man breathe. He marveled that the dull-witted creature had not long since been alarmed; but the fellow sat there as ignorant of the presence of another as though that other had not existed.

Korak moved scarcely more than an inch at a time, then he would stand motionless for a moment. Thus was he worming his way behind the guard when the latter straightened up, opened his cavernous mouth in a wide yawn, and stretched his arms above his head. Korak stood rigid as stone. Another step and he would be within the hut. The black lowered his arms and relaxed. Behind him was the frame work of the doorway. Often before had it supported his sleepy head, and now he leaned back to enjoy the forbidden pleasure of a cat nap.

But instead of the door frame his head and shoulders came in contact with the warm flesh of a pair of living legs. The exclamation of surprise that almost burst from his lips was throttled in his throat by steel-thewed fingers that closed about his windpipe with the suddenness of thought. The black struggled to arise—to turn upon the creature that had seized him—to wriggle from its hold; but all to no purpose. As he had been held in a mighty vise of iron he could not move. He could not scream. Those awful fingers at his throat but closed more and more tightly. His eyes bulged from their sockets. His face turned an ashy blue. Presently he relaxed once more—this time in the final dissolution from which there is no quickening. Korak propped the dead body against the door frame. There it sat, lifelike in the gloom. Then the ape-man turned and glided into the Stygian darkness of the hut's interior.

"Meriem!" he whispered.

"Korak! My Korak!" came an answering cry, subdued by fear of alarming her captors, and half stifled by a sob of joyful welcome.

The youth knelt and cut the bonds that held the girl's wrists and ankles. A moment later he had lifted her to her feet, and grasping her by the hand led her towards the entrance. Outside the grim sentinel of death kept his grisly vigil. Sniffing at his dead feet whined a mangy native cur. At sight of the two emerging from the hut the beast gave an ugly snarl and an instant later as it caught the scent of the strange white man it raised a series of excited yelps. Instantly the warriors at the near-by fire were attracted. They turned their heads in the direction of the commotion. It was impossible that they should fail to see the white skins of the fugitives.

Korak slunk quickly into the shadows at the hut's side, drawing Meriem with him; but he was too late. The blacks had seen enough to arouse their suspicions and a dozen of them were now running to investigate. The yapping cur was still at Korak's heels leading the searchers unerringly in pursuit. The youth struck viciously at the brute with his long spear; but, long accustomed to dodging blows, the wily creature made a most uncertain target.

Other blacks had been alarmed by the running and shouting of their companions and now the entire population of the village was swarming up the street to assist in the search. Their first discovery was the dead body of the sentry, and a moment later one of the bravest of them had entered the hut and discovered the absence of the prisoner. These startling announcements filled the blacks with a combination of terror and rage; but, seeing no foe in evidence they were enabled to permit their rage to get the better of their terror, and so the leaders, pushed on by those behind them, ran rapidly around the hut in the direction of the yapping of the mangy cur. Here they found a single white warrior making away with their captive, and recognizing him as the author of numerous raids and indignities and believing that they had him cornered and at a disadvantage, they charged savagely upon him.

Korak, seeing that they were discovered, lifted Meriem to his shoulder and ran for the tree which would give them egress from the village. He was handicapped in his flight by the weight of the girl whose legs would but scarce bear her weight, to say nothing of maintaining her in rapid flight, for the tightly drawn bonds that had been about her ankles for so long had stopped circulation and partially paralyzed her extremities.

Had this not been the case the escape of the two would have been a feat of little moment, since Meriem was scarcely a whit less agile than Korak, and fully as much at home in the trees as he. But with the girl on his shoulder Korak could not both run and fight to advantage, and the result was that before he had covered half the distance to the tree a score of native curs attracted by the yelping of their mate and the yells and shouts of their masters had closed in upon the fleeing white man, snapping at his legs and at last succeeding in tripping him. As he went down the hyena-like brutes were upon him, and as he struggled to his feet the blacks closed in.

A couple of them seized the clawing, biting Meriem, and subdued her—a blow upon the head was sufficient. For the ape-man they found more drastic measures would be necessary. Weighted down as he was by dogs and warriors he still managed to struggle to his feet. To right and left he swung crushing blows to the faces of his human antagonists—to the dogs he paid not the slightest attention other than to seize the more persistent and wring their necks with a single quick movement of the wrist.

A knob stick aimed at him by an ebon Hercules he caught and wrested from his antagonist, and then the blacks experienced to the full the possibilities for punishment that lay within those smooth flowing muscles beneath the velvet brown skin of the strange, white giant. He rushed among them with all the force and ferocity of a bull elephant gone mad. Hither and thither he charged striking down the few who had the temerity to stand against him, and it was evident that unless a chance spear thrust brought him down he would rout the entire village and regain his prize. But old Kovudoo was not to be so easily robbed of the ransom which the girl represented, and seeing that their weakness lay in the undisciplined method of their attack which had up to now resulted in a series of individual combats with the white warrior, he called his tribesmen off, and forming them in a compact body about the girl and the two who watched over her bid them do nothing more than repel the assaults of the ape-man.

Again and again Korak rushed against this human barricade bristling with spear points. Again and again he was repulsed, often with severe wounds to caution him to greater wariness. From head to foot he was red with his own blood, and at last, weakening from the loss of it, he came to the bitter realization that alone he could do no more to succor his Meriem.

Presently an idea flashed through his brain. He called aloud to the girl. She had regained consciousness now and replied.

"Korak goes," he shouted; "but he will return and take you from the Gomangani. Good-bye, my Meriem. Korak will come for you again."

"Good-bye!" cried the girl. "Meriem will look for you until you come."

Like a flash, and before they could know his intention or prevent him, Korak wheeled, raced across the village and with a single leap disappeared into the foliage of the great tree that was his highroad to the village of Kovudoo. A shower of spears followed him, but their only harvest was a taunting laugh flung back from out the darkness of the jungle.

CHAPTER 13

MERIEM, AGAIN BOUND and under heavy guard in Kovudoo's own hut, saw the night pass and the new day come without bringing the momentarily looked for return of Korak. She had no doubt but that he would come back and less still that he would easily free her from her captivity. To her Korak was little short of omnipotent. He embodied for her all that was finest and strongest and best in her savage world. She gloried in his prowess and worshipped him for the tender thoughtfulness that always had marked his treatment of her. No other within the ken of her memory had ever accorded her the love and gentleness that was his daily offering to her. Most of the gentler attributes of his early childhood had long since been forgotten in the fierce battle for existence which the customs of the mysterious jungle had forced upon him. He was more often savage and bloodthirsty than tender and kindly. His other friends of the wild looked for no gentle tokens of his affection. That he would hunt with them and fight for them was sufficient. If he growled and showed his fighting fangs when they trespassed upon his inalienable rights to the fruits of his kills they felt no anger toward him—only greater respect for the efficient and the fit—for him who could not only kill but protect the flesh of his kill.

But toward Meriem he always had shown more of his human side. He killed primarily for her. It was to the feet of Meriem that he brought the fruits of his labors. It was for Meriem more than for himself that he squatted beside his flesh and growled ominously at whosoever dared sniff too closely to it. When he was cold in the dark days of rain, or thirsty in a prolonged drouth, his discomfort engendered first of all thoughts of Meriem's welfare—after she had been made warm, after her thirst had been slaked, then he turned to the affair of ministering to his own wants.

The softest skins fell gracefully from the graceful shoulders of his Meriem. The sweetest-scented grasses lined her bower where other soft, furry pelts made hers the downiest couch in all the jungle.

What wonder then that Meriem loved her Korak? But she loved

him as a little sister might love a big brother who was very good to her. As yet she knew naught of the love of a maid for a man.

So now as she lay waiting for him she dreamed of him and of all that he meant to her. She compared him with The Sheik, her father, and at thought of the stern, grizzled, old Arab she shuddered. Even the savage blacks had been less harsh to her than he. Not understanding their tongue she could not guess what purpose they had in keeping her a prisoner. She knew that man ate man, and she had expected to be eaten; but she had been with them for some time now and no harm had befallen her. She did not know that a runner had been dispatched to the distant village of The Sheik to barter with him for a ransom. She did not know, nor did Kovudoo, that the runner had never reached his destination— that he had fallen in with the *safari* of Jenssen and Malbihn and with the talkativeness of a native to other natives had unfolded his whole mission to the black servants of the two Swedes. These had not been long in retailing the matter to their masters, and the result was that when the runner left their camp to continue his journey he had scarce passed from sight before there came the report of a rifle and he rolled lifeless into the underbrush with a bullet in his back.

A few moments later Malbihn strolled back into the encampment, where he went to some pains to let it be known that he had had a shot at a fine buck and missed. The Swedes knew that their men hated them, and that an overt act against Kovudoo would quickly be carried to the chief at the first opportunity. Nor were they sufficiently strong in either guns or loyal followers to risk antagonizing the wily old chief.

Following this episode came the encounter with the baboons and the strange, white savage who had allied himself with the beasts against the humans. Only by dint of masterful maneuvering and the expenditure of much powder had the Swedes been able to repulse the infuriated apes, and even for hours afterward their camp was constantly besieged by hundreds of snarling, screaming devils.

The Swedes, rifles in hand, repelled numerous savage charges which lacked only efficient leadership to have rendered them as effective in results as they were terrifying in appearance. Time and time again the two men thought they saw the smooth-skinned body of the wild ape-man moving among the baboons in the forest, and the belief that he might head a charge upon them proved most disquieting. They would have given much for a clean shot at him, for to him they attributed the loss of their specimen and the ugly attitude of the baboons toward them.

"The fellow must be the same we fired on several years ago," said Malbihn. "That time he was accompanied by a gorilla. Did you get a good look at him, Carl?"

"Yes," replied Jenssen. "He was not five paces from me when I fired at him. He appears to be an intelligent looking European—and not much more than a lad. There is nothing of the imbecile or degenerate in his features or expression, as is usually true in similar cases, where some lunatic escapes into the woods and by living in filth and nakedness wins the title of wild man among the peasants of the neighborhood. No, this fellow is of different stuff—and so infinitely more to be feared. As much as I should like a shot at him I hope he stays away. Should he ever deliberately lead a charge against us I wouldn't give much for our chances if we happened to fail to bag him at the first rush."

But the white giant did not appear again to lead the baboons against them, and finally the angry brutes themselves wandered off into the jungle leaving the frightened *safari* in peace.

The next day the Swedes set out for Kovudoo's village bent on securing possession of the person of the white girl whom Kovudoo's runner had told them lay captive in the chief's village. How they were to accomplish their end they did not know. Force was out of the question, though they would not have hesitated to use it had they possessed it. In former years they had marched rough shod over enormous areas, taking toll by brute force even when kindliness or diplomacy would have accomplished more; but now they were in bad straits—so bad that they had shown their true colors scarce twice in a year and then only when they came upon an isolated village, weak in numbers and poor in courage.

Kovudoo was not as these, and though his village was in a way remote from the more populous district to the north his power was such that he maintained an acknowledged suzerainty over the thin thread of villages which connected him with the savage lords to the north. To have antagonized him would have spelled ruin for the Swedes. It would have meant that they might never reach civilization by the northern route. To the west, the village of The Sheik lay directly in their path, barring them effectually. To the east the trail was unknown to them, and to the south there was no trail. So the two Swedes approached the village of Kovudoo with friendly words upon their tongues and deep craft in their hearts.

Their plans were well made. There was no mention of the white prisoner—they chose to pretend that they were not aware that Kovudoo had a white prisoner. They exchanged gifts with the old chief, haggling with his plenipotentiaries over the value of what they were to receive for what they gave, as is customary and proper when one has no ulterior motives. Unwarranted generosity would have aroused suspicion.

During the palaver which followed they retailed the gossip of the villages through which they had passed, receiving in exchange such news as Kovudoo possessed. The palaver was long and tiresome, as these native ceremonies always are to Europeans. Kovudoo made no mention of his prisoner and from his generous offers of guides and presents seemed anxious to assure himself of the speedy departure of his guests. It was Malbihn who, quite casually, near the close of their talk, mentioned the fact that The Sheik was dead. Kovudoo evinced interest and surprise.

"You did not know it?" asked Malbihn. "That is strange. It was during the last moon. He fell from his horse when the beast stepped in a hole. The horse fell upon him. When his men came up The Sheik was quite dead."

Kovudoo scratched his head. He was much disappointed. No Sheik meant no ransom for the white girl. Now she was worthless, unless he utilized her for a feast or—a mate. The latter thought aroused him. He spat at a small beetle crawling through the dust before him. He eyed Malbihn appraisingly. These white men were peculiar. They traveled far from their own villages without women. Yet he knew that they cared for women. But how much did they care for them?—that was the question that disturbed Kovudoo.

"I know where there is a white girl," he said, unexpectedly. "If you wish to buy her she may be had cheap."

Malbihn shrugged. "We have troubles enough, Kovudoo," he said, "without burdening ourselves with an old she-hyena, and as for paying for one—" Malbihn snapped his fingers in derision.

"She is young," said Kovudoo, "and good looking."

The Swedes laughed. "There are no good-looking white women in the jungle, Kovudoo," said Jenssen. "You should be ashamed to try to make fun of old friends."

Kovudoo sprang to his feet. "Come," he said, "I will show you that she is all I say."

Malbihn and Jenssen rose to follow him and as they did so their eyes met, and Malbihn slowly drooped one of his lids in a sly wink. Together they followed Kovudoo toward his hut. In the dim interior they discerned the figure of a woman lying bound upon a sleeping mat.

Malbihn took a single glance and turned away. "She must be a thousand years old, Kovudoo," he said, as he left the hut.

"She is young," cried the savage. "It is dark in here. You cannot see. Wait, I will have her brought out into the sunlight," and he commanded the two warriors who watched the girl to cut the bonds from her ankles and lead her forth for inspection.

Malbihn and Jenssen evinced no eagerness, though both were fairly bursting with it—not to see the girl but to obtain possession of her. They cared not if she had the face of a marmoset, or the figure of pot-bellied Kovudoo himself. All that they wished to know was that she was the girl who had been stolen from The Sheik several years before. They thought that they would recognize her for such if she was indeed the same, but even so the testimony of the runner Kovudoo had sent to The Sheik was such as to assure them that the girl was the one they had once before attempted to abduct.

As Meriem was brought forth from the darkness of the hut's interior the two men turned with every appearance of disinterestedness to glance at her. It was with difficulty that Malbihn suppressed an ejaculation of astonishment. The girl's beauty fairly took his breath from him; but instantly he recovered his poise and turned to Kovudoo.

"Well?" he said to the old chief.

"Is she not both young and good looking?" asked Kovudoo.

"She is not old," replied Malbihn; "but even so she will be a burden. We did not come from the north after wives—there are more than enough there for us."

Meriem stood looking straight at the white men. She expected nothing from them—they were to her as much enemies as the black men. She hated and feared them all. Malbihn spoke to her in Arabic.

"We are friends," he said. "Would you like to have us take you away from here?"

Slowly and dimly as though from a great distance recollection of the once familiar tongue returned to her.

"I should like to go free," she said, "and go back to Korak."

Meriem was brought forth into the sunlight.

"You would like to go with us?" persisted Malbihn.

"No," said Meriem.

Malbihn turned to Kovudoo. "She does not wish to go with us," he said.

"You are men," returned the black. "Can you not take her by force?"

"It would only add to our troubles," replied the Swede. "No, Kovudoo, we do not wish her; though, if you wish to be rid of her, we will take her away because of our friendship for you."

Now Kovudoo knew that he had made a sale. They wanted her. So he commenced to bargain, and in the end the person of Meriem passed from the possession of the black chieftain into that of the two Swedes in consideration of six yards of Amerikan, three empty brass cartridge shells and a shiny, new jack knife from New Jersey. And all but Meriem were more than pleased with the bargain.

Kovudoo stipulated but a single condition and that was that the Europeans were to leave his village and take the girl with them as early the next morning as they could get started. After the sale was consummated he did not hesitate to explain his reasons for this demand. He told them of the strenuous attempt of the girl's savage mate to rescue her, and suggested that the sooner they got her out of the country the more likely they were to retain possession of her.

Meriem was again bound and placed under guard, but this time in the tent of the Swedes. Malbihn talked to her, trying to persuade her to accompany them willingly. He told her that they would return her to her own village; but when he discovered that she would rather die than go back to the old sheik he assured her that they would not take her there, nor, as a matter of fact, had they had an intention of so doing. As he talked with the girl the Swede feasted his eyes upon the beautiful lines of her face and figure. She had grown tall and straight and slender toward maturity since he had seen her in The Sheik's village on that long gone day. For years she had represented to him a certain fabulous reward. In his thoughts she had been but the personification of the pleasures and luxuries that many francs would purchase. Now as she stood before him pulsing with life and loveliness she suggested other seductive and alluring possibilities. He came closer to her and laid his hand upon her. The girl shrank from him. He seized her and she struck him heavily in the mouth as he sought to kiss her. Then Jenssen entered the tent.

"Malbihn!" he almost shouted. "You fool!"

Sven Malbihn released his hold upon the girl and turned toward his companion. His face was red with mortification.

"What the devil are you trying to do?" growled Jenssen. "Would you throw away every chance for the reward? If we maltreat her we not only couldn't collect a sou, but they'd send us to prison for our pains. I thought you had more sense, Malbihn."

"I'm not a wooden man," growled Malbihn.

"You'd better be," rejoined Jenssen, "at least until we have delivered her over in safety and collected what will be coming to us."

"Oh, hell," cried Malbihn. "What's the use? They'll be glad enough to have her back, and by the time we get there with her she'll be only too glad to keep her mouth shut. Why not?"

"Because I say not," growled Jenssen. "I've always let you boss things, Sven; but here's a case where what I say has got to go—because I'm right and you're wrong, and we both know it."

"You're getting damned virtuous all of a sudden," growled Malbihn. "Perhaps you think I have forgotten about the inn keeper's daughter, and little Celella, and that nigger at—"

"Shut up!" snapped Jenssen. "It's not a matter of virtue and you are as well aware of that as I. I don't want to quarrel with you, but so help me God, Sven, you're not going to harm this girl if I have to kill you to prevent it. I've suffered and slaved and been nearly killed forty times in the last nine or ten years trying to accomplish what luck has thrown at our feet at last, and now I'm not going to be robbed of the fruits of success because you happen to be more of a beast than a man. Again I warn you, Sven—" and he tapped the revolver that swung in its holster at his hip.

Malbihn gave his friend an ugly look, shrugged his shoulders, and left the tent. Jenssen turned to Meriem.

"If he bothers you again, call me," he said. "I shall always be near."

The girl had not understood the conversation that had been carried on by her two owners, for it had been in Swedish; but what Jenssen had just said to her in Arabic she understood and from it grasped an excellent idea of what had passed between the two. The expressions upon their faces, their gestures, and Jenssen's final tapping of his revolver before Malbihn had left the tent had all been eloquent of the seriousness of their altercation. Now, toward Jenssen she looked for friendship, and with the innocence of youth she threw herself upon his mercy, begging him to set her free, that she might return to Korak and her jungle life; but she was doomed to another disappointment, for the man only laughed at her roughly and told her that if she tried to escape she would be punished by the very thing that he had just saved her from.

All that night she lay listening for a signal from Korak. All about the jungle life moved through the darkness. To her sensitive ears came sounds that the others in the camp could not hear— sounds that she interpreted as we might interpret the speech of a friend, but not once came a single note that reflected the presence of Korak. But she knew that he would come. Nothing short of death itself could prevent her Korak from returning for her. What delayed him though?

When morning came again and the night had brought no succoring Korak, Meriem's faith and loyalty were still unshaken though misgivings began to assail her as to the safety of her friend. It seemed unbelievable that serious mishap could have overtaken her wonderful Korak who daily passed unscathed through all the terrors of the jungle. Yet morning came, the morning meal was eaten, the camp broken and the disreputable *safari* of the Swedes was on the move northward with still no sign of the rescue the girl momentarily expected.

All that day they marched, and the next and the next, nor did Korak even so much as show himself to the patient little waiter moving, silently and stately, beside her hard captors.

Malbihn remained scowling and angry. He replied to Jenssen's friendly advances in curt monosyllables. To Meriem he did not speak, but on several occasions she discovered him glaring at her from beneath half closed lids—greedily. The look sent a shudder through her. She hugged Geeka closer to her breast and doubly regretted the knife that they had taken from her when she was captured by Kovudoo.

It was on the fourth day that Meriem began definitely to give up hope. Something had happened to Korak. She knew it. He would never come now, and these men would take her far away. Presently they would kill her. She would never see her Korak again.

On this day the Swedes rested, for they had marched rapidly

and their men were tired. Malbihn and Jenssen had gone from camp to hunt, taking different directions. They had been gone about an hour when the door of Meriem's tent was lifted and Malbihn entered. The look of a beast was on his face.

CHAPTER 14

WITH WIDE EYES fixed upon him, like a trapped creature horrified beneath the mesmeric gaze of a great serpent, the girl watched the approach of the man. Her hands were free, the Swedes having secured her with a length of ancient slave chain fastened at one end to an iron collar padlocked about her neck and at the other to a long stake driven deep into the ground.

Slowly Meriem shrank inch by inch toward the opposite end of the tent. Malbihn followed her. His hands were extended and his fingers half-opened—claw-like—to seize her. His lips were parted, and his breath came quickly, pantingly.

The girl recalled Jenssen's instructions to call him should Malbihn molest her; but Jenssen had gone into the jungle to hunt. Malbihn had chosen his time well. Yet she screamed, loud and shrill, once, twice, a third time, before Malbihn could leap across the tent and throttle her alarming cries with his brute fingers. Then she fought him, as any jungle she might fight, with tooth and nail. The man found her no easy prey. In that slender, young body, beneath the rounded curves and the fine, soft skin, lay the muscles of a young lioness. But Malbihn was no weakling. His character and appearance were brutal, nor did they belie his brawn. He was of giant stature and of giant strength. Slowly he forced the girl back upon the ground, striking her in the face when she hurt him badly either with teeth or nails. Meriem struck back, but she was growing weaker from the choking fingers at her throat.

Out in the jungle Jenssen had brought down two bucks. His hunting had not carried him far afield, nor was he prone to permit it to do so. He was suspicious of Malbihn. The very fact that his companion had refused to accompany him and elected instead to hunt alone in another direction would not, under ordinary circumstances, have seemed fraught with sinister suggestion; but Jenssen knew Malbihn well, and so, having secured meat, he turned immediately back toward camp, while his boys brought in his kill.

He had covered about half the return journey when a scream came faintly to his ears from the direction of camp. He halted to listen. It was repeated twice. Then silence. With a muttered curse Jenssen broke into a rapid run. He wondered if he would be too late. What a fool Malbihn was indeed to thus chance jeopardizing a fortune!

Further away from camp than Jenssen and upon the opposite side another heard Meriem's screams—a stranger who was not even aware of the proximity of white men other than himself— a hunter with a handful of sleek, black warriors. He, too, listened intently for a moment. That the voice was that of a woman in distress he could not doubt, and so he also hastened at a run in the direction of the affrighted voice; but he was much further away than Jenssen so that the latter reached the tent first. What the Swede found there roused no pity within his calloused heart, only anger against his fellow scoundrel. Meriem was still fighting off her attacker. Malbihn still was showering blows upon her. Jenssen, streaming foul curses upon his erstwhile friend, burst into the tent. Malbihn, interrupted, dropped his victim and turned to meet Jenssen's infuriated charge. He whipped a revolver from his hip. Jenssen, anticipating the lightning move of the other's hand, drew almost simultaneously, and both men fired at once. Jenssen was still moving toward Malbihn at the time, but at the flash of the explosion he stopped. His revolver dropped from nerveless fingers. For a moment he staggered drunkenly. Deliberately Malbihn put two more bullets into his friend's body at close range. Even in the midst of the excitement and her terror Meriem found herself wondering at the tenacity of life which the hit man displayed. His eyes were closed, his head dropped forward upon his breast, his hands hung limply before him. Yet still he stood there upon his feet, though he reeled horribly. It was not until the third bullet had found its mark within his body that he lunged forward upon his face. Then Malbihn approached him, and with an oath kicked him viciously. Then he returned once more to Meriem. Again he seized her, and at the same instant the flaps of the tent opened silently and a tall white man stood in the aperture. Neither Meriem nor Malbihn saw the newcomer. The latter's back was toward him while his body hid the stranger from Meriem's eyes.

He crossed the tent quickly, stepping over Jenssen's body. The first intimation Malbihn had that he was not to carry out his design without further interruption was a heavy hand upon his shoulder. He wheeled to face an utter stranger—a tall, black-haired, gray-eyed stranger clad in khaki and pith helmet. Malbihn reached for his gun again, but another hand had been quicker than his and he saw the weapon tossed to the ground at the side of the tent—out of reach.

"What is the meaning of this?" the stranger addressed his question to Meriem in a tongue she did not understand. She shook her head and spoke in Arabic. Instantly the man changed his question to that language.

"These men are taking me away from Korak," explained the girl. "This one would have harmed me. The other, whom he has just killed, tried to stop him. They were both very bad men; but this one is the worse. If my Korak were here he would kill him. I suppose you are like them, so you will not kill him."

The stranger smiled. "He deserves killing?" he said. "There is no doubt of that. Once I should have killed him; but not now. I will see, though, that he does not bother you any more."

He was holding Malbihn in a grasp the giant Swede could not break, though he struggled to do so, and he was holding him as easily as Malbihn might have held a little child, yet Malbihn was a huge man, mightily thewed. The Swede began to rage and curse. He struck at his captor, only to be twisted about and held at arm's length. Then he shouted to his boys to come and kill the stranger. In response a dozen strange blacks entered the tent. They, too, were powerful, clean-limbed men, not at all like the mangy crew that followed the Swedes.

"We have had enough foolishness," said the stranger to Malbihn. "You deserve death, but I am not the law. I know now who you are. I have heard of you before. You and your friend here bear a most unsavory reputation. We do not want you in our country. I shall let you go this time; but should you ever return I shall take the law into my own hands. You understand?"

Malbihn blustered and threatened, finishing by applying a most uncomplimentary name to his captor. For this he received a shaking that rattled his teeth. Those who know say that the most painful punishment that can be inflicted upon an adult male, short of injuring him, is a good, old fashioned shaking. Malbihn received such a shaking.

"Now get out," said the stranger, "and next time you see me

remember who I am," and he spoke a name in the Swede's ear—
a name that more effectually subdued the scoundrel than many
beatings—then he gave him a push that carried him bodily through
the tent doorway to sprawl upon the turf beyond.

"Now," he said, turning toward Meriem, "who has the key to
this thing about your neck?"

The girl pointed to Jenssen's body. "He carried it always," she
said.

The stranger searched the clothing on the corpse until he came
upon the key. A moment more Meriem was free.

"Will you let me go back to my Korak?" she asked.

"I will see that you are returned to your people," he replied.
"Who are they and where is their village?"

He had been eyeing her strange, barbaric garmenture wonderingly. From her speech she was evidently an Arab girl; but he
had never before seen one thus clothed.

"Who are your people? Who is Korak?" he asked again.

"Korak! Why Korak is an ape. I have no other people. Korak
and I live in the jungle alone since A'ht went to be king of the
apes." She had always thus pronounced Akut's name, for so it
had sounded to her when first she came with Korak and the ape.
"Korak could have been king, but he would not."

A questioning expression entered the stranger's eyes. He looked
at the girl closely.

"So Korak is an ape?" he said. "And what, pray, are you?"

"I am Meriem. I, also, am an ape."

"M-m," was the stranger's only oral comment upon this startling
announcement; but what he thought might have been partially
interpreted through the pitying light that entered his eyes. He
approached the girl and started to lay his hand upon her forehead.
She drew back with a savage little growl. A smile touched his lips.

"You need not fear me," he said. "I shall not harm you. I only
wish to discover if you have fever—if you are entirely well. If
you are we will set forth in search of Korak."

Meriem looked straight into the keen gray eyes. She must have
found there an unquestionable assurance of the honorableness of
their owner, for she permitted him to lay his palm upon her
forehead and feel her pulse. Apparently she had no fever.

"How long have you been an ape?" asked the man.

"Since I was a little girl, many, many years ago, and Korak
came and took me from my father who was beating me. Since

then I have lived in the trees with Korak and A'ht."

"Where in the jungle lives Korak?" asked the stranger.

Meriem pointed with a sweep of her hand that took in, generously, half the continent of Africa.

"Could you find your way back to him?"

"I do not know," she replied; "but he will find his way to me."

"Then I have a plan," said the stranger. "I live but a few marches from here. I shall take you home where my wife will look after you and care for you until we can find Korak or Korak finds us. If he could find you here he can find you at my village. Is it not so?"

Meriem thought that it was so; but she did not like the idea of not starting immediately back to meet Korak. On the other hand the man had no intention of permitting this poor, insane child to wander further amidst the dangers of the jungle. From whence she had come, or what she had undergone he could not guess, but that her Korak and their life among the apes was but a figment of a disordered mind he could not doubt. He knew the jungle well, and he knew that men had lived alone and naked among the savage beasts for years; but a frail and slender girl! No, it was not possible.

Together they went outside. Malbihn's boys were striking camp in preparation for a hasty departure. The stranger's blacks were conversing with them. Malbihn stood at a distance, angry and glowering. The stranger approached one of his own men.

"Find out where they got this girl," he commanded.

The negro thus addressed questioned one of Malbihn's followers. Presently he returned to his master.

"They bought her from old Kovudoo," he said. "That is all that this fellow will tell me. He pretends that he knows nothing more, and I guess that he does not. These two white men were very bad men. They did many things that their boys knew not the meanings of. It would be well, Bwana, to kill the other."

"I wish that I might; but a new law is come into this part of the jungle. It is not as it was in the old days, Muviri," replied the master.

The stranger remained until Malbihn and his *safari* had disappeared into the jungle toward the north. Meriem, trustful now, stood at his side, Geeka clutched in one slim, brown hand. They talked together, the man wondering at the faltering Arabic of the girl, but attributing it finally to her defective mentality. Could he

have known that years had elapsed since she had used it until
she was taken by the Swedes he would not have wondered that
she had half forgotten it. There was yet another reason why the
language of The Sheik had thus readily eluded her; but of that
reason she herself could not have guessed the truth any better
than could the man.

He tried to persuade her to return with him to his "village" as
he called it, or *douar,* in Arabic; but she was insistent upon
searching immediately for Korak. As a last resort he determined
to take her with him by force rather than sacrifice her life to the
insane hallucination which haunted her; but, being a wise man,
he determined to humor her first and then attempt to lead her
as he would have her go. So when they took up their march it
was in the direction of the south, though his own ranch lay almost
due east.

By degrees he turned the direction of their way more and more
eastward, and greatly was he pleased to note that the girl failed
to discover that any change was being made. Little by little she
became more trusting. At first she had had but her intuition to
guide her belief that this big Tarmangani meant her no harm, but
as the days passed and she saw that his kindness and consideration
never faltered she came to compare him with Korak, and to be
very fond of him; but never did her loyalty to her ape-man flag.

On the fifth day they came suddenly upon a great plain and
from the edge of the forest the girl saw in the distance fenced
fields and many buildings. At the sight she drew back in astonishment.

"Where are we?" she asked, pointing.

"We could not find Korak," replied the man, "and as our way
led near my *douar* I have brought you here to wait and rest with
my wife until my men can find your ape, or he finds you. It is
better thus, little one. You will be safer with us, and you will be
happier."

"I am afraid, Bwana," said the girl. "In thy douar they will
beat me as did The Sheik, my father. Let me go back into the
jungle. There Korak will find me. He would not think to look
for me in the douar of a white man."

"No one will beat you, child," replied the man. "I have not
done so, have I? Well, here all belong to me. They will treat you
well. Here no one is beaten. My wife will be very good to you,

and at last Korak will come, for I shall send men to search for him."

The girl shook her head. "They could not bring him, for he would kill them, as all men have tried to kill him. I am afraid. Let me go, Bwana."

"You do not know the way to your own country. You would be lost. The leopards or the lions would get you the first night, and after all you would not find your Korak. It is better that you stay with us. Did I not save you from the bad man? Do you not owe me something for that? Well, then remain with us for a few weeks at least until we can determine what is best for you. You are only a little girl—it would be wicked to permit you to go alone into the jungle."

Meriem laughed. "The jungle," she said, "is my father and my mother. It has been kinder to me than have men. I am not afraid of the jungle. Nor am I afraid of the leopard or the lion. When my time comes I shall die. It may be that a leopard or a lion shall kill me, or it may be a tiny bug no bigger than the end of my littlest finger. When the lion leaps upon me, or the little bug stings me I shall be afraid—oh, then I shall be terribly afraid, I know; but life would be very miserable indeed were I to spend it in terror of the thing that has not yet happened. If it be the lion my terror shall be short of life; but if it be the little bug I may suffer for days before I die. And so I fear the lion least of all. He is great and noisy. I can hear him, or see him, or smell him in time to escape; but any moment I may place a hand or foot on the little bug, and never know that he is there until I feel his deadly sting. No, I do not fear the jungle. I love it. I should rather die than leave it forever; but your *douar* is close beside the jungle. You have been good to me. I will do as you wish, and remain here for a while to wait the coming of my Korak."

"Good!" said the man, and he led the way down toward the flower-covered bungalow behind which lay the barns and outhouses of a well-ordered African farm.

As they came nearer a dozen dogs ran barking toward them— gaunt wolf hounds, a huge great Dane, a nimble-footed collie and a number of yapping, quarrelsome fox terriers. At first their appearance was savage and unfriendly in the extreme; but once they recognized the foremost black warriors, and the white men behind them their attitude underwent a remarkable change. The collie and the fox terriers became frantic with delirious joy, and while the wolf hounds and the great Dane were not a whit less delighted at the return of their master their greetings were of a more dignified nature. Each in turn sniffed at Meriem who displayed not the slightest fear of any of them.

The wolf hounds bristled and growled at the scent of wild beasts that clung to her garment; but when she layed her hand upon their heads and her soft voice murmured caressingly they half-closed their eyes, lifting their upper lips in contented canine smiles. The man was watching them and he too smiled, for it was seldom that these savage brutes took thus kindly to strangers. It was as though in some subtile way the girl had breathed a message of kindred savagery to their savage hearts.

With her slim fingers grasping the collar of a wolf hound upon either side of her Meriem walked on toward the bungalow upon the porch of which a woman dressed in white waved a welcome to her returning lord. There was more fear in the girl's eyes now than there had been in the presence of strange men or savage beasts. She hesitated, turning an appealing glance toward the man.

"That is my wife," he said. "She will be glad to welcome you."

The woman came down the path to meet them. The man kissed her, and turning toward Meriem introduced them, speaking in the Arab tongue the girl understood.

"This is Meriem, my dear," he said, and he told the story of the jungle waif in so far as he knew it.

Meriem saw that the woman was beautiful. She saw that sweetness and goodness were stamped indelibly upon her countenance. She no longer feared her, and when her brief story had been narrated and the woman came and put her arms about her and kissed her and called her "poor little darling" something snapped in Meriem's little heart. She buried her face on the bosom of this new friend in whose voice was the mother tone that Meriem had not heard for so many years that she had forgotten its very existence. She buried her face on the kindly bosom and wept as she had not wept before in all her life—tears of relief and joy that she could not fathom.

And so came Meriem, the savage little Mangani, out of her beloved jungle into the midst of a home of culture and refinement. Already "Bwana" and "My Dear," as she first heard them called and continued to call them, were as father and mother to her. Once her savage fears allayed, she went to the opposite extreme of trustfulness and love. Now she was willing to wait here until they found Korak, or Korak found her. She did not give up that thought—Korak, her Korak always was first.

CHAPTER 15

AND OUT IN the jungle, far away, Korak, covered with wounds, stiff with clotted blood, burning with rage and sorrow, swung back upon the trail of the great baboons. He had not found them where he had last seen them, nor in any of their usual haunts; but he sought them along the well-marked spoor they had left behind them, and at last he overtook them. When first he came upon them they were moving slowly but steadily southward in one of those periodic migrations the reasons for which the baboon himself is best able to explain. At sight of the white warrior who came upon them from down wind the herd halted in response to the warning cry of the sentinel that had discovered him. There was much growling and muttering; much stiff-legged circling on the part of the bulls. The mothers, in nervous, high pitched tones, called their young to their sides, and with them moved to safety behind their lords and masters.

Korak called aloud to the king, who, at the familiar voice, advanced slowly, warily, and still stiff-legged. He must have the confirmatory evidence of his nose before venturing to rely too implicitly upon the testimony of his ears and eyes. Korak stood perfectly still. To have advanced then might have precipitated an immediate attack, or, as easily, a panic of flight. Wild beasts are creatures of nerves. It is a relatively simple thing to throw them into a species of hysteria which may induce either a mania for murder, or symptoms of apparent abject cowardice—it is a question, however, if a wild animal ever is actually a coward.

The king baboon approached Korak. He walked around him in an ever decreasing circle—growling, grunting, sniffling. Korak spoke to him.

"I am Korak," he said. "I opened the cage that held you. I saved you from the Termangani. I am Korak, The Killer. I am your friend."

"Huh," grunted the king. "Yes, you are Korak. My ears told me that you were Korak. My eyes told me that you were Korak. Now my nose tells me that you are Korak. My nose is never wrong. I am your friend. Come, we shall hunt together."

"Korak cannot hunt now," replied the ape-man. "The Gom-angani have stolen Meriem. They have tied her in their village. They will not let her go. Korak, alone, was unable to set her free. Korak set you free. Now will you bring your people and set Korak's Meriem free?"

"The Gomangani have many sharp sticks which they throw. They pierce the bodies of my people. They kill us. The Gomangani are bad people. They will kill us all if we enter their village."

"The Tarmangani have sticks that make a loud noise and kill at a great distance," replied Korak. "They had these when Korak set you free from their trap. If Korak had run away from them you would now be a prisoner among the Tarmangani."

The baboon scratched his head. In a rough circle about him and the ape-man squatted the bulls of his herd. They blinked their eyes, shouldered one another about for more advantageous positions, scratched in the rotting vegetation upon the chance of unearthing a toothsome worm, or sat listlessly eyeing their king and the strange Mangani, who called himself thus but who more closely resembled the hated Tarmangani. The king looked at some of the older of his subjects, as though inviting suggestion.

"We are too few," grunted one.

"There are the baboons of the hill country," suggested another. "They are as many as the leaves of the forest. They, too, hate the Gomangani. They love to fight. They are very savage. Let us ask them to accompany us. Then can we kill all the Gomangani in the jungle." He rose and growled horribly, bristling his stiff hair.

"That is the way to talk," cried The Killer, "but we do not need the baboons of the hill country. We are enough. It will take a long time to fetch them. Meriem may be dead and eaten before we could free her. Let us set out at once for the village of the Gomangani. If we travel very fast it will not take long to reach it. Then, all at the same time, we can charge into the village, growling and barking. The Gomangani will be very frightened and will run away. While they are gone we can seize Meriem and carry her off. We do not have to kill or be killed—all that Korak wishes is his Meriem."

"We are too few," croaked the old ape again.

"Yes, we are too few," echoed others.

Korak could not persuade them. They would help him, gladly;

but they must do it in their own way and that meant enlisting the services of their kinsmen and allies of the hill country. So Korak was forced to give in. All he could do for the present was to urge them to haste, and at his suggestion the king baboon with a dozen of his mightiest bulls agreed to go to the hill country with Korak, leaving the balance of the herd behind.

Once enlisted in the adventure the baboons became quite enthusiastic about it. The delegation set off immediately. They traveled swiftly; but the ape-man found no difficulty in keeping up with them. They made a tremendous racket as they passed through the trees in an endeavor to suggest to enemies in their front that a great herd was approaching, for when the baboons travel in large numbers there is no jungle creature who cares to molest them. When the nature of the country required much travel upon the level, and the distance between trees was great, they moved silently, knowing that the lion and the leopard would not be fooled by noise when they could see plainly for themselves that only a handful of baboons were on the trail.

For two days the party raced through the savage country, passing out of the dense jungle into an open plain, and across this to timbered mountain slopes. Here Korak never before had been. It was a new country to him and the change from the monotony of the circumscribed view in the jungle was pleasing. But he had little desire to enjoy the beauties of nature at this time. Meriem, his Meriem was in danger. Until she was freed and returned to him he had little thought for aught else.

Once in the forest that clothed the mountain slopes the baboons advanced more slowly. Constantly they gave tongue to a plaintive note of calling. Then would follow silence while they listened. At last, faintly from the distance straight ahead came an answer.

The baboons continued to travel in the direction of the voices that floated through the forest to them in the intervals of their own silence. Thus, calling and listening, they came closer to their kinsmen, who, it was evident to Korak, were coming to meet them in great numbers; but when, at last, the baboons of the hill country came in view the ape-man was staggered at the reality that broke upon his vision.

What appeared a solid wall of huge baboons rose from the ground through the branches of the trees to the loftiest terrace to which they dared entrust their weight. Slowly they were approaching, voicing their weird, plaintive call, and behind them, as far as

Korak's eyes could pierce the vendure, rose solid walls of their fellows treading close upon their heels. There were thousands of them. The ape-man could not but think of the fate of his little party should some untoward incident arouse even momentarily the rage of fear of a single one of all these thousands.

But nothing such befell. The two kings approached one another, as was their custom, with much sniffing and bristling. They satisfied themselves of each other's identity. Then each scratched the other's back. After a moment they spoke together. Korak's friend explained the nature of their visit, and for the first time Korak showed himself. He had been hiding behind a bush. The excitement among the hill baboons was intense at sight of him. For a moment Korak feared that he should be torn to pieces; but his fear was for Meriem. Should he die there would be none to succor her.

The two kings, however, managed to quiet the multitude, and Korak was permitted to approach. Slowly the hill baboons came closer to him. They sniffed at him from every angle. When he spoke to them in their own tongue they were filled with wonder and delight. They talked to him and listened while he spoke. He told them of Meriem, and of their life in the jungle where they were the friends of all the ape folk from little Manu to Mangani, the great ape.

"The Gomangani, who are keeping Meriem from me, are no friends of yours," he said. "They kill you. The baboons of the low country are too few to go against them. They tell me that you are very many and very brave—that your numbers are as the numbers of the grasses upon the plains or the leaves within the forest, and that even Tantor, the elephant, fears you, so brave are you. They told me that you would be happy to accompany us to the village of the Gomangani and punish these bad people while I, Korak, The Killer, carry away my Meriem."

The king ape puffed out his chest and strutted about very stiff-legged indeed. So also did many of the other great bulls of his nation. They were pleased and flattered by the words of the strange Tarmangani, who called himself Mangani and spoke the language of the hairy progenitors of man.

"Yes," said one, "we of the hill country are mighty fighters. Tantor fears us. Numa fears us. Sheeta fears us. The Gomangani of the hill country are glad to pass us by in peace. I, for one, will come with you to the village of the Gomangani of the low places. I am the king's first he-child. Alone can I kill all the

Gomangani of the low country," and he swelled his chest and strutted proudly back and forth, until the itching back of a comrade commanded his industrious attention.

"I am Goob," cried another. "My fighting fangs are long. They are sharp. They are strong. Into the soft flesh of many a Gomangani have they been buried. Alone I slew the sister of Sheeta. Goob will go to the low country with you and kill so many of the Gomangani that there will be none left to count the dead," and then he, too, strutted and pranced before the admiring eyes of the shes and the young.

Korak looked at the king, questioningly.

"Your bulls are very brave," he said; "but braver than any is the king."

Thus addressed, the shaggy bull, still in his prime—else he had been no longer king—growled ferociously. The forest echoed to his lusty challenges. The little baboons clutched fearfully at their mother's hairy necks. The bulls, electrified, leaped high in air and took up the roaring challenge of their king. The din was terrific.

Korak came close to the king and shouted in his ear, "Come!" Then he started off through the forest toward the plain that they must cross on their long journey back to the village of Kovudoo, the Gomangani. The king, still roaring and shrieking, wheeled and followed him. In their wake came the handful of low country baboons and the thousands of the hill clan—savage, wiry, dog-like creatures, athirst for blood.

And so they came, upon the second day, to the village of Kovudoo. It was mid-afternoon. The village was sunk in the quiet of the great equatorial sun-heat. The mighty herd traveled quietly now. Beneath the thousands of padded feet the forest gave forth no greater sound than might have been produced by the increased soughing of a stronger breeze through the leafy branches of the trees.

Korak and the two kings were in the lead. Close beside the village they halted until the stragglers had closed up. Now utter silence reigned. Korak, creeping stealthily, entered the tree that overhung the palisade. He glanced behind him. The pack were close upon his heels. The time had come. He had warned them continuously during the long march that no harm must befall the white she who lay a prisoner within the village. All others were their legitimate prey. Then, raising his face toward the sky, he gave voice to a single cry. It was the signal.

In response three thousand hairy bulls leaped screaming and barking into the village of the terrified blacks. Warriors poured from every hut. Mothers gathered their babes in their arms and fled toward the gates as they saw the horrid horde pouring into the village street. Kovudoo marshaled his fighting men about him and, leaping and yelling to arouse their courage, offered a bristling, spear tipped front to the charging horde.

Korak, as he had led the march, led the charge. The blacks were struck with horror and dismay at the sight of this white-skinned youth at the head of a pack of hideous baboons. For an instant they held their ground, hurling their spears once at the advancing multitude; but before they could fit arrows to their bows they wavered, gave, and turned in terrified rout. Into their ranks, upon their backs, sinking strong fangs into the muscles of their necks sprang the baboons and first among them, most ferocious, most bloodthirsty, most terrible was Korak, The Killer.

At the village gates, through which the blacks poured in panic, Korak left them to the tender mercies of his allies and turned himself eagerly toward the hut in which Meriem had been a prisoner. It was empty. One after another the filthy interiors revealed the same disheartening fact—Meriem was in none of them. That she had not been taken by the blacks in their flight from the village Korak knew for he had watched carefully for a glimpse of her among the fugitives.

To the mind of the ape-man, knowing as he did the proclivities of the savages, there was but a single explanation—Meriem had been killed and eaten. With the conviction that Meriem was dead there surged through Korak's brain a wave of blood red rage against those he believed to be her murderer. In the distance he could hear the snarling of the baboons mixed with the screams of their victims, and towards this he made his way. When he came upon them the baboons had commenced to tire of the sport of battle, and the blacks in a little knot were making a new stand, using their knob sticks effectively upon the few bulls who still persisted in attacking them.

Among these broke Korak from the branches of a tree above them—swift, relentless, terrible, he hurled himself upon the savage warriors of Kovudoo. Blind fury possessed him. Too, it protected him by its very ferocity. Like a wounded lioness he was here, there, everywhere, striking terrific blows with hard fists and with the precision and timeliness of the trained fighter. Again and again he buried his teeth in the flesh of a foeman. He was upon one and gone again to another before an effective blow could be dealt him. Yet, though great was the weight of his execution in determining the result of the combat, it was outweighed by the terror which he inspired in the simple, superstitious minds of his foeman. To them this white warrior, who consorted with the great apes and the fierce baboons, who growled and snarled and snapped like a beast, was not human. He was a demon of the forest—a fearsome god of evil whom they had offended, and who had come out of his lair deep in the jungle to punish them. And because of this belief there were many who offered but little defense, feeling as they did the futility of pitting their puny mortal strength against that of a deity.

Those who could fled, until at last there were no more to pay the penalty for a deed, which, while not beyond them, they were, nevertheless, not guilty of. Panting and bloody, Korak paused for want of further victims. The baboons gathered about him, sated themselves with blood and battle. They lolled upon the ground, fagged.

In the distance Kovudoo was gathering his scattered tribesmen, and taking account of injuries and losses. His people were panic stricken. Nothing could prevail upon them to remain longer in this country. They would not even return to the village for their belongings. Instead they insisted upon continuing their flight until they had put many miles between themselves and the stamping ground of the demon who had so bitterly attacked them. And thus it befell that Korak drove from their homes the only people who might have aided him in a search for Meriem, and cut off the only connecting link between him and her from whomsoever might come in search of him from the *douar* of the kindly Bwana who had befriended his little jungle sweetheart.

It was a sour and savage Korak who bade farewell to his baboon allies upon the following morning. They wished him to accompany them; but the ape-man had no heart for the society of any. Jungle life had encouraged taciturnity in him. His sorrow had deepened this to a sullen moroseness that could not brook even the savage companionship of the ill-natured baboons.

Brooding and despondent he took his solitary way into the deepest jungle. He moved along the ground when he knew that Numa was abroad and hungry. He took to the same trees that harbored Sheeta, the panther. He courted death in a hundred ways and a hundred forms. His mind was ever occupied with reminiscences of Meriem and the happy years that they had spent together. He realized now to the full what she had meant to him. The sweet face, the tanned, supple, little body, the bright smile that always had welcomed his return from the hunt haunted him continually.

Inaction soon threatened him with madness. He must be on the go. He must fill his days with labor and excitement that he might forget—that night might find him so exhausted that he should sleep in blessed unconsciousness of his misery until a new day had come.

Had he guessed that by any possibility Meriem might still live he would at least have had hope. His days could have been devoted to searching for her; but he implicitly believed that she was dead.

For a long year he led his solitary, roaming life. Occasionally he fell in with Akut and his tribe, hunting with them for a day or two; or he might travel to the hill country where the baboons had come to accept him as a matter of course; but most of all was he with Tantor, the elephant—the great gray battle ship of the jungle—the super-dreadnaught of his savage world.

The peaceful quiet of the monster bulls, the watchful solicitude of the mother cows, the awkward playfulness of the calves rested, interested, and amused Korak. The life of the huge beasts took his mind, temporarily from his own grief. He came to iove them as he loved not even the great apes, and there was one gigantic tusker in particular of which he was very fond—the lord of the herd—a savage beast that was wont to charge a stranger upon the slightest provocation, or upon no provocation whatsoever. And to Korak this mountain of destruction was docile and affectionate as a lap dog.

He came when Korak called. He wound his trunk about the ape-man's body and lifted him to his broad neck in response to a gesture, and there would Korak lie at full length kicking his toes affectionately into the thick hide and brushing the flies from about the tender ears of his colossal chum with a leafy branch torn from a nearby tree by Tantor for the purpose.

And all the while Meriem was scarce a hundred miles away.

CHAPTER 16

To MERIEM, IN her new home, the days passed quickly. At first she was all anxiety to be off into the jungle searching for her Korak. Bwana, as she insisted upon calling her benefactor, dissuaded her from making the attempt at once by dispatching a head man with a party of blacks to Kovudoo's village with instructions to learn from the old savage how he came into possession of the white girl and as much of her antecedents as might be culled from the black chieftain. Bwana particularly charged his head men with the duty of questioning Kovudoo relative to the strange character whom the girl called Korak, and of searching for the ape-man if he found the slightest evidence upon which to ground a belief in the existence of such an individual. Bwana was more than fully convinced that Korak was a creature of the girl's disordered imagination. He believed that the terrors and hardships she had undergone during captivity among the blacks and her frightful experience with the two Swedes had unbalanced her mind but as the days passed and he became better acquainted with her and able to observe her under the ordinary conditions of the quiet of his African home he was forced to admit that her strange tale puzzled him not a little, for there was no other evidence whatever that Meriem was not in full possession of her normal faculties.

The white man's wife, whom Meriem had christened "My Dear" from having first heard her thus addressed by Bwana, took not only a deep interest in the little jungle waif because of her forlorn and friendless state, but grew to love her as well for her sunny disposition and natural charm of temperament. And Meriem, similarly impressed by like attributes in the gentle, cultured woman, reciprocated the other's regard and affection.

And so the days flew by while Meriem waited the return of the head man and his party from the country of Kovudoo. They were short days, for into them were crowded many hours of insidious instruction of the unlettered child by the lonely woman. She commenced at once to teach the girl English without forcing it upon her as a task. She varied the instruction with lessons in sewing and deportment, nor once did she let Meriem guess that it was not all play. Nor was this difficult, since the girl was avid to learn. Then there were pretty dresses to be made to take the

353

place of the single leopard skin and in this she found the child as responsive and enthusiastic as any civilized miss of her acquaintance.

A month passed before the head man returned—a month that had transformed the savage, half-naked little tarmangani into a daintly frocked girl of at least outward civilization. Meriem had progressed rapidly with the intricacies of the English language, for Bwana and My Dear had persistently refused to speak Arabic from the time they had decided that Meriem must learn English, which had been a day or two after her introduction into their home.

The report of the head man plunged Meriem into a period of despondency, for he had found the village of Kovudoo deserted nor, search as he would, could he discover a single native anywhere in the vicinity. For some time he had camped near the village, spending the days in a systematic search of the environs for traces of Meriem's Korak; but in this quest, too, had he failed. He had seen neither apes nor ape-man. Meriem at first insisted upon setting forth herself in search of Korak, but Bwana prevailed upon her to wait. He would go himself, he assured her, as soon as he could find the time, and at last Meriem consented to abide by his wishes; but it was months before she ceased to mourn almost hourly for her Korak.

My Dear grieved with the grieving girl and did her best to comfort and cheer her. She told her that if Korak lived he would find her; but all the time she believed that Korak had never existed beyond the child's dreams. She planned amusements to distract Meriem's attention from her sorrow, and she instituted a well-designed campaign to impress upon the child the desirability of civilized life and customs. Nor was this difficult, as she was soon to learn, for it rapidly became evident that beneath the uncouth savagery of the girl was a bed rock of innate refinement—a nicety of taste and predilection that quite equaled that of her instructor.

My Dear was delighted. She was lonely and childless, and so she lavished upon this little stranger all the mother love that would have gone to her own had she had one. The result was that by the end of the first year none might have guessed that Meriem ever had existed beyond the lap of culture and luxury.

She was sixteen now, though she easily might have passed for nineteen, and she was very good to look upon, with her black hair and her tanned skin and all the freshness and purity of health and innocence. Yet she still nursed her secret sorrow, though she no longer mentioned it to My Dear. Scarce an hour passed that did not bring its recollection of Korak, and its poignant yearning to see him again.

Meriem spoke English fluently now, and read and wrote it as well. One day My Dear spoke jokingly to her in French and to her surprise Meriem replied in the same tongue—slowly, it is true, and haltingly; but none the less in excellent French, such, though, as a little child might use. Thereafter they spoke a little French each day, and My Dear often marveled that the girl learned this language with a facility that was at times almost uncanny. At first Meriem had puckered her narrow, arched, little eye brows as though trying to force recollection of something all but forgotten which the new words suggested, and then, to her own astonishment as well as to that of her teacher she had used other French words than those in the lessons—used them properly and with a pronunciation that the English woman knew was more perfect than her own; but Meriem could neither read nor write what she spoke so well, and as My Dear considered a knowledge of correct English of the first importance, other than conversational French was postponed for a later day.

"You doubtless heard French spoken at times in your father's *douar*," suggested My Dear, as the most reasonable explanation.

Meriem shook her head.

"It may be," she said, "but I do not recall ever having seen a Frenchman in my father's company—he hated them and would have nothing whatever to do with them, and I am quite sure that I never heard any of these words before, yet at the same time I find them all familiar. I cannot understand it."

"Neither can I," agreed My Dear.

It was about this time that a runner brought a letter that, when she learned the contents, filled Meriem with excitement. Visitors were coming! A number of English ladies and gentlemen had accepted My Dear's invitation to spend a month of hunting and exploring with them. Meriem was all expectancy. What would these strangers be like? Would they be as nice to her as had Bwana and My Dear, or would they be like the other white folk she had known—cruel and relentless. My Dear assured her that they all were gentle folk and that she would find them kind, considerate and honorable.

To My Dear's surprise there was none of the shyness of the

wild creature in Meriem's anticipation of the visit of strangers.

She looked forward to their coming with curiosity and with a certain pleasurable anticipation when once she was assured that they would not bite her. In fact she appeared no different than would any pretty young miss who had learned of the expected coming of company.

Korak's image was still often in her thoughts, but it aroused now a less well-defined sense of bereavement. A quiet sadness pervaded Meriem when she thought of him; but the poignant grief of her loss when it was young no longer goaded her to desperation. Yet she was still loyal to him. She still hoped that some day he would find her, nor did she doubt for a moment but that he was searching for her if he still lived. It was this last suggestion that caused her the greatest perturbation. Korak might be dead. It scarce seemed possible that one so well-equipped to meet the emergencies of jungle life should have succumbed so young; yet when she had last seen him he had been beset by a horde of armed warriors, and should he have returned to the village again, as she well knew he must have, he may have been killed. Even her Korak could not, single handed, slay an entire tribe.

At last the visitors arrived. There were three men and two women—the wives of the two older men. The youngest member of the party was Hon. Morison Baynes, a young man of considerable wealth who, having exhausted all the possibilities for pleasure offered by the capitals of Europe, had gladly seized upon this opportunity to turn to another continent for excitement and adventure.

He looked upon all things un-European as rather more than less impossible, still he was not at all averse to enjoying the novelty of unaccustomed places, and making the most of strangers indigenous thereto, however unspeakable they might have seemed to him at home. In manner he was suave and courteous to all—if possible a trifle more punctilious toward those he considered of meaner clay than toward the few he mentally admitted to equality.

Nature had favored him with a splendid physique and a handsome face, and also with sufficient good judgment to appreciate that while he might enjoy the contemplation of his superiority to the masses, there was little likelihood of the masses being equally entranced by the same cause. And so he easily maintained the reputation of being a most democratic and likable fellow, and indeed he was likable. Just a shade of his egotism was occasionally apparent—never sufficient to become a burden to his associates. And this, briefly, was the Hon. Morison Baynes of luxurious European civilization. What would be the Hon. Morison Baynes of central Africa it were difficult to guess.

Meriem, at first, was shy and reserved in the presence of the strangers. Her benefactors had seen fit to ignore mention of her strange past, and so she passed as their ward whose antecedents not having been mentioned were not to be inquired into. The guests found her sweet and unassuming, laughing, vivacious and a never exhausted storehouse of quaint and interesting jungle lore.

She had ridden much during her year with Bwana and My Dear. She knew each favorite clump of concealing reeds along the river that the buffalo loved best. She knew a dozen places where lions laired, and every drinking hole in the drier country twenty-five miles back from the river. With unerring precision that was almost uncanny she could track the largest or the smallest beast to his hiding place. But the thing that baffled them all was her instant consciousness of the presence of carnivora that others, exerting their faculties to the utmost, could neither see nor hear.

The Hon. Morison Baynes found Meriem a most beautiful and charming companion. He was delighted with her from the first. Particularly so, it is possible, because he had not thought to find companionship of this sort upon the African estate of his London friends. They were together a great deal as they were the only unmarried couple in the little company. Meriem, entirely unaccustomed to the companionship of such as Baynes, was fascinated by him. His tales of the great, gay cities with which he was familiar filled her with admiration and with wonder. If the Hon Morison always shone to advantage in these narratives Meriem saw in that fact but a most natural consequence to his presence upon the scene of his story—wherever Morison might be he must be a hero; so thought the girl.

With the actual presence and companionship of the young Englishman the image of Korak became less real. Where before it had been an actuality to her she now realized that Korak was but a memory. To that memory she still was loyal; but what weight has a memory in the presence of a fascinating reality?

Meriem had never accompanied the men upon a hunt since the arrival of the guests. She never had cared particularly for the sport of killing. The tracking she enjoyed; but the mere killing for the sake of killing she could not find pleasure in—little savage that she had been, and still, to some measure, was. When Bwana had gone forth to shoot for meat she had always been his enthusiastic companion; but with the coming of the London guests the hunting had deteriorated into mere killing. Slaughter the host would not permit; yet the purpose of the hunts were for heads and skins and not for food. So Meriem remained behind and spent her days either with My Dear upon the shaded verandah, or riding her favorite pony across the plains or to the forest edge. Here she would leave him untethered while she took to the trees for the moment's unalloyed pleasures of a return to the wild, free existence of her earlier childhood.

Then would come again visions of Korak, and, tired at last of leaping and swinging through the trees, she would stretch herself comfortably upon a branch and dream. And presently, as today, she found the features of Korak slowly dissolve and merge into those of another, and the figure of a tanned, half-naked tarmangani become a khaki clothed Englishman astride a hunting pony.

And while she dreamed there came to her ears from a distance, faintly, the terrified bleating of a kid. Meriem was instantly alert. You or I, even had we been able to hear the pitiful wail at so great distance, could not have interpreted it; but to Meriem it meant a species of terror that afflicts the ruminant when a carnivore is near and escape impossible.

It had been both a pleasure and a sport of Korak's to rob Numa of his prey whenever possible, and Meriem too had often joyed in the thrill of snatching some dainty morsel almost from the very jaws of the king of beasts. Now, at the sound of the kid's bleat, all the well remembered thrills recurred. Instantly she was all excitement to play again the game of hide and seek with death.

Quickly she loosened her riding skirt and tossed it aside—it was a heavy handicap to successful travel in the trees. Her boots and stockings followed the skirt, for the bare sole of the human foot does not slip upon dry or even wet bark as does the hard leather of a boot. She would have liked to discard her riding breeches also, but the motherly admonitions of My Dear had convinced Meriem that it was not good form to go naked through the world.

At her hip hung a hunting knife. Her rifle was still in its boot at her pony's withers. Her revolver she had not brought.

The kid was still bleating as Meriem started rapidly in its direction, which she knew was straight toward a certain water hole which had once been famous as a rendezvous for lions. Of late there had been no evidence of carnivora in the neighborhood of this drinking place; but Meriem was positive that the bleating of the kid was due to the presence of either lion or panther.

But she would soon know, for she was rapidly approaching the terrified animal. She wondered as she hastened onward that the sounds continued to come from the same point. Why did the kid not run away? And then she came in sight of the little animal and knew. The kid was tethered to a stake beside the waterhole.

Meriem paused in the branches of a near-by tree and scanned the surrounding clearing with quick, penetrating eyes. Where was the hunter? Bwana and his people did not hunt thus. Who could have tethered this poor little beast as a lure to Numa? Bwana never countenanced such acts in his country and his word was law among those who hunted within a radius of many miles of his estate.

Some wandering savages, doubtless, thought Meriem; but where were they? Not even her keen eyes could discover them. And where was Numa? Why had he not long since sprung upon this delicious and defenseless morsel? That he was close by was attested by the pitiful crying of the kid. Ah! Now she saw him. He was lying close in a clump of brush a few yards to her right. The kid was down wind from him and getting the full benefit of his terrorizing scent, which did not reach Meriem.

To circle to the opposite side of the clearing where the trees approached closer to the kid. To leap quickly to the little animal's side and cut the tether that held him would be the work of but a moment. In that moment Numa might charge, and then there would be scarce time to regain the safety of the trees, yet it might be done. Meriem had escaped from closer quarters than that many times before.

The doubt that gave her momentary pause was caused by fear of the unseen hunters more than by fear of Numa. If they were stranger blacks the spears that they held in readiness for Numa might as readily be loosed upon whomever dared release their bait as upon the prey they sought thus to trap. Again the kid struggled to be free. Again his piteous wail touched the tender heart strings of the girl. Tossing discretion aside, she commenced to circle the clearing. Only from Numa did she attempt to conceal her presence. At last she reached the opposite trees. An instant she paused to look toward the great lion, and at the same moment she saw the huge beast rise slowly to his full height. A low roar betokened that he was ready.

Meriem loosened her knife and leaped to the ground. A quick run brought her to the side of the kid. Numa saw her. He lashed his tail against his tawny sides. He roared terribly; but, for an instant, he remained where he stood—surprised into inaction, doubtless, by the strange apparition that had sprung so unexpectedly from the jungle.

Other eyes were upon Meriem, too—eyes in which were no less surprise than that reflected in the yellow-green orbs of the carnivore. A white man, hiding in a thorn boma, half rose as the young girl leaped into the clearing and dashed toward the kid. He saw Numa hesitate. He raised his rifle and covered the beast's breast. The girl reached the kid's side. Her knife flashed, and the little prisoner was free. With a parting bleat it dashed off into the jungle. Then the girl turned to retreat toward the safety of the tree from which she had dropped so suddenly and unexpectedly into the surprised view of the lion, the kid and the man.

As she turned the girl's face was turned toward the hunter. His eyes went wide as he saw her features. He gave a little gasp of surprise; but now the lion demanded all his attention—the baffled, angry beast was charging. His breast was still covered by the motionless rifle. The man could have fired and stopped the charge at once; but for some reason, since he had seen the girl's face, he hesitated. Could it be that he did not care to save her? Or, did he prefer, if possible, to remain unseen by her? It must have been the latter cause which kept the trigger finger of the steady hand from exerting the little pressure that would have brought the great beast to at least a temporary pause.

Like an eagle the man watched the race for life the girl was making. A second or two measured the time which the whole exciting event consumed from the moment that the lion broke into his charge. Nor once did the rifle sights fail to cover the broad breast or the tawny sire as the lion's course took him a little to the man's left. Once, at the very last moment, when escape seemed impossible, the hunter's finger tightened ever so little upon the trigger, but almost coincidentally the girl leaped for an over hanging branch and seized it. The lion leaped too; but the nimble Meriem had swung herself beyond his reach without a second or an inch to spare.

The man breathed a sigh of relief as he lowered his rifle. He saw the girl fling a grimace at the angry, roaring, maneater beneath her, and then, laughing, speed away into the forest. For an hour the lion remained about the water hole. A hundred times could the hunter have bagged his prey. Why did he fail to do so? Was he afraid that the shot might attract the girl and cause her to return?

At last Numa, still roaring angrily, strode majestically into the jungle. The hunter crawled from his boma, and half an hour later was entering a little camp snugly hidden in the forest. A handful of black followers greeted his return with sullen indifference. He was a great bearded man, a huge, yellow-bearded giant, when he entered his tent. Half an hour later he emerged smooth shaven.

His blacks looked at him in astonishment.

"Would you know me?" he asked.

"The hyena that bore you would not know you, Bwana," replied one.

The man aimed a heavy fist at the black's face; but long experience in dodging similar blows saved the presumptuous one.

CHAPTER 17

MERIEM RETURNED SLOWLY toward the tree in which she had left her skirt, her shoes and her stockings. She was singing blithely; but her song came to a sudden stop when she came within sight of the tree, for there, disporting themselves with glee and pulling and hauling upon her belongings, were a number of baboons. When they saw her they showed no signs of terror. Instead they bared their fangs and growled at her. What was there to fear in a single she-Tarmangani? Nothing, absolutely nothing.

In the open plain beyond the forest the hunters were returning from the day's sport. They were widely separated, hoping to raise a wandering lion on the homeward journey across the plain. The Hon. Morison Baynes rode closest to the forest. As his eyes wandered back and forth across the undulating, shrub sprinkled ground they fell upon the form of a creature close beside the thick jungle where it terminated abruptly at the plain's edge.

He reined his mount in the direction of his discovery. It was yet too far away for his untrained eyes to recognize it; but as he came closer he saw that it was a horse, and was about to resume the original direction of his way when he thought that he discerned a saddle upon the beast's back. He rode a little closer. Yes, the animal was saddled. The Hon. Morison approached yet nearer, and as he did so his eyes expressed a pleasurable emotion of anticipation, for they had now recognized the pony as the special favorite of Meriem.

He galloped to the animal's side. Meriem must be within the wood. The man shuddered a little at the thought of an unprotected girl alone in the jungle that was still, to him, a fearful place of terrors and stealthily stalking death. He dismounted and left his horse beside Meriem's. On foot he entered the jungle. He knew that she was probably safe enough and he wished to surprise her by coming suddenly upon her.

He had gone but a short distance into the wood when he heard a great jabbering in a near-by tree. Coming closer he saw a band of baboons snarling over something. Looking intently he saw that one of them held a woman's riding skirt and that others had boots and stockings. His heart almost ceased to beat as he quite naturally placed the most direful explanation upon the scene. The baboons had killed Meriem and stripped this clothing from her body. Morison shuddered.

He was about to call aloud in the hope that after all the girl still lived when he saw her in a tree close beside that occupied by the baboons, and now he saw that they were snarling and jabbering at her. To his amazement he saw the girl swing, ape-like, into the tree below the huge beasts. He saw her pause upon a branch but a few feet from the nearest baboon. He was about to raise his rifle and put a bullet through the hideous creature that seemed about to leap upon her when he heard the girl speak. He almost dropped his rifle from surprise as a strange jabbering, identical with that of the apes broke from Meriem's lips.

The baboons stopped their snarling and listened. It was quite evident that they were as much surprised as the Hon. Morison Baynes. Slowly and one by one they approached the girl. She gave not the slightest evidence of fear of them. They quite surrounded her now so that Baynes could not have fired without endangering the girl's life; but he no longer desired to fire. He was consumed with curiosity.

For several minutes the girl carried on what could be nothing less than a conversation with the baboons, and then with seeming alacrity every article of her apparel in their possession was

Slowly and one by one they approached the girl.

handed over to her. The baboons still crowded eagerly about her as she donned them. They chattered to her and she chattered back. The Hon. Morison Baynes sat down at the foot of a tree and mopped his perspiring brow. Then he rose and made his way back to his mount.

When Meriem emerged from the forest a few minutes later she found him there, and he eyed her with wide eyes in which were both wonder and a sort of terror.

"I saw your horse here," he explained, "and thought that I would wait and ride home with you—you do not mind?"

"Of course not," she replied. "It will be lovely."

As they made their way stirrup to stirrup across the plain the Hon. Morison caught himself many times watching the girl's regular profile and wondering if his eyes had deceived him or if, in truth, he really had seen this lovely creature consorting with grotesque baboons and conversing with them as fluently as she conversed with him. The thing was uncanny—impossible; yet he had seen it with his own eyes.

And as he watched her another thought persisted in obtruding itself into his mind. She was most beautiful and very desirable; but what did he know of her? Was she not altogether impossible? Was the scene that he had but just witnessed not sufficient proof of her impossibility? A woman who climbed trees and conversed with the baboons of the jungle! It was quite horrible!

Again the Hon. Morison mopped his brow. Meriem glanced toward him.

"You are warm," she said. "Now that the sun is setting I find it quite cool. Why do you perspire now?"

He had not intended to let her know that he had seen her with the baboons; but quite suddenly, before he realized what he was saying, he had blurted it out.

"I perspire from emotion," he said. "I went into the jungle when I discovered your pony. I wanted to surprise you; but it was I who was surprised. I saw you in the trees with the baboons."

"Yes?" she said quite unemotionally, as though it was a matter of little moment that a young girl should be upon intimate terms with savage jungle beasts.

"It was horrible!" ejaculated the Hon. Morison.

"Horrible?" repeated Meriem, puckering her brows in bewilderment. "What was horrible about it? They are my friends. Is it horrible to talk with one's friends?"

"You were really talking with them, then?" cried the Hon. Morison. "You understood them and they understood you?"

"Certainly."

"But they are hideous creatures—degraded beasts of a lower order. How could you speak the language of beasts?"

"They are not hideous, and they are not degraded," replied Meriem. "Friends are never that. I lived among them for years before Bwana found me and brought me here. I scarce knew any other tongue than that of the mangani. Should I refuse to know them now simply because I happen, for the present, to live among humans?"

"For the present!" ejaculated the Hon. Morison. "You cannot mean that you expect to return to live among them? Come, come, what foolishness are we talking! The very idea! You are spoofing me, Miss Meriem. You have been kind to these baboons here and they know you and do not molest you; but that you once lived among them—no, that is preposterous."

"But I did, though," insisted the girl, seeing the real horror that the man felt in the presence of such an idea reflected in his tone and manner, and rather enjoying baiting him still further. "Yes, I lived, almost naked, among the great apes and the lesser apes. I dwelt among the branches of the trees. I pounced upon the smaller prey and devoured it—raw. With Korak and A'ht I hunted the antelope and the boar, and I sat upon a tree limb and made faces at Numa, the lion, and threw sticks at him and annoyed him until he roared so terribly in his rage that the earth shook.

"And Korak built me a lair high among the branches of a mighty tree. He brought me fruits and flesh. He fought for me and was kind to me—until I came to Bwana and My Dear I do not recall that any other than Korak was ever kind to me." There was a wistful note in the girl's voice now and she had forgotten that she was bantering the Hon. Morison. She was thinking of Korak. She had not thought of him a great deal of late.

For a time both were silently absorbed in their own reflections as they rode on toward the bungalow of their host. The girl was thinking of a god-like figure, a leopard skin half concealing his smooth, brown hide as he leaped nimbly through the trees to lay an offering of food before her on his return from a successful hunt. Behind him, shaggy and powerful, swung a huge anthropoid ape, while she, Meriem, laughing and shouting her welcome, swung upon a swaying limb before the entrance to her sylvan bower. It was a pretty picture as she recalled it. The other side seldom obtruded itself upon her memory—the long, black nights—the chill, terrible jungle nights—the cold and damp and discomfort of the rainy season—the hideous mouthings of the savage carnivora as they prowled through the Stygian darkness beneath—the constant menace of Sheeta, the panther, and Histah, the snake—the stinging insects—the loathsome vermin. For, in truth, all these had been outweighed by the happiness of the sunny days, the freedom of it all, and, most, the companionship of Korak.

The man's thoughts were rather jumbled. He had suddenly realized that he had come mighty near falling in love with this girl of whom he had known nothing up to the previous moment when she had voluntarily revealed a portion of her past to him. The more he thought upon the matter the more evident it became to him that he had given her his love—that he had been upon the verge of offering her his honorable name. He trembled a little at the narrowness of his escape. Yet, he still loved her. There was no objection to that according to the ethics of the Hon. Morison Baynes and his kind. She was of meaner clay than he. He could no more have taken her in marriage than he could have taken one of her baboon friends, nor would she, of course, expect such an offer from him. To have his love would be sufficient honor for her—his name he would, naturally, bestow upon one in his own elevated social sphere.

A girl who had consorted with apes, who, according to her own admission, had lived almost naked among them, could have no considerable sense of the finer qualities of virtue. The love that he would offer her, then, would, far from offending her, probably cover all that she might desire or expect.

The more the Hon. Morison Baynes thought upon the subject the more fully convinced he became that he was contemplating a most chivalrous and unselfish act. Europeans will better understand his point of view than Americans, poor, benighted provincials, who are denied a true appreciation of caste and of the fact that "the king can do no wrong." He did not even have to argue the point that she would be much happier amidst the luxuries of a London apartment, fortified as she would be by both his love and his bank account, than lawfully wed to such a one as her social position warranted. There was one question however, which he wished to have definitely answered before he committed himself even to the program he was considering.

"Who were Korak and A'ht?" he asked.

"A'ht was a Mangani," replied Meriem, "and Korak a Tarmangani."

"And what, pray, might a Mangani be, and a Tarmangani?" The girl laughed.

"You are a Tarmangani," she replied. "The Mangani are covered with hair—you would call them apes."

"Then Korak was a white man?" he asked.

"Yes."

"And he was—ah—your—er—your—?" He paused, for he found it rather difficult to go on with that line of questioning while the girl's clear, beautiful eyes were looking straight into his.

"My what?" insisted Meriem, far too unsophisticated in her unspoiled innocence to guess what the Hon. Morison was driving at.

"Why—ah—your brother?" he stumbled.

"No, Korak was not my brother," she replied.

"Was he your husband, then?" he finally blurted.

Far from taking offense, Meriem, broke into a merry laugh.

"My husband!" she cried. "Why how old do you think I am? I am too young to have a husband. I had never thought of such a thing. Korak was—why—," and now she hesitated, too, for she never before had attempted to analyse the relationship that existed between herself and Korak—"why, Korak was just Korak," and again she broke into a gay laugh as she realized the illuminating quality of her description.

Looking at her and listening to her the man beside her could not believe that depravity of any sort or degree entered into the girl's nature, yet he wanted to believe that she had not been virtuous, for otherwise his task was less a sinecure—the Hon. Morison was not entirely without conscience.

For several days the Hon. Morison made no appreciable progress toward the consummation of his scheme. Sometimes he almost abandoned it for he found himself time and again wondering how slight might be the provocation necessary to trick him into making a bona-fide offer of marriage to Meriem if he permitted himself to fall more deeply in love with her, and it was difficult to see her daily and not love her. There was a quality about her which, all unknown to the Hon. Morison, was making his task an extremely difficult one—it was that quality of innate goodness and cleanness which is a good girl's stoutest bulwark and protection—

an impregnable barrier that only degeneracy has the affrontery to assail. The Hon. Morison Baynes would never be considered a degenerate.

He was sitting with Meriem upon the verandah one evening after the others had retired. Earlier they had been playing tennis— a game in which the Hon. Morison shone to advantage, as, in truth, he did in most all manly sports. He was telling Meriem stories of London and Paris, of balls and banquets, of the wonderful women and their wonderful gowns, of the pleasures and pastimes of the rich and powerful. The Hon. Morison was a past master in the art of insidious boasting. His egotism was never flagrant or tiresome—he was never crude in it, for crudeness was a plebeianism that the Hon. Morison studiously avoided, yet the impression derived by a listener to the Hon. Morison was one that was not at all calculated to detract from the glory of the house of Baynes, or from that of its representative.

Meriem was entranced. His tales were like fairy stories to this little jungle maid. The Hon. Morison loomed large and wonderful and magnificent in her mind's eye. He fascinated her, and when he drew closer to her after a short silence and took her hand she thrilled as one might thrill beneath the touch of a deity—a thrill of exaltation not unmixed with fear.

He bent his lips close to her ear.

"Meriem!" he whispered. "My little Meriem! May I hope to have the right to call you 'my little Meriem'?"

The girl turned wide eyes upward to his face; but it was in shadow. She trembled but she did not draw away. The man put an arm about her and drew her closer.

"I love you!" he whispered.

She did not reply. She did not know what to say. She knew nothing of love. She had never given it a thought; but she did know that it was very nice to be loved, whatever it meant. It was nice to have people kind to one. She had known so little of kindness or affection.

"Tell me," he said, "that you return my love."

His lips came steadily closer to hers. They had almost touched when a vision of Korak sprang like a miracle before her eyes. She saw Korak's face close to hers, she felt his lips hot against her lips, and then for the first time in her life she guessed what love meant. She drew away, gently.

"I am not sure," she said, "that I love you. Let us wait. There is plenty of time. I am too young to marry yet, and I am not sure that I should be happy in London or Paris—they rather frighten me."

How easily and naturally she had connected his avowal of love with the idea of marriage! The Hon. Morison was perfectly sure that he had not mentioned marriage—he had been particularly careful not to do so. And then she was not sure that she loved him! That, too, came rather in the nature of a shock to his vanity. It seemed incredible that this little barbarian should have any doubts whatever as to the desirability of the Hon. Morison Baynes.

The first flush of passion cooled, the Hon. Morison was enabled to reason more logically. The start had been all wrong. It would be better now to wait and prepare her mind gradually for the only proposition which his exalted estate would permit him to offer her. He would go slow. He glanced down at the girl's profile. It was bathed in the silvery light of the great tropic moon. The Hon. Morison Baynes wondered if it were to be so easy a matter to "go slow." She was most alluring.

Meriem rose. The vision of Korak was still before her.

"Good night," she said. "It is almost too beautiful to leave," she waved her hand in a comprehensive gesture which took in the starry heavens, the great moon, the broad, silvered plain, and the dense shadows in the distance, that marked the jungle. "Oh, how I love it!"

"You would love London more," he said earnestly. "And London would love you. You would be a famous beauty in any capital of Europe. You would have the world at your feet, Meriem."

"Good night!" she repeated, and left him.

The Hon. Morison selected a cigarette from his crested case, lighted it, blew a thin line of blue smoke toward the moon, and smiled.

CHAPTER 18

MERIEM AND BWANA were sitting on the verandah together the following day when a horseman appeared in the distance riding across the plain toward the bungalow. Bwana shaded his eyes with his hand and gazed out toward the oncoming rider. He was puzzled. Strangers were few in Central Africa. Even the blacks for a distance of many miles in every direction were well known to him. No white man came within a hundred miles that word of his coming did not reach Bwana long before the stranger. His every move was reported to the big Bwana—just what animals he killed and how many of each species, how he killed them, too, for Bwana would not permit the use of prussic acid or strychnine; and how he treated his "boys."

Several European sportsmen had been turned back to the coast by the big Englishman's orders because of unwarranted cruelty to their black followers, and one, whose name had long been heralded in civilized communities as that of a great sportsman, was driven from Africa with orders never to return when Bwana found that his big bag of fourteen lions had been made by the diligent use of poisoned bait.

The result was that all good sportsmen and all the natives loved and respected him. His word was law where there had never been law before. There was scarce a head man from coast to coast who would not heed the big Bwana's commands in preference to those of the hunters who employed them, and so it was easy to turn back any undesirable stranger—Bwana had simply to threaten to order his boys to desert him.

But here was evidently one who had slipped into the country unheralded. Bwana could not imagine who the approaching horseman might be. After the manner of frontier hospitality the globe round he met the newcomer at the gate, welcoming him even before he had dismounted. He saw a tall, well knit man of thirty or over, blonde of hair and smooth shaven. There was a tantalizing familiarity about him that convinced Bwana that he should be able to call the visitor by name, yet he was unable to do so. The newcomer was evidently of Scandinavian origin—both his appearance and accent denoted that. His manner was rough but open. He made a good impression upon the Englishman, who was wont to accept strangers in this wild and savage country at their own valuation, asking no questions and assuming the best of them until they proved themselves undeserving of his friendship and hospitality.

"It is rather unusual that a white man comes unheralded," he said, as they walked together toward the field into which he had suggested that the traveler might turn his pony. "My friends, the natives, keep us rather well-posted."

"It is probably due to the fact that I came from the south," explained the stranger, "that you did not hear of my coming. I have seen no village for several marches."

"No, there are none to the south of us for many miles," replied Bwana. "Since Kovudoo deserted his country I rather doubt that one could find a native in that direction under two or three hundred miles."

Bwana was wondering how a lone white man could have made his way through the savage, unhospitable miles that lay toward the south. As though guessing what must be passing through the other's mind, the stranger vouchsafed an explanation.

"I came down from the north to do a little trading and hunting," he said, "and got way off the beaten track. My head man, who was the only member of the *safari* who had ever before been in the country, took sick and died. We could find no natives to guide us, and so I simply swung back straight north. We have been living on the fruits of our guns for over a month. Didn't have an idea there was a white man within a thousand miles of us when we camped last night by a water hole at the edge of the plain. This morning I started out to hunt and saw the smoke from your chimney, so I sent my gun bearer back to camp with the good news and rode straight over here myself. Of course I've heard of you—everybody who comes into Central Africa does— and I'd be mighty glad of permission to rest up and hunt around here for a couple of weeks."

"Certainly," replied Bwana. "Move your camp up close to the river below my boys' camp and make yourself at home."

They had reached the verandah now and Bwana was introducing the stranger to Meriem and My Dear, who had just come from the bungalow's interior.

"This is Mr. Hanson," he said, using the name the man had given him. "He is a trader who has lost his way in the jungle to the south."

My Dear and Meriem bowed their acknowledgments of the introduction. The man seemed rather ill at ease in their presence. His host attributed this to the fact that his guest was unaccustomed to the society of cultured women, and so found a pretext to quickly extricate him from his seemingly unpleasant position and lead him away to his study and the brandy and soda which were evidently much less embarrassing to Mr. Hanson.

When the two had left them Meriem turned toward My Dear.

"It is odd," she said, "but I could almost swear that I had

known Mr. Hanson in the past. It is odd, but quite impossible," and she gave the matter no further thought.

Hanson did not accept Bwana's invitation to move his camp closer to the bungalow. He said his boys were inclined to be quarrelsome, and so were better off at a distance; and he, himself, was around but little, and then always avoided coming into contact with the ladies. A fact which naturally aroused only laughing comment on the rough trader's bashfulness. He accompanied the men on several hunting trips where they found him perfectly at home and well versed in all the finer points of big game hunting. Of an evening he often spent much time with the white foreman of the big farm, evidently finding in the society of this rougher man more common interests than the cultured guests of Bwana possessed for him. So it came that his was a familiar figure about the premises by night. He came and went as he saw fit, often wandering along in the great flower garden that was the especial pride and joy of My Dear and Meriem. The first time that he had been surprised there he apologized gruffly, explaining that he had always been fond of the good old blooms of northern Europe which My Dear had so successfully transplanted in African soil.

Was it, though, the ever beautiful blossoms of hollyhocks and phlox that drew him to the perfumed air of the garden, or that other infinitely more beautiful flower who wandered often among the blooms beneath the great moon—the black-haired, sun-tanned Meriem?

For three weeks Hanson had remained. During this time he said that his boys were resting and gaining strength after their terrible ordeals in the untracked jungle to the south; but he had not been as idle as he appeared to have been. He divided his small following into two parties, entrusting the leadership of each to men whom he believed that he could trust. To them he explained his plans and the rich reward that they would win from him if they carried his designs to a successful conclusion. One party he moved very slowly northward along the trail that connects with the great caravan routes entering the Sahara from the south. The other he ordered straight westward with orders to halt and go into permanent camp just beyond the great river which marks the natural boundary of the country that the big Bwana rightfully considers almost his own.

To his host he explained that he was moving his *safari* slowly toward the north—he said nothing of the party moving westward.

Then, one day, he announced that half his boys had deserted, for a hunting party from the bungalow had come across his northerly camp and he feared that they might have noticed the reduced numbers of his following.

And thus matters stood when, one hot night, Meriem, unable to sleep, rose and wandered out into the garden. The Hon. Morison had been urging his suit once more that evening, and the girl's mind was in such a turmoil that she had been unable to sleep.

The wide heavens above her seemed to promise a greater freedom from doubt and questioning. Baynes had urged her to tell him that she loved him. A dozen times she thought that she might honestly give him the answer that he demanded. Korak fast was becoming but a memory. That he was dead she had come to believe, since otherwise he would have sought her out. She did not know that he had even better reason to believe her dead, and that it was because of that belief he had made no effort to find her after his raid upon the village of Kovudoo.

Behind a great flowering shrub Hanson lay gazing at the stars and waiting. He had lain thus and there many nights before. For what was he waiting, or for whom? He heard the girl approaching, and half raised himself to his elbow. A dozen paces away, the reins looped over a fence post, stood his pony.

Meriem, walking slowly, approached the bush behind which the waiter lay. Hanson drew a large bandanna handkerchief from his pocket and rose stealthily to his knees. A pony neighed down at the corrals. Far out across the plain a lion roared. Hanson changed his position until he squatted upon both feet, ready to come erect quickly.

Again the pony neighed—this time closer. There was the sound of his body brushing against shrubbery. Hanson heard and wondered how the animal had gotten from the corral, for it was evident that he was already in the garden. The man turned his head in the direction of the beast. What he saw sent him to the ground, huddled close beneath the shrubbery—a man was coming, leading two ponies.

Meriem heard now and stopped to look and listen. A moment later the Hon. Morison Baynes drew near, the two saddled mounts at his heels.

Meriem looked up at him in surprise. The Hon. Morison grinned sheepishly.

"I couldn't sleep," he explained, "and was going for a bit of a ride when I chanced to see you out here, and I thought you'd like to join me. Ripping good sport, you know, night riding. Come on."

Meriem laughed. The adventure appealed to her.

"All right," she said.

Hanson swore beneath his breath. The two led their horses from the garden to the gate and through it. There they discovered Hanson's mount.

"Why here's the trader's pony," remarked Baynes.

"He's probably down visiting with the foreman," said Meriem.

"Pretty late for him, isn't it?" remarked the Hon. Morison. "I'd hate to have to ride back through that jungle at night to his camp."

As though to give weight to his apprehensions the distant lion roared again. The Hon. Morison shivered and glanced at the girl to note the effect of the uncanny sound upon her. She appeared not to have noticed it.

A moment later the two had mounted and were moving slowly across the moon-bathed plain. The girl turned her pony's head straight toward the jungle. It was in the direction of the roaring of the hungry lion.

"Hadn't we better steer clear of that fellow?" suggested the Hon. Morison. "I guess you didn't hear him."

"Yes, I heard him," laughed Meriem. "Let's ride over and call on him."

The Hon. Morison laughed uneasily. He didn't care to appear at a disadvantage before this girl, nor did he care, either, to approach a hungry lion too closely at night. He carried his rifle in his saddle boot; but moonlight is an uncertain light to shoot by, nor ever had he faced a lion alone—even by day. The thought gave him a distinct nausea. The beast ceased his roaring now. They heard him no more and the Hon. Morison gained courage accordingly. They were riding down wind toward the jungle. The lion lay in a little swale to their right. He was old. For two nights he had not fed, for no longer was his charge as swift or his spring as mighty as in the days of his prime when he spread terror among the creatures of his wild domain. For two nights and days he had gone empty, and for long time before that he had fed only upon carrion. He was old; but he was yet a terrible engine of destruction.

At the edge of the forest the Hon. Morison drew rein. He had no desire to go further. Numa, silent upon his padded feet, crept into the jungle beyond them. The wind, now, was blowing gently between him and his intended prey. He had come a long way in search of man, for even in his youth he had tasted human flesh and while it was poor stuff by comparison with eland and zebra it was less difficult to kill. In Numa's estimation man was a slow-witted, slow-footed creature which commanded no respect unless accompanied by the acrid odor which spelled to the monarch's sensitive nostrils the great noise and the blinding flash of an express rifle.

He caught the dangerous scent tonight; but he was ravenous to madness. He would face a dozen rifles, if necessary, to fill his empty belly. He circled about into the forest that he might again be down wind from his victims, for should they get his scent he could not hope to overtake them. Numa was famished; but he was old and crafty.

Deep in the jungle another caught faintly the scent of man and of Numa both. He raised his head and sniffed. He cocked it upon one side and listened.

"Come on," said Meriem, "let's ride in a way—the forest is wonderful at night. It is open enough to permit us to ride."

The Hon. Morison hesitated. He shrank from revealing his fear in the presence of the girl. A braver man, sure of his own position, would have had the courage to have refused uselessly to expose the girl to danger. He would not have thought of himself at all; but the egotism of the Hon. Morison required that he think always of self first. He had planned the ride to get Meriem away from the bungalow. He wanted to talk to her alone and far enough away so should she take offense at his purposed suggestion he would have time in which to attempt to right himself in her eyes before they reached home. He had little doubt, of course, but that he should succeed; but it is to his credit that he did have some slight doubts.

"You needn't be afraid of the lion," said Meriem, noting his slight hesitancy. "There hasn't been a man eater around here for two years, Bwana says, and the game is so plentiful that there is no necessity to drive Numa to human flesh. Then, he has been so often hunted that he rather keeps out of man's way."

"Oh, I'm not afraid of lions," replied the Hon. Morison. "I was just thinking what a beastly uncomfortable place a forest is to ride in. What with the underbrush and the low branches and all that, you know, it's not exactly cut out for pleasure riding."

"Let's go a-foot then," suggested Meriem, and started to dismount.

"Oh, no," cried the Hon. Morison, aghast at this suggestion. "Let's ride," and he reined his pony into the dark shadows of the wood. Behind him came Meriem and in front, prowling ahead awaiting a favorable opportunity, skulked Numa, the lion.

Out upon the plain a lone horseman muttered a low curse as he saw the two disappear from sight. It was Hanson. He had followed them from the bungalow. Their way led in the direction of his camp, so he had a ready and plausible excuse should they discover him; but they had not seen him for they had not turned their eyes behind.

Now he turned directly toward the spot at which they had entered the jungle. He no longer cared whether he was observed or not. There were two reasons for his indifference. The first was that he saw in Baynes' act a counterpart of his own planned abduction of the girl. In some way he might turn the thing to his own purposes. At least he would keep in touch with them and make sure that Baynes did not get her. His other reason was based on his knowledge of an event that had transpired at his camp the previous night—an event which he had not mentioned at the bungalow for fear of drawing undesired attention to his movements and bringing the blacks of the big Bwana into dangerous intercourse with his own boys. He had told at the bungalow that half his men had deserted. That story might be quickly disproved should his boys and Bwana's grow confidential.

The event that he had failed to mention and which now urged him hurriedly after the girl and her escort had occurred during his absence early the preceding evening. His men had been sitting around their camp fire, entirely encircled by a high, thorn *boma,* when, without the slightest warning, a huge lion had leaped amongst them and seized one of their number. It had been solely due to the loyalty and courage of his comrades that his life had been saved, and then only after a battle royal with the hunger-enraged beast had they been able to drive him off with burning brands, spears, and rifles.

From this Hanson knew that a man eater had wandered into the district or been developed by the aging of one of the many lions who ranged the plains and hills by night, or lay up in the cool wood by day. He had heard the roaring of a hungry lion not half an hour before, and there was little doubt in his mind

but that the man eater was stalking Meriem and Baynes. He cursed
the Englishman for a fool, and spurred rapidly after them.

Meriem and Baynes had drawn up in a small, natural clearing.
A hundred yards beyond them Numa lay crouching in the underbrush, his yellow-green eyes fixed upon his prey, the tip of his
sinuous tail jerking spasmodically. He was measuring the distance
between him and them. He was wondering if he dared venture a
charge, or should he wait yet a little longer in the hope that they
might ride straight into his jaws. He was very hungry; but also
was he very crafty. He could not chance losing his meat by a
hasty and ill-considered rush. Had he waited the night before until
the blacks slept he would not have been forced to go hungry for
another twenty-four hours.

Behind him the other that had caught his scent and that of
man together came to a sitting posture upon the branch of a tree
in which he had reposed himself for slumber. Beneath him a
lumbering gray hulk swayed to and fro in the darkness. The beast
in the tree uttered a low guttural and dropped to the back of the
gray mass. He whispered a word in one of the great ears and
Tantor, the elephant, raised his trunk aloft, swinging it high and
low to catch the scent that the word had warned him of. There
was another whispered word—was it a command?—and the lumbering beast wheeled into an awkward, yet silent shuffle, in the
direction of Numa, the lion, and the stranger Tarmangani his
rider had scented.

Onward they went, the scent of the lion and his prey becoming
stronger and stronger. Numa was becoming impatient. How much
longer must he wait for his meat to come his way? He lashed his
tail viciously now. He almost growled. All unconscious of their
danger the man and the girl sat talking in the little clearing.

Their horses were pressed side by side. Baynes had found Meriem's hand and was pressing it as he poured words of love into
her ear, and Meriem was listening.

"Come to London with me," urged the Hon. Morison. "I can
gather a *safari* and we can be a whole day upon the way to the
coast before they guess that we have gone."

"Why must we go that way?" asked the girl. "Bwana and My
Dear would not object to our marriage."

"I cannot marry you just yet," explained the Hon. Morison,
"there are some formalities to be attended to first—you do not
understand. It will be all right. We will go to London. I cannot

wait. If you love me you will come. What of the apes you lived with? Did they bother about marriage? They love as we love. Had you stayed among them you would have mated as they mate. It is the law of nature—no man-made law can abrogate the laws of God. What difference does it make if we love one another? What do we care for anyone in the world besides ourselves? I would give my life for you—will you give nothing for me?"

"You love me?" she asked. "You will marry me when we have reached London?"

"I swear it," he cried.

"I will go with you," she whispered, "though I do not understand why it is necessary." She leaned toward him and he took her in his arms and bent to press his lips to hers.

At the same instant the head of a huge tusker poked through the trees that fringed the clearing. The Hon. Morison and Meriem, with eyes and ears for one another alone, did not see or hear; but Numa did. The man upon Tantor's broad head saw the girl in the man's arms. It was Korak; but in the trim figure of the neatly garbed girl he did not recognize his Meriem. He only saw a Tarmangani with his she. And then Numa charged.

With a frightful roar, fearful lest Tantor had come to frighten away his prey, the great beast leaped from his hiding place. The earth trembled to his mighty voice. The ponies stood for an instant transfixed with terror. The Hon. Morison Baynes went white and cold. The lion was charging toward them full in the brilliant light of the magnificent moon. The muscles of the Hon. Morison no longer obeyed his will—they flexed to the urge of a greater power— the power of Nature's first law. They drove his spurred heels deep into his pony's flanks, they bore the rein against the brute's neck that wheeled him with an impetuous drive toward the plain and safety.

The girl's pony, squealing in terror, reared and plunged upon the heels of his mate. The lion was close upon him. Only the girl was cool—the girl and the half-naked savage who bestrode the neck of his mighty mount and grinned at the exciting spectacle chance had staked for his enjoyment.

To Korak here were but two strange Tarmangani pursued by Numa, who was empty. It was Numa's right to prey; but one was a she. Korak felt an intuitive urge to rush to her protection. Why, he could not guess. All Tarmangani were enemies now. He had lived too long a beast to feel strongly the humanitarian impulses that were inherent in him—yet feel them he did, for the girl at least.

He urged Tantor forward. He raised his heavy spear and hurled it at the flying target of the lion's body. The girl's pony had reached the trees upon the opposite side of the clearing. Here he would become easy prey to the swiftly moving lion; but Numa, infuriated, preferred the woman upon his back. It was for her he leaped.

Korak gave an exclamation of astonishment and approval as Numa landed upon the pony's rump and at the same instant the girl swung free of her mount to the branches of a tree above her.

Korak's spear struck Numa in the shoulder, knocking him from his precarious hold upon the frantically plunging horse. Freed of the weight of both girl and lion the pony raced ahead toward safety. Numa tore and struck at the missile in his shoulder but could not dislodge it. Then he resumed the chase.

Korak guided Tantor into the seclusion of the jungle. He did not wish to be seen, nor had he.

Hanson had almost reached the wood when he heard the lion's terrific roars, and knew that the charge had come. An instant later the Hon. Morison broke upon his vision, racing like mad for safety. The man lay flat upon his pony's back hugging the animal's neck tightly with both arms and digging the spurs into his sides. An instant later the second pony appeared—riderless.

Hanson groaned as he guessed what had happened out of sight in the jungle. With an oath he spurred on in the hope of driving the lion from his prey—his rifle was ready in his hand. And then the lion came into view behind the girl's pony. Hanson could not understand. He knew that if Numa had succeeded in seizing the girl he would not have continued in pursuit of the others.

He drew in his own mount, took quick aim and fired. The lion stopped in his tracks, turned and bit at his side, then rolled over dead. Hanson rode on into the forest, calling aloud to the girl.

"Here I am," came a quick response from the foliage of the trees just ahead. "Did you hit him?"

"Yes," replied Hanson. "Where are you? You had a mighty narrow escape. It will teach you to keep out of the jungle at night."

Together they returned to the plain where they found the Hon. Morison riding slowly back toward them. He explained that his pony had bolted and that he had had hard work stopping him at all. Hanson grinned, for he recalled the pounding heels that he had seen driving sharp spurs into the flanks of Baynes' mount; but he said nothing of what he had seen. He took Meriem up behind him and the three rode in silence toward the bungalow.

CHAPTER 19

BEHIND THEM KORAK emerged from the jungle and recovered his spear from Numa's side. He still was smiling. He had enjoyed the spectacle exceedingly. There was one thing that troubled him— the agility with which the she had clambered from her pony's back into the safety of the tree *above* her. That was more like a mangani—more like his lost Meriem. He sighed. His lost Meriem! His little, dead Meriem! He wondered if this she stranger resembled his Meriem in other ways. A great longing to see her overwhelmed him. He looked after the three figures moving steadily across the plain. He wondered where might lie their destination. A desire to follow them came over him, but he only stood there watching until they had disappeared in the distance. The sight of the civilized girl and the dapper, khaki clad Englishman had aroused in Korak memories long dormant.

Once he had dreamed of returning to the world of such as these; but with the death of Meriem hope and ambition seemed to have deserted him. He cared now only to pass the remainder of his life in solitude, as far from man as possible. With a sigh he turned slowly back into the jungle.

Tantor, nervous by nature, had been far from reassured by close proximity to the three strange whites, and with the report of Hanson's rifle had turned and ambled away at his long, swinging shuffle. He was nowhere in sight when Korak returned to look for him. The ape-man, however, was little concerned by the absence of his friend. Tantor had a habit of wandering off unexpectedly. For a month they might not see one another, for Korak seldom took the trouble to follow the great pachyderm, nor did he upon this occasion. Instead he found a comfortable perch in a large tree and was soon asleep.

At the bungalow Bwana had met the returning adventurers on the veranda. In a moment of wakefulness he had heard the report of Hanson's rifle far out across the plain, and wondered what it

Meriem's leap saved her from a horrible death.

might mean. Presently it had occurred to him that the man whom he considered in the light of a guest might have met with an accident on his way back to camp, so he had arisen and gone to his foreman's quarters where he had learned that Hanson had been there earlier in the evening but had departed several hours before. Returning from the foreman's quarters Bwana had noticed that the corral gate was open and further investigation revealed the fact that Meriem's pony was gone and also the one most often used by Baynes. Instantly Bwana assumed that the shot had been fired by Hon. Morison, and had again aroused his foreman and was making preparations to set forth in investigation when he had seen the party approaching across the plain.

Explanations on the part of the Englishman met a rather chilly reception from his host. Meriem was silent. She saw that Bwana was angry with her. It was the first time and she was heart broken.

"Go to your room, Meriem," he said; "and Baynes, if you will step into my study, I'd like to have a word with you in a moment."

He stepped toward Hanson as the others turned to obey him. There was something about Bwana even in his gentlest moods that commanded instant obedience.

"How did you happen to be with them, Hanson?" he asked.

"I'd been sitting in the garden," replied the trader, "after leaving Jervis' quarters. I have a habit of doing that as your lady probably knows. Tonight I fell asleep behind a bush, and was awakened by them two spooning. I couldn't hear what they said, but presently Baynes brings two ponies and they ride off. I didn't like to interfere for it wasn't any of my business, but I knew they hadn't ought to be ridin' about that time of night, leastways not the girl—it wasn't right and it wasn't safe. So I follows them and it's just as well I did. Baynes was gettin' away from the lion as fast as he could, leavin' the girl to take care of herself, when I got a lucky shot into the beast's shoulder that fixed him."

Hanson paused. Both men were silent for a time. Presently the trader coughed in an embarrassed manner as though there was something on his mind he felt in duty bound to say, but hated to.

"What is it, Hanson?" asked Bwana. "You were about to say something weren't you?"

"Well, you see it's like this," ventured Hanson. "Bein' around here evenings a good deal I've seen them two together a lot, and, beggin' your pardon, sir, but I don't think Mr. Baynes means the girl any good. I've overheard enough to make me think he's tryin' to get her to run off with him." Hanson, to fit his own ends, hit nearer the truth than he knew. He was afraid that Baynes would interfere with his own plans, and he had hit upon a scheme to both utilize the young Englishman and get rid of him at the same time.

"And I thought," continued the trader, "that inasmuch as I'm about due to move you might like to suggest to Mr. Baynes that he go with me. I'd be willin' to take him north to the caravan trails as a favor to you, sir."

Bwana stood in deep thought for a moment. Presently he looked up.

"Of course, Hanson, Mr. Baynes is my guest," he said, a grim twinkle in his eye. "Really I cannot accuse him of planning to run away with Meriem on the evidence that we have, and as he is my guest I should hate to be so discourteous as to ask him to leave; but, if I recall his words correctly, it seems to me that he has spoken of returning home, and I am sure that nothing would delight him more than going north with you—you say you start tomorrow? I think Mr. Baynes will accompany you. Drop over in the morning, if you please, and now good night, and thank you for keeping a watchful eye on Meriem."

Hanson hid a grin as he turned and sought his saddle. Bwana stepped from the veranda to his study, where he found the Hon. Morison pacing back and forth, evidently very ill at ease.

"Baynes," said Bwana, coming directly to the point, "Hanson is leaving for the north tomorrow. He has taken a great fancy to you, and just asked me to say to you that he'd be glad to have you accompany him. Good night, Baynes."

At Bwana's suggestion Meriem kept to her room the following morning until after the Hon. Morison Baynes had departed. Hanson had come for him early—in fact he had remained all night with the foreman, Jervis, that they might get an early start.

The farewell exchanges between the Hon. Morison and his host were of the most formal type, and when at last the guest rode away Bwana breathed a sigh of relief. It had been an unpleasant duty and he was glad that it was over; but he did not regret his action. He had not been blind to Baynes' infatuation for Meriem, and knowing the young man's pride in caste he had never for a moment believed that his guest would offer his name to this nameless Arab girl, for, extremely light in color though she was for a full blood Arab, Bwana believed her to be such.

He did not mention the subject again to Meriem, and in this he made a mistake, for the young girl, while realizing the debt of gratitude she owed Bwana and My Dear, was both proud and sensitive, so that Bwana's action in sending Baynes away and giving her no opportunity to explain or defend hurt and mortified her. Also it did much toward making a martyr of Baynes in her eyes and arousing in her breast a keen feeling of loyalty toward him.

What she had half-mistaken for love before, she now wholly mistook for love. Bwana and My Dear might have told her much of the social barriers that they only too well knew Baynes must feel existed between Meriem and himself, but they hesitated to wound her. It would have been better had they inflicted this lesser sorrow, and saved the child the misery that was to follow because of her ignorance.

As Hanson and Baynes rode toward the former's camp the Englishman maintained a morose silence. The other was attempting to formulate an opening that would lead naturally to the proposition he had in mind. He rode a neck behind his companion, grinning as he noted the sullen scowl upon the other's patrician face.

"Rather rough on you, wasn't he?" he ventured at last, jerking his head back in the direction of the bungalow as Baynes turned his eyes upon him at the remark. "He thinks a lot of the girl," continued Hanson, "and don't want nobody to marry her and take her away; but it looks to me as though he was doin' her more harm than good in sendin' you away. She ought to marry some time, and she couldn't do better than a fine young gentleman like you."

Baynes, who had at first felt inclined to take offense at the mention of his private affairs by this common fellow, was mollified by Hanson's final remark, and immediately commenced to see in him a man of fine discrimination.

"He's a darned bounder," grumbled the Hon. Morison; "but I'll get even with him. He may be the whole thing in Central Africa but I'm as big as he is in London, and he'll find it out when he comes home."

"If I was you," said Hanson, "I wouldn't let any man keep me from gettin' the girl I want. Between you and me I ain't got no use for him either, and if I can help you any way just call on me."

"It's mighty good of you, Hanson," replied Baynes, warming up a bit; "but what can a fellow do here in this God-forsaken hole?"

"I know what I'd do," said Hanson. "I'd take the girl along with me. If she loves you she'll go, all right."

"It can't be done," said Baynes. "He bosses this whole blooming country for miles around. He'd be sure to catch us."

"No he wouldn't, not with me running things," said Hanson. "I've been trading and hunting here for ten years and I know as much about the country as he does. If you want to take the girl along I'll help you, and I'll guarantee that there won't nobody catch up with us before we reach the coast. I'll tell you what, you write her a note and I'll get it to her by my head man. Ask her to meet you to say good-bye—she won't refuse that. In the meantime we can be movin' camp a little further north all the time and you can make arrangements with her to be all ready on a certain night. Tell her I'll meet her then while you wait for us in camp. That'll be better for I know the country well and can cover it quicker than you. You can take charge of the *safari* and be movin' along slow toward the north and the girl and I'll catch up to you."

"But suppose she won't come?" suggested Baynes.

"Then make another date for a last good-bye," said Hanson, "and instead of you I'll be there and I'll bring her along anyway. She'll have to come, and after it's all over she won't feel so bad about it—especially after livin' with you for two months while we're makin' the coast."

A shocked and angry protest rose to Baynes' lips; but he did not utter it, for almost simultaneously came the realization that this was practically the same thing he had been planning upon himself. It had sounded brutal and criminal from the lips of the rough trader; but nevertheless the young Englishman saw that with Hanson's help and his knowledge of African travel the possibilities of success would be much greater than as though the Hon. Morison were to attempt the thing single handed. And so he nodded a glum assent.

The balance of the long ride to Hanson's northerly camp was made in silence, for both men were occupied with their own thoughts, most of which were far from being either complimentary or loyal to the other. As they rode through the wood the sounds of their careless passage came to the ears of another jungle wayfarer. The Killer had determined to come back to the place where he had seen the white girl who took to the trees with the agility of long habitude. There was a compelling something in the recollection of her that drew him irresistibly toward her. He wished to see her by the light of day, to see her features, to see the color of her eyes and hair. It seemed to him that she must bear a strong resemblance to his lost Meriem, and yet he knew that the chances were that she did not. The fleeting glimpse that he had had of her in the moonlight as she swung from the back of her plunging pony into the branches of the tree above her had shown him a girl of about the same height as his Meriem; but of a more rounded and developed femininity.

Now he was moving lazily back in the direction of the spot where he had seen the girl when the sounds of the approaching horsemen came to his sharp ears. He moved stealthily through the branches until he came within sight of the riders. The younger man he instantly recognized as the same he had seen with his arms about the girl in the moonlit glade just the instant before Numa charged. The other he did not recognize though there was a familiarity about his carriage and figure that puzzled Korak.

The ape-man decided that to find the girl again he would but have to keep in touch with the young Englishman, and so he fell in behind the pair, following them to Hanson's camp. Here the Hon. Morison penned a brief note, which Hanson gave into the keeping of one of his boys who started off forthwith toward the south.

Korak remained in the vicinity of the camp, keeping a careful watch upon the Englishman. He had half expected to find the girl at the destination of the two riders and had been disappointed when no sign of her materialized about the camp.

Baynes was restless, pacing back and forth beneath the trees when he should have been resting against the forced marches of the coming flight. Hanson lay in his hammock and smoked. They spoke but little. Korak lay stretched upon a branch among the dense foliage above them. Thus passed the balance of the afternoon. Korak became hungry and thirsty. He doubted that either of the men would leave camp now before morning, so he withdrew, but toward the south, for there it seemed most likely the girl still was.

In the garden beside the bungalow Meriem wandered thoughtfully in the moonlight. She still smarted from Bwana's, to her, unjust treatment of the Hon. Morison Baynes. Nothing had been explained to her, for both Bwana and My Dear had wished to spare her the mortification and sorrow of the true explanation of Baynes' proposal. They knew, as Meriem did not, that the man had had no intention of marrying her, else he would have come directly to Bwana, knowing full well that no objection would be interposed if Meriem really cared for him.

Meriem loved them both and was grateful to them for all that they had done for her; but deep in her little heart surged the savage love of liberty that her years of untrameled freedom in the jungle had made part and parcel of her being. Now, for the first time since she had come to them, Meriem felt like a prisoner in the bungalow of Bwana and My Dear.

Like a caged tigress the girl paced the length of the enclosure. Once she paused near the outer fence, her head upon one side— listening. What was it she had heard? The pad of naked human feet just beyond the garden. She listened for a moment. The sound was not repeated. Then she resumed her restless walking. Down to the opposite end of the garden she passed, turned and retraced her steps toward the upper end. Upon the sward near the bushes that hid the fence, full in the glare of the moonlight, lay a white envelope that had not been there when she had turned almost upon the very spot a moment before.

Meriem stopped short in her tracks, listening again, and sniffing—more than ever the tigress; alert, ready. Beyond the bushes a naked black runner squatted, peering through the foliage. He saw her take a step closer to the letter. She had seen it. He rose quietly and following the shadows of the bushes that ran down to the corral was soon gone from sight.

Meriem's trained ears heard his every move. She made no attempt to seek closer knowledge of his identity. Already she had guessed that he was a messenger from the Hon. Morison. She stooped and picked up the envelope. Tearing it open she easily read the contents by the moon's brilliant light. It was, as she had guessed, from Baynes.

"I cannot go without seeing you again," it read. "Come to the clearing early tomorrow morning and say good-bye to me. Come alone."

There was a little more—words that made her heart beat faster and a happy flush mount her cheek.

CHAPTER 20

IT WAS STILL dark when the Hon. Morison Baynes set forth for the trysting place. He insisted upon having a guide, saying that he was not sure that he could find his way back to the little clearing. As a matter of fact the thought of that lonely ride through the darkness before the sun rose had been too much for his courage, and he craved company. A black, therefore, preceded him on foot. Behind and above him came Korak, whom the noise in the camp had awakened.

It was nine o'clock before Baynes drew rein in the clearing. Meriem had not yet arrived. The black lay down to rest. Baynes lolled in his saddle. Korak stretched himself comfortably upon a lofty limb, where he could watch those beneath him without being seen.

An hour passed. Baynes gave evidence of nervousness. Korak had already guessed that the young Englishman had come here to meet another, nor was he at all in doubt as to the identity of that other. The Killer was perfectly satisfied that he was soon again to see the nimble she who had so forcefully reminded him of Meriem.

Presently the sound of an approaching horse came to Korak's ears. She was coming! She had almost reached the clearing before Baynes became aware of her presence, and then as he looked up, the foliage parted to the head and shoulders of her mount and Meriem rode into view. Baynes spurred to meet her. Korak looked searchingly down upon her, mentally anathematizing the broad-brimmed hat that hid her features from his eyes. She was abreast the Englishman now. Korak saw the man take both her hands and draw her close to his breast. He saw the man's face concealed for a moment beneath the same broad brim that hid the girl's. He could imagine their lips meeting, and a twinge of sorrow and sweet recollection combined to close his eyes for an instant in that involuntary muscular act with which we attempt to shut out from the mind's eye harrowing reflections.

When he looked again they had drawn apart and were conversing earnestly. Korak could see the man urging something. It was equally evident that the girl was holding back. There were many of her gestures, and the way in which she tossed her head up and

Korak looked searchingly down.

to the right, tip-tilting her chin, that reminded Korak still more strongly of Meriem. And then the conversation was over and the man took the girl in his arms again to kiss her good-bye. She turned and rode toward the point from which she had come. The man sat on his horse watching her. At the edge of the jungle she turned to wave him a final farewell.

"Tonight!" she cried, throwing back her head as she called the words to him across the little distance which separated them— throwing back her head and revealing her face for the first time to the eyes of The Killer in the tree above. Korak started as though pierced through the heart with an arrow. He trembled and shook like a leaf. He closed his eyes, pressing his palms across them, and then he opened them again and looked—but the girl was gone—only the waving foliage of the jungle's rim marked where she had disappeared. It was impossible! It could not be true! And yet, with his own eyes he had seen his Meriem—older a little, with figure more rounded by nearer maturity, and subtly changed in other ways; more beautiful than ever, yet still his little Meriem. Yes, he had seen the dead alive again; he had seen his Meriem in the flesh. She lived! She had not died! He had seen her—he had seen his Meriem—*in the arms of another man!* And that man sat below him now, within easy reach. Korak, The Killer, fondled his heavy spear. He played with the grass rope dangling from his geestring. He stroked the hunting knife at his hip. And the man beneath him called to his drowsy guide, bent the rein to his pony's neck and moved off toward the north. Still sat Korak, The Killer, alone among the trees. Now his hands hung idly at his sides. His weapons and what he had intended were forgotten for the moment. Korak was thinking. He had noted that subtle change in Meriem. When last he had seen her she had been his little, half-naked Mangani—wild, savage, and uncouth. She had not seemed uncouth to him then; but now, in the change that had come over her, he knew that such she had been; yet no more uncouth than he, and he was still uncouth.

In her had taken place the change. In her he had just seen a sweet and lovely flower of refinement and civilization, and he shuddered as he recalled the fate that he himself had planned for her—to be the mate of an ape-man, his mate, in the savage jungle. Then he had seen no wrong in it, for he had loved her, and the way he had planned had been the way of the jungle which they two had chosen as their home; but now, after having seen the

Meriem of civilized attire, he realized the hideousness of his once cherished plan, and he thanked his God that chance and the blacks of Kovudoo had thwarted him.

Yet he still loved her, and jealousy seared his soul as he recalled the sight of her in the arms of the dapper young Englishman. What were his intentions toward her? Did he really love her? How could one not love her? And she loved him, of that Korak had had ample proof. Had she not loved him she would not have accepted his kisses. His Meriem loved another! For a long time he let that awful truth sink deep, and from it he tried to reason out his future plan of action. In his heart was a great desire to follow the man and slay him; but ever there rose in his consciousness the thought: She loves him. Could he slay the creature Meriem loved? Sadly he shook his head. No, he could not. Then came a partial decision to follow Meriem and speak with her. He half started, and then glanced down at his nakedness and was ashamed. He, the son of a British peer, had thus thrown away his life, had thus degraded himself to the level of a beast that he was ashamed to go to the woman he loved and lay his love at her feet. He was ashamed to go to the little Arab maid who had been his jungle playmate, for what had he to offer her?

For years circumstances had prevented a return to his father and mother, and at last pride had stepped in and expunged from his mind the last vestige of any intention to return. In a spirit of boyish adventure he had cast his lot with the jungle ape. The killing of the crook in the coast inn had filled his childish mind with terror of the law, and driven him deeper into the wilds. The rebuffs that he had met at the hands of men, both black and white, had had their effect upon his mind while yet it was in a formative state, and easily influenced.

He had come to believe that the hand of man was against him, and then he had found in Meriem the only human association he required or craved. When she had been snatched from him his sorrow had been so deep that the thought of ever mingling again with human beings grew still more unutterably distasteful. Finally and for all time, he thought, the die was cast. Of his own volition he had become a beast, a beast he had lived, a beast he would die.

Now, that it was too late, he regretted it. For now Meriem, still living, had been revealed to him in a guise of progress and advancement that had carried her completely out of his life. Death itself could not have further removed her from him. In her new world she loved a man of her own kind. And Korak knew that it was right. She was not for him—not for the naked, savage ape. No, she was not for him; but he still was hers. If he could not have her and happiness, he would at least do all that lay in his power to assure happiness to her. He would follow the young Englishman. In the first place he would know that he meant Meriem no harm, and after that, though jealousy wrenched his heart, he would watch over the man Meriem loved, for Meriem's sake; but God help that man if he thought to wrong her!

Slowly he aroused himself. He stood erect and stretched his great frame, the muscles of his arms gliding sinuously beneath his tanned skin as he bent his clenched fists behind his head. A movement on the ground beneath caught his eye. An antelope was entering the clearing. Immediately Korak became aware that he was empty—again he was a beast. For a moment love had lifted him to sublime heights of honor and renunciation.

The antelope was crossing the clearing. Korak dropped to the ground upon the opposite side of the tree, and so lightly that not even the sensitive ears of the antelope apprehended his presence. He uncoiled his grass rope—it was the latest addition to his armament, yet he was proficient with it. Often he traveled with nothing more than his knife and his rope—they were light and easy to carry. His spear and bow and arrows were cumbersome and he usually kept one or all of them hidden away in a private cache.

Now he held a single coil of the long rope in his right hand, and the balance in his left. The antelope was but a few paces from him. Silently Korak leaped from his hiding place swinging the rope free from the entangling shrubbery. The antelope sprang away almost instantly; but instantly, too, the coiled rope, with its sliding noose, flew through the air above him. With unerring precision it settled about the creature's neck. There was a quick wrist movement of the thrower, the noose tightened. The Killer braced himself with the rope across his hip, and as the antelope taunted the singing strands in a last frantic bound for liberty he was thrown over upon his back.

Then, instead of approaching the fallen animal as a roper of the western plains might do, Korak dragged his captive to himself, pulling him in hand over hand, and when he was within reach leaping upon him even as Sheeta the panther might have done, and burying his teeth in the animal's neck while he found its heart with the point of his hunting knife. Recoiling his rope, he cut a few generous strips from his kill and took to the trees again, where he ate in peace. Later he swung off in the direction of a nearby water hole, and then he slept.

In his mind, of course, was the suggestion of another meeting between Meriem and the young Englishman that had been borne to him by the girl's parting: "Tonight!"

He had not followed Meriem because he knew from the direction from which she had come and in which she returned that wheresoever she had found an asylum it lay out across the plains, and not wishing to be discovered by the girl he had not cared to venture into the open after her. It would do as well to keep in touch with the young man, and that was precisely what he intended doing.

To you or me the possibility of locating the Hon. Morison in the jungle after having permitted him to get such a considerable start might have seemed remote; but to Korak it was not at all so. He guessed that the white man would return to his camp; but should he have done otherwise it were a simple matter to The Killer to trail a mounted man accompanied by another on foot. Days might pass and still such a spoor would be sufficiently plain to lead Korak unfalteringly to its end; while a matter of a few hours only left it as clear to him as though the makers themselves were still in plain sight.

And so it came that a few minutes after the Hon. Morison Baynes entered the camp to be greeted by Hanson, Korak slipped noiselessly into a near-by tree. There he lay until late afternoon and still the young Englishman made no move to leave camp. Korak wondered if Meriem were coming there. A little later Hanson and one of his black boys rode out of camp. Korak merely noted the fact. He was not particularly interested in what any other member of the company than the young Englishman did.

Darkness came and still the young man remained. He ate his evening meal, afterward smoking numerous cigarettes. Presently he began to pace back and forth before his tent. He kept his boy busy replenishing the fire. A lion coughed and he went into his tent to reappear with an express rifle. Again he admonished the boy to throw more brush upon the fire. Korak saw that he was nervous and afraid, and his lip curled in a sneer of contempt.

Was this the creature who had supplanted him in the heart of his Meriem? Was this a man, who trembled when Numa coughed? How could such as he protect Meriem from the countless dangers of the jungle? Ah, but he would not have to. They would live in the safety of European civilization, where men in uniforms were hired to protect them. What need had a European of prowess to protect his mate? Again the sneer curled Korak's lip.

Hanson and his boy had ridden directly to the clearing. It was already dark when they arrived. Leaving the boy there Hanson rode to the edge of the plain, leading the boy's horse. There he waited. It was nine o'clock before he saw a solitary figure galloping toward him from the direction of the bungalow. A few moments later Meriem drew in her mount beside him. She was nervous and flushed. When she recognized Hanson she drew back, startled.

"Mr. Baynes' horse fell on him and sprained his ankle," Hanson hastened to explain. "He couldn't very well come so he sent me to meet you and bring you to camp."

The girl could not see in the darkness the gloating, triumphant expression on the speaker's face.

"We had better hurry," continued Hanson, "for we'll have to move along pretty fast if we don't want to be overtaken."

"Is he hurt badly?" asked Meriem.

"Only a little sprain," replied Hanson. "He can ride all right; but we both thought he'd better lie up tonight, and rest, for he'll have plenty hard riding in the next few weeks."

"Yes," agreed the girl.

Hanson swung his pony about and Meriem followed him. They rode north along the edge of the jungle for a mile and then turned straight into it toward the west. Meriem, following, payed little attention to directions. She did not know exactly where Hanson's camp lay and so she did not guess that he was not leading her toward it. All night they rode, straight toward the west. When morning came, Hanson permitted a short halt for breakfast, which he had provided in well-filled saddle bags before leaving his camp. Then they pushed on again, nor did they halt a second time until in the heat of the day he stopped and motioned the girl to dismount.

"We will sleep here for a time and let the ponies graze," he said.

"I had no idea the camp was so far away," said Meriem.

"I left orders that they were to move on at day break," explained the trader, "so that we could get a good start. I knew that you and I could easily overtake a laden *safari*. It may not be until tomorrow that we'll catch up with them."

But though they traveled part of the night and all the following day no sign of the *safari* appeared ahead of them. Meriem, an adept in jungle craft, knew that none had passed ahead of them for many days. Occasionally she saw indications of an old spoor, a very old spoor, of many men. For the most part they followed this well-marked trail along elephant paths and through park-like groves. It was an ideal trail for rapid traveling.

Meriem at last became suspicious. Gradually the attitude of the man at her side had begun to change. Often she surprised him devouring her with his eyes. Steadily the former sensation of previous acquaintanceship urged itself upon her. Somewhere, sometime before she had known this man. It was evident that he had not shaved for several days. A blonde stubble had commenced to cover his neck and cheeks and chin, and with it the assurance that he was no stranger continued to grow upon the girl.

It was not until the second day, however, that Meriem rebelled. She drew in her pony at last and voiced her doubts. Hanson assured her that the camp was but a few miles further on.

"We should have overtaken them yesterday," he said. "They must have marched much faster than I had believed possible."

"They have not marched here at all," said Meriem. "The spoor that we have been following is weeks old."

Hanson laughed.

"Oh, that's it, is it?" he cried. "Why didn't you say so before? I could have easily explained. We are not coming by the same route; but we'll pick up their trail sometime today, even if we don't overtake them."

Now, at last, Meriem knew that the man was lying to her. What a fool he must be to think that anyone could believe such a ridiculous explanation? Who was so stupid as to believe that they could have expected to overtake another party, and he had certainly assured her that momentarily he expected to do so, when that party's route was not to meet theirs for several miles yet?

She kept her own counsel however, planning to escape at the first opportunity when she might have a sufficient start of her captor, as she now considered him, to give her some assurance of outdistancing him. She watched his face continually when she could without being observed. Tantalizingly the placing of his familiar features persisted in eluding her. Where had she known him? Under what conditions had they met before she had seen him about the farm of Bwana? She ran over in her mind all the few white men she ever had known. There were some who had come to her father's *douar* in the jungle. Few it is true, but there had been some. Ah, now she had it! She had seen him there! She almost seized upon his identity and then, in an instant, it had slipped from her again.

It was mid afternoon when they suddenly broke out of the jungle upon the banks of a broad and placid river. Beyond, upon the opposite shore, Meriem described a camp surrounded by a high, thorn *boma.*

"Here we are at last," said Hanson. He drew his revolver and fired in the air. Instantly the camp across the river was astir. Black men ran down to the river's bank. Hanson hailed them. But there was no sign of the Hon. Morison Baynes.

In accordance with their master's instructions the blacks manned a canoe and rowed across. Hanson placed Meriem in the little craft and entered it himself, leaving two boys to watch the horses, which the canoe was to return for and swim across to the camp side of the river.

Once in the camp Meriem asked for Baynes. For the moment her fears had been allayed by the sight of the camp, which she had come to look upon as more or less of a myth. Hanson pointed toward the single tent that stood in the center of the enclosure.

"There," he said, and preceded her toward it. At the entrance he held the flap aside and motioned her within. Meriem entered and looked about. The tent was empty. She turned toward Hanson. There was a broad grin on his face.

"Where is Mr. Baynes?" she demanded.

"He ain't here," replied Hanson. "Leastwise I don't see him, do you? But I'm here, and I'm a damned sight better man than that thing ever was. You don't need him no more—you got me," and he laughed uproariously and reached for her.

Meriem struggled to free herself. Hanson encircled her arms and body in his powerful grip and bore her slowly backward toward the pile of blankets at the far end of the tent. His face was bent close to hers. His eyes were narrowed to two slits of heat and passion and desire. Meriem was looking full into his face as she fought for freedom when there came over her a sudden recollection of a similar scene in which she had been a participant and with it full recognition of her assailant. He was the Swede

Malbihn who had attacked her once before, who had shot his companion who would have saved her, and from whom she had been rescued by Bwana. His smooth face had deceived her; but now with the growing beard and the similarity of conditions recognition came swift and sure.

But today there would be no Bwana to save her.

CHAPTER 21

THE BLACK BOY whom Malbihn had left awaiting him in the clearing with instructions to remain until he returned sat crouched at the foot of a tree for an hour when he was suddenly startled by the coughing grunt of a lion behind him. With celerity born of the fear of death the boy clambered into the branches of the tree, and a moment later the king of beasts entered the clearing and approached the carcass of an antelope which, until now, the boy had not seen.

Until daylight the beast fed, while the black clung, sleepless, to his perch, wondering what had become of his master and the two ponies. He had been with Malbihn for a year, and so was fairly conversant with the character of the white. His knowledge presently led him to believe that he had been purposely abandoned. Like the balance of Malbihn's followers, this boy hated his master cordially—fear being the only bond that held him to the white man. His present uncomfortable predicament but added fuel to the fires of his hatred.

As the sun rose the lion withdrew into the jungle and the black descended from his tree and started upon his long journey back to camp. In his primitive brain revolved various fiendish plans for a revenge that he would not have the courage to put into effect when the test came and he stood face to face with one of the dominant race.

A mile from the clearing he came upon the spoor of two ponies crossing his path at right angles. A cunning look entered the black's eyes. He laughed uproariously and slapped his thighs.

Negroes are tireless gossipers, which, of course, is but a roundabout way of saying that they are human. Malbihn's boys had been no exception to the rule and as many of them had been with him at various times during the past ten years there was little about his acts and life in the African wilds that was not known directly or by hearsay to them all.

And so, knowing his master and many of his past deeds, knowing, too, a great deal about the plans of Malbihn and Baynes that had been overheard by hmself, or other servants; and knowing well from the gossip of the head-men that half of Malbihn's party lay in camp by the great river far to the west, it was not difficult for the boy to put two and two together and arrive at four as the sum—the four being represented by a firm conviction that his master had deceived the other white man and taken the latter's woman to his western camp, leaving the other to suffer capture and punishment at the hands of the Big Bwana whom all feared. Again the boy bared his rows of big, white teeth and laughed aloud. Then he resumed his northward way, traveling at a dogged trot that ate up the miles with marvelous rapidity.

In the Swede's camp the Hon. Morison had spent an almost sleepless night of nervous apprehension and doubts and fears. Toward morning he had slept, utterly exhausted It was the head-man who awoke him shortly after sun rise to remind him that they must at once take up their northward journey. Baynes hung back. He wanted to wait for "Hanson" and Meriem. The head-man urged upon him the danger that lay in loitering. The fellow knew his master's plans sufficiently well to understand that he had done something to arouse the ire of the Big Bwana and that it would fare ill with them all if they were overtaken in Big Bwana's country. At the suggestion Baynes took alarm.

What if the Big Bwana, as the head-man called him, had surprised "Hanson" in his nefarious work. Would he not guess the truth and possibly be already on the march to overtake and punish him? Baynes had heard much of his host's summary method of dealing out punishment to malefactors great and small who transgressed the laws or customs of his savage little world which lay beyond the outer ramparts of what men are pleased to call frontiers. In this savage world where there was no law the Big Bwana was law unto himself and all who dwelt about him. It was even rumored that he had exacted the death penalty from a white man who had maltreated a native girl.

Baynes shuddered at the recollection of this piece of gossip as he wondered what his host would exact of the man who had attempted to steal his young, white ward. The thought brought him to his feet.

THE SON OF TARZAN

"Yes," he said, nervously, "we must get away from here at once. Do you know the trail to the north?"

The head-man did, and he lost no time in getting the *safari* upon the march.

It was noon when a tired and sweat-covered runner overtook the trudging little column. The man was greeted with shouts of welcome from his fellows, to whom he imparted all that he knew and guessed of the actions of their master, so that the entire *safari* was aware of matters before Baynes, who marched close to the head of the column, was reached and acquainted with the facts and the imaginings of the black boy whom Malbihn had deserted in the clearing the night before.

When the Hon. Morison had listened to all that the boy had to say and realized that the trader had used him as a tool whereby he himself might get Meriem into his possession, his blood ran hot with rage and he trembled with apprehension for the girl's safety.

That another contemplated no worse a deed than he had contemplated in no way palliated the hideousness of the other's offense. At first it did not occur to him that he would have wronged Meriem no less than he believed "Hanson" contemplated wronging her. Now his rage was more the rage of a man beaten at his own game and robbed of the prize that he had thought already his.

"Do you know where your master has gone?" he asked the black.

"Yes, Bwana," replied the boy. "He has gone to the other camp beside the big *afi* that flows far toward the setting sun."

"Can you take me to him?" demanded Baynes.

The boy nodded affirmatively. Here he saw a method of revenging himself upon his hated Bwana and at the same time of escaping the wrath of the Big Bwana whom all were positive would first follow after the northerly *safari*.

"Can you and I, alone, reach his camp?" asked the Hon. Morison.

"Yes, Bwana," assured the black.

Baynes turned toward the head-man. He was conversant with "Hanson's" plans now. He understood why he had wished to move the northern camp as far as possible toward the northern boundary of the Big Bwana's country—it would give him far more time to make his escape toward the West Coast while the Big

Bwana was chasing the northern contingent. Well, he would utilize the man's plans to his own ends. He, too, must keep out of the clutches of his host.

"You may take the men north as fast as possible," he said to the head-man. "I shall return and attempt to lead the Big Bwana to the west."

The negro assented with a grunt. He had no desire to follow this strange white man who was afraid at night; he had less to remain at the tender mercies of the Big Bwana's lusty warriors, between whom and his people there was long-standing blood feud; and he was more than delighted, into the bargain, for a legitimate excuse for deserting his much hated Swede master. He knew a way to the north and his own country that the white men did not know—a short cut across an arid plateau where lay water holes of which the white hunters and explorers that had passed from time to time the fringe of the dry country had never dreamed. He might even elude the Big Bwana should he follow them, and with this thought uppermost in his mind he gathered the remnants of Malbihn's *safari* into a semblance of order and moved off toward the north. And toward the southwest the black boy led the Hon. Morison Baynes into the jungles.

Korak had waited about the camp, watching the Hon. Morison until the *safari* had started north. Then, assured that the young Englishman was going in the wrong direction to meet Meriem he had abandoned him and returned slowly to the point where he had seen the girl, for whom his heart yearned, in the arms of another.

So great had been his happiness at seeing Meriem alive that, for the instant, no thought of jealousy had entered his mind. Later these thoughts had come—dark, bloody thoughts that would have made the flesh of the Hon. Morison creep could he have guessed that they were revolving in the brain of a savage creature creeping stealthily among the branches of the forest giants beneath which he waited the coming of "Hanson" and the girl.

And with passing of the hours had come subdued reflection in which he had weighed himself against the trimly clad English gentleman and—found that he was wanting. What had he to offer her by comparison with that which the other might offer? What was his "mess of pottage" to the birthright that the other had preserved? How could he dare go, naked and unkempt, to that fair thing who had once been his jungle-fellow and propose the thing that had been in his mind when first the realization of his love had swept over him? He shuddered as he thought of the irreparable wrong that his love would have done the innocent child but for the chance that had snatched her from him before it was too late. Doubtless she knew now the horror that had been in his mind. Doubtless she hated and loathed him as he hated and loathed himself when he let his mind dwell upon it. He had lost her. No more surely had she been lost when he thought her dead than she was in reality now that he had seen her living—living in the guise of a refinement that had transfigured and sanctified her.

He had loved her before, now he worshiped her. He knew that he might never possess her now, but at least he might see her. From a distance he might look upon her. Perhaps he might serve her; but never must she guess that he had found her or that he lived.

He wondered if she ever thought of him—if the happy days that they had spent together never recurred to her mind. It seemed unbelievable that such could be the case, and yet, too, it seemed almost equally unbelievable that this beautiful girl was the same disheveled, half naked, little sprite who skipped nimbly among the branches of the trees as they ran and played in the lazy, happy days of the past. It could not be that her memory held more of the past than did her new appearance.

It was a sad Korak who ranged the jungle near the plain's edge waiting for the coming of his Meriem—the Meriem who never came.

But there came another—a tall, broad-shouldered man in khaki at the head of a swarthy crew of ebon warriors. The man's face was set in hard, stern lines and the marks of sorrow were writ deep about his mouth and eyes—so deep that the set expression of rage upon his features could not obliterate them.

Korak saw the man pass beneath him where he hid in the great tree that had harbored him before upon the edge of that fateful little clearing. He saw him come and he set rigid and frozen and suffering above him. He saw him search the ground with his keen eyes, and he only sat there watching with eyes that glazed from the intensity of his gaze. He saw him sign to his men that he had come upon that which he sought and he saw him pass out of sight toward the north, and still Korak sat like a graven image, with a heart that bled in dumb misery. An hour later Korak moved slowly away, back into the jungle toward the west. He went listlessly, with bent head and stooped shoulders, like an old man who bore upon his back the weight of a great sorrow.

Baynes, following his black guide, battled his way through the dense underbrush, riding stooped low over his horse's neck, or often he dismounted where the low branches swept too close to earth to permit him to remain in the saddle. The black was taking him the shortest way, which was no way at all for a horseman, and after the first day's march the young Englishman was forced to abandon his mount, and follow his nimble guide entirely on foot.

During the long hours of marching the Hon. Morison had much time to devote to thought, and as he pictured the probable fate of Meriem at the hands of the Swede his rage against the man became the greater. But presently there came to him a realization of the fact that his own base plans had led the girl into this terrible predicament, and that even had she escaped "Hanson" she would have found but little better deserts awaiting her with him.

There came too, the realization that Meriem was infinitely more precious to him than he had imagined. For the first time he commenced to compare her with other women of his acquaintance—women of birth and position—and almost to his surprise—he discovered that the young Arab girl suffered less than they by the comparison. And then from hating "Hanson" he came to look upon himself with hate and loathing—to see himself and his perfidious act in all their contemptible hideousness.

Thus, in the crucible of shame amidst the white heat of naked truths, the passion that the man had felt for the girl he had considered his social inferior was transmuted into love. And as he staggered on there burned within him beside his newborn love another great passion—the passion of hate urging him on to the consummation of revenge.

A creature of ease and luxury, he had never been subjected to the hardships and tortures which now were his constant companions, yet, his clothing torn, his flesh scratched and bleeding, he urged the black to greater speed, though with every dozen steps he himself fell from exhaustion.

It was revenge which kept him going—that and a feeling that in his suffering he was partially expiating the great wrong he had done the girl he loved—for hope of saving her from the fate into which he had trapped her had never existed. "Too late! Too late!"

was the dismal accompaniment of thought to which he marched. "Too late! Too late to save; but not too late to avenge!" That kept him up.

Only when it became too dark to see would he permit of a halt. A dozen times in the afternoon he had threatened the black with instant death when the tired guide insisted upon resting. The fellow was terrified. He could not understand the remarkable change that had so suddenly come over the white man who had been afraid in the dark the night before. He would have deserted this terrifying master had he had the opportunity; but Baynes guessed that some such thought might be in the other's mind, and so gave the fellow none. He kept close to him by day and slept touching him at night in the rude thorn *boma* they constructed as a slight protection against prowling carnivora.

That the Hon. Morison could sleep at all in the midst of the savage jungle was sufficient indication that he had changed considerably in the past twenty-four hours, and that he could lie close beside a none-too-fragrant black man spoke of possibilities for democracy within him yet all undreamed of.

Morning found him stiff and lame and sore, but none the less determined to push on in pursuit of "Hanson" as rapidly as possible. With his rifle he brought down a buck at a ford in a small stream shortly after they broke camp, breakfastless. Begrudgingly he permitted a halt while they cooked and ate, and then on again through the wilderness of trees and vines and underbrush.

And in the meantime Korak wandered slowly westward, coming upon the trail of Tantor, the elephant, whom he overtook browsing in the deep shade of the jungle. The ape-man, lonely and sorrowing, was glad of the companionship of his huge friend. Affectionately the sinuous trunk encircled him, and he was swung to the mighty back where so often before he had lolled and dreamed the long afternoons away.

Far to the north the Big Bwana and his black warriors clung tenaciously to the trail of the fleeing *safari* that was luring them further and further from the girl they sought to save, while back at the bungalow the woman who had loved Meriem as though she had been her own waited impatiently and in sorrow for the return of the rescuing party and the girl she was positive her invincible lord and master would bring back with him.

CHAPTER 22

As MERIEM STRUGGLED with Malbihn, her hands pinioned to her sides by his brawny grip, hope died within her. She did not utter a sound for she knew that there was none to come to her assistance, and, too, the jungle training of her earlier life had taught her the futility of appeals for succor in the savage world of her up-bringing.

But as she fought to free herself one hand came in contact with the butt of Malbihn's revolver where it rested in the holster at his hip. Slowly he was dragging her toward the blankets, and slowly her fingers encircled the coveted prize and drew it from its resting place.

Then, as Malbihn stood at the edge of the disordered pile of blankets, Meriem suddenly ceased to draw away from him, and as quickly hurled her weight against him with the result that he was thrown backward, his feet stumbled against the bedding and he was hurled to his back. Instinctively his hands flew out to save himself and at the same instant Meriem leveled the revolver at his breast and pulled the trigger.

But the hammer fell futilely upon an empty shell, and Malbihn was again upon his feet clutching at her. For a moment she eluded him, and ran toward the entrance to the tent, but at the very doorway his heavy hand fell upon her shoulder and dragged her back. Wheeling upon him with the fury of a wounded lioness Meriem grasped the long revolver by the barrel, swung it high above her head and crashed it down full in Malbihn's face.

With an oath of pain and rage the man staggered backward, releasing his hold upon her and then sank unconscious to the ground. Without a backward look Meriem turned and fled into the open. Several of the blacks saw her and tried to intercept her flight, but the menace of the empty weapon kept them at a distance. And so she won beyond the encircling boma and disappeared into the jungle to the south.

Straight into the branches of a tree she went, true to the arboreal instincts of the little mangani she had been, and here she stripped off her riding skirt, her shoes and her stockings, for she knew that she had before her a journey and a flight which would not brook the burden of these garments. Her riding breeches and jacket would have to serve as protection from cold and thorns, nor would they hamper her over much; but a skirt and shoes were impossible among the trees.

She had not gone far before she commenced to realize how slight were her chances for survival without means of defense or a weapon to bring down meat. Why had she not thought to strip the cartridge belt from Malbihn's waist before she had left his tent! With cartridges for the revolver she might hope to bag small game, and to protect herself from all but the most ferocious of the enemies that would beset her way back to the beloved hearth-stone of Bwana and My Dear.

With the thought came determination to return and obtain the coveted ammunition. She realized that she was taking great chances of recapture; but without means of defense and of obtaining meat she felt that she could never hope to reach safety. And so she turned her face back toward the camp from which she had but just escaped.

She thought Malbihn dead, so terrific a blow had she dealt him, and she hoped to find an opportunity after dark to enter the camp and search his tent for the cartridge belt; but scarcely had she found a hiding place in a great tree at the edge of the *boma* where she could watch without danger of being discovered, than she saw the Swede emerge from his tent, wiping blood from his face, and hurling a volley of oaths and questions at his terrified followers.

Shortly after the entire camp set forth in search of her and when Meriem was positive that all were gone she descended from her hiding place and ran quickly across the clearing to Malbihn's tent. A hasty survey of the interior revealed no ammunition; but in one corner was a box in which were packed the Swede's personal belongings that he had sent along by his head-man to this westerly camp.

Meriem seized the receptacle as the possible container of extra ammunition. Quickly she loosed the cords that held the canvas covering about the box, and a moment later had raised the lid and was rummaging through the heterogeneous accumulation of odds and ends within. There were letters and papers and cuttings from old newspapers, and among other things the photograph of a little girl upon the back of which was pasted a cutting from a Paris daily—a cutting that she could not read, yellowed and dimmed by age and handling—but something about the photo-graph of the little girl which was also reproduced in the newspaper cutting held her attention. Where had she seen that picture before?

And then, quite suddenly, it came to her that this was a picture of herself as she had been years and years before.

Where had it been taken? How had it come into the possession of this man? Why had it been reproduced in a newspaper? What was the story that the faded type told of it?

Meriem was baffled by the puzzle that her search for ammunition had revealed. She stood gazing at the faded photograph for a time and then bethought herself of the ammunition for which she had come. Turning again to the box she rummaged to the bottom and there in a corner she came upon a little box of cartridges. A single glance assured her that they were intended for the weapon she had thrust inside the band of her riding breeches, and slipping them into her pocket she turned once more for an examination of the baffling likeness of herself that she held in her hand.

As she stood thus in vain endeavor to fathom this inexplicable mystery the sound of voices broke upon her ears. Instantly she was all alert. They were coming closer! A second later she recognized the lurid profanity of the Swede. Malbihn, her persecutor, was returning! Meriem ran quickly to the opening of the tent and looked out. It was too late! She was fairly cornered! The white man and three of his black henchmen were coming straight across the clearing toward the tent. What was she to do? She slipped the photograph into her waist. Quickly she slipped a cartridge into each of the chambers of the revolver. Then she backed toward the end of the tent, keeping the entrance covered by her weapon. The men stopped outside, and Meriem could hear Malbihn profanely issuing instructions. He was a long time about it, and while he talked in his bellowing, brutish voice, the girl sought some avenue of escape. Stooping, she raised the bottom of the canvas and looked beneath and beyond. There was no one in sight upon that side. Throwing herself upon her stomach she wormed beneath the tent wall just as Malbihn, with a final word to his men, entered the tent.

Meriem heard him cross the floor, and then she rose and, stooping low, ran to a native hut directly behind. Once inside this she turned and glanced back. There was no one in sight. She had not been seen. And now from Malbihn's tent she heard a great cursing. The Swede had discovered the rifling of his box. He was shouting to his men, and as she heard them reply Meriem darted from the hut and ran toward the edge of the boma furthest from Malbihn's tent. Overhanging the *boma* at this point was a tree that had been too large, in the eyes of the rest-loving blacks, to cut down. So they had terminated the *boma* just short of it. Meriem was thankful for whatever circumstance had resulted in the leaving of that particular tree where it was, since it gave her the much-needed avenue of escape which she might not otherwise have had.

From her hiding place she saw Malbihn again enter the jungle, this time leaving a guard of three of his boys in the camp. He went toward the south, and after he had disappeared Meriem skirted the outside of the enclosure and made her way to the river. Here lay the canoes that had been used in bringing the party from the opposite shore. They were unwieldy things for a lone girl to handle, but there was no other way and she must cross the river.

The landing place was in full view of the guard at the camp. To risk the crossing under their eyes would have meant undoubted capture. Her only hope lay in waiting until darkness had fallen, unless some fortuitous circumstance should arise before. For an hour she lay watching the guard, one of whom seemed always in a position where he would immediately discover her should she attempt to launch one of the canoes.

Presently Malbihn appeared, coming out of the jungle, hot and puffing. He ran immediately to the river where the canoes lay and counted them. It was evident that it had suddenly occurred to him that the girl must cross here if she wished to return to her protectors. The expression of relief on his face when he found that none of the canoes was gone was ample evidence of what was passing in his mind. He turned and spoke hurriedly to the head man who had followed him out of the jungle and with whom were several other blacks.

Following Malbihn's instructions they launched all the canoes but one. Malbihn called to the guards in the camp and a moment later the entire party had entered the boats and were paddling up stream.

Meriem watched them until a bend in the river directly above the camp hid them from her sight. They were gone! She was alone, and they had left a canoe in which lay a paddle! She could scarce believe the good fortune that had come to her. To delay now would be suicidal to her hopes. Quickly she ran from her hiding place and dropped to the ground. A dozen yards lay between her and the canoe.

Up stream, beyond the bend, Malbihn ordered his canoes in to shore. He landed with his head man and crossed the little point slowly in search of a spot where he might watch the canoe he had left at the landing place. He was smiling in anticipation of the almost certain success of his stratagem—sooner or later the girl would come back and attempt to cross the river in one of their canoes. It might be that the idea would not occur to her for some time. They might have to wait a day, or two days; but that she would come if she lived or was not captured by the men he had scouting the jungle for her Malbihn was sure. That she would come so soon, however, he had not guessed, and so when he topped the point and came again within sight of the river he saw that which drew an angry oath from his lips—his quarry already was half way across the river.

Turning, he ran rapidly back to his boats, the head man at his heels. Throwing themselves in Malbihn urged his paddlers to their most powerful efforts. The canoes shot out into the stream and down with the current toward the fleeing quarry. She had almost completed the crossing when they came in sight of her. At the same instant she saw them, and redoubled her efforts to reach the opposite shore before they should overtake her. Two minutes' start of them was all Meriem cared for. Once in the trees she knew that she could outdistance and elude them. Her hopes were high—they could not overtake her now—she had too good a start of them.

Malbihn, urging his men onward with a stream of hideous oaths and blows from his fists, realized that the girl was again slipping from his clutches. The leading canoe, in the bow of which he stood, was yet a hundred yards behind the fleeing Meriem when she ran the point of her craft beneath the overhanging trees on the shore of safety.

Malbihn screamed to her to halt. He seemed to have gone mad with rage at the realization that he could not overtake her, and then he threw his rifle to his shoulder, aimed carefully at the slim figure scrambling into the trees, and fired.

Malbihn was an excellent shot. His misses at so short a distance were practically non-existent, nor would he have missed this time but for an accident occurring at the very instant that his finger tightened upon the trigger—an accident to which Meriem owed her life—the providential presence of a water-logged tree trunk, one end of which was embedded in the mud of the river bottom and the other end of which floated just beneath the surface where the prow of Malbihn's canoe ran upon it as he fired. The slight deviation of the boat's direction was sufficient to throw the muzzle of the rifle out of aim. The bullet whizzed harmlessly by Meriem's head and an instant later she had disappeared into the foliage of the tree.

There was a smile on her lips as she dropped to the ground to cross a little clearing where once had stood a native village surrounded by its fields. The ruined huts still stood in crumbling decay. The rank vegetation of the jungle overgrew the cultivated ground. Small trees already had sprung up in what had been the village street; but desolation and loneliness hung like a pall above the scene. To Meriem, however, it presented but a place denuded of large trees which she must cross quickly to regain the jungle upon the opposite side before Malbihn should have landed.

The deserted huts were, to her, all the better because they were deserted—she did not see the keen eyes watching her from a dozen points, from tumbling doorways, from behind tottering granaries. In utter unconsciousness of impending danger she started up the village street because it offered the clearest pathway to the jungle.

A mile away toward the east, fighting his way through the jungle along the trail taken by Malbihn when he had brought Meriem to his camp, a man in torn khaki—filthy, haggard, unkempt— came to a sudden stop as the report of Malbihn's rifle resounded faintly through the tangled forest. The black man just ahead of him stopped, too.

"We are almost there, Bwana," he said. There was awe and respect in his tone and manner.

The white man nodded and motioned his ebon guide forward once more. It was the Hon. Morison Baynes—the fastidious—the exquisite. His face and hands were scratched and smeared with dried blood from the wounds he had come by in thorn and thicket. His clothes were tatters. But through the blood and the dirt and the rags a new Baynes shone forth—a handsomer Baynes than the dandy and the fop of yore.

In the heart and soul of every son of woman lies the germ of manhood and honor. Remorse for a scurvy act, and an honorable desire to right the wrong he had done the woman he now knew he really loved had excited these germs to rapid growth in Morison Baynes—and the metamorphosis had taken place.

Onward the two stumbled toward the point from which the

single rifle shot had come. The black was unarmed—Baynes, fearing his loyalty had not dared trust him even to carry the rifle which the white man would have been glad to be relieved of many times upon the long march; but now that they were approaching their goal, and knowing as he did that hatred of Malbihn burned hot in the black man's brain, Baynes handed him the rifle, for he guessed that there would be fighting—he intended that there should, for he had come to avenge. Himself, an excellent revolver shot, would depend upon the smaller weapon at his side.

As the two forged ahead toward their goal they were startled by a volley of shots ahead of them. Then came a few scattering reports, some savage yells, and silence. Baynes was frantic in his endeavors to advance more rapidly, but here the jungle seemed a thousand times more tangled than before. A dozen times he tripped and fell. Twice the black followed a blind trail and they were forced to retrace their steps; but at last they came out into a little clearing near the big *afi*—a clearing that once had held a thriving village, but lay somber and desolate in decay and ruin.

In the jungle vegetation that overgrew what had once been the main village street lay the body of a black man, pierced through the heart with a bullet, and still warm. Baynes and his companion looked about in all directions; but no sign of living being could they discover. They stood in silence listening intently.

What was that! Voices and the dip of paddles out upon the river?

Baynes ran across the dead village toward the fringe of jungle upon the river's brim. The black was at his side. Together they forced their way through the screening foliage until they could obtain a view of the river, and there, almost to the other shore, they saw Malbihn's canoes making rapidly for camp. The black recognized his companions immediately.

"How can we cross?" asked Baynes.

The black shook his head. There was no canoe and the crocodiles made it equivalent to suicide to enter the water in an attempt to swim across. Just then the fellow chanced to glance downward. Beneath him, wedged among the branches of a tree, lay the canoe in which Meriem had escaped. The negro grasped Baynes' arm and pointed toward his find. The Hon. Morison could scarce repress a shout of exultation. Quickly the two slid down the drooping branches into the boat. The black seized the paddle and Baynes shoved them out from beneath the tree. A second later the canoe shot out upon the bosom of the river and headed toward the opposite shore and the camp of the Swede. Baynes squatted in the bow, straining his eyes after the men pulling the other canoes upon the bank across from him. He saw Malbihn step from the bow of the foremost of the little craft. He saw him turn and glance back across the river. He could see his start of surprise as his eyes fell upon the pursuing canoe, and called the attention of his followers to it.

Then he stood waiting, for there was but one canoe and two men—little danger to him and his followers in that. Malbihn was puzzled. Who was this white man? He did not recognize him though Baynes' canoe was now in mid stream and the features of both its occupants plainly discernible to those on shore. One of Malbihn's blacks it was who first recognized his fellow black in the person of Baynes' companion. Then Malbihn guessed who the white man must be, though he could scarce believe his own reasoning. It seemed beyond the pale of wildest conjecture to suppose that the Hon. Morison Baynes had followed him through the jungle with but a single companion—and yet it was true. Beneath the dirt and dishevelment he recognized him at last, and in the necessity of admitting that it was he, Malbihn was forced to recognize the incentive that had driven Baynes, the weakling and coward, through the savage jungle upon his trail.

The man had come to demand an accounting and to avenge. It seemed incredible, and yet there could be no other explanation. Malbihn shrugged. Well, others had sought Malbihn for similar reasons in the course of a long and checkered career. He fingered his rifle, and waited.

Now the canoe was within easy speaking distance of the shore. "What do you want?" yelled Malbihn, raising his weapon threateningly.

The Hon. Morison Baynes leaped to his feet.

"You, damn you!" he shouted, whipping out his revolver and firing almost simultaneously with the Swede.

As the two reports rang out Malbihn dropped his rifle, clutched frantically at his breast, staggered, fell first to his knees and then lunged upon his face. Baynes stiffened. His head flew back spasmodically. For an instant he stood thus, and then crumpled very gently into the bottom of the boat.

The black paddler was at a loss as to what to do. If Malbihn really were dead he could continue on to join his fellows without fear; but should the Swede only be wounded he would be safer upon the far shore. Therefore he hesitated, holding the canoe in mid-stream. He had come to have considerable respect for his new master and was not unmoved by his death. As he sat gazing at the crumpled body in the bow of the boat he saw it move. Very feebly the man essayed to turn over. He still lived. The black moved forward and lifted him to a sitting position. He was standing in front of him, his paddle in one hand, asking Baynes where he was hit when there was another shot from shore and the negro pitched headlong overboard, his paddle still clutched in his dead fingers—shot through the forehead.

Baynes turned weakly in the direction of the shore to see Malbihn drawn up upon his elbows levelling his rifle at him. The Englishman slid to the bottom of the canoe as a bullet whizzed above him. Malbihn, sore hit, took longer in aiming, nor was his aim as sure as formerly. With difficulty Baynes turned himself over on his belly and grasping his revolver in his right hand drew himself up until he could look over the edge of the canoe.

Malbihn saw him instantly and fired; but Baynes did not flinch or duck. With painstaking care he aimed at the target upon the shore from which he now was drifting with the current. His finger closed upon the trigger—there was a flash and a report, and Malbihn's giant frame jerked to the impact of another bullet.

But he was not yet dead. Again he aimed and fired, the bullet splintering the gunwale of the canoe close by Baynes face. Baynes fired again as his canoe drifted further down stream and Malbihn answered from the shore where he lay in a pool of his own blood. And thus, doggedly, the two wounded men continued to carry on their weird duel until the winding African river had carried the Hon. Morison Baynes out of sight around a wooded point.

CHAPTER 23

MERIEM HAD TRAVERSED half the length of the village street when a score of white-robed negroes and half-castes leaped out upon her from the dark interiors of surrounding huts. She turned to flee, but heavy hands seized her, and when she turned at last to plead with them her eyes fell upon the face of a tall, grim, old man glaring down upon her from beneath the folds of his burnous.

At sight of him she stggered back in shocked and terrified surprise. It was The Sheik!

Instantly all the old fears and terrors of her childhood returned upon her. She stood trembling before this horrible old man, as a murderer before the judge about to pass sentence of death upon him. She knew that The Sheik recognized her. The years and the changed raiment had not altered her so much but what one who had known her features so well in childhood would know her now.

"So you have come back to your people, eh?" snarled The Sheik. "Come back begging for food and protection, eh?"

"Let me go," cried the girl. "I ask nothing of you, but that you let me go back to the Big Bwana."

"The Big Bwana?" almost screamed The Sheik, and then followed a stream of profane, Arabic invective against the white man whom all the transgressors of the jungle feared and hated. "You would go back to the Big Bwana, would you? So that is where you have been since you ran away from me, is it? And who comes now across the river after you—the Big Bwana?"

"The Swede whom you once chased away from your country when he and his companion conspired with Nbeeda to steal me from you," replied Meriem.

The Sheik's eyes blazed, and he called his men to approach the shore and hide among the bushes that they might ambush and annihilate Malbihn and his party; but Malbihn already had landed and crawling through the fringe of jungle was at that very moment looking with wide and incredulous eyes upon the scene being enacted in the street of the deserted village. He recognized The Sheik the moment his eyes fell upon him. There were two men in the world that Malbihn feared as he feared the devil. One was the Big Bwana and the other The Sheik. A single glance he took at that gaunt, familiar figure and then he turned tail and scurried back to his canoe calling his followers after him. And so it happened that the party was well out in the stream before The Sheik reached the shore, and after a volley and a few parting shots that were returned from the canoes the Arab called his men off and securing his prisoner set off toward the South.

One of the bullets from Malbihn's force had struck a black standing in the village street where he had been left with another to guard Meriem, and his companions had left him where he had fallen, after appropriating his apparel and belongings. His was the body that Baynes had discovered when he had entered the village.

The Sheik and his party had been marching southward along the river when one of them, dropping out of line to fetch water, had seen Meriem paddling desperately from the opposite shore. The fellow had called The Sheik's attention to the strange sight— a white woman alone in Central Africa—and the old Arab had hidden his men in the deserted village to capture her when she landed, for thoughts of ransom were always in the mind of The Sheik. More than once before had glittering gold filtered through his fingers from a similar source. It was easy money and The Sheik had none too much easy money since the Big Bwana had so circumscribed the limits of his ancient domain that he dared not even steal ivory from natives within two hundred miles of the Big Bwana's *douar*. And when at last the woman had walked into the trap he had set for her and he had recognized her as the same little girl he had brutalized and mal-treated years before his gratification had been huge. Now he lost no time in establishing the old relations of father and daughter that had existed between them in the past. At the first opportunity he struck her a heavy blow across the face. He forced her to walk when he might have dismounted one of his men instead, or had her carried on a horse's rump. He seemed to revel in the discovery of new methods for torturing or humiliating her, and among all his followers she found no single one to offer her sympathy, or who dared defend her, even had they had the desire to do so.

A two days' march brought them at last to the familiar scenes of her childhood, and the first face upon which she set her eyes as she was driven through the gates into the strong stockade was that of the toothless, hideous Mabunu, her one time nurse. It was as though all the years that had intervened were but a dream. Had it not been for her clothing and the fact that she had grown in stature she might well have believed it so. All was there as she had left it—the new faces which supplanted some of the old were of the same bestial, degraded type. There were a few young Arabs who had joined The Sheik since she had been away. Otherwise all was the same—all but one. Geeka was not there, and she found herself missing Geeka as though the ivory-headed one had been a flesh and blood intimate and friend. She missed her ragged little confidante, into whose deaf ears she had been wont to pour her many miseries and her occasional joys—Geeka, of the splinter limbs and the ratskin torso—Geeka the disreputable—Geeka the beloved.

For a time the inhabitants of The Sheik's village who had not been upon the march with him amused themselves by inspecting the strangely clad white girl, whom some of them had known as a little child. Mabunu pretended great joy at her return, baring her toothless gums in a hideous grimace that was intended to be indicative of rejoicing. But Meriem could but shudder as she recalled the cruelties of this terrible old hag in the years gone by.

Among the Arabs who had come in her absence was a tall young fellow of twenty—a handsome, sinister looking youth— who stared at her in open admiration until The Sheik came and ordered him away, and Abdul Kamak went, scowling.

At last, their curiosity satisfied, Meriem was alone. As of old, she was permitted the freedom of the village, for the stockade was high and strong and the only gates were well-guarded by day and by night; but as of old she cared not for the companionship of the cruel Arabs and the degraded blacks who formed the following of The Sheik, and so, as had been her wont in the sad days of her childhood, she slunk down to an unfrequented corner of the enclosure where she had often played at housekeeping with her beloved Geeka beneath the spreading branches of the great tree that had overhung the palisade; but now the tree was gone, and Meriem guessed the reason. It was from this tree that Korak had descended and struck down The Sheik the day that he had rescued her from the life of misery and torture that had been her lot for so long that she could remember no other.

There were low bushes growing within the stockade, however, and in the shade of these Meriem sat down to think. A little glow of happiness warmed her heart as she recalled her first meeting with Korak and then the long years that he had cared for and protected her with the solicitude and purity of an elder brother. For months Korak had not so occupied her thoughts as he did today. He seemed closer and dearer now than ever he had before, and she wondered that her heart had drifted so far from loyalty to his memory. And then came the image of the Hon. Morison, the exquisite, and Meriem was troubled. Did she really love the flawless young Englishman? She thought of the glories of London, of which he had told her in such glowing language. She tried to picture herself admired and honored in the midst of the gayest society of the great capital. The pictures she drew were the pictures that the Hon. Morison had drawn for her. They were alluring pictures, but through them all the brawny, half-naked figure of the giant Adonis of the jungle persisted in obtruding itself.

Meriem pressed her hand above her heart as she stifled a sigh, and as she did so she felt the hard outlines of the photograph she had hidden there as she slunk from Malbihn's tent. Now she drew it forth and commenced to re-examine it more carefully than she had had time to do before. She was sure that the baby face was hers. She studied every detail of the picture. Half hidden in the lace of the dainty dress rested a chain and locket. Meriem puckered her brows. What tantalizing half-memories it awakened! Could this flower of evident civilization be the little Arab Meriem, daughter of The Sheik? It was impossible, and yet that locket? Meriem knew it. She could not refute the conviction of her memory. She had seen that locket before and it had been hers. What strange mystery lay buried in her past?

As she sat gazing at the picture she suddenly became aware that she was not alone—that someone was standing close behind her—some one who had approached her noiselessly. Guiltily she thrust the picture back into her waist. A hand fell upon her shoulder. She was sure that it was The Sheik and she awaited in dumb terror the blow that she knew would follow.

No blow came and she looked upward over her shoulder—into the eyes of Abdul Kamak, the young Arab.

"I saw," he said, "the picture that you have just hidden. It is you when you were a child—a very young child. May I see it again?"

Meriem drew away from him.

"I will give it back," he said. "I have heard of you and I know that you have no love for The Sheik, your father. Neither have I. I will not betray you. Let me see the picture."

Friendless among cruel enemies, Meriem clutched at the straw that Abdul Kamak held out to her. Perhaps in him she might find the friend she needed. Anyway he had seen the picture and if he was not a friend he could tell The Sheik about it and it would be taken away from her. So she might as well grant his request and hope that he had spoken fairly, and would deal fairly. She drew the photograph from its hiding place and handed it to him.

Abdul Kamak examined it carefully, comparing it, feature by feature with the girl sitting on the ground looking up into his face. Slowly he nodded his head.

"Yes," he said, "it is you, but where was it taken? How does it happen that The Sheik's daughter is clothed in the garments of the unbeliever?"

"I do not know," replied Meriem. "I never saw the picture until a couple of days ago, when I found it in the tent of the Swede, Malbihn."

Abdul Kamak raised his eyebrows. He turned the picture over and as his eyes fell upon the old newspaper cutting they went wide. He could read French, with difficulty, it is true; but he could read it. He had been to Paris. He had spent six months there with a troupe of his desert fellows, upon exhibition, and he had improved his time, learning many of the customs, some of the language, and most of the vices of his conquerors. Now he put his learning to use. Slowly, laboriously he read the yellowed cutting. His eyes were no longer wide. Instead they narrowed to two slits of cunning. When he had done he looked at the girl.

"You have read this?" he asked.

"It is French," she replied, "and I do not read French."

Abdul Kamak stood long in silence looking at the girl. She was very beautiful. He desired her, as had many other men who had seen her. At last he dropped to one knee beside her.

A wonderful idea had sprung to Abdul Kamak's mind. It was an idea that might be furthered if the girl were kept in ignorance of the contents of that newspaper cutting. It would certainly be doomed should she learn its contents.

"Meriem," he whispered, "never until today have my eyes beheld you, yet at once they told my heart that it must ever be your servant. You do not know me, but I ask that you trust me. I can help you. You hate The Sheik—so do I. Let me take you away from him. Come with me, and we will go back to the great desert where my father is a sheik mightier than is yours. Will you come?"

Meriem sat in silence. She hated to wound the only one who had offered her protection and friendship; but she did not want Abdul Kamak's love. Deceived by her silence the man seized her and strained her to him; but Meriem struggled to free herself.

"I do not love you," she cried. "Oh, please do not make me hate you. You are the only one who has shown kindness toward me, and I want to like you, but I cannot love you."

Abdul Kamak drew himself to his full height.

"You will learn to love me," he said, "for I shall take you

whether you will or no. You hate The Sheik and so you will not tell him, for if you do I will tell him of the picture. I hate The Sheik, and—"

"You hate The Sheik?" came a grim voice from behind them.

Both turned to see The Sheik standing a few paces from them. Abdul still held the picture in his hand. Now he thrust it within his burnous.

"Yes," he said, "I hate The Sheik," and as he spoke he sprang toward the older man, felled him with a blow and dashed on across the village to the line where his horse was picketed, saddled and ready, for Abdul Kamak had been about to ride forth to hunt when he had seen the stranger girl alone by the bushes.

Leaping into the saddle Abdul Kamak dashed for the village gates. The Sheik, momentarily stunned by the blow that had felled him, now staggered to his feet, shouting lustily to his followers to stop the escaping Arab. A dozen blacks leaped forward to intercept the horseman, only to be ridden down or brushed aside by the muzzle of Abdul Kamak's long musket, which he lashed from side to side about him as he spurred on toward the gate. But here he must surely be intercepted. Already the two blacks stationed there were pushing the unwieldy portals to. Up flew the barrel of the fugitive's weapon. With reins flying loose and his horse at a mad gallop the son of the desert fired once—twice; and both the keepers of the gate dropped in their tracks. With a wild whoop of exultation, twirling his musket high above his head and turning in his saddle to laugh back into the faces of his pursuers Abdul Kamak dashed out of the village of The Sheik and was swallowed up by the jungle.

Foaming with rage The Sheik ordered immediate pursuit, and then strode rapidly back to where Meriem sat huddled by the bushes where he had left her.

"The picture!" he cried. "What picture did the dog speak of? Where is it? Give it to me at once!"

"He took it," replied Meriem, dully.

"What was it?" again demanded The Sheik, seizing the girl roughly by the hair and dragging her to her feet, where he shook her venomously. "What was it a picture of?"

"Of me," said Meriem, "when I was a little girl. I stole it from Malbihn, the Swede—it had printing on the back cut from an old newspaper."

The Sheik went white with rage.

"What said the printing?" he asked in a voice so low that she but barely caught his words.

"I do not know. It was in French and I cannot read French."

The Sheik seemed relieved. He almost smiled, nor did he again strike Meriem before he turned and strode away with the parting admonition that she speak never again to any other than Mabunu and himself. And along the caravan trail galloped Abdul Kamak toward the north.

As his canoe drifted out of sight and range of the wounded Swede the Hon. Morison sank weakly to its bottom where he lay for long hours in partial stupor.

It was night before he fully regained consciousness. And then he lay for a long time looking up at the stars and trying to recollect where he was, what accounted for the gently rocking motion of the thing upon which he lay, and why the position of the stars changed so rapidly and miraculously. For a while he thought he was dreaming, but when he would have moved to shake sleep from him the pain of his wound recalled to him the events that had led up to his present position. Then it was that he realized that he was floating down a great African river in a native canoe—alone, wounded, and lost.

Painfully he dragged himself to a sitting position. He noticed that the wound pained him less than he had imagined it would. He felt of it gingerly—it had ceased to bleed. Possibly it was but a flesh wound after all, and nothing serious. If it totally incapacitated him even for a few days it would mean death, for by that time he would be too weakened by hunger and pain to provide food for himself.

From his own troubles his mind turned to Meriem's. That she had been with the Swede at the time he had attempted to reach the fellow's camp he naturally believed; but he wondered what would become of her now. Even if Hanson died of his wounds would Meriem be any better off? She was in the power of equally villainous men—brutal savages of the lowest order. Baynes buried his face in his hands and rocked back and forth as the hideous picture of her fate burned itself into his consciousness. And it was he who had brought this fate upon her! His wicked desire had snatched a pure and innocent girl from the protection of those who loved her to hurl her into the clutches of the bestial Swede and his outcast following! And not until it had become too late had he realized the magnitude of the crime he himself had planned and contemplated. Not until it had become too late had he realized that greater than his desire, greater than his lust, greater than any passion he had ever felt before was the newborn love that burned within his breast for the girl he would have ruined.

The Hon. Morison Baynes did not fully realize the change that had taken place within him. Had one suggested that he ever had been aught than the soul of honor and chivalry he would have taken umbrage forthwith. He knew that he had done a vile thing when he had plotted to carry Meriem away to London, yet he excused it on the ground of his great passion for the girl having temporarily warped his moral standards by the intensity of its heat. But, as a matter of fact, a new Baynes had been born. Never again could this man be bent to dishonor by the intensity of a desire. His moral fiber had been strengthened by the mental suffering he had endured. His mind and his soul had been purged by sorrow and remorse.

His one thought now was to atone—win to Meriem's side and lay down his life, if necessary, in her protection. His eyes sought the length of the canoe in search of the paddle, for a determination had galvanized him to immediate action despite his weakness and his wound. But the paddle was gone. He turned his eyes toward the shore. Dimly through the darkness of a moonless night he saw the awful blackness of the jungle, yet it touched no responsive chord of terror within him now as it had done in the past. He did not even wonder that he was unafraid, for his mind was entirely occupied with thoughts of another's danger.

Drawing himself to his knees he leaned over the edge of the canoe and commenced to paddle vigorously with his open palm. Though it tired and hurt him he kept assiduously at his self imposed labor for hours. Little by little the drifting canoe moved nearer and nearer the shore. The Hon. Morison could hear a lion roaring directly opposite him and so close that he felt he must be almost to the shore. He drew his rifle closer to his side; but he did not cease to paddle.

After what seemed to the tired man an eternity of time he felt the brush of branches against the canoe and heard the swirl of the water about them. A moment later he reached out and clutched a leafy limb. Again the lion roared—very near it seemed now, and Baynes wondered if the brute could have been following along the shore waiting for him to land.

He tested the strength of the limb to which he clung. It seemed strong enough to support a dozen men. Then he reached down and lifted his rifle from the bottom of the canoe, slipping the sling over his shoulder. Again he tested the branch, and then reaching upward as far as he could for a safe hold he drew himself painfully and slowly upward until his feet swung clear of the canoe, which, released, floated silently from beneath him to be lost forever in the blackness of the dark shadows down stream.

He had burned his bridges behind him. He must either climb aloft or drop back into the river; but there had been no other way. He struggled to raise one leg over the limb, but found himself scarce equal to the effort, for he was very weak. For a time he hung there feeling his strength ebbing. He knew that he must gain the branch above at once or it would be too late.

Suddenly the lion roared almost in his ear. Baynes glanced up. He saw two spots of flame a short distance from and above him. The lion was standing on the bank of the river glaring at him, and—waiting for him. Well, thought the Hon. Morison, let him wait. Lions can't climb trees, and if I get into this one I shall be safe enough from him.

The young Englishman's feet hung almost to the surface of the water—closer than he knew, for all was pitch dark below as above him. Presently he heard a slight commotion in the river beneath him and something banged against one of his feet, followed almost instantly by a sound that he felt he could not have mistaken— the click of great jaws snapping together.

"By George!" exclaimed the Hon. Morison, aloud. "The beggar nearly got me," and immediately he struggled again to climb higher and to comparative safety; but with that final effort he knew that it was futile. Hope that had survived persistently until now began to wane. He felt his tired, numbed fingers slipping from their hold—he was dropping back into the river—into the jaws of the frightful death that awaited him there.

And then he heard the leaves above him rustle to the movement of a creature among them. The branch to which he clung bent beneath an added weight—and no light weight, from the way it sagged; but still Baynes clung desperately—he would not give up voluntarily either to the death above or the death below.

He felt a soft, warm pad upon the fingers of one of his hands where they circled the branch to which he clung, and then some-

thing reached down out of the blackness above and dragged him
up among the branches of the tree.

CHAPTER 24

SOMETIMES LOLLING UPON Tantor's back, sometimes roaming the
jungle in solitude, Korak made his way slowly toward the West
and South. He made but a few miles a day, for he had a whole
lifetime before him and no place in particular to go. Possibly he
would have moved more rapidly but for the thought which continually haunted him that each mile he traversed carried him
further and further away from Meriem—no longer his Meriem,
as of yore, it is true! but still as dear to him as ever.

Thus he came upon the trail of The Sheik's band as it traveled
down river from the point where The Sheik had captured Meriem
to its own stockaded village. Korak pretty well knew who it was
that had passed, for there were few in the great jungle with whom
he was not familiar, though it had been years since he had come
this far north. He had no particular business, however, with the
old Sheik and so he did not purpose following him—the further
from men he could stay the better pleased he would be—he wished
that he might never see a human face again. Men always brought
him sorrow and misery.

The river suggested fishing and so he dawdled upon its shores,
catching fish after a fashion of his own devising and eating them
raw. When night came he curled up in a great tree beside the
stream—the one from which he had been fishing during the
afternoon—and was soon asleep. Numa, roaring beneath him,
awoke him. He was about to call out in anger to his noisy neighbor
when something else caught his attention. He listened. Was there
something in the tree beside himself? Yes, he heard the noise of
something below him trying to clamber upward. Presently he heard
the click of a crocodile's jaws in the waters beneath, and then,
low but distinct: "By George! The begger nearly got me." The
voice was familiar.

Korak glanced downward toward the speaker. Outlined against
the faint luminosity of the water he saw the figure of a man
clinging to a lower branch of the tree. Silently and swiftly the
ape-man clambered downward. He felt a hand beneath his foot.

He reached down and clutched the figure beneath him and dragged it up among the branches. It struggled weakly and struck at him; but Korak paid no more attention than Tantor to an ant. He lugged his burden to the higher safety and greater comfort of a broad crotch, and there he propped it in a sitting position against the bole of the tree. Numa still was roaring beneath them, doubtless in anger that he had been robbed of his prey. Korak shouted down at him, calling him, in the language of the great apes, "Old green-eyed eater of carrion," "Brother of Dango," the hyena, and other choice appellations of jungle approbrium.

The Hon. Morison Baynes, listening, felt assured that a gorilla had seized upon him. He felt for his revolver, and as he was drawing it stealthily from its holster a voice asked in perfectly good English: "Who are you?"

Baynes started so that he nearly fell from the branch.

"My God!" he exclaimed. "Are you a man?"

"What did you think I was?" asked Korak.

"A gorilla," replied Baynes, honestly.

Koral laughed.

"Who are you?" he repeated.

"I'm an Englishman by the name of Baynes; but who the devil are you?" asked the Hon. Morison.

"They call me The Killer," replied Korak, giving the English translation of the name that Akut had given him. And then after a pause during which the Hon. Morison attempted to pierce the darkness and catch a glimpse of the features of the strange being into whose hands he had fallen, "You are the same whom I saw kissing the girl at the edge of the great plain to the East, that time that the lion charged you?"

"Yes," replied Baynes.

"What are you doing here?"

"The girl was stolen—I am trying to rescue her."

"Stolen!" The word was shot out like a bullet from a gun. "Who stole her?"

"The Swede trader, Hanson," replied Baynes.

"Where is he?"

Baynes related to Korak all that had transpired since he had come upon Hanson's camp. Before he was done the first gray dawn had relieved the darkness. Korak made the Englishman comfortable in the tree. He filled his canteen from the river and fetched him fruits to eat. Then he bid him good-bye.

"I am going to the Swede's camp," he announced. "I will bring the girl back to you here."

"I shall go, too, then," insisted Baynes. "It is my right and my duty, for she was to have become my wife."

Korak winced. "You are wounded. You could not make the trip," he said. "I can go much faster alone."

"Go, then," replied Baynes; "but I shall follow. It is my right and duty."

"As you will," replied Korak, with a shrug. If the man wanted to be killed it was none of his affair. He wanted to kill him himself, but for Meriem's sake he would not. If she loved him then he must do what he could to preserve him, but he could not prevent his following him, more than to advise him against it, and this he did, earnestly.

And so Korak set out rapidly toward the North, and limping slowly and painfully along, soon far to the rear, came the tired and wounded Baynes. Korak had reached the river bank opposite Malbihn's camp before Baynes had covered two miles. Late in the afternoon the Englishman was still plodding wearily along, forced to stop often for rest when he heard the sound of the galloping feet of a horse behind him. Instinctively he drew into the concealing foliage of the underbrush and a moment later a white-robed Arab dashed by. Baynes did not hail the rider. He had heard of the nature of the Arabs who penetrate thus far to the South, and what he had heard had convinced him that a snake or a panther would as quickly befriend him as one of these villainous renegades from the Northland.

When Abdul Kamak has passed out of sight toward the North Baynes resumed his weary march. A half hour later he was again surprised by the unmistakable sound of galloping horses. This time there were many. Once more he sought a hiding place; but it chanced that he was crossing a clearing which offered little opportunity for concealment. He broke into a slow trot—the best that he could do in his weakened condition; but it did not suffice to carry him to safety and before he reached the opposite side of the clearing a band of white-robed horsemen dashed into view behind him.

At sight of him they shouted in Arabic, which, of course, he could not understand, and then they closed about him, threatening and angry. Their questions were unintelligible to him, and no more could they interpret his English. At last, evidently out of patience, the leader ordered two of his men to seize him, which they lost no time in doing. They disarmed him and ordered him to climb to the rump of one of the horses, and then the two who had been detailed to guard him turned and rode back toward the South, while the others continued their pursuit of Abdul Kamak.

As Korak came out upon the bank of the river across from which he could see the camp of Malbihn he was at a loss as to how he was to cross. He could see men moving about among the huts inside the *boma*—evidently Hanson was still there. Korak did not know the true identity of Meriem's abductor.

How was he to cross. Not even he would dare the perils of the river—almost certain death. For a moment he thought, then wheeled and sped away into the jungle, uttering a peculiar cry, shrill and piercing. Now and again he would halt to listen as though for an answer to his weird call, then on again, deeper and deeper into the wood.

At last his listening ears were rewarded by the sound they craved—the trumpeting of a bull elephant, and a few moments later Korak broke through the trees into the presence of Tantor, standing with upraised trunk, waving his great ears.

"Quick, Tantor!" shouted the ape man, and the beast swung him to his head. "Hurry!" and the mighty pachyderm lumbered off through the jungle, guided by kicking of naked heels against the sides of his head.

Toward the northwest Korak guided his huge mount, until they came out upon the river a mile or more above the Swede's camp, at a point where Korak knew that there was an elephant ford. Never pausing the ape-man urged the beast into the river, and with trunk held high Tantor forged steadily toward the opposite bank. Once an unwary crocodile attacked him but the sinuous trunk dove beneath the surface and grasping the amphibian about the middle dragged it to light and hurled it a hundred feet down stream. And so, in safety, they made the opposite shore, Korak perched high and dry above the turgid flood.

Then back toward the South Tantor moved, steadily, relentlessly, and with a swinging gait which took no heed of any obstacle other than the larger jungle trees. At times Korak was forced to abandon the broad head and take to the trees above, so close the branches raked the back of the elephant; but at last they came to the edge of the clearing where lay the camp of the renegade Swede, nor even then did they hesitate or halt. The gate lay upon the east side of the camp, facing the river. Tantor and Korak approached from the north. There was no gate there; but what cared Tantor or Korak for gates.

At a word from the ape man and raising his tender trunk high above the thorns Tantor breasted the *boma,* walking through it as though it had not existed. A dozen blacks squatted before their huts looked up at the noise of his approach. With sudden howls of terror and amaze they leaped to their feet and fled for the open gates. Tantor would have pursued. He hated man, and he thought that Korak had come to hunt these; but the ape man held him back, guiding him toward a large, canvas tent that rose in the center of the clearing—there should be the girl and her abductor.

Malbihn lay in a hammock beneath canopy before his tent. His wounds were painful and he had lost much blood. He was very weak. He looked up in surprise as he heard the screams of his men and saw them running toward the gate. And then from around the corner of his tent loomed a huge bulk, and Tantor, the great tusker, towered above him. Malbihn's boy, feeling neither affection nor loyalty for his master, broke and ran at the first glimpse of the beast, and Malbihn was left alone and helpless.

The elephant stopped a couple of paces from the wounded man's hammock. Malbihn cowered, moaning. He was too weak to escape. He could only lie there with staring eyes gazing in horror into the blood rimmed, angry little orbs fixed upon him, and await his death.

Then, to his astonishment, a man slid to the ground from the elephant's back. Almost at once Malbihn recognized the strange figure as that of the creature who consorted with apes and baboons—the white warrior of the jungle who had freed the king baboon and led the whole angry horde of hairy devils upon him and Jenssen. Malbihn cowered still lower.

"Where is the girl?" demanded Korak, in English.

"What girl?" asked Malbihn. "There is no girl here—only the women of my boys. Is it one of them you want?"

"The white girl," replied Korak. "Do not lie to me—you lured her from her friends. You have her. Where is she?"

"It was not I," cried Malbihn. "It was an Englishman who hired me to steal her. He wished to take her to London with him. She was willing to go. His name is Baynes. Go to him, if you want to know where the girl is."

"I have just come from him," said Korak. "He sent me to you.

The girl is not with him. Now stop your lying and tell me the truth. Where is she?" Korak took a threatening step toward the Swede.

Malbihn shrank from the anger in the other's face.

"I will tell you," he cried. "Do not harm me and I will tell you all that I know. I had the girl here; but it was Baynes who persuaded her to leave her friends—he had promised to marry her. He does not know who she is; but I do, and I know that there is a great reward for whoever takes her back to her people. It was only the reward I wanted. But she escaped and crossed the river in one of my canoes. I followed her, but The Sheik was there, God knows how, and he captured her and attacked me and drove me back. Then came Baynes, angry because he had lost the girl, and shot me. If you want her, go to The Sheik and ask him for her—she has passed as his daughter since childhood."

"She is not The Sheik's daughter?" asked Korak.

"She is not," replied Malbihn.

"Who is she then?" asked Korak.

Here Malbihn saw his chance. Possibly he could make use of his knowledge after all—it might even buy back his life for him. He was not so credulous as to believe that this savage ape-man would have any compunctions about slaying him.

"When you find her I will tell you," he said, "if you will promise to spare my life and divide the reward with me. If you kill me you will never know, for only The Sheik knows and he will never tell. The girl herself is ignorant of her origin."

"If you have told me the truth I will spare you," said Korak. "I shall go now to The Sheik's village and if the girl is not there I shall return and slay you. As for the other information you have, if the girl wants it when we have found her we will find a way to purchase it from you."

The look in The Killer's eyes and his emphasis of the word "purchase" were none too reassuring to Malbihn. Evidently, unless he found means to escape, this devil would have both his secret and his life before he was done with him. He wished he would be gone and take his evil-eyed companion away with him. The swaying bulk towering high above him, and the ugly little eyes of the elephant watching his every move made Malbihn nervous.

Korak stepped into the Swede's tent to assure himself that Meriem was not hid there. As he disappeared from view Tantor, his eyes still fixed upon Malbihn took a step nearer the man. An elephant's eyesight is none too good; but the great tusker evidently had harbored suspicions of this yellow-bearded white man from the first. Now he advanced his snake-like trunk toward the Swede, who shrank still deeper into his hammock.

The sensitive member felt and smelled back and forth along the body of the terrified Malbihn. Tantor uttered a low, rumbling sound. His little eyes blazed. At last he had recognized the creature who had killed his mate long years before. Tantor, the elephant, never forgets and never forgives. Malbihn saw in the demoniacal visage above him the murderous purpose of the beast. He shrieked aloud to Korak. "Help! Help! The devil is going to kill me!"

Korak ran from the tent just in time to see the enraged elephant's trunk encircle the beast's victim, and then hammock, canopy and man were swung high above Tantor's head. Korak leaped before the animal, commanding him to put down his prey unharmed; but as well might he have ordered the eternal river to reverse its course. Tantor wheeled around like a cat, hurled Malbihn to the earth and kneeled upon him with the quickness of a cat. Then he gored the prostrate thing through and through with his mighty tusks, trumpeting and roaring in his rage, and at last, convinced that no slightest spark of life remained in the crushed and lacerated flesh, he lifted the shapeless clay that had been Sven Malbihn far aloft and hurled the bloody mass, still entangled in canopy and hammock, over the *boma* and out into the jungle.

Korak stood looking sorrowfully on at the tragedy he gladly would have averted. He had no love for the Swede, in fact only hatred; but he would have preserved the man for the sake of the secret he possessed. Now that secret was gone forever unless The Sheik could be made to divulge it; but in that possibility Korak placed little faith.

The ape-man, as unafraid of the mighty Tantor as though he had not just witnessed his shocking murder of a human being, signalled the beast to approach and lift him to its head, and Tantor came as he was bid, docile as a kitten, and hoisted The Killer tenderly aloft.

From the safety of their hiding places in the jungle Malbihn's boys had witnessed the killing of their master, and now, with wide, frightened eyes, they saw the strange white warrior, mounted upon the head of his ferocious charger, disappear into the jungle at the point from which he had emerged upon their terrified vision.

CHAPTER 25

THE SHEIK GLOWERED at the prisoner which his two men brought back to him from the North. He had sent the party after Abdul Kamak, and he was wroth that instead of his erstwhile lieutenant they had sent back a wounded and useless Englishman. Why had they not dispatched him where they had found him? He was some penniless beggar of a trader who had wandered from his own district and became lost. He was worthless. The Sheik scowled terribly upon him.

"Who are you?" he asked in French.

"I am the Hon. Morison Baynes of London," replied his prisoner.

The title sounded promising, and at once the wily old robber had visions of ransom. His intentions, if not his attitude toward the prisoner underwent a change—he would investigate further.

"What are you doing poaching in my country?" growled he.

"I was not aware that you owned Africa," replied the Hon. Morison. "I was searching for a young woman who had been abducted from the home of a friend. The abductor wounded me and I drifted down river in a canoe—I was on my way back to his camp when your men seized me."

"A young woman?" asked The Sheik. "Is that she?" and he pointed to his left over toward a clump of bushes near the stockade.

Baynes looked in the direction indicated and his eyes went wide, for there, sitting cross-legged upon the ground, her back toward them, was Meriem.

"Meriem!" he shouted, starting toward her; but one of his guards grasped his arm and jerked him back. The girl leaped to her feet and turned toward him as she heard her name.

"Morison!" she cried.

"Be still, and stay where you are," snapped The Sheik, and then to Baynes. "So you are the dog of a Christian who stole my daughter from me?"

"Your daughter?" ejaculated Baynes. "She is your daughter?"

"She is my daughter," growled the Arab, "and she is not for any unbeliever. You have earned death, Englishman, but if you can pay for your life I will give it to you."

Baynes eyes were still wide at the unexpected sight of Meriem here in the camp of the Arab when he had thought her in Hanson's

429

power. What had happened? How had she escaped the Swede? Had the Arab taken her by force from him, or had she escaped and come voluntarily back to the protection of the man who called her "daughter"? He would have given much for a word with her. If she was safe here he might only harm her by antagonizing the Arab in an attempt to take her away and return her to her English friends. No longer did the Hon. Morison harbor thoughts of luring the girl to London.

"Well?" asked The Sheik.

"Oh," exclaimed Baynes; "I beg your pardon—I was thinking of something else. Why yes, of course, glad to pay, I'm sure. How much do you think I'm worth?"

The Sheik named a sum that was rather less exorbitant than the Hon. Morison had anticipated. The latter nodded his head in token of his entire willingness to pay. He would have promised a sum far beyond his resources just as readily, for he had no intention of paying anything—his one reason for seeming to comply with The Sheik's demands was that the wait for the coming of the ransom money would give him the time and the opportunity to free Meriem if he found that she wished to be freed. The Arab's statement that he was her father naturally raised the question in the Hon. Morison's mind as to precisely what the girl's attitude toward escape might be. It seemed, of course, preposterous that this fair and beautiful young woman should prefer to remain in the filthy *douar* of an illiterate old Arab rather than return to the comforts, luxuries, and congenial associations of the hospitable African bungalow from which the Hon. Morison had tricked her. The man flushed at the thought of his duplicity which these recollections aroused—thoughts which were interrupted by The Sheik, who instructed the Hon. Morison to write a letter to the British consul at Algiers, dictating the exact phraseology of it with a fluency that indicated to his captive that this was not the first time the old rascal had had occasion to negotiate with English relatives for the ransom of a kinsman. Baynes demurred when he saw that the letter was addressed to the consul at Algiers, saying that it would require the better part of a year to get the money back to him; but The Sheik would not listen to Baynes' plan to send a messenger directly to the nearest coast town, and from there communicate with the nearest cable station, sending the Hon. Morison's request for funds straight to his own solicitors. No, The Sheik was cautious and wary. He knew his own plan had worked well in the past. In the other were too many untried elements. He was in no hurry for the money—he could wait a year, or two years if necessary; but it should not require over six months. He turned to one of the Arabs who had been standing behind him and gave the fellow instructions in relation to the prisoner.

Baynes could not understand the words, spoken in Arabic, but the jerk of the thumb toward him showed that he was the subject of conversation. The Arab addressed by The Sheik bowed to his master and beckoned Baynes to follow him. The Englishman looked toward The Sheik for confirmation. The latter nodded impatiently, and the Hon. Morison rose and followed his guide toward a native hut which lay close beside one of the outside goatskin tents. In the dark, stifling interior his guard led him, then stepped to the doorway and called to a couple of black boys squatting before their own huts. They came promptly and in accordance with the Arab's instructions bound Baynes' wrists and ankles securely. The Englishman objected strenuously; but as neither the blacks nor the Arab could understand a word he said his pleas were wasted. Having bound him they left the hut. The Hon. Morison lay for a long time contemplating the frightful future which awaited him during the long months which must intervene before his friends learned of his predicament and could get succor to him. Now he hoped that they would send the ransom—he would gladly pay all that he was worth to be out of this hole. At first it had been his intention to cable his solicitors to send no money but to communicate with the British West African authorities and have an expedition sent to his aid.

His patrician nose wrinkled in disgust as his nostrils were assailed by the awful stenches of the hut. The nasty grasses upon which he lay exuded the effluvium of sweaty bodies, of decayed animal matter and of offal. But worse was yet to come. He had lain in the uncomfortable position in which they had thrown him for but a few minutes when he became distinctly conscious of an acute itching sensation upon his hands, his neck and scalp. He wriggled to a sitting posture horrified and disgusted. The itching rapidly extended to other parts of his body—it was torture, and his hands were bound securely at his back!

He tugged and pulled at his bonds until he was exhausted; but not entirely without hope, for he was sure that he was working enough slack out of the knot to eventually permit of his withdrawing one of his hands. Night came. They brought him neither food nor drink. He wondered if they expected him to live on nothing for a year. The bites of the vermin grew less annoying though not less numerous. The Hon. Morison saw a ray of hope in this indication of future immunity through inoculation. He still worked weakly at his bonds, and then the rats came. If the vermin were disgusting the rats were terrifying. They scurried over his body, squealing and fighting. Finally one commenced to chew at one of his ears. With an oath, the Hon. Morison struggled to a sitting posture. The rats retreated. He worked his legs beneath him and came to his knees, and then, by superhuman effort, rose to his feet. There he stood, reeling drunkenly, dripping with cold sweat.

"God!" he muttered, "what have I done to deserve—" He paused. What had he done? He thought of the girl in another tent in that accursed village. He was getting his deserts. He set his jaws firmly with the realization. He would never complain again! At that moment he became aware of voices raised angrily in the goatskin tent close beside the hut in which he lay. One of them was a woman's. Could it be Meriem's? The language was probably Arabic—he could not understand a word of it; but the tones were hers.

He tried to think of some way of attracting her attention to his near presence. If she could remove his bonds they might escape together—if she wished to escape. That thought bothered him. He was not sure of her status in the village. If she were the petted child of the powerful Sheik then she would probably not care to escape. He must know, definitely.

At the bungalow he had often heard Meriem sing God Save the King, as My Dear accompanied her on the piano. Raising his voice he now hummed the tune. Immediately he heard Meriem's voice from the tent. She spoke rapidly.

"Good bye, Morison," she cried. "If God is good I shall be dead before morning, for if I still live I shall be worse than dead after tonight."

Then he heard an angry exclamation in a man's voice, followed by the sounds of a scuffle. Baynes went white with horror. He struggled frantically again with his bonds. They were giving. A moment later one hand was free. It was but the work of an instant then to loose the other. Stooping, he untied the rope from his ankles, then he straightened and started for the hut doorway bent on reaching Meriem's side. As he stepped out into the night the figure of a huge black rose and barred his progress.

When speed was required of him Korak depended upon no other muscles than his own, and so it was that the moment Tantor had landed him safely upon the same side of the river as lay the village of The Sheik, the ape-man deserted his bulky comrade and took to the trees in a rapid race toward the south and the spot where the Swede had told him Meriem might be. It was dark when he came to the palisade, strengthened considerably since the day that he had rescued Meriem from her pitiful life within its cruel confines. No longer did the giant tree spread its branches above the wooden rampart; but ordinary man-made defenses were scarce considered obstacles by Korak. Loosening the rope at his waist he tossed the noose over one of the sharpened posts that composed the palisade. A moment later his eyes were above the level of the obstacle taking in all within their range beyond. There was no one in sight close by, and Korak drew himself to the top and dropped lightly to the ground within the enclosure.

Then he commenced his stealthy search of the village. First toward the Arab tents he made his way, sniffing and listening. He passed behind them searching for some sign of Meriem. Not even the wild Arab curs heard his passage, so silently he went—a shadow passing through shadows. The odor of tobacco told him that the Arabs were smoking before their tents. The sound of laughter fell upon his ears, and then from the opposite side of the village came the notes of a once familiar tune: God Save the King. Korak halted in perplexity. Who might it be—the tones were those of a man. He recalled the young Englishman he had left on the river trail and who had disappeared before he returned. A moment later there come to him a woman's voice in reply—it was Meriem's, and The Killer, quickened into action, slunk rapidly in the direction of these two voices.

The evening meal over Meriem had gone to her pallet in the women's quarters of The Sheik's tent, a little corner screened off in the rear by a couple of priceless Persian rugs to form a partition. In these quarters she had dwelt with Mabunu alone, for The Sheik had no wives. Nor were conditions altered now after the years of her absence—she and Mabunu were alone in the women's quarters.

Presently The Sheik came and parted the rugs. He glared through the dim light of the interior.

"Meriem!" he called. "Come hither."

The girl arose and came into the front of the tent. There the light of a fire illuminated the interior. She saw Ali ben Kadin, The Sheik's half brother, squatted upon a rug, smoking. The Sheik was standing. The Sheik and Ali ben Kadin had had the same father, but Ali ben Kadin's mother had been a slave—a West Coast negress. Ali ben Kadin was old and hideous and almost black. His nose and part of one cheek were eaten away by disease. He looked up and grinned as Meriem entered.

The Sheik jerked his thumb toward Ali ben Kadin and addressed Meriem.

"I am getting old," he said. "I shall not live much longer. Therefore I have given you to Ali ben Kadin, my brother."

That was all. Ali ben Kadin rose and came toward her. Meriem shrank back, horrified. The man seized her wrist.

"Come!" he commanded, and dragged her from The Sheik's tent and to his own.

After they had gone The Sheik chuckled. "When I send her north in a few months," he soliloquized, "they will know the reward for slaying the son of the sister of Amor ben Khatour."

And in Ali ben Kadin's tent Meriem plead and threatened, but all to no avail. The hideous old half-caste spoke soft words at first, but when Meriem loosed upon him the vials of her horror and loathing he became enraged, and rushing upon her seized her in his arms. Twice she tore away from him, and in one of the intervals during which she managed to elude him she heard Baynes' voice humming the tune that she knew was meant for her ears. At her reply Ali ben Kadin rushed upon her once again. This time he dragged her back into the rear apartment of his tent where three negresses looked up in stolid indifference to the tragedy being enacted before them.

As the Hon. Morison saw his way blocked by the huge frame of the giant black his disappointment and rage filled him with a bestial fury that transformed him into a savage beast. With an oath he leaped upon the man before him, the momentum of his body hurling the black to the ground. There they fought, the black to draw his knife, the white to choke the life from the black.

Baynes' fingers shut off the cry for help that the other would have been glad to voice; but presently the negro succeeded in drawing his weapon, and an instant later Baynes felt the sharp steel in his shoulder. Again and again the weapon fell. The white man removed one hand from its choking grip upon the black throat. He felt around upon the ground beside him searching for some missile, and at last his fingers touched a stone and closed upon it. Raising it above his antagonist's head the Hon. Morison drove home a terrific blow. Instantly the black relaxed—stunned. Twice more Baynes struck him. Then he leaped to his feet and ran for the goat skin tent from which he had heard the voice of Meriem in distress.

But before him was another. Naked but for his leopard skin and his loin cloth, Korak, The Killer, slunk into the shadows at the back of Ali ben Kadin's tent. The half-caste had just dragged Meriem into the rear chamber as Korak's sharp knife slit a six foot opening in the tent wall, and Korak, tall and mighty, sprang through upon the astonished visions of the inmates.

Meriem saw and recognized him the instant that he entered the apartment. Her heart leaped in pride and joy at the sight of the noble figure for which it had hungered for so long.

"Korak!" she cried.

"Meriem!" He uttered the single word as he hurled himself upon the astonished Ali ben Kadin. The three negresses leaped from their sleeping mats, screaming. Meriem tried to prevent them from escaping; but before she could succeed the terrified blacks had darted through the hole in the tent wall made by Korak's knife, and were gone screaming through the village.

The Killer's fingers closed once upon the throat of the hideous Ali. Once his knife plunged into the putrid heart—and Ali ben Kadin lay dead upon the floor of his tent. Korak turned toward Meriem and at the same moment a bloody and disheveled apparition leaped into the apartment.

"Morison!" cried the girl.

Korak turned and looked at the new comer. He had been about to take Meriem in his arms, forgetful of all that might have transpired since last he had seen her. Then the coming of the young Englishman recalled the scene he had witnessed in the little clearing, and a wave of misery swept over the ape man.

Already from without came the sounds of the alarm that the three negresses had started. Men were running toward the tent of Ali ben Kadin. There was no time to be lost.

"Quick!" cried Korak, turning toward Baynes, who had scarce yet realized whether he was facing a friend or foe. "Take her to the palisade, following the rear of the tents. Here is my rope.

With it you can scale the wall and make your escape."

"But you, Korak?" cried Meriem.

"I will remain," replied the ape-man. "I have business with The Sheik."

Meriem would have demurred, but The Killer seized them both by the shoulders and hustled them through the slit wall and out into the shadows beyond.

"Now run for it," he admonished, and turned to meet and hold those who were pouring into the tent from the front.

The ape-man fought well—fought as he had never fought before; but the odds were too great for victory, though he won that which he most craved—time for the Englishman to escape with Meriem. Then he was overwhelmed by numbers, and a few minutes later, bound and guarded, he was carried to The Sheik's tent.

The old man eyed him in silence for a long time. He was trying to fix in his own mind some form of torture that would gratify his rage and hatred toward this creature who twice had been the means of his losing possession of Meriem. The killing of Ali ben Kadin caused him little anger—always had he hated the hideous son of his father's hideous slave. The blow that this naked white warrior had once struck him added fuel to his rage. He could think of nothing adequate to the creature's offense.

And as he sat there looking upon Korak the silence was broken by the trumpeting of an elephant in the jungle beyond the palisade. A half smile touched Korak's lips. He turned his head a trifle in the direction from which the sound had come and then there broke from his lips a low, weird call. One of the blacks guarding him struck him across the mouth with the haft of his spear; but none there knew the significance of his cry.

In the jungle Tantor cocked his ears as the sound of Korak's voice fell upon them. He approached the palisade and lifting his trunk above it, sniffed. Then he placed his head against the wooden logs and pushed; but the palisade was strong and only gave a little to the pressure.

In The Sheik's tent The Sheik rose at last, and, pointing toward the bound captive, turned to one of his lieutenants.

"Burn him," he commanded. "At once. The stake is set."

The guard pushed Korak from The Sheik's presence. They dragged him to the open space in the center of the village, where a high stake was set in the ground. It had not been intended for burnings, but offered a convenient place to tie up refractory slaves that they might be beaten—ofttimes until death relieved their agonies.

To this stake they bound Korak. Then they brought brush and piled about him, and The Sheik came and stood by that he might watch the agonies of his victim. But Korak did not wince even after they had fetched a brand and the flames had shot up among the dry tinder.

Once, then, he raised his voice in the low call that he had given in The Sheik's tent, and now, from beyond the palisade, came again the trumpeting of an elephant.

Old Tantor had been pushing at the palisade in vain. The sound of Korak's voice calling him, and the scent of man, his enemy, filled the great beast with rage and resentment against the dumb barrier that held him back. He wheeled and shuffled back a dozen paces, then he turned, lifted his trunk and gave voice to a mighty roaring, trumpet-call of anger, lowered his head and charged like a huge battering ram of flesh and bone and muscle straight for the mighty barrier.

The palisade sagged and splintered to the impact, and through the breach rushed the infuriated bull. Korak heard the sounds that the others heard, and he interpreted them as the others did not. The flames were creeping closer to him when one of the blacks, hearing a noise behind him turned to see the enormous bulk of Tantor lumbering toward them. The man screamed and fled, and then the bull elephant was among them tossing negroes and Arabs to right and left as he tore through the flames he feared to the side of the comrade he loved.

The Sheik, calling orders to his followers, ran to his tent to get his rifle. Tantor wrapped his trunk about the body of Korak and the stake to which it was bound, and tore it from the ground. The flames were searing his sensitive hide—sensitive for all its thickness—so that in his frenzy to both rescue his friend and escape the hated fire he all but crushed the life from the ape-man.

Lifting his burden high above his head the giant beast wheeled and raced for the breach that he had just made in the palisade. The Sheik, rifle in hand, rushed from his tent directly into the path of the maddened brute. He raised his weapon and fired once, the bullet missed its mark, and Tantor was upon him, crushing him beneath those gigantic feet as he raced over him as you or

I might crush out the life of an ant that chanced to be in our pathway.

And then, bearing his burden carefully, Tantor, the elephant, entered the blackness of the jungle.

CHAPTER 26

MERIEM, DAZED BY the unexpected sight of Korak whom she had long given up as dead, permitted herself to be led away by Baynes. Among the tents he guided her safely to the palisade, and there, following Korak's instructions, the Englishman pitched a noose over the top of one of the upright logs that formed the barrier. With difficulty he reached the top and then lowered his hand to assist Meriem to his side.

"Come!" he whispered. "We must hurry." And then, as though she had awakened from a sleep, Meriem came to herself. Back there, fighting her enemies, alone, was Korak—her Korak. Her place was by his side, fighting with him and for him. She glanced up at Baynes.

"Go!" she called. "Make your way back to Bwana and bring help. My place is here. You can do no good remaining. Get away while you can and bring the Big Bwana back with you."

Silently the Hon. Morison Baynes slid to the ground inside the palisade to Meriem's side.

"It was only for you that I left him," he said, nodding toward the tents they had just left. "I knew that he could hold them longer than I and give you a chance to escape that I might not be able to have given you. It was I though who should have remained. I heard you call him Korak and so I know now who he is. He befriended you. I would have wronged you. No—don't interrupt. I'm going to tell you the truth now and let you know just what a beast I have been. I planned to take you to London, as you know; but I did not plan to marry you. Yes, shrink from me—I deserve it. I deserve your contempt and loathing; but I didn't know then what love was. Since I have learned that I have learned something else—what a cad and what a coward I have been all my life. I looked down upon those whom I considered my social inferiors. I did not think you good enough to bear my name. Since Hanson tricked me and took you for himself I have been through hell; but it has made a man of me, though too late. Now I can come to you with an offer of honest love, which will realize the honor of having such as you share my name with me."

For a moment Meriem was silent, buried in thought. Her first question seemed irrelevant.

"How did you happen to be in this village?" she asked.

He told her all that had transpired since the black had told him of Hanson's duplicity.

"You say that you are a coward," she said, "and yet you have done all this to save me? The courage that it must have taken to tell me the things that you told me but a moment since, while courage of a different sort, proves that you are no moral coward, and the other proves that you are not a physical coward. I could not love a coward."

"You mean that you love me?" he gasped in astonishment, taking a step toward her as though to gather her into his arms; but she placed her hand against him and pushed him gently away, as much as to say, not yet. What she did mean she scarcely knew. She thought that she loved him, of that there can be no question; nor did she think that love for this young Englishman was disloyalty to Korak, for her love for Korak was undiminished—the love of a sister for an indulgent brother. As they stood there for the moment of their conversation the sounds of tumult in the village subsided.

"They have killed him," whispered Meriem.

The statement brought Baynes to a realization of the cause of their return.

"Wait here," he said. "I will go and see. If he is dead we can do him no good. If he lives I will do my best to free him."

"We will go together," replied Meriem. "Come!" And she led the way back toward the tent in which they last had seen Korak. As they went they were often forced to throw themselves to the ground in the shadow of a tent or hut, for people were passing hurriedly to and fro now—the whole village was aroused and moving about. The return to the tent of Ali ben Kadin took much longer than had their swift flight to the palisade. Cautiously they crept to the slit that Korak's knife had made in the rear wall. Meriem peered within—the rear apartment was empty. She crawled through the aperture, Baynes at her heels, and then silently crossed the space to the rugs that partitioned the tent into two rooms. Parting the hangings Meriem looked into the front room. It, too, was deserted. She crossed to the door of the tent and looked out. Then she gave a little gasp of horror. Baynes at her shoulder looked past her to the sight that had startled her, and he, too, exclaimed; but his was an oath of anger.

A hundred feet away they saw Korak bound to a stake—the brush piled about him already alight. The Englishman pushed Meriem to one side and started to run for the doomed man. What he could do in the face of scores of hostile blacks and Arabs he did not stop to consider. At the same instant Tantor broke through the palisade and charged the group. In the face of the maddened beast the crowd turned and fled, carrying Baynes backward with them. In a moment it was all over, and the elephant had disappeared with his prize; but pandemonium reigned throughout the village. Men, women and children ran helter skelter for safety. Curs fled, yelping. The horses and camels and donkeys, terrorized by the trumpeting of the pachyderm, kicked and pulled at their tethers. A dozen or more broke loose, and it was the galloping of these past him that brought a sudden idea into Baynes' head. He turned to search for Meriem only to find her at his elbow.

"The horses!" he cried. "If we can get a couple of them!"

Filled with the idea Meriem led him to the far end of the village.

"Loosen two of them," she said, "and lead them back into the shadows behind those huts. I know where there are saddles. I will bring them and the bridles," and before he could stop her she was gone.

Baynes quickly untied two of the restive animals and led them to the point designated by Meriem. Here he waited impatiently for what seemed an hour; but was, in reality, but a few minutes. Then he saw the girl approaching beneath the burden of two saddles. Quickly they placed these upon the horses. They could see by the light of the torture fire that still burned that the blacks and Arabs were recovering from their panic. Men were running about gathering in the loose stock, and two or three were already leading their captives back to the end of the village where Meriem and Baynes were busy with the trappings of their mounts.

Now the girl flung herself into the saddle.

"Hurry!" she whispered. "We shall have to run for it. Ride through the gap that Tantor made," and as she saw Baynes swing his leg over the back of his horse, she shook the reins free over her mount's neck. With a lunge, the nervous beast leaped forward.

The shortest path led straight through the center of the village, and this Meriem took. Baynes was close behind her, their horses running at full speed.

So sudden and impetuous was their dash for escape that it carried them half-way across the village before the surprised inhabitants were aware of what was happening. Then an Arab recognized them, and, with a cry of alarm, raised his rifle and fired. The shot was a signal for a volley, and amid the rattle of musketry Meriem and Baynes leaped their flying mounts through the breach in the palisade and were gone up the well-worn trail toward the north.

And Korak?

Tantor carried him deep into the jungle, nor paused until no sound from the distant village reached his keen ears. Then he laid his burden gently down. Korak struggled to free himself from his bonds, but even his great strength was unable to cope with the many strands of hard-knotted cord that bound him. While he lay there, working and resting by turns, the elephant stood guard above him, nor was there jungle enemy with the hardihood to tempt the sudden death that lay in that mighty bulk.

Dawn came, and still Korak was no nearer freedom than before. He commenced to believe that he should die there of thirst and starvation with plenty all about him, for he knew that Tantor could not unloose the knots that held him.

And while he struggled through the night with his bonds, Baynes and Meriem were riding rapidly northward along the river. The girl had assured Baynes that Korak was safe in the jungle with Tantor. It had not occurred to her that the ape-man might not be able to burst his bonds. Baynes had been wounded by a shot from the rifle of one of the Arabs, and the girl wanted to get him back to Bwana's home, where he could be properly cared for.

"Then," she said, "I shall get Bwana to come with me and search for Korak. He must come and live with us."

All night they rode, and the day was still young when they came suddenly upon a party hurrying southward. It was Bwana himself and his sleek, black warriors. At sight of Baynes the big Englishman's brows contracted in a scowl; but he waited to hear Meriem's story before giving vent to the long pent anger in his breast. When she had finished he seemed to have forgotten Baynes. His thoughts were occupied with another subject.

"You say that you found Korak?" he asked. "You really saw him?"

"Yes," replied Meriem; "as plainly as I see you, and I want you to come with me, Bwana, and help me find him again."

"Did you see him?" He turned toward the Hon. Morison.

"Yes, sir," replied Baynes; "very plainly."

"What sort of appearing man is he?" continued Bwana. "About how old, should you say?"

"I should say he was an Englishman, about my own age," replied Baynes; "though he might be older. He is remarkably muscled, and exceedingly tanned."

"His eyes and hair, did you notice them?" Bwana spoke rapidly, almost excitedly. It was Meriem who answered him.

"Korak's hair is black and his eyes are gray," she said.

Bwana turned to his headman.

"Take Miss Meriem and Mr. Baynes home," he said. "I am going into the jungle."

"Let me go with you, Bwana," cried Meriem. "You are going to search for Korak. Let me go, too."

Bwana turned sadly but firmly upon the girl.

"Your place," he said, "is beside the man you love."

Then he motioned to his head-man to take his horse and commence the return journey to the farm. Meriem slowly mounted the tired Arab that had brought her from the village of The Sheik. A litter was rigged for the now feverish Baynes, and the little cavalcade was soon slowly winding off along the river trail.

Bwana stood watching them until they were out of sight. Not once had Meriem turned her eyes backward. She rode with bowed head and drooping shoulders. Bwana sighed. He loved the little Arab girl as he might have loved an own daughter. He realized that Baynes had redeemed himself, and so he could interpose no objections now if Meriem really loved the man; but, somehow, some way, Bwana could not convince himself that the Hon. Morison was worthy of his little Meriem. Slowly he turned toward a nearby tree. Leaping upward he caught a lower branch and drew himself up among the branches. His movements were cat-like and agile. High into the tree he made his way and there commenced to divest himself of his clothing. From the game bag slung across one shoulder he drew a long strip of doe-skin, a neatly coiled rope, and a wicked looking knife. The doe-skin he fashioned into a loin cloth, the rope he looped over one shoulder, and the knife he thrust into the belt formed by his gee string.

When he stood erect, his head thrown back and his great chest expanded a grim smile touched his lips for a moment. His nostrils dilated as he sniffed the jungle odors. His gray eyes narrowed. He crouched and leaped to a lower limb and was away through the trees toward the southeast, bearing away from the river. He moved swiftly, stopping only occasionally to raise his voice in a weird and piercing scream, and to listen for a moment after for a reply.

He had traveled thus for several hours when, ahead of him and a little to his left, he heard, far off in the jungle, a faint response— the cry of a bull ape answering his cry. His nerves tingled and his eyes lighted as the sound fell upon his ears. Again he voiced his hideous call, and sped forward in the new direction.

Korak, finally becoming convinced that he must die if he remained where he was, waiting for the succor that could not come, spoke to Tantor in the strange tongue that the great beast understood. He commanded the elephant to lift him and carry him toward the northeast. There, recently, Korak had seen both white men and black. If he could come upon one of the latter it would be a simple matter to command Tantor to capture the fellow, and then Korak could get him to release him from the stake. It was worth trying at least—better than lying there in the jungle until he died. As Tantor bore him along through the forest Korak called aloud now and then in the hope of attracting Akut's band of anthropoids, whose wanderings often brought them into this neighborhood. Akut, he thought, might possibly be able to negotiate the knots—he had done so upon that other occasion when the Russian had bound Korak years before; and Akut, to the south of him, heard his calls faintly, and came. There was another who heard them, too.

After Bwana had left his party, sending them back toward the farm, Meriem had ridden for a short distance with bowed head. What thoughts passed through that active brain who may say? Presently she seemed to come to a decision. She called the headman to her side.

"I am going back with Bwana," she announced.

The black shook his head. "No!" he announced. "Bwana says I take you home. So I take you home."

"You refuse to let me go?" asked the girl.

The black nodded, and fell to the rear where he might better watch her. Meriem half smiled. Presently her horse passed beneath a low-hanging branch, and the black headman found himself gazing at the girl's empty saddle. He ran forward to the tree into which she had disappeared. He could see nothing of her. He called; but there was no response, unless it might have been a low, taunting laugh far to the right. He sent his men into the jungle to search for her; but they came back empty handed. After a while he resumed his march toward the farm, for Baynes, by this time, was delirious with fever.

Meriem raced straight back toward the point she imagined Tantor would make for—a point where she knew the elephants often gathered deep in the forest due east of The Sheik's village. She moved silently and swiftly. From her mind she had expunged all thoughts other than that she must reach Korak and bring him back with her. It was her place to do that. Then, too, had come the tantalizing fear that all might not be well with him. She upbraided herself for not thinking of that before—of letting her desire to get the wounded Morison back to the bungalow blind her to the possibilities of Korak's need for her. She had been traveling rapidly for several hours without rest when she heard ahead of her the familiar cry of a great ape calling to his kind.

She did not reply, only increased her speed until she almost flew. Now there came to her sensitive nostrils the scent of Tantor and she knew that she was on the right trail and close to him she sought. She did not call out because she wished to surprise him, and presently she did, breaking into sight of them as the great elephant shuffled ahead balancing the man and the heavy stake upon his head, holding them there with his upcurled trunk.

"Korak!" cried Meriem from the foliage above him.

Instantly the bull swung about, lowered his burden to the ground and, trumpeting savagely, prepared to defend his comrade. The ape-man, recognizing the girl's voice, felt a sudden lump in his throat.

"Meriem!" he called back to her.

Happily the girl clambered to the ground and ran forward to release Korak; but Tantor lowered his head ominously and trumpeted a warning.

"Go back! Go back!" cried Korak. "He will kill you."

Meriem paused. "Tantor!" she called to the huge brute. "Don't you remember me? I am little Meriem. I used to ride on your broad back;" but the bull only rumbled in his throat and shook his tusks in angry defiance. Then Korak tried to placate him.

He commanded the elephant to lift him and carry him.

Tried to order him away, that the girl might approach and release him; but Tantor would not go. He saw in every human being other than Korak an enemy. He thought the girl bent upon harming his friend and he would take no chances. For an hour the girl and the man tried to find some means whereby they might circumvent the beast's ill directed guardianship, but all to no avail; Tantor stood his ground in grim determination to let no one approach Korak.

Presently the man hit upon a scheme. "Pretend to go away," he called to the girl. "Keep down wind from us so that Tantor won't get your scent, then follow us. After a while I'll have him put me down, and find some pretext for sending him away. While he is gone you can slip up and cut my bonds—have you a knife?"

"Yes, I have a knife," she replied. "I'll go now—I think we may be able to fool him; but don't be too sure—Tantor invented cunning."

Korak smiled, for he knew that the girl was right. Presently she had disappeared. The elephant listened, and raised his trunk to catch her scent. Korak commanded him to raise him to his head once more and proceed upon their way. After a moment's hesitation he did as he was bid. It was then that Korak heard the distant call of an ape.

"Akut!" he thought. "Good! Tantor knew Akut well. He would let him approach." Raising his voice Korak replied to the call of the ape; but he let Tantor move off with him through the jungle; it would do no harm to try the other plan. They had come to a clearing and plainly Korak smelled water. Here was a good place and a good excuse. He ordered Tantor to lay him down, and go and fetch him water in his trunk. The big beast deposited him upon the grass in the center of the clearing, then he stood with cocked ears and attentive trunk, searching for the slightest indication of danger—there seemed to be none and he moved away in the direction of the little brook that Korak knew was some two or three hundred yards away. The ape-man could scarce help smiling as he thought how cleverly he had tricked his friend; but well as he knew Tantor he little guessed the guile of his cunning brain. The animal ambled off across the clearing and disappeared in the jungle beyond in the direction of the stream; but scarce had his great bulk been screened by the dense foliage than he wheeled about and came cautiously back to the edge of the clearing where he could see without being seen. Tantor, by nature, is suspicious. Now he still feared the return of the she Tarmangani who had attempted to attack his Korak. He would just stand there for a moment and assure himself that all was well before he continued on toward the water. Ah! It was well that he did! There she was now dropping from the branches of a tree across the clearing and running swiftly toward the ape-man. Tantor waited. He would let her reach Korak before he charged—that would ensure that she had no chance of escape. His little eyes blazed savagely. His tail was elevated stiffly. He could scarce restrain a desire to trumpet forth his rage to the world. Meriem was almost at Korak's side when Tantor saw the long knife in her hand, and then he broke forth from the jungle, bellowing horribly, and charged down upon the frail girl.

CHAPTER 27

KORAK SCREAMED COMMANDS to his huge protector, in an effort to halt him; but all to no avail. Meriem raced toward the bordering trees with all the speed that lay in her swift, little feet; but Tantor, for all his huge bulk, drove down upon her with the rapidity of an express train.

Korak lay where he could see the whole frightful tragedy. The cold sweat broke out upon his body. His heart seemed to have stopped its beating. Meriem might reach the trees before Tantor overtook her, but even her agility would not carry her beyond the reach of that relentless trunk—she would be dragged down and tossed. Korak could picture the whole frightful scene. Then Tantor would follow her up, goring the frail, little body with his relentless tusks, or trampling it into an unrecognizable mass beneath his ponderous feet.

He was almost upon her now. Korak wanted to close his eyes, but he could not. His throat was dry and parched. Never in all his savage existence had he suffered such blighting terror—never before had he known what terror meant. A dozen more strides and the brute would seize her. What was that? Korak's eyes started from their sockets. A strange figure had leaped from the tree the shade of which Meriem already had reached—leaped beyond the girl straight into the path of the charging elephant. It was a naked white giant. Across his shoulder a coil of rope was looped. In the band of his gee string was a hunting knife. Otherwise he was unarmed. With naked hands he faced the maddened Tantor. A sharp command broke from the stranger's lips—the great beast halted in his tracks—and Meriem swung herself upward into the tree to safety. Korak breathed a sigh of relief not unmixed with wonder. He fastened his eyes upon the face of Meriem's deliverer and as recognition slowly filtered into his understanding they went wide in incredulity and surprise.

Tantor, still rumbling angrily, stood swaying to and fro close before the giant white man. Then the latter stepped straight beneath the upraised trunk and spoke a low word of command. The great beast ceased his muttering. The savage light died from his eyes, and as the stranger stepped forward toward Korak, Tantor trailed docilely at his heels.

Meriem was watching, too, and wondering. Suddenly the man turned toward her as though recollecting her presence after a moment of forgetfulness. "Come! Meriem," he called, and then she recognized him with a startled: "Bwana!" Quickly the girl dropped from the tree and ran to his side. Tantor cocked a questioning eye at the white giant, but receiving a warning word let Meriem approach. Together the two walked to where Korak lay, his eyes wide with wonder and filled with a pathetic appeal for forgiveness, and, mayhap, a glad thankfulness for the miracle that had brought these two of all others to his side.

"Jack!" cried the white giant, kneeling at the ape-man's side.

"Father!" came chokingly from The Killer's lips. "Thank God that it was you. No one else in all the jungle could have stopped Tantor."

Quickly the man cut the bonds that held Korak, and as the youth leaped to his feet and threw his arms about his father, the older man turned toward Meriem.

"I thought," he said, sternly, "that I told you to return to the farm."

Korak was looking at them wonderingly. In his heart was a great yearning to take the girl in his arms; but in time he remembered the other—the dapper young English gentleman—and that he was but a savage, uncouth ape-man.

Meriem looked up pleadingly into Bwana's eyes.

"You told me," she said, in a very small voice, "that my place was beside the man I loved," and she turned her eyes toward Korak all filled with the wonderful light that no other man had

With naked hands he faced the maddened Tantor.

yet seen in them, and that none other ever would.

The Killer started toward her with outstretched arms; but suddenly he fell upon one knee before her, instead, and lifting her hand to his lips kissed it more reverently than he could have kissed the hand of his country's queen.

A rumble from Tantor brought the three, all jungle bred, to instant alertness. Tantor was looking toward the trees behind them, and as their eyes followed his gaze the head and shoulders of a great ape appeared amidst the foliage. For a moment the creature eyed them, and then from its throat rose a loud scream of recognition and of joy, and a moment later the beast had leaped to the ground, followed by a score of bulls like himself, and was waddling toward them, shouting in the primordial tongue of the anthropoid:

"Tarzan has returned! Tarzan, Lord of the Jungle!"

It was Akut, and instantly he commenced leaping and bounding about the trio, uttering hideous shrieks and mouthings that to any other human beings might have indicated the most ferocious rage; but these three knew that the king of the apes was doing homage to a king greater than himself. In his wake leaped his shaggy bulls, vying with one another as to which could spring the highest and which utter the most uncanny sounds.

Korak laid his hand affectionately upon his father's shoulder.

"There is but one Tarzan," he said. "There can never be another."

Two days later the three dropped from the trees on the edge of the plain across which they could see the smoke rising from the bungalow and the cook house chimneys. Tarzan of the Apes had regained his civilized clothing from the tree where he had hidden it, and as Korak refused to enter the presence of his mother in the savage half-raiment that he had worn so long and as Meriem would not leave him, for fear, as she explained, that he would change his mind and run off into the jungle again, the father went on ahead to the bungalow for horses and clothes.

My Dear met him at the gate, her eyes filled with questioning and sorrow, for she saw that Meriem was not with him.

"Where is she?" she asked, her voice trembling. "Muviri told me that she disobeyed your instructions and ran off into the jungle after you had left them. Oh, John, I cannot bear to lose her, too!" And Lady Greystoke broke down and wept, as she pillowed her head upon the broad breast where so often before she had found comfort in the great tragedies of her life.

Lord Greystoke raised her head and looked down into her eyes, his own smiling and filled with the light of happiness.

"What is it, John?" she cried. "You have good news—do not keep me waiting for it."

"I want to be quite sure that you can stand hearing the best news that ever came to either of us," he said.

"Joy never kills," she cried. "You have found—her?" She could not bring herself to hope for the impossible.

"Yes, Jane," he said, and his voice was husky with emotion; "I have found her, and—*him!*"

"Where is he? Where are they?" she demanded.

"Out there at the edge of the jungle. He wouldn't come to you in his savage leopard skin and his nakedness—he sent me to fetch him civilized clothing."

She clapped her hands in ecstasy, and turned to run toward the bungalow. "Wait!" she cried over her shoulder. "I have all his little suits—I have saved them all. I will bring one to you."

Tarzan laughed and called to her to stop.

"The only clothing on the place that will fit him," he said, "is mine—if it isn't too small for him—your little boy has grown, Jane."

She laughed, too; she felt like laughing at everything, or at nothing. The world was all love and happiness and joy once more—the world that had been shrouded in the gloom of her great sorrow for so many years. So great was her joy that for the moment she forgot the sad message that awaited Meriem. She called to Tarzan after he had ridden away to prepare her for it, but he did not hear and rode on without knowing himself what the event was to which his wife referred.

And so, an hour later, Korak, The Killer, rode home to his mother—the mother whose image had never faded in his boyish heart—and found in her arms and her eyes the love and forgiveness that he plead for.

And then the mother turned toward Meriem, an expression of pitying sorrow erasing the happiness from her eyes.

"My little girl," she said, "in the midst of our happiness a great sorrow awaits you—Mr. Baynes did not survive his wound."

The expression of sorrow in Meriem's eyes expressed only what she sincerely felt; but it was not the sorrow of a woman bereft of her best beloved.

"I am sorry," she said, quite simply. "He would have done me a great wrong; but he amply atoned before he died. Once I thought that I loved him. At first it was only fascination for a type that was new to me—then it was respect for a brave man who had the moral courage to admit a sin and the physical courage to face death to right the wrong he had committed. But it was not love. I did not know what love was until I knew that Korak lived," and she turned toward The Killer with a smile.

Lady Greystoke looked quickly up into the eyes of her son— the son who one day would be Lord Greystoke. No thought of the difference in the stations of the girl and her boy entered her mind. To her Meriem was fit for a king. She only wanted to know that Jack loved the little Arab waif. The look in his eyes answered the question in her heart, and she threw her arms about them both and kissed them each a dozen times.

"Now," she cried, "I shall really have a daughter!"

It was several weary marches to the nearest mission; but they only waited at the farm a few days for rest and preparation for the great event before setting out upon the journey, and after the marriage ceremony had been performed they kept on to the coast to take passage for England. Those days were the most wonderful of Meriem's life. She had not dreamed even vaguely of the marvels that civilization held in store for her. The great ocean and the commodious steamship filled her with awe. The noise, and bustle and confusion of the English railway station frightened her.

"If there was a good-sized tree at hand," she confided to Korak, "I know that I should run to the very top of it in terror of my life."

"And make faces and throw twigs at the engine?" he laughed back.

"Poor old Numa," sighed the girl. "What will he do without us?"

"Oh, there are others to tease him, my little Mangani," assured Korak.

The Greystoke town house quite took Meriem's breath away; but when strangers were about none might guess that she had not been to the manner born.

They had been home but a week when Lord Greystoke received a message from his friend of many years, D'Arnot.

It was in the form of a letter of introduction brought by one General Armand Jacot. Lord Greystoke recalled the name, as who familiar with modern French history would not, for Jacot was in reality the Prince de Cadrenet—that intense republican who refused to use, even by courtesy, a title that had belonged to his family for four hundred years.

"There is no place for princes in a republic," he was wont to say.

Lord Greystoke received the hawk-nosed, gray mustached soldier in his library, and after a dozen words the two men had formed a mutual esteem that was to endure through life.

"I have come to you," explained General Jacot, "because our dear Admiral tells me that there is no one in all the world who is more intimately acquainted with Central Africa than you.

"Let me tell you my story from the beginning. Many years ago my little daughter was stolen, presumably by Arabs, while I was serving with the Foreign Legion in Algeria. We did all that love and money and even government resources could do to discover her; but all to no avail. Her picture was published in the leading papers of every large city in the world, yet never did we find a man or woman who ever had seen her since the day she mysteriously disappeared.

"A week since there came to me in Paris a swarthy Arab, who called himself Abdul Kamak. He said that he had found my daughter and could lead me to her. I took him at once to Admiral d'Arnot, whom I knew had traveled some in Central Africa. The man's story led the Admiral to believe that the place where the white girl the Arab supposed to be my daughter was held in captivity was not far from your African estates, and he advised that I come at once and call upon you—that you would know if such a girl were in your neighborhood."

"What proof did the Arab bring that she was your daughter?" asked Lord Greystoke.

"None," replied the other. "That is why we thought best to consult you before organizing an expedition. The fellow had only an old photograph of her on the back of which was pasted a newspaper cutting describing her and offering a reward. We feared that having found this somewhere it had aroused his cupidity and led him to believe that in some way he could obtain the reward, possibly by foisting upon us a white girl on the chance that so many years had elapsed that we would not be able to recognize an imposter as such."

"Have you the photograph with you?" asked Lord Greystoke. The General drew an envelope from his pocket, took a yellowed photograph from it and handed it to the Englishman.

Tears dimmed the old warrior's eyes as they fell again upon the pictured features of his lost daughter.

Lord Greystoke examined the photograph for a moment. A queer expression entered his eyes. He touched a bell at his elbow, and an instant later a footman entered.

"Ask my son's wife if she will be so good as to come to the library," he directed.

The two men sat in silence. General Jacot was too well bred to show in any way the chagrin and disappointment he felt in the summary manner in which Lord Greystoke had dismissed the subject of his call. As soon as the young lady had come and he had been presented he would make his departure. A moment later Meriem entered.

Lord Greystoke and General Jacot rose and faced her. The Englishman spoke no word of introduction—he wanted to mark the effect of the first sight of the girl's face on the Frenchman, for he had a theory—a heaven-born theory that had leaped into his mind the moment his eyes had rested on the baby face of Jeanne Jacot.

General Jacot took one look at Meriem, then he turned toward Lord Greystoke.

"How long have you known it?" he asked, a trifle accusingly.

"Since you showed me that photograph a moment ago," replied the Englishman.

"It is she," said Jacot, shaking with suppressed emotion; "but she does not recognize me—of course she could not." Then he turned to Meriem. "My child," he said, "I am your—"

But she interrupted him with a quick, glad cry, as she ran toward him with outstretched arms.

"I know you! I know you!" she cried. "Oh, now I remember," and the old man folded her in his arms.

Jack Clayton and his mother were summoned, and when the story had been told them they were only glad that little Meriem had found a father and a mother.

"And really you didn't marry an Arab waif after all," said Meriem. "Isn't it fine!"

"You are fine," replied The Killer. "I married my little Meriem, and I don't care, for my part, whether she is an Arab, or just a little Tarmangani."

"She is neither, my son," said General Armand Jacot. "She is a princess in her own right."

Tarzan at the Earth's Core

Frontispiece by J. Allen St. John

Overleaf: *Lifting her to his shoulder, he leaped to the low branch of a nearby tree.*

FOREWORD

PELLUCIDAR, AS EVERY schoolboy knows, is a world within a world, lying, as it does, upon the inner surface of the hollow sphere, which is the Earth.

It was discovered by David Innes and Abner Perry upon the occasion when they made the trial trip upon the mechanical prospector invented by Perry, wherewith they hoped to locate new beds of anthracite coal. Owing, however, to their inability to deflect the nose of the prospector, after it had started downward into the Earth's crust, they bored straight through for five hundred miles, and upon the third day, when Perry was already unconscious owing to the consumption of their stock of oxygen, and David was fast losing consciousness, the nose of the prospector broke through the crust of the inner world and the cabin was filled with fresh air.

In the years that have intervened, weird adventures have befallen these two explorers. Perry has never returned to the outer crust, and Innes but once—upon that occasion when he made the difficult and dangerous return trip in the prospector for the purpose of bringing back to the empire he had founded in the inner world the means to bestow upon his primitive people of the stone age the civilization of the twentieth century.

But what with battles with primitive men and still more primitive beasts and reptiles, the advance of the empire of Pellucidar toward civilization has been small; and in so far as the great area of the inner world is concerned, or the countless millions of its teeming life of another age than ours, David Innes and Abner Perry might never have existed.

When one considers that these land and water areas upon the surface of Pellucidar are in opposite relationship to the same areas upon the outer crust, some slight conception of the vast extent of this mighty world within a world may be dreamed.

The land area of the outer world comprises some fifty-three million square miles, or one-quarter of the total area of the earth's surface; while within Pellucidar three-quarters of the surface is land, so that jungle, mountain, forest and plain stretch interminably over 124,110,000 square miles; nor are the oceans with their area of 41,370,000 square miles of any mean or niggardly extent.

Thus, considering the land area only, we have the strange anomaly of a larger world within a smaller one, but then Pellucidar is a world of deviation from what we of the outer crust have come to accept as unalterable laws of nature.

In the exact center of the earth hangs Pellucidar's sun, a tiny orb compared with ours, but sufficient to illuminate Pellucidar and flood her teeming jungles with warmth and life-giving rays. Her sun hanging thus perpetually at zenith, there is no night upon Pellucidar, but always an endless eternity of noon.

There being no stars and no apparent movement of the sun, Pellucidar has no points of compass; nor has she any horizon since her surface curves always upward in all directions from the observer, so that far above one's line of vision, plain or sea or distant mountain range go onward and upward until lost in the haze of the distance. And again, in a world where there is no sun, no stars and no moon, such as we know, there can be no such thing as time, as we know it. And so, in Pellucidar, we have a timeless world which must necessarily be free from those pests who are constantly calling our attention to "the busy little bee" and to the fact that "time is money." While time may be "the soul of this world" and the "essence of contracts," in the beatific existence of Pellucidar it is nothing and less than nothing.

Thrice in the past have we of the outer world received communication from Pellucidar. We know that Perry's first great gift of civilization to the stone age was gunpowder. We know that he followed this with repeating rifles, small ships of war upon which were mounted guns of no great caliber, and finally we know that he perfected a radio.

Knowing Perry as something of an empiric, we were not surprised to learn that his radio could not be tuned in upon any known wave or wave length of the outer world, and it remained for young Jason Gridley of Tarzana, experimenting with his newly discovered Gridley Wave, to pick up the first message from Pellucidar.

The last word that we received from Perry before his messages faltered and died out was to the effect that David Innes, first Emperor of Pellucidar, was languishing in a dark dungeon in the land of the Korsars, far across continent and ocean from his beloved land of Sari, which lies upon a great plateau not far inland from the Lural Az.

CHAPTER 1

The O-220

TARZAN OF THE apes paused to listen and to sniff the air. Had you been there you could not have heard what he heard, or had you you could not have interpreted it. You could have smelled nothing but the mustiness of decaying vegetation, which blended with the aroma of growing things.

The sounds that Tarzan heard came from a great distance and were faint even to his ears; nor at first could he definitely ascribe them to their true source, though he conceived the impression that they heralded the coming of a party of men.

Buto the rhinoceros, Tantor the elephant or Numa the lion might come and go through the forest without arousing more than the indifferent interest of the Lord of the Jungle, but when man came Tarzan investigated, for man alone of all creatures brings change and dissension and strife wheresoever he first sets foot.

Reared to manhood among the great apes without knowledge of the existence of any other creatures like himself, Tarzan had since learned to anticipate with concern each fresh invasion of his jungle by these two-footed harbingers of strife. Among many races of men he had found friends, but this did not prevent him from questioning the purposes and the motives of whosoever entered his domain. And so today he moved silently through the middle terrace of his leafy way in the direction of the sounds that he had heard.

As the distance closed between him and those he went to investigate, his keen ears cataloged the sound of padding, naked feet and the song of native carriers as they swung along beneath their heavy burdens. And then to his nostrils came the scent spoor of black men and with it, faintly, the suggestion of another scent, and Tarzan knew that a white man was on safari before the head of the column came in view along the wide, well marked game trail, above which the Lord of the Jungle waited.

Near the head of the column marched a young white man, and when Tarzan's eyes had rested upon him for a moment as he swung along the trail they impressed their stamp of approval of the stranger within the ape-man's brain, for in common with many savage beasts and primitive men Tarzan possessed an uncanny instinct in judging aright the characters of strangers whom he met.

Turning about, Tarzan moved swiftly and silently through the trees until he was some little distance ahead of the marching safari, then he dropped down into the trail and awaited its coming.

Rounding a curve in the trail the leading askari came in sight of him and when they saw him they halted and commenced to jabber excitedly, for these were men recruited in another district— men who did not know Tarzan of the Apes by sight.

"I am Tarzan," announced the ape-man. "What do you in Tarzan's country?"

Immediately the young man, who had halted abreast of his askari, advanced toward the ape-man. There was a smile upon his eager face. "You are Lord Greystoke?" he asked.

"Here, I am Tarzan of the Apes," replied the foster son of Kala.

"Then luck is certainly with me," said the young man, "for I have come all the way from Southern California to find you."

"Who are you," demanded the ape-man, "and what do you want of Tarzan of the Apes?"

"My name is Jason Gridley," replied the other. "And what I have come to talk to you about will make a long story. I hope that you can find the time to accompany me to our next camp and the patience to listen to me there until I have explained my mission."

Tarzan nodded. "In the jungle," he said, "we are not often pressed for time. Where do you intend making camp?"

"The guide that I obtained in the last village complained of being ill and turned back an hour ago, and as none of my own men is familiar with this country we do not know whether there is a suitable camp-site within one mile or ten."

"There is one within half a mile," replied Tarzan, "and with good water."

"Good," said Gridley; and the safari resumed its way, the porters laughing and singing at the prospect of an early camp.

It was not until Jason and Tarzan were enjoying their coffee that evening that the ape-man reverted to the subject of the American's visit.

"And now," he said, "what has brought you all the way from Southern California to the heart of Africa?"

Gridley smiled. "Now that I am actually here," he said, "and face to face with you, I am suddenly confronted with the conviction that after you have heard my story it is going to be difficult to convince you that I am not crazy, and yet in my own mind I am so thoroughly convinced of the truth of what I am going to tell you that I have already invested a considerable amount of money and time to place my plan before you for the purpose of enlisting your personal and financial support, and I am ready and willing to invest still more money and all of my time. Unfortunately I cannot wholly finance the expedition that I have in mind from my personal resources, but that is not primarily my reason for coming to you. Doubtless I could have raised the necessary money elsewhere, but I believe that you are peculiarly fitted to lead such a venture as I have in mind."

"Whatever the expedition may be that you are contemplating," said Tarzan, "the potential profits must be great indeed if you are willing to risk so much of your own money."

"On the contrary," replied Gridley, "there will be no financial profit for anyone concerned in so far as I now know."

"And you are an American?" asked Tarzan, smiling.

"We are not all money mad," replied Gridley.

"Then what is the incentive? Explain the whole proposition to me."

"Have you ever heard of the theory that the earth is a hollow sphere, containing a habitable world within its interior?"

"The theory that has been definitely refuted by scientific investigation," replied the ape-man.

"But has it been refuted satisfactorily?" asked Gridley.

"To the satisfaction of the scientists," replied Tarzan.

"And to my satisfaction, too," replied the American, "until I recently received a message direct from the inner world."

"You surprise me," said the ape-man.

"And I, too, was surprised, but the fact remains that I have been in radio communication with Abner Perry in the inner world of Pellucidar and I have brought a copy of that message with me and also an affidavit of its authenticity from a man with whose name you are familiar and who was with me when I received the message; in fact, he was listening in at the same time with me. Here they are."

From a portfolio he took a letter which he handed to Tarzan and a bulky manuscript bound in board covers.

"I shall not take the time to read you all of the story of Tanar of Pellucidar," said Gridley, "because there is a great deal in it that is not essential to the exposition of my plan."

"As you will," said Tarzan. "I am listening."

For half an hour Jason Gridley read excerpts from the manuscript before him. "This," he said, when he had completed the reading, "is what convinced me of the existence of Pellucidar, and it is the unfortunate situation of David Innes that impelled me to come to you with the proposal that we undertake an expedition whose first purpose shall be to rescue him from the dungeon of the Korsars."

"And how do you think this may be done?" asked the ape-man. "Are you convinced of the correctness of Innes' theory that there is an entrance to the inner world at each pole?"

"I am free to confess that I do not know what to believe," replied the American. "But after I received this message from Perry I commenced to investigate and I discovered that the theory of an inhabitable world at the center of the earth with openings leading into it at the north and south poles is no new one and that there is much evidence to support it. I found a very complete exposition of the theory in a book written about 1830 and in another work of more recent time. Therein I found what seemed to be a reasonable explanation of many well known phenomena that have not been satisfactorily explained by any hypothesis endorsed by science."

"What, for example?" asked Tarzan.

"Well, for example, warm winds and warm ocean currents coming from the north and encountered and reported by practically all arctic explorers; the presence of the limbs and branches of trees with green foliage upon them floating southward from the far north, far above the latitude where any such trees are found upon the outer crust; then there is the phenomenon of the northern lights, which in the light of David Innes' theory may easily be explained as rays of light from the central sun of the inner world, breaking occasionally through the fog and cloud banks above the polar opening. Again there is the pollen, which often thickly covers the snow and ice in portions of the polar regions. This pollen could not come from elsewhere than the inner world. And in addition to all this is the insistence of the far northern tribes of Eskimos that their forefathers came from a country to the north."

"Did not Amundson and Ellsworth in the Norge expedition definitely disprove the theory of a north polar opening in the earth's crust, and have not airplane flights been made over a considerable portion of the hitherto unexplored regions near the pole?" demanded the ape-man.

"The answer to that is that the polar opening is so large that a ship, a dirigible or an airplane could dip down over the edge into it a short distance and return without ever being aware of the fact, but the most tenable theory is that in most instances explorers have merely followed around the outer rim of the orifice, which would largely explain the peculiar and mystifying action of compasses and other scientific instruments at points near the so-called north pole—matters which have greatly puzzled all arctic explorers."

"You are convinced then that there is not only an inner world but that there is an entrance to it at the north pole?" asked Tarzan.

"I am convinced that there is an inner world, but I am not convinced of the existence of a polar opening," replied Gridley. "I can only say that I believe there is sufficient evidence to warrant the organization of an expedition such as I have suggested."

"Assuming that a polar opening into an inner world exists, by just what means do you purpose accomplishing the discovery and exploration of it?"

"The most practical means of transportation that exists today for carrying out my plan would be a specially constructed rigid airship, built along the lines of the modern Zeppelin. Such a ship, using helium gas, would show a higher factor of safety than any other means of transportation at our disposal. I have given the matter considerable thought and I feel sure that if there is such a polar opening, the obstacles that would confront us in an attempt to enter the inner world would be far less than those encountered by the Norge in its famous trip across the pole to Alaska, for there is no question in my mind but that it made a wide detour in following the rim of the polar orifice and covered a far greater distance than we shall have to cover to reach a reasonably safe anchorage below the cold, polar sea that David Innes discovered north of the land of the Korsars before he was finally taken prisoner by them.

"The greatest risk that we would have to face would be a possible inability to return to the outer crust, owing to the depletion of our helium gas that might be made necessary by the maneuvering of the ship. But that is only the same chance of life or death that every explorer and scientific investigator must be willing to assume in the prosecution of his labors. If it were but possible to build a hull sufficiently light, and at the same time sufficiently strong, to withstand atmospheric pressure, we could dispense with both the dangerous hydrogen gas and the rare and expensive helium gas and have the assurance of the utmost safety and maximum of buoyancy in a ship supported entirely by vacuum tanks."

"Perhaps even that is possible," said Tarzan, who was now evincing increasing interest in Gridley's proposition.

The American shook his head. "It may be possible some day," he said, "but not at present with any known material. Any receptacle having sufficient strength to withstand the atmospheric pressure upon a vacuum would have a weight far too great for the vacuum to lift."

"Perhaps," said Tarzan, "and, again, perhaps not."

"What do you mean?" inquired Gridley.

"What you have just said," replied Tarzan, "reminds me of something that a young friend of mine recently told me. Erich von Harben is something of a scientist and explorer himself, and the last time that I saw him he had just returned from a second expedition into the Wiramwazi Mountains, where he told me that he had discovered a lake-dwelling tribe using canoes made of a metal that was apparently as light as cork and stronger than steel. He brought some samples of the metal back with him, and at the time I last saw him he was conducting some experiments in a little laboratory he has rigged up at his father's mission."

"Where is this man?" demanded Gridley.

"Dr. von Harben's mission is in the Urambi country," replied the ape-man, "about four marches west of where we now are."

Far into the night the two men discussed plans for the project, for Tarzan was now thoroughly interested, and the next day they turned back toward the Urambi country and von Harben's mission, where they arrived on the fourth day and were greeted by Dr. von Harben and his son, Erich, as well as by the latter's wife, the beautiful Favonia of Castrum Mare.

It is not my intention to weary you with a recital of the details of the organization and equipment of the Pellucidarian expedition, although that portion of it which relates to the search for and discovery of the native mine containing the remarkable metal now known as Harbenite, filled as it was with adventure and excitement, is well worth a volume by itself.

While Tarzan and Erich von Harben were locating the mine and transporting the metal to the seacoast, Jason Gridley was in Friedrichshafen in consultation with the engineers of the company he had chosen to construct the specially designed airship in which the attempt was to be made to reach the inner world.

Exhaustive tests were made of the samples of Harbenite brought to Friedrichshafen by Jason Gridley. Plans were drawn, and by the time the shipment of the ore arrived everything was in readiness to commence immediate construction, which was carried on secretly. And six months later, when the O-220, as it was officially known, was ready to take the air, it was generally considered to be nothing more than a new design of the ordinary type of rigid airship, destined to be used as a common carrier upon one of the already numerous commercial airways of Europe.

The great cigar-shaped hull of the O-220 was 997 feet in length and 150 feet in diameter. The interior of the hull was divided into six large, air-tight compartments, three of which, running the full length of the ship, were above the medial line and three below. Inside the hull and running along each side of the ship, between the upper and lower vacuum tanks, were long corridors in which were located the engines, motors and pumps, in addition to supplies of gasoline and oil.

The internal location of the engine room was made possible by the elimination of fire risk, which is an ever-present source of danger in airships which depend for their lifting power upon hydrogen gas, as well as to the absolutely fireproof construction of the O-220; every part of which, with the exception of a few cabin fittings and furniture, was of Harbenite, this metal being used throughout except for certain bushings and bearings in motors, generators and propellers.

Connecting the port and starboard engine and fuel corridors

were two transverse corridors, one forward and one aft, while bisecting these transverse corridors were two climbing shafts extending from the bottom of the ship to the top.

The upper end of the forward climbing shaft terminated in a small gun and observation cabin at the top of the ship, along which was a narrow walking-way extending from the forward cabin to a small turret near the tail of the ship, where provision had been made for fixing a machine gun.

The main cabin, running along the keel of the ship, was an integral part of the hull, and because of this entirely rigid construction, which eliminated the necessity for cabins suspended below the hull, the O-220 was equipped with landing gear in the form of six, large, heavily tired wheels projecting below the bottom of the main cabin. In the extreme stern of the keel cabin a small scout monoplane was carried in such a way that it could be lowered through the bottom of the ship and launched while the O-220 was in flight.

Eight air-cooled motors drove as many propellers, which were arranged in pairs upon either side of the ship and staggered in such a manner that the air from the forward propellers would not interfere with those behind.

The engines, developing 5600 horsepower, were capable of driving the ship at a speed of 105 miles per hour.

In the O-220 the ordinary axial wire, which passes the whole length of the ship through the center, consisted of a tubular shaft of Harbenite from which smaller tubular braces radiated, like the spokes of a wheel, to the tubular girders, to which the Harbenite plates of the outer envelope were welded.

Owing to the extreme lightness of Harbenite, the total weight of the ship was 75 tons, while the total lift of its vacuum tanks was 225 tons.

For purposes of maneuvering the ship and to facilitate landing, each of the vacuum tanks was equipped with a bank of eight air valves operated from the control cabin at the forward end of the keel; while six pumps, three in the starboard and three in the port engine corridors, were designed to expel the air from the tanks when it became necessary to renew the vacuum. Special rudders and elevators were also operated from the forward control cabin as well as from an auxiliary position aft in the port engine corridor, in the event that the control cabin steering gear should break down.

In the main keel cabin were located the quarters for the officers and crew, gun and ammunition room, provision room, galley, additional gasoline and oil storage tanks, and water tanks, the latter so constructed that the contents of any of them might be emptied instantaneously in case of an emergency, while a proportion of the gasoline and oil tanks were slip tanks that might be slipped through the bottom of the ship in cases of extreme emergency when it was necessary instantaneously to reduce the weight of the load.

This, then, briefly, was the great, rigid airship in which Jason Gridley and Tarzan of the Apes hoped to discover the north polar entrance to the inner world and rescue David Innes, Emperor of Pellucidar, from the dungeons of the Korsars.

CHAPTER 2

Pellucidar

JUST BEFORE DAYBREAK of a clear June morning, the O-220 moved slowly from its hangar under its own power. Fully loaded and equipped, it was to make its test flight under load conditions identical with those which would obtain when it set forth upon its long journey. The three lower tanks were still filled with air and she carried an excess of water ballast sufficient to overcome her equilibrium, so that while she moved lightly over the ground she moved with entire safety and could be maneuvered almost as handily as an automobile.

As she came into the open her pumps commenced to expel the air from the three lower tanks, and at the same time a portion of her excess water ballast was slowly discharged, and almost immediately the huge ship rose slowly and gracefully from the ground.

The entire personnel of the ship's company during the test flight was the same that had been selected for the expedition. Zuppner, who had been chosen as captain, had been in charge of the construction of the ship and had a considerable part in its designing. There were two mates, Von Horst and Dorf, who had been officers in the Imperial air forces, as also had the navigator, Lieutenant Hines. In addition to these there were twelve engineers and eight mechanics, a negro cook and two Filipino cabin-boys.

Tarzan was commander of the expedition, with Jason Gridley as his lieutenant, while the fighting men of the ship consisted of Muviro and nine of his Waziri warriors.

As the ship rose gracefully above the city, Zuppner, who was at the controls, could scarce restrain his enthusiasm.

"The sweetest thing I ever saw!" he exclaimed. "She responds to the lightest touch."

"I am not surprised at that," said Hines; "I knew she'd do it. Why we've got twice the crew we need to handle her."

"There you go again, Lieutenant," said Tarzan, laughing; "but do not think that my insistence upon a large crew was based upon any lack of confidence in the ship. We are going into a strange world. We may be gone a long time. If we reach our destination we shall have fighting, as each of you men who volunteered has been informed many times, so that while we may have twice as many men as we need for the trip in, we may yet find ourselves short handed on the return journey, for not all of us will return."

"I suppose you are right," said Hines; "but with the feel of this ship permeating me and the quiet peacefulness of the scene below, danger and death seem remote."

"I hope they are," returned Tarzan, "and I hope that we shall return with every man that goes out with us, but I believe in being prepared and to that end Gridley and I have been studying navigation and we want you to give us a chance at some practical experience before we reach our destination."

Zuppner laughed. "They have you marked already, Hines," he said.

The Lieutenant grinned. "I'll teach them all I know," he said; "but I'll bet the best dinner that can be served in Berlin that if this ship returns I'll still be her navigator."

"That is a case of heads-I-win, tails-you-lose," said Gridley.

"And to return to the subject of preparedness," said Tarzan, "I am going to ask you to let my Waziri help the mechanics and engineers. They are highly intelligent men, quick to learn, and if some calamity should overtake us we cannot have too many men familiar with the engines and other machinery of the ship."

"You are right," said Zuppner, "and I shall see that it is done."

The great, shining ship sailed majestically north; Ravensburg fell astern and half an hour later the somber gray ribbon of the

Danube lay below them.

The longer they were in the air the more enthusiastic Zuppner became. "I had every confidence in the successful outcome of the trial flight," he said; "but I can assure you that I did not look for such perfection as I find in this ship. It marks a new era in aeronautics, and I am convinced that long before we cover the four hundred miles to Hamburg that we shall have established the entire air worthiness of the O-220 to the entire satisfaction of each of us."

"To Hamburg and return to Friedrichshafen was to have been the route of the trial trip," said Tarzan, "but why turn back at Hamburg?"

The others turned questioning eyes upon him as the purport of his query sank home.

"Yes, why?" demanded Gridley.

Zuppner shrugged his shoulders. "We are fully equipped and provisioned," he said.

"Then why waste eight hundred miles in returning to Friedrichshafen?" demanded Hines.

"If you are all agreeable we shall continue on toward the north," said Tarzan. And so it was that the trial trip of the O-220 became an actual start upon its long journey toward the interior of the earth, and the secrecy that was desired for the expedition was insured.

The plan had been to follow the Tenth Meridian east of Greenwich north to the pole. But to avoid attracting unnecessary notice a slight deviation from this course was found desirable, and the ship passed to the west of Hamburg and out across the waters of the North Sea, and thus due north, passing to the west of Spitzbergen and out across the frozen polar wastes.

Maintaining an average cruising speed of about 75 miles per hour, the O-220 reached the vicinity of the north pole about midnight of the second day, and excitement ran high when Hines announced that in accordance with his calculation they should be directly over the pole. At Tarzan's suggestion the ship circled slowly at an altitude of a few hundred feet above the rough, snow-covered ice.

"We ought to be able to recognize it by the Italian flags," said Zuppner, with a smile. But if any reminders of the passage of the Norge remained below them, they were effectually hidden by the mantle of many snows.

The ship made a single circle above the desolate ice pack before she took up her southerly course along the 170th East Meridian.

From the moment that the ship struck south from the pole Jason Gridley remained constantly with Hines and Zuppner eagerly and anxiously watching the instruments, or gazing down upon the bleak landscape ahead. It was Gridley's belief that the north polar opening lay in the vicinity of 85 north latitude and 170 east longitude. Before him were compass, aneroids, bubble statoscope, air speed indicator, inclinometers, rise and fall indicator, bearing plate, clock and thermometers; but the instrument that commanded his closest attention was the compass, for Jason Gridley held a theory and upon the correctness of it depended their success in finding the north polar opening.

For five hours the ship flew steadily toward the south, when she developed an apparent tendency to fall off toward the west.

"Hold her steady, Captain," cautioned Gridley, "for if I am correct we are now going over the lip of the polar opening, and the deviation is in the compass only and not in our course. The further we go along this course the more erratic the compass will become and if we were presently to move upward, or in other words, straight out across the polar opening toward its center, the needle would spin erratically in a circle. But we could not reach the center of the polar opening because of the tremendous altitude which this would require. I believe that we are now on the eastern verge of the opening and if whatever deviation from the present course you make is to the starboard we shall slowly spiral downward into Pellucidar, but your compass will be useless for the next four to six hundred miles."

Zuppner shook his head, dubiously. "If this weather holds, we may be able to do it," he said, "but if it commences to blow I doubt my ability to keep any sort of a course if I am not to follow the compass."

"Do the best you can," said Gridley, "and when in doubt put her to starboard."

So great was the nervous strain upon all of them that for hours at a time scarcely a word was exchanged.

"Look!" exclaimed Hines suddenly. "There is open water just ahead of us."

"That, of course, we might expect," said Zuppner, "even if there is no polar opening, and you know that I have been skeptical about that ever since Gridley first explained his theory to me."

"I think," said Gridley, with a smile, "that really I am the only one in the party who has had any faith at all in the theory, but please do not call it my theory for it is not, and even I should not have been surprised had the theory proven to be a false one. But if any of you has been watching the sun for the last few hours, I think that you will have to agree with me that even though there may be no polar opening into an inner world, there must be a great depression at this point in the earth's crust and that we have gone down into it for a considerable distance, for you will notice that the midnight sun is much lower than it should be and that the further we continue upon this course the lower it drops—eventually it will set completely, and if I am not much mistaken we shall soon see the light of the eternal noonday sun of Pellucidar."

Suddenly the telephone rang and Hines put the receiver to his ear. "Very good, sir," he said, after a moment, and hung up. "It was Von Horst, Captain, reporting from the observation cabin. He has sighted land dead ahead."

"Land!" exclaimed Zuppner. "The only land our chart shows in this direction is Siberia."

"Siberia lies over a thousand miles south of 85, and we cannot be over three hundred miles south of 85," said Gridley.

"Then we have either discovered a new arctic land, or we are approaching the northern frontiers of Pellucidar," said Lieutenant Hines.

"And that is just what we are doing," said Gridley. "Look at your thermometer."

"The devil!" exclaimed Zuppner. "It is only twenty degrees above zero Fahrenheit."

"You can see the land plainly now," said Tarzan. "It looks desolate enough, but there are only little patches of snow here and there."

"This corresponds with the land Innes described north of Korsar," said Gridley.

Word was quickly passed around the ship to the other officers and the crew that there was reason to believe that the land below them was Pellucidar. Excitement ran high, and every man who could spare a moment from his duties was aloft on the walking-way, or peering through portholes for a glimpse of the inner world.

Steadily the O-220 forged southward and just as the rim of the midnight sun disappeared from view below the horizon astern, the glow of Pellucidar's central sun was plainly visible ahead.

The nature of the landscape below was changing rapidly. The barren land had fallen astern, the ship had crossed a range of wooded hills and now before it lay a great forest that stretched on and on seemingly curving upward to be lost eventually in the haze of the distance. This was indeed Pellucidar—the Pellucidar of which Jason Gridley had dreamed.

Beyond the forest lay a rolling plain dotted with clumps of trees, a well-watered plain through which wound numerous streams, which emptied into a large river at its opposite side.

Great herds of game were grazing in the open pasture land and nowhere was there sight of man.

"This looks like heaven to me," said Tarzan of the Apes. "Let us land, Captain."

Slowly the great ship came to earth as air was taken into the lower vacuum tanks.

Short ladders were run out, for the bottom of the cabin was only six feet above the ground, and presently the entire ship's company, with the exception of a watch of an officer and two men, were knee deep in the lush grasses of Pellucidar.

"I thought we might get some fresh meat," said Tarzan, "but the ship has frightened all the game away."

"From the quantity of it I saw, we shall not have to go far to bag some," said Dorf.

"What we need most right now, however, is rest," said Tarzan. "For weeks every man has been working at high pitch in completing the preparation for the expedition and I doubt if one of us has had over two hours sleep in the last three days. I suggest that we remain here until we are all thoroughly rested and then take up a systematic search for the city of Korsar."

The plan met with general approval and preparations were made for a stay of several days.

"I believe," said Gridley to Captain Zuppner, "that it would be well to issue strict orders that no one is to leave the ship, or rather its close vicinity, without permission from you and that no one be allowed to venture far afield except in parties commanded by an officer, for we have every assurance that we shall meet with savage men and far more savage beasts everywhere within Pellucidar."

"I hope that you will except me from that order," said Tarzan, smiling.

"I believe that you can take care of yourself in any country," said Zuppner.

"And I can certainly hunt to better effect alone than I can with a party," said the ape-man.

"In any event," continued Zuppner, "the order comes from you as commander, and no one will complain if you exempt yourself from its provisions since I am sure that none of the rest of us is particularly anxious to wander about Pellucidar alone."

Officers and men, with the exception of the watch, which changed every four hours, slept the clock around.

Tarzan of the Apes was the first to complete his sleep and leave the ship. He had discarded the clothing that had encumbered and annoyed him since he had left his own African jungle to join in the preparation of the O-220, and it was no faultlessly attired Englishman that came from the cabin and dropped to the ground below, but instead an almost naked and primitive warrior, armed with hunting knife, spear, a bow and arrows, and the long rope which Tarzan always carried, for in the hunt he preferred the weapons of his youth to the firearms of civilization.

Lieutenant Dorf, the only officer on duty at the time, saw him depart and watched with unfeigned admiration as the black-haired jungle lord moved across the open plain and disappeared in the forest.

There were trees that were familiar to the eyes of the ape-man, and trees such as he had never seen before, but it was a forest and that was enough to lure Tarzan of the Apes and permit him to forget the last few weeks that had been spent amidst the distasteful surroundings of civilization. He was happy to be free from the ship, too, and, while he liked all his companions, he was yet glad to be alone.

In the first flight of his new-found freedom Tarzan was like a boy released from school. Unhampered by the hated vestments of civilization, out of sight of anything that might even remotely remind him of the atrocities with which man scars the face of nature, he filled his lungs with the free air of Pellucidar, leaped into a nearby tree and swung away through the forest, his only concern for the moment the joyousness of exultant vitality and life. On he sped through the primeval forest of Pellucidar. Strange birds, startled by his swift and silent passage, flew screaming from his path, and strange beasts slunk to cover beneath him. But Tarzan did not care; he was not hunting; he was not even searching for the new in this new world. For the moment he was only living.

While this mood dominated him Tarzan gave no thought to the passage of time any more than he had given thought to the timelessness of Pellucidar, whose noonday sun, hanging perpetually at zenith, gives a lie to us of the outer crust who rush frantically through life in mad and futile effort to beat the earth in her revolutions. Nor did Tarzan reckon upon distance or direction, for such matters were seldom the subjects of conscious consideration upon the part of the ape-man, whose remarkable ability to meet every and any emergency he unconsciously attributed to powers that lay within himself, not stopping to consider that in his own jungle he relied upon the friendly sun and moon and stars as guides by day and night, and to the myriad familiar things that spoke to him in a friendly, voiceless language that only the jungle people can interpret.

As his mood changed Tarzan reduced his speed, and presently he dropped to the ground in a well-marked game trail. Now he let his eyes take in the new wonders all about him. He noticed the evidences of great age as betokened by the enormous size of the trees and the hoary stems of the great vines that clung to many of them—suggestions of age that made his own jungle seem modern—and he marvelled at the gorgeous flowers that bloomed in riotous profusion upon every hand, and then of a sudden something gripped him about the body and snapped him high into the air.

Tarzan of the Apes had nodded. His mind occupied with the wonders of this new world had permitted a momentary relaxation of that habitual wariness that distinguishes creatures of the wild.

Almost in the instant of its occurrence the ape-man realized what had befallen him. Although he could easily imagine its disastrous sequel, the suggestion of a smile touched his lips—a rueful smile—and one that was perhaps tinged with disgust for himself, for Tarzan of the Apes had been caught in as primitive a snare as was ever laid for unwary beasts.

A rawhide noose, attached to the downbent limb of an overhanging tree, had been buried in the trail along which he had been passing and he had struck the trigger—that was the whole story. But its sequel might have had less unfortunate possibilities had the noose not pinioned his arms to his sides as it closed about him.

He hung about six feet above the trail, caught securely about the hips, the noose imprisoning his arms between elbows and wrists and pinioning them securely to his sides. And to add to his discomfort and helplessness, he swung head downward, spinning dizzily like a human plumb-bob.

He tried to draw an arm from the encircling noose so that he might reach his hunting knife and free himself, but the weight of his body constantly drew the noose more tightly about him and every effort upon his part seemed but to strengthen the relentless grip of the rawhide that was pressing deep into his flesh.

He knew that the snare meant the presence of men and that doubtless they would soon come to inspect their noose, for his own knowledge of primitive hunting taught him that they would not leave their snares long untended, since in the event of a catch, if they would have it at all, they must claim it soon lest it fall prey to carnivorous beasts or birds. He wondered what sort of people they were and if he might not make friends with them, but whatever they were he hoped that they would come before the beasts of prey came. And while such thoughts were running through his mind, his keen ears caught the sound of approaching footsteps, but they were not the steps of men. Whatever was approaching was approaching across the wind and he could detect no scent spoor; nor, upon the other hand, he realized, could the beast scent him. It was coming leisurely and as it neared him, but before it came in sight along the trail, he knew that it was a hoofed animal and, therefore, that he had little reason to fear its approach unless, indeed, it might prove to be some strange Pellucidarian creature with characteristics entirely unlike any that he knew upon the outer crust.

But even as he permitted these thoughts partially to reassure him, there came strongly to his nostrils a scent that always caused the short hairs upon his head to rise, not in fear but in natural reaction to the presence of an hereditary enemy. It was not an odor that he had ever smelled before. It was not the scent spoor of Numa the lion, nor Sheeta the leopard, but it was the scent spoor of some sort of great cat. And now he could hear its almost silent approach through the underbrush and he knew that it was coming down toward the trail, lured either by knowledge of his presence or by that of the beast whose approach Tarzan had been awaiting.

It was the latter who came first into view—a great ox-like animal with wide-spread horns and shaggy coat—a huge bull that advanced several yards along the trail after Tarzan discovered it before it saw the ape-man dangling in front of it. It was the thag of Pellucidar, the Bos Primigenus of the paleontologist of the outer crust, a long extinct progenitor of the bovine races of our own world.

For a moment it stood eyeing the man dangling in its path.

Tarzan remained very quiet. He did not wish to frighten it away for he realized that one of them must be the prey of the carnivore sneaking upon them, but if he expected the thag to be frightened he soon realized his error in judgment for, uttering low grumblings, the great bull pawed the earth with a front foot, and then, lowering his massive horns, gored it angrily, and the ape-man knew that he was working his short temper up to charging pitch; nor did it seem that this was to take long for already he was advancing menacingly to the accompaniment of thunderous bellowing. His tail was up and his head down as he broke into the trot that preluded the charge.

The ape-man realized that if he was ever struck by those massive horns or that heavy head, his skull would be crushed like an eggshell.

The dizzy spinning that had been caused by the first stretching of the rawhide to his weight had lessened to a gentle turning motion, so that sometimes he faced the thag and sometimes in the opposite direction. The utter helplessness of his position galled the ape-man and gave him more concern than any consideration of impending death. From childhood he had walked hand in hand with the Grim Reaper and he had looked upon death in so many forms that it held no terror for him. He knew that it was the final experience of all created things, that it must as inevitably come to him as to others and while he loved life and did not wish to die, its mere approach induced within him no futile hysteria. But to die without a chance to fight for life was not such an end as Tarzan of the Apes would have chosen. And now, as his body slowly revolved and his eyes were turned away from the charging thag, his heart sank at the thought that he was not even to be vouchsafed the meager satisfaction of meeting death face to face.

In the brief instant that he waited for the impact, the air was rent by as horrid a scream as had ever broken upon the ears of the ape-man and the bellowing of the bull rose suddenly to a higher pitch and mingled with that other awesome sound.

Once more the dangling body of the ape-man revolved and his eyes fell upon such a scene as had not been vouchsafed to men of the outer world for countless ages.

Upon the massive shoulders and neck of the great thag clung a tiger of such huge proportions that Tarzan could scarce credit the testimony of his own eyes. Great saber-like tusks, projecting from the upper jaw, were buried deep in the neck of the bull, which, instead of trying to escape, had stopped in its tracks and was endeavoring to dislodge the great beast of prey, swinging its huge horns backward in an attempt to rake the living death from its shoulders, or again shaking its whole body violently for the same purpose and all the while bellowing in pain and rage.

Gradually the saber-tooth changed its position until it had attained a hold suited to its purpose. Then with lightning-like swiftness it swung back a great forearm and delivered a single, terrific blow on the side of the thag's head—a titanic blow that crushed that mighty skull and dropped the huge bull dead in its tracks. And then the carnivore settled down to feast upon its kill.

During the battle the saber-tooth had not noticed the ape-man; nor was it until after he had commenced to feed upon the thag that his eye was attracted by the revolving body swinging above the trail a few yards away. Instantly the beast stopped feeding; his head lowered and flattened, his upper lip turned back in a hideous snarl. He watched the ape-man. Low, menacing growls rumbled from his cavernous throat; his long, sinuous tail lashed angrily as slowly he arose from the body of his kill and advanced toward Tarzan of the Apes.

CHAPTER 3

The Great Cats

THE EBBING TIDE of the great war had left human flotsam stranded upon many an unfamiliar beach. In its full flow it had lifted Robert Jones, high private in the ranks of a labor battalion, from uncongenial surroundings and landed him in a prison camp behind the enemy line. Here his good nature won him friends and favors, but neither one nor the other served to obtain his freedom. Robert

Jones seemed to have been lost in the shuffle. And finally, when the evacuation of the prison had been completed, Robert Jones still remained, but he was not downhearted. He had learned the language of his captors and had made many friends among them. They found him a job and Robert Jones of Alabama was content to remain where he was. He had been graduated from body servant to cook of an officers' mess and it was in this capacity that he had come under the observation of Captain Zuppner, who had drafted him for the O-220 expedition.

Robert Jones yawned, stretched, turned over in his narrow berth aboard the O-220, opened his eyes and sat up with an exclamation of surprise. He jumped to the floor and stuck his head out of an open port.

"Lawd, niggah!" he exclaimed; "you all suah done overslep' yo'sef."

For a moment he gazed up at the noonday sun shining down upon him and then, hastily dressing, hurried into his galley.

" 'S funny," he soliloquized; "dey ain't no one stirrin'—mus' all of overslep' demsef." He looked at the clock on the galley wall. The hour hand pointed to six. He cocked his ear and listened. "She ain't stopped," he muttered. Then he went to the door that opened from the galley through the ship's side and pushed it back. Leaning far out he looked up again at the sun. Then he shook his head. "Dey's sumpin wrong," he said. "Ah dunno whether to cook breakfas', dinner or supper."

Jason Gridley, emerging from his cabin, sauntered down the narrow corridor toward the galley. "Good morning, Bob!" he said, stopping in the open doorway. "What's the chance for a bite of breakfast?"

"Did you all say breakfas', suh?" inquired Robert.

"Yes," replied Gridley; "just toast and coffee and a couple of eggs—anything you have handy."

"Ah knew it!" exclaimed the black. "Ah knew dat ol' clock couldn't be wrong, but Mistah Sun he suah gone hay wire."

Gridley grinned. "I'll drop down and have a little walk," he said. "I'll be back in fifteen minutes. Have you seen anything of Lord Greystoke?"

"No suh, Ah ain't seen nothin' o' Massa Ta'zan sence yesterday."

"I wondered," said Gridley; "he is not in his cabin."

For fifteen minutes Gridley walked briskly about in the vicinity of the ship. When he returned to the mess room he found Zuppner and Dorf awaiting breakfast and greeted them with a pleasant "good morning."

"I don't know whether it's good morning or good evening," said Zuppner.

"We have been here twelve hours," said Dorf, "and it is just the same time that it was when we arrived. I have been on watch for the last four hours and if it hadn't been for the chronometer I could not swear that I had been on fifteen minutes or that I had not been on a week."

"It certainly induces a feeling of unreality that is hard to explain," said Gridley.

"Where is Greystoke?" asked Zuppner. "He is usually an early riser."

"I was just asking Bob," said Gridley, "but he has not seen him."

"He left the ship shortly after I came on watch," said Dorf. "I should say about three hours ago, possibly longer. I saw him cross the open country and enter the forest."

"I wish he had not gone out alone," said Gridley.

"He strikes me as a man who can take care of himself," said Zuppner.

"I have seen some things during the last four hours," said Dorf, "that make me doubt whether any man can take care of himself alone in this world, especially one armed only with the primitive weapons that Greystoke carried with him."

"You mean that he carried no firearms?" demanded Zuppner.

"He was armed with a bow and arrows, a spear and a rope," said Dorf, "and I think he carried a hunting knife as well. But he might as well have had nothing but a pea-shooter if he met some of the things I have seen since I went on watch."

"What do you mean?" demanded Zuppner. "What have you seen?"

Dorf grinned sheepishly. "Honestly, Captain, I hate to tell you," he said, "for I'm damned if I believe it myself."

"Well, out with it," exclaimed Zuppner. "We will make allowances for your youth and for the effect that the sun and horizon of Pellucidar may have had upon your eyesight or your veracity."

"Well," said Dorf, "about an hour ago a bear passed within a hundred yards of the ship."

"There is nothing remarkable about that," said Zuppner.

"There was a great deal that was remarkable about the bear, however," said Dorf.

"In what way?" asked Gridley.

"It was fully as large as an ox," said Dorf, "and if I were going out after bear in this country I should want to take along field artillery."

"Was that all you saw—just a bear?" asked Zuppner.

"No," said Dorf, "I saw tigers, not one but fully a dozen, and they were as much larger than our Bengal tigers as the bear was larger than any bear of the outer crust that I have ever seen. They were perfectly enormous and they were armed with the most amazing fangs you ever saw—great curved fangs that extended from their upper jaws to lengths of from eight inches to a foot. They came down to this stream here to drink and then wandered away, some of them toward the forest and some down toward that big river yonder."

"Greystoke couldn't do much against such creatures as those even if he had carried a rifle," said Zuppner.

"If he was in the forest, he could escape them," said Gridley.

Zuppner shook his head. "I don't like the looks of it," he said. "I wish that he had not gone out alone."

"The bear and the tigers were bad enough," continued Dorf, "but I saw another creature that to me seemed infinitely worse."

Robert, who was more or less a privileged character, had entered from the galley and was listening with wide-eyed interest to Dorf's account of the creatures he had seen, while Victor, one of the Filipino cabin-boys, served the officers.

"Yes," continued Dorf, "I saw a mighty strange creature. It flew directly over the ship and I had an excellent view of it. At first I thought that it was a bird, but when it approached more closely I saw that it was a winged reptile. It had a long, narrow head and it flew so close that I could see its great jaws, armed with an infinite number of long, sharp teeth. Its head was elongated above the eyes and came to a sharp point. It was perfectly immense and must have had a wing spread of at least twenty feet. While I was watching it, it dropped suddenly to earth only a short distance beyond the ship, and when it arose again it was carrying in its talons some animal that must have been fully as large as a good sized sheep, with which it flew away without apparent effort. That the creature is carnivorous is evident as is also the fact that it has sufficient strength to carry away a man."

Robert Jones covered his large mouth with a pink palm and with hunched and shaking shoulders turned and tip-toed from the room. Once in the galley with the door closed, he gave himself over to unrestrained mirth.

"What is the matter with you?" asked Victor.

"Lawd-a-massy!" exclaimed Robert. "Ah allus thought some o'dem gem'n in dat dere Adventurous Club in Bummingham could lie some, but, shucks, dey ain't in it with this Lieutenant Dorf. Did you all heah him tell about dat flyin' snake what carries off sheep?"

But back in the mess room the white men took Dorf's statement more seriously.

"That would be a pterodactyl," said Zuppner.

"Yes," replied Dorf. "I classified it as a Pteranodon."

"Don't you think we ought to send out a search party?" asked Gridley.

"I am afraid Greystoke would not like it," replied Zuppner.

"It could go out under the guise of a hunting party," suggested Dorf.

"If he has not returned within an hour," said Zuppner, "we shall have to do something of the sort."

Hines and Von Horst now entered the mess room, and when they learned of Tarzan's absence from the ship and had heard from Dorf a description of some of the animals that he might have encountered, they were equally as apprehensive as the others of his safety.

"We might cruise around a bit, sir," suggested Von Horst to Zuppner.

"But suppose he returns to this spot during our absence?" asked Gridley.

"Could you return the ship to this anchorage again?" inquired Zuppner.

"I doubt it," replied the Lieutenant. "Our instruments are almost worthless under the conditions existing in Pellucidar."

"Then we had better remain where we are," said Gridley, "until he returns."

"But if we send a searching party after him on foot, what assurance have we that it will be able to find its way back to the ship?" demanded Zuppner.

"That will not be so difficult," said Gridley. "We can always blaze our trail as we go and thus easily retrace our steps."

"Yes, that is so," agreed Zuppner.

"Suppose," said Gridley, "that Von Horst and I go out with Muviro and his Waziri. They are experienced trackers, prime fighting men and they certainly know the jungle."

"Not this jungle," said Dorf.

"But at least they know any jungle better than the rest of us," insisted Gridley.

"I think your plan is a good one," said Zuppner, "and anyway as you are in command now, the rest of us gladly place ourselves under your orders."

"The conditions that confront us here are new to all of us," said Gridley. "Nothing that anyone of us can suggest or command can be based upon any personal experience or knowledge that the rest do not possess, and in matters of this kind I think that we had better reach our decision after full discussion rather than to depend blindly upon official priority of authority."

"That has been Greystoke's policy," said Zuppner, "and it has made it very easy and pleasant for all of us. I quite agree with you, but I can think of no more feasible plan than that which you have suggested."

"Very good," said Gridley. "Will you accompany me, Lieutenant?" he asked, turning to Von Horst.

The officer grinned. "Will I?" he exclaimed. "I should never have forgiven you if you had left me out of it."

"Fine," said Gridley. "And now, I think, we might as well make our preparations at once and get as early a start as possible. See that the Waziri have eaten, Lieutenant, and tell Muviro that I want them armed with rifles. These fellows can use them all right, but they rather look with scorn upon anything more modern than their war spears and arrows."

"Yes, I discovered that," said Hines. "Muviro told me a few days ago that his people consider firearms as something of an admission of cowardice. He told me that they use them for target practice, but when they go out after lions or rhino they leave their rifles behind and take their spears and arrows."

"After they have seen what I saw," said Dorf, "they will have more respect for an express rifle."

"See that they take plenty of ammunition, Von Horst," said Gridley, "for from what I have seen in this country we shall not have to carry any provisions."

"A man who could not live off this country would starve to

death in a meat market," said Zuppner.

Von Horst left to carry out Gridley's orders while the latter returned to his cabin to prepare for the expedition.

The officers and crew remaining with the O-220 were all on hand to bid farewell to the expedition starting out in search of Tarzan of the Apes, and as the ten stalwart Waziri warriors marched away behind Gridley and Von Horst, Robert Jones, watching from the galley door, swelled with pride. "Dem niggahs is sho nuf hot babies," he exclaimed. "All dem flyin' snakes bettah clear out de country now." With the others Robert watched the little party as it crossed the plain and until it had disappeared within the dark precincts of the forest upon the opposite side. Then he glanced up at the noonday sun, shook his head, elevated his palms in resignation and turned back into his galley.

Almost immediately after the party had left the ship, Gridley directed Muviro to take the lead and watch for Tarzan's trail since, of the entire party, he was the most experienced tracker; nor did the Waziri chieftain have any difficulty in following the spoor of the ape-man across the plain and into the forest, but here, beneath a great tree, it disappeared.

"The Big Bwana took to the trees here," said Muviro, "and no man lives who can follow his spoor through the lower, the middle or the upper terraces."

"What do you suggest, then, Muviro?" asked Gridley.

"If this were his own jungle," replied the warrior, "I should feel sure that when he took to the trees he would move in a straight line toward the place he wished to go; unless he happened to be hunting, in which case his direction would be influenced by the sign and scent of game."

"Doubtless he was hunting here," said Von Horst.

"If he was hunting," said Muviro, "he would have moved in a straight line until he caught the scent spoor of game or came to a well-beaten game trail."

"And then what would he do?" asked Gridley.

"He might wait above the trail," replied Muviro, "or he might follow it. In a new country like this, I think he would follow it, for he has always been interested in exploring every new country he entered."

"Then let us push straight into the forest in this same direction until we strike a game trail," said Gridley.

Muviro and three of his warriors went ahead, cutting brush

where it was necessary and blazing the trees at frequent intervals that they might more easily retrace their steps to the ship. With the aid of a small pocket compass Gridley directed the line of advance, which otherwise it would have been difficult to hold accurately beneath that eternal noonday sun, whose warm rays filtered down through the foliage of the forest.

"God! What a forest!" exclaimed Von Horst. "To search for a man here is like the proverbial search for the needle in a haystack."

"Except," said Gridley, "that one might stand a slight chance of finding the needle."

"Perhaps we had better fire a shot occasionally," suggested Von Horst.

"Excellent," said Gridley. "The rifles carry a much heavier charge and make a louder report than our revolvers."

After warning the others of his intention, he directed one of the blacks to fire three shots at intervals of a few seconds, for neither Gridley nor Von Horst was armed with rifles, each of the officers carrying two .45 caliber Colts. Thereafter, at intervals of about half an hour, a single shot was fired, but as the searching party forced its way on into the forest each of its members became gloomily impressed with the futility of their search.

Presently the nature of the forest changed. The trees were set less closely together and the underbrush, while still forming an almost impenetrable screen, was less dense than it had been heretofore and here they came upon a wide game trail, worn by countless hoofs and padded feet to a depth of two feet or more below the surface of the surrounding ground, and here Jason Gridley blundered.

"We won't bother about blazing the trees as long as we follow this trail," he said to Muviro, "except at such places as it may fork or be crossed by other trails."

It was, after all, a quite natural mistake since a few blazed trees along the trail would not serve any purpose in following it back when they wished to return.

The going here was easier and as the Waziri warriors swung along at a brisk pace, the miles dropped quickly behind them and already had the noonday sun so cast its spell upon them that the element of time seemed not to enter into their calculations, while the teeming life about them absorbed the attention of blacks and whites alike.

Strange monkeys, some of them startlingly manlike in appearance and of large size, watched them pass. Birds of both gay and somber plumage scattered protestingly before their advance, and again dim bulks loomed through the undergrowth and the sound of padded feet was everywhere.

At times they would pass through a stretch of forest as silent as the tomb, and then again they seemed to be surrounded by a bedlam of hideous growls and roars and screams.

"I'd like to see some of those fellows," said Von Horst, after a particularly savage outburst of sound.

"I am surprised that we haven't," replied Gridley; "but I imagine that they are a little bit leery of us right now, not alone on account of our numbers but because of the, to them strange and unfamiliar, odors which must surround us. These would naturally increase the suspicion which must have been aroused by the sound of our shots."

"Have you noticed," said Von Horst, "that most of the noise seems to come from behind us; I mean the more savage, growling sounds. I have heard squeals and noises that sounded like the trumpeting of elephants to the right and to the left and ahead, but only an occasional growl or roar seems to come from these directions and then always at a considerable distance."

"How do you account for it?" asked Gridley.

"I can't account for it," replied Von Horst. "It is as though we were moving along in the center of a procession with all the savage carnivores behind us."

"This perpetual noonday sun has its compensations," remarked Gridley with a laugh, "for at least it insures that we shall not have to spend the night here."

At that instant the attention of the two men was attracted by an exclamation from one of the Waziri behind them. "Look, Bwana! Look!" cried the man, pointing back along the trail. Following the direction of the Waziri's extended finger, Gridley and Von Horst saw a huge beast slinking slowly along the trail in their rear.

"God!" exclaimed Von Horst, "and I thought Dorf was exaggerating."

"It doesn't seem possible," exclaimed Gridley, "that five hundred miles below our feet automobiles are dashing through crowded streets lined by enormous buildings; that there the telegraph, the telephone and the radio are so commonplace as to excite no comment; that countless thousands live out their entire lives without ever having to use a weapon in self-defense, and yet at the same instant we stand here facing a saber-tooth tiger in surroundings that may not have existed upon the outer crust for a million years."

"Look at them!" exclaimed Von Horst. "If there is one there are a dozen of them."

"Shall we fire, Bwana?" asked one of the Waziri.

"Not yet," said Gridley. "Close up and be ready. They seem to be only following us."

Slowly the party fell back, a line of Waziri in the rear facing the tigers and backing slowly away from them. Muviro dropped back to Gridley's side.

"For a long time, Bwana," he said, "there has been the spoor of many elephants in the trail, or spoor that looked like the spoor of elephants, though it was different. And just now I sighted some of the beasts ahead. I could not make them out distinctly, but if they are not elephants they are very much like them."

"We seem to be between the devil and the deep sea," said Von Horst.

"And there are either elephants or tigers on each side of us," said Muviro. "I can hear them moving through the brush."

Perhaps the same thought was in the minds of all these men, that they might take to the trees, but for some reason no one expressed it. And so they continued to move slowly along the trail until suddenly it broke into a large, open area in the forest, where the ground was scantily covered with brush and there were few trees. Perhaps a hundred acres were included in the clearing and then the forest commenced again upon all sides.

And into the clearing, along numerous trails that seemed to center at this spot, came as strange a procession as the eyes of these men had ever rested upon. There were great ox-like creatures with shaggy coats and wide-spreading horns. There were red deer and sloths of gigantic size. There were mastodon and mammoth, and a huge, elephantine creature that resembled an elephant and yet did not seem to be an elephant at all. Its great head was four feet long and three feet wide. It had a short, powerful trunk and from its lower jaw mighty tusks curved downward, their points bending inward toward the body. At the shoulder it stood at least ten feet above the ground, and in length it must have been fully twenty feet. But what resemblance it bore to an elephant was lessened by its small, pig-like ears.

The two white men, momentarily forgetting the tigers behind them in their amazement at the sight ahead, halted and looked with wonder upon the huge gathering of creatures within the clearing.

"Did you ever see anything like it?" exclaimed Gridley.

"No, nor anyone else," replied Von Horst.

"I could catalog a great many of them," said Gridley, "although practically all are extinct upon the outer crust. But that fellow there gets me," and he pointed to the elephantine creature with the downward pointing tusks.

"A Dinotherium of the Miocene," said Von Horst.

Muviro had stopped beside the two whites and was gazing in wide-eyed astonishment at the scene before him.

"Well," asked Gridley, "what do you make of it, Muviro?"

"I think I understand now, Bwana," replied the black, "and if we are ever going to escape our one chance is to cross that clearing as quickly as possible. The great cats are herding these creatures here and presently there will be such a killing as the eyes of man have never before seen. If we are not killed by the cats, we shall be trampled to death by these beasts in their efforts to escape or to fight the tigers."

"I believe you are right, Muviro," said Gridley.

"There is an opening just ahead of us," said Von Horst.

Gridley called the men around him and pointed out across the clearing to the forest upon the opposite side. "Apparently our only chance now," he said, "is to cross before the cats close in on these beasts. We have already come into the clearing too far to try to take refuge in the trees on this side for the saber-tooths are too close. Stick close together and fire at nothing unless we are charged."

"Look!" exclaimed Von Horst. "The tigers are entering the clearing from all sides. They have surrounded their quarry."

"There is still the one opening ahead of us, Bwana," said Muviro.

Already the little party was moving slowly across the clearing, which was covered with nervous beasts moving irritably to and fro, their whole demeanor marked by nervous apprehension. Prior to the advent of the tigers the animals had been moving quietly about, some of them grazing on the short grass of the clearing or upon the leaves and twigs of the scattered trees growing in it; but with the appearance of the first of the carnivores their attitude changed. A huge, bull mastodon raised his trunk and trumpeted shrilly, and instantly every herbivore was on the alert. And as eyes or nostrils detected the presence of the great cats, or the beasts became excited by the excitement of their fellows, each added his voice to the pandemonium that now reigned. To the squealing, trumpeting and bellowing of the quarry were added the hideous growls and roars of the carnivores.

"Look at those cats!" cried Von Horst. "There must be hundreds of them." Nor was his estimate an exaggeration for from all sides of the clearing, with the exception of a single point opposite them, the cats were emerging from the forest and starting to circle the herd. That they did not rush it immediately evidenced their respect for the huge beasts they had corraled, the majority of which they would not have dared to attack except in superior numbers.

Now a mammoth, a giant bull with tail raised and ears up-cocked, curled his trunk above his head and charged. But a score of the great cats, growling hideously, sprang to meet him, and the bull, losing his nerve, wheeled in a wide circle and returned to the herd. Had he gone through that menacing line of fangs and talons, as with his great size and weight and strength he might have done, he would have opened a hole through which a stampede of the other animals would have carried the bulk of them to safety.

The frightened herbivores, their attention centered upon the menacing tigers, paid little attention to the insignificant man-things passing among them. But there were some exceptions. A thag, bellowing and pawing the earth directly in their line of march, terrified by the odor of the carnivores and aroused and angered by the excited trumpeting and squealing of the creatures about him, seeking to vent his displeasure upon something, lowered his head and charged them. A Waziri warrior raised his rifle to his shoulder and fired, and a prehistoric Bos Primigenus crashed to the impact of a modern bullet.

As the report of the rifle sounded above the other noises of the clearing, the latter were momentarily stilled, and the full attention of hunters and hunted was focused upon the little band of men, so puny and insignificant in the presence of the mighty beasts of another day. A dinotherium, his little ears upcocked, his tail stiffly erect, walked slowly toward them. Almost immediately others followed his example until it seemed that the whole aggregation was converging upon them. The forest was yet a hundred yards away as Jason Gridley realized the seriousness of the emergency that now confronted them.

"We shall have to run for it," he said. "Give them a volley, and then beat it for the trees. If they charge, it will have to be every man for himself."

The Waziri wheeled and faced the slowly advancing herd and then, at Gridley's command, they fired. The thunderous volley had its effect upon the advancing beasts. They hesitated and then turned and retreated; but behind them were the carnivores. And once again they swung back in the direction of the men, who were now moving rapidly toward the forest.

"Here they come!" cried Von Horst. And a backward glance revealed the fact that the entire herd, goaded to terror by the tigers behind them, had broken into a mad stampede. Whether or not it was a direct charge upon the little party of men is open to question, but the fact that they lay in its path was sufficient to seal their doom if they were unable to reach the safety of the forest ahead of the charging quadrupeds.

"Give them another volley!" cried Gridley. And again the Waziri turned and fired. A dinotherium, a thag and two mammoths stumbled and fell to the ground, but the remainder of the herd did not pause. Leaping over the carcasses of their fallen comrades they thundered down upon the fleeing men.

It was now, in truth, every man for himself, and so close pressed were they that even the brave Waziri threw away their rifles as useless encumbrances to flight.

Several of the red deer, swifter in flight than the other members of the herd, had taken the lead, and, stampeding through the party, scattered them to left and right.

Gridley and Von Horst were attempting to cover the retreat of the Waziri and check the charge of the stampeding animals with their revolvers. They succeeded in turning a few of the leaders, but presently a great, red stag passed between them, forcing them to jump quickly apart to escape his heavy antlers, and behind him swept a nightmare of terrified beasts forcing them still further apart.

Not far from Gridley grew a single, giant tree, a short distance from the edge of the clearing, and finding himself alone and cut off from further retreat, the American turned and ran for it, while Von Horst was forced to bolt for the jungle which was now almost within reach.

Bowled over by a huge sloth, Gridley scrambled to his feet,

and, passing in front of a fleeing mastodon, reached the tree just as the main body of the stampeding herd closed about it. Its great bole gave him momentary protection and an instant later he had scrambled among its branches.

Instantly his first thought was for his fellows, but where they had been a moment before was now only a solid mass of leaping, plunging, terrified beasts. No sign of a human being was anywhere to be seen and Gridley knew that no living thing could have survived the trampling of those incalculable tons of terrified flesh.

Some of them, he knew, must have reached the forest, but he doubted that all had come through in safety and he feared particularly for Von Horst, who had been some little distance in rear of the Waziri.

The eyes of the American swept back over the clearing to observe such a scene as probably in all the history of the world had never before been vouchsafed to the eyes of man. Literally thousands of creatures, large and small, were following their leaders in a break for life and liberty, while upon their flanks and at their rear hundreds of savage saber-tooth tigers leaped upon them, dragging down the weaker, battling with the stronger, leaving the maimed and crippled behind that they might charge into the herd again and drag down others.

The mad rush of the leaders across the clearing had been checked as they entered the forest, and now those in the rear were forced to move more slowly, but in their terror they sought to clamber over the backs of those ahead. Red deer leaped upon the backs of mastodons and fled across the heaving bodies beneath them, as a mountain goat might leap from rock to rock. Mammoths raised their huge bulks upon lesser animals and crushed them to the ground. Tusks and horns were red with gore as the maddened beasts battled for their lives. The scene was sickening in its horror, and yet fascinating in its primitive strength and savagery—and everywhere were the great, savage cats.

Slowly they were cutting into the herd from both sides in an effort to encircle a portion of it and at last they were successful, though within the circle there remained but a few scattered beasts that were still unmaimed or uncrippled. And then the great tigers turned upon these, closing in and drawing tighter their hideous band of savage fury.

In twos and threes and scores they leaped upon the remaining beasts and dragged them down until the sole creature remaining alive within their circle was a gigantic bull mammoth. His shaggy coat was splashed with blood and his tusks were red with gore. Trumpeting, he stood at bay, a magnificent picture of primordial power, of sagacity, of courage.

The heart of the American went out to that lone warrior trumpeting his challenge to overwhelming odds in the face of certain doom.

By hundreds the carnivores were closing in upon the great bull; yet it was evident that even though they outnumbered him so overwhelmingly, they still held him in vast respect. Growling and snarling, a few of them slunk in stealthy circles about him, and as he wheeled about with them, three of them charged him from the rear. With a swiftness that matched their own, the pachyderm wheeled to meet them. Two of them he caught upon his tusks and tossed them high into the air, and at the same instant a score of others rushed him from each side and from the rear and fastened themselves to his back and flanks. Down he went as though struck by lightning, squatting quickly upon his haunches and rolling over backward, crushing a dozen tigers before they could escape.

Gridley could scarce repress a cheer as the great fellow staggered to his feet and threw himself again upon the opposite side to the accompaniment of hideous screams of pain and anger from the tigers he pinioned beneath him. But now he was gushing blood from a hundred wounds, and other scores of the savage carnivores were charging him.

Though he put up a magnificent battle the end was inevitable and at last they dragged him down, tearing him to pieces while he yet struggled to rise again and battle with them.

And then commenced the aftermath as the savage beasts fought among themselves for possession of their prey. For even though there was flesh to more than surfeit them all, in their greed, jealousy and ferocity, they must still battle one with another.

That they had paid heavily for their meat was evident by the carcasses of the tigers strewn about the clearing and as the survivors slowly settled down to feed, there came the jackals, the hyaenodons and the wild dogs to feast upon their leavings.

CHAPTER 4

The Sagoths

As THE GREAT cat slunk toward him, Tarzan of the Apes realized that at last he faced inevitable death, yet even in that last moment of life the emotion which dominated him was one of admiration for the magnificent beast drawing angrily toward him.

Tarzan of the Apes would have preferred to die fighting, if he must die; yet he felt a certain thrill as he contemplated the magnificence of the great beast that Fate had chosen to terminate his earthly career. He felt no fear, but a certain sense of anticipation of what would follow after death. The Lord of the Jungle subscribed to no creed. Tarzan of the Apes was not a church man; yet like the majority of those who have always lived close to nature he was, in a sense, intensely religious. His intimate knowledge of the stupendous forces of nature, of her wonders and her miracles had impressed him with the fact that their ultimate origin lay far beyond the conception of the finite mind of man, and thus incalculably remote from the farthest bounds of science. When he thought of God he liked to think of Him primitively, as a personal God. And while he realized that he knew nothing of such matters, he liked to believe that after death he would live again.

Many thoughts passed quickly through his mind as the saber-tooth advanced upon him. He was watching the long, glistening fangs that so soon were to be buried in his flesh when his attention was attracted by a sound among the trees about him. That the great cat had heard too was evident, for it stopped in its tracks and gazed up into the foliage of the trees above. And then Tarzan heard a rustling in the branches directly overhead, and looking up he saw what appeared to be a gorilla glaring down upon him.

Two more savage faces showed through the foliage above him and then in other trees about he caught glimpses of similar shaggy forms and fierce faces. He saw that they were like gorillas, and yet unlike them; that in some respects they were more man than gorilla, and in others more gorilla than man. He caught glimpses of great clubs wielded by hairy hands, and when his eyes returned to the saber-tooth he saw that the great beast had hesitated in its advance and was snarling and growling angrily as its eyes roved upward and around at the savage creatures glaring down upon it.

It was only for a moment that the cat paused in its advance upon the ape-man. Snarling angrily, it moved forward again and as it did so, one of the creatures in the tree above Tarzan reached down, and, seizing the rope that held him dangling in mid-air, drew him swiftly upward. Then several things occurred simultaneously—the saber-tooth leaped to retrieve its prey and a dozen heavy cudgels hurtled through the air from the surrounding trees, striking the great cat heavily upon head and body with the result that the talons that must otherwise have inevitably been imbedded in the flesh of the ape-man grazed harmlessly by him, and an instant later he was drawn well up among the branches of the tree, where he was seized by three hairy brutes whose attitude suggested that he might have been as well off had he been left to the tender mercies of the saber-tooth.

Two of them, one on either side, seized an arm and the third grasped him by the throat with one hand while he held his cudgel poised above his head in the other. And then from the lips of the creature facing him came a sound that fell as startlingly upon the ears of the ape-man as had the first unexpected roar of the saber-tooth, but with far different effect.

"Ka-goda!" said the creature facing Tarzan.

In the language of the apes of his own jungle Ka-goda may be roughly interpreted according to its inflection as a command to surrender, or as an interrogation, "do you surrender?" or as a declaration of surrender.

This word, coming from the lips of a hairy gorilla man of the inner world, suggested possibilities of the most startling nature. For years Tarzan had considered the language of the great apes as the primitive root language of created things. The great apes, the lesser apes, the gorillas, the baboons and the monkeys utilized this with various degrees of refinement and many of its words were understood by jungle animals of other species and by many of the birds; but, perhaps, after the fashion that our domestic animals have learned many of the words in our vocabulary, with this difference that the language of the great apes has doubtless persisted unchanged for countless ages.

That these gorilla men of the inner world used even one word of this language suggested one of two possibilities—either they held an origin in common with the creatures of the outer crust, or else that the laws of evolution and progress were so constant that this was the only form of primitive language that could have been possible to any creatures emerging from the lower orders toward the estate of man. But the suggestion that impressed Tarzan most vividly was that this single word, uttered by the creature grasping him by the throat, postulated familiarity on the part of his fierce captors with the entire ape language that he had used since boyhood.

"Ka-goda?" inquired the bull.

"Ka-goda," said Tarzan of the Apes.

The brute, facing Tarzan, half lowered his cudgel as though he were surprised to hear the prisoner answer in his own tongue. "Who are you?" he demanded in the language of the great apes.

"I am Tarzan—mighty hunter, mighty fighter," replied the ape-man.

"What are you doing in M'wa-lot's country?" demanded the gorilla man.

"I come as a friend," replied Tarzan. "I have no quarrel with your people."

The fellow had lowered his club now, and from other trees had come a score more of the shaggy creatures until the surrounding limbs sagged beneath their weight.

"How did you learn the language of the Sagoths?" demanded the bull. "We have captured gilaks in the past, but you are the first one who ever spoke or understood our language."

"It is the language of my people," replied Tarzan. "As a little balu, I learned it from Kala and other apes of the tribe of Kerchak."

"We never heard of the tribe of Kerchak," said the bull.

"Perhaps he is not telling the truth," said another. "Let us kill him; he is only a gilak."

"No," said a third. "Take him back to M'wa-lot that the whole tribe of M'wa-lot may join in the killing."

"That is good," said another. "Take him back to the tribe, and while we are killing him we shall dance."

The language of the great apes is not like our language. It sounds to man like growling and barking and grunting, punctuated at times by shrill screams, and it is practically untranslatable to any tongue known to man; yet it carried to Tarzan and the Sagoths the sense that we have given it. It is a means of communicating thought and there its similarity to the languages of men ceases.

Having decided upon the disposition of their prisoner, the Sagoths now turned their attention to the saber-tooth, who had returned to his kill, across the body of which he was lying. He was not feeding, but was gazing angrily up into the trees at his tormentors.

While three of the gorilla men secured Tarzan's wrists behind his back with a length of buckskin thong, the others renewed their attention to the tiger. Three or four of them would cast well-aimed cudgels at his face at intervals so nicely timed that the great beast could do nothing but fend off the missiles as they sped toward him. And while he was thus occupied, the other Sagoths, who had already cast their clubs, sprang to the ground and retrieved them with an agility and celerity that would have done credit to the tiniest monkey of the jungle. The risk that they took bespoke great self-confidence and high courage since often they were compelled to snatch their cudgels from almost beneath the claws of the saber-tooth.

Battered and bruised, the great cat gave back inch by inch until, unable to stand the fusillade longer, it suddenly turned tail and bounded into the underbrush, where for some time the sound of its crashing retreat could be distinctly heard. And with the departure of the carnivore, the gorilla men leaped to the ground and fell upon the carcass of the thag. With heavy fangs they tore its flesh, oftentimes fighting among themselves like wild beasts for some particularly choice morsel; but unlike many of the lower orders of man upon similar occasions they did not gorge themselves; and having satisfied their hunger they left what remained to the jackals and wild dogs that had already gathered.

Tarzan of the Apes, silent spectator of this savage scene, had an opportunity during the feast to examine his captors more closely. He saw that they were rather lighter in build than the gorillas he had seen in his own native jungle, but even though they were not as heavy as Bolgani, they were yet mighty creatures. Their arms and legs were of more human conformation and proportion than those of a gorilla, but the shaggy brown hair covering their entire body increased their beast-like appearance, while their faces were even more brutal than that of Bolgani himself, except that the development of the skull denoted a brain capacity seemingly as great as that of man.

They were entirely naked, nor was there among them any suggestion of ornamentation, while their only weapons were clubs. These, however, showed indications of having been shaped by some sharp instrument as though an effort had been made to insure a firm grip and a well-balanced weapon.

Their feeding completed, the Sagoths turned back along the game trail in the same direction that Tarzan had been going when he had sprung the trigger of the snare. But before departing several of them reset the noose, covered it carefully with earth and leaves and set the trigger that it might be sprung by the first passing animal.

So sure were all their movements and so deft their fingers, Tarzan realized that though these creatures looked like beasts they had long since entered the estate of man. Perhaps they were still low in the scale of evolution, but unquestionably they were men with the brains of men and the faces and skins of gorillas.

As the Sagoths moved along the jungle trail they walked erect as men walk, but in other ways they reminded Tarzan of the great apes who were his own people, for they were given neither to laughter nor song and their taciturnity suggested the speechlessness of the alali. That certain of their sense faculties were more highly developed than in man was evidenced by the greater dependence they placed upon their ears and noses than upon their eyes in their unremitting vigil against surprise by an enemy.

While by human standards they might have been judged ugly and even hideous, they did not so impress Tarzan of the Apes, who recognized in them a certain primitive majesty of bearing and mien such as might well have been expected of pioneers upon the frontiers of humanity.

It is sometimes the custom of theorists to picture our primordial progenitors as timid, fearful creatures, fleeing from the womb to the grave in constant terror of the countless, savage creatures that beset their entire existence. But as it does not seem reasonable that a creature so poorly equipped for offense and defense could have survived without courage, it seems far more consistent to assume that with the dawning of reason came a certain superiority complex—a vast and at first stupid egotism—that knew caution, perhaps, but not fear; nor is any other theory tenable unless we are to suppose that from the loin of a rabbit-hearted creature sprang men who hunted the bison, the mammoth and the cave bear with crude spears tipped with stone.

The Sagoths of Pellucidar may have been analogous in the scale of evolution to the Neanderthal men of the outer crust, or they may, indeed, have been even a step lower; yet in their bearing there was nothing to suggest to Tarzan that they had reached this stage in evolution through the expedience of flight. Their bearing as they trod the jungle trail bespoke assurance and even truculence, as though they were indeed the lords of creation, fearing nothing. Perhaps Tarzan understood their attitude better than another might have since it had been his own always in the jungle—unquestioning fearlessness—with which a certain intelligent caution was not inconsistent.

They had come but a short distance from the scene of Tarzan's capture when the Sagoths stopped beside a hollow log, the skeleton of a great tree that had fallen beside the trail. One of the creatures tapped upon the log with his club—one, two; one, two; one, two, three. And then, after a moment's pause, he repeated the same tapping. Three times the signal boomed through the jungle and then the signaler paused, listening, while others stooped and put their ears against the ground.

Faintly through the air, more plainly through the ground, came an answering signal—one, two; one, two; one, two, three.

The creatures seemed satisfied and climbing into the surrounding trees, disposed themselves comfortably as though settling down to a wait. Two of them carried Tarzan easily aloft with them, as with his hands bound behind his back he could not climb unassisted.

Since they had started on the march Tarzan had not spoken, but now he turned to one of the Sagoths near him. "Remove the bonds from my wrists," he said. "I am not an enemy."

"Tar-gash," said he whom Tarzan had addressed, "the gilak wants his bonds removed."

Tar-gash, a large bull with noticeably long, white canine fangs, turned his savage eyes upon the ape-man. For a long time he glared unblinkingly at the prisoner and it seemed to Tarzan that the mind of the half-brute was struggling with a new idea. Presently he turned to the Sagoth who had repeated Tarzan's request. "Take them off," he said.

"Why?" demanded another of the bulls. The tone was challenging.

"Because I, Tar-gash, say 'take them off,'" growled the other.

"You are not M'wa-lot. He is king. If M'wa-lot says take them off, we will take them off."

"I am not M'wa-lot, To-yad; I am Tar-gash, and Tar-gash says 'take them off.'"

To-yad swung to Tarzan's side. "M'wa-lot will come soon," he said. "If M'wa-lot says take them off, we shall take them off. We do not take orders from Tar-gash."

Like a panther, quickly, silently Tar-gash sprang straight for the throat of To-yad. There was no warning, not even an instant of hesitation. In this Tarzan saw that Tar-gash differed from the great apes with whom the Lord of the Jungle had been familiar upon the outer crust, for among them two bulls ordinarily must need have gone through a long preliminary of stiff-legged strutting and grumbled invective before either one launched himself upon the other in deadly combat. But the mind of Tar-gash had functioned with man-like celerity, so much so that decision and action had appeared to be almost simultaneous.

The impact of the heavy body of Tar-gash toppled To-yad from the branch upon which he had been standing, but so naturally arboreal were the two great creatures that even as they fell they reached out and seized the same branch and still fighting, each with his free hand and his heavy fangs, they hung there a second breaking their fall, and then dropped to the ground. They fought almost silently except for low growls, Tar-gash seeking the jugular of To-yad with those sharp, white fangs that had given him his name. To-yad, his every faculty concentrated upon defense, kept the grinning jaws from his flesh and suddenly twisting quickly around, tore loose from the powerful fingers of his opponent and sought safety in flight. But like a football player, Tar-gash launched himself through the air; his long hairy arms encircled the legs of the fleeing To-yad, bringing him heavily to the ground, and an instant later the powerful aggressor was on the back of his opponent and To-yad's jugular was at the mercy of his foe, but the great jaws of Tar-gash did not close.

"Ka-goda?" he inquired.

"Ka-goda," growled To-yad, and instantly Tar-gash arose from the body of the other bull.

With the agility of a monkey the victor leaped back into the branches of the tree. "Remove the bonds from the wrists of the gilak," he said, and at the same time he glared ferociously about him to see if there was another so mutinously minded as To-yad; but none spoke and none objected as one of the Sagoths who had dragged Tarzan up into the tree untied the bonds that secured his wrists.

"If he tries to run away from us," said Tar-gash, "kill him."

When his bonds were removed Tarzan expected that the Sagoths would take his knife away from him. He had lost his spear and bow and most of his arrows at the instant that the snare had snapped him from the ground, but though they had lain in plain view in the trail beneath the snare the Sagoths had paid no attention to them; nor did they now pay any attention to his knife. He was sure they must have seen it and he could not understand their lack of concern regarding it, unless they were ignorant of its purpose or held him in such contempt that they did not consider it worth the effort to disarm him.

Presently To-yad sneaked back into the tree, but he huddled sullenly by himself, apart from the others.

Faintly, from a distance, Tarzan heard something approaching. He heard it just a moment before the Sagoths heard it.

"They come!" announced Tar-gash.

"M'wa-lot comes," said another, glancing at To-yad. Now Tarzan knew why the primitive drum had been sounded, but he wondered why they were gathering.

At last they arrived, nor was it difficult for Tarzan to recognize M'wa-lot, the king among the others. A great bull walked in front—a bull with so much gray among the hairs on his face that the latter had a slightly bluish complexion, and instantly the ape-man saw how the king had come by his name.

As soon as the Sagoths with Tarzan were convinced of the identity of the approaching party, they descended from the trees to the ground and when M'wa-lot had approached within twenty paces of them, he halted. "I am M'wa-lot," he announced. "With me are the people of my tribe."

"I am Tar-gash," replied the bull who seemed to be in charge of the other party. "With me are other bulls of the tribe of M'wa-lot."

This precautionary preliminary over, M'wa-lot advanced, followed by the bulls, the shes and the balus of his tribe.

"What is that?" demanded M'wa-lot, as his fierce eyes espied Tarzan.

"It is a gilak that we found caught in our snare," replied Tar-gash.

"That is the feast that you called us to?" demanded M'wa-lot, angrily. "You should have brought it to the tribe. It can walk."

"This is not the food of which the drum spoke," replied Tar-gash. "Nearby is the body of a thag that was killed by a tarag close by the snare in which this gilak was caught."

"Ugh!" grunted M'wa-lot. "We can eat the gilak later."

"We can have a dance," suggested one of Tarzan's captors. "We have eaten and slept many times since we have danced, M'wa-lot."

As the Sagoths, guided by Tar-gash, proceeded along the trail towards the body of the thag, the shes with balus growled savagely when one of the little ones chanced to come near to Tarzan. The bulls eyed him suspiciously and all seemed uneasy because of his presence. In these and in other ways the Sagoths were reminiscent of the apes of the tribe of Kerchak and to such an extent was this true that Tarzan, although a prisoner among them, felt strangely at home in this new environment.

A short distance ahead of the ape-man walked M'wa-lot, king of the tribe, and at M'wa-lot's elbow was To-yad. The two spoke in low tones and from the frequent glances they cast at Tar-gash, who walked ahead of them, it was evident that he was the subject of their conversation, the effect of which upon M'wa-lot seemed to be highly disturbing.

Tarzan could see that the shaggy chieftain was working himself into a frenzy of rage, the inciting cause of which was evidently the information that To-yad was imparting to him. The latter seemed to be attempting to goad him to greater fury, a fact which seemed to be now apparent to every member of the tribe with the exception of Tar-gash, who was walking in the lead, ahead of M'wa-lot and To-yad, for practically every other eye was turned upon the king, whose evident excitement had imparted a certain fierce restlessness to the other members of his party. But it was not until they had come within sight of the body of the thag that the storm broke and then, without warning, M'wa-lot swung his heavy club and leaped forward toward Tar-gash with the very evident intention of braining him from behind.

If the life of the ape-man in his constant battle for survival had taught him to act quickly, it also had taught him to think quickly. He knew that in all this savage company he had no friends, but he also knew that Tar-gash, from very stubbornness and to spite To-yad, might alone be expected to befriend him and now it appeared that Tar-gash himself might need a friend, for it was evident that no hand was to be raised in defense of him nor any voice in warning. And so Tarzan of the Apes, prompted both by considerations of self-interest and fair play, took matters into his own hands with such suddenness that he had already acted before any hand could be raised to stop him.

"Kreeg-ah, Tar-gash!" he cried, and at the same instant he sprang quickly forward, brushing To-yad aside with a single sweep of a giant arm that sent the Sagoth headlong into the underbrush bordering the trail.

At the warning cry of "Kreeg-ah," which in the language of the great apes is synonymous to beware, Tar-gash wheeled about to see the infuriated M'wa-lot with upraised club almost upon him and then he saw something else which made his savage eyes widen in surprise. The strange gilak, whom he had taken prisoner, had leaped close to M'wa-lot from behind. A smooth, bronzed arm slipped quickly about the king's neck and tightened. The gilak turned and stooped and surging forward with the king across his hip threw the great, hairy bull completely over his head and sent him sprawling at the feet of his astonished warriors. Then the gilak leaped to Tar-gash's side and, wheeling, faced the tribe with Tar-gash.

Instantly a score of clubs were raised against the two.

"Shall we remain and fight, Tar-gash?" demanded the ape-man.

"They will kill us," said Tar-gash. "If you were not a gilak, we might escape through the trees, but as you cannot escape we shall have to remain and fight."

"Lead the way," said Tarzan. "There is no Sagoth trail that Tarzan cannot follow."

"Come then," said Tar-gash, and as he spoke he hurled his club into the faces of the oncoming warriors and, turning, fled along the trail. A dozen mighty bounds he took and then leaped to the branch of an overhanging tree, and close behind him came the hairless gilak.

M'wa-lot's hairy warrior bulls pursued the two for a short distance and then gave up the chase as Tarzan was confident that they would, since among his own people it had usually been considered sufficient to run a recalcitrant bull out of the tribe and, unless he insisted upon returning, no particular effort was made to molest him.

As soon as it became evident that pursuit had been abandoned the Sagoth halted among the branches of a huge tree. "I am Tar-gash," he said, as Tarzan stopped near him.

"I am Tarzan," replied the ape-man.

"Why did you warn me?" asked Tar-gash.

"I told you that I did not come among you as an enemy," replied Tarzan, "and when I saw that To-yad had succeeded in urging M'wa-lot to kill you, I warned you because it was you that kept the bulls from killing me when I was captured."

"What were you doing in the country of the Sagoths?" asked Tar-gash.

"I was hunting," replied Tarzan.

"Where do you want to go now?" asked the Sagoth.

"I shall return to my people," replied Tarzan.

"Where are they?"

Tarzan of the Apes hesitated. He looked upward toward the sun, whose rays were filtering down through the foliage of the forest. He looked about him—everywhere was foliage. There was nothing in the foliage nor upon the boles or branches of the trees to indicate direction. Tarzan of the Apes was lost!

CHAPTER 5

Brought Down

JASON GRIDLEY, LOOKING down from the branches of the tree in which he had found sanctuary, was held by a certain horrible fascination as he watched the feast of the great cats.

The scene that he had just witnessed—this stupendous spectacle of savagery—suggested to him something of what life upon the outer crust must have been at the dawn of humanity.

The suggestion was borne in upon him that perhaps this scene which he had witnessed might illustrate an important cause of the extinction of all of these animals upon the outer crust.

The action of the great saber-tooth tigers of Pellucidar in rounding up the other beasts of the forest and driving them to this clearing for slaughter evidenced a development of intelligence far beyond that attained by the carnivores of the outer world of the present day, such concerted action by any great number for the common good being unknown.

Gridley saw the vast number of animals that had been slaughtered and most of them uselessly, since there was more flesh there than the surviving tigers could consume before it reached a stage of putrefaction that would render it unpalatable even to one of the great cats. And this fact suggested the conviction that the cunning of the tigers had reached a plane where it might reasonably be expected to react upon themselves and eventually cause their extinction, for in their savage fury and lust for flesh they had slaughtered indiscriminately males and females, young and old. If this slaughter went on unchecked for ages, the natural prey of the tigers must become extinct and then, goaded by starvation, they would fall upon one another.

The last stage of the ascendancy of the great cats upon the outer crust must have been short and terrible and so eventually it would prove here in Pellucidar.

And just as the great cats may have reached a point where their mental development had spelled their own doom, so in the preceding era the gigantic, carnivorous dinosaurs of the Jurassic may similarly have caused the extinction of their own contemporaries and then of themselves. Nor did Jason Gridley find it difficult to apply the same line of reasoning to the evolution of man upon the outer crust and to his own possible extinction in the not far remote future. In fact, he recalled quite definitely that statisticians had shown that within two hundred years or less the human race would have so greatly increased and the natural resources of the outer world would have been so depleted that the last generation must either starve to death or turn to cannibalism to prolong its hateful existence for another short period.

Perhaps, thought Gridley, in nature's laboratory each type that had at some era dominated all others represented an experiment in the eternal search for perfection. The invertebrate had given way to fishes, the fishes to the reptiles, the reptiles to the birds and mammals, and these, in turn, had been forced to bow to the greater intelligence of man.

What would be next? Gridley was sure that there would be something after man, who is unquestionably the Creator's greatest blunder, combining as he does all the vices of preceding types from invertebrates to mammals, while possessing few of their virtues.

As such thoughts were forced upon his mind by the scene below him they were accompanied by others of more immediate importance, first of which was concern for his fellows.

Nowhere about the clearing did he see any sign of a human being alive or dead. He called aloud several times but received no reply, though he realized that it was possible that above the roaring and the growling of the feeding beasts his voice might not carry to any great distance. He began to have hopes that his companions had all escaped, but he was still greatly worried over the fate of Von Horst.

The subject of second consideration was that of his own escape and return to the O-220. He had it in his mind that at nightfall the beasts might retire and unconsciously he glanced upward at the sun to note the time, when the realization came to him that there would never be any night, that forever throughout all eternity it would be noon here. And then he began to wonder how long he had been gone from the ship, but when he glanced at his watch he realized that that meant nothing. The hour hand might have made an entire circle since he had last looked at it, for in the excitement of all that had transpired since they had left the O-220 how might the mind of man, unaided, compute time?

But he knew that eventually the beasts must get their fill and leave. After them, however, there would be the hyænodons and the jackals with their fierce cousins, the wild dogs. As he watched these, sitting at a respectful distance from the tigers or slinking hungrily in the background, he realized that they might easily prove as much of a bar to his escape as the saber-tooth tigers themselves.

The hyænodons especially were most discouraging to contemplate. Their bodies were as large as that of a full grown mastiff. They walked upon short, powerful legs and their broad jaws were massive and strong. Dark, shaggy hair covered their backs and sides, turning to white upon their breasts and bellies.

Gnawing hunger assailed Jason Gridley and also an overpowering desire to sleep, convincing him that he must have been many hours away from the O-220, and yet the beasts beneath him continued to feed.

A dead thag lay at the foot of the tree in which the American kept his lonely vigil. So far it had not been fed upon and the nearest tiger was fifty yards away. Gridley was hungry, so hungry that he eyed the thag covetously. He glanced about him, measuring the distance from the tree to the nearest tiger and trying to compute the length of time that it would take him to clamber back to safety should he descend to the ground. He had seen the tigers in action and he knew how swiftly they could cover ground and that one of them could leap almost as high as the branch upon which he sat.

Altogether the chance of success seemed slight for the plan he had in mind in the event that the nearest tiger took exception to it. But great though the danger was, hunger won. Gridley drew his hunting knife and lowered himself gently to the ground, keeping an alert eye upon the nearest tiger. Quickly he sliced several long strips of flesh from the thag's hind quarter.

The tarag feeding fifty yards away looked up. Jason sliced another strip, returned his knife to its sheath and climbed quickly back to safety. The tarag lowered its head upon its kill and closed its eyes.

The American gathered dead twigs and small branches that still clung to the living tree and with them he built a small fire in a great crotch.

Here he cooked some of the meat of the thag; the edges were charred, the inside was raw, but Jason Gridley could have sworn that never before in his life had he tasted such delicious food.

How long his culinary activities employed him, he did not know, but when he glanced down again at the clearing he saw that most of the tigers had quitted their kills and were moving leisurely toward the forest, their distended bellies proclaiming how well they had surfeited themselves. And as the tigers retired, the hyænodons, the wild dogs and the jackals closed in to the feast.

The hyænodons kept the others away and Gridley saw another long wait ahead of him; nor was he mistaken. And when the hyænodons had had their fill and gone, the wild dogs came and kept the jackals away.

In the meantime Gridley had fashioned a rude platform among the branches of the tree, and here he had slept, awakening refreshed but assailed by a thirst that was almost overpowering.

The wild dogs were leaving now and Gridley determined to wait no longer. Already the odor of decaying flesh was warning him of worse to come and there was the fear too that the tigers might return to their kills.

Descending from the tree he skirted the clearing, keeping close to the forest and searching for the trail by which his party had entered the clearing. The wild dogs, slinking away, turned to growl at him, baring menacing fangs. But knowing how well their bellies were filled, he entertained little fear of them; while for the jackals he harbored that contempt which is common among all creatures.

Gridley was dismayed to note that many trails entered the clearing; nor could he recognize any distinguishing mark that might suggest the one by which he had come. Whatever footprints his party had left had been entirely obliterated by the pads of the carnivores.

He tried to reconstruct his passage across the clearing to the tree in which he had found safety and by this means he hit upon a trail to follow, although he had no assurance that it was the right trail. The baffling noonday sun shining down upon him seemed to taunt him with his helplessness.

As he proceeded alone down the lonely trail, realizing that at any instant he might come face to face with some terrible beast of a long dead past, Jason Gridley wondered how the ape-like progenitors of man had survived to transmit any of their characteristics however unpleasant to a posterity. That he could live to reach the O-220 he much doubted. The idea that he might live to take a mate and raise a family was preposterous.

While the general aspect of the forest through which he was passing seemed familiar, he realized that this might be true no matter what trail he was upon and now he reproached himself for not having had the trees along the trail blazed. What a stupid ass he had been, he thought; but his regrets were not so much for himself as for the others, whose safety had been in his hands.

Never in his life had Jason Gridley felt more futile or helpless. To trudge ceaselessly along that endless trail, having not the slightest idea whether it led toward the O-220 or in the opposite direction was depressing, even maddening; yet there was naught else to do. And always that damned noonday sun staring unblinkingly down upon him—the cruel sun that could see his ship, but would not lead him to it.

His thirst was annoying, but not yet overpowering, when he came to a small stream that was crossed by the trail. Here he drank and rested for a while, built a small fire, cooked some more of his thag meat, drank again and took up his weary march—but much refreshed.

Aboard the O-220, as the hours passed and hope waned, the spirit of the remaining officers and members of the crew became increasingly depressed as apprehension for the safety of their absent comrades increased gradually until it became eventually an almost absolute conviction of disaster.

"They have been gone nearly seventy-two hours now," said Zuppner, who, with Dorf and Hines, spent most of his time in the upper observation cabin or pacing the narrow walkingway along the ship's back. "I never felt helpless before in my life," he continued ruefully, "but I am free to admit that I don't know what in the devil to do."

"It just goes to show," said Hines, "how much we depend upon habit and custom and precedence in determining all our action even in the face of what we are pleased to call emergency. Here there is no custom, habit or precedence to guide us."

"We have only our own resources to fall back upon," said Dorf, "and it is humiliating to realize that we have no resources."

"Not under the conditions that surround us," said Zuppner. "On the outer crust there would be no question but that we should cruise around in search of the missing members of our party. We could make rapid excursions, returning to our base often; but here in Pellucidar if we should lose sight of our base there is not one of us who believes he could return the ship to this same anchorage. And that is a chance we cannot take for the only hope those men have is that the ship shall be here when they return."

One hundred and fifty feet below them Robert Jones leaned far out of the galley doorway in an effort to see the noonday sun shining down upon the ship. His simple, good-natured face wore a puzzled expression not untinged with awe, and as he drew back into the galley he extracted a rabbit's foot from his trousers pocket. Gently he touched each eye with it and then rubbed it vigorously upon the top of his head at the same time muttering incoherently below his breath.

From the vantage point of the walkingway far above, Lieutenant Hines scanned the landscape in all directions through powerful glasses as he had done for so long that it seemed he knew every shrub and tree and blade of grass within sight. The wild life of savage Pellucidar that crossed and re-crossed the clearing had long since become an old story to these three men. Again and again as one animal or another had emerged from the distant forest the glasses had been leveled upon it until it could be identified as other than man; but now Hines voiced a sudden, nervous exclamation.

"What is it?" demanded Zuppner. "What do you see?"

"It's a man!" exclaimed Hines. "I'm sure of it."

"Where?" asked Dorf, as he and Zuppner raised their glasses to their eyes.

"About two points to port."

"I see it," said Dorf. "It's either Gridley or Von Horst, and whoever it is he is alone."

"Take ten of the crew at once, Lieutenant," said Zuppner, turning to Dorf. "See that they are well armed and go out and meet him. Lose no time," he shouted after the Lieutenant, who had already started down the climbing shaft.

The two officers upon the top of the O-220 watched Dorf and his party as it set out to meet the man they could see trudging steadily toward the ship. They watched them as they approached one another, though, owing to the contour of the land, which was rolling, neither Dorf nor the man he had gone to meet caught sight of one another until they were less than a hundred yards apart. It was then that the Lieutenant recognized the other as Jason Gridley.

As they hastened forward and clasped hands it was typical of the man that Gridley's first words were an inquiry relative to the missing members of the party.

Dorf shook his head. "You are the only one that has returned," he said.

The eager light died out of Gridley's eyes and he suddenly looked very tired and much older as he greeted the engineers and mechanics who made up the party that had come to escort him back to the ship.

"I have been within sight of the ship for a long time," he said. "How long, I do not know. I broke my watch back in the forest a way trying to beat a tiger up a tree. Then another one treed me just on the edge of the clearing in plain view of the ship. It seems as though I have been there a week. How long have I been gone, Dorf?"

"About seventy-two hours."

Gridley's face brightened. "Then there is no reason to give up hope yet for the others," he said. "I honestly thought I had been gone a week. I have slept several times, I never could tell how long; and then I have gone for what seemed long periods without sleep because I became very tired and excessively hungry and thirsty."

During the return march to the ship Jason insisted upon hearing a detailed account of everything that had happened since his departure, but it was not until they had joined Zuppner and Hines that he narrated the adventures that had befallen him and his companions during their ill-fated expedition.

"The first thing I want," he told them after he had been greeted by Zuppner and Hines, "is a bath, and then if you will have Bob cook a couple of cows I'll give you the details of the expedition while I am eating them. A couple of handfuls of Bos Primigenus and some wild fruit have only whetted my appetite."

A half hour later, refreshed by a bath, a shave and fresh clothing, he joined them in the mess room.

As the three men seated themselves, Robert Jones entered from the galley, his black face wreathed in smiles.

"Ah'm suttinly glad to see you all, Mas' Jason," said Robert. "Ah knew sumpin was a-goin' to happen though—Ah knew we was a-goin' to have good luck."

"Well, I'm glad to be back, Bob," said Gridley, "and I don't know of anyone that I am any happier to see than you, for I sure have missed your cooking. But what made you think that we're going to have good luck?"

"Ah jes had a brief conversation with mah rabbit's foot. Dat ole boy he never fails me. We suah be out o' luck if Ah lose him."

"Oh, I've seen lots of rabbits around, Bob," said Zuppner. "We can get you a bushel of them in no time."

"Yes suh, Cap'n, but you cain't get 'em in de dahk of de moon where dey ain't no dahk an' dey ain't no moon, an' othe'wise dey lacks efficiency."

"It's a good thing, then, that we brought you along," said Jason, "and a mighty good thing for Pellucidar, for she never has had a really effective rabbit's foot before in all her existence. But I can see where you're going to need that rabbit's foot pretty badly yourself in about a minute, Bob."

"How's dat, suh?" demanded Robert.

"The spirits tell me that something is going to happen to you if you don't get food onto this table in a hurry," laughed Gridley.

"Yes suh, comin' right up," exclaimed the black as he hastened into the galley.

As Gridley ate, he went over the adventures of the last seventy-two hours in careful detail and the three men sought to arrive at some definite conjecture as to the distance he had covered from the ship and the direction.

"Do you think that you could lead another party to the clearing where you became separated from Von Horst and the Waziri?" asked Zuppner.

"Yes, of course I could," replied Gridley, "because from the point that we entered the forest we blazed the trees up to the time we reached the trail, which we followed to the left. In fact I would not be needed at all and if we decide to send out such a party, I shall not accompany it."

The other officers looked at him in surprise and for a moment there was an embarrassed silence.

"I have what I consider a better plan," continued Gridley. "There are twenty-seven of us left. In the event of absolute necessity, twelve men can operate the ship. That will leave fifteen to form a new searching party. Leaving me out, you would have fourteen, and after you have heard my plan, if you decide upon sending out such a party, I suggest that Lieutenant Dorf command it, leaving you, Captain Zuppner, and Hines to navigate the ship in the event that none of us returns, or that you finally decide to set out in search of us."

"But I thought that you were not going," said Zuppner.

"I am not going with the searching party. I am going alone in the scout plane, and my advice would be that you send out no searching party for at least twenty-four hours after I depart, for in that time I shall either have located those who are missing or have failed entirely."

Zuppner shook his head, dubiously. "Hines, Dorf and I have discussed the feasibility of using the scout plane," he said. "Hines was very anxious to make the attempt, although he realizes better than any of us that once a pilot is out of sight of the O-220 he may never be able to locate it again, for you must remember that we know nothing concerning any of the landmarks of the country in the direction that our search must be prosecuted."

"I have taken all that into consideration," replied Gridley, "and I realize that it is at best but a forlorn hope."

"Let me undertake it," said Hines. "I have had more flying experience than any of you with the possible exception of Captain Zuppner, and it is out of the question that we should risk losing him."

"Any one of you three is probably better fitted to undertake such a flight than I," replied Gridley; "but that does not relieve me of the responsibility. I am more responsible than any other member of this party for our being where we are and, therefore, my responsibility for the safety of the missing members of the expedition is greater than that of any of the rest of you. Under the circumstances, then, I could not permit anyone else to undertake this flight. I think that you will all understand and appreciate how I feel and that you will do me the favor to interpose no more objection."

It was several minutes thereafter before anyone spoke, the four seeming to be immersed in the business of sipping their coffee and smoking their cigarettes. It was Zuppner who broke the silence.

"Before you undertake this thing," he said, "you should have a long sleep, and in the meantime we will get the plane out and have it gone over thoroughly. You must have every chance for success that we can give you."

"Thank you!" said Gridley. "I suppose you are right about the sleep. I hate to waste the time, but if you will call me the moment that the ship is ready I shall go to my cabin at once and get such sleep as I can in the meantime."

While Gridley slept, the scout plane, carried aft in the keel cabin, was lowered to the ground, where it underwent a careful inspection and test by the engineers and officers of the O-220.

Even before the plane was ready Gridley appeared at the cabin door of the O-220 and descended to the ground.

"You did not sleep long," said Zuppner.

"I do not know how long," said Gridley, "but I feel rested and anyway I could not have slept longer, knowing that those fellows are out there somewhere waiting and hoping for succor."

"What route do you expect to follow," asked Zuppner, "and how are you planning to insure a reasonable likelihood of your being able to return?"

"I shall fly directly over the forest as far as I think it at all likely that they could have marched in the time that they have been absent, assuming that they became absolutely confused and have traveled steadily away from the ship. As soon as I have gained sufficient altitude to make any observation I shall try and spot some natural landmark, like a mountain or a body of water, near the ship and from time to time, as I proceed, I shall make a note of similar landmarks. I believe that in this way I can easily find my way back, since at the furthest I cannot proceed over two hundred and fifty miles from the O-220 and return to it with the fuel that I can carry.

"After I have reached the furthest possible limits that I think the party could have strayed, I shall commence circling, depending upon the noise of the motor to attract their attention and, of course, assuming that they will find some means of signaling their presence to me, which they can do even in wooded country by building smudges."

"You expect to land?" inquired Zuppner, nodding at the heavy rifle which Gridley carried.

"If I find them in open country, I shall land; but even if I do not find them it may be necessary for me to come down and my recent experiences have taught me not to venture far in Pellucidar without a rifle."

After a careful inspection, Gridley shook hands with the three remaining officers and bid farewell to the ship's company, all of whom were anxious observers of his preparation for departure.

"Good-bye, old man," said Zuppner, "and may God and luck go with you."

Gridley pressed the hand of the man he had come to look upon as a staunch and loyal friend, and then took his seat in the open cockpit of the scout plane. Two mechanics spun the propeller, the motor roared and a moment later the block was kicked away and the plane rolled out across the grassy meadowland towards the forest at the far side. The watchers saw it rise swiftly and make a great circle and they knew that Gridley was looking for a landmark. Twice it circled above the open plain and then darted away across the forest.

It had not been until he had made that first circle that Jason Gridley had realized the handicap that this horizonless landscape of Pellucidar had placed upon his chances of return. He had thought of a mountain standing boldly out against the sky, for such a landmark would have been almost constantly within the range of his vision during the entire flight.

There were mountains in the distance, but they stood out against no background of blue sky nor upon any horizon. They simply merged with the landscape beyond them, curving upward in the distance. Twice he circled, his keen eyes searching for any outstanding point in the topography of the country beneath him, but there was nothing that was more apparent than the grassy plain upon which the O-220 rested.

He felt that he could not waste time and fuel by searching longer for a landmark that did not exist, and while he realized that the plain would be visible for but a comparatively short distance he was forced to accept it as his sole guide in lieu of a better one.

Roaring above the leafy roof of the primeval forest, all that transpired upon the ground below was hidden from him and it was tantalizing to realize that he might have passed directly over the heads of the comrades he sought, yet there was no other way. Returning, he would either circle or hold an exaggerated zig-zag course, watching carefully for sign of a signal.

For almost two hours Jason Gridley held a straight course, passing over forest, plain and rolling, hilly country, but nowhere did he see any sign of those he sought. Already he had reached the limit of the distance he had planned upon coming when there loomed ahead of him in the distance a range of lofty mountains. These alone would have determined him to turn back, since his judgment told him that the lost members of the party, should they have chanced to come this far, would by now have realized that they were traveling in the wrong direction.

As he banked to turn he caught a glimpse out of the corner of an eye of something in the air above him and looking quickly back, Jason Gridley caught his breath in astonishment.

Hovering now, almost above him, was a gigantic creature, the enormous spread of whose wings almost equalled that of the plane he was piloting. The man had a single glimpse of tremendous jaws, armed with mighty teeth, in the very instant that he realized that this mighty anachronism was bent upon attacking him.

Gridley was flying at an altitude of about three thousand feet when the huge pteranodon launched itself straight at the ship. Jason sought to elude it by diving. There was a terrific crash, a roar, a splintering of wood and a grinding of metal as the pteranodon swooped down upon its prey and full into the propeller.

What happened then, happened so quickly that Jason Gridley could not have reconstructed the scene five seconds later.

The plane turned completely over and at the same instant Gridley jumped. He jerked the rip cord of his parachute. Something struck him on the head and he lost consciousness.

CHAPTER 6

A Phororhacos of the Miocene

"WHERE ARE YOUR people?" Tar-gash asked again.

Tarzan shook his head. "I do not know," he said.

"Where is your country?" asked Tar-gash.

"It is a long way off," replied the ape-man. "It is not in

Pellucidar;" but that the Sagoth could not understand any more than he could understand that a creature might be lost at all, for inherent in him was that same homing instinct that marked all the creatures of Pellucidar and which constitutes a wise provision of nature in a world without guiding celestial bodies.

Had it been possible to transport Tar-gash instantly to any point within that mighty inner world, elsewhere than upon the surface of an ocean, he could have unerringly found his way to the very spot where he was born, and because that power was instinctive he could not understand why Tarzan did not possess it.

"I know where there is a tribe of men," he said, presently. "Perhaps they are your people. I shall lead you to them."

As Tarzan had no idea as to the direction in which the ship lay and as it was remotely possible that Tar-gash was referring to the members of the O-220 expedition, he felt that he was as well off following where Tar-gash led as elsewhere, and so he signified his readiness to accompany the Sagoth.

"How long since you saw this tribe of men," he asked after a while, "and how long have they lived where you saw them?"

Upon the Sagoth's reply to these questions, the ape-man felt that he might determine the possibility of the men to whom Tar-gash referred being the members of his own party, for if they were newcomers in the district then the chances were excellent that they were the people he sought; but his questions elicited no satisfactory reply for the excellent reason that time meant nothing to Tar-gash. And so the two set out upon a leisurely seach for the tribe of men that Tar-gash knew of. It was leisurely because for Tar-gash time did not exist; nor had it ever been a very important factor in the existence of the ape-man, except in occasional moments of emergency.

They were a strangely assorted pair—one a creature just standing upon the threshold of humanity, the other an English Lord in his own right, who was, at the same time, in many respects as primitive as the savage, shaggy bull into whose companionship chance had thrown him.

At first Tar-gash had been inclined to look with contempt upon this creature of another race, which he considered far inferior to his own in strength, agility, courage and woodcraft, but he soon came to hold the ape-man in vast respect. And because he could respect his prowess he became attached to him in bonds of loyalty that were as closely akin to friendship as the savage nature of his primitive mind permitted.

They hunted together and fought together. They swung through the trees when the great cats hunted upon the ground, or they followed game trails ages old beneath the hoary trees of Pellucidar or out across her rolling, grassy, flower-spangled meadowland.

They lived well upon the fat of the land for both were mighty hunters.

Tarzan fashioned a new bow and arrows and a stout spear, and these, at first, the Sagoth refused even to notice, but presently when he saw how easily and quickly they brought game to their larder he evinced a keen interest and Tarzan taught him how to use the weapons and later how to fashion them.

The country through which they traveled was well watered and was alive with game. It was partly wooded with great stretches of open land, where tremendous herds of herbivores grazed beneath the eternal noonday sun, and because of these great herds the beasts of prey were numerous—and such beasts!

Tarzan had thought that there was no world like his own world and no jungle like his own jungle, but the more deeply he dipped into the wonders of Pellucidar the more enamored he became of this savage, primitive world, teeming with the wild life he loved best. That there were few men was Pellucidar's chiefest recommendation. Had there been none the ape-man might have considered this the land of ultimate perfection, for who is there more conversant with the cruelty and inconsideration of man than the savage beasts of the jungle?

The friendship that had developed between Tarzan and the Sagoth—and that was primarily based upon the respect which each felt for the prowess of the other—increased as each seemed to realize other admirable, personal qualities and characteristics in his companion, not the least of which being a common taciturnity. They spoke only when conversation seemed necessary, and that, in reality, was seldom.

If man spoke only when he had something worth while to say and said that as quickly as possible, ninety-eight per cent. of the human race might as well be dumb, thereby establishing a heavenly harmony from pate to tonsil.

And so the companionship of Tar-gash, coupled with the romance of strange sights and sounds and odors in this new world, acted upon the ape-man as might a strong drug, filling him with exhilaration and dulling his sense of responsibility, so that the necessity of finding his people dwindled to a matter of minor importance. Had he known that some of them were in trouble his attitude would have changed immediately, but this he did not know. On the contrary he was only aware that they had every facility for insuring their safety and their ultimate return to the outer world and that his absence would not handicap them in any particular. However, when he did give the matter thought he knew that he must return to them, that he must find them, and that sooner or later he must go back with them to the world from which they had come.

But all such considerations were quite remote from his thoughts as he and Tar-gash were crossing a rolling, tree-dotted plain in their search for the tribe of men to which the Sagoth was guiding him. By comparison with other plains they had crossed, this one seemed strangely deserted, but the reason for this was evident in the close-cropped grass which suggested that great herds had grazed it off before moving on to new pastures. The absence of life and movement was slightly depressing and Tarzan found himself regretting the absence of even the dangers of the teeming land through which they had just come.

They were well out toward the center of the plain and could see the solid green of a great forest curving upward into the hazy distance when the attention of both was attracted by a strange, droning noise that brought them to a sudden halt. Simultaneously both turned and looked backward and up into the sky from which the sound seemed to come.

Far above and just emerging from the haze of the distance was a tiny speck. "Quick!" exclaimed Tar-gash. "It is a thipdar," and motioning Tarzan to follow him he ran swiftly to concealment beneath a large tree.

"What is a thipdar?" asked Tarzan, as the two halted beneath the friendly shade.

"A thipdar," said the Sagoth, "is a thipdar;" nor could he describe it more fully other than to add that the thipdars were sometimes used by the Mahars either to protect them or to hunt their food.

"Is the thipdar a living thing?" demanded Tarzan.

"Yes," replied Tar-gash. "It lives and is very strong and very fierce."

"Then that is not a thipdar," said Tarzan.

"What is it then?" demanded the Sagoth.

"It is an aeroplane," replied Tarzan.

"What is that?" inquired the Sagoth.

"It would be hard to explain it to you," replied the ape-man. "It is something that the men of my world build and in which they fly through the air," and as he spoke he stepped out into the opening, where he might signal the pilot of the plane, which he was positive was the one carried by the O-220 and which, he assumed, was prosecuting a search for him.

"Come back," exclaimed Tar-gash. "You cannot fight a thipdar. It will swoop down and carry you off if you are out in the open."

"It will not harm me," said Tarzan. "One of my friends is in it."

"And you will be in it, too, if you do not come back under the tree," replied Tar-gash.

As the plane approached, Tarzan ran around in a small circle to attract the pilot's attention, stopping occasionally to wave his arms, but the plane sped on above him and it was evident that its pilot had not seen him.

Until it faded from sight in the distance, Tarzan of the Apes stood upon the lonely plain, watching the ship that was bearing his comrade away from him.

The sight of the ship awakened Tarzan to a sense of his responsibility. He realized now that someone was risking his life to save him and with this thought came a determination to exert every possible effort to locate the O-220.

The passage of the plane opened many possibilities for conjecture. If it was circling, which was possible, the direction of its flight as it passed over him would have no bearing upon the direction of the O-220, and if it were not circling, then how was he to know whether it was traveling away from the ship in the beginning of its quest, or was returning to it having concluded its flight.

"That was not a thipdar," said Tar-gash, coming from beneath the tree and standing at Tarzan's side. "It is a creature that I have never seen before. It is larger and must be even more terrible than a thipdar. It must have been very angry, for it growled terribly all the time."

"It is not alive," said Tarzan. "It is something that the men of my country build that they may fly through the air. Riding in it is one of my friends. He is looking for me."

The Sagoth shook his head. "I am glad he did not come down," he said. "He was either very angry or very hungry, otherwise he would not have growled so loudly."

It was apparent to Tarzan that Tar-gash was entirely incapable of comprehending his explanation of the aeroplane and that he would always believe it was a huge, flying reptile; but that was of no importance—the thing that troubled Tarzan being the question of the direction in which he should now prosecute his search for the O-220, and eventually he determined to follow in the direction taken by the airship, for as this coincided with the direction in which Tar-gash assured him he would find the tribe of human beings for which they were searching, it seemed after all the wisest course to pursue.

The drone of the motor had died away in the distance when Tarzan and Tar-gash took up their interrupted journey across the plain and into broken country of low, rocky hills.

The trail, which was well marked and which Tar-gash said led through the hills, followed the windings of a shallow canyon, which was rimmed on one side by low cliffs, in the face of which there were occasional caves and crevices. The bottom of the canyon was strewn with fragments of rock of various sizes. The vegetation was sparse and there was every indication of an aridity such as Tarzan had not previously encountered since he left the O-220, and as it seemed likely that both game and water would be scarce here, the two pushed on at a brisk, swinging walk.

It was very quiet and Tarzan's ears were constantly upon the alert to catch the first sound of the hum of the motor of the returning aeroplane, when suddenly the silence was shattered by the sound of hoarse screeching which seemed to be coming from a point further up the canyon.

Tar-gash halted. "Dyal," he said.

Tarzan looked at the Sagoth questioningly.

"It is a Dyal," repeated Tar-gash, "and it is angry."

"What is a Dyal?" asked Tarzan.

"It is a terrible bird," replied the Sagoth; "but its meat is good, and Tar-gash is hungry."

That was enough. No matter how terrible the Dyal might be, it was meat and Tar-gash was hungry, and so the two beasts of prey crept warily forward, stalking their quarry. A vagrant breeze, wafting gently down the canyon, brought to the nostrils of the ape-man a strange, new scent. It was a bird scent, slightly suggestive of the scent of an ostrich, and from its volume Tarzan guessed that it might come from a very large bird, a suggestion that was borne out by the loud screeching of the creature, intermingled with which was a scratching and a scraping sound.

Tar-gash, who was in the lead and who was taking advantage of all the natural shelter afforded by the fragments of rock with which the canyon bed was strewn, came to a halt upon the lower side of a great boulder, behind which he quickly withdrew, and as Tarzan joined him he signalled the ape-man to look around the corner of the boulder.

Following the suggestion of his companion, Tarzan saw the author of the commotion that had attracted their attention. Being a savage jungle beast, he exhibited no outward sign of the astonishment he felt as he gazed upon the mighty creature that was clawing frantically at a crevice in the cliffside.

To Tarzan it was a nameless creature of another world. To Tar-gash it was simply a Dyal. Neither knew that he was looking upon a Phororhacos of the Miocene. They saw a huge creature whose crested head, larger than that of a horse, towered eight feet above the ground. Its powerful, curved beak gaped wide as it screeched in anger. It beat its short, useless wing in a frenzy of rage as it struck with its mighty three-toed talons at something just within the fissure before it. And then it was that Tarzan saw that the thing at which it struck was a spear, held by human hands—a pitifully inadequate weapon with which to attempt to ward off the attack of the mighty Dyal.

As Tarzan surveyed the creature he wondered how Tar-gash, armed only with his puny club, might hope to pit himself in successful combat against it. He saw the Sagoth creep stealthily out from behind their rocky shelter and move slowly to another closer to the Dyal and behind it, and so absorbed was the bird in its attack upon the man within the fissure that it did not notice the approach of the enemy in its rear.

The moment that Tar-gash was safely concealed behind the new shelter, Tarzan followed him and now they were within fifty feet of the great bird.

The Sagoth, grasping his club firmly by the small end, arose and ran swiftly from his concealment, straight toward the giant Dyal, and Tarzan followed, fitting an arrow to his bow.

Tar-gash had covered but half the distance when the sound of his approach attracted the attention of the bird. Wheeling about, it discovered the two rash creatures who dared to interfere with its attack upon its quarry, and with a loud screech and wide distended beak it charged them.

The instant that the Dyal had turned and discovered them, Tar-gash had commenced whirling his club about his head and as the bird charged he launched it at one of those mighty legs, and on the instant Tarzan understood the purpose of the Sagoth's method of attack. The heavy club, launched by the mighty muscles of the beast man, would snap the leg bone that it struck, and then the enormous fowl would be at the mercy of the Sagoth. But if it did not strike the leg, what then? Almost certain death for Tar-gash.

Tarzan had long since had reason to appreciate his companion's savage disregard of life in the pursuit of flesh, but this seemed the highest pinnacle to which rashness might ascend and still remain within the realm of sanity.

And, indeed, there happened that which Tarzan had feared— the club missed its mark. Tarzan's bow sang and an arrow sank deep into the breast of the Dyal. Tar-gash leaped swiftly to one side, eluding the charge, and another arrow pierced the bird's feathers and hide. And then the ape-man sprang quickly to his right as the avalanche of destruction bore down upon him, its speed undiminished by the force of the two arrows buried so deeply within it.

Before the Dyal could turn to pursue either of them, Tar-gash hurled a rock, many of which were scattered upon the ground about them. It struck the Dyal upon the side of the head, momentarily dazing him, and Tarzan drove home two more arrows. As he did so, the Dyal wheeled drunkenly toward him and as he faced about a great spear drove past Tarzan's shoulder and plunged deep into the breast of the maddened creature, and to the impact of this last missile it went down, falling almost at the feet of the ape-man.

Ignorant though he was of the strength and the methods of attack and defense of this strange bird, Tarzan nevertheless hes-itated not an instant and as the Dyal fell he was upon it with drawn hunting knife.

So quickly was he in and out that he had severed its windpipe and was away again before he could become entangled in its death struggle, and then it was that for the first time he saw the man who had cast the spear.

Standing erect, a puzzled expression upon his face, was a tall, stalwart warrior, his slightly bronzed skin gleaming in the sunlight, his shaggy head of hair bound back by a deerskin band.

For weapons, in addition to his spear, he carried a stone knife, thrust into the girdle that supported his G-string. His eyes were well set and intelligent. His features were regular and well cut. Altogether he was as splendid a specimen of manhood as Tarzan had ever beheld.

Tar-gash, who had recovered his club, was advancing toward the stranger. "I am Tar-gash," he said. "I kill."

The stranger drew his stone knife and waited, looking first at Tar-gash and then at Tarzan.

The ape-man stepped in front of Tar-gash. "Wait," he commanded. "Why do you kill?"

"He is a gilak," replied the Sagoth.

"He saved you from the Dyal," Tarzan reminded Tar-gash. "My arrows would not stop the bird. Had it not been for his spear, one or both of us must have died."

The Sagoth appeared puzzled. He scratched his head in perplexity. "But if I do not kill him, he will kill me," he said finally.

Tarzan turned toward the stranger. "I am Tarzan," he said. "This is Tar-gash," and he pointed at the Sagoth and waited.

"I am Thoar," said the stranger.

"Let us be friends," said Tarzan. "We have no quarrel with you."

Again the stranger looked puzzled.

"Do you understand the language of the Sagoths?" asked Tarzan, thinking that possibly the man might not have understood him.

Thoar nodded. "A little," he said; "but why should we be friends?"

"Why should we be enemies?" countered the ape-man.

Thoar shook his head. "I do not know," he said. "It is always thus."

"Together we have slain the Dyal," said Tarzan. "Had we not come it would have killed you. Had you not cast your spear it would have killed us. Therefore, we should be friends, not enemies. Where are you going?"

"Back to my own country," replied Thoar, nodding in the direction that Tarzan and Tar-gash had been travelling.

"We, too, are going in that direction," said Tarzan. "Let us go together. Six hands are better than four."

Thoar glanced at the Sagoth.

"Shall we all go together as friends, Tar-gash?" demanded Tarzan.

"It is not done," said the Sagoth, precisely as though he had behind him thousands of years of civilization and culture.

Tarzan smiled one of his rare smiles. "We shall do it, then," he said. "Come!"

As though taking it for granted that the others would obey his command, the ape-man turned to the body of the Dyal and, drawing his hunting knife, fell to work cutting off portions of the meat. For a moment Thoar and Tar-gash hesitated, eyeing each other suspiciously, and then the bronzed warrior walked over to assist Tarzan and presently Tar-gash joined them.

Thoar exhibited keen interest in Tarzan's steel knife, which slid so easily through the flesh while he hacked and hewed laboriously with his stone implement; while Tar-gash seemed not particularly to notice either of the implements as he sunk his strong fangs into the breast of the Dyal and tore away a large hunk of the meat, which he devoured raw. Tarzan was about to do the same, having been raised exclusively upon a diet of raw meat, when he saw Thoar preparing to make fire, which he accomplished by the primitive expedient of friction. The three ate in silence, the Sagoth carrying his meat to a little distance from the others, perhaps because in him the instinct of the wild beast was stronger.

When they had finished they followed the trail upward toward the pass through which it led across the hills, and as they went Tarzan sought to question Thoar concerning his country and its people, but so limited is the primitive vocabulary of the Sagoths and so meager Thoar's knowledge of this language that they found communication difficult and Tarzan determined to master Thoar's tongue.

Considerable experience in learning new dialects and languages rendered the task far from difficult and as the ape-man never for a moment relinquished a purpose he intended to achieve, nor ever abandoned a task that he had set himself until it had been successfully concluded, he made rapid progress which was greatly facilitated by the interest which Thoar took in instructing him.

As they reached the summit of the low hills, they saw, hazily in the far distance, what appeared to be a range of lofty mountains.

"There," said Thoar, pointing, "lies Zoram."

"What is Zoram?" asked Tarzan.

"It is my country," replied the warrior. "It lies in the Mountains of the Thipdars."

This was the second time that Tarzan had heard a reference to thipdars. Tar-gash had said the aeroplane was a thipdar and now Thoar spoke of the Mountains of the Thipdars. "What is a thipdar?" he asked.

Thoar looked at him in astonishment. "From what country do you come," he demanded, "that you do not know what a thipdar is and do not speak the language of the gilaks?"

"I am not of Pellucidar," said Tarzan.

"I could believe that," said Thoar, "if there were any other place from which you could be, but there is not, except Molop Az, the flaming sea upon which Pellucidar floats. But the only inhabitants of the Molop Az are the little demons, who carry the dead who are buried in the ground, piece by piece, down to Molop Az, and while I have never seen one of these little demons I am sure that they are not like you."

"No," said Tarzan, "I am not from Molop Az, yet sometimes I have thought that the world from which I come is inhabited by demons, both large and small."

As they hunted and ate and slept and marched together, these three creatures found their confidence in one another increasing so that even Tar-gash looked no longer with suspicion upon Thoar, and though they represented three distinct periods in the ascent of man, each separated from the other by countless thousands of years, yet they had so much in common that the advance which man had made from Tar-gash to Tarzan seemed scarcely a fair recompense for the time and effort which Nature must have expended.

Tarzan could not even conjecture the length of time he had been absent from the O-220, but he was confident that he must be upon the wrong trail, yet it seemed futile to turn back since he could not possibly have any idea as to what direction he should take. His one hope was that either he might be sighted by the pilot of the plane, which he was certain was hunting for him, or that the O-220, in cruising about, would eventually pass within signalling distance of him. In the meantime he might as well be with Tar-gash and Thoar as elsewhere.

The three had eaten and slept again and were resuming their journey when Tarzan's keen eyes espied from the summit of a low hill something lying upon an open plain at a considerable distance ahead of them. He did not know what it was, but he was sure that whatever it was, it was not a part of the natural landscape, there being about it that indefinable suggestion of discord, or, more properly, lack of harmony with its surroundings that every man whose perception has not been dulled by city dwelling will understand. And as it was almost instinctive with Tarzan to investigate anything that he did not understand, he turned his footsteps in the direction of the thing that he had seen.

The object that had aroused his curiosity was hidden from him almost immediately after he started the descent of the hill upon which he had stood when he discovered it; nor did it come again within the range of his vision until he was close upon it, when to his astonishment and dismay he saw that it was the wreck of an aeroplane.

CHAPTER 7

The Red Flower of Zoram

JANA, THE RED Flower of Zoram, paused and looked back across the rocky crags behind and below her. She was very hungry and it had been long since she had slept, for behind her, dogging her trail, were the four terrible men from Pheli, which lies at the foot of the Mountains of the Thipdars, beyond the land of Zoram.

For just an instant she stood erect and then she threw herself prone upon the rough rock, behind a jutting fragment that partially concealed her, and here she looked back along the way she had come, across a pathless waste of tumbled granite. Mountain-bred, she had lived her life among the lofty peaks of the Mountains of the Thipdars, considering contemptuously the people of the lowland to which those who pursued her belonged. Perchance, if they followed her here she might be forced to concede them some measure of courage and possibly to look upon them with a slightly lessened contempt, yet even so she would never abate her effort to escape them.

Bred in the bone of The Red Flower was loathing of the men of Pheli, who ventured occasionally into the fastnesses of the Mountains of the Thipdars to steal women, for the pride and the fame of the mountain people lay in the beauty of their girls, and so far had this fame spread that men came from far countries, out of the vast river basin below their lofty range, and risked a hundred deaths in efforts to steal such a mate as Jana, The Red Flower of Zoram.

The girl's sister, Lana, had been thus stolen, and within her memory two other girls of Zoram, by the men from the lowland, and so the fear, as well as the danger, was ever present. Such a fate seemed to The Red Flower worse than death, since not only would it take her forever from her beloved mountains, but make her a low-country woman and her children low-country children than which, in the eyes of the mountain people, there could be no deeper disgrace, for the mountain men mated only with mountain women, the men of Zoram, and Clovi, and Daroz taking mates from their own tribes or stealing them from their neighbors.

Jana was beloved by many of the young warriors of Zoram, and though, as yet, there had been none who had fired her own heart to love she knew that some day she would mate with one of them, unless in the meantime she was stolen by a warrior from another tribe.

Were she to fall into the hands of one from either Clovi or Daroz she would not be disgraced and she might even be happy, but she was determined to die rather than to be taken by the men from Pheli.

Long ago, it seemed to her now, who had no means for measuring time, she had been searching for thipdar eggs among the lofty crags above the caverns that were the home of her people when a great hairy man leaped from behind a rock and endeavored to seize her. Active as a chamois, she eluded him with ease, but he stood between her and the village and when she sought to circle back she discovered that he had three companions who effectually barred her way, and then had commenced the flight and the pursuit that had taken her far from Zoram among lofty peaks where she had never been before.

Not far below her, four squat, hairy men had stopped to rest. "Let us turn back," growled one. "You can never catch her, Skruk, in country like this, which is fit only for thipdars and no place for men."

Skruk shook his bullet head. "I have seen her," he said, "and I shall have her if I have to chase her to the shores of Molop Az."

"Our hands are torn by the sharp rock," said another. "Our

sandals are almost gone and our feet bleed. We cannot go on. We shall die."

"You may die," said Skruk, "but until then you shall go on. I am Skruk, the chief, and I have spoken."

The others growled resentfully, but when Skruk took up the pursuit again they followed him. Being from a low country they found strenuous exertion in these high altitudes exhausting, it is true, but the actual basis for their disinclination to continue the pursuit was the terror which the dizzy heights inspired in them and the perilous route along which The Red Flower of Zoram was leading them.

From above Jana saw them ascending, and knowing that they were again upon the right trail she stood erect in plain view of them. Her single, soft garment made from the pelt of tarag cubs, whipped about her naked legs, half revealing, half concealing the rounded charms of her girlish figure. The noonday sun shown down upon her light, bronzed skin, glistening from the naked contours of a perfect shoulder and imparting golden glints to her hair that was sometimes a lustrous brown and again a copper bronze. It was piled loosely upon her head and held in place by slender, hollow bones of the dimorphodon, a little long-tailed cousin of the thipdar. The upper ends of these bone pins were ornamented with carving and some of them were colored. A fillet of soft skin ornamented in colors encircled her brow and she wore bracelets and anklets made of the vertebrae of small animals, strung upon leather thongs. These, too, were carved and colored. Upon her feet were stout, little sandals, soled with the hide of the mastodon and from the center of her headband rose a single feather. At her hip was a stone knife and in her right hand a light spear.

She stooped and picking up a small fragment of rock hurled it down at Skruk and his companions. "Go back to your swamps, jaloks of the low country," she cried. "The Red Flower of Zoram is not for you," and then she turned and sped away across the pathless granite.

To her left lay Zoram, but there was a mighty chasm between her and the city. Along its rim she made her way, sometimes upon its very verge, but unshaken by the frightful abyss below her. Constantly she sought for a means of descent, since she knew that if she could cross it she might circle back toward Zoram, but the walls rose sheer for two thousand feet offering scarce a handhold in a hundred feet.

As she rounded the shoulder of the peak she saw a vast country stretching away below her—a country that she had never seen before—and she knew that she had crossed the mighty range and was looking on the land that lay beyond. The fissure that she had been following she could see widening below her into a great canyon that led out through foothills to a mighty plain. The slopes of the lower hills were wooded and beyond the plain were forests. This was a new world to Jana of Zoram, but it held no lure for her; it did not beckon to her for she knew that savage beasts and savage men of the low countries roamed its plains and forests.

To her right rose the mountains she had rounded; to her left was the deep chasm, and behind her were Skruk and his three companions.

For a moment she feared that she was trapped, but after advancing a few yards she saw that the sheer wall of the abyss had given way to a tumbled mass of broken ledges. But whether there were any means of descent, even here, she did not know—she could only hope.

From pausing often to search for a way down into the gorge, Jana had lost precious time and now she became suddenly aware that her pursuers were close behind her. Again she sprang forward, leaping from rock to rock, while they redoubled their speed and stumbled after her in pursuit, positive now that they were about to capture her.

Jana glanced below, and a hundred feet beneath her she saw a tumbled mass of granite that had fallen from above and formed a wide ledge. Just ahead the mountain jutted out forming an overhanging cliff.

She glanced back. Skruk was already in sight. He was stumbling awkwardly along in a clumsy run and breathing heavily, but he was very near and she must choose quickly.

There was but one way—over the edge of the cliff lay temporary escape or certain death. A leather thong, attached a foot below the point of her spear, she fastened around her neck, letting the spear hang down her back, threw herself upon the ground and slid over the edge of the cliff. Perhaps there were handholds; perhaps not. She glanced down. The face of the cliff was rough and not perpendicular, leaning in a little toward the mountain. She felt about with her toes and finally she located a protuberance that would hold her weight. Then she relinquished her hold upon the top of the cliff with one hand and searched about for a crevice in which to insert her fingers, or a projection to which she could cling.

She must work quickly for already the footsteps of the Phelians were sounding above her. She found a hold to which she might cling with scarcely more than the tips of her fingers, but it was something and the horror of the lowland was just above her and only death below.

She relinquished her hold upon the cliff edge with her other hand and lowered herself very slowly down the face of the cliff, searching with her free foot for another support. One foot, two, three she descended, and then attracted by a noise above her she glanced up and saw the hairy face of Skruk just above her.

"Hold my legs," he shouted to his companions, at the same time throwing himself prone at the edge of the cliff, and as they obeyed his command he reached down a long, hairy arm to seize Jana, and the girl was ready to let go all holds and drop to the jagged rocks beneath when Skruk's hand should touch her. Still looking upward she saw the fist of the Phelian but a few inches from her face.

The outstretched fingers of the man brushed the hair of the girl. One of her groping feet found a tiny ledge and she lowered herself from immediate danger of capture. Skruk was furious, but that one glance into the upturned face of the girl so close beneath him only served to add to his determination to possess her. No lengths were too far now to go to achieve his heart's desire, but as he glanced down that frightful escarpment his savage heart was filled with fear for the safety of his prize. It seemed incredible that she had descended as far as she had without falling and she had only commenced the descent. He knew that he and his companions could not follow the trail that she was blazing and he realized, too, that if they menaced her from above she might be urged to a greater haste that would spell her doom.

With these thoughts in his mind Skruk arose to his feet and turned to his companions. "We shall seek an easier way down," he said in a low voice, and then leaning over the cliff edge, he called down to Jana. "You have beaten me, mountain girl," he said. "I go back now to Pheli in the lowland. But I shall return and then I shall take you with me as my mate."

"May the thipdars catch you and tear out your heart before ever you reach Pheli again," cried Jana. But Skruk made no reply and she saw that they were going back the way that they had come, but she did not know that they were merely looking for an easier way into the bottom of the gorge toward which she was descending, or that Skruk's words had been but a ruse to throw her off her guard.

The Red Flower of Zoram, relieved of immediate necessity for haste, picked her way cautiously down the face of the cliff to the first ledge of tumbled granite. Here, by good fortune, she found the egg of a thipdar, which furnished her with both food and drink.

It was a long, slow descent to the bottom of the gorge, but finally the girl accomplished it, and in the meantime Skruk and his companions had found an easier way and had descended into the gorge several miles above her.

For a moment after she reached the bottom Jana was undecided as to what course to pursue. Instinct urged her to turn upward along the gorge in the general direction of Zoram, but her judgment prompted her to descend and skirt the base of the mountain to the left in search of an easier route back across them. And so she came leisurely down toward the valley, while behind her followed the four men from Pheli.

The canyon wall at her left, while constantly lessening in height as she descended, still presented a formidable obstacle, which it seemed wiser to circumvent than to attempt to surmount, and so she continued on downward toward the mouth of the canyon, where it debauched upon a lovely valley.

Never before in all her life had Jana approached the lowland so closely. Never before had she dreamed how lovely the lowland country might be, for she had always been taught that it was a horrid place and no fit abode for the stalwart tribes of the mountains.

The lure of the beauties and the new scenes unfolding before her, coupled with a spirit of exploration which was being born within her, led her downward into the valley much farther than necessity demanded.

Suddenly her attention was attracted by a strange sound coming suddenly from on high—a strange, new note in the diapason of her savage world, and glancing upward she finally descried the creature that must be the author of it.

A great thipdar, it appeared to be, moaning dismally far above her head—but what a thipdar! Never in her life had she seen one as large as this.

As she watched she saw another thipdar, much smaller, soaring above it. Suddenly the lesser one swooped upon its intended prey. Faintly she heard sounds of shattering and tearing and then the two combatants plunged earthward. As they did so she saw something separate itself from the mass and as the two creatures, partially supported by the wings of the larger, fell in a great, gliding spiral a most remarkable thing happened to the piece that had broken loose. Something shot out of it and unfolded above it in the air—something that resembled a huge toadstool, and as it did so the swift flight of the falling body was arrested and it floated slowly earthward, swinging back and forth as she had seen a heavy stone do when tied at the end of a buckskin thong.

As the strange thing descended nearer, Jana's eyes went wide in surprise and terror as she recognized the dangling body as that of a man.

Her people had few superstitions, not having advanced sufficiently in the direction of civilization to have developed a priesthood, but here was something that could be explained according to no natural logic. She had seen two great, flying reptiles meet in battle, high in air and out of one of them had come a man. It was incredible, but more than all it was terrifying. And so The Red Flower of Zoram, reacting in the most natural way, turned and fled.

Back toward the canyon she raced, but she had gone only a short distance when, directly in front of her, she saw Skruk and his three companions.

They, too, had seen the battle in mid-air and they had seen the thing floating downward toward the ground, and while they had not recognized it for what it was they had been terrified and were themselves upon the point of fleeing when Skruk descried Jana running toward them. Instantly every other consideration was submerged in his desire to have her and growling commands to his terrified henchmen he led them toward the girl.

When Jana discovered them she turned to the right and tried to circle about them, but Skruk sent one to intercept her and when she turned in the opposite direction, the four spread out across her line of retreat so as to effectually bar her escape in that direction.

Choosing any fate rather than that which must follow her capture by Skruk, Jana turned again and fled down the valley and in pursuit leaped the four squat, hairy men of Pheli.

At the instant that Jason Gridley had pulled the rip cord of his parachute a fragment of the broken propeller of his plane had struck him a glancing blow upon the head, and when he regained consciousness he found himself lying upon a bed of soft grasses at the head of a valley, where a canyon, winding out of lofty mountains, opened onto leveller land.

Disgusted by the disastrous end of his futile search for his companions, Gridley arose and removed the parachute harness. He was relieved to discover that he had suffered no more serious injury than a slight abrasion of the skin upon one temple.

His first concern was for his ship and though he knew that it must be a total wreck he hoped against hope that he might at least salvage his rifle and ammunition from it. But even as the thought entered his mind it was forced into the background by a chorus of savage yelps and growls that caused him to turn his eyes quickly to the right. At the summit of a little rise of ground a short distance away he saw four of the ferocious wolf dogs of Pellucidar. As hyænodons they were known to the paleontologists of the outer crust, and as jaloks to the men of the inner world. As large as full grown mastiffs they stood there upon their short, powerful legs, their broad, strong jaws parted in angry growls, their snarling lips drawn back to reveal their powerful fangs.

As he discovered them Jason became aware that their attention was not directed upon him—that they seemed not as yet to have discovered him—and as he looked in the direction that they were looking he was astounded to see a girl running swiftly toward them, and at a short distance behind the girl four men, who were apparently pursuing her.

As the vicious growls of the jaloks broke angrily upon the comparative silence of the scene, the girl paused and it was evident that she had not before been aware of the presence of this new menace. She glanced at them and then back at her pursuers.

The hyænodons advanced toward her at an easy trot. In piteous bewilderment she glanced about her. There was but one way open for escape and then as she turned to flee in that direction her eyes fell upon Jason Gridley, straight ahead in her path of flight and again she hesitated.

To the man came an intuitive understanding of her quandary. Menaced from the rear and upon two sides by known enemies, she was suddenly faced by what might indeed be another, cutting off all hope of retreat.

Acting impulsively and in accordance with the code that dominates his kind, Gridley ran toward the girl, shouting words of encouragement and motioning her to come to him.

Skruk and his companions were closing in upon her from behind and from her right, while upon her left came the jaloks. For just an instant longer, she hesitated and then seemingly determined to place her fate in the hands of an unknown, rather than surrender it to the inevitable doom which awaited her either at the hands of the Phelians or the fangs of the jaloks, she turned and sped toward Gridley, and behind her came the four beasts and the four men.

As Gridley ran forward to meet the girl he drew one of his revolvers, a heavy .45 caliber Colt.

The hyænodons were charging now and the leader was close behind her, and at that instant Jana tripped and fell, and simultaneously Jason reached her side, but so close was the savage beast that when Jason fired the hyænodon's body fell across the body of the girl.

The shot, a startling sound to which none of them was accustomed, brought the other hyænodons to a sudden stop, as well as the four men, who were racing rapidly forward under Skruk's command in an effort to save the girl from the beasts.

Quickly rolling the body of the jalok from its intended victim, Jason lifted the girl to her feet and as he did so she snatched her stone knife from its scabbard. Jason Gridley did not know how near he was to death at that instant. To Jana, every man except the men of Zoram was a natural enemy. The first law of nature prompted her to kill lest she be killed, but in the instant before she struck the blade home she saw something in the eyes of this man, something in the expression upon his face that she had never seen in the eyes or face of any man before. As plainly as though it had been spoken in words she understood that this stranger was prompted by solicitousness for her safety; that he was prompted by a desire to befriend rather than to harm her, and though in common with the jaloks and the Phelians she had been terrified by the loud noise and the smoke that had burst from the strange stick in his hand she knew that this had been the means that he had taken to protect her from the jaloks.

Her knife hand dropped to her side, and, as a slow smile lighted

the face of the stranger, The Red Flower of Zoram smiled back
in response.

They stood as they had when he had lifted her from the ground,
his left arm about her shoulders supporting her and he maintained
this unconscious gesture of protection as he turned to face the
girl's enemies, who, after their first fright, seemed on the point of
returning to the attack.

Two of the hyænodons, however, had transferred their attention
to Skruk and his companions, while the third was slinking bare
fanged, toward Jason and Jana.

The men of Pheli stood ready to receive the charge of the
hyænodons, having taken positions in line, facing their attackers,
and at sufficient intervals to permit them properly to wield their
clubs. As the beasts charged two of the men hurled their weapons,
each singling out one of the fierce carnivores. Skruk hurled his
weapon with the greater accuracy, breaking one of the forelegs of
the beast attacking him, and as it went down the Phelian standing
next to Skruk leaped forward and rained heavy blows upon its
skull.

The cudgel aimed at the other beast struck it a glancing blow
upon the shoulder, but did not stop it and an instant later it was
upon the Phelian whose only defense now was his crude stone
knife. But his companion, who had reserved his club for such an
emergency, leaped in and swung lustily at the savage brute, while
Skruk and the other, having disposed of their adversary, came to
the assistance of their fellows.

The savage battle between men and beast went unnoticed by
Jason, whose whole attention was occupied by the fourth wolfdog
as it moved forward to attack him and his companion.

Jana, fully aware that the attention of each of the men was
fully centered upon the attacking beasts, realized that now was
the opportune moment to make a break for freedom. She felt the
arm of the stranger about her shoulders, but it rested there lightly—
so lightly that she might easily disengage herself by a single, quick
motion. But there was something in the feel of that arm about
her that imparted to her a sense of greater safety than she had
felt since she had left the caverns of her people—perhaps the
protective instinct which dominated the man subconsciously exerted its natural reaction upon the girl to the end that instead of
fleeing she was content to remain, sensing greater safety where
she was than elsewhere.

And then the fourth hyænodon charged, growling, to be met by the roaring bark of the Colt. The creature stumbled and went down, stopped by the force of the heavy charge—but only for an instant—again it was up, maddened by pain, desperate in the face of death. Bloody foam crimsoned its jowls as it leaped for Jason's throat.

Again the Colt spoke, and then the man went down beneath the heavy body of the wolf dog, and at the same instant the Phelians dispatched the second of the beasts which had attacked them.

Jason Gridley was conscious of a great weight upon him as he was borne to the ground and he sought to fend those horrid jaws from his throat by interposing his left forearm, but the jaws never closed and when Gridley struggled from beneath the body of the beast and scrambled to his feet he saw the girl tugging upon the shaft of her crude, stonetipped spear in an effort to drag it from the body of the jalok.

Whether his last bullet or the spear had dispatched the beast the man did not know, and he was only conscious of gratitude and admiration for the brave act of the slender girl, who had stood her ground at his side, facing the terrible beast without loss of poise or resourcefulness.

The four jaloks lay dead, but Jason Gridley's troubles were by no means over, for scarcely had he arisen after the killing of the second beast when the girl seized him by the arm and pointed toward something behind him.

"They are coming," she said. "They will kill you and take me. Oh, do not let them take me!"

Jason did not understand a word that she had said, but it was evident from her tone of voice and from the expression upon her beautiful face that she was more afraid of the four men approaching them than she had been of the hyænodons, and as he turned to face them he could not wonder, for the men of Pheli looked quite as brutal as the hyænodons and there was nothing impressive or magnificent in their appearance as there had been in the mien of the savage carnivores—a fact which is almost universally noticeable when a comparison is made between the human race and the so-called lower orders.

Gridley raised his revolver and levelled it at the leading Phelian, who happened to be another than Skruk. "Beat it!" he said. "Your faces frighten the young lady."

"I am Gluf," said the Phelian. "I kill."

"If I could understand you I might agree with you," replied Jason, "but your exuberant whiskers and your diminutive forehead suggest that you are all wet."

He did not want to kill the man, but he realized that he could not let him approach too closely. But if he had any compunction in the matter of manslaughter, it was evident that the girl did not for she was talking volubly, evidently urging him to some action, and when she realized that he could not understand her she touched his pistol with a brown forefinger and then pointed meaningly at Gluf.

The fellow was now within fifteen paces of them and Jason could see that his companions were starting to circle them. He knew that something must be done immediately and prompted by humanitarian motives he fired his Colt, aiming above the head of the approaching Phelian. The sharp report stopped all four of them, but when they realized that none of them was injured they broke into a torrent of taunts and threats, and Gluf, inspired only by a desire to capture the girl so that they might return to Pheli, resumed his advance, at the same time commencing to swing his club menacingly. Then it was that Jason Gridley regretfully shot, and shot to kill. Gluf stopped in his tracks, stiffened, whirled about and sprawled forward upon his face.

Wheeling upon the others, Gridley fired again, for he realized that those menacing clubs were almost as effective at short range as was his Colt. Another Phelian dropped in his tracks, and then Skruk and his remaining companion turned and fled.

"Well," said Gridley, looking about him at the bodies of the four hyænodons and the corpses of the two men, "this is a great little country, but I'll be gosh-darned if I see how anyone grows up to enjoy it."

The Red Flower of Zoram stood looking at him admiringly. Everything about this stranger aroused her interest, piqued her curiosity and stimulated her imagination. In no particular was he like any other man she had ever seen. Not one item of his strange apparel corresponded to anything that any other human being of her acquaintance wore. The remarkable weapon, which spat smoke and fire to the accompaniment of a loud roar, left her dazed with awe and admiration; but perhaps the outstanding cause for astonishment, when she gave it thought, was the fact that she was not afraid of this man. Not only was the fear of strangers inherent in her, but from earliest childhood she had been taught to expect only the worst from men who were not of her own tribe and to flee from them upon any and all occasions. Perhaps it was his smile that had disarmed her, or possibly there was something in his friendly, honest eyes that had won her immediate trust and confidence. Whatever the cause, however, the fact remained that The Red Flower of Zoram made no effort to escape from Jason Gridley, who now found himself completely lost in a strange world, which in itself was quite sad enough without having added to it responsibilities for the protection of a strange, young woman, who could understand nothing that he said to her and whom, in turn, he could not understand.

CHAPTER 8

Jana and Jason

TAR-GASH AND THOAR looked with wonder upon the wreckage of the plane and Tarzan hastily searched it for the body of the pilot. The ape-man experienced at least temporary relief when he discovered that there was no body there, and a moment later he found footprints in the turf upon the opposite side of the plane— the prints of a booted foot which he recognized immediately as having been made by Jason Gridley—and this evidence assured him that the American had not been killed and apparently not even badly injured by the fall. And then he discovered something else which puzzled him exceedingly. Mingling with the footprints of Gridley and evidently made at the same time were those of a small sandaled foot.

A further brief examination revealed the fact that two persons, one of them Gridley and the other apparently a female or a youth of some Pellucidarian tribe, who had accompanied him, had approached the plane after it had crashed, remained in its vicinity for a short time and then returned in the direction from which they had come. With the spoor plain before him there was nothing for Tarzan to do other than to follow it.

The evidence so far suggested that Gridley had been forced to abandon the plane in air and that he had safely made a parachute descent, but where and under what circumstances he had picked up his companion, Tarzan could not even hazard a guess.

He found it difficult to get Thoar away from the aeroplane, the strange thing having so fired his curiosity and imagination that he must need remain near it and ask a hundred questions concerning it.

With Tar-Gash, however, the reaction was entirely different. He had glanced at it with only a faint show of curiosity or interest, and then he had asked one question, "What is it?"

"This is the thing that passed over us and which you said was a flying reptile," replied Tarzan. "I told you at that time that one of my friends was in it. Something happened and the thing fell, but my friend escaped without injury."

"It has no eyes," said Tar-gash. "How could it see to fly?"

"It was not alive," replied Tarzan.

"I heard it growl," said the Sagoth; nor was he ever convinced that the thing was not some strange form of living creature.

They had covered but a short distance along the trail made by Gridley and Jana, after they had left the aeroplane, when they came upon the carcass of a huge pteranodon. Its head was crushed and battered and almost severed from its body and a splinter of smooth wood projected from its skull—a splinter that Tarzan recognized as a fragment of an aeroplane propeller—and instantly he knew the cause of Gridley's crash.

Half a mile further on the three discovered further evidence, some of it quite startling. An opened parachute lay stretched upon the ground where it had fallen and at short distances from it lay the bodies of four hyænodons and two hairy men.

An examination of the bodies revealed the fact that both of the men and two of the hyænodons had died from bullet wounds. Everywhere upon the trampled turf appeared the imprints of the small sandals of Jason's companion. It was evident to the keen eyes of Tarzan that two other men, both natives, had taken part in the battle which had been waged here. That they were of the same tribe as the two that had fallen was evidenced by the imprints of their sandals, which were of identical make, while those of Jason's companion differed materially from all the others.

As he circled about, searching for further evidence, he saw that the two men who had escaped had run rapidly for some distance toward the mouth of a large canyon, and that, apparently following their retreat, Jason and his companion had set out in search of the plane. Later they had returned to the scene of the battle, and when they had departed they also had gone toward the mountains, but along a line considerably to the right of the trail made by the fleeing natives.

Thoar, too, was much interested in the various tracks that the participants in the battle by the parachute had left, but he said nothing until after Tarzan had completed his investigation.

"There were four men and either a woman or a youth here with my friend," said Tarzan.

"Four of them were low countrymen from Pheli," said Thoar, "and the other was a woman of Zoram."

"How do you know?" asked Tarzan, who was always anxious to add to his store of woodcraft.

"The low country sandals are never shaped to the foot as closely as are those of the mountain tribes," replied Thoar, "and the soles are much thinner, being made usually of the hides of the thag, which is tough enough for people who do not walk often upon anything but soft grasses or in soggy marshland. The sandals of the mountain tribes are soled with the thick hide of Maj, the cousin of Tandor. If you will look at the spoor you will see that they are not worn at all, while there are holes in the sandals of these dead men of Pheli."

"Are we near Zoram?" asked Tarzan.

"No," replied Thoar. "It lies across the highest range ahead of us."

"When we first met, Thoar, you told me that you were from Zoram."

"Yes, that is my country," replied Thoar.

"Then, perhaps, this woman is someone whom you know?"

"She is my sister," replied Thoar.

Tarzan of the Apes looked at him in surprise. "How do you know?" he demanded.

"I found an imprint where there was no turf, only soft earth, and there the spoor was so distinct that I could recognize the sandals as hers. So familiar with her work am I that I could recognize the stitching alone, where the sole is joined to the upper part of the sandal, and in addition there are the notches, which indicate the tribe. The people of Zoram have three notches in the underside of the sole at the toe of the left sandal."

"What was your sister doing so far from her own country and how is it that she is with my friend?"

"It is quite plain," replied Thoar. "These men of Pheli sought to capture her. One of them wanted her for his mate, but she eluded them and they pursued her across the Mountains of the Thipdars and down into this valley, where she was set upon by jaloks. The man from your country came and killed the jaloks and two of the Phelians and drove the other two away. It is evident that my sister could not escape him, and he captured her."

Tarzan of the Apes smiled. "The spoor does not indicate that she ever made any effort to escape him," he said.

Thoar scratched his head. "That is true," he replied, "and I cannot understand it, for the women of my tribe do not care to mate with the men of other tribes and I know that Jana, my sister, would rather die than mate outside the Mountains of the Thipdars. Many times has she said so and Jana is not given to idle talk."

"My friend would not take her by force," said Tarzan. "If she has gone with him, she has gone with him willingly. And I think that when we find them you will discover that he is simply accompanying her back to Zoram, for he is the sort of man who would not permit a woman to go alone and unprotected."

"We shall see," said Thoar, "but if he has taken Jana against her wishes, he must die."

As Tarzan, Tar-gash and Thoar followed the spoor of Jason and Jana a disheartened company of men rounded the end of the great Mountains of the Thipdars, fifty miles to the east of them, and entered the Gyor Cors, or great Plains of the Gyors.

The party consisted of ten black warriors and a white man, and, doubtless, never in the history of mankind had eleven men been more completely and hopelessly lost than these.

Muviro and his warriors, than whom no better trackers ever lived, were totally bewildered by their inability even to back-track successfully.

The stampeding of the maddened beasts, from which they had barely escaped with their lives and then only by what appeared nothing short of a miracle, had so obliterated all signs of the party's former spoor that though they were all confident that they had gone but a short distance from the clearing, into which the beasts had been herded by the tarags, they had never again been able to locate the clearing, and now they were wandering hopelessly and, in accordance with Von Horst's plans, keeping as much in the open as possible in the hope that the cruising O-220 might thus discover them, for Von Horst was positive that eventually his companions would undertake a search for them.

Aboard the O-220 the grave fear that had been entertained for the safety of the thirteen missing members of the ship's company had developed into a conviction of disaster when Gridley failed to return within the limit of the time that he might reasonably be able to keep the scout plane in the air.

Then it was that Zuppner had sent Dorf out with another searching party, but at the end of seventy hours they had returned to report absolute failure. They had followed the trail to a clearing where jackals fed upon rotting carrion, but beyond this there was no sign of spoor to suggest in what direction their fellows had wandered.

Going and coming they had been beset by savage beasts and so ruthless and determined had been the attacks of the giant tarags that Dorf reported to Zuppner that he was confident that all of the missing members of the party must by this time have been destroyed by these great cats.

"Until we have proof of that, we must not give up hope," replied Zuppner, "nor may we relinquish our efforts to find them, whether dead or alive, and that we cannot do by remaining here."

There was nothing now to delay the start. While the motors were warming up, the anchor was drawn in and the air expelled from the lower vacuum tanks. As the giant ship rose from the ground Robert Jones jotted down a brief note in a greasy memorandum book: "We sailed from here at noon."

When Skruk and his companion had left the field to the victorious Jason, the latter had returned his six-gun to its holster and faced the girl. "Well," he inquired, "what now?"

She shook her head. "I cannot understand you," she said. "You do not speak the language of gilaks."

Jason scratched his head. "That being the case," he said, "and as it is evident that we are never going to get anywhere on conversation which neither one of us understands, I am going to have a look around for my ship, in the meantime, praying to all the gods that my thirty-thirty and ammunition are safe. It's a cinch that she did not burn for she must have fallen close by and I could have seen the smoke."

Jana listened attentively and shook her head.

"Come on," said Jason, and started off in the direction that he thought the ship might lie.

"No, not that way," exclaimed Jana, and running forward she seized his arm and tried to stop him, pointing back to the tall peaks of the Mountains of the Thipdars, where Zoram lay.

Jason essayed the difficult feat of explaining in a weird sign language of his own invention that he was looking for an aeroplane that had crashed somewhere in the vicinity, but the conviction soon claimed him that that would be a very difficult thing to accomplish even if the person to whom he was trying to convey the idea knew what an aeroplane was, and so he ended up by grinning good naturedly, and, seizing the girl by the hand, gently leading her in the direction he wished to go.

Again that charming smile disarmed The Red Flower of Zoram and though she knew that this stranger was leading her away from the caverns of her people, yet she followed docilely, though her brow was puckered in perplexity as she tried to understand why she was not afraid, or why she was willing to go with this stranger, who evidently was not even a gilak, since he could not speak the language of men.

A half hour's search was rewarded by the discovery of the wreck of the plane, which had suffered far less damage than Jason had expected.

It was evident that in its plunge to earth it must have straightened out and glided to a landing. Of course, it was wrecked beyond repair, even if there had been any facilities for repairs, but it had not burned and Jason recovered his thirty-thirty and all his ammunition.

Jana was intensely interested in the plane and examined every portion of it minutely. Never in her life had she wished so much to ask questions, for never in her life had she seen anything that had so aroused her wonder. And here was the one person in all the world who could answer her questions, but she could not make him understand one of them. For a moment she almost hated him, and then he smiled at her and pressed her hand, and she forgave him and smiled back.

"And now," said Jason, "where do we go from here? As far as I am concerned one place is as good as another."

Being perfectly well aware that he was hopelessly lost, Jason Gridley felt that the only chance he had of being reunited with his companions lay in the possibility that the O-220 might chance to cruise over the very locality where he happened to be, and no matter whither he might wander, whether north or south or east or west, that chance was as slender in one direction as another, and, conversely, equally good. In an hour the O-220 would cover a distance fully as great as he could travel in several days of outer earthly time. And so even if he chanced to be moving in a direction that led away from the ship's first anchorage, he could never go so far that it might not easily and quickly overtake him, if its search should chance to lead it in his direction. Therefore he turned questioningly to the girl, pointing first in one direction, and then in another, while he looked inquiringly at her, attempting thus to convey to her the idea that he was ready and willing to go in any direction she chose, and Jana, sensing his meaning, pointed toward the lofty Mountains of the Thipdars.

"There," she said, "lies Zoram, the land of my people."

"Your logic is unassailable," said Jason, "and I only wish I could understand what you are saying, for I am sure that anyone with such beautiful teeth could never be uninteresting."

Jana did not wait to discuss the matter, but started forthwith for Zoram and beside her walked Jason Gridley of California.

Jana's active mind had been working rapidly and she had come to the conclusion that she could not for long endure the constantly increasing pressure of unsatisfied curiosity. She must find some means of communicating with this interesting stranger and to the accomplishment of this end she could conceive of no better plan than teaching the man her language. But how to commence! Never in her experience or that of her people had the necessity arisen for teaching a language. Previously she had not dreamed of the existence of such a means. If you can feature such a state, which is doubtful, you must concede to this primitive girl of the stone age a high degree of intelligence. This was no accidental blowing off of the lid of the teapot upon which might be built a theory. It required, as a matter of fact, a greater reasoning ability. Give a steam engine to a man who had never heard of steam and ask him to make it go—Jana's problem was almost as difficult. But the magnitude of the reward spurred her on, for what will one not do to have one's curiosity satisfied, especially if one happens to be a young and beautiful girl and the object of one's curiosity an exceptionally handsome young man. Skirts may change, but human nature never.

And so The Red Flower of Zoram pointed at herself with a slim, brown forefinger and said, "Jana." She repeated this several times and then she pointed at Jason, raising her eyebrows in interrogation.

"Jason," he said, for there was no misunderstanding her meaning. And so the slow, laborious task began as the two trudged upward toward the foothills of the Mountains of the Thipdars.

There lay before them a long, hard climb to the higher altitudes, but there was water in abundance in the tumbling brooks, dropping down the hillside, and Jana knew the edible plants, and nuts, and fruits which grew in riotous profusion in many a dark, deep ravine, and there was game in plenty to be brought down, when they needed meat, by Jason's thirty-thirty.

As they proceeded in their quest for Zoram, Jason found greater opportunity to study his companion and he came to the conclusion that nature had attained the pinnacle of physical perfection with the production of this little savage. Every line and curve of that lithe, brown body sang of symmetry, for The Red Flower of Zoram was a living poem of beauty. If he had thought that her teeth were beautiful he was forced to admit that they held no advantage in that respect over her eyes, her nose or any other of her features. And when she fell to with her crude stone knife and helped him skin a kill and prepare the meat for cooking, when he saw the deftness and celerity with which she made fire with the simplest and most primitive of utensils, when he witnessed the almost uncanny certitude with which she located nests of eggs and edible fruit and vegetables, he was conscious that her perfections were not alone physical and he became more than ever anxious to acquire a sufficient understanding of her tongue to be able to communicate with her, though he realized that he might doubtless suffer a rude awakening and disillusionment when, through an understanding of her language, he might be able to judge the limitations of her mind.

When Jana was tired she went beneath a tree, and, making a bed of grasses, curled up and fell asleep immediately, and, while she slept, Gridley watched, for the dangers of this primitive land were numerous and constant. Fully as often as he shot for food he shot to protect them from some terrible beast, until the encounters became as prosaic and commonplace as does the constant eluding of death by pedestrians at congested traffic corners in cities of the outer crust.

When Jason felt the need of sleep, Jana watched and sometimes they merely rested without sleeping, usually beneath a tree for there they found the greatest protection from their greatest danger, the fierce and voracious thipdars from which the mountains took their name. These hideous, flying reptiles were a constant menace, but so thoroughly had nature developed a defense against them that the girl could hear their wings at a greater distance than either of them could see the creatures.

Jason had no means for determining how far they had travelled, or how long they had been upon their way, but he was sure that considerable outer earthly time must have elapsed since he had met the girl, when they came to a seemingly insurmountable obstacle, for already he had made considerable progress toward mastering her tongue and they were exchanging short sentences, much to Jana's delight, her merry laughter, often marking one of Jason's more flagrant errors in pronunciation or construction.

And now they had come to a deep chasm with overhanging walls that not even Jana could negotiate. To Jason it resembled a stupendous fault that might have been caused by the subsidence of the mountain range for it paralleled the main axis of the range. And if this were true he knew that it might extend for hundreds of miles, effectually barring the way across the mountains by the route they were following.

For a long time Jana sought a means of descent into the crevice. She did not want to turn to the left as that route might lead her eventually back to the canyon that she had descended when pursued by Skruk and his fellows and she well knew how almost unscalable were the perpendicular sides of this terrific gorge. Another thing, perhaps, which decided her against the left hand route was the possibility that in that direction they might again come in contact with the Phelians, and so she led Jason toward the right and always she searched for a way to the bottom of the rift.

Jason realized that they were consuming a great deal of time in trying to cross, but he became also aware of the fact that time meant nothing in timeless Pellucidar. It was never a factor with which to reckon for the excellent reason that it did not exist, and when he gave the matter thought he was conscious of a mild surprise that he, who had been always a slave of time, so easily and naturally embraced the irresponsible existence of Pellucidar. It was not only the fact that time itself seemed not to matter but that the absence of this greatest of all task masters singularly affected one's outlook upon every other consideration of existence. Without time there appeared to be no accountability for one's acts since it is to the future that the slaves of time have learned to look for their reward or punishment. Where there is no time, there is no future. Jason Gridley found himself affected much as Tarzan had been in that the sense of his responsibility for the welfare of his fellows seemed deadened. What had happened to them had happened and no act of his could alter it. They were not there with him and so he could not be of assistance to them, and as it was difficult to visualize the future beneath an eternal noonday sun how might one plan ahead for others or for himself?

Jason Gridley gave up the riddle with a shake of his head and found solace in contemplation of the profile of The Red Flower of Zoram.

"Why do you look at me so much?" demanded the girl; for by now they could make themselves understood to one another.

Jason Gridley flushed slightly and looked quickly away. Her question had been very abrupt and surprising and for the first time he realized that he had been looking at her a great deal. He started to answer, hesitated and stopped. Why *had* he been looking at her so much? It seemed silly to say that it was because she was beautiful.

"Why do you not say it, Jason?" she inquired.

"Say what?" he demanded.

"Say the thing that is in your eyes when you look at me," she replied.

Gridley looked at her in astonishment. No one but an imbecile could have misunderstood her meaning, and Jason Gridley was no imbecile.

Could it be possible that he had been looking at her *that* way? Had he gone stark mad that he was even subconsciously entertaining such thoughts of this little barbarian who seized her meat in both hands and tore pieces from it with her flashing, white teeth, who went almost as naked as the beasts of the field and with all their unconsciousness of modesty? Could it be that his eyes had told this untutored savage that he was harboring thoughts of love for her? The artificialities of a thousand years of civilization rose up in horror against such a thought.

Upon the screen of his memory there was flashed a picture of the haughty Cynthia Furnois of Hollywood, daughter of the famous director, Abelard Furnois, né Abe Fink. He recalled Cynthia's meticulous observance of the minutest details of social usages and the studied perfection of her deportment that had sometimes awed him. He saw, too, the aristocratic features of Barbara Green, daughter of old John Green, the Los Angeles realtor, from Texas. It is true that old John was no purist and that his total disregard of the social precedence of forks often shocked the finer sensibilities that Mrs. Green and Barbara had laboriously achieved in the universities of Montmarte and Cocoanut Grove, but Barbara had had two years at Marlborough and knew her suffixes and her hardware.

Of course Cynthia was a rotten little snob, not only on the surface but to the bottom of her shallow, selfish soul, while Barbara's snobbishness, he felt, was purely artificial, the result of mistaking for the genuine the silly artificialities and affectations of the almost celebrities and sudden rich that infest the public places of Hollywood.

But nevertheless these two did, after a fashion, reflect the social environment to which he was accustomed and as he tried to answer Jana's question he could not but picture her seated at dinner with a company made up of such as these. Of course, Jana was a bully companion upon an adventure such as that in which they were engaged, but modern man cannot go adventuring forever in the Stone Age. If his eyes had carried any other message to Jana than that of friendly comradeship he felt sorry, for he realized that in fairness to her, as well as to himself, there could never be anything more than this between them.

As Jason hesitated for a reply, the eyes of The Red Flower of Zoram searched his soul and slowly the half expectant smile faded from her lips. Perhaps she was a savage little barbarian of the Stone Age, but she was no fool and she was a woman.

Slowly she drew her slender figure erect as she turned away from him and started back along the rim of the rift toward the great gorge through which she had descended from the higher peaks when Skruk and his fellows had been pursuing her.

"Jana," he exclaimed, "don't be angry. Where are you going?"

She stopped and with her haughty little chin in air turned a withering look back upon him across a perfect shoulder. "Go your way, jalok," she said, "and Jana will go hers."

CHAPTER 9

To the Thipdar's Nest

HEAVY CLOUDS FORMED about the lofty peaks of the Mountains of the Thipdars—black, angry clouds that rolled down the northern slopes, spreading far to east and west.

"The waters have come again," said Thoar. "They are falling upon Zoram. Soon they will fall here too."

It looked very dark up there above them and presently the clouds swept out across the sky, blotting out the noonday sun.

It was a new landscape upon which Tarzan looked—a sullen, bleak and forbidding landscape. It was the first time that he had seen Pellucidar in shadow and he did not like it. The effect of the change was strikingly apparent in Thoar and Tar-gash. They seemed depressed, almost fearful. Nor was it man alone that was so strangely affected by the blotting out of the eternal sunlight, for presently from the upper reaches of the mountains the lower animals came, pursuing the sunlight. That they, too, were strangely affected and filled with terror was evidenced by the fact that the carnivores and their prey trotted side by side and that none of them paid any attention to the three men.

"Why do they not attack us, Thoar?" asked Tarzan.

"They know that the water is about to fall," he replied, "and they are afraid of the falling water. They forget their hunger and their quarrels as they seek to escape the common terror."

"Is the danger so great then?" asked the ape-man.

"Not if we remain upon high ground," replied Thoar. "Sometimes the gulleys and ravines fill with water in an instant, but the only danger upon the high land is from the burning spears that are hurled from the black clouds. But if we stay in the open, even these are not dangerous for, as a rule, they are aimed at trees. Do not go beneath a tree while the clouds are hurling their spears of fire."

As the clouds shut off the sunlight, the air became suddenly cold. A raw wind swept down from above and the three men shivered in their nakedness.

"Gather wood," said Tarzan. "We shall build a fire for warmth." And so the three gathered firewood and Tarzan made fire and they sat about it, warming their naked hides; while upon either side of them the brutes passed on their way down toward the sunlight.

The rain came. It did not fall in drops, but in great enveloping blankets that seemed to beat them down and smother them. Inches deep it rolled down the mountainside, filling the depressions and the gulleys, turning the canyons into raging torrents.

The wind lashed the falling water into a blinding maelstrom that the eye could not pierce a dozen feet. Terrified animals stampeded blindly, constituting themselves the greatest menace of the storm. The lightning flashed and the thunder roared, and the beasts progressed from panic to an insanity of fear.

Above the roar of the thunder and the howling of the wind rose the piercing shrieks and screams of the monsters of another day, and in the air above flapped shrieking reptiles fighting toward the sunlight against the pounding wrath of the elements. Giant pteranodons, beaten to the ground, staggered uncertainly upon legs unaccustomed to the task, and through it all the three beast-men huddled at the spot where their fire had been, though not even an ash remained.

It seemed to Tarzan that the storm lasted a great while, but like the others he was enured to the hardships and discomforts of primitive life. Where a civilized man might have railed against fate and cursed the elements, the three beast-men sat in stoic silence, their backs hunched against the storm, for each knew that it would not last forever and each knew that there was nothing he could say or do to lessen its duration or abate its fury.

Had it not been for the example set by Tarzan and Thoar, Targash would have fled toward the sunlight with the other beasts, not that he was more fearful than they, but that he was influenced more by instinct than by reason. But where they stayed, he was content to stay, and so he squatted there with them, in dumb misery, waiting for the sun to come again.

The rain lessened; the howling wind died down; the clouds passed on and the sun burst forth upon a steaming world. The three beast-men arose and shook themselves.

"I am hungry," said Tarzan.

Thoar pointed about them to where lay the bodies of lesser beasts that had been crushed in the mad stampede for safety.

Now even Thoar was compelled to eat his meat raw, for there was no dry wood wherewith to start a fire, but to Tarzan and

Tar-gash this was no hardship. As Tarzan ate, the suggestion of a smile smoldered in his eyes. He was recalling a fussy old nobleman with whom he had once dined at a London club and who had almost suffered a stroke of apoplexy because his bird had been slightly underdone.

When the three had filled their bellies, they arose to continue their search for Jana and Jason, only to discover that the torrential rain had effectually erased every vestige of the spoor that they had been following.

"We cannot pick up their trail again," said Thoar, "until we reach the point where they continued on again after the waters ceased to fall. To the left is a deep canyon, whose walls are difficult to scale. In front of us is a fissure, which extends along the base of the mountains for a considerable distance in both directions. But if we go to the right we shall find a place where we can descend into it and cross it. This is the way that they should have gone. Perhaps there we shall pick up their trail again." But though they continued on and crossed the fissure and clambered upward toward the higher peaks, they found no sign that Jana or Jason had come this way.

"Perhaps they reached your country by another route," suggested Tarzan.

"Perhaps," said Thoar. "Let us continue on to Zoram. There is nothing else that we can do. There we can gather the men of my tribe and search the mountains for them."

In the ascent toward the summit Thoar sometimes followed trails that for countless ages the rough pads of the carnivores had followed, or again he led them over trackless wastes of granite, taking such perilous chances along dizzy heights that Tarzan was astonished that any of them came through alive.

Upon a bleak summit they had robbed a thipdar's nest of its eggs and the three were eating when Thoar became suddenly alert and listening. To the ears of the ape-man came faintly a sound that resembled the dismal flapping of distant wings.

"A thipdar," said Thoar, "and there is no shelter for us."

"There are three of us," said Tarzan. "What have we to fear?"

"You do not know them," said Thoar. "They are hard to kill and they are never defeated until they are killed. Their brains are very small. Sometimes when we have cut them open it has been difficult to find the brain at all, and having no brain they have no fear of anything, not even death, for they cannot know what death is; nor do they seem to be affected much by pain, it merely angers them, making them more terrible. Perhaps we can kill it, but I wish that there were a tree."

"How do you know that it will attack us?" asked Tarzan.

"It is coming in this direction. It cannot help but see us, and whatever living thing they see they attack."

"Have you ever been attacked by one?" asked Tarzan.

"Yes," replied Thoar; "but only when there was no tree or cave. The men of Zoram are not ashamed to admit that they fear the mighty thipdars."

"But if you have killed them in the past, why may we not kill this one?" demanded the ape-man.

"We may," replied Thoar, "but I have never chanced to have an encounter with one, except when there were a number of my tribesmen with me. The lone hunter who goes forth and never returns is our reason for fearing the thipdar. Even when there are many of us to fight them, always there are some killed and many injured."

"It comes," said Tar-gash, pointing.

"It comes," said Thoar, grasping his spear more firmly.

Down to their ears came a sound resembling the escaping of steam through a petcock.

"It has seen us," said Thoar.

Tarzan laid his spear upon the ground at his feet, plucked a handful of arrows from his quiver and fitted one to his bow. Tar-gash swung his club slowly to and fro and growled.

On came the giant reptile, the dismal flapping of its wings punctuated occasionally by a loud and angry hiss. The three men waited, poised, ready, expectant.

There were no preliminaries. The mighty pteranodon drove straight toward them. Tarzan loosed a bolt which drove true to its mark, burying its head in the breast of the pterodactyl. The hiss became a scream of anger and then in rapid succession three more arrows buried themselves in the creature's flesh.

That this was a warmer reception than it had expected was evidenced by the fact that it rose suddenly upward, skimmed above their heads as though to abandon the attack, and then, quite suddenly and with a speed incomprehensible in a creature of its tremendous size, wheeled like a sparrow hawk and dove straight at Tarzan's back.

So quickly did the creature strike that there could be no defense.

The ape-man felt sharp talons half buried in his naked flesh and simultaneously he was lifted from the ground.

Thoar raised his spear and Tar-gash swung his cudgel, but neither dared strike for fear of wounding their comrade. And so they were forced to stand there futilely inactive and watch the monster bear Tarzan of the Apes away across the tops of the Mountains of the Thipdars.

In silence they stood watching until the creature passed out of sight beyond the summit of a distant peak, the body of the ape-man still dangling in its talons. Then Tar-gash turned and looked at Thoar.

"Tarzan is dead," said the Sagoth. Thoar of Zoram nodded sadly. Without another word Tar-gash turned and started down toward the valley from which they had ascended. The only bond that had united these two hereditary enemies had parted, and Tar-gash was going his way back to the stamping grounds of his tribe.

For a moment Thoar watched him, and then, with a shrug of his shoulders, he turned his face toward Zoram.

As the pteranodon bore him off across the granite peaks, Tarzan hung limply in its clutches, realizing that if Fate held in store for him any hope of escape it could not come in midair and if he were to struggle against his adversary, or seek to battle with it, death upon the jagged rocks below would be the barren reward of success. His one hope lay in retaining consciousness and the power to fight when the creature came to the ground with him. He knew that there were birds of prey that kill their victims by dropping them from great heights, but he hoped that the pteranodons of Pellucidar had never acquired this disconcerting habit.

As he watched the panorama of mountain peaks passing below him, he realized that he was being carried a considerable distance from the spot at which he had been seized; perhaps twenty miles.

The flight at last carried them across a frightful gorge and a short distance beyond the pteranodon circled a lofty granite peak, toward the summit of which it slowly dropped, and there, below him, Tarzan of the Apes saw a nest of small thipdars, eagerly awaiting with wide distended jaws the flesh that their savage parent was bringing to them.

The nest rested upon the summit of a lofty granite spire, the entire area of the summit encompassing but a few square yards, the walls dropping perpendicularly hundreds of feet to the rough granite of the lofty peak the spire surmounted. It was, indeed, a precarious place at which to stage a battle for life.

Cautiously, Tarzan of the Apes drew his keen hunting knife from its sheath. Slowly his left hand crept upward against his body and passed over his left shoulder until his fingers touched the thipdar's leg. Cautiously, his fingers encircled the scaly, birdlike ankle just above the claws.

The reptile was descending slowly toward its nest. The hideous demons below were screeching and hissing in anticipation. Tarzan's feet were almost in their jaws when he struck suddenly upward with his blade at the breast of the thipdar.

It was no random thrust. What slender chance for life the ape-man had depended upon the accuracy and the strength of that single blow. The giant pteranodon emitted a shrill scream, stiffened convulsively in mid-air and, as it collapsed, relaxed its hold upon its prey, dropping the ape-man into the nest among the gaping jaws of its frightful brood.

Fortunately for Tarzan there were but three of them and they were still very young, though their teeth were sharp and their jaws strong.

Striking quickly to right and left with his blade he scrambled from the nest with only a few minor cuts and scratches upon his legs.

Lying partially over the edge of the spire was the body of the dead thipdar. Tarzan gave it a final shove and watched it as it fell three hundred feet to the rocks below. Then he turned his attention to a survey of his surroundings, but almost hopelessly since the view that he had obtained of the spire while the thipdar was circling it assured him that there was little or no likelihood that he could find any means of descent.

The young thipdars were screaming and hissing, but they had made no move to leave their nest as Tarzan started a close investigation of the granite spire upon the lofty summit of which it seemed likely that he would terminate his adventurous career.

Lying flat upon his belly he looked over the edge, and thus moving slowly around the periphery of the lofty aerie he examined the walls of the spire with minute attention to every detail.

Again and again he crept around the edge until he had catalogued within his memory every projection and crevice and possible handhold that he could see from above.

Several times he returned to one point and then he removed the coils of his grass rope from about his shoulders and holding the two ends in one hand, lowered the loop over the edge of the spire. Carefully he noted the distance that it descended from the summit and what a pitiful span it seemed—that paltry twenty-five feet against the three hundred that marked the distance from base to apex.

Releasing one end of the rope, he let that fall to its full length, and when he saw where the lower end touched the granite wall he was satisfied that he could descend at least that far, and below that another twenty-five feet. But it was difficult to measure distances below that point and from there on he must leave everything to chance.

Drawing the rope up again he looped the center of it about a projecting bit of granite, permitting the ends to fall over the edge of the cliff. Then he seized both strands of the rope tightly in one hand and lowered himself over the edge. Twenty feet below was a projection that gave him precarious foothold and a little crevice into which he could insert the fingers of his left hand. Almost directly before his face was the top of a buttress-like projection and below him he knew that there were many more similar to it. It was upon these that he had based his slender hope of success.

Gingerly he pulled upon one strand of the rope with his right hand. So slender was his footing upon the rocky escarpment that he did not dare draw the rope more than a few inches at a time lest the motion throw him off his balance. Little by little he drew it in until the upper end passed around the projection over which the rope had been looped at the summit and fell upon him. And as it descended he held his breath for fear that even this slight weight might topple him to the jagged rocks below.

And now came the slow process of drawing the rope unaided through one hand, fingering it slowly an inch at a time until the center was in his grasp. This he looped over the top of the projection in front of him, seating it as securely as he could, and then he grasped both strands once more in his right hand and was ready to descend another twenty-five feet.

This stage of the descent was the most appalling of all, since the rope was barely seated upon a shelving protuberance from which he was aware it might slip at any instant. And so it was with a sense of unspeakable relief that he again found foothold near the end of the frail strands that were supporting him.

At this point the surface of the spire became much rougher. It was broken by fissures and horizontal cracks that had not been visible from above, with the result that compared with the first fifty feet the descent from here to the base was a miracle of ease, and it was not long before Tarzan stood again squarely upon his two feet and level ground. And now for the first time he had an opportunity to take stock of his injuries.

His legs were scratched and cut by the teeth and talons of the young thipdars, but these wounds were as nothing to those left by the talons of the adult reptile upon his back and shoulders. He could feel the deep wounds, but he could not see them; nor the clotted blood that had dried upon his brown skin.

The wounds pained and his muscles were stiff and sore, but his only fear lay in the possibility of blood poisoning and that did not greatly worry the ape-man, who had been repeatedly torn and mauled by carnivores since childhood.

A brief survey of his position showed him that it would be practically impossible for him to recross the stupendous gorge that yawned between him and the point at which he had been so ruthlessly torn from his companions. And with that discovery came the realization that there was little or no likelihood that the people toward which Tar-gash had been attempting to guide him could be the members of the O-220 expedition. Therefore it seemed useless to attempt the seemingly impossible feat of finding Thoar and Tar-gash again among this maze of stupendous peaks, gorges and ravines. And so he determined merely to seek a way out of the mountains and back to the forests and plains that held a greater allure for him than did the rough and craggy contours of inhospitable hills. And to the accomplishment of this end he decided to follow the line of least resistance, seeking always the easiest avenues of descent.

Below him, in various directions, he could see the timber line and toward this he hastened to make his way.

As he descended the way became easier, though on several occasions he was again compelled to resort to his rope to lower himself from one level to another. Then the steep crags gave place to leveller land upon the shoulders of the mighty range and here, where earth could find lodgment, vegetation commenced. Grasses and shrubs, at first, then stunted trees and finally what was almost a forest, and here he came upon a trail.

It was a trail that offered infinite variety. For a while it wound through a forest and then climbed to a ledge of rock that projected from the face of a cliff and overhung a stupendous canyon.

He could not see the trail far ahead for it was continually rounding the shoulders of jutting crags.

As he moved along it, sure-footed, silent, alert, Tarzan of the Apes became aware that somewhere ahead of him other feet were treading probably the same trail.

What wind there was was eddying up from the canyon below and carrying the scent spoor of the creature ahead of him as well as his own up toward the mountain top, so that it was unlikely that either might apprehend the presence of the other by scent; but there was something in the sound of the footsteps that even at a distance assured Tarzan that they were not made by man, and it was evident too that they were going in the same direction as he for they were not growing rapidly more distinct, but very gradually as though he was slowly overhauling the author of them.

The trail was narrow and only occasionally, where it crossed some ravine or shallow gulley, was there a place where one might either descend or ascend from it.

To meet a savage beast upon it, therefore, might prove, to say the least, embarrassing but Tarzan had elected to go this way and he was not in the habit of turning back whatever obstacles in the form of man or beast might bar his way. And, too, he had the advantage over the creature ahead of him whatever it might be, since he was coming upon it from behind and was quite sure that it had no knowledge of his presence, for Tarzan well knew that no creature could move with greater silence than he, when he elected to do so, and now he passed along that trail as noiselessly as the shadow of a shadow.

Curiosity caused him to increase his speed that he might learn the nature of the thing ahead, and as he did so and the sound of its footsteps increased in volume, he knew that he was stalking some heavy, four-footed beast with padded feet—that much he could tell, but beyond that he had no idea of the identity of the creature; nor did the winding trail at any time reveal it to his view. Thus the silent stalker pursued his way until he knew that he was but a short distance behind his quarry when there suddenly broke upon his ears the horrid snarling and growling of an enraged beast just ahead of him.

There was something in the tone of that awful voice that increased the ape-man's curiosity. He guessed from the volume of the sound that it must come from the throat of a tremendous beast, for the very hills seemed to shake to the thunder of its roars.

Guessing that it was attacking or was about to attack some other creature, and spurred, perhaps, entirely by curiosity, Tarzan hastened forward at a brisk trot, and as he rounded the shoulder of a buttressed crag his eyes took in a scene that galvanized him into instant action.

A hundred feet ahead the trail ended at the mouth of a great cave, and in the entrance to the cave stood a boy—a lithe, handsome youth of ten or twelve—while between the boy and Tarzan a huge cave bear was advancing angrily upon the former.

The boy saw Tarzan and at the first glance his eyes lighted with hope, but an instant later, evidently recognizing that the newcomer was not of his own tribe, the expression of hopelessness that had been there before returned to his face, but he stood his ground bravely, his spear and his crude stone knife ready.

The scene before the ape-man told its own story. The bear, returning to its cave, had unexpectedly discovered the youth emerging from it, while the latter, doubtless equally surprised, found himself cornered with no avenue of escape open to him.

By the primitive jungle laws that had guided his youth, Tarzan of the Apes was under no responsibility to assume the dangerous rôle of savior, but there had always burned within his breast the flame of chivalry, bequeathed him by his English parents, that more often than not found him jeopardizing his own life in the interests of others. This child of a nameless tribe in an unknown world might hold no claim upon the sympathy of a savage beast, or even of savage men who were not of his tribe. And perhaps Tarzan of the Apes would not have admitted that the youth had any claim upon him, yet in reality he exercised a vast power over the ape-man—a power that lay solely in the fact that he was a child and that he was helpless.

One may analyze the deeds of a man of action and speculate upon them, whereas the man himself does not appear to do so at all—he merely acts; and thus it was with Tarzan of the Apes. He saw an emergency confronting him and he was ready to meet it, for since the moment that he had known that there was a beast upon the trail ahead of him he had had his weapons in readiness, years of experience with primitive men and savage beasts having taught him the value of preparedness.

His grass rope was looped in the hollow of his left arm and in the fingers of his left hand were grasped his spear, his bow and three extra arrows, while a fourth arrow was ready in his right hand.

One glance at the beast ahead of him had convinced him that only by a combination of skill and rare luck could he hope to destroy this titanic monster with the relatively puny weapons with which he was armed, but he might at least divert its attention from the lad and by harassing it draw it away until the boy could find some means of escape. And so it was that within the very instant that his eyes took in the picture his bow twanged and a heavy arrow sank deeply into the back of the bear close to its spine, and at the same time Tarzan voiced a savage cry intended to apprise the beast of an enemy in its rear.

Maddened by the pain and surprised by the voice behind it, the creature evidently associated the two, instantly whirling about on the narrow ledge.

Tarzan's first impression was that in all his life he had never gazed upon such a picture of savage bestial rage as was depicted upon the snarling countenance of the mighty cave bear as its fiery eyes fell upon the author of its hurt.

In quick succession three arrows sank into its chest as it charged, howling, down upon the ape-man.

For an instant longer Tarzan held his ground. Poising his heavy spear he carried his spear hand far back behind his right shoulder, and then with all the force of those giant muscles, backed by the weight of his great body, he launched the weapon.

At the instant that it left his hand the bear was almost upon him and he did not wait to note the effect of his throw, but turned and leaped swiftly down the trail; while close behind him the savage growling and the ponderous footfalls of the carnivore proved the wisdom of his strategy.

He was sure that upon this narrow, rocky ledge, if no obstacle interposed itself, he could outdistance the bear, for only Ara, the lightning, is swifter than Tarzan of the Apes.

There was the possibility that he might meet the bear's mate coming up to their den, and in that event his position would be highly critical, but that, of course, was only a remote possibility and in the meantime he was sure that he had inflicted sufficiently severe wounds upon the great beast to sap its strength and eventually to prove its total undoing. That it possessed an immense reserve of vitality was evidenced by the strength and savagery of its pursuit. The creature seemed tireless and although Tarzan was equally so he found fleeing from an antagonist peculiarly irksome and to a considerable degree obnoxious to his self esteem. And so he cast about him for some means of terminating the flight and to that end he watched particularly the cliff walls rising above the trail down which he sped, and at last he saw that for which he had hoped—a jutting granite projection protruding from the cliff about twenty-five feet above the trail.

His coiled rope was ready in his left hand, the noose in his right, and as he came within throwing distance of the projection, he unerringly tossed the latter about it. The bear tore down the trail behind him. The ape-man pulled heavily once upon the end of the rope to assure himself that it was safely caught above, and then with the agility of Manu, the monkey, he clambered upward.

CHAPTER 10

Only a Man May Go

It REQUIRED NO Sherlockian instinct to deduce that Jana was angry, and Jason was not so dense as to be unaware of the cause of her displeasure, which he attributed to natural feminine vexation induced by the knowledge that she had been mistaken in assuming that her charms had effected the conquest of his heart. He judged Jana by his own imagined knowledge of feminine psychology. He knew that she was beautiful and he knew that she knew it, too. She had told him of the many men of Zoram who had wanted to take her as their mate, and he had saved her from one suitor, who had pursued her across the terrible Mountains of the Thipdars, putting his life constantly in jeopardy to win her. He felt that it was only natural, therefore, that Jana should place a high valuation upon her charms and believe that any man might fall a victim to their spell, but he saw no reason why she should be angry because she had not succeeded in enthralling him. They had been very happy together. He could not recall when ever before he had been for so long a time in the company of any girl, or so enjoyed the companionship of one of her sex. He was sorry that anything had occurred to mar the even tenor of their friendship and he quickly decided that the manly thing to do was to ignore her tantrum and go on with her as he had before, until she came to her senses. Nor was there anything else that he might do for he certainly could not permit Jana to continue her journey to Zoram without protection. Of course it was not very nice of her to have called him a jalok, which he knew to be a Pellucidarian epithet of high insult, but he would overlook that for the present and eventually she would relent and ask his forgiveness.

And so he followed her, but he had taken scarcely a dozen steps when she wheeled upon him like a young tiger, whipping her stone knife from its sheath. "I told you to go your way," she cried. "I do not want to see you again. If you follow me I shall kill you."

"I cannot let you go on alone, Jana," he said quietly.

"The Red Flower of Zoram wants no protection from such as you," she replied haughtily.

"We have been such good friends, Jana," he pleaded. "Let us go on together as we have in the past. I cannot help it if—" He hesitated and stopped.

"I do not care that you do not love me," she said. "I hate you. I hate you because your eyes lie. Sometimes lips lie and we are not hurt because we have learned to expect that from lips, but when eyes lie then the heart lies and the whole man is false. I cannot trust you. I do not want your friendship. I want nothing more of you. Go away."

"You do not understand, Jana," he insisted.

"I understand that if you try to follow me I will kill you," she said.

"Then you will have to kill me," he replied, "for I shall follow you. I cannot let you go on alone, no matter whether you hate me or not," and as he ceased speaking he advanced toward her.

Jana stood facing him, her little feet firmly planted, her crude stone dagger grasped in her right hand, her eyes flashing angrily.

His hands at his sides, Jason Gridley walked slowly up to her as though offering his breast as a target for her weapon. The stone blade flashed upward. It poised a moment above her shoulder and then The Red Flower of Zoram turned and fled along the rim of the rift.

She ran very swiftly and was soon far ahead of Jason, who was weighted down by clothes, heavy weapons and ammunition. He called after her once or twice, begging her to stop, but she did not heed him and he continued doggedly along her trail, making the best time that he could. He felt hurt and angry, but after all the emotion which dominated him was one of regret that their sweet friendship had been thus wantonly blasted.

Slowly the realization was borne in upon him that he had been very happy with Jana and that she had occupied his thoughts almost to the exclusion of every other consideration of the past or future. Even the memory of his lost comrades had been relegated to the hazy oblivion of temporary forgetfulness in the presence of the responsibility which he had assumed for the safe conduct of the girl to her home land.

"Why, she has made a regular monkey out of me," he mused. "Odysseus never met a more potent Circe. Nor one half so lovely," he added, as he regretfully recalled the charms of the little barbarian.

And what a barbarian she had proven herself—whipping out her stone knife and threatening to kill him. But he could not help but smile when he realized how in the final extremity she had proven herself so wholly feminine. With a sigh he shook his head and plodded on after The Red Flower of Zoram.

Occasionally Jason caught a glimpse of Jana as she crossed a ridge ahead of him and though she did not seem to be travelling as fast as at first, yet he could not gain upon her. His mind was constantly harassed by the fear that she might be attacked by some savage beast and destroyed before he could come to her rescue with his rifle. He knew that sooner or later she would have to stop and rest and then he was hopeful of overtaking her, when he might persuade her to forget her anger and resume their former friendly comradeship.

But it seemed that The Red Flower of Zoram had no intention of resting, though the American had long since reached a state of fatigue that momentarily threatened to force him to relinquish the pursuit until outraged nature could recuperate. Yet he plodded on doggedly across the rough ground, while the weight of his arms and ammunition seemed to increase until his rifle assumed the ponderous proportions of a field gun. Determined not to give up, he staggered down one hill and struggled up the next, his legs seeming to move mechanically as though they were some detached engine of torture over which he had no control and which were bearing him relentlessly onward, while every fiber of his being cried out for rest.

Added to the physical torture of fatigue, were hunger and thirst, and knowing that only thus might time be measured, he was confident that he had covered a great distance since they had last rested and then he topped the summit of a low rise and saw Jana directly ahead of him.

She was standing on the edge of the rift where it opened into a mighty gorge that descended from the mountains and it was evident that she was undecided what course to pursue. The course which she wished to pursue was blocked by the rift and gorge. To her left the way led back down into the valley in a direction opposite to that in which lay Zoram, while to retrace her steps would entail another encounter with Jason.

She was looking over the edge of the precipice, evidently searching for some avenue of descent when she became aware of Jason's approach.

She wheeled upon him angrily. "Go back," she cried, "or I shall jump."

"Please, Jana," he pleaded, "let me go with you. I shall not annoy you. I shall not even speak to you unless you wish it, but let me go with you to protect you from the beasts."

The girl laughed. "You protect me!" she exclaimed, her tone caustic with sarcasm. "You do not even know the dangers which beset the way. Without your strange spear, which spits fire and death, you would be helpless before the attack of even one of the lesser beasts, and in the high Mountains of the Thipdars there are beasts so large and so terrible that they would devour you and your fire spear in a single gulp. Go back to your own people, man of another world; go back to the soft women of which you have told me. Only a man may go where The Red Flower of Zoram goes."

"You half convince me," said Jason with a rueful smile, "that I am only a caterpillar, but nevertheless even a caterpillar must have guts of some sort and so I am going to follow you, Red Flower of Zoram, until some goggle-eyed monstrosity of the Jurassic snatches me from this vale of tears."

"I do not know what you are talking about," snapped Jana; "but if you follow me you will be killed. Remember what I told you—only a man may go where goes The Red Flower of Zoram," and as though to prove her assertion she turned and slid quickly over the edge of the precipice, disappearing from his view.

Running quickly forward to the edge of the chasm, Jason Gridley looked down and there, a few yards below him, clinging to the perpendicular face of the cliff, Jana was working her way slowly downward. Jason held his breath. It seemed incredible that any creature could find hand or foothold upon that dizzy escarpment. He shuddered and cold sweat broke out upon him as he watched the girl.

Foot by foot she worked her way downward, while the man, lying upon his belly, his head projecting over the edge of the cliff, watched her in silence. He dared not speak to her for fear of distracting her attention and when, after what seemed an eternity, she reached the bottom, he fell to trembling like a leaf and for the first time realized the extent of the nervous strain he had been undergoing.

"God!" he murmured. "What a magnificent display of nerve and courage and skill!"

The Red Flower of Zoram did not look back or upward once as she resumed her way, following the gorge upward, searching for some point where she might clamber out of it above the rift.

Jason Gridley looked down into the terrible abyss. " 'Only a man may go where goes The Red Flower of Zoram,' " he mused.

He watched the girl until she disappeared behind a mass of fallen rock, where the gorge curved to the right, and he knew that unless he could descend into the gorge she had passed out of his life forever.

"Only a man may go where goes The Red Flower of Zoram!"

Jason Gridley arose to his feet. He readjusted the leather sling upon his rifle so that he could carry the weapon hanging down the center of his back. He slipped the holsters of both of his six-guns to the rear so that they, too, were entirely behind him. He removed his boots and dropped them over the edge of the cliff. Then he lay upon his belly and lowered his body slowly downward, and from a short distance up the gorge two eyes watched him from behind a pile of tumbled granite. There was anger in them at first, then skepticism, then surprise, and then terror.

As gropingly the man sought for some tiny foothold and then lowered himself slowly a few inches at a time, the eyes of the girl, wide in horror, never left him for an instant.

"Only a man may go where goes The Red Flower of Zoram!"

Cautiously, Jason Gridley groped for each handhold and foothold—each precarious support from which it seemed that even his breathing might dislodge him. Hunger, thirst and fatigue were forgotten as he marshalled every faculty to do the bidding of his iron nerve.

Hugging close to the face of the cliff he did not dare turn his head sufficiently to look downward and though it seemed he had clung there, lowering himself inch by inch, for an eternity, yet he had no idea how much further he had to descend. And so impossible of accomplishment did the task that he had set himself appear that never for an instant did he dare to hope for a successful conclusion. Never for an instant did any new hold impart to him a feeling of security, but each one seemed, if possible, more precarious than its predecessor, and then he reached a point where, grope as he would, he could find no foothold. He could not move to right or left; nor could he ascend. Apparently he had reached the end of his resources, but still he did not give up. Replacing his torn and bleeding feet upon the last, slight hold that they had found, he cautiously sought for new handholds lower down, and when he had found them—mere protuberances of rough granite— he let his feet slip slowly from their support as gradually he lowered his body to its full length, supported only by his fingers, where they clutched at the tiny projections that were his sole support.

As he clung there, desperately searching about with his feet for some slight projection, he reproached himself for not having discarded his heavy weapons and ammunition. And why? Because his life was in jeopardy and he feared to die? No, his only thought was that because of them he would be unable to cling much longer to the cliff and that when his hands slipped from their holds and he was dashed into eternity, his last, slender hope of ever again seeing The Red Flower of Zoram would be gone. It is remarkable, perhaps, that as he clung thus literally upon the brink of eternity, no visions of Cynthia Furnois or Barbara Green impinged themselves upon his consciousness.

He felt his fingers weakening and slipping from their hold. The end came suddenly. The weight of his body dragged one hand loose and instantly the other slipped from the tiny knob it had ben clutching, and Jason Gridley dropped downward, perhaps eighteen inches, to the bottom of the cliff.

As he came to a stop, his feet on solid rock, Jason could not readily conceive the good fortune that had befallen him. Almost afraid to look, he glanced downward and then the truth dawned upon him—he had made the descent in safety. His knees sagged beneath him and as he sank to the ground, a girl, watching him from up the gorge, burst into tears.

A short distance below him a spring bubbled from the canyon side, forming a little brooklet which leaped downward in the sunlight toward the bottom of the canyon and the valley, and after he had regained his composure he found his boots and hobbled down to the water. Here he satisfied his thirst and washed his feet, cleansing the cuts as best he could, bandaged them crudely with strips torn from his handkerchief, pulled his boots on once more and started up the canyon after Jana.

Far above, near the summit of the stupendous range, he saw ominous clouds gathering. They were the first clouds that he had seen in Pellucidar, but only for this reason did they seem remarkable or important. That they presaged rain, he could well imagine; but how could he dream of the catastrophic proportions of their menace.

Far ahead of him The Red Flower of Zoram was clambering upward along a precarious trail that gave promise of leading eventually over the rim of the gorge to the upper reaches that she wished to gain. When she had seen Jason's life in imminent jeopardy, she had been filled with terror and remorse, but when he had safely completed the descent her mood changed, and with the perversity of her sex she still sought to elude him. She had almost gained the summit of the escarpment when the storm broke and with it came a realization that the man behind her was ignorant of the danger which now more surely menaced him than had the descent of the cliff.

Without an instant's hesitation The Red Flower of Zoram turned and fled swiftly down the steep trail she had just so laboriously ascended. She must reach him before the waters reached him. She must guide him to some high place upon the canyon's wall, for she knew that the bottom of this great gorge would soon be a foaming, boiling torrent, spreading from side to side, its waters, perhaps, two hundred feet in depth. Already the water was running deep in the canyon far below her and spilling over the rim above her, racing downward in torrents and cataracts and waterfalls that carried earth and stone with them. Never in her life had Jana witnessed a storm so terrible. The thunder roared and the lightning flashed; the wind howled and the water fell in blinding sheets, and yet constantly menaced by instant death the girl groped her way blindly downward upon her hopeless errand of mercy. How hopeless it was she was soon to see, for the waters in the gorge had risen, she saw them just below her now, nor was the end in sight. Nothing down there could have survived. The man must long since have been washed away.

Jason was dead! The Red Flower of Zoram stood for an instant looking at the rising waters below her. There came to her an urge to throw herself into them. She did not want to live, but something stayed her; perhaps it was the instinct of primeval man, whose whole existence was a battle against death, who knew no other state and might not conceive voluntary surrender to the enemy, and so she turned and fought her way upward as the waters rising below her climbed to overtake her and the waters from above sought to hurl her backward to destruction.

Jason Gridley had witnessed cloudbursts in California and Arizona and he knew how quickly gulleys and ravines may be transformed into raging torrents. He had seen a river a mile wide formed in a few hours in the San Simon Flats, and when he saw the sudden rush of waters in the bottom of the gorge below him and realized that no storm that he had ever previously witnessed could compare in magnitude with this, he lost no time in seeking higher ground; but the sides of the canyon were steep and his upward progress discouragingly slow, as he saw the waters rising rapidly behind him. Yet there was hope, for just ahead and above him he saw a gentle acclivity rising toward the summit of the canyon rim.

As he struggled toward safety the boiling torrent rose and lapped his feet, while from above the torrential rain thundered down upon him, beating him backward so that often for a full minute at a time he could make no headway.

The raging waters that were filling the gorge reached his knees and for an instant he was swept from his footing. Clutching at the ground above him with his hands, he lost his rifle, but as it slid into the turgid waters he clambered swiftly upward and regained momentary safety.

Onward and upward he fought until at last he reached a spot above which he was confident the flood could not reach and there he crouched in the partial shelter of an overhanging granite ledge as Tarzan and Thoar and Tar-gash were crouching in another part of the mountains, waiting in dumb misery for the storm to spend its wrath.

He wondered if Jana had escaped the flood and so much

confidence did he have in her masterful ability to cope with the vagaries of savage Pellucidarian life that he harbored few fears for her upon the score of the storm.

In the cold and the dark and the wet he tried to plan for the future. What chance had he to find The Red Flower of Zoram in this savage chaos of stupendous peaks when he did not even know the direction in which her country lay and where there were no roads or trails and where even the few tracks that she might have left must have been wholly obliterated by the torrents of water that had covered the whole surface of the ground?

To stumble blindly on, then, seemed the only course left open to him, since he knew neither the direction of Zoram, other than in a most general way, nor had any idea as to the whereabouts of his fellow members of the O-220 expedition.

At last the rain ceased; the sun burst forth upon a steaming world and beneath the benign influence of its warm rays Jason felt the cold ashes of hope rekindled within his breast. Revivified, he took up the search that but now had seemed so hopeless.

Trying to bear in mind the general direction in which Jana had told him Zoram lay, he set his face toward what appeared to be a low saddle between two lofty peaks, which appeared to surmount the summit of the range. Thirst no longer afflicted him and the pangs of hunger had become deadened. Nor did it seem at all likely that he might soon find food since the storm seemed to have driven all animal life from the higher hills, but fortune smiled upon him. In a water worn rocky hollow he found a nest of eggs that had withstood the onslaught of the elements. The nature of the creature that had laid them he did not know; nor whether they were the eggs of fowl or reptile did he care. They were fresh and they were food and so large were they that the contents of two of them satisfied his hunger.

A short distance from the spot where he had found them grew a low stunted tree, and having eaten he carried the three remaining eggs to this meager protection from the prying eyes of soaring reptiles and birds of prey. Here he removed his clothing, hanging it upon the branches of the tree where the sunlight might dry it, and then he lay down beneath the tree to sleep, and in the warmth of Pellucidar's eternal noon he found no discomfort.

How long a time he slept he had no means of estimating, but when he awoke he was completely rested and refreshed. He was imbued with a new sense of self-confidence as he arose, stretching luxuriously, to don his clothes. His stretch half completed, he froze with consternation—his clothes were gone! He looked hastily about for them or for some sign of the creature that had purloined them, but never again did he see the one, nor ever the other.

Upon the ground beneath the tree lay a shirt that, having fallen, evidently escaped the eye of the marauder. That, his revolvers and belts of ammunition, which had lain close to him while he slept, were all that remained to him.

The temperature of Pellucidar is such that clothing is rather a burden than a necessity, but so accustomed is civilized man to the strange apparel with which he has encumbered himself for generations that, bereft of it, his efficiency, self-reliance and resourcefulness are reduced to a plane approximating the vanishing point.

Never in his life had Jason Gridley felt so helpless and futile as he did this instant as he contemplated the necessity which stared him in the face of going forth into this world clothed only in a torn shirt and an ammunition belt. Yet he realized that with the exception of his boots he had lost nothing that was essential either to his comfort or his efficiency, but perhaps he was appalled most by the realization of the effect that this misfortune would have upon the pursuit of the main object of his quest—how could he prosecute the search for The Red Flower of Zoram thus scantily appareled?

Of course The Red Flower had not been overburdened with wearing apparel; yet in her case this seemed no reflection upon her modesty, but the anticipation of finding her was now dampened by a realization of the ridiculousness of the figure he would cut, and already the mere contemplation of such a meeting caused a flush to overspread him.

In his dreams he had sometimes imagined himself walking abroad in some ridiculous state of undress, but now that such a dream had become an actuality he appreciated that in the figment of the subconscious mind he had never fully realized such complete embarrassment and loss of self-confidence as the actuality entailed.

Ruefully he tore his shirt into strips and devised a G-string; then he buckled his ammunition belt around him and stepped forth into the world, an Adam armed with two Colts.

As he proceeded upon his search for Zoram he found that the greatest hardship which the loss of his clothing entailed was the pain and discomfort attendant upon travelling barefoot on soles already lacerated by his descent of the rough granite cliff. This discomfort, however, he eventually partially overcame when with the return of the game to the mountains he was able to shoot a small reptile, from the hide of which he fashioned two crude sandals.

The sun, beating down upon his naked body, had no such effect upon his skin as would the sun of the outer world under like conditions, but it did impart to him a golden bronze color, which gave him a new confidence similar to that which he would have felt had he been able to retrieve his lost apparel, and in this fact he saw what he believed to be the real cause of his first embarrassment at his nakedness—it had been the whiteness of his skin that had made him seem so naked by contrast with other creatures, for this whiteness had suggested softness and weakness, arousing within him a disturbing sensation of inferiority; but now as he took on his heavy coat of tan and his feet became hardened and accustomed to the new conditions, he walked no longer in constant realization of his nakedness.

He slept and ate many times and was conscious, therefore, that considerable outer earthly time had passed since he had been separated from Jana. As yet he had seen no sign of her or any other human being, though he was often menaced by savage beasts and reptiles, but experience had taught him how best to elude these without recourse to his weapons, which he was determined to use only in extreme emergencies for he could not but anticipate with misgivings the time, which must sometime come, when the last of his ammunition would have been exhausted.

He had crossed the summit of the range and found a fairer country beyond. It was still wild and tumbled and rocky, but the vegetation grew more luxuriantly and in many places the mountain slopes were clothed in forests that reached far upward toward the higher peaks. There were more streams and a greater abundance of smaller game, which afforded him relief from any anxiety upon the score of food.

For the purpose of economizing his precious ammunition he had fashioned other weapons; the influence of his association with Jana being reflected in his spear, while to Tarzan of the Apes and the Waziri he owed his crude bow and arrows. Before he had mastered the intricacies of either of his new weapons he might have died of starvation had it not been for his Colts, but eventually he achieved a sufficient degree of adeptness to insure him a full larder at all times.

Jason Gridley had long since given up all hope of finding his ship or his companions and had accepted with what philosophy he could command the future lot from which there seemed no escape, in which he visioned a lifetime spent in Pellucidar, battling with his primitive weapons for survival amongst the savage creatures of the inner world.

Most of all he missed human companionship and he looked forward to the day that he might find a tribe of men with which he could cast his lot. Although he was quite aware from the information that he had gleaned from Jana that it might be extremely difficult, if not impossible, for him to win either the confidence or the friendship of any Pellucidarian tribe whose attitude towards strangers was one of habitual enmity; yet he did not abandon hope and his eyes were always on the alert for a sign of man; nor was he now to have long to wait.

He had lost all sense of direction in so far as the location of Zoram was concerned and was wandering aimlessly from camp to camp in the idle hope that some day he would stumble upon Zoram, when a breeze coming from below brought to his nostrils the acrid scent of smoke. Instantly his whole being was surcharged with excitement, for smoke meant fire and fire meant man.

Moving cautiously down the mountain in the direction from which the wind was blowing, his eager, searching eyes were presently rewarded by sight of a thin wisp of smoke arising from a canyon just ahead. It was a rocky canyon with precipitous walls, those upon the opposite side from him being lofty, while that which he was approaching was much lower and in many places so broken down by erosion or other natural causes as to give ready ingress to the canyon bottom below.

Creeping stealthily to the rim Jason Gridley peered downward into the canyon. Along the center of its grassy floor tumbled a mountain torrent. Giant trees grew at intervals, lending a park-like appearance to the scene; a similarity which was further accentuated by the gorgeous blooms which starred the sward or blossomed in the trees themselves.

Beside a small fire at the edge of a brook squatted a bronzed warrior, his attention centered upon a fowl which he was roasting above the fire. Jason, watching the warrior, deliberated upon the best method of approaching him, that he might convince him of his friendly intentions and overcome the natural suspicion of strangers that he knew to be inherent in these savage tribesmen. He had decided that the best plan would be to walk boldly down to the stranger, his hands empty of weapons, and he was upon the point of putting his plan into action when his attention was attracted to the summit of the cliff upon the opposite side of the narrow canyon.

There had been no sound that had been appreciable to his ears and the top of the opposite cliff had not been within the field of his vision while he had been watching the man in the bottom of the canyon. So what had attracted his attention he did not know, unless it had been the delicate powers of perception inherent in that mysterious attribute of the mind which we are sometimes pleased to call a sixth sense.

But be that as it may, his eyes moved directly to a spot upon the summit of the opposite cliff where stood such a creature as no living man upon the outer crust had ever looked upon before— a giant armored dinosaur it was, a huge reptile that appeared to be between sixty and seventy feet in length, standing at the rump, which was its highest point, fully twenty-five feet above the ground. Its relatively small, pointed head resembled that of a lizard. Along its spine were thin, horny plates arranged alternately, the largest of which were almost three feet high and equally as long, but with a thickness of little more than an inch. The stout tail, which terminated in a long, horny spine, was equipped with two other such spines upon the upper side and toward the tip. Each of these spines was about three feet in length. The creature walked upon four lizard-like feet, its short, front legs bringing its nose close to the ground, imparting to it an awkward and ungainly appearance.

It appeared to be watching the man in the canyon, and suddenly, to Jason's amazement, it gathered its gigantic hind legs beneath it and launched itself straight from the top of the lofty cliff.

Jason's first thought was that the gigantic creature would be dashed to pieces upon the ground in the canyon bottom, but to his vast astonishment he saw that it was not falling but was gliding swiftly through the air, supported by its huge spinal plates, which it had dropped to a horizontal position, transforming itself into a gigantic animate glider.

The swish of its passage through the air attracted the attention of the warrior squatting over his fire. The man leaped to his feet, snatching up his spear as he did so, and simultaneously Jason

Gridley sprang over the edge of the cliff and leaped down the rough declivity toward the lone warrior, at the same time whipping both his six-guns from their holsters.

CHAPTER 11

The Cavern of Clovi

AS TARZAN SWARMED up the rope the bear, almost upon his heels and running swiftly, squatted upon its haunches to overcome its momentum and came to a stop directly beneath him. And then it was that there occurred one of those unforeseen accidents which no one might have guarded against.

It chanced that the granite projection across which Tarzan had cast his noose was at a single point of knife-like sharpness upon its upper edge, and with the weight of the man dragging down upon it the rope parted where it rested upon this sharp bit of granite, and the Lord of the Jungle was precipitated upon the back of the cave bear.

With such rapidity had these events transpired it is a matter of question as to whether the bear or Tarzan was the more surprised, but primitive creatures who would survive cannot permit surprise to disconcert them. In this instance both of the creatures accepted the happening as though it had been planned and expected.

The bear reared up and shook itself in an effort to dislodge the man-thing from its back, while Tarzan slipped a bronzed arm around the shaggy neck and clung desperately to his hold while he dragged his hunting knife from its sheath. It was a precarious place in which to stage a struggle for life. On one side the cliff rose far above them, and upon the other it dropped away dizzily into the depth of a gloomy gorge, and here the efforts of the cave bear to dislodge its antagonist momentarily bade fair to plunge them both into eternity.

The growls and roars of the quadruped reverberated among the mighty peaks of the Mountains of the Thipdars, but the ape-man battled silently, driving his blade repeatedly into the back of the lunging beast, which was seeking by every means at its command to dislodge him, though ever wary against precipitating itself over the brink into the chasm.

But the battle could not go on forever and at last the blade found the spinal cord. The creature stiffened spasmodically and Tarzan slipped quickly from its back. He found safe footing upon the ledge as the mighty carcass stumbled forward and rolled over the edge to hurtle downward to the gorge's bottom, carrying with it four of Tarzan's arrows and his spear.

The ape-man found his rope lying upon the ledge where it had fallen, and gathering it up he started back along the trail in search of the bow that he had been forced to discard in his flight, as well as to find the boy.

He had taken only a few steps when, upon rounding the shoulder of a crag, he came face to face with the youth. At sight of him the latter stopped, his spear ready, his stone knife loosened in its sheath. He had been carrying Tarzan's bow, but at sight of the ape-man he dropped it at his feet, the better to defend himself in the event that he was attacked by the stranger.

"I am Tarzan of the Apes," said the Lord of the Jungle. "I come as a friend, and not to kill."

"I am Ovan," said the boy. "If you did not come to our country to kill, then you came to steal a mate, and thus it is the duty of every warrior of Clovi to kill you."

"Tarzan seeks no mate," said the ape-man.

"Then why is he in Clovi?" demanded the youth.

"He is lost," replied the ape-man. "Tarzan comes from another world that is beyond Pellucidar. He has become separated from his friends and he cannot find his way back to them. He would be friend with the people of Clovi."

"Why did you attack the bear?" demanded Ovan, suddenly.

"If I had not attacked it it would have killed you," replied the ape-man.

Ovan scratched his head. "It seemed to me," he said presently, "that there could be no other reason. It is what one of the men of my own tribe would have done, but you are not of my tribe. You are an enemy and so I could not understand why you did it. Do you tell me that though I am not of your tribe you would have saved my life?"

"Certainly," replied Tarzan.

Ovan looked long and steadily at the handsome giant standing before him. "I believe you," he said presently, "although I do not understand. I never heard of such a thing before, but I do not know that the men of my tribe will believe. Even after I have told them what you have done for me they may still wish to kill you, for they believe that it is never safe to trust an enemy."

"Where is your village?" asked Tarzan.

"It is not at a great distance," replied Ovan.

"I will go there with you," said Tarzan, "and talk with your chief."

"Very well," said the boy. "You may talk with Avan the chief. He is my father. And if they decide to kill you I shall try to help you, for you saved my life when the ryth would have destroyed me."

"Why were you in the cave?" demanded Tarzan. "It was plainly apparent that it was the den of a wild beast."

"You, too, were upon the same trail," said the boy, "while you chanced to be behind the ryth. It was my misfortune that I was in front of it."

"I did not know where the trail led," said the ape-man.

"Neither did I," said Ovan. "I have never hunted before except in the company of older men, but now I have reached an age when I would be a warrior myself, and so I have come out of the caves of my people to make my first kill alone, for only thus may a man hope to become a warrior. I saw this trail and, though I did not know where it led, I followed it; nor had I been long upon it when I heard the footsteps of the ryth behind me and when I came to the cave and saw that the trail ended there, I knew that I should never again see the caves of my people, that I should never become a warrior. When the great ryth came and saw me standing there he was very angry, but I should have fought him. Perhaps I might have killed him, though I do not believe that that is at all likely.

"And then you came and with this bent stick cast a little spear into the back of the ryth, which so enraged him that he forgot me and turned to pursue you as you knew that he would. They must indeed be brave warriors who come from the land from which you come. Tell me about your country. Where is it? Are your warriors great hunters and is your chief powerful in the land?"

Tarzan tried to explain that his country was not in Pellucidar, but that was beyond Ovan's powers of conception, and so Tarzan turned the conversation from himself to the youth and as they followed a winding trail toward Clovi, Ovan discoursed upon the bravery of the men of his tribe and the beauty of its women.

"Avan, my father, is a great chief," he said, "and the men of my tribe are mighty warriors. Often we battle with the men of Zoram and we have even gone as far as Daroz, which lies beyond Zoram, for always there are more men than women in our tribe and the warriors must seek their mates in Zoram and Daroz. Even now Carb has gone to Zoram with twenty warriors to steal women. The women of Zoram are very beautiful. When I am a little larger I shall go to Zoram and steal a mate."

"How far is it from Clovi to Zoram?" asked Tarzan.

"Some say that it is not so far, and others that it is farther," replied Ovan. "I have heard it said that going to Zoram is much farther than returning inasmuch as the warriors usually eat six times on the journey from Clovi to Zoram, but returning a strong man may make the journey eating only twice and still retain his strength."

"But why should the distance be shorter returning than going?" demanded the ape-man.

"Because when they are returning they are usually pursued by the warriors of Zoram," replied Ovan.

Inwardly Tarzan smiled at the naïveté of Ovan's reasoning, while it again impressed upon him the impossibility of measuring distances or computing time under the anomalous condition obtaining in Pellucidar.

As the two made their way toward Clovi, the boy gradually abandoned his suspicious attitude toward Tarzan and presently seemed to accept him quite as he would have a member of his own tribe. He noticed the wound made by the talons of the thipdar on Tarzan's back and shoulders and when he had wormed the story from his companion he marvelled at the courage, resourcefulness and strength that had won escape for this stranger from what a Pellucidarian would have considered an utterly hopeless situation.

Ovan saw that the wounds were inflamed and realized that they must be causing Tarzan considerable pain and discomfort, and so when first their way led near a brook he insisted upon cleansing them thoroughly, and collecting the leaves of a particular shrub he crushed them and applied the juices to the open wounds.

The pain of the inflammation had been as nothing compared to the acute agony caused by the application thus made by Ovan and yet the boy noticed that not even by the tremor of a single muscle did the stranger evidence the agony that Ovan well knew he was enduring, and once again his admiration for his new-found companion was increased.

"It may hurt," he said, "but it will keep the wounds from rotting and afterward they will heal quickly."

For a short time after they resumed their march the pain continued to be excruciating, but it lessened gradually until it finally disappeared, and thereafter the ape-man felt no discomfort.

The way led to a forest where there were straight, tough, young saplings, and here Tarzan tarried long enough to fashion a new spear and to split and scrape half a dozen additional arrows.

Ovan was much interested in Tarzan's steel-bladed knife and in his bow and arrows, although secretly he looked with contempt upon the latter, which he referred to as little spears for young children. But when they became hungry and Tarzan bowled over a mountain sheep with a single shaft, the lad's contempt was changed to admiration and thereafter he not only evinced great respect for the bow and arrows, but begged to be taught how to make and to use them.

The little Clovian was a lad after the heart of the ape-man and the two became fast friends as they made their way toward the land of Clovi, for Ovan possessed the quiet dignity of the wild beast; nor was he given to that garrulity which is at once the pride and the curse of civilized man—there were no boy orators in the peaceful Pliocene.

"We are almost there," announced Ovan, halting at the brink of a canyon. "Below lie the caves of the Clovi. I hope that Avan, the chief, will receive you as a friend, but that I cannot promise. Perhaps it might be better for you to go your way and not come to the caves of the Clovi. I do not want you to be killed."

"They will not kill me," said Tarzan. "I come as a friend." But in his heart he knew that the chances were that these primitive savages might never accept a stranger among them upon an equal or a friendly footing.

"Come, then," said Ovan, as he started the descent into the canyon. Part way down the trail turned up along the canyon side in the direction of the head of the gorge. It was a level trail here, well kept and much used, with indications that no little engineering skill had entered into its construction. It was by no means the haphazard trail of beasts, but rather the work of intelligent, even though savage and primitive men.

They had proceeded no great distance along the trail when Ovan sounded a low whistle, which, a moment later, was answered from around the bend in the trail ahead, and when the two had passed this turn Tarzan saw before him a wide, natural ledge of rock entirely overhung by beetling cliffs and in the depth of the recess thus formed in the cliffside he saw the dark mouth of a cavern.

Upon the flat surface of the ledge, which comprised some two acres, were congregated fully a hundred men, women and children.

All eyes were turned in their direction as they came into view and on sight of Tarzan the warriors sprang to their feet, seizing spears and knives. The women called their children to them and moved quickly toward the entrance to the cavern.

"Do not fear," cried the boy. "It is only Ovan and his friend, Tarzan."

"We kill," growled some of the warriors.

"Where is Avan the chief?" demanded the boy.

"Here is Avan the chief," announced a deep gruff voice, and Tarzan shifted his gaze to the figure of a stalwart, brawny savage emerging from the mouth of the cavern.

"What have you there, Ovan?" demanded the chief. "If you have brought a prisoner of war, you should have disarmed him first."

"He is no prisoner," replied Ovan. "He is a stranger in Pellucidar and he comes as a friend and not as an enemy."

"He is a stranger," replied Avan, "and you should have killed him. He has learned the way to the caverns of Clovi and if we do not kill him he will return to his people and lead them against us."

"He has no people and he does not know how to return to his own country," said the boy.

"Then he does not speak true words, for that is not possible," said Avan. "There can be no man who does not know the way to his own country. Come! Stand aside, Ovan, while I destroy him."

The lad drew himself stiffly erect in front of Tarzan. "Who would kill the friend of Ovan," he said, "must first kill Ovan."

A tall warrior, standing near the chief, laid his hand upon Avan's arm. "Ovan has always been a good boy," he said. "There is none in Clovi near his age whose words are as full of wisdom as his. If he says that this stranger is his friend and if he does not wish us to kill him, he must have a reason and we should listen to him before we decide to destroy the stranger."

"Very well," said the chief; "perhaps you are right, Ulan. We shall see. Speak, boy, and tell us why we should not kill the stranger."

"Because at the risk of his life he saved mine. Hand to hand he fought with a great ryth from which I could not have escaped had it not been for him; nor did he offer to harm me, and what enemy of the Clovi is there, even among the people of Zoram or Daroz who are of our own blood, that would not slay a Clovi youth who was so soon to become a warrior? Not only is he very brave, but he is a great hunter. It would be well for the tribe of Clovi if he came to live with us as a friend."

Avan bowed his head in thought. "When Carb returns we shall call a council and decide what to do," he said. "In the meantime the stranger must remain here as a prisoner."

"I shall not remain as a prisoner," said Tarzan. "I came as a friend and I shall remain as a friend, or I shall not remain at all."

"Let him stay as a friend," said Ulan. "He has marched with Ovan and has not harmed him. Why should we think that he will harm us when we are many and he only one?"

"Perhaps he has come to steal a woman," suggested Avan.

"No," said Ovan, "that is not so. Let him remain and with my life I will guarantee that he will harm no one."

"Let him stay," said some of the other warriors, for Ovan had long been the pet of the tribe so that they were accustomed to humoring him and so unspoiled was he that they still found pleasure in doing so.

"Very well," said Avan. "Let him remain. But Ovan and Ulan shall be responsible for his conduct."

There were only a few of the Clovians who accepted Tarzan without suspicion, and among these was Maral, the mother of Ovan, and Rela, his sister. These two accepted him without question because Ovan had accepted him. Ulan's friendship, too, had been apparent from the first; nor was it without great value for Ulan, because of his intelligence, courage and ability was a force in the councils of the Clovi.

Tarzan, accustomed to the tribal life of primitive people, took his place naturally among them, paying no attention to those who paid no attention to him, observing scrupulously the ethics of tribal life and conforming to the customs of the Clovi in every detail of his relations with them. He liked to talk with Maral because of her sunny disposition and her marked intelligence. She told him that she was from Zoram, having been captured by Avan when, as a young warrior, he had decided to take a mate. And to her nativity he attributed her great beauty, for it seemed to be an accepted fact among the Clovis that the women of Zoram were the most beautiful of all women.

Ulan he had liked from the first, being naturally attracted to him because he had been the first of the Clovians to champion his cause. In many ways Ulan differed from his fellows. He seemed to have been the first among his people to discover that a brain may be used for purposes other than securing the bare necessities of existence. He had learned to dream and to exercise his brain along pleasant paths that gave entertainment to himself and others— fantastic stories that sometimes amused and sometimes awed his eager audiences; and, too, he was a maker of pictures and these he exhibited to Tarzan with no small measure of pride. Leading the ape-man into the rocky cavern that was the shelter, the storehouse and the citadel of the tribe, he lighted a crude torch which illuminated the walls, revealing the pictures that Ulan had drawn there. Mammoth and saber-tooth and cave bear were depicted, with the red deer, the hyænodon and other familiar beasts, and in addition thereto were some with which Tarzan was unfamiliar and one that he had never seen elsewhere than in Pal-ul-don, where it had been known as a gryf. Ulan told him that it was a gyor and that it was found upon the Gyor Cors, or Gyor Plains, which lie at the end of the range of the Mountains of the Thipdars beyond Clovi.

The drawings were in outline and were well executed. The other members of the tribe thought they were very wonderful for Ulan was the first ever to have made them and they could not understand how he did it. Perhaps if he had been a weakling he would have lost caste among them because of this gift, but inasmuch as he was also a noted hunter and warrior his talents but added to his fame and the esteem in which he was held by all.

But though these and a few others were friendly toward him, the majority of the tribe looked upon Tarzan with suspicion, for never within the memory of one of them had a strange warrior entered their village other than as an enemy. They were waiting for the return of Carb and the warriors who had accompanied him, when, the majority of them hoped, the council would sentence the stranger to death.

As they became better acquainted with Tarzan, however, others among them were being constantly won to his cause and this was particularly true when he accompanied them upon their hunts, his skill and his prowess winning their admiration, and his strange weapons which they had at first viewed with contempt, soon commanding their unqualified respect.

And so it was that the longer that Carb remained away the better Tarzan's chances became of being accepted into the tribe upon an equal footing with its other members; a contingency for which he hoped since it would afford him a base from which to prosecute his search for his fellows and allies familiar with the country, whose friendly services he could enlist to aid him in his search.

He was confident that Jason Gridley, if he still lived, was lost somewhere among these stupendous mountains and if he could but find him they might eventually, with the assistance of the Clovians, locate the camp of the O-220.

He had eaten and slept with the Clovi many times and had accompanied them upon several hunts. It had been noon when he arrived and it was still noon, so whether a day or a month had passed he did not know. He was squatting by the cook-fire of Maral, talking with her and with Ulan, when from down the gorge there sounded the whistled signal of the Clovians announcing the approach of a friendly party and an instant later a youth rounded the shoulder of the cliff and entered the village.

"It is Tomar," announced Maral. "Perhaps he brings news of Carb."

The youth ran to the center of the ledge upon which the village stood and halted. For a moment he stood there dramatically with upraised hand, commanding silence, and then he spoke. "Carb is returning," he cried. "The victorious warriors of Clovi are returning with the most beautiful woman of Zoram. Great is Carb! Great are the warriors of Clovi!"

Cook fires and the routine occupations of the moment were abandoned as the tribe advanced to await the coming of the victorious war party.

Presently it came into sight, rounding the shoulder of the cliff and filing on to the ledge—twenty warriors led by Carb and among them a girl, her wrists bound behind her back, a rawhide leash around her neck, the free end held by a brawny warrior.

The ape-man's greatest interest lay in Carb, for his position in the tribe, perhaps even his life itself might rest with the decision of this man, whose influence, he had learned, was great in the councils of his people.

Carb was evidently a man of great physical strength; his regular features imparted to him much of the physical beauty that is an attribute of his people, but an otherwise handsome countenance was marred by thin, cruel lips and cold, unsympathetic eyes.

From contemplation of Carb the ape-man's eyes wandered to the face of the prisoner, and there they were arrested by the startling beauty of the girl. Well, indeed, thought Tarzan, might she be acclaimed the most beautiful woman of Zoram, for it was doubtful that there existed many in this world or the outer who might lay claim to greater pulchritude than she.

Avan, the chief, standing in the center of the ledge, received the returning warriors. He looked with favor upon the prize and listened attentively while Carb narrated the more important details of the expedition.

"We shall hold the council at once," announced Avan, "to decide who shall possess the prisoner, and at the same time we may settle another matter that has been awaiting the return of Carb and his warriors."

"What is that?" demanded Carb.

Avan pointed at Tarzan. "There is a stranger who would come into the tribe and be as one of us."

Carb turned his cold eyes in the direction of the ape-man and his face clouded. "Why has he not been destroyed?" he asked. "Let us do away with him at once."

"That is not for you to decide," said Avan, the chief. "The warriors in council alone may say what shall be done."

Carb shrugged. "If the council does not destroy him, I shall kill him myself," he said. "I, Carb, will have no enemy living in the village where I live."

"Let us hold the council at once, then," said Ulan, "for if Carb is greater than the council of the warriors we should know it." There was a note of sarcasm in his voice.

"We have marched for a long time without food or sleep," said Carb. "Let us eat and rest before the council is held, for matters may arise in the council which will demand all of our strength," and he looked pointedly at Ulan.

The other warriors, who had accompanied Carb, also wished to eat and rest before the council was held, and Avan, the chief, acceded to their just demands.

The girl captive had not spoken since she had arrived in the village and she was now turned over to Maral, who was instructed to feed her and permit her to sleep. The bonds were removed from her wrists and she was brought to the cook-fire of the chief's mate, where she stood with an expression of haughty disdain upon her beautiful face.

None of the women revealed any inclination to abuse the prisoner—an attitude which rather surprised Tarzan until the reason for it had been explained to him, for he had upon more than one occasion witnessed the cruelties inflicted upon female prisoners by the women of native African tribes into whose hands the poor creatures had fallen.

Maral, in particular, was kind to the girl. "Why should I be otherwise?" she asked when Tarzan commented upon the fact. "Our daughters, or even anyone of us, may at any time be captured by the warriors of another tribe, and if it were known that we had been cruel to their women, they would doubtless repay us in kind; nor, aside from this, is there any reason why we should be other than kind to a woman who will live among us for the rest of her life. We are few in numbers and we are constantly together. If we harbored enmities and if we quarreled our lives would be less happy. Since you have been here you have never seen quarreling among the women of Clovi; nor would you if you remained here for the rest of your life. There have been quarrelsome women among us, just as at some time there have been crippled children, but as we destroy the one for the good of the tribe we destroy the others."

She turned to the girl. "Sit down," she said pleasantly. "There is meat in the pot. Eat, and then you may sleep. Do not be afraid; you are among friends. I, too, am from Zoram."

At that the girl turned her eyes upon the speaker. "You are from Zoram?" she asked. "Then you must have felt as I feel. I want to go back to Zoram. I would rather die than live elsewhere."

"You will get over that," said Maral. "I felt the same way, but when I became acquainted I found that the people of Clovi are much like the people of Zoram. They have been kind to me; they will be kind to you, and you will be happy as I have been. When they have given you a mate you will look upon life very differently."

"I shall not mate with one of them," cried the girl, stamping her sandaled foot. "I am Jana, The Red Flower of Zoram, and

I choose my own mate."

Maral shook her head sadly. "Thus spoke I once," she said; "but I have changed, and so will you."

"Not I," said the girl. "I have seen but one man with whom I would mate and I shall never mate with another."

"You are Jana," asked Tarzan, "the sister of Thoar?"

The girl looked at him in surprise, and as though she had noticed him now for the first time her eyes quickly investigated him. "Ah," she said, "you are the stranger whom Carb would destroy."

"Yes," replied the ape-man.

"What do you know of Thoar, my brother?"

"We hunted together. We were travelling back to Zoram when I became separated from him. We were following the tracks made by you and a man who was with you when a storm came and obliterated them. Your companion was the man whom I was seeking."

"What do you know of the man who was with me?" demanded the girl.

"He is my friend," replied Tarzan. "What has become of him?"

"He was caught in a canyon during the storm and he must have been drowned," replied Jana sadly. "You are from his country?"

"Yes."

"How did you know he was with me?" she demanded.

"I recognized his tracks and Thoar recognized yours."

"He was a great warrior," she said, "and a very brave man."

"Are you sure that he is dead?" asked Tarzan.

"I am sure," replied The Red Flower of Zoram.

For a time they were silent, both occupied with thoughts of Jason Gridley. "You were his friend," said Jana. She had moved close to him and had seated herself at his side. Now she leaned still closer. "They are going to kill you," she whispered. "I know the people of these tribes better than you and I know Carb. He will have his way. You were Jason's friend and so was I. If we can escape I can lead the way back to Zoram, and if you are Thoar's friend and mine the people of Zoram will have to accept you."

"Why do you whisper?" asked a gruff voice behind them, and turning they saw Avan, the chief. Without waiting for a reply, he turned to Maral. "Take the woman to the cavern," he said. "She will remain there until the council has decided who shall have her as mate, and in the meantime I will place warriors at the entrance to the cavern to see that she does not escape."

As Maral motioned Jana toward the cavern, the latter arose, and as she did so she cast an appealing glance at Tarzan. The ape-man, who was already upon his feet, looked quickly about him. Perhaps a hundred members of the tribe were scattered about the ledge, while near the opening to the trail which led down the canyon and which afforded the only avenue of escape, fully a dozen warriors loitered. Alone he might have won his way through, but with the girl it would have been impossible. He shook his head and his lips, which were turned away from Avan, formed the word, "Wait," and a moment later The Red Flower of Zoram had entered the dark cavern of the Clovians.

"And as for you, man of another country," said Avan, addressing Tarzan, "until the council has decided upon your fate, you are a prisoner. Go, therefore, into the cavern and remain there until the council of warriors has spoken."

A dozen warriors barred his way to freedom now, but they were lolling idly, expecting no emergency. A bold dash for freedom might carry him beyond them before they could realize that he was attempting escape. He was confident that the voice of the council would be adverse to him and when its decision was announced he would be surrounded by all the warriors of Clovi, alert and ready to prevent his escape. Now, therefore, was the most propitious moment; but Tarzan of the Apes made no break for liberty; instead he turned and strode toward the entrance to the cavern, for The Red Flower of Zoram had appealed to him for aid and he would not desert the sister of Thoar and the friend of Jason.

CHAPTER 12

The Phelian Swamp

As JASON GRIDLEY leaped down the canyon side toward the lone warrior who stood facing the attack of the tremendous reptile gliding swiftly through the air from the top of the opposite cliff side, there flashed upon the screen of his recollection the picture of a restoration of a similar extinct reptile and he recognized the creature as a stegosaurus of the Jurassic; but how inadequately had the picture that he had seen carried to his mind the colossal proportions of the creature, or but remotely suggested its terrifying aspect.

Jason saw the lone warrior standing there facing inevitable doom, but in his attitude there was no outward sign of fear. In his right hand he held his puny spear, and in his left his crude stone knife. He would die, but he would give a good account of himself. There was no panic of terror, no futile flight.

The distance between Jason and the stegosaurus was over great for a revolver shot, but the American hoped that he might at least divert the attention of the reptile from its prey and even, perhaps, frighten it away by the unaccustomed sound of the report of the weapon, and so he fired twice in rapid succession as he leaped downward toward the bottom of the canyon. That at least one of the shots struck the reptile was evidenced by the fact that it veered from its course, simultaneously emitting a loud, screaming sound.

Attracted to Jason by the report of the revolver and evidently attributing its hurt to this new enemy, the reptile, using its tail as a rudder and tilting its spine plates up on one side, veered in the direction of the American.

As the two shots shattered the silence of the canyon, the warrior turned his eyes in the direction of the man leaping down the declivity toward him, and then he saw the reptile veer in the direction of the newcomer.

Heredity and training, coupled with experience, had taught this primitive savage that every man's hand was against him, unless that man was a member of his own tribe. Only upon a single occasion in his life had experience controverted these teachings, and so it seemed inconceivable that this stranger, whom he immediately recognized as such, was deliberately risking his life in an effort to succor him; yet there seemed no other explanation, and so the perplexed warrior, instead of seeking to escape now that the attention of the reptile was diverted from him, ran swiftly toward Jason to join forces with him in combatting the attack of the creature.

From the instant that the stegosaurus had leaped from the summit of the cliff, it had hurtled through the air with a speed which seemed entirely out of proportion to its tremendous bulk, so that all that had transpired in the meantime had occupied but a few moments of time, and Jason Gridley found himself facing this onrushing death almost before he had had time to speculate upon the possible results of his venturesome interference.

With wide distended jaws and uttering piercing shrieks, the terrifying creature shot toward him, but now at last it presented an easy target and Jason Gridley was entirely competent to take advantage of the altered situation.

He fired rapidly with both weapons, trying to reach the tiny brain, at the location of which he could only guess and for which his bullets were searching through the roof of the opened mouth. His greatest hope, however, was that the beast could not for long face that terrific fusillade of shots, and in this he was right. The strange and terrifying sound and the pain and shock of the bullets tearing into its skull proved too much for the stegosaurus. Scarcely half a dozen feet from Gridley it swerved upward and passed over his head, receiving two or three bullets in its belly as it did so.

Still shrieking with rage and pain it glided to the ground beyond him.

Almost immediately it turned to renew the attack. This time it came upon its four feet, and Jason saw that it was likely to prove fully as formidable upon the ground as it had been in the air, for considering its tremendous bulk it moved with great agility and speed.

As he stood facing the returning creature, the warrior reached his side.

"Get on that side of him," said the warrior, "and I will attack him on this. Keep out of the way of his tail. Use your spear; you cannot frighten a dyrodor away by making a noise."

Jason Gridley leaped quickly to one side to obey the suggestions of the warrior, smiling inwardly at the naive suggestion of the other that his Colt had been used solely to frighten the creature.

The warrior took his place upon the opposite side of the approaching reptile, but before he had time to cast his spear or Jason to fire again the creature stumbled forward, its nose dug into the ground and it rolled over upon its side dead.

"It is dead!" said the warrior in a surprised tone. "What could have killed it? Neither one of us has cast a spear."

Jason slipped his Colts into their holsters. "These killed it," he said, tapping them.

"Noises do not kill," said the warrior skeptically. "It is not the bark of the jalok or the growl of the ryth that rends the flesh of man. The hiss of the thipdar kills no one."

"It was not the noise that killed it," said Jason, "but if you will examine its head and especially the roof of its mouth you will see what happened when my weapons spoke."

Following Jason's suggestion the warrior examined the head and mouth of the dyrodor and when he had seen the gaping wounds he looked at Jason with a new respect. "Who are you," he asked, "and what are you doing in the land of Zoram?"

"My God!" exclaimed Jason. "Am I in Zoram?"

"You are."

"And you are one of the men of Zoram?" demanded the American.

"I am; but who are you?"

"Tell me, do you know Jana, The Red Flower of Zoram?" insisted Jason.

"What do you know of The Red Flower of Zoram, stranger?" demanded the other. And then suddenly his eyes widened to a new thought. "Tell me," he cried, "by what name do they call you in the country from which you come?"

"My name is Gridley," replied the American; "Jason Gridley."

"Jason!" exclaimed the other; "yes, Jason Gridley, that is it. Tell me, man, where is The Red Flower of Zoram? What did you with her?"

"That is what I am asking you," said Jason. "We became separated and I have been searching for her. But what do you know of me?"

"I followed you for a long time," replied the other, "but the waters fell and obliterated your tracks."

"Why did you follow me?" asked Jason.

"I followed because you were with The Red Flower of Zoram," replied the other. "I followed to kill you, but he said you would not harm her; he said that she went with you willingly. Is that true?"

"She came with me willingly for a while," replied Jason, "and then she left me; but I did not harm her."

"Perhaps he was right then," said the warrior. "I shall wait until I find her and if you have not harmed her, I shall not kill you."

"Whom do you mean by 'he'?" asked Jason. "There is no one in Pellucidar who could possibly know anything about me, except Jana."

"Do you not know Tarzan?" asked the warrior.

"Tarzan!" exclaimed Jason. "You have seen Tarzan? He is alive?"

"I saw him. We hunted together and we followed you and Jana, but he is not alive now; he is dead."

"Dead! You are sure that he is dead?"

"Yes, he is dead."

"How did it happen?"

"We were crossing the summit of the mountains when he was seized by a thipdar and carried away."

Tarzan dead! He had feared as much and yet now that he had proof it seemed unbelievable. His mind could scarcely grasp the significance of the words that he had heard as he recalled the strength and vitality of that man of steel. It seemed incredible that that giant frame should cease to pulsate with life; that those mighty muscles no longer rolled beneath the sleek, bronzed hide; that that courageous heart no longer beat.

"You were very fond of him?" asked the warrior, noticing the silence and dejection of the other.

"Yes," said Jason.

"So was I," said the warrior; "but neither Tar-gash nor I could save him, the thipdar struck so swiftly and was gone before we could cast a weapon."

"Who is Tar-gash?" asked Jason.

"A Sagoth—one of the hairy men," replied the warrior. "They live in the forest and are often used as warriors by the Mahars."

"And he was with you and Tarzan?" inquired Jason.

"Yes. They were together when I first saw them, but now Tarzan is dead and Tar-gash has gone back to his own country and I must proceed upon my search for The Red Flower of Zoram. You have saved my life, man from another country, but I do not know that you have not harmed Jana. Perhaps you have slain her. How am I to know? I do not know what I should do."

"I, too, am looking for Jana," said Jason. "Let us look for her together."

"Then if we find her, she shall tell me whether or not I shall kill you," said the warrior.

Jason could not but recall how angry Jana had been with him. She had almost killed him herself. Perhaps she would find it easier to permit this warrior to kill him. Doubtless the man was her sweetheart and if he knew the truth he would need no urging to destroy a rival, but neither by look nor word did he reveal any apprehension as he replied.

"I will go with you," he said, "and if I have harmed The Red Flower of Zoram you may kill me. What is your name?"

"Thoar," replied the warrior.

Jana had spoken of her brother to Jason, but if she had ever mentioned his name, the American had forgotten it, and so he continued to think that Thoar was the sweetheart and possibly the mate of The Red Flower and his reaction to this belief was unpleasant; yet why it should have been he could not have explained. The more he thought of the matter the more certain he was that Thoar was Jana's mate, for who was there who might more naturally desire to kill one who had wronged her. Yes, he was sure that the man was Jana's mate. The thought made him angry for she had certainly led him to believe that she was not mated. That was just like a woman, he meditated; they were all flirts; they would make a fool of a man merely to pass an idle hour, but she had not made a fool of him. He had not fallen victim to her lures, that is why she had been so angry—her vanity had been piqued—and being a very primitive young person the first thought that had come to her mind had been to kill him. What a little devil she was to try to get him to make love to her when she already had a mate, and thus Jason almost succeeded in working himself into a rage until his sense of humor came to his rescue; yet even though he smiled, way down deep within him something hurt and he wondered why.

"Where did you last see Jana?" asked Thoar. "We can return there and try and locate her tracks."

"I do not know that I can explain," replied Jason. "It is very difficult for me to locate myself or anything else where there are no points of compass."

"We can start together at the point where we found your tracks with Jana's," said Thoar.

"Perhaps that will not be necessary if you are familiar with the country on the other side of the range," said Jason. "Returning toward the mountains from the spot where I first saw Jana, there was a tremendous gorge upon our left. It was toward this gorge that the two men of the four that had been pursuing her ran after I had killed two of their number. Jana tried to find a way to the summit, far to the right of this gorge, but our path was blocked by a deep rift which paralleled the base of the mountains, so that she was compelled to turn back again toward the gorge, into which she descended. The last I saw of her she was going up the gorge, so that if you know where this gorge lies it will not be necessary for us to go all the way back to the point at which I first met her."

"I know the gorge," said Thoar, "and if the two Phelians entered it it is possible that they captured her. We will search in the direction of the gorge then and if we do not find any trace of her, we shall drop down to the country of the Phelians in the lowland."

Through a maze of jagged peaks Thoar led the way. To him time meant nothing; to Jason Gridley it was little more than a memory. When they found food they ate; when they were tired they slept, and always just ahead there were perilous crags to skirt and stupendous cliffs to scale. To the American it would have seemed incredible that a girl ever could find her way here had he not had occasion to follow where The Red Flower of Zoram led.

Occasionally they were forced to take a lower route which led into the forests that climbed high along the slopes of the mountains, and here they found more game and with Thoar's assistance Jason fashioned a garment from the hide of a mountain goat. It was at best but a sketchy garment; yet it sufficed for the purpose for which it was intended and left his arms and legs free. Nor was it long before he realized its advantages and wondered why civilized man of the outer crust should so encumber himself with useless clothing, when the demands of temperature did not require it.

As Jason became better acquainted with Thoar he found his regard for him changing from suspicion to admiration, and finally to a genuine liking for the savage Pellucidarian, in spite of the fact that this sentiment was tinged with a feeling that, while not positive animosity, was yet akin to it. It was difficult for Jason to fathom the sentiment which seemed to animate him. There could be no rivalry between him and this primitive warrior and yet Jason's whole demeanor and attitude toward Thoar was such as might be scrupulously observed by any honorable man toward an honorable opponent or rival.

They seldom, if ever, spoke of Jana; yet thoughts of her were uppermost in the mind of each of them. Jason often found himself reviewing every detail of his association with her; every little characteristic gesture and expression was indelibly imprinted upon his memory, as were the contours of her perfect figure and the radiant loveliness of her face. Not even the bitter words with which she had parted with him could erase the memory of her joyous comradeship. Never before in his life had he missed the companionship of any woman. At times he tried to crowd her from his thoughts by recalling incidents of his friendship with Cynthia Furnois or Barbara Green, but the vision of The Red Flower of Zoram remained persistently in the foreground, while that of Cynthia and Barbara always faded gradually into forgetfulness.

This state of mental subjugation to the personality of an untutored savage, however beautiful, annoyed his ego and he tried to escape it by dwelling upon the sorrow entailed by the death of Tarzan; but somehow he never could convince himself that Tarzan was dead. It was one of those things that it was simply impossible to conceive.

Failing in this, he would seek to occupy his mind with conjectures concerning the fate of Von Horst, Muviro and the Waziri warriors, or upon what was transpiring aboard the great dirigible in search of which his eyes were often scanning the cloudless Pellucidarian sky. But travel where it would, even to his remote Tarzana hills in far off California, it would always return to hover around the girlish figure of The Red Flower of Zoram.

Thoar, upon his part, found in the American a companion after his own heart—a dependable man of quiet ways, always ready to assume his share of the burden and responsibilities of the savage trail they trod.

So the two came at last to the rim of the great gorge and though they followed it up and down for a great distance in each direction they found no trace of Jana, nor any sign that she had passed that way.

"We shall go down to the lowlands," said Thoar, "to the country that is called Pheli and even though we may not find her, we shall avenge her."

The idea of primitive justice suggested by Thoar's decision aroused no opposing question of ethics in the mind of the civilized American; in fact, it seemed quite the most natural thing in the world that he and Thoar should constitute themselves a court of justice as well as the instrument of its punishment, for thus easily does man slough off the thin veneer of civilization, which alone differentiates him from his primitive ancestors.

Thus a gap of perhaps a hundred thousand years which yawned between Thoar of Zoram, and Jason Gridley of Tarzana was closed. Imbued with the same hatred, they descended the slopes of the Mountains of the Thipdars toward the land of Pheli, and the heart of each was hot with the lust to kill. No greedy munitions manufacturer was needed here to start a war.

Down through stately forests and across rolling foothills went Thoar and Jason toward the land of Pheli. The country teemed with game of all descriptions and their way was beset by fierce carnivores, by stupid, irritable herbivores of ponderous weight and short tempers or by gigantic reptiles beneath whose charging feet the earth trembled. It was by the exercise of the superior intelligence of man combined with a considerable share of luck that they passed unscathed to the swamp land where Pheli lies. Here the world seemed dedicated to the reptilia. They swarmed in countless thousands and in all sizes and infinite varieties. Aquatic and amphibious, carnivorous and herbivorous, they hissed and screamed and fought and devoured one another constantly, so that Jason wondered in what intervals they found the time to propagate their kind and he marvelled that the herbivores among them could exist at all. A terrific orgy of extermination seemed to constitute the entire existence of a large proportion of the species and yet the tremendous size of many of them, including several varieties of the herbivores, furnished ample evidence that considerable numbers of them lived to a great age, for unlike mammals, reptiles never cease to grow while they are living.

The swamp, in which Thoar believed the villages of the Phelians were to be found, supported a tremendous forest of gigantic trees and so interlaced were their branches that oftentimes the two men found it expedient to travel among them rather than upon the treacherous, boggy ground. Here, too, the reptiles were smaller, though scarcely less numerous. Among these, however, there were exceptions, and those which caused them the greatest anxiety were snakes of such titanic proportions that when he first encountered one Jason could not believe the testimony of his own eyes. They came upon the creature suddenly as it was in the act of swallowing a trachodon that was almost as large as an elephant. The huge herbivorous dinosaur was still alive and battling bravely to extricate itself from the jaws of the serpent, but not even its giant strength nor its terrific armament of teeth, which included a reserve supply of over four hundred in the lower jaw alone, availed it in its unequal struggle with the colossal creature that was slowly swallowing it alive.

Perhaps it was their diminutive size as much as their brains or luck that saved the two men from the jaws of these horrid creatures. Or, again, it may have been the dense stupidity of the reptiles themselves, which made it comparatively easy for the men to elude them.

Here in this dismal swamp of horrors not even the giant tarags or the equally ferocious lions and leopards of Pellucidar dared venture, and how man existed there it was beyond the power of Jason to conceive. In fact he doubted that the Phelians or any other race of men made their homes here.

"Men could not exist in such a place," he said to Thoar. "Pheli must lie elsewhere."

"No," said his companion, "members of my tribe have come down here more than once in the memory of man to avenge the stealing of a woman and the stories that they have brought back have familiarized us all with the conditions existing in the land of Pheli. This is indeed it."

"You may be right," said Jason, "but, like these snakes that we have seen, I shall have to see the villages of the Phelians before I will believe that they exist here and even then I won't know whether to believe it or not."

"It will not be long now," said Thoar, "before you shall see the Phelians in their own village."

"What makes you think so?" asked Jason.

"Look down below you and you will see what I have been searching for," replied Thoar, pointing.

Jason did as he was bid and discovered a small stream meandering through the swamp. "I see nothing but a brook," he said.

"That is what I have been searching for," replied Thoar. "All of my people who have been here say that Phelians live upon the banks of a river that runs through the swamp. In places the land is high and upon these hills the Phelians build their homes. They do not live in caverns as do we, but they make houses of great trees so strong that not even the largest reptiles can break into them."

"But why should anyone choose to live in such a place?" demanded the American.

"To eat and to breed in comparative peace and contentment," replied Thoar. "The Phelians, unlike the mountain people, are not a race of warriors. They do not like to fight and so they have hidden their villages away in this swamp where no man would care to come and thus they are practically free from human enemies. Also, here, meat abounds in such quantities that food lies always at their doors. For them then the conditions are ideal and here, more than elsewhere in Pellucidar, may they find contentment."

As they advanced now they exercised the greatest caution, knowing that any moment they might come within sight of a Phelian village. Nor was it long before Thoar halted and drew back behind the bole of a tree through which they were passing, then he pointed forward. Jason, looking, saw a bare hill before them, just a portion of which was visible through the trees. It was evident that the hill had been cleared by man, for many stumps remained. Within the range of his vision was but a single house, if such it might be called.

It was constructed of logs, a foot or two in diameter. Three or four of these logs, placed horizontally and lying one upon the other, formed the wall that was presented to Jason's view. The other side wall paralleled it at a distance of five or six feet, and across the top of the upper logs were laid sections of smaller trees, about six inches in diameter, and placed not more than a foot apart. These supported the roof, which consisted of several logs, a little longer than the logs constituting the walls. The roof logs were laid close together, the interstices being filled with mud. The front of the building was formed by shorter logs set upright in the ground, a single small aperture being left to form a doorway. But the most noticeable feature of Phelian architecture consisted of long pointed stakes, which protruded diagonally from the ground at an angle of about forty-five degrees, pointing outward from the base of the walls entirely around the building at intervals of about eighteen inches. The stakes themselves were six or eight inches in diameter and about ten feet long, being sharpened at the upper end, and forming a barrier against which few creatures, however brainless they might be, would venture to hurl themselves.

Drawing closer the two men had a better view of the village, which contained upon that side of the hill they were approaching and upon the top four buildings similar to that which they had first discovered. Close about the base of the hill grew the dense forest, but the hill itself had been entirely denuded of vegetation so that nothing, either large or small, could approach the habitation of the Phelians without being discovered.

No one was in sight about the village, but that did not deceive

Thoar, who guessed that anything which transpired upon the hillside would be witnessed by many eyes peering through the openings between the wall logs from the dim interiors of the long buildings, beneath whose low ceilings Phelians must spend their lives either squatting or lying down, since there was not sufficient headroom to permit an adult to stand erect.

"Well," said Jason, "here we are. Now, what are we going to do?"

Thoar looked longingly at Jason's two Colts. "You have refused to use those for fear of wasting the deaths which they spit from their blue mouths," he said, "but with one of those we might soon find Jana if she was here or quickly avenge her if she is not."

"Come on then," said Jason. "I would sacrifice more than my ammunition for The Red Flower of Zoram." As he spoke he descended from the tree and started toward the nearest Phelian dwelling. Close behind him was Thoar and neither saw the eyes that watched them from among the trees that grew thickly upon the river side of the hill—cruel eyes that gleamed from whiskered faces.

CHAPTER 13

The Horibs

AVAN, CHIEF OF the Clovi, had placed warriors before the entrance to the cavern and as Tarzan approached it to enter they halted him.

"Where are you going?" demanded one.

"Into the cavern," replied Tarzan.

"Why?" asked the warrior.

"I wish to sleep," replied the ape-man. "I have entered often before and no one has ever stopped me."

"Avan has issued orders that no strangers are to enter or leave the cavern until after the council of the warriors," exclaimed the guard.

At this juncture Avan approached. "Let him enter," he said. "I sent him hither, but do not let him come out again."

Without a word of comment or question the Lord of the Jungle passed into the interior of the gloomy cavern of Clovi. It was several moments before his eyes became accustomed to the subdued light within and permitted him to take account of his surroundings.

That portion of the cavern which was visible and with which he was familiar was of considerable extent. He could see the walls on either side, and, very vaguely, a portion of the rear wall, but adjoining that was utter darkness, suggesting that the cavern extended further into the mountainside. Against the walls upon pallets of dry grasses covered with hide lay many warriors and a few women and children, almost all of whom were wrapped in slumber. In the greater light near the entrance a group squatted engaged in whispered conversation as, silently, he moved about the cavern searching for the girl from Zoram. It was she who recognized him first, attracting his attention by a low whistle.

"You have a plan of escape?" she asked as Tarzan seated himself upon a skin beside her.

"No," he said, "all that we may do is to await developments and take advantage of any opportunity that may present itself."

"I should think that it would be easy for you to escape," said the girl; "they do not treat you as a prisoner; you go about among them freely and they have permitted you to retain your weapons."

"I am a prisoner now," he replied. "Avan just instructed the warriors at the entrance not to permit me to leave here until after the council of warriors had decided my fate."

"Your future does not look very bright then," said Jana, "and as for me I already know my fate, but they shall not have me, Carb nor any other!"

They talked together in low tones with many periods of long silence, but when Jana turned the conversation upon the world from which Jason had come, the silences were few and far between. She would not let Tarzan rest, but plied him with questions, the answers to many of which were far beyond her powers to understand. Steam and electricity and all the countless activities of civilized existence which are dependent upon them were utterly beyond her powers of comprehension, as were the heavenly bodies or musical instruments or books, and yet despite what appeared to be the darkest depth of ignorance, to the very bottom of which she had plumbed, she was intelligent and when she spoke of those things pertaining to her own world with which she was familiar, she was both interesting and entertaining.

Presently a warrior near them opened his eyes, sat up and stretched. He looked about him and then he arose to his feet. He walked around the apartment awakening the other warriors.

"Awaken," he said to each, "and attend the council of the warriors."

When he approached Tarzan and Jana he recognized the former and stopped to glare down at him.

"What are you doing here?" he demanded.

Tarzan arose and faced the Clovian warrior, but he did not reply to the other's question.

"Answer me," growled Carb. "Why are you here?"

"You are not the chief," said Tarzan. "Go and ask your question of women and children."

Carb sputtered angrily. "Go!" said Tarzan, pointing toward the exit. For an instant the Clovian hesitated, then he continued on around the apartment, awakening the remaining warriors.

"Now he will see that you are killed," said the girl.

"He had determined on that before," replied Tarzan. "We are no worse off than we were."

Now they lapsed into silence, each waiting for the doom that was to be pronounced upon them. They knew that outside upon the ledge the warriors were sitting in a great circle and that there would be much talking and boasting and argument before any decision was reached, most of it unnecessary, for that has been the way with men who make laws from time immemorial, a great advantage, however, lying with our modern lawmakers in that they know more words than the first ape-men.

As Tarzan and Jana waited a youth entered the cavern. He bore a torch in the light of which he searched about the interior. Presently he discovered Tarzan and came swiftly toward him. It was Ovan.

"The council has reached its decision," he said. "They will kill you and the girl goes to Carb."

Tarzan of the Apes rose to his feet. "Come," he said to Jana, "now is as good a time as any. If we can cross the ledge and reach the trail only a swift warrior can overtake us. And if you are my friend," he continued, turning to Ovan, "and you have said that you are, you will remain silent and give us our chance."

"I am your friend," replied the youth; "that is why I am here, but you would never live to cross the ledge to the trail, there are too many warriors and they are all prepared. They know that you are armed and they expect that you will try to escape."

"There is no other way," said Tarzan.

"There is another way," replied the boy, "and I have come to show it to you."

"Where?" asked Jana.

"Follow me," replied Ovan, and he started back into the remote recesses of the cavern, which were fitfully illumined by his flickering torch, while behind him followed Jana and the ape-man.

The walls of the cavern narrowed, the floor rose steeply ahead of them, so that in places it was only with considerable difficulty that they ascended in the semi-darkness. At last Ovan halted and held his torch high above his head, revealing a small, natural chamber, at the far end of which there was a dark fissure.

"In that dark hole," he said, "lies a trail that leads to the summit of the mountains. Only the chief and the chief's first son ever know of this trail. If my father learns that I have shown it to you, he will have to kill me, but he shall never know for when next they find me I shall be asleep upon a skin in the cavern far below. The trail is steep and rough, but it is the only way. Go now. This is the return I make you for having saved my life." With that he dashed the torch to the floor, leaving them in utter darkness. He did not speak again, but Tarzan heard the soft falls of his sandaled feet groping their way back down toward the cavern of the Clovi.

The ape-man reached out through the darkness and found Jana's hand. Carefully he led her through the stygian darkness toward the mouth of the fissure. Feeling his way step by step, groping forward with his free hand, the ape-man finally discovered the entrance to the trail.

Clambering upward over broken masses of jagged granite through utter darkness, it seemed to the two fugitives that they made no progress whatever. If time could be measured by muscular effort and physical discomfort, the two might have guessed that they passed an eternity in this black fissure, but at length the darkness lessened and they knew that they were approaching the opening in the summit of the mountains; nor was it long thereafter before they emerged into the brilliant light of the noonday sun.

"And now," said Tarzan, "in which direction lies Zoram?"

The girl pointed. "But we cannot reach it by going back that way," she said, "for every trail will be guarded by Carb and his fellows. Do not think that they will let us escape so easily. Perhaps in searching for us they may even find the fissure and follow us here."

"This is your world," said Tarzan. "You are more familiar with it than I. What, then, do you suggest?"

"We should descend the mountains, going directly away from Clovi," replied Jana, "for it is in the mountains that they will look for us. When we have reached the lowland we can turn back along the foot of the range until we are below Zoram, but not until then should we come back to the mountains."

The descent of the mountains was slow because neither of them was familiar with this part of the range. Oftentimes, their way barred by yawning chasms, they were compelled to retrace their steps to find another way around. They ate many times and slept thrice and thus only could Tarzan guess that they had consumed considerable time in the descent, but what was time to them?

During the descent Tarzan had caught glimpses of a vast plain, stretching away as far as the eye could reach. The last stage of their descent was down a long, winding canyon, and when, at last, they came to its mouth they found themselves upon the edge of the plain that Tarzan had seen. It was almost treeless and from where he stood it looked as level as a lake.

"This is the Gyor Cors," said Jana, "and may we not have the bad fortune to meet a Gyor."

"And what is a Gyor?" asked Tarzan.

"Oh, it is a terrible creature," replied Jana. "I have never seen one, but some of the warriors of Zoram have been to the Gyor Cors and they have seen them. They are twice the size of a tandor and their length is more than that of four tall men, lying upon the ground. They have a curved beak and three great horns, two above their eyes and one above their nose. Standing upright at the backs of their heads is a great collar of bony substance covered with thick, horny hide, which protects them from the horns of their fellows and spears of men. They do not eat flesh, but they are irritable and short tempered, charging every creature that they see and thus keeping the Gyor Cors for their own use."

"Theirs is a vast domain," said Tarzan, letting his eyes sweep the illimitable expanse of pasture land that rolled on and on, curving slowly upward into the distant haze, "and your description of them suggests that they have few enemies who would care to dispute their dominion."

"Only the Horibs," replied Jana. "They hunt them for their flesh and hide."

"What are Horibs?" asked Tarzan.

The girl shuddered. "The snake people," she whispered in an awed tone.

"Snake people," repeated Tarzan, "and what are they?"

"Let us not speak of them. They are horrible. They are worse than the Gyors. Their blood is cold and men say that they have no hearts, for they do not possess any of the characteristics that men admire, knowing not friendship or sympathy or love."

Along the bottom of the canyon through which they had descended a mountain torrent had cut a deep gorge, the sides of which were so precipitous that they found it expedient to follow the stream down into the plain in order to discover an easier crossing, since the stream lay between them and Zoram.

They had proceeded for about a mile below the mouth of the canyon; around them were low, rolling hills which gradually merged with the plain below; here and there were scattered clumps of trees; to their knees grew the gently waving grasses that rendered the Gyor Cors a paradise for the huge herbivorous dinosaurs. The noonday sun shown down upon a scene of peace and quiet, yet Tarzan of the Apes was restless. The apparent absence of animal life seemed almost uncanny to one familiar with the usual teeming activity of Pellucidar; yet the ape-man knew that there were creatures about and it was the strange and unfamiliar scent spoors carried to his nostrils that aroused within him a foreboding of ill omen. Familiar odors had no such effect upon him, but here were scents that he could not place, strangely disagreeable in the nostrils of man. They suggested the scent spoor of Histah the snake, but they were not his.

For Jana's sake Tarzan wished that they might quickly find a crossing and ascend again to the higher levels on their journey to Zoram, for there the creatures would be well known to them, and the dangers which they portended familiar dangers with which they were prepared to cope, but the vertical banks of the raging torrent as yet offered no means of descent and now they saw that the appearance of flatness which distance had imparted to the great Gyor Cors was deceptive, since it was cut by ravines and broken by depressions, some of which were of considerable extent and depth. Presently a lateral ravine, opening into the now comparatively shallow gorge of the river, necessitated a detour which took them directly away from Zoram. They had proceeded for about a mile in this direction when they discovered a crossing and as they emerged upon the opposite side the girl touched Tarzan's arm and pointed. The thing that she saw he had seen simultaneously.

"A Gyor," whispered the girl. "Let us lie down and hide in this tall grass."

"He has not seen us yet," said Tarzan, "and he may not come in this direction."

No description of the beast looming tremendously before them could convey an adequate impression of its titanic proportions or its frightful mien. At the first glance Tarzan was impressed by its remarkable likeness to the Gryfs of Pal-ul-don. It had the two large horns above the eyes, a medial horn on the nose, a horny beak and a great, horny hood or transverse crest over the neck, and its coloration was similar but more subdued, the predominant note being a slaty gray with yellowish belly and face. The blue bands around the eyes were less well marked and the red of the hood and the bony protuberances along the spine were less brilliant than in the Gryf. That it was herbivorous, a fact that he had learned from Jana, convinced him that he was looking upon an almost unaltered type of the gigantic triceratop that had, with its fellow dinosaurs, ruled the ancient Jurassic world.

Jana had thrown herself prone among the grasses and was urging Tarzan to do likewise. Crouching low, his eyes just above the grasses, Tarzan watched the huge dinosaur.

"I think he has caught our scent," he said. "He is standing with his head up, looking about him; now he is trotting around in a circle. He is very light on his feet for a beast of such enormous size. There, he has caught a scent, but it is not ours; the wind is not in the right direction. There is something approaching from our left, but it is still at a considerable distance. I can just hear it, a faint suggestion of something moving. The Gyor is looking in that direction now. Whatever is coming is coming swiftly. I can tell by the rapidly increasing volume of sound, and there are more than one—there are many. He is moving forward now to investigate, but he will pass at a considerable distance to our left." Tarzan watched the Gyor and listened to the sound coming from the, as yet, invisible creatures that were approaching. "Whatever is approaching is coming along the bottom of the ravine we just crossed," he whispered. "They will pass directly behind us."

Jana remained hiding low in the grasses. She did not wish to tempt Fate by revealing even the top of her head to attract the attention of the Gyor. "Perhaps we had better try to crawl away while his attention is attracted elsewhere," she suggested.

"They are coming out of the ravine," whispered Tarzan. "They are coming up over the edge—a number of men—but in the name of God what is it that they are riding?"

Jana raised her eyes above the level of the grasses and looked in the direction that Tarzan was gazing. She shuddered. "They are not men," she said; "they are the Horibs and the things upon the backs of which they ride are Gorobors. If they see us we are lost. Nothing in the world can escape the Gorobors, for there is nothing in all Pellucidar so swift as they. Lie still. Our only chance is that they may not discover us."

At sight of the Horibs the Gyor emitted a terrific bellow that shook the ground and, lowering his head, he charged straight for them. Fully fifty of the Horibs on their horrid mounts had emerged from the ravine. Tarzan could see that the riders were armed with long lances—pitiful and inadequate weapons, he thought, with which to face an enraged triceratop. But it soon became apparent that the Horibs did not intend to meet that charge head-on. Wheeling to their right they formed in single file behind their leader and then for the first time Tarzan had an exhibition of the phenomenal speed of the huge lizards upon which they were mounted, which is comparable only to the lightning-like rapidity of a tiny desert lizard known as a swift.

Following tactics similar to those of the plains Indians of western America, the Horibs were circling their prey. The bellowing Gyor, aroused to a frenzy of rage, charged first in one direction and then another, but the Gorobors darted from his path so swiftly that he never could overtake them. Panting and blowing, he presently came to bay and then the Horibs drew their circle closer, whirling dizzily about him, while Tarzan watched the amazing scene, wondering by what means they might ever hope to dispatch the ten tons of incarnate fury that wheeled first this way and then that at the center of their circle.

Presently a Horib darted in close to the Gyor at such speed that the mount and the rider were little more than a blur. The Gyor wheeled to meet him, head down, the three terrible horns set to impale him, and then two other Horibs darted in from the rear upon either side.

As swiftly as they had darted in all three wheeled and were out again, part of the racing circle, but in the sides of the Gyor they had left two lances deeply imbedded. The fury of the wounded triceratop transcended any of his previous demonstrations. His bellowing became a hoarse, coughing scream as once again he lowered his head and charged.

This time he did not turn and charge in another direction as he had in the past, but kept on in a straight line, possibly in the hope of breaking through the encircling Horibs, and to his dismay the ape-man saw that he and Jana were directly in the path of the charging beast. If the Horibs did not turn him, they were lost.

A dozen of the reptile-men darted in upon the rear of the Gyor. A dozen more lances sank deeply into its body, proving sufficient to turn him in an effort to avenge himself upon those who had inflicted these new hurts.

This charge had carried the Gyor within fifty feet of Tarzan and Jana. It had given the ape-man an uncomfortable moment, but its results were almost equally disastrous for it brought the circling Horibs close to their position.

The Gyor stood now with lowered head, breathing heavily and bleeding from more than a dozen wounds. A Horib now rode slowly toward him, approaching him directly from in front. The attention of the triceratop was centered wholly upon this single adversary as two more moved toward him diagonally from the rear, one on either side, but in such a manner that they were concealed from his view by the great transverse crest encircling his neck behind the horns and eyes. The three approached thus to within about fifty feet of the brute and then those in the rear darted forward simultaneously at terrific speed, leaning well forward upon their mounts, their lances lowered. At the same instant each struck heavily upon either side of the Gyor, driving their spears far in. So close did they come to their prey that their mounts struck the shoulders of the Gyor as they turned and darted out again.

For an instant the great creature stood reeling in its tracks and then it slumped forward heavily and rolled over upon its side— the final lances had pierced its heart.

Tarzan was glad that it was over as he had momentarily feared discovery by the circling Horibs and he was congratulating himself upon their good fortune when the entire band of snake-men wheeled their mounts and raced swiftly in the direction of their hiding place. Once more they formed their circle, but this time Tarzan and Jana were at its center. Evidently the Horibs had seen them, but had temporarily ignored them until after they had dispatched the Gyor.

"We shall have to fight," said Tarzan, and as concealment was no longer possible he arose to his feet.

"Yes," said Jana, arising to stand beside him. "We shall have to fight, but the end will be the same. There are fifty of them and we are but two."

Tarzan fitted an arrow to his bow. The Horibs were circling slowly about them inspecting their new prey. Finally they came closer and halted their mounts, facing the two.

Now for the first time Tarzan was able to obtain a good view of the snake-men and their equally hideous mounts. The conformation of the Horibs was almost identical to man insofar as the torso and extremities were concerned. Their three-toed feet and five-toed hands were those of reptiles. The head and face resembled a snake, but pointed ears and two short horns gave a grotesque appearance that was at the same time hideous. The arms were better proportioned than the legs, which were quite shapeless. The entire body was covered with scales, although those upon the hands, feet and face were so minute as to give the impression of bare skin, a resemblance which was further emphasized by the fact that these portions of the body were a much lighter color, approximating the shiny dead whiteness of a snake's belly. They wore a single apron-like garment fashioned from a piece of very heavy hide, apparently that of some gigantic reptile. This garment was really a piece of armor, its sole purpose being, as Tarzan later learned, to cover the soft, white bellies of the Horibs. Upon the breast of each garment was a strange device—an eight-pronged cross with a circle in the center. Around his waist each Horib wore a leather belt, which supported a scabbard in which was inserted a bone knife. About each wrist and above each elbow was a band or bracelet. These completed their apparel and or-naments. In addition to his knife each Horib carried a long lance shod with bone. They sat on their grotesque mounts with their toes locked behind the elbows of the Gorobors, anomodont reptiles of the Triassic, known to paleontologists as Pareiasuri. Many of these creatures measured ten feet in length, though they stood low upon squat and powerful legs.

As Tarzan gazed in fascination upon the Horibs, whose "blood ran cold and who had no hearts," he realized that he might be gazing upon one of the vagaries of evolution, or possibly upon a replica of some form that had once existed upon the outer crust and that had blazed the trail that some, to us, unknown creature must have blazed from the age of reptiles to the age of man. Nor did it seem to him, after reflection, any more remarkable that a man-like reptile might evolve from reptiles than that birds should have done so or, as scientific discoveries are now demonstrating, mammals must have.

These thoughts passed quickly, almost instantaneously, through his mind as the Horibs sat there with their beady, lidless eyes fastened upon them, but if Tarzan had been astounded by the appearance of these creatures the emotion thus aroused was nothing compared with the shock he received when one of them spoke, addressing him in the common language of the gilaks of Pellucidar.

"You cannot escape," he said. "Lay down your weapons."

CHAPTER 14

Through the Dark Forest

JASON GRIDLEY RAN swiftly up the hill toward the Phelian village in which he hoped to find The Red Flower of Zoram and at his side was Thoar, ready with spear and knife to rescue or avenge his sister, while behind them, concealed by the underbrush that grew beneath the trees along the river's bank, a company of swarthy, bearded men watched the two.

To Thoar's surprise no defending warriors rushed from the building they were approaching, nor did any sound come from the interior. "Be careful," he cautioned Jason, "we may be running into a trap," and the American, profiting by the advice of his companion, advanced more cautiously. To the very entrance of the building they came and as yet no opposition to their advance had manifested itself.

Jason stopped and looked through the low doorway, then, stooping, he entered with Thoar at his heels.

"There is no one here," said Jason; "the building is deserted."

"Better luck in the next one then," said Thoar; but there was no one in the next building, nor in the next, nor in any of the buildings of the Phelian village.

"They have all gone," said Jason.

"Yes," replied Thoar, "but they will return. Let us go down among the trees at the riverside and wait for them there in hiding."

Unconscious of danger, the two walked down the hillside and entered the underbrush that grew luxuriantly beneath the trees. They followed a narrow trail, worn by Phelian sandals.

Scarcely had the foliage closed about them when a dozen men sprang upon them and bore them to the ground. In an instant they were disarmed and their wrists bound behind their backs; then they were jerked roughly to their feet and Jason Gridley's eyes went wide as they got the first glimpse of his captors.

"Well, for Pete's sake!" he exclaimed. "I have learned to look with comparative composure upon woolly rhinoceroses, mammoths, trachodons, pterodactyls and dinosaurs, but I never expected to see Captain Kidd, Lafitte and Sir Henry Morgan in the heart of Pellucidar."

In his surprise he reverted to his native tongue, which, of course, none of the others understood.

"What language is that?" demanded one of their captors. "Who are you and from what country do you come?"

"That is good old American, from the U.S.A.," replied Jason; "but who the devil are you and why have you captured us?" and then turning to Thoar, "these are not the Phelians, are they?"

"No," replied Thoar. "These are strange men, such as I have never before seen."

"We know who you are," said one of the bearded men. "We know the country from which you come. Do not try to deceive us."

"Very well, then, if you know, turn me loose, for you must know that we haven't a war on with anyone."

"Your country is always at war with Korsar," replied the speaker. "You are a Sarian. I know it by the weapons that you carry. The moment I saw them, I knew that you were from distant Sari. The Cid will be glad to have you and so will Bulf. Perhaps," he added, turning to one of his fellows, "this is Tanar, himself. Did you see him when he was a prisoner in Korsar?"

"No, I was away upon a cruise," replied the other. "I did not see him, but if this is indeed he we shall be well rewarded."

"We might as well return to the ship now," said the first speaker. "There is no use waiting any longer for these flat-footed natives with but one chance in a thousand of finding a good looking woman among them."

"They told us further down the river that these people sometimes captured women from Zoram. Perhaps it would be well to wait."

"No," said the other, "I should like well enough to see one of these women from Zoram that I have heard of all my life, but the natives will not return as long as we are in the vicinity. We have been gone from the ship too long now and if I know the captain, he will be wanting to slit a few throats by the time we get back."

Moored to a tree along the shore and guarded by five other Korsars was a ship's longboat, but of a style that was reminiscent of Jason's boyhood reading as were the bearded men with their bizarre costumes, their great pistols and cutlasses and their ancient arquebuses.

The prisoners were bundled into the boat, the Korsars entered and the craft was pushed off into the stream, which here was narrow and swift.

As the current bore them rapidly along Jason had an opportunity to examine his captors. They were as villainous a looking crew as he had ever imagined outside of fiction and were more typically piratical than the fiercest pirates of his imagination. What with earrings and, in some instances, nose rings of gold, with the gay handkerchiefs bound about their heads and body sashes around their waists, they would have presented a gorgeous and colorful picture at a distance sufficiently great to transform their dirt and patches into a pleasing texture.

Although in the story of Tanar of Pellucidar that Jason had received by radio from Perry, he had become familiar with the appearance and nature of the Korsars, yet he now realized that heretofore he had accepted them more as he had accepted the pirates of history and of his boyhood reading—as fictionary or, at best, legendary—and not men of flesh and bone such as he saw before him, their mouths filled with oaths and coarse jokes, the grim and filth of reality marking them as real human beings.

In these savage Korsars, their boat, their apparel and their ancient firearms, Jason saw conclusive proof of their descent from men of the outer crust and realized how they must have carried to the mind of David Innes an overwhelming conviction of the existence of a polar opening leading from Pellucidar to the outer world.

While Thoar was disheartened by the fate that had thrown them into the hands of these strange people, Jason was not at all sure but that it might prove a stroke of fortune for himself, as from the conversation and comments that he had heard since their capture it seemed reasonable to assume that they were to be taken to Korsar, the city in which David Innes was confined and which was, therefore, the first goal of their expedition to effect the rescue of the Emperor of Pellucidar.

That he would arrive there alone and a prisoner were not in themselves causes for rejoicing; yet, on the whole, he would be no worse off than to remain wandering aimlessly through a country filled with unknown dangers without the faintest shadow of a hope of ever being able to locate his fellows. Now, at least, he was almost certain of being transported to a place that they also were attempting to reach and thus the chances of a reunion were so much the greater.

The stream down which they floated wound through a swampy forest, crossing numerous lagoons that sometimes were of a size that raised them to the dignity of lakes. Everywhere the waters and the banks teemed with reptilian life, suggesting to Jason Gridley that he was reviewing a scene such as might have been enacted in a Mesozoic paradise countless ages before upon the outer crust. So numerous and oftentimes so colossal and belligerent were the savage reptiles that the descent of the river became a running fight, during which the Korsars were constantly upon the alert and frequently were compelled to discharge their arquebuses in defense of their lives. More often than not the noise of the weapons frightened off the attacking reptiles, but occasionally one would persist in its attack until it had been killed; nor was the possibility ever remote that in one of these encounters some fierce and brainless saurian might demolish their craft and with its fellows devour the crew.

Jason and Thoar had been placed in the middle of the boat, where they squatted upon the bottom, their wrists still secured behind their backs. Close to Jason was a Korsar whose fellows addressed him as Lajo. There was something about this fellow that attracted Jason's particular attention. Perhaps it was his more open countenance or a less savage and profane demeanor. He had not joined the others in the coarse jokes that were directed against their captives; in fact, he paid little attention to anything other than the business of defending the boat against the attacking monsters.

There seemed to be no one in command of the party, all matters being discussed among them and in this way a decision arrived at; yet Jason had noticed that the others listened attentively when Lajo spoke, which was seldom, though always intelligently and to the point. Guided by the result of these observations he selected Lajo as the most logical Korsar through whom to make a request. At the first opportunity, therefore, he attracted the man's attention.

"What do you want?" asked Lajo.

"Who is in command here?" asked Jason.

"No one," replied the Korsar. "Our officer was killed on the way up. Why do you ask?"

"I want the bonds removed from our wrists," replied Jason. "We cannot escape. We are unarmed and outnumbered and, therefore, cannot harm you; while in the event that the boat is destroyed or capsized by any of these reptiles we shall be helpless with our wrists tied behind our backs."

Lajo drew his knife.

"What are you going to do?" asked one of the other Korsars who had been listening to the conversation.

"I am going to cut their bonds," replied Lajo. "There is nothing to be gained by keeping them bound."

"Who are you to say that their bonds shall be cut?" demanded the other belligerently.

"Who are you to say that they shall not?" returned Lajo quietly, moving toward the prisoners.

"I'll show you who I am," shouted the other, whipping out his knife and advancing toward Lajo.

There was no hesitation. Like a panther Lajo swung upon his adversary, striking up the other's knife-hand with his left forearm and at the same time plunging his villainous looking blade to the hilt in the other's breast. Voicing a single bloodcurdling scream the man sank lifeless to the bottom of the boat. Lajo wrenched his knife from the corpse, wiped it upon his adversary's shirt and quietly cut the bonds that confined the wrists of Thoar and Jason. The other Korsars looked on, apparently unmoved by the killing of their fellow, except for a coarse joke or two at the expense of the dead man and a grunt of approbation for Lajo's act.

The killer removed the weapons from the body of the dead man and cast them aft out of reach of the prisoners, then he motioned to the corpse. "Throw it overboard," he commanded, addressing Jason and Thoar.

"Wait," cried another member of the crew. "I want his boots."

"His sash is mine," cried another, and presently half a dozen of them were quarreling over the belongings of the corpse like a pack of dogs over a bone. Lajo took no part in this altercation and presently the few wretched belongings that had served to cover the nakedness of the dead man were torn from his corpse and divided among them by the simple expedient of permitting the stronger to take what they could; then Jason and Thoar eased the naked body over the side, where it was immediately seized upon by voracious denizens of the river.

Interminable, to an unknown destination, seemed the journey to Jason. They ate and slept many times and still the river wound through the endless swamp. The luxuriant vegetation and flowering blooms which lined the banks long since had ceased to interest, their persistent monotony making them almost hateful to the eyes.

Jason could not but wonder at the superhuman efforts that must have been necessary to row this large, heavy boat upstream in the face of all the terrific assaults which must have been launched upon it by the reptilian hordes that contested every mile of the downward journey.

But presently the landscape changed, the river widened and the low swamp gave way to rolling hills. The forests, which still lined the banks, were freer from underbrush, suggesting that they might be the feeding grounds of droves of herbivorous animals, a theory that was soon substantiated by sight of grazing herds, among which Jason recognized red deer, bison, bos and several other species of herbivorous animals. The forest upon the right bank was open and sunny and with its grazing herds presented a cheerful aspect of warmth and life, but the forest upon the left bank was dark and gloomy. The foliage of the trees, which grew to tremendous proportions, was so dense as practically to shut out the sunlight, the space between the boles giving the impression of long, dark aisles, gloomy and forbidding.

There were fewer reptiles in the stream here, but the Korsars appeared unusually nervous and apprehensive of danger after they entered this stretch of the river. Previously they had been drifting with the current, using but a single oar, scull fashion, from the stern to keep the nose of the boat pointed downstream, but now they manned the oars, pressing Jason and Thoar into service to row with the others. Loaded arquebuses lay beside the oarsmen, while in the bow and stern armed men were constantly upon watch. They paid little attention to the right bank of the river, but toward the dark and gloomy left bank they directed their nervous, watchful gaze. Jason wondered what it was that they feared, but he had no opportunity to inquire and there was no respite from the rowing, at least not for him or Thoar, though the Korsars alternated between watching and rowing.

Between oars and current they were making excellent progress, though whether they were close to the end of the danger zone or not, Jason had no means of knowing any more than he could guess the nature of the menace which must certainly threaten them if aught could be judged by the attitude of the Korsars.

The two prisoners were upon the verge of exhaustion when Lajo noticed their condition and relieved them from the oars. How long they had been rowing, Jason could not determine, although he knew that while no one had either eaten or slept, since they had entered this stretch of the river, the time must have been considerable. The distance they had come he estimated roughly at something over a hundred miles, and he and Thoar had been continuously at the oars during the entire period, without food or sleep, but they had barely thrown themselves to the bottom of the boat when a cry, vibrant with excitement, arose from the bow. "There they are!" shouted the man, and instantly all was excitement aboard the boat.

"Keep to the oars!" shouted Lajo. "Our best chance is to run through them."

Although almost too spent with fatigue to find interest even in impending death, Jason dragged himself to a sitting position that raised his eyes above the level of the gunwales of the boat. At first he could not even vaguely classify the horde of creatures swimming out upon the bosom of the placid river with the evident intention of intercepting them, but presently he saw that they were man-like creatures riding upon the backs of hideous reptiles. They bore long lances and their scaly mounts sped through the waters at incredible speed. As the boat approached them he saw that the creatures were not men, though they had the forms of men, but were grotesque and horrid reptiles with the heads of lizards to whose naturally frightful mien, pointed ears and short horns added a certain horrid grotesquery.

"My God!" he exclaimed. "What are they?"

Thoar, who had also dragged himself to a sitting posture, shuddered. "They are the Horibs," he said. "It is better to die than to fall into their clutches."

Carried downward by the current and urged on by the long sweeps and its own terrific momentum, the heavy boat shot straight toward the hideous horde. The distance separating them was rapidly closing; the boat was almost upon the leading Horib when an arquebus in the bow spoke. Its loud report broke the menacing silence that had overhung the river like a pall. Directly in front of the boat's prow the horde of Horibs separated and a moment later they were racing along on either side of the craft. Arquebuses were belching smoke and fire, scattering the bits of iron and pebbles with which they were loaded among the hissing enemy, but for every Horib that fell there were two to take its place.

Now they withdrew to a little distance, but with apparently no effort whatever their reptilian mounts kept pace with the boat and then, one after another on either side, a rider would dart in and cast his lance; nor apparently ever did one miss its mark. So deadly was their aim that the Korsars were compelled to abandon their oars and drop down into the bottom of the boat, raising themselves above the gunwales only long enough to fire their arquebuses, when they would again drop down into concealment to reload. But even these tactics could not preserve them for long, since the Horibs, darting in still closer to the side of the boat, could reach over the edge and lance the inmates. Straight to the muzzles of the arquebuses they came, apparently entirely devoid of any conception of fear; great holes were blown entirely through the bodies of some, others were decapitated, while more than a score lost a hand or an arm, yet still they came.

Presently one succeeded in casting the noose of a long leather rope over a cleat upon the gunwale and instantly several of the Horibs seized it and headed their mounts toward the river's bank.

Practically exhausted and without weapons to defend themselves, Jason and Thoar had remained lying upon the bottom of the boat almost past caring what fate befell them. Half covered by the corpses of the Korsars that had fallen, they lay in a pool of blood. About them arquebuses still roared amid screams and curses, and above all rose the shrill, hissing screech that seemed to be the war cry of the Horibs.

The boat was dragged to shore and the rope made fast about the bole of a tree, though three times the Korsars had cut the line and three times the Horibs had been forced to replace it.

There was only a handful of the crew who had not been killed or wounded when the Horibs left their mounts and swarmed over the gunwales to fall upon their prey. Cutlasses, knives and arquebuses did their deadly work, but still the slimy snake-men came, crawling over the bodies of their dead to fall upon the survivors until the latter were practically buried by greater numbers.

When the battle was over there were but three Korsars who had escaped death or serious wounds—Lajo was one of them. The Horibs bound their wrists and took them ashore, after which they started unloading the dead and wounded from the boat, killing the more seriously wounded with their knives. Coming at last upon Jason and Thoar and finding them unwounded, they bound them as they had the living Korsars and placed them with the other prisoners on the shore.

The battle over, the prisoners secured, the Horibs now fell upon the corpses of the dead, nor did they rest until they had devoured them all, while Jason and his fellow prisoners sat nauseated with horror during the grizzly feast. Even the Korsars, cruel and heartless as they were, shuddered at the sight.

"Why do you suppose they are saving us?" asked Jason.

Lajo shook his head. "I do not know," he said.

"Doubtless to feed us to their women and children," said Thoar. "They say that they keep their human prisoners and fatten them."

"You know what they are? You have seen them before?" Lajo asked Thoar.

"Yes, I know what they are," said Thoar, "but these are the first that I have ever seen. They are the Horibs, the snake people. They dwell between the Rela Am and the Gyor Cors."

As Jason watched the Horibs at their grizzly feast, he became suddenly conscious of a remarkable change that was taking place in their appearance. When he had first seen them and all during the battle they had been of a ghastly bluish color, the hands, feet and faces being several shades paler than the balance of the body, but as they settled down to their gory repast this hue gradually faded to be replaced by a reddish tinge, which varied in intensity in different individuals, the faces and extremities of a few of whom became almost crimson as the feast progressed.

If the appearance and blood-thirsty ferocity of the creatures appalled him, he was no less startled when he first heard them converse in the common language of the men of Pellucidar.

The general conformation of the creatures, their weapons, which consisted of long lances and stone knives, the apron-like apparel which they wore and the evident attempt at ornamentation as exemplified by the insignia upon the breasts of their garments and the armlets which they wore, all tended toward establishing a suggestion of humanity that was at once grotesque and horrible, but when to these other attributes was added human speech the likeness to man created an impression that was indescribably repulsive.

So powerful was the fascination that the creatures aroused in the mind of Jason that he could divert neither his thoughts nor his eyes from them. He noticed that while the majority of them were about six feet in height, there were many much smaller, ranging downward to about four feet, while there was one tremendous individual that must have been fully nine feet tall; yet all were proportioned identically and the difference in height did not have the appearance of being at all related to a difference in age, except that the scales upon the largest of them were considerably thicker and coarser. Later, however, he was to learn that differences in size predicated differences in age, the growth of these creatures being governed by the same law which governs the growth of reptiles, which, unlike mammals, continue to grow throughout the entire duration of their lives.

When they had gorged themselves upon the flesh of the Korsars, the Horibs lay down, but whether to sleep or not Jason never knew since their lidless eyes remained constantly staring. And now a new phenomenon occurred. Gradually the reddish tinge faded from their bodies to be replaced by a dull brownish gray, which harmonized with the ground upon which they lay.

Exhausted by his long tour at the oars and by the horrors that he had witnessed, Jason gradually drifted off into deep slumber, which was troubled by hideous dreams in which he saw Jana in the clutches of a Horib. The creature was attempting to devour The Red Flower of Zoram, while Jason struggled with the bonds that secured him.

He was awakened by a sharp pain in his shoulder and opening his eyes he saw one of the homosaurians, as he had mentally dubbed them, standing over him, prodding him with the point of his sharp lance. "Make less noise," said the creature, and Jason realized that he must have been raving in his sleep.

The other Horibs were rising from the ground, voicing strange whistling hisses, and presently from the waters of the river and from the surrounding aisles of the gloomy forest their hideous mounts came trooping in answer to the summons.

"Stand up!" said the Horib who had awakened Jason. "I am going to remove your bonds," he continued. "You cannot escape. If you try to you will be killed. Follow me," he then commanded after he had removed the thongs which secured Jason's wrists.

Jason accompanied the creature into the midst of the herd of periosauri that was milling about, snapping and hissing, along the shore of the river.

Although the Gorobors all looked alike to Jason, it was evident that the Horibs differentiated between individuals among them for he who was leading Jason threaded his way through the mass of slimy bodies until he reached the side of a particular individual.

"Get up," he said, motioning Jason to mount the creature. "Sit well forward on its neck."

It was with a sensation of the utmost disgust that Jason vaulted onto the back of the Gorobor. The feel of its cold, clammy, rough hide against his naked legs sent a chilly shudder up his spine. The reptile-man mounted behind him and presently the entire company was on the march, each of the other prisoners being mounted in front of a Horib.

Into the gloomy forest the strange cavalcade marched, down dark, winding corridors overhung with dense vegetation, much of which was of a dead pale cast through lack of sunlight. A clammy chill, unusual in Pellucidar, pervaded the atmosphere and a feeling of depression weighed heavily upon all the prisoners.

"What are you going to do with us?" asked Jason after they had proceeded in silence for some distance.

"You will be fed upon eggs until you are fit to be eaten by the females and the little ones," replied the Horib. "They tire of fish and Gyor flesh. It is not often that we get as much gilak meat as we have just had."

Jason relapsed into silence, discovering that, as far as he was concerned, the Horib was conversationally a total loss and for long after the horror of the creature's reply weighed upon his mind. It was not that he feared death; it was the idea of being fattened for slaughter that was peculiarly abhorrent.

As they rode between the never ending trees he tried to speculate as to the origin of these grewsome creatures. It seemed to him that they might constitute a supreme effort upon the part of Nature to reach a higher goal by a less devious route than that which evolution had pursued upon the outer crust from the age of reptiles upwards to the age of man.

During the march Jason caught occasional glimpses of Thoar and the other prisoners, though he had no opportunity to exchange words with them, and after what seemed an interminable period of time the cavalcade emerged from the forest into the sunlight and Jason saw in the distance the shimmering blue waters of an inland lake. As they approached its shores he discerned throngs of Horibs, some swimming or lolling in the waters of the lake, while others lay or squatted upon the muddy bank. As the company arrived among them they showed only a cold, reptilian interest in the returning warriors, though some of the females and young evinced a suggestive interest in the prisoners.

The adult females differed but slightly from the males. Aside from the fact that they were hornless and went naked, Jason could discover no other distinguishing feature. He saw no signs of a village, nor any indication of arts or crafts other than those necessary to produce their crude weapons and the simple apron-like armor that the warriors wore to protect the soft skin of their bellies.

The prisoners were now dragged from their mounts and herded together by several of the warriors, who conducted them along the edge of the lake toward a slightly higher bank.

On the way they passed a number of females laying eggs, which they deposited in the soft, warm mud just above the water line, covering them lightly with mud, afterwards pushing a slender stake into the ground at the spot to mark the nest. All along the shore at this point were hundreds of such stakes and further on Jason saw several tiny Horibs, evidently but just hatched, wriggling upward out of the mud. No one paid the slightest attention to them as they stumbled and reeled about trying to accustom themselves to the use of their limbs, upon all four of which they went at first, like tiny, grotesque lizards.

Arrived at the higher bank the warrior in charge of Thoar, who was in the lead, suddenly clapped his hand over the prisoner's mouth, pinching Thoar's nose tightly between his thumb and first finger, and, without other preliminaries, dove head foremost into the waters of the lake carrying his victim with him.

Jason was horrified as he saw his friend and companion disappear beneath the muddy waters, which, after a moment of violent agitation, settled down again, leaving only an ever widening circular ripple to mark the spot where the two had disappeared. An instant later another Horib dove in with Lajo and in rapid succession the other two Korsars shared a similar fate.

With a superhuman effort Jason sought to tear himself free from the clutches of his captor, but the cold, clammy hands held him tightly. One of them was suddenly clapped over his mouth and nose and an instant later he felt the warm waters of the lake close about him.

Still struggling to free himself he was conscious that the Horib was carrying him swiftly beneath the surface. Presently he felt slimy mud beneath him, along which his body was being dragged. His lungs cried out in tortured agony for air, his senses reeled and momentarily all went black before him, though no blacker than the stygian darkness of the hole into which he was being dragged, and then the hand was removed from his mouth and nose; mechanically his lungs gasped for air and as consciousness slowly returned Jason realized that he was not drowned, but that he was lying upon a bed of mud inhaling air and not water.

Total darkness surrounded him; he felt a clammy body scrape against his, and then another and another. There was a sound of splashing, gurgling water and then silence—the silence of the tomb.

CHAPTER 15

Prisoners

STANDING UPON THE edge of the great Gyor plains surrounded by armed creatures, who had but just demonstrated their ability to destroy one of the most powerful and ferocious creatures that evolution has ever succeeded in producing, Tarzan of the Apes was yet loath to lay down his weapons as he had been instructed and surrender, without resistance, to an unknown fate.

"What do you intend to do with us?" he demanded of the Horib who had ordered him to lay down his weapons.

"We shall take you to our village where you will be well fed," replied the creature. "You cannot escape us; no one escapes the Horibs."

The ape-man hesitated. The Red Flower of Zoram moved closer to his side. "Let us go with them," she whispered. "We cannot escape them now; there are too many of them. Possibly if we go with them we shall find an opportunity later."

Tarzan nodded and then he turned to the Horib. "We are ready," he said.

Mounted upon the necks of Gorobors, each in front of a Horib warrior, they were carried across a corner of the Gyor Cors to the same gloomy forest through which Jason and Thoar had been taken, though they entered it from a different direction.

Rising at the east end of the Mountains of the Thipdars, a river flows in a southeasterly direction entering upon its course the gloomy forest of the Horibs, through which it runs down to the Rela Am, or River of Darkness. It was near the confluence of these two rivers that the Korsars had been attacked by the Horibs and it was along the upper reaches of the same river that Tarzan and Jana were being conducted down stream toward the village of the lizard-men.

The lake of the Horibs lies at a considerable distance from the eastern end of the Mountains of the Thipdars, perhaps five hundred miles, and where there is no time and distances are measured by food and sleep it makes little difference whether places are separated by five miles or five hundred. One man might travel a thousand miles without mishap, while another, in attempting to go one mile, might be killed, in which event the one mile would be much further than the thousand miles, for, in fact, it would have proved an interminable distance to him who had essayed it in this instance.

As Tarzan and Jana rode through the dismal forest, hundreds of miles away Jason Gridley drew himself to a sitting position in such utter darkness that he could almost feel it. "God!" he exclaimed.

"Who spoke?" asked a voice out of the darkness, and Jason recognized the voice as Thoar's.

"It is I, Jason," replied Gridley.

"Where are we?" demanded another voice. It was Lajo.

"It is dark. I wish they had killed us," said a fourth voice.

"Don't worry," said a fifth, "we shall be killed soon enough."

"We are all here," said Jason. "I thought we were all done for when I saw them drag you into the water one by one."

"Where are we?" demanded one of the Korsars. "What sort of hole is this into which they have put us?"

"In the world from which I come," said Jason, "there are huge reptiles, called crocodiles, who build such nests or retreats in the banks of rivers, just above the water line, but the only entrance leads down below the waters of the river. It is such a hole as that into which we have been dragged."

"Why can't we swim out again?" asked Thoar.

"Perhaps we could," replied Jason, "but they would see us and bring us back again."

"Are we going to lie here in the mud and wait to be slaughtered?" demanded Lajo.

"No," said Jason; "but let us work out a reasonable plan of escape. It will gain us nothing to act rashly."

For some time the men sat in silence, which was finally broken by the American. "Do you think we are alone here?" he asked in a low tone. "I have listened carefully, but I have heard no sound other than our own breathing."

"Nor I," said Thoar.

"Come closer then," said Jason, and the five men groped through the darkness and arranged themselves in a circle, where they squatted leaning forward till their heads touched. "I have a plan," continued Jason. "When they were bringing us here I noticed that the forest grew close to the lake at this point. If we can make a tunnel into the forest, we may be able to escape."

"Which way is the forest?" asked Lajo.

"That is something that we can only guess at," replied Jason. "We may guess wrong, but we must take the chance. But I think that it is reasonable to assume that the direction of the forest is directly opposite the entrance through which we were carried into this hole."

"Let us start digging at once," exclaimed one of the Korsars.

"Wait until I locate the entrance," said Thoar.

He crawled away upon his hands and knees, groping through the darkness and the mud. Presently he announced that he had found the opening, and from the direction of his voice the others knew where to start digging.

All were filled with enthusiasm, for success seemed almost within the range of possibility, but now they were confronted with the problem of the disposal of the dirt which they excavated from their tunnel. Jason instructed Lajo to remain at the point where they intended excavating and then had the others crawl in different directions in an effort to estimate the size of the chamber in which they were confined. Each man was to crawl in a straight line in the direction assigned him and count the number of times that his knees touched the ground before he came to the end of the cavern.

By this means they discovered that the cave was long and narrow and, if they were correct in the directions they had assumed, it ran parallel to the lake shore. For twenty feet it extended in one direction and for over fifty in the other.

It was finally decided that they should distribute the earth equally over the floor of the chamber for a while and then carry it to the further end, piling it against the further wall uniformly so as not to attract unnecessary attention in the event that any of the Horibs visited them.

Digging with their fingers was slow and laborious work, but they kept steadily at it, taking turns about. The man at work would push the dirt behind him and the others would gather it up and distribute it, so that at no time was there a fresh pile of earth upon the ground to attract attention should a Horib come. Horibs did come; they brought food, but the men could hear the splash of their bodies in the water as they dove into the lake to reach the tunnel leading to the cave and being thus warned they grouped themselves in front of the entrance to their tunnel effectually hiding it from view. The Horibs who came into the chamber at no time gave any suggestion of suspicion that all was not right. While it was apparent that they could see in the dark it was also quite evident that they could not discern things clearly and thus the greatest fear that their plot might be discovered was at least partially removed.

After considerable effort they had succeeded in excavating a tunnel some three feet in diameter and about ten feet long when Jason, who was excavating at the time, unearthed a large shell, which greatly facilitated the process of excavation. From then on their advance was more rapid, yet it seemed to them all that it was an endless job; nor was there any telling at what moment the Horibs would come to take them for the feast.

It was Jason's wish to get well within the forest before turning their course upward toward the surface, but to be certain of this he knew that they must first encounter roots of trees and pass beyond them, which might necessitate a detour and delay; yet to come up prematurely would be to nullify all that they had accomplished so far and to put a definite end to all hope of escape.

And while the five men dug beneath the ground in the dark hole that was stretching slowly out beneath the dismal forest of the Horibs a great ship rode majestically high in air above the northern slopes of the Mountains of the Thipdars.

"They never passed this way," said Zuppner. "Nothing short of a mountain goat could cross this range."

"I quite agree with you, sir," said Hines. "We might as well search in some other direction now."

"God!" exclaimed Zuppner, "if I only knew in what direction to search."

Hines shook his head. "One direction is as good as another, sir," he said.

"I suppose so," said Zuppner, and, obeying his light touch upon the helm, the nose of the great dirigible swung to port. Following an easterly course she paralleled the Mountains of the Thipdars and sailed out over the Gyor Cors. A slight turn of the wheel would have carried her to the southeast, across the dismal forest through whose gloomy corridors Tarzan and Jana were being borne to a horrible fate. But Captain Zuppner did not know and so the O-220 continued on toward the east, while the Lord of the Jungle and The Red Flower of Zoram rode silently toward their doom.

From almost the moment that they had entered the forest Tarzan had known that he might escape. It would have been the work of but an instant to have leaped from the back of the Gorobor upon which he was riding to one of the lower branches of the forest, some of which barely grazed their heads as they passed beneath, and once in the trees he knew that no Horib nor any Gorobor could catch him, but he could not desert Jana; nor could he acquaint her with his plans for they were never sufficiently close together for him to whisper to her unheard by the Horibs. But even had he been able to lay the whole thing before her, he doubted her ability to reach the safety of the trees before the Horibs recaptured her.

If he could but get near enough to take hold of her, he was confident that he could effect a safe escape for both of them and so he rode on in silence, hoping against hope that the opportunity he so desired would eventually develop.

They had reached the upper end of the lake and were skirting its western shore and, from remarks dropped by the Horibs in their conversations, which were far from numerous, the ape-man guessed that they were almost at their destination, and still escape seemed as remote as ever.

Chafing with impatience Tarzan was on the point of making a sudden break for liberty, trusting that the unexpectedness of his act would confuse the lizard-men for just the few seconds that would be necessary for him to throw Jana to his shoulder and swing to the lower terrace that beckoned invitingly from above.

The nerves and muscles of Tarzan of the Apes are trained to absolute obedience to his will; they are never surprised into any revelation of emotion, nor are they often permitted to reveal what is passing in the mind of the ape-man when he is in the presence of strangers or enemies, but now, for once, they were almost shocked into revealing the astonishment that filled him as a vagrant breeze carried to his nostrils a scent spoor that he had never thought to know again.

The Horibs were moving almost directly up wind so that Tarzan knew that the authors of the familiar odors that he had sensed were somewhere ahead of them. He thought quickly now, but not without weighing carefully the plan that had leaped to his mind the instant that that familiar scent spoor had impinged upon his nostrils. His major consideration was for the safety of the girl, but in order to rescue her he must protect himself. He felt that it would be impossible for them both to escape simultaneously, but there was another way now—a way which seemed to offer excellent possibilities for success. Behind him, upon the Gorobor, and so close that their bodies touched, sat a huge Horib. In one hand he carried a lance, but the other hand was free. Tarzan must move so quickly that the fellow could not touch him with his free hand before he was out of reach. To do this would require agility of an almost superhuman nature, but there are few creatures who can compare in this respect with the ape-man. Low above them swung the branches of the dismal forest; Tarzan waited, watching for the opportunity he sought. Presently he saw it—a sturdy branch with ample head room above it—a doorway in the ceiling of somber foliage. He leaned forward, his hands resting lightly upon the neck of the Gorobor. They were almost beneath the branch he had selected when he sprang lightly to his feet and almost in the same movement sprang upward into the tree. So quickly had he accomplished the feat that he was gone before the Horib that had been guarding him realized it. When he did it was too late—the prisoner had gone. With others, who had seen the escape, he raised a cry of warning to those ahead, but neither by sight nor sound could they locate the fugitive, for Tarzan travelled through the upper terrace and all the foliage beneath hid him from the eyes of his enemies.

Jana, who had been riding a little in the rear of Tarzan, saw his escape and her heart sank for in the presence of the Horibs The Red Flower of Zoram had come as near to experiencing fear as she ever had in her life. She had derived a certain sense of comfort from the presence of Tarzan and now that he was gone she felt very much alone. She did not blame him for escaping when he had the opportunity, but she was sure in her own heart that Jason would not thus have deserted her.

Following the scent spoor that was his only guide, Tarzan of the Apes moved rapidly through the trees. At first he climbed high to the upper terraces and here he found a new world—a world of sunlight and luxuriant foliage, peopled by strange birds of gorgeous plumage which darted swiftly hither and thither. There were flying reptiles, too, and great gaudy moths. Snakes coiled upon many a branch and because they were of varieties unknown to him, he did not know whether they constituted a real menace or not. It was at once a beautiful and a repulsive world, but the feature of it which attracted him most was its silence, for its denizens seemed to be voiceless. The presence of the snakes and the dense foliage rendered it an unsatisfactory world for one who wished to travel swiftly and so the ape-man dropped to a lower level, and here he found the forest more open and the scent spoor clearer in his nostrils.

Not once had he doubted the origin of that scent, although it seemed preposterously unbelievable that he should discover it here in this gloomy wood in vast Pellucidar.

He was moving very rapidly for he wished, if possible, to reach his destination ahead of the Horibs. He hoped that his escape might delay the lizard-men and this was, in fact, the case, for they had halted immediately while a number of them had climbed into the trees searching for Tarzan. There was little in their almost expressionless faces to denote their anger, but the sickly bluish cast which overspread their scales denoted their mounting rage at the ease with which this gilak prisoner had escaped them, and when, finally, thwarted in their search, they resumed their interrupted march, they were in a particularly ugly mood.

Far ahead of them now Tarzan of the Apes dropped to the lower terraces. Strong in his nostrils was the scent spoor he had been following, telling him in a language more dependable than words that he had but little farther to go to find those he sought, and a moment later he dropped down into one of the gloomy aisles of the forest, dropping as from heaven into the astonished view of ten stalwart warriors.

For an instant they stood looking at him in wide-eyed amazement and then they ran forward and threw themselves upon their knees about him, kissing his hands as they shed tears of happiness. "Oh, Bwana, Bwana," they cried; "it is indeed you! Mulungu has been good to his children; he has given their Big Bwana back to them alive."

"And now I have work for you, my children," said Tarzan; "the snake people are coming and with them is a girl whom they have captured. I thank God that you are armed with rifles and I hope that you have plenty of ammunition."

"We have saved it, Bwana, using our spears and our arrows whenever we could."

"Good," said Tarzan; "we shall need it now. How far are we from the ship?"

"I do not know," said Muviro.

"You do not know?" repeated Tarzan.

"No, Bwana, we are lost. We have been lost for a long while," replied the chief of the Waziri.

"What were you doing away from the ship alone?" demanded Tarzan.

"We were sent out with Gridley and Von Horst to search for you, Bwana."

"Where are they?" asked Tarzan.

"A long time ago, I do not know how long, we became separated from Gridley and never saw him again. At that time it was savage beasts that separated us, but how Von Horst became separated from us we do not know. We had found a cave and had gone into it to sleep; when we awoke Von Horst was gone; we never saw him again."

"They are coming!" warned Tarzan.

"I hear them, Bwana," replied Muviro.

"Have you seen them—the snake people?" asked Tarzan.

"No, Bwana, we have seen no people for a long time; only beasts—terrible beasts."

"You are going to see some terrible men now," Tarzan warned them; "but do not be frightened by their appearance. Your bullets will bring them down."

"When, Bwana, have you seen a Waziri frightened?" asked Muviro proudly.

The ape-man smiled. "One of you let me take his rifle," he said, "and then spread out through the forest. I do not know exactly where they will pass, but the moment that any of you makes contact with them commence shooting and shoot to kill, remembering, however, that the girl rides in front of one of them. Be careful that you do not harm her."

He had scarcely ceased speaking when the first of the Horibs rode into view. Tarzan and the Waziri made no effort to seek concealment and at sight of them the leading Horib gave voice to a shrill cry of pleasure. Then a rifle spoke and the leading Horib writhed convulsively and toppled sideways to the ground. The others in the lead, depending upon the swiftness of their mounts, darted quickly toward the Waziri and the tall, white giant who led them, but swifter than the Gorobors were the bullets of the outer world. As fast as Tarzan and the Waziri could fire the Horibs fell. Never before had they known defeat. They blazed blue with rage, which faded to a muddy gray when the bullets found their hearts and they rolled dead upon the ground.

So swiftly did the Gorobors move and so rapidly did Tarzan and the Waziri fire that the engagement was decided within a few minutes of its inception, and now the remaining Horibs, discovering that they could not hope to overcome and capture gilaks armed with these strange weapons that hit them more swiftly than they could hurl their lances, turned and scattered in an effort to pass around the enemy and continue on their way.

As yet Tarzan had not caught a glimpse of Jana, though he knew that she must be there somewhere in the rear of the remaining Horibs, and then he saw her as she flashed by in the distance, borne swiftly upon the back of a fleet Gorobor. What appeared to be the only chance to save her now was to shoot down the swift beast upon which she was being borne away. Tarzan swung his rifle to his shoulder and at the same instant a riderless Gorobor struck him in the back and sent him sprawling upon the ground. By the time he had regained his feet, Jana and her captor were out of sight, hidden by the boles of intervening trees.

Milling near the Waziri were a number of terrified, riderless Gorobors. It was from this number that the fellow had broken who had knocked Tarzan down. The beasts seemed to be lost without the guidance of their masters, but when they saw one of their number start in pursuit of the Horibs who had ridden away, the others followed and in their mad rush these savage beasts constituted as great a menace as the Horibs themselves.

Muviro and his warriors leaped nimbly behind the boles of large trees to escape them, but to the mind of the ape-man they carried a new hope, offering as they did the only means whereby he might overtake the Horib who was bearing away The Red Flower of Zoram, and then, to the horror and astonishment of the Waziri, Tarzan leaped to the back of one of the great lizards as it scuttled abreast of him. Locking his toes beneath its elbows, as he had seen the Horibs do, he was carried swiftly in the mad rush of the creature to overtake its fellows and its masters. No need to urge it on, if he had known what means to employ to do so, for probably still terrified and excited by the battle it darted with incredible swiftness among the boles of the gray trees, outstripping its fellows and leaving them behind.

Presently, just ahead of him, Tarzan saw the Horib who was bearing Jana away and he saw, too, that he would soon overtake him, but so swiftly was his own mount running that it seemed quite likely that he would be carried past Jana without being able to accomplish anything toward her rescue, and with this thought came the realization that he must stop the Horib's mount.

There was just an instant in which to decide and act, but in that instant he raised his rifle and fired. Perhaps it was a wonderful bit of marksmanship, or perhaps it was just luck, but the bullet struck the Gorobor in the spine and a moment later its hind legs collapsed and it rolled over on its side, pitching Jana and the Horib heavily to the ground. Simultaneously Tarzan's mount swept by and the ape-man, risking a bad fall, slipped from its back to go tumbling head over heels against the carcass of the Horib's mount.

Leaping to his feet, he faced the lizard-man and as he did so the ground gave way beneath him and he dropped suddenly into a hole, almost to his armpits. As he was struggling to extricate himself something seized him by the ankles and dragged him downward—cold fingers that clung relentlessly to him dragging him into a dark, subterranean hole.

CHAPTER 16

Escape

THE O-220 CRUISED slowly above the Gyor Cors, watchful eyes scanning the ground below, but the only living things they saw were huge dinosaurs. Disturbed by the motors of the dirigible, the great beasts trotted angrily about in circles and occasionally an individual, sighting the ship above him, would gallop after it, bellowing angrily, or again one might charge the elliptical shadow that moved along the ground directly beneath the O-220.

"Sweet tempered little fellows," remarked Lieutenant Hines, who had been watching them from a messroom port.

"Jes' which *am* dem bad dreams, Lieutenant?" asked Robert Jones.

"Triceratops," replied the officer.

"Ah'll try most anything once, suh, but not dem babies," replied Robert.

Unknown to the bewildered navigating officer, the ship was taking a southeasterly course. Far away, on its port side, loomed a range of mountains, hazily visible in the up-curving distance, and now a river cut the plain—a river that came down from the distant mountains—and this they followed, knowing that men lost in a strange country are prone to follow the course of a river, if they are so fortunate as to find one.

They had followed the river for some distance when Lieutenant Dorf telephoned down from the observation cabin. "There is a considerable body of water ahead, sir," he reported to Captain Zuppner. "From its appearance I should say that we might be approaching the shore of a large ocean."

All eyes were now strained ahead and presently a large body of water became visible to all on board. The ship cruised slowly up and down the coast for a short distance, and as it had been some time since they had had fresh water or fresh meat, Zuppner decided to land and make camp, selecting a spot just north of the river they had been following, where it emptied into the sea. And as the great ship settled gently to rest upon a rolling, grassy meadow, Robert Jones made an entry in his little black diary.

"Arrived here at noon."

While the great ship settled down beside the shore of the silent Pellucidarian sea, Jason Gridley and his companions, hundreds of miles to the west, pushed their tunnel upward toward the surface of the ground. Jason was in front, laboriously pushing the earth backward a few handfuls at a time to those behind him. They were working frantically now because the length of the tunnel already was so great that it was with difficulty that they could return to the cavern in time to forestall discovery when they heard Horibs approaching.

As Jason scraped away at the earth above him, there broke suddenly upon his ears what sounded like the muffled reverberation of rifle shots. He could not believe that they were such, and yet what else could they be? For so long had he been separated from his fellows that it seemed impossible that any freak of circumstance had brought them to this gloomy corner of Pellucidar, and though hope ran high yet he cast this idea from his mind, substituting for it a more natural conclusion—that the shots had come from the arquebuses of Korsars, who had come up from the ship that Lajo had told him was anchored somewhere below in the Rela Am. Doubtless the captain had sent an expedition in search of the missing members of his crew, but even the prospects of falling again into the hands of the fierce Korsars appeared a heavenly one by comparison to the fate with which they were confronted.

Now Jason redoubled his efforts, working frantically to drive his narrow shaft upward toward the surface. The sound of the shots, which had lasted but a few minutes, had ceased, to be followed by the rapidly approaching thunder of many feet, as though heavy animals were racing in his direction. He heard them passing almost directly overhead and they seemed so close that he was positive he must be near the surface of the ground. Another shot sounded almost directly above him; he heard the thud of a heavy body and the earth about him shook to the impact of its fall. Jason's excitement had arisen to the highest pitch when suddenly the earth gave way above him and something dropped into the shaft upon his head.

His mind long imbued with the fear that their plan for escape would be discovered by the Horibs, Jason reacted instinctively to the urge of self-preservation, the best chance for the accomplishment of which seemed to be to drag the discoverer of their secret out of sight as quickly as possible, and with this end in view he backed quickly into the tunnel, dragging the interloper with him, and to a certain point this was not difficult, but it so happened that Tarzan had clung to his rifle. The rifle chanced to strike the ground in a horizontal position, as the ape-man was dragged into the tunnel, and the muzzle and butt lodged upon opposite sides of the opening, thus forming a rigid bar across the mouth of the aperture, to which the ape-man clung as Jason dragged frantically upon his ankles, and then slowly the steel thews of the Jungle Lord tensed and as he drew himself upward, he drew Jason Gridley with him. Strain and struggle as he would, the American could not overcome the steady pull of those giant thews. Slowly, irresistibly, he was dragged into the shaft and upward toward the surface of the ground.

By this time, of course, he knew that the creature to which he clung was no Horib, for his fingers were closed upon the smooth skin of a human being, and not upon the scaly hide of a lizard-man, but yet he felt that he must not let the fellow escape.

The Horib, who had been expecting Tarzan's attack, had seen him disappear mysteriously into the ground; nor did he wait to investigate the miracle, but seizing Jana by the wrist he hurried after his fellows, dragging the struggling girl with him.

The two were just disappearing among the boles of the trees down a gloomy aisle of the somber forest when Tarzan, emerging from the shaft, caught a single fleeting glimpse of them. It was almost the growl of an enraged beast that escaped his lips as he realized that this last calamity might have definitely precluded the possibility of effecting the girl's rescue. Chafing at the restraint of the clutching fingers clinging desperately to his ankles, the ape-man kicked violently in an effort to dislodge them and with such good effect that he sent Jason tumbling back into his tunnel, while he leaped to the solid ground and freedom to spring into pursuit of the Horib and The Red Flower of Zoram.

Calling back to his companions to hurry after him, Jason clambered swiftly to the surface of the ground just in time to see a half-naked bronzed giant before he disappeared from view behind the bole of a large tree, but that single glimpse awakened familiar memories and his heart leaped within him at the suggestion it implied. But how could it be? Had not Thoar seen the Lord of the Jungle carried to his doom? Whether the man was Tarzan or not was of less import than the reason for his haste. Was he escaping or pursuing? But in either event something seemed to tell Jason Gridley that he should not lose sight of him; at least he was not a Horib, and if not a Horib, then he must be an enemy of the lizard-men. So rapidly had events transpired that Jason was confused in his own mind as to the proper course to pursue; yet something seemed to urge him not to lose sight of the stranger and acting upon this impulse, he followed at a brisk run.

Through the dark wood ran Tarzan of the Apes, guided only by the delicate and subtle aroma that was the scent spoor of The Red Flower of Zoram and which would have been perceptible to no other human nostrils than those of the Lord of the Jungle. Strong in his nostrils, also, was the sickening scent of the Horibs and fearful lest he come upon them unexpectedly in numbers, he swung lightly into the trees and, with undiminished speed, raced in the direction of his quarry; nor was it long before he saw them beneath him—a single Horib dragging the still-struggling Jana.

There was no hesitation, there was no diminution in his speed as he launched himself like a living projectile straight for the ugly back of the Horib. With such force he struck the creature that it was half stunned as he bore it to the ground. A sinewy arm encircled its neck as Tarzan arose dragging the creature up with him. Turning quickly and bending forward, Tarzan swung the body over his head and hurled it violently to the ground, still retaining his hold about its neck. Again and again he whipped the mighty body over his head and dashed it to the gray earth, while the girl, wide-eyed with astonishment at this exhibition of Herculean strength, looked on.

At last, satisfied that the creature was dead or stunned, Tarzan released it. Quickly he appropriated its stone knife and picked up its fallen lance, then he turned to Jana. "Come," he said, "there is but one safe place for us," and lifting her to his shoulder he leaped to the low hanging branch of a nearby tree. "Here, at least," he said, "you will be safe from Horibs, for I doubt if any Gorobor can follow us here."

"I always thought that there were no warriors like the warriors of Zoram," said Jana, "but that was before I had known you and Jason;" nor could she, as Tarzan well knew, have voiced a more sincere appreciation of what he had done for her, for to the primitive woman there are no men like her own men. "I wish," she continued sadly after a pause, "that Jason had lived. He was a great man and a mighty warrior, but above all he was a kind man. The men of Zoram are never cruel to their women, but they are not always thoughtful and considerate. Jason seemed always to think of my comfort before everything except my safety."

"You were very fond of him, were you not?" asked Tarzan.

The Red Flower of Zoram did not answer. There were tears in her eyes and in her throat so that she could only nod her head.

Once in the trees, Tarzan had lowered Jana to her feet, presently discovering that she could travel quite without assistance, as might have been expected of one who could leap lightly from crag to crag upon the dizzy slopes of Thipdars' heights. They moved without haste back to the point where they had last seen Muviro, and his Waziri warriors, but as the way took them down wind Tarzan could not hope to pick up the scent spoor of his henchmen and so his ears were constantly upon the alert for any slightest sound that might reveal their whereabouts. Presently they were rewarded by the sound of footsteps hurrying through the forest toward them.

The ape-man drew the girl behind the bole of a large tree and waited, silent, motionless, for all footfalls are not the footfalls of friends.

They had waited for but a moment when there came into view upon the ground below them an almost naked man clothed in a bit of filthy goatskin, which was almost undistinguishable as such beneath a coating of mud, while the original color of his skin was hidden beneath a similar covering. A great mass of tousled black hair surmounted his head. He was quite the filthiest appearing creature that Tarzan had ever looked upon, but he was evidently no Horib and he was unarmed. What he was doing there alone in the grim forest, the ape-man could not imagine, so he dropped to the ground immediately in front of the surprised wayfarer.

At sight of the ape-man, the other stopped, his eyes wide with astonishment and incredulity. "Tarzan!" he exclaimed. "My God, it is really you. You are not dead. Thank God you are not dead."

It was an instant before the ape-man could recognize the speaker, but not so the girl hiding in the tree above. The instant that she had heard his voice she had known him.

A slow smile overspread the features of the Lord of the Jungle. "Gridley!" he exclaimed. "Jason Gridley! Jana told me that you were dead."

"Jana!" exclaimed Jason. "You know her? You have seen her? Where is she?"

"She is here with me," replied Tarzan.

Lifting her to his shoulder, he leaped to the low branch of a nearby tree.

The Red Flower of Zoram had slipped to the ground upon the opposite side of the tree and now she stepped from behind its trunk.

"Jana!" cried Jason, coming eagerly toward her.

The girl drew herself to her full height and turned a shoulder toward him. "Jalok!" she cried contemptuously. "Must I tell you again to keep away from The Red Flower of Zoram?"

Jason halted in his tracks, his arms dropped limply to his sides, his attitude one of utter dejection.

Tarzan looked silently on, his brows momentarily revealing his perplexity; but it was not his way to interfere in affairs that were wholly the concern of others. "Come," he said, "we must find the Waziri."

Suddenly loud voices just ahead apprised them of the presence of other men and in the babel of excited voices Tarzan recognized the tones of his Waziri. Hurrying forward the three came upon a scene that was momentarily ludicrous, but which might soon have developed into tragedy had they not arrived in time.

Ten Waziri warriors armed with rifles had surrounded Thoar and the three Korsars and each party was jabbering volubly in a language unknown to the other.

The Pellucidarians, never before having seen human beings of the rich, deep, black color of the Waziri and assuming that all strangers were enemies, apprehended only the worst and were about to make a concerted effort to escape their captors, while Muviro, believing that these men might have some sinister connection with the disappearance of his master, was determined to hold and question them; nor would he have hesitated to kill them had they resisted him. It was, therefore, a relief to both parties when Tarzan, Jason and Jana appeared, and the Waziri saw their Big Bwana greet one of their captives with every indication of friendship.

Thoar was even more surprised to find Tarzan alive than Jason had been, and when he saw Jana the natural reserve which ordinarily marked his bearing was dissipated by the joy and relief which he felt in finding her safe and well; nor any less surprised and happy was Jana as she rushed forward and threw herself into her brother's arms.

His breast filled with emotion such as he had never experienced before, Jason Gridley stood apart, a silent witness of this loving reunion, and then, probably for the first time, there came to him an acute realization of the fact that the sentiment which he entertained for this little barbarian was nothing less than love.

It galled him even to admit it to himself and he felt that he was contemptible to harbor jealousy of Thoar, not only because Thoar was his friend, but because he was only a primitive savage, while he, Jason Gridley, was the product of ages of culture and civilization.

Thoar, Lajo and the other two Korsars were naturally delighted when they found that the strange warriors whom they had looked upon as enemies were suddenly transformed into friends and allies, and when they heard the story of the battle with the Horibs they knew that the greatest danger which threatened them was now greatly minimized because of the presence of these warriors armed with death-dealing weapons that made the ancient arquebuses of the Korsars appear as inadequate as sling shots, and that escape from this horrible country was as good as accomplished.

Resting after their recent exertion, each party briefly narrated the recent adventures that had befallen them and attempts were made to formulate plans for the future, but here difficulties arose. Thoar wished to return to Zoram with Jana. Tarzan, Jason and the Waziri desired only to find the other members of their expedition; while Lajo and his two fellows were principally concerned with getting back to their ship.

Tarzan and Jason, realizing that it might not be expedient to acquaint the Korsars with the real purpose of their presence in Pellucidar and finding that the men were familiar with the story of Tanar, gave them to believe that they were merely searching for Sari in order to pay a friendly visit to Tanar and his people.

"Sari is a long way," said Lajo. "He who would go to Sari from here must sleep over a hundred times upon the journey, which would take him across the Korsar Az and then through strange countries filled with enemies, even as far as The Land of Awful Shadow. Maybe one would never reach it."

"Is there no way overland?" asked Tarzan.

"Yes," replied Lajo, "and if we were at Korsar, I might direct you, but that, too, would be a terrible journey, for no man knows what savage tribes and beasts beset the long marches that must lie between Korsar and Sari."

"And if we went to Korsar," said Jason, "we could not hope to be received as friends. Is this not true, Lajo?"

The Korsar nodded. "No," he said. "You would not be received as friends."

"Nevertheless," said Tarzan to Jason, "I believe that if we are ever to find the O-220 again our best chance is to look for it in the vicinity of Korsar."

Jason nodded in acquiescence. "But that will not accord with Thoar's plans," he said, "for, if I understand it correctly, we are much nearer to Zoram now than we are to Korsar and if we decide to go to Korsar, our route will lead directly away from Zoram. But unless we accompany them with the Waziri, I doubt if Thoar and Jana could live to reach Zoram if they returned by the route that he and I have followed since we left the Mountains of the Thipdars."

Tarzan turned to Thoar. "If you will come with us, we can return you very quickly to Zoram if we find our ship. If we do not find it within a reasonable time, we will accompany you back to Zoram. In either event you would have a very much better chance of reaching your own country than you would if you and Jana set out alone from here."

"We will accompany you, then," said Thoar, and then his brow clouded as some thought seemed suddenly to seize upon his mind. He looked for a moment at Jason, and then he turned to Jana. "I had almost forgotten," he said. "Before we can go with these people as friends, I must know if this man offered you any injury or harm while you were with him. If he did, I must kill him."

Jana did not look at Jason as she replied. "You need not kill him," she said. "Had that been necessary The Red Flower of Zoram would have done it herself."

"Very well," said Thoar, "I am glad because he is my friend. Now we may all go together."

"Our boat is probably in the river where the Horibs left it after they captured us," said Lajo. "If it is we can soon drop down to our ship, which is anchored in the lower waters of the Rela Am."

"And be taken prisoners by your people," said Jason. "No, Lajo, the tables are turned now and if you go with us, it is you who will be the prisoners."

The Korsar shrugged. "I do not care," he said. "We will doubtless get a hundred lashes apiece when the captain finds that we have been unsuccessful, that we have brought back nothing and that he has lost an officer and many members of his crew."

It was finally decided that they would return to the Rela Am and look for the longboat of the Korsars. If they found it they would float down in search of the ship, when they would at least make an effort to persuade the captain to receive them as friends and transport them to the vicinity of Korsar.

On the march back to the Rela Am they were not molested by the Horibs, who had evidently discovered that they had met their masters in the Waziri. During the march Jason made it a point to keep as far away from Jana as possible. The very sight of her reminded him of his hopeless and humiliating infatuation, and to be very near her constituted a form of refined agony which he could not endure. Her contempt, which she made no effort to conceal galled him bitterly, though it was no greater than his own self-contempt when he realized that in spite of every reason that he had to dislike her, he still loved her—loved her more than he had thought it was possible for him to love any woman.

The American was glad when a glimpse of the broad waters of the Rela Am ahead of them marked the end of this stage of their journey, which his own unhappy thoughts, combined with the depressing influence of the gloomy forest, had transformed into one of the saddest periods of his life.

To the relief of all, the boat was found still moored where the Horibs had left it; nor did it take them long to embark and push out upon the waters of the River of Darkness.

The river widened as they floated down toward the sea until it became possible to step a mast and set sail, after which their progress was still more rapid. Though the way was often beset by dangers in the form of angry and voracious saurians, the rifles of the Waziri proved adequate protection when other means of defense had failed.

The river became very wide so that but for the current they might have considered it an arm of the sea and at Lajo's direction they kept well in toward the left bank, near which, he said, the ship was anchored. Dimly visible in the distance was the opposite shore, but only so because the surface of Pellucidar curved upward. At the same distance upon the outer crust, it would have been hidden by the curvature of the earth.

As they neared the sea it became evident that Lajo and the two other Korsars were much concerned because they had not sighted their ship.

"We have passed the anchorage," said Lajo at last. "That wooded hill, which we just passed, was directly opposite the spot where the ship lay. I cannot be mistaken because I noted it particularly and impressed it upon my memory as a landmark against the time when we should return from our expedition up the river."

"He has sailed away and left us," growled one of the Korsars, applying a vile epithet to the captain of the departed ship.

Continuing on down to the ocean they sighted a large island directly off the mouth of the river, which Lajo told them afforded good hunting with plenty of fresh water and as they were in need of meat they landed there and made camp. It was an ideal spot inasmuch as that part of the island at which they had touched seemed to be peculiarly free from the more dangerous forms of carnivorous mammals and reptiles; nor did they see any sign of the presence of man. Game, therefore, was abundant.

Discussing their plans for the future, it was finally decided that they would push on toward Korsar in the longboat, for Lajo assured them that it lay upon the coast of the same landmass that loomed plainly from their island refuge. "What lies in that direction," he said, pointing south, "I do not know, but there lies Korsar, upon this same coast," and he pointed in a direction a little east of north. "Otherwise I am not familiar with this sea, or with this part of Pellucidar, since never before has an expedition come as far as the Rela Am."

In preparation for the long cruise to Korsar, great quantities of meat were cut into strips and dried in the sun, or smoked over slow fires, after which it was packed away in bladders that had been carefully cleaned and dried. These were stowed in the boat together with other bladders filled with fresh water, for, although it was their intention to hug the coast on the way to Korsar, it might not always be expedient to land for water or food and there was always the possibility that a storm arising they might be blown out to sea.

At length, all preparations having been made, the strangely assorted company embarked upon their hazardous journey toward distant Korsar.

Jana had worked with the others preparing the provisions and the containers and though she had upon several occasions worked side by side with Jason, she had never relaxed toward him; nor appeared to admit that she was cognizant of his presence.

"Can't we be friends, Jana?" he asked once. "I think we would both be very much happier if we were."

"I am as happy as I can be," she replied lightly, "until Thoar takes me back to Zoram."

CHAPTER 17

Reunited

As FAVORABLE WINDS carried the longboat and its company up the sunlit sea, the O-220, following the same route, made occasional wide circles inland upon what Zuppner now considered an almost hopeless quest for the missing members of the expedition, and not only was he hopeless upon this score, but he also shared the unvoiced hopelessness of the balance of the company with regard to the likelihood of their ever being able to find the polar opening and return again to the outer world. With them, he knew that even their tremendous reserve of fuel and oil would not last indefinitely and if they were unable to find the polar opening, while they still had sufficient in reserve to carry them back to civilization, they must resign themselves to remaining in Pellucidar for the rest of their lives.

Lieutenant Hines finally broached this subject and the two officers, after summoning Lieutenant Dorf to their conference, decided that before their fuel was entirely exhausted they would try to locate some district where they might be reasonably free from attacks by savage tribesmen, or the even more dangerous menace of the mighty carnivores of Pellucidar.

While the remaining officers of the O-220 pondered the serious problems that confronted them, the great ship moved serenely through the warm Pellucidarian sunlight and the members of the crew went quietly and efficiently about their various duties.

Robert Jones of Alabama, however, was distressed. He seemed never to be able to accustom himself to the changed conditions of Pellucidar. He often mumbled to himself, shaking his head vehemently, and frequently he wound a battered alarm clock or took it down from the hook upon which it hung and held it to his ear.

Below the ship there unrolled a panorama of lovely sea coast, indented by many beautiful bays and inlets. There were rolling hills and plains and forests and winding rivers blue as turquoise.

It was a scene to inspire the loftiest sentiments in the lowliest heart nor was it without its effect upon the members of the ship's company, which included many adventurous spirits, who would experience no regret should it develop that they must remain forever in this, to them, enchanted land. But there were others who had left loved ones at home and these were already beginning to discuss the possibilities and the probabilities of the future. With few exceptions, they were keen and intelligent men and fully as cognizant of the possible plight of the O-220 as was its commander, but they had been chosen carefully and there was not one who waivered even momentarily in loyalty to Zuppner, for they well knew that whatever fate was to be theirs, he would share it with them and, too, they had confidence that if any man could extricate them from their predicament, it was he. And so the great ship rode its majestic way between the sun and earth and each part, whether mechanical or human, functioned perfectly.

The Captain and his Lieutenant discussed the future as Robert Jones laboriously ascended the climbing shaft to the walkingway upon the ship's back, a hundred and fifty feet above his galley. He did not come entirely out of the climbing shaft onto the walkingway, but merely looked about the blue heaven and when his gaze had completed the circle, he hesitated a moment and then looked straight up, where, directly overhead, hung the eternal noonday sun of Pellucidar.

Robert Jones blinked his eyes and retreated into the shaft, closing the hatch after him. Muttering to himself, he descended carefully to the galley, crossed it, took the clock off its hook and, walking to an open port, threw it overboard.

To the occupants of the longboat dancing over the blue waves, without means of determining either time or distance, the constant expectation of nearing their journey's end lessened the monotony as did the oft recurring attacks of the frightful denizens of this Mesozoic sea. To the highly civilized American the utter time-lessness of Pellucidarian existence brought a more marked nervous reaction than to the others. To a lesser degree Tarzan felt it, while the Waziri were only slightly conscious of the anomalous conditions. Upon the Pellucidarians, accustomed to no other state, it had no effect whatever. It was apparent when Tarzan and Jason discussed the matter with them that they had practically no conception of the meaning of time.

But time did elapse, leagues of ocean passed beneath them and conditions changed.

As they moved along the coast their course changed; though without instruments or heavenly bodies to guide them they were not aware of it. For a while they had moved northeast and then, for a long distance, to the east, where the coast curved gradually until they were running due north.

Instinct told the Korsars that they had come about three quarters of the distance from the island where they had outfitted to their destination. A land breeze was blowing stiffly and they were tacking briskly up the coast at a good clip. Lajo was standing erect in the bow apparently sniffing the air, as might a hunting dog searching out a scent spoor. Presently he turned to Tarzan.

"We had better put in to the coast," he said. "We are in for a stiff blow." But it was too late, the wind and the sea mounted to such proportions that finally they had to abandon the attempt and turn and flee before the storm. There was no rain nor lightning, for there were no clouds—just a terrific wind that rose to hurricane violence and stupendous seas that threatened momentarily to engulf them.

The Waziri were frankly terrified, for the sea was not their element. The mountain girl and her brother seemed awed, but if they felt fear they gave no outward indication of it. Tarzan and Jason were convinced that the boat could not live and the latter made his way to where Jana sat huddled upon a thwart. The howling of the wind made speech almost impossible, but he bent low placing his lips close to her ear.

"Jana," he said, "it is impossible for this small boat to ride out such a storm. We are going to die, but before we die, whether you hate me or not, I am going to tell you that I love you," and then before she could reply, before she could humiliate him further, he turned away and moved forward to where he had been before.

He knew that he had done wrong; he knew that he had no right to tell Thoar's sweetheart that he loved her; it had been an act of disloyalty and yet a force greater than loyalty, greater than pride, had compelled him to speak those words—he could not die with them unspoken. Perhaps it had been a little easier because he could not help but have noticed the seemingly platonic relationship which existed between Thoar and Jana and being unable to picture Jana as platonic in love, he had assumed that Thoar did not appreciate her. He was always kind to her and always pleasant, but he had never been quite as thoughtful of her as Jason thought that he should have been. He felt that perhaps it was one of the strange inflections of Pellucidarian character, but it was difficult to know either Jana or Thoar and also to believe that, for they were evidently quite as normal human beings as was he, and though they had much of the natural primitive reserve and dignity that civilized man now merely affects; yet it seemed unlikely that either one of them could have been for so long a time in close association without inadvertently, at least, having given some indication of their love. "Why," mused Jason, "they might be brother and sister from the way they act."

By some miracle of fate the boat lived through the storm, but when the wind diminished and the seas went down there were only tumbling waters to be seen on every hand; nor any sign of land.

"Now that we have lost the coast, Lajo, how are we going to set our course for Korsar?" asked Tarzan.

"It will not be easy," replied Lajo. "The only guide that we have is the wind. We are well out on the Korsar Az and I know from which direction the wind usually blows. By keeping always on the same tack we shall eventually reach land and probably not far from Korsar."

"What is that?" asked Jana, pointing, and all eyes turned in the direction that she indicated.

"It is a sail," said Lajo presently. "We are saved."

"But suppose the ship is manned by unfriendly people?" asked Jason.

"It is not," said Lajo. "It is manned by Korsars, for no other ships sail the Korsar Az."

"There is another," exclaimed Jana. "There are many of them."

"Come about and run for it," said Tarzan; "perhaps they have not seen us yet."

"Why should we try to escape?" asked Lajo.

"Because we have not enough men to fight them," replied Tarzan. "They may not be your enemies, but they will be ours."

Lajo did as he was bid, nor had he any alternative since the Korsars aboard were only three unarmed men, while there were ten Waziri with rifles.

All eyes watched the sails in the distance and it soon became apparent that they were coming closer, for the longboat, with its small sail, was far from fast. Little by little the distance between them and the ships decreased until it was evident that they were being pursued by a considerable fleet.

"Those are no Korsars," said Lajo. "I have never seen ships like those before."

The longboat wallowed through the sea making the best headway that it could, but the pursuing ships, stringing out as far as the eye could reach until their numbers presented the appearance of a vast armada, continued to close up rapidly upon it.

The leading ship was now closing up so swiftly upon them that the occupants of the longboat had an excellent view of it. It was short and broad of beam with rather a high bow. It had two sails and in addition was propelled by oars, which protruded through ports along each side, there being some fifty oars all told. Above the line of oars, over the sides of the ship, were hung the shields of the warriors.

"Lord!" exclaimed Jason to Tarzan; "Pellucidar not only boasts Spanish pirates, but vikings as well, for if those are not viking ships they certainly are an adaptation of them."

"Slightly modernized, however," remarked the Lord of the Jungle. "There is a gun mounted on a small deck built in the bow."

"So there is," exclaimed Jason, "and I think we had better come about. There is a fellow up there turning it on us now."

Presently another man appeared upon the elevated bow deck of the enemy. "Heave to," he cried, "or I'll blow you out of the water."

"Who are you?" demanded Jason.

"I am Ja of Anoroc," replied the man, "and this is the fleet of David I, Emperor of Pellucidar."

"Come about," said Tarzan to Lajo.

"Someone in this boat must have been born on Sunday," exclaimed Jason. "I never knew there was so much good luck in the world."

"Who are you?" demanded Ja as the longboat came slowly about.

"We are friends," replied Tarzan.

"The Emperor of Pellucidar can have no friends upon the Korsar Az," replied Ja.

"If Abner Perry is with you, we can prove that you are wrong," replied Jason.

"Abner Perry is not with us," said Ja; "but what do you know of him?"

By this time the two boats were alongside and the bronzed Mezop warriors of Ja's crew were gazing down curiously upon the occupants of the boat.

"This is Jason Gridley," said Tarzan to Ja, indicating the American. "Perhaps you have heard Abner Perry speak of him. He organized an expedition in the outer world to come here to rescue David Innes from the dungeons of the Korsars."

The three Korsars of the longboat made Ja suspicious, but when a full explanation had been made and especially when he had examined the rifles of the Waziri, he became convinced of the truth of their statements and welcomed them warmly aboard his ship, about which were now gathered a considerable number of the armada. When word was passed among them that two of the strangers were friends from the outer world who had come to assist in the rescue of David Innes, a number of the captains of other ships came aboard Ja's flagship to greet Tarzan and Jason. Among these captains were Dacor the Strong One, brother of Dian the Beautiful, Empress of Pellucidar; Kolk, son of Goork, who is chief of the Thurians; and Tanar, son of Ghak, the Hairy One, King of Sari.

From these Tarzan and Jason learned that this fleet was on its way to effect the rescue of David. It had been building for a great while, so long that they had forgotten how many times they had eaten and slept since the first keel was laid, and then they had had to find a way into the Korsar Az from the Lural Az, where the ships were built upon the island of Anoroc.

"Far down the Sojar Az beyond the Land of Awful Shadow we found a passage that led to the Korsar Az. The Thurians had heard of it and while the fleet was building they sent warriors out to see if it was true and they found the passage and soon we shall be before the city of Korsar."

"How did you expect to rescue David with only a dozen men?" asked Tanar.

"We are not all here," said Tarzan. "We became separated from our companions and have been unable to find them. However, there were not very many men in our expedition. We depended upon other means than manpower to effect the rescue of your Emperor."

At this moment a great cry arose from one of the ships. The excitement rose and spread. The warriors were all looking into the air and pointing. Already some of them were elevating the muzzles of their cannons and all were preparing their rifles, and as Tarzan and Jason looked up they saw the O-220 far above them.

The dirigible had evidently discovered the fleet and was descending toward it in a wide spiral.

"Now I *know* someone was born on Sunday," said Jason. "That is our ship. Those are our friends," he added, turning to Ja.

All that transpired on board the flagship passed quickly from ship to ship until every member of the armada knew that the great thing hovering above them was no gigantic flying reptile, but a ship of the air in which were friends of Abner Perry and their beloved Emperor, David I.

Slowly the great ship settled toward the surface of the sea and as it did so Jason Gridley borrowed a spear from one of the warriors and tied Lajo's head handkerchief to its tip. With this improvised flag he signalled, "O-220 ahoy! This is the war fleet of David I, Emperor of Pellucidar, commanded by Ja of Anoroc; Lord Greystoke, ten Waziri and Jason Gridley aboard."

A moment later a gun boomed from the rear turret of the O-220, marking the beginning of the first international salute of twenty-one guns that had ever reverberated beneath the eternal sun of Pellucidar, and when the significance of it was explained to Ja he returned the salute with the bow gun of his flagship.

The dirigible dropped lower until it was within speaking distance of the flagship.

"Are you all well aboard?" asked Tarzan.

"Yes," came back the reassuring reply in Zuppner's booming tone.

"Is Von Horst with you?" asked Jason.

"No," replied Zuppner.

"Then he alone is missing," said Jason sadly.

"Can you drop a sling and take us aboard?" asked Tarzan.

Zuppner maneuvered the dirigible to within fifty feet of the deck of Ja's flagship, a sling was lowered and one after another the members of the party were taken on board the O-220, the Waziri first and then Jana and Thoar, followed by Jason and Tarzan, the three Korsars being left prisoners with Ja with the understanding that they were to be treated humanely.

Before Tarzan left the deck of the flagship he told Ja that if he would proceed toward Korsar, the dirigible would keep in touch with him and in the meantime they would be perfecting plans for the rescue of David Innes.

As Thoar and Jana were hoisted aboard the O-220, they were filled with a boundless amazement. To them such a creation as the giant dirigible was inconceivable. As Jana expressed it afterward; "I knew that I was dreaming, but yet at the same time I knew that I could not dream about such a thing as this because no such thing existed."

Jason introduced Jana and Thoar to Zuppner and Hines, but Lieutenant Dorf did not come to the cabin until after Tarzan had boarded the ship, and it was the latter who introduced them to Dorf.

He presented Lieutenant Dorf to Jana and then, indicating Thoar, "This is Thoar, the brother of The Red Flower of Zoram."

As those words broke upon the ears of Jason Gridley he reacted almost as to the shock of a physical blow. He was glad that no one chanced to be looking at him at the time and instantly he regained his composure, but it left him with a distinct feeling of injury. They had all known it and none of them had told him. He was almost angry at them until it occurred to him that they had all probably assumed that he had known it too, and yet try as he would he could not quite forgive Jana. But, really, what difference did it make, for, whether sister or mate of Thoar or another, he knew that The Red Flower of Zoram was not for him. She had made that definitely clear in her attitude toward him, which had convinced him even more definitely than had her bitter words.

The reunited officers of the expedition had much to discuss and many reminiscences to narrate as the O-220 followed above the slowly moving fleet. It was a happy reunion, clouded only by the absence of Von Horst.

As the dirigible moved slowly above the waters of the Korsar Az, Zuppner dropped occasionally to within speaking distance of Ja of Anoroc, and when the distant coast of Korsar was sighted a sling was lowered and Ja was taken aboard the O-220, where plans for the rescue of David were discussed, and when they were perfected Ja was returned to his ship, and Lajo and the two other Korsars were taken aboard the dirigible.

The three prisoners were filled with awe and consternation as Jason and Tarzan personally conducted them throughout the giant craft. They were shown the armament, which was carefully explained to them, special stress being laid upon the destructive power of the bombs which the O-220 carried.

"One of these," said Jason to Lajo, "would blow The Cid's palace a thousand feet into the air and as you see, we have many of them. We could destroy all of Korsar and all the Korsar ships."

While Ja's fleet was still a considerable distance off the coast, the O-220 raced ahead at full speed toward Korsar, for the plan which they had evolved was such that, if successful, David's release would be effected without the shedding of blood—a plan which was especially desirable since if it was necessary to attack Korsar either from the sea or the air, the Emperor's life would be placed in jeopardy from the bombs and cannons of his friends, as well as from a possible spirit of vengeance which might animate The Cid.

As the dirigible glided almost silently over the city of Korsar, the streets and courtyards filled with people staring upward in awe-struck wonder.

Three thousand feet above the city the ship stopped and Tarzan sent for the three Korsar prisoners.

"As you know," he said to them, "we are in a position to destroy Korsar. You have seen the great fleet coming to the rescue of the Emperor of Pellucidar. You know that every warrior manning those ships is armed with a weapon far more effective than your best; even with their knives and spears and their bows and arrows they might take Korsar without their rifles, but they have the rifles and they have better ammunition than yours and in each ship of the fleet cannons are mounted. Alone the fleet could reduce Korsar, but in addition to the fleet there is this airship. Your shots could never reach it as it sailed back and forth above Korsar, dropping bombs upon the city. Do you think, Lajo, that we can take Korsar?"

"I know it," replied the Korsar.

"Very well," said Tarzan. "I am going to send you with a message to The Cid. Will you tell him the truth?"

"I will," replied Lajo.

"The message is simple," continued Tarzan. "You may tell him that we have come to effect the release of the Emperor of Pellucidar. You may explain to him the means that we have to enforce our demands, and then you may say to him that if he will place the Emperor upon a ship and take him out to our fleet and deliver him unharmed to Ja of Anoroc, we will return to Sari without firing a shot. Do you understand?"

"I do," said Lajo.

"Very well, then," said Tarzan. He turned to Dorf, "Lieutenant, will you take him now?" he asked.

Dorf approached with a bundle in his hand. "Slip into this," he said.

"What is it?" asked Lajo.

"It is a parachute," said Dorf.

"What is that?" demanded Lajo.

"Here," said Dorf, "put your arms through here." A moment later he had the parachute adjusted upon the Korsar.

"Now," said Jason, "a great distinction is going to be conferred upon you—you are going to make the first parachute jump that has ever been witnessed in Pellucidar."

"I don't understand what you mean," said Lajo.

"You will presently," said Jason. "You are going to take Lord Greystoke's message to The Cid."

"But you will have to bring the ship down to the ground before I can," objected Lajo.

"On the contrary we are going to stay right where we are," said Jason; "you are going to jump overboard."

"What?" exclaimed Lajo. "You are going to kill me?"

"No," said Jason with a laugh. "Listen carefully to what I tell you and you will land safely. You have seen some wonderful things on board this ship so you must have some conception of what we of the outer world can do. Now you are going to have a demonstration of another very wonderful invention and you may take my word for it that no harm will befall you if you do precisely as I tell you to. Here is an iron ring," and he touched the ring opposite Lajo's left breast; "take hold of it with your right hand. After you jump from the ship, pull it; give it a good jerk and you will float down to the ground as lightly as a feather."

"I will be killed," objected Lajo.

"If you are a coward," said Jason, "perhaps one of these other men is braver than you. I tell you that you will not be hurt."

"I am not afraid," said Lajo. "I will jump."

"Tell The Cid," said Tarzan, "that if we do not presently see a ship sail out alone to meet the fleet, we shall start dropping bombs upon the city."

Dorf led Lajo to a door in the cabin and flung it open. The man hesitated.

"Do not forget to jerk the ring," said Dorf, and at the same time he gave Lajo a violent push that sent him headlong through the doorway and a moment later the watchers in the cabin saw the white folds of the parachute streaming in the air. They saw it open and they knew that the message of Tarzan would be delivered to The Cid.

What went on in the city below we may not know, but presently a great crowd was seen to move from the palace down toward the river, where the ships were anchored, and a little later one of the ships weighed anchor and as it drifted slowly with the current its sails were set and presently it was moving directly out to sea toward the fleet from Sari.

The O-220 followed above it and Ja's flagship moved forward to meet it, and thus David Innes, Emperor of Pellucidar, was returned to his people.

As the Korsar ship turned back to port the dirigible dropped low above the flagship of the Sarian fleet and greetings were exchanged between David and his rescuers—men from another world whom he had never seen.

The Emperor was half starved and very thin and weak from his long period of confinement, but otherwise he had been unharmed, and great was the rejoicing aboard the ships of Sari as they turned back to cross the Korsar Az toward their own land.

Tarzan was afraid to accompany the fleet back to Sari for fear that their rapidly diminishing store of fuel would not be sufficient to complete the trip and carry them back to the outer world. He followed the fleet only long enough to obtain from David explicit directions for reaching the polar opening from the city of Korsar.

"We have another errand to fulfill first," said Jason to Tarzan. "We must return Thoar and Jana to Zoram."

"Yes," said the ape-man, "and drop these two Korsars off near their city. I have thought of all that and we shall have fuel enough for that purpose."

"I am not going to return with you," said Jason. "I wish to be put aboard Ja's flagship."

"What?" exclaimed Tarzan. "You are going to remain here?"

"This expedition was undertaken at my suggestion. I feel responsible for the life and safety of every man in it and I shall never return to the outer world while the fate of Lieutenant Von Horst remains a mystery."

"But how can you find Von Horst if you go back to Sari with the fleet?" asked Tarzan.

"I shall ask David Innes to equip an expedition to go in search of him," replied Jason, "and with such an expedition made up of native Pellucidarians I shall stand a very much better chance of finding him than we would in the O-220."

"I quite agree with you," said Tarzan, "and if you are unalterably determined to carry out your project, we will lower you to Ja's ship immediately."

As the O-220 dropped toward Ja's flagship and signalled it to heave to, Jason gathered what belongings he wished to take with him, including rifles and revolvers and plenty of ammunition. These were lowered first to Ja's ship, while Jason bid farewell to his companions of the expedition.

"Good-bye, Jana," he said, after he had shaken hands with the others.

The girl made no reply, but instead turned to her brother.

"Good-bye, Thoar," she said.

"Good-bye?" he asked. "What do you mean?"

"I am going to Sari with the man I love," replied The Red Flower of Zoram.

Tarzan
Triumphant

Illustrated by Studley Burroughs

Overleaf: *Sheeta plunged to the earth dead, slain by the spear.*

PROLOGUE

TIME IS THE warp of the tapestry which is life. It is eternal, constant, unchanging. But the woof is gathered together from the four corners of the earth and the twenty-eight seas and out of the air and the minds of men by that master artist, Fate, as she weaves the design that is never finished.

A thread from here, a thread from there, another from out of the past that has waited years for the companion thread without which the picture must be incomplete.

But Fate is patient. She waits a hundred or a thousand years to bring together two strands of thread whose union is essential to the fabrication of her tapestry, to the composition of the design that was without beginning and is without end.

A matter of some one thousand eight hundred sixty-five years ago (scholars do not agree as to the exact year), Paul of Tarsus suffered martyrdom at Rome.

That a tragedy so remote should seriously affect the lives and destinies of an English aviatrix and an American professor of geology, neither of whom was conscious of the existence of the other at the time this narrative begins—when it does begin, which is not yet, since Paul of Tarsus is merely by way of prologue—may seem remarkable to us, but not to Fate, who has been patiently waiting these nearly two thousand years for these very events I am about to chronicle.

But there is a link between Paul and these two young people. It is Angustus the Ephesian. Angustus was a young man of moods and epilepsy, a nephew of the house of Onesiphorus. Numbered was he among the early converts to the new faith when Paul of Tarsus first visited the ancient Ionian city of Ephesus.

Inclined to fanaticism, from early childhood an epileptic, and worshipping the apostle as the representative of the Master on earth, it is not strange that news of the martyrdom of Paul should have so affected Angustus as to seriously imperil his mental balance.

Conjuring delusions of persecution, he fled Ephesus, taking ship for Alexandria; and here we might leave him, wrapped in his robe, huddled, sick and frightened, on the deck of the little vessel, were it not for the fact that at the Island of Rhodus, where the ship touched, Angustus, going ashore, acquired in some manner (whether by conversion or purchase we know not) a fair haired slave girl from some far northern barbarian tribe.

And here we bid Angustus and the days of the Caesars adieu, and not without some regrets upon my part for I can well imagine adventure, if not romance, in the flight of Angustus and the fair haired slave girl down into Africa from the storied port of Alexandria, through Memphis and Thebae into the great unknown.

CHAPTER 1

Gathering the Threads

AS FAR AS I know the first Earl of Whimsey has nothing to do with this story, and so we are not particularly interested in the fact that it was not so much the fine grade of whiskey that he manufactured that won him his earldom as the generous contribution he made to the Liberal party at the time that it was in power a number of years ago.

Being merely a simple historian and no prophet, I cannot say whether we shall see the Earl of Whimsey again or not. But if we do not find the Earl particularly interesting, I can assure you that the same may not be said of his fair daughter, Lady Barbara Collis.

The African sun, still an hour high, was hidden from the face of the earth by solid cloud banks that enveloped the loftier peaks of the mysterious, impenetrable fastnesses of the forbidding Ghenzi Mountain range that frowned perpetually upon a thousand valleys little known to man.

From far above this seeming solitude, out of the heart of the densely banked clouds, there came to whatever ears there might be to hear a strange and terrifying droning, suggesting the presence of a preposterous Gargantuan bumble-bee circling far above the jagged peaks of Ghenzi. At times it grew in volume until it attained terrifying proportions; and then gradually it diminished until it was only a suggestion of a sound, only to grow once again in volume and to again retreat.

For a long time, invisible and mysterious, it had been describing its great circles deep in the concealing vapors that hid it from the earth and hid the earth from it.

Lady Barbara Collis was worried. Her petrol was running low. At the crucial moment her compass had failed her, and she had been flying blind through the clouds looking for an opening for what now seemed an eternity of hours to her.

She had known that she must cross a lofty range of mountains, and she had kept at a considerable altitude above the clouds for this purpose; but presently they had risen to such heights that she could not surmount them; and, foolishly, rather than turn back and give up her projected non-stop flight from Cairo to the Cape, she had risked all in an effort to penetrate them.

For an hour Lady Barbara had been indulging in considerable high powered thinking, intermingled with the regret that she had not started thinking a little more heavily before she had taken off, as she had, against the explicit command of her sire. To say that she was terrified in the sense that fear had impaired any of her faculties would not be true. However, she was a girl of keen intelligence, fully competent to understand the grave danger of her situation; and when there loomed suddenly close to the tip of her left wing a granite escarpment that was lost immediately above and below her in the all enveloping vapor, it is no reflection upon her courage that she involuntarily caught her breath in a quick gasp and simultaneously turned the nose of her ship upwards until her altimeter registered an altitude that she knew must be far higher than the loftiest peak that reared its head above any part of Africa.

Rising in a wide spiral, she was soon miles away from that terrifying menace that had seemingly leaped out of the clouds to seize her. Yet even so, her plight was still as utterly hopeless as it well could be. Her fuel was practically exhausted. To attempt to drop below the cloud banks, now that she knew positively that she was among lofty mountains, would be utter madness; and so she did the only thing that remained to her.

Alone in the cold wet clouds, far above an unknown country, Lady Barbara Collis breathed a little prayer as she bailed out. With the utmost meticulosity she counted ten before she jerked the rip cord of her chute.

At that same instant Fate was reaching out to gather other threads—far flung threads—for this tiny fragment of her tapestry.

Kabariga, chief of the Bangalo people of Bungalo, knelt before

Tarzan of the Apes many weary marches to the south of the Ghenzi Mountain.

In Moscow, Leon Stabutch entered the office of Stalin, the dictator of Red Russia.

Ignorant of the very existence of Kabariga, the black chief, or of Leon Stabutch or Lady Barbara Collis, Lafayette Smith, A.M., Ph.D., Sc.D., professor of geology at the Phil Sheridan Military Academy, boarded a steamship in the harbor of New York.

Mr. Smith was a quiet, modest, scholarly looking young man with horn rimmed spectacles, which he wore not because of any defect of eyesight but in the belief that they added a certain dignity and semblance of age to his appearance. That his spectacles were fitted with plain glass was known only to himself and his optician.

Graduated from college at seventeen the young man had devoted four additional years to acquiring further degrees, during which time he optimistically expected the stamp of dignified maturity to make itself evident in his face and bearing; but, to his intense dismay, his appearance seemed quite as youthful at twenty-one as it had at seventeen.

Lafe Smith's great handicap to the immediate fulfillment of his ambition (to occupy the chair of geology in some university of standing) lay in his possession of the unusual combination of brilliant intellect and retentive memory with robust health and a splendid physique. Do what he might he could not look sufficiently mature and scholarly to impress any college board. He tried whiskers, but the result was humiliating; and then he conceived the idea of horn rimmed spectacles and pared his ambition down, temporarily, from a university to a prep school.

For a school year, now, he had been an instructor in an inconspicuous western military academy, and now he was about to achieve another of his cherished ambitions—he was going to Africa to study the great rift valleys of the Dark Continent, concerning the formation of which there are so many theories propounded and acclaimed by acknowledged authorities on the subject as to leave the layman with the impression that a fundamental requisite to success in the science of geology is identical to that required by weather forecasters.

But be that as it may, Lafayette Smith was on his way to Africa with the financial backing of a wealthy father and the wide experience that might be gained from a number of week-end field excursions into the back pastures of accommodating farmers, plus considerable ability as a tennis player and a swimmer.

We may leave him now, with his note books and seasickness, in the hands of Fate, who is leading him inexorably toward sinister situations from which no amount of geological knowledge nor swimming nor tennis ability may extricate him.

When it is two hours before noon in New York it is an hour before sunset in Moscow and so it was that as Lafe Smith boarded the liner in the morning, Leon Stabutch, at the same moment, was closeted with Stalin late in the afternoon.

"That is all," said Stalin; "you understand?"

"Perfectly," replied Stabutch. "Peter Zveri shall be avenged, and the obstacle that thwarted our plans in Africa shall be removed."

"The latter is most essential," emphasized Stalin, "but do not belittle his abilities. He may be, as you have said, naught but an ape-man; but he utterly routed a well organized Red expedition that might have accomplished much in Abyssinia and Egypt but for his interference. And," he added, "I may tell you, comrade, that we contemplate another attempt; but it will not be made until we have a report from you that—the obstacle has been removed."

Stabutch swelled his great chest. "Have I ever failed?" he asked.

Stalin rose and laid a hand upon the other's shoulder. "Red Russia does not look to the OGPU for failures," he said. Only his lips smiled as he spoke.

That same night Leon Stabutch left Moscow. He thought that he left secretly and alone, but Fate was at his side in the compartment of the railway carriage.

As Lady Barbara Collis bailed out in the clouds above the Ghenzi range, and Lafayette Smith trod the gangplank leading aboard the liner, and Stabutch stood before Stalin, Tarzan, with knitted brows, looked down upon the black kneeling at his feet.

"Rise!" he commanded, and then; "Who are you and why have you sought Tarzan of the Apes?"

"I am Kabariga, O Great Bwana," replied the black. "I am chief of the Bangalo people of Bungalo. I come to the Great Bwana because my people suffer much sorrow and great fear and our neighbors, who are related to the Gallas, have told us that you are the friend of those who suffer wrongs at the hands of bad men."

"And what wrongs have your people suffered?" demanded Tarzan, "and at whose hands?"

"For long we lived at peace with all men," explained Kabariga; "we did not make war upon our neighbors. We wished only to plant and harvest in security. But one day there came into our country from Abyssinia a band of *shiftas* who had been driven from their own country. They raided some of our villages, stealing our grain, our goats and our people, and these they sold into slavery in far countries.

"They do not take everything, they destroy nothing; but they do not go away out of our country. They remain in a village they have built in inaccessible mountains, and when they need more provisions or slaves they come again to other villages of my people.

"And so they permit us to live and plant and harvest that they may continue to take toll of us."

"But why do you come to me?" demanded the ape-man. "I do not interfere among tribes beyond the boundaries of my own country, unless they commit some depredation against my own people."

"I come to you, Great Bwana," replied the black chief, "because you are a white man and these *shiftas* are led by a white man. It is known among all men that you are the enemy of bad white men."

"That," said Tarzan, "is different. I will return with you to your country."

And thus Fate, enlisting the services of the black chief, Kabariga, led Tarzan of the Apes out of his own country, toward the north. Nor did many of his own people know whither he had gone nor why—not even little Nkima, the close friend and confidant of the ape-man.

CHAPTER 2

The Land of Midian

ABRAHAM, THE SON of Abraham, stood at the foot of the towering cliff that is the wall of the mighty crater of a long extinct volcano. Behind and above him were the dwellings of his people, carved from the soft volcanic ash that rose from the bottom of the crater part way up the encircling cliffs; and clustered about him were the men and women and children of his tribe.

One and all, they stood with faces raised toward the heavens, upon each countenance reflected the particular emotion that the occasion evoked—wonder, questioning, fear, and always rapt, tense listening, for from the low clouds hanging but a few hundred feet above the rim of the great crater, the floor of which stretched away for fully five miles to its opposite side, came a strange, ominous droning sound, the like of which not one of them had ever heard before.

The sound grew in volume until it seemed to hover just above them, filling all the heavens with its terrifying threat; and then it diminished gradually until it was only a suggestion of a sound that might have been no more than a persistent memory rumbling in their heads; and when they thought that it had gone it grew again in volume until once more it thundered down upon them where they stood in terror or in ecstasy, as each interpreted the significance of the phenomenon.

And upon the opposite side of the crater a similar group, actuated by identical fears and questionings, clustered about Elija, the son of Noah.

In the first group a woman turned to Abraham, the son of Abraham. "What is it, Father?" she asked. "I am afraid."

"Those who trust in the Lord," replied the man, "know no fear. You have revealed the wickedness of your heresy, woman."

The face of the questioner blenched and now, indeed, did she tremble. "Oh, Father, you know that I am no heretic!" she cried piteously.

"Silence, Martha!" commanded Abraham. "Perhaps this is the Lord Himself, come again to earth as was prophesied in the days of Paul, to judge us all." His voice was high and shrill, and he trembled as he spoke.

A half grown child, upon the outskirts of the assemblage, fell to the ground, where he writhed, foaming at the mouth. A woman screamed and fainted.

"Oh, Lord, if it is indeed Thee, Thy chosen people await to receive Thy blessing and Thy commands," prayed Abraham; "but," he added, "if it is not Thee, we beseech that Thou savest us whole from harm."

"Perhaps it is Gabriel!" suggested another of the long bearded men.

"And the sound of his trump," wailed a woman—"the trump of doom!"

"Silence!" shrilled Abraham, and the woman shrank back in fear.

Unnoticed, the youth floundered and gasped for breath as, with eyes set as in death, he struggled in the throes of agony; and then another lurched and fell and he, too, writhed and foamed.

And now they were dropping on all sides—some in convulsions and others in deathlike faints—until a dozen or more sprawled upon the ground, where their pitiable condition elicited no attention from their fellows unless a stricken one chanced to fall against a neighbor or upon his feet, in which case the latter merely stepped aside without vouchsafing so much as a glance at the poor unfortunate.

With few exceptions those who suffered the violent strokes were men and boys, while it was the women who merely fainted; but whether man, woman or child, whether writhing in convulsions or lying quietly in coma, no one paid the slightest attention to any of them. As to whether this seeming indifference was customary, or merely induced by the excitement and apprehension of the moment, as they stood with eyes, ears, and minds focussed on the clouds above them, only a closer acquaintance with these strange people may enlighten us.

Once more the terrifying sound, swollen to hideous proportions, swept toward them; it seemed to stop above them for a moment and then—

Out of the clouds floated a strange apparition—a terrifying thing—a great, white thing above, below which there swung to and fro a tiny figure. At sight of it, dropping gently toward them, a dozen of the watchers collapsed, frothing, in convulsions.

Abraham, the son of Abraham, dropped to his knees, raising his hands in supplication toward the heavens. His people, those of them who were still upon their feet, followed his example. From his lips issued a torrent of strange sounds—a prayer perhaps, but if so not in the same language as that in which he had previously spoken to his people nor in any language known to man, and as he prayed, his followers knelt in terrified silence.

Closer and closer floated the mysterious apparition until, at length, expectant eyes recognized in the figure floating beneath the small, white cloud the outlines of a human form.

A great cry arose as recognition spread—a cry that was a mingling of terror born wail and ecstatic hosanna. Abraham was among the last to recognize the form of the dangling figure for what it was, or, perhaps, among the last to admit the testimony of his eyes. When he did he toppled to the ground, his muscles twitching and jerking his whole body into horrid contortions, his eyes rolled upward and set as in death, his breath expelled in painful gasps between lips flecked with foam.

Abraham, the son of Abraham, never an Adonis, was at this moment anything but a pretty sight; but no one seemed to notice him any more than they had the score or more of lesser creatures who had succumbed to the nervous excitation of the experiences of the past half hour.

Some five hundred people, men, women and children, of which thirty, perhaps, lay quietly or writhed in convulsions upon the ground, formed the group of watchers toward which Lady Barbara Collis gently floated. As she landed in, if the truth must be told (and we historians are proverbially truthful, except when we are chronicling the lives of our national heroes, or living rulers within whose grasp we may be, or of enemy peoples with whom our country has been at war, and upon other occasions)—but, as I was recording, as Lady Barbara landed in an awkward sprawl within a hundred yards of the assemblage all those who had remained standing up to this time went down upon their knees.

Hastily scrambling to her feet, the girl disengaged the harness of her parachute and stood gazing in perplexity upon the scene about her. A quick glance had revealed the towering cliffs that formed the encircling walls of the gigantic crater, though at the time she did not suspect the true nature of the valley spreading before her. It was the people who claimed her surprised attention.

They were white! In the heart of Africa she had landed in the midst of a settlement of whites. But this thought did not wholly reassure her. There was something strange and unreal about these prone and kneeling figures; but at least they did not appear ferocious or unfriendly—their attitudes, in fact, were quite the opposite, and she saw no evidence of weapons among them.

She approached them, and, as she did so, many of them began to wail and press their faces against the ground, while others raised their hands in supplication—some toward the heavens and others toward her.

She was close enough now to see their features and her heart sank within her, for she had never conceived the existence of an entire village of people of such unprepossessing appearance, and

Lady Barbara was one of those who are strongly impressed by externals.

The men were particularly repulsive. Their long hair and beards seemed as little acquainted with soap, water and combs as with shears and razors.

There were two features that impressed her most strongly and unfavorably—the huge noses and receding chins of practically the entire company. The noses were so large as to constitute a deformity, while in many of those before her, chins were almost nonexistent.

And then she saw two things that had diametrically opposite effects upon her—the score of epileptics writhing upon the ground and a singularly beautiful, golden haired girl who had risen from the prostrate herd and was slowly approaching her, a questioning look in her large grey eyes.

Lady Barbara Collis looked the girl full in the eyes and smiled, and when Lady Barbara smiled stone crumbled before the radiant vision of her face—or so a poetic and enthralled admirer had once stated in her hearing. The fact that he lisped, however, had prejudiced her against his testimony.

The girl returned the smile with one almost as gorgeous, but quickly she erased it from her features, at the same time glancing furtively about her as though fearful that some one had detected her in the commission of a crime; but when Lady Barbara extended both her hands toward her, she came forward and placed her own within the grasp of the English girl's.

"Where am I?" asked Lady Barbara. "What country is this? Who are these people?"

The girl shook her head. "Who are you?" she asked. "Are you an angel that the Lord God of Hosts has sent to His chosen people?"

It was now the turn of Lady Barbara to shake her head to evidence her inability to understand the language of the other.

An old man with a long white beard arose and came toward them, having seen that the apparition from Heaven had not struck the girl dead for her temerity.

"Get thee gone, Jezebel!" cried the old man to the girl. "How durst thou address this Heavenly visitor?"

The girl stepped back, dropping her head; and though Lady Barbara had understood no word that the man spoke, his tone and gesture, together with the action of the girl, told her what had transpired between them.

She thought quickly. She had realized the impression that her
miraculous appearance had made upon these seemingly ignorant
people, and she guessed that their subsequent attitude toward her
would be governed largely by the impression of her first acts; and
being English, she held to the English tradition of impressing upon
lesser people the authority of her breed. It would never do, therefore, to let this unkempt patriarch order the girl from her if Lady
Barbara chose to retain her; and, after glancing at the faces about
her, she was quite sure that if she must choose a companion from
among them the fair haired beauty would be her nominee.

With an imperious gesture, and a sinking heart, she stepped
forward and took the girl by the arm, and, as the latter turned a
surprised glance upon her, drew her to her side.

"Remain with me," she said, although she knew her words were
unintelligible to the girl.

"What did she say, Jezebel?" demanded the old man.

The girl was about to reply that she did not know, but something
stopped her. Perhaps the very strangeness of the question gave
her pause, for it must have been obvious to the old man that the
stranger spoke in a tongue unknown to him and, therefore, unknown to any of them.

She thought quickly, now. Why should he ask such a question
unless he might entertain a belief that she might have understood?
She recalled the smile that the stranger had brought to her lips
without her volition, and she recalled, too, that the old man had
noted it.

The girl called Jezebel knew the price of a smile in the land
of Midian, where any expression of happiness is an acknowledg-
ment of sin; and so, being a bright girl among a people who were
almost uniformly stupid, she evolved a ready answer in the hope
that it might save her from punishment.

She looked the ancient one straight in the eye. "She said, Jobab,"
she replied, "that she cometh from Heaven with a message for
the chosen people and that she will deliver the message through
me and through no other."

Now much of this statement had been suggested to Jezebel by
the remarks of the elders and the apostles as they had watched
the strange apparition descending from the clouds and had sought
to find some explanation for the phenomenon. In fact, Jobab
himself had volunteered the very essence of this theory and was,

therefore, the more ready to acknowledge belief in the girl's statement.

Lady Barbara stood with an arm about the slim shoulders of the golden haired Jezebel, her shocked gaze encompassing the scene before her—the degraded, unkempt people huddled stupidly before her, the inert forms of those who had fainted, the writhing contortions of the epileptics. With aversion she appraised the countenance of Jobab, noting the watery eyes, the huge monstrosity of his nose, the long, filthy beard that but half concealed his weak chin. With difficulty she stemmed the involuntary shudder that was her natural nervous reaction to the sight before her.

Jobab stood staring at her, an expression of awe on his stupid, almost imbecile face. From the crowd behind him several other old men approached, almost fearfully, halting just behind him. Jobab looked back over his shoulder. "Where is Abraham, the son of Abraham?" he demanded.

"He still communeth with Jehovah," replied one of the ancients.

"Perhaps even now Jehovah revealeth to him the purpose of this visitation," suggested another hopefully.

"She hath brought a message," said Jobab, "and she will deliver it only through the girl called Jezebel. I wish Abraham, the son of Abraham, was through communing with Jehovah," he added; but Abraham, the son of Abraham, still writhed upon the ground, foaming at the mouth.

"Verily," said another old man, "if this be indeed a messenger from Jehovah let us not stand thus idly staring, lest we arouse the anger of Jehovah, that he bring a plague upon us, even of flies or of lice."

"Thou speaketh true words, Timothy," agreed Jobab, and, turning to the crowd behind them; "Get thee hence quickly and fetch offerings that may be good in the sight of Jehovah, each in accordance with his ability."

Stupidly the assemblage turned away toward the caves and hovels that constituted the village, leaving the small knot of ancients facing Lady Barbara and the golden Jezebel and, upon the ground, the stricken ones, some of whom were evidencing symptoms of recovery from their seizures.

Once again a feeling of revulsion gripped the English girl as she noted the features and carriages of the villagers. Almost without exception they were disfigured by enormous noses and chins so small and receding that in many instances the chin seemed to be lacking entirely. When they walked they ordinarily leaned forward, giving the impression that they were upon the verge of pitching headlong upon their faces.

Occasionally among them appeared an individual whose countenance suggested a much higher mentality than that possessed by the general run of the villagers, and without exception these had blond hair, while the hair of all the others was black.

So striking was this phenomenon that Lady Barbara could not but note it almost in her first brief survey of these strange creatures, yet she was never to discover an indisputable explanation, for there was none to tell her of Angustus and the fair haired slave girl from some barbarian horde of the north, none who knew that Angustus had had a large nose, a weak chin and epilepsy, none to guess the splendid mind and the radiant health of that little slave girl, dead now for almost nineteen centuries, whose blood, even now, arose occasionally above the horrid decadence of all those long years of enforced inbreeding to produce such a creature as Jezebel in an effort, however futile, to stem the tide of degeneracy.

Lady Barbara wondered now why the people had gone to their dwellings—what did it portend? She looked at the old men who had remained behind; but their stupid, almost imbecile faces revealed nothing. Then she turned to the girl. How she wished that they might understand one another. She was positive that the girl was actively friendly, but she could not be so sure of these others. Everything about them repelled her, and she found it impossible to have confidence in their intentions toward her.

But how different was the girl! She, too, doubtless, was an alien among them; and that fact gave the English girl hope, for she had seen nothing to indicate that the golden haired one was being threatened or mistreated; and at least she was alive and uninjured. Yes, she must be of another breed. Her simple, and scant, apparel, fabricated apparently from vegetable fibre, was clean, as were those parts of her body exposed to view, while the garments of all the others, especially the old men, were filthy beyond words, as were their hair and beards and every portion of their bodies not concealed by the mean garments that scarce half covered their nakedness.

As the old men whispered among themselves, Lady Barbara turned slowly to look about her in all directions. She saw precipitous cliffs completely hemming a small circular valley, near the center of which was a lake. Nowhere could she see any indication of a break in the encircling walls that rose hundreds of feet above the floor of the valley; and yet she felt that there must be an entrance from the outer world, else how had these people gained entrance?

Her survey suggested that the valley lay at the bottom of the crater of a great volcano, long extinct, and if that were true the path to the outer world must cross the summit of those lofty walls; yet these appeared, insofar as she could see, utterly unscalable. But how account for the presence of these people? The problem vexed her, but she knew that it must remain unsolved until she had determined the attitude of the villagers and discovered whether she were to be a guest or a prisoner.

Now the villagers were returning, and she saw that many of them carried articles in their hands. They came slowly, timidly nearer her, exhorted by the ancients, until at her feet they deposited the burdens they had carried—bowls of cooked food, raw vegetables and fruits, fish, and pieces of the fibre cloth such as that from which their crude garments were fabricated, the homely offerings of a simple people.

As they approached her many of them displayed symptoms of great nervousness and several sank to the ground, victims of the convulsive paroxysms that marked the seizures to which so many of them appeared to be subject.

To Lady Barbara it appeared that these simple folk were either bringing gifts attesting their hospitality or were offering their wares, in barter, to the stranger within their gates; nor did the truth once occur to her at the moment—that the villagers were, in fact, making votive offerings to one they believed the messenger of God, or even, perhaps, a goddess in her own right. When, after depositing their offerings at her feet, they turned and hastened away, the simple faces of some evidencing fear caused her to abandon the idea that the goods were offered for sale; and she determined that, if not gifts of hospitality, they might easily be considered as tribute to appease the wrath of a potential enemy.

Abraham, the son of Abraham, had regained consciousness. Slowly he raised himself to a sitting position and looked about him. He was very weak. He always was after these seizures. It required a minute or two before he could collect his wits and recall the events immediately preceding the attack. He saw the last of those bringing offerings to Lady Barbara deposit them at her feet. He saw the stranger. And then he recalled the strange droning that had come out of the heavens and the apparition that he had seen floating down toward them.

Abraham, the son of Abraham, arose. It was Jobab, among the ancients, who saw him first. "Hallelujah!" he exclaimed. "Abraham, the son of Abraham, walketh no longer with Jehovah. He hath returned to our midst. Let us pray!" Whereupon the entire assemblage, with the exception of Lady Barbara and the girl called Jezebel, dropped to its knees. Among them, Abraham, the son of Abraham, moved slowly, as though in a trance, toward the stranger, his mind still lethargic from the effects of his seizure. About him arose a strange, weird babel as the ancients prayed aloud without concord or harmony, interrupted by occasional cries of "Hallelujah" and "Amen."

Tall and thin, with a long grey beard still flecked with foam and saliva, his scant robe ragged and filthy, Abraham, the son of Abraham, presented a most repulsive appearance to the eyes of the English girl as, at last, he stopped before her.

Now his mind was clearing rapidly, and as he halted he seemed to note the presence of the girl, Jezebel, for the first time. "What doest thou here, wanton?" he demanded. "Why art thou not upon thy knees praying with the others?"

Lady Barbara was watching the two closely. She noted the stern and accusing attitude and tones of the man, and she saw the appealing glance that the girl cast toward her. Instantly she threw an arm about the latter's shoulders. "Remain here!" she said, for she feared that the man was ordering the girl to leave her.

If Jezebel did not understand the words of the strange, heavenly visitor, she could not mistake the detaining gesture; and, anyway, she did not wish to join the others in prayer. Perhaps it was only that she might cling a few brief minutes longer to the position of importance to which the incident had elevated her out of a lifetime of degradation and contempt to which her strange inheritance of beauty had condemned her.

And so, nerved by the pressure of the arm about her, she faced Abraham, the son of Abraham, resolutely, although, withal, a trifle fearfully, since who knew better than she what a terrible man Abraham, the son of Abraham, might become when crossed by anyone.

"Answer me, thou—thou—" Abraham, the son of Abraham,

could not find an epithet sufficiently excoriating to meet the emergency.

"Let not thy anger blind thee to the will of Jehovah," warned the girl.

"What meanest thou?" he demanded.

"Canst thou not see that His messenger hath chosen me to be her mouthpiece?"

"What sacrilege is this, woman?"

"It is no sacrilege," she replied sturdily. "It is the will of Jehovah, and if thou believest me not, ask Jobab, the apostle."

Abraham, the son of Abraham, turned to where the ancients prayed. "Jobab!" he cried in a voice that arose above the din of prayer.

Instantly the devotions ceased with a loud "Amen!" from Jobab. The old men arose, their example being followed by those others of the villagers who were not held earth-bound by epilepsy; and Jobab, the apostle, approached the three who were now the goal of every eye.

"What transpired while I walked with Jehovah?" demanded Abraham, the son of Abraham.

"There came this messenger from heaven," replied Jobab, "and we did her honor, and the people brought offerings, each according to his ability, and laid them at her feet, and she did not seem displeased—nor either did she seem pleased," he added. "And more than this we knew not what to do."

"But this daughter of Satan!" cried Abraham, the son of Abraham. "What of her?"

"Verily I say unto you that she speaks with the tongue of Jehovah," replied Jobab, "for He hath chosen her to be the mouthpiece of His messenger."

"Jehovah be praised," said Abraham, the son of Abraham; "the ways of the Almighty passeth understanding." He turned now to Jezebel, but when he spoke there was a new note in his tones— a conciliatory note—and, perhaps, not a little of fear in his eyes. "Beseech the messenger to look upon us poor servants of Jehovah with mercy and forgiveness; beg of her that she open her mouth to us poor sinners and divulge her wishes. We await her message, trembling and fearful in the knowledge of our unworthiness."

Jezebel turned to Lady Barbara.

"But wait!" cried Abraham, the son of Abraham, as a sudden questioning doubt assailed his weak mind. "How can you converse with her? You speak only the language of the land of Midian. Verily, if thou canst speak with her, why may not I, the Prophet of Paul, the son of Jehovah?"

Jezebel had a brain worth fifty such brains as that possessed by the Prophet of Paul; and now she used it to advantage, though, if the truth were known, not without some misgivings as to the outcome of her rash proposal, for, although she had a bright and resourceful mind, she was none the less the ignorant child of an ignorant and superstitious people.

"Thou hast a tongue, Prophet," she said. "Speak thou then to the messenger of Jehovah, and if she answers thee in the language of the land of Midian thou canst understand her as well as I."

"That," said Abraham, the son of Abraham, "is scarce less than an inspiration."

"A miracle!" exclaimed Jobab. "Jehovah must have put the words in her mouth."

"I shall address the messenger," said the Prophet. "O angel of light!" he cried, turning toward Lady Barbara, "look with compassion upon an old man, upon Abraham, the son of Abraham, the Prophet of Paul, the son of Jehovah, and deign to make known to him the wishes of Him who sent you to us."

Lady Barbara shook her head. "There is something that one does when one is embarrassed," she said. "I have read it repeatedly in the advertising sections of American periodicals, but I haven't that brand. However, any port in a storm," and she extracted a gold cigarette case from a pocket of her jacket and lighted one of the cigarettes.

"What didst she say, Jezebel?" demanded the Prophet—"and, in the name of Paul, what miracle is this? 'Out of his nostrils goeth smoke' is said of the behemoth of holy writ. What can be the meaning of this?"

"It is a warning," said Jezebel, "because thou didst doubt my words."

"Nay, nay," exclaimed Abraham, the son of Abraham, "I doubted thee not. Tell her that I did not doubt thee, and then tell me what she said."

"She said," replied Jezebel, "that Jehovah is not pleased with thee or thy people. He is angry because thou so mistreat Jezebel. His anger is terrible because thou dost make her work beyond her strength, nor give her the best food, and that thou dost punish her when she would laugh and be happy."

"Tell her," said the Prophet, "that we knew not that thou wert overworked and that we shall make amends. Tell her that we lovest thee and thou shalt have the best of food. Speak to her, O Jezebel, and ask if she has further commands for her poor servants."

Jezebel looked into the eyes of the English girl, and upon her countenance rested an expression of angelic guilelessness, while from her lips issued a stream of meaningless jargon which was as unintelligible to Jezebel as to Lady Barbara or the listening villagers of the land of Midian.

"My dear child," said Lady Barbara, when Jezebel eventually achieved a period, "what you say is as Greek to me, but you are very beautiful and your voice is musical. I am sorry that you can understand me no better than I understand you."

"What saith she?" demanded Abraham, the son of Abraham.

"She says that she is tired and hungry and that she wishes the offerings brought by the people to be taken to a cave—a clean cave—and that I accompany her and that she be left in peace, as she is tired and would rest; and she wishes no one but Jezebel to be with her."

Abraham, the son of Abraham, turned to Jobab. "Send women to make clean the cave next to mine," he commanded, "and have others carry the offerings to the cave, as well as clean grasses for a bed."

"For two beds," Jezebel corrected him.

"Yea, even for two beds," agreed the Prophet, hastily.

And so Lady Barbara and Jezebel were installed in a well renovated cave near the bottom of the cliff, with food enough to feed a numerous company. The English girl stood at the entrance to her strange, new abode looking out across the valley as she sought to evolve some plan whereby she might get word of her predicament and her whereabouts to the outside world. In another twenty-four hours she knew the apprehension of her friends and her family would be aroused and soon many an English plane would be roaring over the Cape to Cairo route in search of her, and, as she pondered her unfortunate situation, the girl called Jezebel lay in luxurious idleness upon her bed of fresh grasses and ate from a pile of fruit near her hand, the while a happy smile of contentment illumed her lovely countenance.

The shadows of night were already falling, and Lady Barbara turned back into the cave with but a single practical idea evolved from all her thinking—that she must find the means to communicate with these people, nor could she escape the conviction that only by learning their language might this be accomplished.

As darkness came and chill night air replaced the heat of the day, Jezebel kindled a fire at the mouth of the cave. Near it the two girls sat upon a soft cushion of grass, the firelight playing upon their faces, and there the Lady Barbara commenced the long and tedious task of mastering a new language. The first step consisted in making Jezebel understand what she desired to accomplish, but she was agreeably astonished at the celerity with which the girl grasped the idea. Soon she was pointing to various objects, calling them by their English names and Jezebel was naming them in the language of the land of Midian.

Lady Barbara would repeat the word in the Midian language several times until she had mastered the pronunciation, and she noticed that, similarly, Jezebel was repeating its English equivalent. Thus was Jezebel acquiring an English vocabulary while she taught the Midian to her guest.

An hour passed while they occupied their time with their task. The village lay quiet about them. Faintly, from the distant lake, came the subdued chorus of the frogs. Occasionally a goat bleated somewhere out in the darkness. Far away, upon the opposite side of the valley, shone tiny, flickering lights—the cooking fires of another village, thought Lady Barbara.

A man, bearing a lighted torch, appeared suddenly, coming from a nearby cave. In low, monotonous tones he voiced a chant. Another man, another torch, another voice joined him. And then came others until a procession wound down toward the level ground below the caves.

Gradually the voices rose. A child screamed. Lady Barbara saw it now—a small child being dragged along by an old man.

Now the procession encircled a large boulder and halted, but the chanting did not cease, nor did the screaming of the child. Tall among the others Lady Barbara recognized the figure of the man who had last interrogated her. Abraham, the son of Abraham, the Prophet, stood behind the boulder that rose waist high in front of him. He raised his open palm and the chanting ceased. The child had ceased to scream, but its broken sobs came clearly to the ears of the two girls.

Abraham, the son of Abraham, commenced to speak, his eyes raised toward the heavens. His voice came monotonously across the little span of darkness. His grotesque features were lighted by the flickering torches that played as well upon the equally repulsive faces of his congregation.

Unaccountably, the entire scene assumed an aspect of menace in the eyes of the English girl. Apparently it was only the simple religious service of a simple people and yet, to Barbara Collis, there was something terrible about it, something that seemed fraught with horror.

She glanced at Jezebel. The girl was sitting cross legged, her elbows on her knees, her chin supported in the palms of her hands, staring straight ahead. There was no smile now upon her lips.

Suddenly the air was rent by a childish scream of fear and horror that brought the Lady Barbara's gaze back to the scene below. She saw the child, struggling and fighting, dragged to the top of the boulder; she saw Abraham, the son of Abraham, raise a hand above his head; she saw the torchlight play upon a knife; and then she turned away and hid her face in her hands.

CHAPTER 3

The "Gunner"

DANNY "GUNNER" PATRICK stretched luxuriously in his deck chair. He was at peace with the world—temporarily, at least. In his clothes were 20 G. securely hidden. Beneath his left arm pit, also securely hidden, snuggled a .45 in a specially designed holster. "Gunner" Patrick did not expect to have to use it for a long, long time perhaps; but it was just as well to be prepared. "Gunner" hailed from Chicago where people in his circle of society believe in preparedness.

He had never been a Big Shot, and if he had been content to remain more or less obscure he might have gone along about his business for some time until there arrived the allotted moment when, like many of his late friends and acquaintances, he should be elected to stop his quota of machine gun bullets; but Danny Patrick was ambitious. For years he had been the right hand, and that means the pistol hand, of a Big Shot. He had seen his patron grow rich—"lousy rich," according to Danny's notion—and he had become envious.

So Danny double-crossed the Big Shot, went over to the other side, which, incidentally, boasted a bigger and better Big Shot, and was a party to the hijacking of several truck loads of booze belonging to his former employer.

Unfortunately, on the occasion of the hijacking of the last truck, one of his former pals in the service of the double-crossee recognized him; and Danny, knowing that he had been recognized, sought, quite pardonably, to eliminate this damaging evidence; but his unwilling target eluded him and before he could rectify his ballistic errors the police came.

It is true that they obligingly formed an escort to convoy the truck safely to the warehouse of the bigger and better Big Shot, but the witness to Danny's perfidy escaped.

Now Danny "Gunner" Patrick knew the temper of his erstwhile patron—and who better? Many of the Big Shot's enemies, and several of his friends, had Danny taken for a ride. He knew the power of the Big Shot, and he feared him. Danny did not want to go for a ride himself, but he knew that if he remained in dear old Chi he would go the way of all good gunmen much too soon to suit his plans.

And so, with the 20 G. that had been the price of his perfidy, he had slipped quietly out of town; and, being wise in his day and generation, he had also slipped quietly out of the country, another thread to be woven into Fate's tapestry.

He knew that the Big Shot was slipping (that was one reason he had deserted him); and he also knew that, sooner or later, the Big Shot would have a grand funeral with truck loads of flowers and, at least, a ten thousand dollar casket. So Danny would dally in foreign climes until after the funeral.

Just where he would dally he did not know, for Danny was shy of geographic lore; but he knew he was going at least as far as England, which he also knew to be somewhere in London.

So now he lolled in the sun, at peace with the world that immediately surrounded him; or almost at peace, for there rankled in his youthful breast various snubs that had been aimed in his direction by the few fellow passengers he had accosted. Danny was at a loss to understand why he was *persona non grata*. He was good looking. His clothes had been designed by one of Chicago's most exclusive tailors—they were quiet and in good taste. These things Danny knew, and he also knew that no one aboard ship had any inkling of his profession. Why then, after a few minutes conversation, did they invariably lose interest in him and thereafter look through him as though he did not exist? The "Gunner" was both puzzled and peeved.

It was the third day out, and Danny was already fed up on ocean travel. He almost wished that he were back in Chicago where he knew he could find congenial spirits with whom to foregather, but not quite. Better a temporary isolation above ground than a permanent one below.

A young man whom he had not before noticed among the passengers came and sat down in the chair next to his. He looked over at Danny and smiled. "Good morning," he said. "Lovely weather we're having."

Danny's cold, blue eyes surveyed the stranger. "Are we?" he replied in a tone as cold as his gaze; then he resumed his previous occupation of staring out across the rail at the illimitable expanse of rolling sea.

Lafayette Smith smiled, opened a book, settled himself more comfortably in his chair and proceeded to forget all about his discourteous neighbor.

Later that day Danny saw the young man at the swimming pool and was impressed by one of the few things that Danny could really understand—proficiency in a physical sport. The young man far outshone the other passengers both in swimming and diving, and his sun bronzed body evidenced long hours in a bathing suit.

The following morning when Danny came on deck he found that the young man had preceded him. "Good morning," said Danny pleasantly as he dropped into his chair. "Nice morning."

The young man looked up from his book. "Is it?" he asked and let his eyes fall again to the printed page.

Danny laughed. "Right back at me, eh?" he exclaimed. "You see I thought youse was one of them high hat guys. Then I seen you in the tank. You sure can dive, buddy."

Lafayette Smith, A.M., Ph.D., Sc.D., let his book drop slowly to his lap as he turned to survey his neighbor. Presently a smile stole across his face—a good natured, friendly smile. "Thanks," he said. "You see it is because I like it so well. A fellow who's spent as much time at it as I have ever since I was a little shaver would have to be an awful dub not to be fairly proficient."

"Yeah," agreed Danny. "It's your racket, I suppose."

Lafayette Smith looked about the deck around his chair. He thought, at first, that Danny was referring to a tennis racquet, as that would be the thing that the word would connote to the mind of so ardent a tennis enthusiast as he. Then he caught the intended meaning and smiled. "I am not a professional swimmer, if that is what you mean," he said.

"Pleasure trip?" inquired Danny.

"Well, I hope it will be," replied the other, "but it is largely what might be called a business trip, too. Scientific investigation. I am a geologist."

"Yeah? I never heard of that racket before."

"It is not exactly a racket," said Smith. "There is not enough money in it to raise it to the importance and dignity of a racket."

"Oh, well, I know a lot of little rackets that pay good—especially if a fellow goes it alone and doesn't have to split with a mob. Going to England?"

"I shall be in London a couple of days only," replied Smith.

"I thought maybe you was goin' to England."

Lafayette Smith looked puzzled. "I am," he said.

"Oh, you're goin' there from London?"

Was the young man trying to kid him? Very good! "Yes," he said, "if I can get permission from King George to do so I shall visit England while I am in London."

"Say, does that guy live in England? He's the fellow Big Bill was goin' to punch in the snoot. Geeze, but there is one big bag of hot wind."

"Who, King George?"

"No, I don't know him—I mean Thompson."

"I don't know either of them," admitted Smith; "but I've heard of King George."

"You aint never heard of Big Bill Thompson, mayor of Chicago?"

"Oh, yes; but there are so many Thompsons—I didn't know to which one you referred."

"Do you have to get next to King George to get to England?" demanded Danny, and something in the earnestness of his tone assured Smith that the young man had not been kidding him.

"No," he replied. "You see London is the capital of England. When you are in London you are, of course, in England."

"Geeze!" exclaimed Danny. "I sure was all wet, wasn't I; but you see," he added confidentially, "I aint never been out of America before."

"Are you making a protracted stay in England?"

"A what?"

"Are you going to remain in England for some time?"

"I'll see how I like it," replied Danny.

"I think you'll like London," Smith told him.

"I don't have to stay there," Danny confided; "I can go where I please. Where are you goin'?"

"To Africa."

"Where the smokes come from."

"What? Oh, yes."

"What sort of a burgh is it? I don't think I'd like bein' bossed by a lot of smokes, though most of 'em is regular, at that. I knew some nigger cops in Chi that never looked to frame a guy."

"You wouldn't be bothered by any policeman where I'm going," Smith assured him; "there are none."

"Geeze! you don't say? But get me right, mister, I ain't worried about no cops—they aint got nothin' on me. Though I sure would like to go somewhere where I wouldn't never see none of their ugly mugs. You know, mister," he added confidentially, "I just can't like a cop."

This young man puzzled Lafayette Smith the while he amused him. Being a scholar, and having pursued scholarly ways in a quiet university town, Smith was only aware of the strange underworld of America's great cities to such a sketchy extent as might result from a cursory and disinterested perusal of the daily press. He could not catalog his new acquaintance by any first hand knowledge. He had never talked with exactly such a type before. Outwardly, the young man might be the undergraduate son of a cultured family, but when he spoke one had to revise this first impression.

"Say," exclaimed Danny, after a short silence; "I know about this here Africa, now. I seen a moving pitcher once—lions and elephants and a lot of foolish lookin' deer with funny monickers. So that's where you're goin'? Huntin', I suppose?"

"Not for animals, but for rocks," explained Smith.

"Geeze! Who ain't huntin' for rocks?" demanded Danny. "I know guys would croak their best friends for a rock."

"Not the sort I'm going to look for," Smith assured him.

"You don't mean diamonds then?"

"No, just rock formations that will teach me more about the structure of the earth."

"And you can't cash in on them after you find them?"

"No."

"Geeze, that's a funny racket. You know a lot about this here Africa, don't you?"

"Only what I've read in books," replied Smith.

"I had a book once," said Danny, with almost a verbal swagger.

"Yes?" said Smith politely. "Was it about Africa?"

"I don't know. I never read it. Say, I been thinkin'," he added. "Why don't I go to this here Africa? That pitcher I seen looked like they wasn't many people there, and I sure would like to get away from people for a while—I'm fed up on 'em. How big a place is Africa?"

"Almost four times as large as the United States."

"Geeze! An' no cops?"

"Not where I'm going, nor very many people. Perhaps I shall see no one but the members of my safari for weeks at a time."

"Safari?"

"My people—porters, soldiers, servants."

"Oh, your mob."

"It may be."

"What say I go with you, mister? I don't understand your racket and I don't want to, but I won't demand no cut-in whatever it is. Like the old dame that attended the funeral, I just want to go along for the ride—only I'll pay my way."

Lafayette Smith wondered. There was something about this young man he liked, and he certainly found him interesting as a type. Then, too, there was an indefinable something in his manner and in those cold, blue eyes that suggested he might be a good companion in an emergency. Furthermore, Lafayette Smith had recently been thinking that long weeks in the interior without the companionship of another white man might prove intolerable. Yet he hesitated. He knew nothing about the man. He might be a fugitive from justice. He might be anything. Well, what of it? He had about made up his mind.

"If it's expenses that's worrying you," said Danny, noting the other's hesitation, "forget 'em. I'll pay my share and then some, if you say so."

"I wasn't thinking of that, though the trip will be expensive— not much more for two, though, than for one."

"How much?"

"Frankly, I don't know, but I have been assuming that five thousand dollars should cover everything, though I may be wrong."

Danny Patrick reached into his trousers' pocket and brought forth a great roll of bills—50's and 100's. He counted out three thousand dollars. "Here's three G. to bind the bargain," he said, "and there's more where that came from. I aint no piker. I'll pay my share and part of yours, too."

"No," said Smith, motioning the proffered bills aside. "It is not that. You see we don't know anything about each other. We might not get along together."

"You know as much about me as I do about you," replied Danny, "and I'm game to take a chance. Maybe the less we know the better. Anyhow, I'm goin' to this here Africa, and if you're goin' too, we might as well go together. It'll cut down expenses, and two white fellows is got a better chance than one alone in any bunch of smokes I ever seen. Do we stick or do we split?"

Lafayette Smith laughed. Here, perhaps, was the making of an adventure, and in his scholarly heart he had long held the secret hope that some day he might go adventuring. "We stick," he said.

"Gimme five!" exclaimed "Gunner" Patrick, extending his hand.

"Five what?" asked Lafayette Smith, A.M., Ph.D., Sc.D.

CHAPTER 4

Gathering the Strands

WEEKS ROLLED BY. Trains rattled and chugged. Steamships plowed. Black feet padded well worn trails. Three safaris, headed by white men from far separated parts of the earth, moved slowly along different trails that led toward the wild fastnesses of the Ghenzis. None knew of the presence of the others, nor were their missions in any way related.

From the West came Lafayette Smith and "Gunner" Patrick; from the South, an English big game hunter, Lord Passmore; from the East, Leon Stabutch.

The Russian had been having trouble with his men. They had enlisted with enthusiasm, but their eagerness to proceed had waned as they penetrated more deeply into strange and unknown country.

Recently they had talked with men of a village beside which they had camped, and these men had told them terrifying tales of the great band of *shiftas,* led by a white man, that was terrorizing the country toward which they were marching, killing and raping as they collected slaves to be sold in the north.

Stabutch had halted for the noonday rest upon the southern slopes of the foothills of the Ghenzis. To the north rose the lofty peaks of the main range; to the south, below them, they could see forest and jungle stretching away into the distance; about them were rolling hills, sparsely timbered, and between the hills and the forest an open, grassy plain where herds of antelope and zebra could be seen grazing.

The Russian called his headman to him. "What's the matter with those fellows?" he asked, nodding toward the porters, who were gathered, squatting, in a circle, jabbering in low voices.

"They are afraid, Bwana," replied the black.

"Afraid of what?" demanded Stabutch, though he well knew.

"Afraid of the *shiftas,* Bwana. Three more deserted last night."

"We didn't need them anyway," snapped Stabutch; "the loads are getting lighter."

"More will run away," said the headman. "They are all afraid."

"They had better be afraid of me," blustered Stabutch. "If any more men desert I'll—I'll——"

"They are not afraid of you, Bwana," the headman told him, candidly. "They are afraid of the *shiftas* and the white man who is their chief. They do not want to be sold into slavery, far from their own country."

"Don't tell me you believe in that cock-and-bull story, you black rascal," snapped Stabutch. "It's just an excuse to turn back. They want to get home so they can loaf, the lazy dogs. And I guess you're as bad as the rest of them. Who said you were a headman, anyway? If you were worth a kopeck you'd straighten those fellows out in no time; and we wouldn't have any more talk about turning back, nor any more desertions, either."

"Yes, Bwana," replied the black; but what he thought was his own business.

"Now, listen to me," growled Stabutch, but that to which he would have had the headman listen was never voiced.

The interruption came from one of the porters, who leaped suddenly to his feet, voicing a low cry of warning pregnant with terror. "Look!" he cried, pointing toward the west. "The *shiftas!*"

Silhouetted against the sky, a group of mounted men had reined in their horses upon the summit of a low hill a mile away. The distance was too great to permit the excited watchers in the Russian's camp to distinguish details, but the very presence of a body of horsemen was all the assurance that the blacks needed to convince them that it was composed of members of the *shifta* band of which they had heard terrifying rumors that had filled their simple breasts with steadily increasing dread during the past several days. The white robes fluttering in the breeze at the summit of the distant hill, the barrels of rifles and the shafts of spears that, even at a distance, were sufficiently suggestive of their true nature to permit of no doubt, but served to definitely crystallize the conjectures of the members of Stabutch's safari and augment their panic.

They were standing now, every eye turned toward the menace of that bristling hill top. Suddenly one of the men ran toward the loads that had been discarded during the noonday halt, calling something back over his shoulder to his fellows. Instantly there was a break for the loads.

"What are they doing?" cried Stabutch. "Stop them!"

The headman and the askaris ran quickly toward the porters, many of whom already had shouldered their loads and were starting on the back trail. The headman sought to stop them, but one, a great, burly fellow, felled him with a single blow. Then another, glancing back toward the west, voiced a shrill cry of terror. "Look!" he cried. "They come!"

Those who heard him turned to see the horsemen, their robes fluttering backward in the breeze, reining down the hillside toward them at a gallop.

It was enough. As one man, porters, askaris, and the headman, they turned and fled. Those who had shouldered loads threw them to the ground lest their weight retard the runner's speed.

Stabutch was alone. For an instant he hesitated on the verge of flight, but almost immediately he realized the futility of attempted escape.

With loud yells the horsemen were bearing down upon his camp; and presently, seeing him standing there alone, they drew rein before him. Hard faced, villainous appearing blacks, they presented such an appearance of evil as might have caused the stoutest heart to quail.

Their leader was addressing Stabutch in a strange tongue, but his attitude was so definitely menacing that the Russian had little need of knowledge of the other's language to interpret the threat reflected in the speaker's tones and scowling face; but he dissembled his fears and met the blacks with a cool equanimity that impressed them with the thought that the stranger must be sure of his power. Perhaps he was but the advance guard of a larger body of white men!

The *shiftas* looked about them uneasily as this thought was voiced by one of their number, for they well knew the temper and the arms of white men and feared both. Yet, notwithstanding their doubts, they could still appreciate the booty of the camp, as they cast covetous and appraising eyes upon the abandoned loads of the departed porters, most of whom were still in view as they scurried toward the jungle.

Failing to make himself understood by the white man, the leader of the *shiftas* fell into a heated argument with several of his henchmen and when one, sitting, stirrup to stirrup, beside him, raised his rifle and aimed it at Stabutch the leader struck the weapon up and berated his fellow angrily. Then he issued several orders, with the result that, while two of the band remained to guard Stabutch, the others dismounted and loaded the packs on several of the horses.

A half hour later the *shiftas* rode back in the direction from which they had come, taking with them all of the Russian's belongings and him, also, disarmed and a prisoner.

And, as they rode away, keen grey eyes watched them from the concealing verdure of the jungle—eyes that had been watching every turn of events in the camp of the Russian since Stabutch had called the halt for the disastrous noonday rest.

Though considerable the distance from the jungle to the camp, nothing had escaped the keen eyes of the watcher reclining at ease in the fork of a great tree just at the edge of the plain. What his mental reactions to the happenings he had witnessed none might have guessed by any changing expression upon his stern, emotionless countenance.

He watched the retreating figures of the *shiftas* until they had disappeared from view, and then he sprang lightly to his feet and swung off through the jungle in the opposite direction—in the direction taken by the fleeing members of Stabutch's safari.

Goloba, the headman, trod fearfully the gloomy trails of the jungle; and with him were a considerable number of the other members of Stabutch's safari, all equally fearful lest the *shiftas* pursue them.

The first panic of their terror had abated; and as the minutes sped, with no sign of pursuit, they took greater heart, though there grew in the breast of Goloba another fear to replace that which was fading—it was the fear of the trusted lieutenant who has deserted his bwana. It was something that Goloba would have to explain one day, and even now he was formulating his excuse. "They rode upon us, firing their rifles," he said. "There were many of them—at least a hundred." No one disputed him. "We fought bravely in defense of the Bwana, but we were few and could not repulse them." He paused and looked at those walking near him. He saw that they nodded their heads in assent. "And then I saw the Bwana fall and so, to escape being taken and sold into slavery, we ran away."

"Yes," said one walking at his side, "it is all as Goloba has said. I myself—" but he got no further. The figure of a bronzed white man, naked but for a loin cloth, dropped from the foliage of the trees into the trail a dozen paces ahead of them. As one man they halted, surprise and fear writ large upon their faces.

"Which is the headman?" demanded the stranger in their own dialect, and every eye turned upon Goloba.

"I am," replied the black leader.

"Why did you desert your bwana?"

Goloba was about to reply when the thought occurred to him that here was only a single, primitively armed white without companions, without a safari—a poor creature, indeed, in the jungle—lower than the meanest black.

"Who are you, to question Goloba, the headman?" he demanded, sneeringly. "Get out of my way," and he started forward along the trail toward the stranger.

But the white man did not move. He merely spoke, in low, even tones. "Goloba should know better," he said, "than to speak thus to any white man."

The black hesitated. He was not quite sure of himself, but yet he ventured to hold his ground. "Great bwanas do not go naked and alone through the forests, like the low Bagesu. Where is your safari?"

"Tarzan of the Apes needs no safari," replied the white man.

Goloba was stunned. He had never seen Tarzan of the Apes, for he came from a country far from Tarzan's stamping ground, but he had heard tales of the great bwana—tales that had lost nothing in the telling.

"You are Tarzan?" he asked.

The white man nodded, and Goloba sank, fearfully, to his knees. "Have mercy, great bwana!" he begged. "Goloba did not know."

"Now, answer my question," said Tarzan. "Why did you desert your bwana?"

"We were attacked by a band of *shiftas*," replied Goloba. "They rode upon us, firing their rifles. There were at least a hundred of them. We fought bravely—"

"Stop!" commanded Tarzan. "I saw all that transpired. No shots were fired. You ran away before you knew whether the horsemen were enemies or friends. Speak now, but speak true words."

"We knew that they were enemies," said Goloba, "for we had been warned by villagers, near whom we had camped, that these *shiftas* would attack us and sell into slavery all whom they captured."

"What more did the villagers tell you?" asked the ape-man.

"That the *shiftas* are led by a white man."

"That is what I wished to know," said Tarzan.

"And now may Goloba and his people go?" asked the black. "We fear that the *shiftas* may be pursuing us."

"They are not," Tarzan assured him. "I saw them ride away toward the west, taking your bwana with them. It is of him I would know more. Who is he? What does he here?"

"He is from a country far in the north," replied Goloba. "He called it Russa."

"Yes," said Tarzan. "I know the country. Why did he come here?"

"I do not know," replied Goloba. "It was not to hunt. He did not hunt, except for food."

"Did he speak ever of Tarzan?" demanded the ape-man.

"Yes," replied Goloba. "Often he asked about Tarzan. At every village he asked when they had seen Tarzan and where he was; but none knew."

"That is all," said the ape-man. "You may go."

CHAPTER 5

When the Lion Charged

LORD PASSMORE WAS camped in a natural clearing on the bank of a small river a few miles south of the jungle's northern fringe. His stalwart porters and askaris squatted over their cooking fires laughing and joking among themselves. It was two hours past sunset; and Lord Passmore, faultlessly attired in dinner clothes, was dining, his native boy, standing behind his chair, ready to anticipate his every need.

A tall, well built negro approached the fly beneath which Lord Passmore's camp table had been placed. "You sent for me, bwana?" he asked.

Lord Passmore glanced up into the intelligent eyes of the handsome black. There was just the faintest shadow of a smile lurking about the corners of the patrician mouth of the white man. "Have you anything to report?" he asked.

"No, bwana," replied the black. "Neither to the east nor to the west were there signs of game. Perhaps the bwana had better luck."

"Yes," replied Passmore, "I was more fortunate. To the north I saw signs of game. Tomorrow, perhaps, we shall have better hunting. Tomorrow I shall—" He broke off abruptly. Both men were suddenly alert, straining their ears to a faint sound that rose above the nocturnal voices of the jungle for a few brief seconds.

The black looked questioningly at his master. "You heard it, bwana?" he asked. The white nodded. "What was it, bwana?"

"It sounded deucedly like a machine gun," replied Passmore. "It came from south of us; but who the devil would be firing a machine gun here? and why at night?"

"I do not know, bwana," replied the headman. "Shall I go and find out?"

"No," said the Englishman. "Perhaps tomorrow. We shall see. Go now, and get your sleep."

"Yes, bwana; good night."

"Good night—and warn the askari on sentry duty to be watchful."

"Yes, bwana." The black bowed very low and backed from beneath the fly. Then he moved silently away, the flickering flames of the cook fires reflecting golden high lights from his smooth brown skin, beneath which played the mighty muscles of a giant.

"This," remarked "Gunner" Patrick, "is the life. I aint seen a cop for weeks."

Lafayette Smith smiled. "If cops are the only things you fear, Danny, your mind and your nerves can be at rest for several weeks more."

"What give you the idea I was afraid of cops?" demanded Danny. "I aint never seen the cop I was afraid of. They're a bunch of punks. Anyhow, they aint got nothin' on me. What a guy's got to look out for though is they might frame a guy. But, geeze, out here a guy don't have to worry about nothin'." He settled back easily in his camp chair and exhaled a slowly spiraling column of cigarette smoke that rose lazily in the soft night air of the jungle. "Geeze," he remarked after a brief silence, "I didn't know a guy could feel so peaceful. Say, do you know this is the first time in years I aint packed a rod?"

"A what?"

"A rod, iron, a gat—you know—a gun."

"Why didn't you say so in the first place?" laughed Smith. "Why don't you try talking English once in a while?"

"Geeze!" exclaimed Danny. "You're a great guy to talk about a guy talkin' English! What's that you pulled on me the other day when we was crossin' that open rollin' country? I learned that by heart—'a country of low relief in an advanced stage of mature dissection'—an' you talk about me talkin' English! You and your thrust faults and escarpments, your calderas and solfataras—geeze!"

"Well, you're learning, Danny."

"Learnin' what? Every racket has its own lingo. What good is your line to me? But every guy wants to know what a rod is— if he knows what's good for his health."

"From what Ogonyo tells me it may be just as well to continue 'packing your rod,' " said Smith.

"How come?"

"He says we're getting into lion country. We may even find them near here. They don't often frequent jungles, but we're only about a day's march to more open terrain."

"Whatever that is. Talk English. Geeze! What was that?" A series of coughing grunts rose from somewhere in the solid black wall of jungle that surrounded the camp, to be followed by a thunderous roar that shook the earth.

"Simba!" cried one of the blacks, and immediately a half dozen men hastened to add fuel to the fires.

"Gunner" Patrick leaped to his feet and ran into the tent, emerging a moment later with a Thompson submachine gun. "T'ell with a rod," he said. "When I get that baby on the spot I want a typewriter."

"Are you going to take him for a ride?" inquired Lafayette Smith, whose education had progressed noticeably in the weeks he had spent in the society of Danny "Gunner" Patrick.

"No," admitted Danny, "unless he tries to muscle in on my racket."

Once again the rumbling roar of the lion shattered the quiet of the outer darkness. This time it sounded so close that both men started nervously.

"He appears to be harboring the thought," commented Smith.

"What thought?" demanded the "Gunner."

"About muscling in."

"The smokes got the same hunch," said Danny. "Look at 'em."

The blacks were palpably terrified and were huddled close to the fires, the askaris fingering the triggers of their rifles. The "Gunner" walked over to where they stood straining their eyes out into the impenetrable darkness.

"Where is he?" he asked Ogonyo, the headman. "Have you seen him?"

"Over there," said Ogonyo. "It looks like something moving over there, bwana."

Danny peered into the darkness. He could see nothing, but now he thought he heard a rustling of foliage beyond the fires. He dropped to one knee and aimed the machine gun in the direction of the sound. There was a burst of flame and the sudden rat-a-tat-tat of the weapon as he squeezed the trigger. For a moment the ringing ears of the watchers heard nothing, and then, as their auditory nerves returned to normal, to the keenest ears among them came the sound of crashing among the bushes, diminishing in the distance.

"I guess I nicked him," said Danny to Smith, who had walked over and was standing behind him.

"You didn't kill him," said Smith. "You must have wounded him."

"Simba is not wounded, bwana," said Ogonyo.

"How do you know?" demanded Danny. "You can't see nothin' out there."

"If you had wounded him he would have charged," explained the headman. "He ran away. It was the noise that frightened him."

"Do you think he will come back?" asked Smith.

"I do not know, bwana," replied the negro. "No one knows what Simba will do."

"Of course he won't come back," said Danny. "The old typewriter scared him stiff. I'm goin' to turn in."

Numa, the lion, was old and hungry. He had been hunting in the open country; but his muscles, while still mighty, were not what they had been in his prime. When he reared to seize Pacco, the zebra, or Wappi, the antelope, he was always just a trifle slower than he had been in the past; and his prey eluded him. So Numa, the lion, had wandered into the jungle where the scent of man had attracted him to the camp. The beast fires of the blacks blinded him; but, beyond them, his still keen scent told him there was flesh and blood, and Numa, the lion, was ravenous.

Slowly his hunger was overcoming his inherent urge to avoid the man-things; little by little it drew him closer to the hated fires. Crouched almost upon his belly he moved forward a few inches at a time. In another moment he would charge—and then came the sudden burst of flame, the shattering crash of the machine gun, the shriek of bullets above his head.

The startling suddenness with which this unexpected tumult broke the fear laden silence of the camp and the jungle snapped the taut nerves of the great cat, and his reaction was quite as natural as it was involuntary. Wheeling in his tracks, he bounded away into the forest.

The ears of Numa, the lion, were not the only jungle ears upon which the discord of "Gunner" Patrick's typewriter impinged, for that seeming solitude of impenetrable darkness harbored a myriad life. For an instant it was motionless, startled into immobility; and then it moved on again upon the multitudinous concerns of its varied existence. Some, concerned by the strangeness of the noise, moved farther from the vicinity of the camp of the man-things; but there was at least one that curiosity attracted to closer investigation.

Gradually the camp was settling down for the night. The two bwanas had retired to the seclusion of their tent. The blacks had partially overcome their nervousness, and most of them had lain down to sleep. A few watched the beast fires near which two askaris stood on guard, one on either side of the camp.

Numa stood with low hung head out there, somewhere, in the night. The tattoo of the machine gun had not appeased his appetite, but it had added to his nervous irritability—and to his caution. No longer did he rumble forth his coughing protests against the emptiness of his belly as he watched the flames of the beast fires that now fed the flood of his anger until it submerged his fears.

And as the camp drifted gradually into sleep the tawny body of the carnivore slunk slowly closer to the dancing circle of the beast fires' light. The yellow-green eyes stared in savage fixity at an unsuspecting askari leaning sleepily upon his rifle.

The man yawned and shifted his position. He noted the condition of the fire. It needed new fuel, and the black turned to the pile of branches and dead wood behind him. As he stooped to gather what he required, his back toward the jungle, Numa charged.

The great lion wished to strike swiftly and silently; but something within him, the mark of the ages of charging forebears that had preceded him, raised a low, ominous growl in his throat.

The victim heard and so did "Gunner" Patrick, lying sleepless on his cot. As the askari wheeled to the menace of that awesome warning, the "Gunner" leaped to his feet, seizing the Thompson as he sprang into the open just as Numa rose, towering, above the black. A scream of terror burst from the lips of the doomed man in the instant that the lion's talons buried themselves in his shoulders. Then the giant jaws closed upon his face.

The scream, fraught with the terror of utter hopelessness, awakened the camp. Men, startled into terrified consciousness, sprang to their feet, most of them in time to see Numa, half carrying, half dragging his victim, bounding off into the darkness.

The "Gunner" was the first to see all this and the only one to act. Without waiting to kneel he raised the machine gun to his shoulder. That his bullets must indubitably find the man if they found the lion was of no moment to Danny Patrick, intimate of sudden and violent death. He might have argued that the man was already dead, but he did not waste a thought upon a possibility which was, in any event, of no consequence, so do environment and habitude warp or dull the sensibilities of man.

The lion was still discernible in the darkness when Danny squeezed the trigger of his beloved typewriter, and this time he did not miss—perhaps unfortunately, for a wounded lion is as dangerous an engine of destruction as an all wise Providence can create.

Aroused by the deafening noise of the weapon, enraged by the wound inflicted by the single slug that entered his body, apprehending that he was to be robbed of his prey, and bent upon swift and savage reprisal, Numa dropped the askari, wheeled about, and charged straight for Danny Patrick.

The "Gunner" was kneeling, now, to take better aim. Lafayette Smith stood just behind him, armed only with a nickel plated .32 caliber revolver that some friend had given him years before. A great tree spread above the two men—a sanctuary that Lafayette Smith, at least, should have sought, but his mind was not upon flight, for, in truth, Lafayette was assailed by no fear for his own welfare or that of his companion. He was excited, but not afraid, since he could conceive of no disaster, in the form of man or beast, overwhelming one under the protection of Danny Patrick and his submachine gun. And even in the remote contingency that they should fail, was not he, himself, adequately armed? He grasped the grip of his shiny toy more tightly and with a renewed sensation of security.

The blacks, huddled in small groups, stood wide eyed awaiting the outcome of the event, which was accomplished in a few brief seconds from the instant that one of Danny's slugs struck the fleeing carnivore.

And now as the lion came toward him, not in bounds, but rather in a low gliding rush of incredible speed, several things, surprising things, occurred almost simultaneously. And if there was the element of surprise, there was also, for Danny, at least one cause for embarrassment.

As the lion had wheeled Danny had again squeezed the trigger. The mechanism of the piece was set for a continuous discharge of bullets as long as Danny continued to squeeze and the remainder of the one hundred rounds in the drum lasted; but there was only a brief spurt of fire, and then the gun jammed.

How may one record in slow moving words the thoughts and happenings of a second and impart to the narration any suggestion of the speed and action of the instant?

Did the "Gunner" seek, frantically, to remove the empty cartridge that had caused the jam? Did terror enter his heart, causing his fingers to tremble and bungle? What did Lafayette Smith do?

A scream of terror burst from the lips of the doomed man.

Or rather, what did he contemplate doing? since he had no opportunity to do aught but stand there, a silent observer of events. I do not know.

Before either could formulate a plan wherewith to meet the emergency, a bronzed white man, naked but for a G string, dropped from the branches of the tree above them directly into the path of the charging lion. In the man's hand was a heavy spear, and as he alighted silently upon the soft mold he was already braced to receive the shock of the lion's charge upon the point of his weapon.

The impact of Numa's heavy body would have hurled a lesser man to earth; but this one kept his feet, and the well placed thrust drove into the carnivore's chest a full two feet, while in the same instant the man stepped aside. Numa, intercepted before the completion of his charge, had not yet reared to seize his intended victim. Now, surprised and thwarted by this new enemy, while the other was almost within his grasp, he was momentarily confused; and in that brief moment the strange man-thing leaped upon his back. A giant arm encircled his throat, legs of steel locked around his shrunken waist, and a stout blade was driven into his side.

Spellbound, Smith and Patrick and their blacks stood staring incredulously at the sight before them. They saw Numa turn quickly to seize his tormentor. They saw him leap and bound and throw himself to the ground in an effort to dislodge his opponent. They saw the free hand of the man repeatedly drive home the point of his knife in the tawny side of the raging lion.

From the tangled mass of man and lion there issued frightful snarls and growls, the most terrifying element of which came to the two travellers with the discovery that these bestial sounds issued not alone from the savage throat of the lion but from that of the man as well.

The battle was brief, for the already sorely wounded animal had received the spear thrust directly through its heart, only its remarkable tenacity of life having permitted it to live for the few seconds that intervened between the death blow and the collapse.

As Numa slumped suddenly to his side, the man leaped clear. For a moment he stood looking down upon the death throes of his vanquished foe, while Smith and Patrick remained in awestruck contemplation of the savage, primordial scene; and then he stepped closer; and, placing one foot upon the carcass of his kill, he raised his face to the heavens and gave tongue to a cry so hideous that the black men dropped to the ground in terror while the two whites felt the hair rise upon their scalps.

Once again upon the jungle fell the silence and the paralysis of momentary terror. Then faintly, from the far distance, came an answering challenge. Somewhere out there in the black void of night a bull ape, awakened, had answered the victory cry of his fellow. More faintly, and from a greater distance, came the rumbling roar of a lion.

The stranger stooped and seized the haft of his spear. He placed a foot against Numa's shoulder and withdrew the weapon from the carcass. Then he turned toward the two white men. It was the first intimation he had given that he had been aware of their presence.

"Geeze!" exclaimed "Gunner" Patrick, beyond which his vocabulary failed to meet the situation.

The stranger surveyed them coolly. "Who are you?" he asked. "What are you doing here?"

That he spoke English was both a surprise and a relief to Lafayette Smith. Suddenly he seemed less terrifying. "I am a geologist," he explained. "My name is Smith—Lafayette Smith— and my companion is Mr. Patrick. I am here to conduct some field research work—purely a scientific expedition."

The stranger pointed to the machine gun. "Is that part of the regular field equipment of a geologist?" he asked.

"No," replied Smith, "and I'm sure I don't know why Mr. Patrick insisted on bringing it along."

"I wasn't takin' no chances in a country full of strange smokes," said the "Gunner." "Say, a broad I meets on the boat tells me some of these smokes eats people."

"It would come in handy, perhaps, for hunting," suggested the stranger. "A herd of antelope would make an excellent target for a weapon of that sort."

"Geeze!" exclaimed the "Gunner," "wot do you think I am, Mister, a butcher? I packs this for insurance only. It sure wasn't worth the premium this time though," he added disgustedly; "jammed on me right when I needed it the most. But say, you were there all right. I gotta hand it to you. You're regular, Mister, and if I can ever return the favor—" He made an expansive gesture that completed the sentence and promised all that the most exacting might demand of a reciprocatory nature.

The giant nodded. "Don't use it for hunting," he said, and then, turning to Smith, "Where are you going to conduct your research?"

Suddenly a comprehending light shone in the eyes of the "Gunner," and a pained expression settled definitely upon his face. "Geeze!" he exclaimed disgustedly to Smith. "I might of known it was too good to be true."

"What?" asked Lafayette.

"What I said about there not bein' no cops here."

"Where are you going?" asked the stranger, again.

"We are going to the Ghenzi Mountains now," replied Smith.

"Say, who the hell are you, anyhow?" demanded the "Gunner," "and what business is it of yours where we go?"

The stranger ignored him and turned again toward Smith. "Be very careful in the Ghenzi country," he said. "There is a band of slave raiders working there at present, I understand. If your men learn of it they may desert you."

"Thanks," replied Smith. "It is very kind of you to warn us. I should like to know to whom we are indebted," but the stranger was gone.

As mysteriously and silently as he had appeared, he swung again into the tree above and disappeared. The two whites looked at one another in amazement.

"Geeze," said Danny.

"I fully indorse your statement," said Smith.

"Say, Ogonyo," demanded the "Gunner," "who was that bozo? You or any of your men know?"

"Yes, bwana," replied the headman, "that was Tarzan of the Apes."

CHAPTER 6

The Waters of Chinnereth

LADY BARBARA COLLIS walked slowly along the dusty path leading from the Midian village down to the lake that lay in the bottom of the ancient crater which formed the valley of the Land of Midian. At her right walked Abraham, the son of Abraham, and at her left the golden haired Jezebel. Behind them came the apostles, surrounding a young girl whose sullen countenance was enlivened occasionally by the fearful glances she cast upon the old men who formed her escort or her guard. Following the apostles marched the remainder of the villagers, headed by the elders. Other than these general divisions of the cortege, loosely observed, there was no attempt to maintain a semblance of orderly formation. They moved like sheep, now huddled together, now spewing beyond the limits of the narrow path to spread out on either side, some forging ahead for a few yards only to drop back again.

Lady Barbara was apprehensive. She had learned many things in the long weeks of her virtual captivity among this strange religious sect. Among other things she had learned their language, and the mastery of it had opened to her inquiring mind many avenues of information previously closed. And now she was learning, or she believed she was, that Abraham, the son of Abraham, was nursing in his bosom a growing skepticism of her divinity.

Her first night in Midian had witnessed her introduction to the cruel customs and rites of this degenerate descendant of the earliest Christian Church, and as she acquired a working knowledge of the language of the land and gained an appreciation of the exalted origin the leaders of the people attributed to her, and her position of spokesman for their god, she had used her influence to discourage, and even to prohibit, the more terrible and degrading practices of their religion.

While recollection of the supernatural aspects of her descent from the clouds remained clear in the weak mind of Abraham, the son of Abraham, Lady Barbara had been successful in her campaign against brutality; but daily association with this celestial visitor had tended to dissipate the awe that had at first overwhelmed the prophet of Paul, the son of Jehovah. The interdictions of his heavenly guest were all contrary to the desires of Abraham, the son of Abraham, and to the word of Jehovah as it had been interpreted by the prophets beyond the memory of man. Such were the foundations of the prophet's increasing skepticism, nor was the changing attitude of the old man toward her unrecognized by the English girl.

Today he had ignored her and was even forcing her to accompany them and witness the proof of his apostasy. What would come next? She had had not only ocular proof of the fanatical blood frenzy of the terrible old man, but she had listened for hours to detailed descriptions of orgies of frightfulness from the lips of Jezebel. Yes, Lady Barbara Collis was apprehensive, and not without reason; but she determined to make a last effort to reassert her waning authority.

"Think well Abraham, the son of Abraham," she said to the man walking at her side, "of the wrath of Jehovah when he sees that you have disobeyed him."

"I walk in the path of the prophets," replied the old man. "Always we have punished those who defied the laws of Jehovah, and Jehovah has rewarded us. Why should he be wroth now? The girl must pay the price of her iniquity."

"But she only smiled," argued Lady Barbara.

"A sin in the eyes of Jehovah," replied Abraham, the son of Abraham. "Laughter is carnal, and smiles lead to laughter, which gives pleasure; and all pleasures are the lures of the devil. They are wicked."

"Do not say any more," said Jezebel, in English. "You will only anger him, and when he is angry he is terrible."

"What sayest thou, woman?" demanded Abraham, the son of Abraham.

"I was praying to Jehovah in the language of Heaven," replied the girl.

The Prophet let his scowling gaze rest upon her. "Thou doest well to pray, woman. Jehovah looks not with pleasure upon thee."

"Then I shall continue praying," replied the girl meekly, and to Lady Barbara, in English; "The old devil is already planning my punishment. He has always hated me, just as they always hate us poor creatures who are not created in the same image as they."

The remarkable difference in physical appearance and mentality that set Jezebel apart from the other Midians was an inexplicable phenomenon that had constantly puzzled Lady Barbara and would continue to puzzle her, since she could not know of the little fair haired slave girl whose virile personality still sought to express itself beyond a grave nineteen centuries old. How greatly Jezebel's mentality surpassed that of her imbecilic fellows had been demonstrated to Lady Barbara by the surprising facility with which the girl had learned to speak English while she was teaching Lady Barbara the language of the Midians. How often and how sincerely had she thanked a kindly Providence for Jezebel!

The procession had now arrived at the shore of the lake, which legend asserted to be bottomless, and had halted where a few flat lava rocks of great size overhung the waters. The apostles took their places with Abraham, the son of Abraham, upon one of the rocks, the girl in their midst; and then a half dozen younger men came forward at a signal from Jobab. One of their number carried a fibre net, and two others brought a heavy piece of lava. Quickly they threw the net over the now terrified and screaming girl and secured the lava rock to it.

Abraham, the son of Abraham, raised his hands above his head, and at the signal all knelt. He commenced to pray in that now familiar gibberish that was not Midian, nor, according to Jezebel, any language whatsoever, for she insisted that the Prophet and the Apostles, to whose sole use it was restricted, could not understand it themselves. The girl, kneeling, was weeping softly now, sometimes choking down a muffled sob, while the young men held the net securely.

Suddenly Abraham, the son of Abraham, abandoned the ecclesiastical tongue and spoke in the language of his people. "For as she has sinned so shall she suffer," he cried. "It is the will of Jehovah, in his infinite mercy, that she shall not be consumed by fire, but that she shall be immersed three times in the waters of Chinnereth that her sins may be washed from her. Let us pray that they may be not too grievous, since otherwise she shall not survive." He nodded to the six young men, who seemed well schooled in their parts.

Four of them seized the net and raised it between them, while the remaining two held the ends of long fibre ropes that were attached to it. As the four commenced to swing the body of the girl pendulum like between them, her screams and pleas for mercy rose above the silent waters of Chinnereth in a diapason of horror, mingled with which were the shrieks and groans of those who, excited beyond the capacity of their nervous systems, were falling to the ground in the throes of epileptic seizures.

To and fro, with increasing rapidity, the young men swung their terror crazed burden. Suddenly one of them collapsed to sink, writhing and foaming, to the surface of the great block of lava upon which they stood, dropping the soft body of the girl heavily to the hard rocks. As Jobab signaled to another young man to take the place of him who had fallen, an apostle screamed and dropped in his tracks.

But no one gave heed to those who had succumbed, and a moment later the girl was swinging to and fro out over the waters of Chinnereth, back over the hard face of the lava.

"In the name of Jehovah! In the name of Jehovah!" chanted Abraham, the son of Abraham, to the cadence of the swinging sack. "In the name of Jehovah! In the name of his son—" there was a pause, and as the body of the girl swung again out over the water—"Paul!"

It was the signal. The four young men released their holds upon the net, and the body of the girl shot downward toward the dark waters of the lake. There was a splash. The screaming ceased. The waters closed in above the victim of cruel fanaticism, leaving only a widening circle of retreating wavelets and two fibre ropes extending upward to the altar of castigation.

For a few seconds there was silence and immobility, except for the groans and contortions of the now greatly increased numbers of the victims of the Nemesis of the Midians. Then Abraham, the son of Abraham, spoke again to the six executioners, who immediately laid hold of the two ropes and hauled the girl upward until she swung, dripping and choking, just above the surface of the water.

For a brief interval they held her there; and then, at a word from the Prophet, they dropped her again beneath the waters.

"You murderer!" cried Lady Barbara, no longer able to control her anger. "Order that poor creature drawn ashore before she is drowned."

Abraham, the son of Abraham, turned eyes upon the English girl that almost froze her with horror—the wild, staring eyes of a maniac; piercing pupils rimmed round with white. "Silence, blasphemer!" screamed the man. "Last night I walked with Jehovah, and He told me that you would be next."

"Oh, please," whispered Jezebel, tugging at Lady Barbara's sleeve. "Do not anger him more or you are lost."

The Prophet turned again to the six young men, and again, at his command, the victim was drawn above the surface of the lake. Fascinated by the horror of the situation, Lady Barbara had stepped to the edge of the rock and, looking down, saw the poor creature limp but still gasping in an effort to regain her breath. She was not dead, but another immersion must surely prove fatal.

"Oh, please," she begged, turning to the Prophet, "in the name of merciful God, do not let them lower her again!"

Without a word of reply Abraham, the son of Abraham, gave the signal; and for the third time the now unconscious girl was dropped into the lake. The English girl sank to her knees in an attitude of prayer, and raising her eyes to heaven plead fervently to her Maker to move the heart of Abraham, the son of Abraham, to compassion, or out of the fulness of His own love to save the victim of these misguided creatures from what seemed now certain death. For a full minute she had prayed, and still the girl was left beneath the waters. Then the Prophet commanded that she be raised.

"If she is now pure in the eyes of Jehovah," he cried, "she will emerge alive. If she be dead, it is the will of Jehovah. I have but walked in the paths of the Prophets."

The six young men raised the sagging net to the surface of the rocks where they rolled the limp form of the girl from it close to where Lady Barbara kneeled in prayer. And now the Prophet appeared to notice the attitude and the pleading voice of the English girl for the first time.

"What doest thou?" he demanded.

"I pray to a God whose power and mercy are beyond your understanding," she replied. "I pray for the life of this poor child."

"There is the answer to your prayer," sneered the Prophet contemptuously, indicating the still body of the girl. "She is dead, and Jehovah has revealed to all who may have doubted that Abraham, the son of Abraham, is His prophet and that thou art an impostor."

"We are lost," whispered Jezebel.

Lady Barbara thought as much herself; but she thought quickly, for the emergency was critical. Rising, she faced the Prophet. "Yes, she is dead," she replied, "but Jehovah can resurrect her."

"He can, but He will not," said Abraham, the son of Abraham.

"Not for you, for He is angry with him who dares to call himself His prophet and yet disobeys His commands." She stepped quickly to the side of the lifeless body. "But for me He will resurrect her. Come Jezebel and help me!"

Now Lady Barbara, in common with most modern, athletically inclined young women, was familiar with the ordinary methods for resuscitating the drowned; and she fell to work upon the victim of the Prophet's homicidal mania with a will born not only of compassion, but of vital necessity. She issued curt orders to Jezebel from time to time, orders which broke but did not terminate a constant flow of words which she voiced in chant-like measures. She started with The Charge of the Light Brigade, but after two stanzas her memory failed and she had recourse to Mother Goose, snatches from the verse in Alice in Wonderland, Kipling, Omar Khayyam; and, as the girl after ten minutes of heartbreaking effort commenced to show signs of life, Lady Barbara closed with excerpts from Lincoln's Gettysburg Address.

Crowded about them were the Prophet, the Apostles, the Elders, and the six executioners, while beyond these the villagers pressed as close as they dared to witness the miracle—if such it were to be.

" 'And that government of the people, by the people and for the people shall not perish from the earth,' " chanted Lady Barbara, rising to her feet. "Lay the child in the net," she commanded, turning to the wide eyed young men who had cast her into the lake, "and carry her tenderly back to the cave of her parents. Come Jezebel!" To Abraham, the son of Abraham, she vouchsafed not even a glance.

That night the two girls sat at the entrance of their cave looking out across the uncharted valley of Midian. A full moon silvered the crest of the lofty escarpment of the crater's northern rim. In the middle distance the silent waters of Chinnereth lay like a burnished shield.

"It is beautiful," sighed Jezebel.

"But, oh, how horrible, because of man," replied Lady Barbara, with a shudder.

"At night, when I am alone, and can see only the beautiful things, I try to forget man," said the golden one. "Is there so much cruelty and wickedness in the land from which you come, Barbara?"

"There are cruelty and wickedness everywhere where men are, but in my land it is not so bad as here where the church rules and cruelty is the sole business of the church."

"They say the men over there are very cruel," said Jezebel, pointing across the valley; "but they are beautiful—not like our people."

"You have seen them?"

"Yes. Sometimes they come searching for their strayed goats, but not often. Then they chase us into our caves, and we roll rocks down on them to keep them from coming up and killing us. They steal our goats at such times; and if they catch any of our men they kill them, too. If I were alone I would let them catch me for they are very beautiful, and I do not think they would kill me. I think they would like me."

"I don't doubt it," agreed Lady Barbara, "but if I were you I would not let them catch me."

"Why not? What have I to hope for here? Perhaps some day I shall be caught smiling or singing; and then I shall be killed, and you have not seen all of the ways in which the Prophet can destroy sinners. If I am not killed I shall certainly be taken to his cave by some horrible old man; and there, all my life, I shall be a slave to him and his other women; and the old women are more cruel to such as I than even the men. No, if I were not afraid of what lies between I should run away and go to the land of the North Midians."

"Perhaps your life will be happier and safer here with me since we showed Abraham, the son of Abraham, that we are more powerful than he; and when the time comes that my people find me, or I discover an avenue of escape, you shall come away with me, Jezebel; though I don't know that you will be much safer in England than you are here."

"Why?" demanded the girl.

"You are too beautiful ever to have perfect safety or perfect happiness."

"You think I am beautiful? I always thought so, too. I saw myself when I looked into the lake or into a vessel of water; and I thought that I was beautiful, although I did not look like the other girls of the land of Midian. Yet you are beautiful and I do not look like you. Have you never been safe or happy, Barbara?"

The English girl laughed. "I am not *too* beautiful, Jezebel," she explained.

A footfall on the steep pathway leading to the cave caught their attention. "Someone comes," said Jezebel.

"It is late," said Lady Barbara. "No one should be coming now to our cave."

"Perhaps it is a man from North Midian," suggested Jezebel. "Is my hair arranged prettily?"

"We had better be rolling a rock into position than thinking about our hair," said Lady Barbara, with a short laugh.

"Ah, but they are such beautiful men!" sighed Jezebel.

Lady Barbara drew a small knife from one of her pockets and opened the blade. "I do not like 'beautiful' men," she said.

The approaching footfalls were coming slowly nearer; but the two young women, sitting just within the entrance to their cave, could not see the steep pathway along which the nocturnal visitor was approaching. Presently a shadow fell across their threshold and an instant later a tall old man stepped into view. It was Abraham, the son of Abraham.

Lady Barbara rose to her feet and faced the Prophet. "What brings you to my cave at this time of night?" she demanded. "What is it, of such importance, that could not wait until morning? Why do you disturb me now?"

For a long moment the old man stood glaring at her. "I have walked with Jehovah in the moonlight," he said, presently; "and Jehovah hath spoken in the ear of Abraham, the son of Abraham, Prophet of Paul, the son of Jehovah."

"And you have come to make your peace with me as Jehovah directed?"

"Such are not the commands of Jehovah," replied the Prophet. "Rather He is wroth with thee who didst seek to deceive the Prophet of His son."

"You must have been walking with some one else," snapped Lady Barbara.

"Nay. I walked with Jehovah," insisted Abraham, the son of Abraham. "Thou hast deceived me. With trickery, perhaps even with sorcery, thou didst bring to life her who was dead by the will of Jehovah; and Jehovah is wroth."

"You heard my prayers, and you witnessed the miracle of the resurrection," Lady Barbara reminded him. "Thinkest thou that I am more powerful than Jehovah? It was Jehovah who raised the dead child."

"Thou speakest even as Jehovah prophesied," said the Prophet. "And He spoke in my ear and commanded that I should prove thee false, that all men might see thy iniquity."

"Interesting, if true," commented Lady Barbara; "but not true."

"Thou darest question the word of the Prophet?" cried the man angrily. "But tomorrow thou shalt have the opportunity to prove thy boasts. Tomorrow Jehovah shall judge thee. Tomorrow thou shalt be cast into the waters of Chinnereth in a weighted net, nor will there be cords attached whereby it may be drawn above the surface."

CHAPTER 7

The Slave Raider

LEON STABUTCH, MOUNTED behind one of his captors, riding to an unknown fate, was warrantably perturbed. He had been close to death at the hands of one of the band already, and from their appearance and their attitude toward him it was not difficult for him to imagine that they would require but the slightest pretext to destroy him.

What their intentions might be was highly problematical, though he could conceive of but one motive which might inspire such as they to preserve him. But if ransom were their aim he could not conjecture any method by which these semi-savages might contact with his friends or superiors in Russia. He was forced to admit that his prospects appeared most discouraging.

The *shiftas* were forced to move slowly because of the packs some of their horses were carrying since the looting of the Russian's camp. Nor could they have ridden much more rapidly, under any circumstances, on the trail that they entered shortly following their capture of Stabutch.

Entering a narrow, rocky canyon the trail wound steeply upward to debouch at last upon a small, level mesa, at the upper end of which Stabutch saw what, at a distance, appeared to be a palisaded village nestling close beneath a rocky cliff that bounded the mesa in that direction.

This evidently was the destination of his captors, who were doubtless members of the very band the mere rumor of which had filled his men with terror. Stabutch was only sorry that the balance of the story, postulating the existence of a white leader, was evidently erroneous, since he would have anticipated less difficulty in arranging the terms and collection of a ransom with a European than with these ignorant savages.

As they neared the village Stabutch discovered that their approach had been made beneath the scrutiny of lookouts posted behind the palisade, whose heads and shoulders were now plainly visible above the crude though substantial rampart.

And presently these sentries were shouting greetings and queries to the members of the returning band as the village gate swung slowly open and the savage horsemen entered the enclosure with their captive, who was soon the center of a throng of men, women, and children, curious and questioning—a savage throng of surly blacks.

Although there was nothing actively menacing in the attitude of the savages there was a definite unfriendliness in their demeanor that cast a further gloom of apprehension upon the already depressed spirits of the Russian; and as the cavalcade entered the central compound, about which the huts were grouped, he experienced a sensation of utter hopelessness.

It was at this moment that he saw a short, bearded white man emerge from one of the squalid dwellings; and instantly the depression that had seized him was, partially at least, relieved.

The *shiftas* were dismounting, and now he was roughly dragged from the animal which had borne him from his camp and pushed unceremoniously toward the white man, who stood before the doorway from whence he had appeared surveying the prisoner sullenly, while he listened to the report of the leader of the returning band.

There was no smile upon the face of the bearded man as he addressed Stabutch after the black *shifta* had completed his report. The Russian recognized that the language employed by the stranger was Italian, a tongue which he could neither speak nor understand, and this he explained in Russian; but the bearded one only shrugged and shook his head. Then Stabutch tried English.

"That is better," said the other brokenly. "I understand English a little. Who are you? What was the language you first spoke to me? From what country do you come?"

"I am a scientist," replied Stabutch. "I spoke to you in Russian."

"Is Russia your country?"

"Yes."

The man eyed him intently for some time, as though attempting to read the innermost secrets of his mind, before he spoke again. Stabutch noted the squat, powerful build of the stranger, the cruel lips, only partially concealed by the heavy, black beard, and the hard, crafty eyes, and guessed that he might have fared as well at the hands of the blacks.

"You say you are a Russian," said the man. "Red or white?"

Stabutch wished that he might know how to answer this question. He was aware that Red Russians were not well beloved by all peoples; and that the majority of Italians were trained to hate them, and yet there was something in the personality of this stranger that suggested that he might be more favorably inclined to a Red than to a White Russian. Furthermore, to admit that he was a Red might assure the other that a ransom could be obtained more surely than from a White, whose organization was admittedly weak and poverty stricken. For these reasons Stabutch decided to tell the truth.

"I am a Red," he said.

The other considered him intently and in silence for a moment; then he made a gesture that would have passed unnoticed by any but a Red Communist. Leon Stabutch breathed an inaudible sigh of relief, but his facial expression gave no indication of recognition of this secret sign as he answered it in accordance with the ritual of his organization, while the other watched him closely.

"Your name, comrade?" inquired the bearded one in an altered tone.

"Leon Stabutch," replied the Russian; "and yours, comrade?"

"Dominic Capietro. Come, we will talk inside. I have a bottle there wherewith we may toast the cause and become better acquainted."

"Lead on, comrade," said Stabutch; "I feel the need of something to quiet my nerves. I have had a bad few hours."

"I apologize for the inconvenience to which my men have put you," replied Capietro, leading the way into the hut; "but all shall be made right again. Be seated. As you see, I lead the simple life; but what imperial throne may compare in grandeur with the bosom of Mother Earth!"

"None, comrade," agreed Stabutch, noting the entire absence of chairs, or even stools, that the other's speech had already suggested and condoned. "Especially," he added, "when enjoyed beneath a friendly roof."

Capietro rummaged in an old duffle bag and at last withdrew a bottle which he uncorked and handed to Stabutch. "Golden goblets are for royal tyrants, Comrade Stabutch," he declaimed, "but not for such as we, eh?"

Stabutch raised the bottle to his lips and took a draught of the fiery liquid, and as it burned its way to his stomach and the fumes rose to his head the last of his fears and doubts vanished. "Tell me now," he said, as he passed the bottle back to his host, "why I was seized, who you are, and what is to become of me?"

"My headman told me that he found you alone, deserted by

your safari, and not knowing whether you were friend or enemy he brought you here to me. You are lucky, comrade, that Dongo chanced to be in charge of the scouting party today. Another might have killed you first and inquired later. They are a pack of murderers and thieves, these good men of mine. They have been oppressed by cruel masters, they have felt the heel of the tyrant upon their necks, and their hands are against all men. You cannot blame them.

"But they are good men. They serve me well. They are the man power, I am the brains; and we divide the profits of our operations equally—half to the man power, half to the brains," and Capietro grinned.

"And your operations?" asked Stabutch.

Capietro scowled; then his face cleared. "You are a comrade, but let me tell you that it is not always safe to be inquisitive."

Stabutch shrugged. "Tell me nothing," he said. "I do not care. It is none of my business."

"Good," exclaimed the Italian, "and why you are here in Africa is none of my business, unless you care to tell me. Let us drink again."

While the conversation that ensued, punctuated by numerous drinks, carefully eschewed personalities, the question of the other's occupation was uppermost in the mind of each; and as the natural effects of the liquor tended to disarm their suspicions and urge confidences it also stimulated the curiosity of the two, each of whom was now mellow and genial in his cups.

It was Capietro who broke first beneath the strain of an overpowering curiosity. They were sitting side by side upon a disreputably filthy rug, two empty bottles and a newly opened one before them. "Comrade," he cried, throwing an arm about the shoulders of the Russian affectionately, "I like you. Dominic Capietro does not like many men. This is his motto: Like few men and love all women," whereat he laughed loudly.

"Let us drink to that," suggested Stabutch, joining in the laughter. " 'Like few men and love all women.' That is the idea!"

"I knew the minute I saw you that you were a man after my own heart, comrade," continued Capietro, "and why should there be secrets between comrades?"

"Certainly, why?" agreed Stabutch.

"So I shall tell you why I am here with this filthy band of thieving cutthroats. I was a soldier in the Italian army. My regiment was stationed in Eritrea. I was fomenting discord and mutiny, as a good Communist should, when some dog of a Fascist reported me to the commanding officer. I was arrested. Doubtless, I should have been shot, but I escaped and made my way into Abyssinia, where Italians are none too well liked; but when it was known that I was a deserter I was treated well.

"After a while I obtained employment with a powerful ras to train his soldiers along European lines. There I became proficient in Amharic, the official language of the country, and also learned to speak that of the Gallas, who constituted the bulk of the population of the principality of the ras for whom I worked. Naturally, being averse to any form of monarchistic government, I commenced at once to instill the glorious ideals of Communism into the breasts of the retainers of the old ras; but once again I was frustrated by an informer, and only by chance did I escape with my life.

"This time, however, I succeeded in enticing a number of men to accompany me. We stole horses and weapons from the ras and rode south where we joined a band of *shiftas,* or rather, I should say, absorbed them.

"This organized body of raiders and thieves made an excellent force with which to levy tribute upon chance travellers and caravans, but the returns were small and so we drifted down into this remote country of the Ghenzi where we can ply a lucrative trade in black ivory."

"Black ivory? I never knew there was such a thing."

Capietro laughed. "Two legged ivory," he explained.

Stabutch whistled. "Oh," he said, "I think I understand. You are a slave raider; but where is there any market for slaves, other than the wage slaves of capitalistic countries?"

"You would be surprised, comrade. There are still many markets, including the mandates and protectorates of several highly civilized signatories to world court conventions aimed at the abolition of human slavery. Yes, I am a slave raider—rather a remarkable vocation for a university graduate and the former editor of a successful newspaper."

"And you prefer this?"

"I have no alternative, and I must live. At least I think I must live—a most common form of rationalization. You see, my newspaper was anti-Fascist. And now, comrade, about yourself—what 'scientific' research is the Soviet government undertaking in Africa?"

"Let us call it anthropology," replied Stabutch. "I am looking for a man."

"There are many men in Africa and much nearer the coast than the Ghenzi country. You have travelled far inland looking for a man."

"The man I look for I expected to find somewhere south of the Ghenzies," replied Stabutch.

"Perhaps I can aid you. I know many men, at least by name and reputation, in this part of the world," suggested the Italian.

Stabutch, had he been entirely sober, would have hesitated to give this information to a total stranger, but alcohol induces thoughtless confidences. "I search for an Englishman known as Tarzan of the Apes," he explained.

Capietro's eyes narrowed. "A friend of yours?" he asked.

"I know of no one I would rather see," replied Stabutch.

"You say he is here in the Ghenzi country?"

"I do not know. None of the natives I have questioned knew his whereabouts."

"His country is far south of the Ghenzies," said Capietro.

"Ah, you know of him, then?"

"Yes. Who does not? But what business have you with Tarzan of the Apes?"

"I have come from Moscow to kill him," blurted Stabutch, and in the same instant regretted his rash admission.

Capietro relaxed. "I am relieved," he said.

"Why?" demanded the Russian.

"I feared he was a friend of yours," explained the Italian. "In which case we could not be friends; but if you have come to kill him you shall have nothing but my best wishes and heartiest support."

Stabutch's relief was almost a thing of substance, so considerable and genuine was it. "You, too, have a grievance against him?" he asked.

"He is a constant threat against my little operations in black ivory," replied Capietro. "I should feel much safer if he were out of the way."

"Then perhaps you will help me, comrade?" inquired Stabutch eagerly.

"I have lost no ape-man," replied Capietro, "and if he leaves me alone I shall never look for him. That adventure, comrade, you will not have to share with me."

"But you have taken away my means of carrying out my plans. I cannot seek Tarzan without a safari," complained Stabutch.

"That is right," admitted the raider; "but perhaps the mistake of my men may be rectified. Your equipment and goods are safe. They will be returned to you, and, as for men, who better could find them for you than Dominic Capietro, who deals in men?"

The safari of Lord Passmore moved northward, skirting the western foothills of the Ghenzi Mountains. His stalwart porters marched almost with the precision of trained soldiers, at least in that proper distances were maintained and there were no stragglers. A hundred yards in advance were three askaris and behind these came Lord Passmore, his gun bearer, and his headman. At the head and rear of the column of porters was a detachment of askaris—well armed, efficient appearing men. The whole entourage suggested intelligent organization and experienced supervision. Evidence of willingly observed discipline was apparent, a discipline that seemed to be respected by all with the possible exception of Isaza, Lord Passmore's "boy," who was also his cook.

Isaza marched where his fancy dictated, laughing and joking with first one and then another of the members of the safari— the personification of the good nature that pervaded the whole party and that was constantly manifested by the laughter and singing of the men. It was evident that Lord Passmore was an experienced African traveller and that he knew what treatment to accord his followers.

How different, indeed, this well ordered safari, from another that struggled up the steep slopes of the Ghenzies a few miles to the east. Here the column was strung out for fully a mile, the askaris straggling along among the porters, while the two white men whom they accompanied forged far ahead with a single boy and a gun bearer.

"Geeze," remarked the "Gunner," "you sure picked on a lousy racket! I could of stayed home and climbed up the front of the Sherman Hotel, if I had of wanted to climb, and always been within a spit of eats and drinks."

"Oh, no you couldn't," said Lafayette Smith.

"Why not? Who'd a stopped me?"

"Your friends, the cops."

"That's right; but don't call 'em my friends—the lousy bums.

But wherinel do you think you're going?"

"I think I perceive in this mountain range evidences of upthrust by horizontal compression," replied Lafayette Smith, "and I wish to examine the surface indications more closely than it is possible to do from a distance. Therefore, we must go to the mountains, since they will not come to us."

"And what does it get you?" demanded "Gunner" Patrick. "Not a buck. It's a bum racket."

Lafayette Smith laughed good naturedly. They were crossing a meadowland through which a mountain stream wound. Surrounding it was a forest. "This would make a good camp," he said, "from which to work for a few days. You can hunt, and I'll have a look at the formations in the vicinity. Then we'll move on."

"It's jake with me," replied the "Gunner." "I'm fed up on climbing."

"Suppose you remain with the safari and get camp made," suggested Smith. "I'll go on up a little farther with my boy and see what I can see. It's early yet."

"Oke," assented the "Gunner." "I'll park the mob up near them trees. Don't get lost, and, say, you better take my protection guy with you," he added, nodding in the direction of his gun bearer.

"I'm not going to hunt," replied Smith. "I won't need him."

"Then take my rod here." The "Gunner" started to unbuckle his pistol belt. "You might need it."

"Thanks, I have one," replied Smith, tapping his .32.

"Geeze, you don't call that thing a rod, do you?" demanded the "Gunner," contemptuously.

"It's all I need. I'm looking for rocks, not trouble. Come on Obambi," and he motioned his boy to follow him as he started up the slope toward the higher mountains.

"Geeze," muttered the "Gunner," "I seen pipies what aint as much of a nut as that guy; but," he added, "he's a regular guy at that. You can't help likin' him." Then he turned his attention to the selection of a campsite.

Lafayette Smith entered the forest beyond the meadowland; and here the going became more difficult, for the ground rose rapidly; and the underbrush was thick. He fought his way upward, Obambi at his heels; and at last he reached a higher elevation, where the forest growth was much thinner because of the rocky nature of the ground and the absence of top soil. Here he paused to examine the formation, but only to move on again, this time at right angles to his original direction.

Thus, stopping occasionally to investigate, he moved erratically upward until he achieved the summit of a ridge from which he had a view of miles of rugged mountains in the distance. The canyon that lay before him, separating him from the next ridge, aroused his interest. The formation of the opposite wall, he decided, would bear closer investigation.

Obambi had flung himself to the ground when Smith halted. Obambi appeared exhausted. He was not. He was merely disgusted. To him the bwana was mad, quite mad. Upon no other premises could Obambi explain this senseless climbing, with an occasional pause to examine rocks. Obambi was positive that they might have discovered plenty of rocks at the foot of the mountains had they but searched for them. And then, too, this bwana did not hunt. He supposed all bwanas came to Africa to hunt. This one, being so different, must be mad.

Smith glanced at his boy. It was too bad, he thought, to make Obambi do all this climbing unnecessarily. Certainly there was no way in which the boy might assist him, while seeing him in a constant state of exhaustion reacted unfavorably on Smith. Better by far be alone. He turned to the boy. "Go back to camp, Obambi," he said. "I do not need you here."

Obambi looked at him in surprise. Now he knew the bwana was very mad. However, it would be much more pleasant in camp than climbing about in these mountains. He rose to his feet. "The bwana does not need me?" he asked. "Perhaps he will need me." Obambi's conscience was already troubling him. He knew that he should not leave his bwana alone.

"No, I shan't need you, Obambi," Smith assured him. "You run along back to camp. I'll come in pretty soon."

"Yes, bwana," and Obambi turned back down the mountain side.

Lafayette Smith clambered down into the canyon, which was deeper than he had supposed, and then worked his way up the opposite side that proved to be even more precipitous than it had appeared from the summit of the ridge. However, he found so much to interest him that he considered it well worth the effort, and so deeply absorbed was he that he gave no heed to the passage of time.

It was not until he reached the top of the far side of the canyon that he noted the diminishing light that presaged the approach of night. Even then he was not greatly concerned; but he realized that it would be quite dark before he could hope to recross the canyon, and it occurred to him that by following up the ridge on which he stood he could reach the head of the canyon where it joined the ridge from which he had descended into it, thus saving him a long, arduous climb and shortening the time, if not the distance, back to camp.

As he trudged upward along the ridge, night fell; but still he kept on, though now he could only grope his way slowly, nor did it occur to him for several hours that he was hopelessly lost.

CHAPTER 8

The Baboons

A NEW DAY had dawned, and Africa greeted the age old miracle of Kudu emerging from his lair behind the eastern hills and smiled. With the exception of a few stragglers the creatures of the night had vanished, surrendering the world to their diurnal fellows.

Tongani, the baboon, perched upon his sentinel rock, surveyed the scene and, perhaps, not without appreciation of the beauties; for who are we to say that God touched so many countless of his works with beauty yet gave to but one of these the power of appreciation?

Below the sentinel fed the tribe of Zugash, the king; fierce tongani shes with their balus clinging to their backs, if very young, while others played about, imitating their elders in their constant search for food; surly, vicious bulls; old Zugash himself, the surliest and most vicious.

The keen, close-set eyes of the sentinel, constantly upon the alert down wind, perceived something moving among the little hills below. It was the top of a man's head. Presently the whole head came into view; and then the sentinel saw that it belonged to a tarmangani; but as yet he sounded no alarm, for the tarmangani was still a long way off and might not be coming in the direction of the tribe. The sentinel would watch yet a little longer and make sure, for it was senseless to interrupt the feeding of the tribe if no danger threatened.

Now the tarmangani was in full view. Tongani wished that he

might have the evidence of his keen nose as well as his eyes; then there would be no doubt, for, like many animals, the tonganis preferred to submit all evidence to their sensitive nostrils before accepting the verdict of their eyes; but the wind was in the wrong direction.

Perhaps, too, Tongani was puzzled, for this was such a tarmangani as he had never before seen—a tarmangani who walked almost as naked as Tongani himself. But for the white skin he might have thought him a gomangani. This being a tarmangani, the sentinel looked for the feared thunder stick; and because he saw none he waited before giving the alarm. But presently he saw that the creature was coming directly toward the tribe.

The tarmangani had long been aware of the presence of the baboons, being down wind from them where their strong scent was borne to his keen nostrils. Also, he had seen the sentinel at almost the same instant that the sentinel had seen him; yet he continued upward, swinging along in easy strides that suggested the power and savage independence of Numa, the lion.

Suddenly Tongani, the baboon, sprang to his feet, uttering a sharp bark, and instantly the tribe awoke to action, swarming up the low cliffs at the foot of which they had been feeding. Here they turned and faced the intruder, barking their defiance as they ran excitedly to and fro.

When they saw that the creature was alone and bore no thunder stick they were more angry than frightened, and they scolded noisily at this interruption of their feeding. Zugash and several of the other larger bulls even clambered part way down the cliff to frighten him away; but in this they only succeeded in increasing their own anger, for the tarmangani continued upward toward them.

Zugash, the king, was now beside himself with rage. He stormed and threatened. "Go away!" he barked. "I am Zugash. I kill!"

And now the stranger halted at the foot of the cliff and surveyed him. "I am Tarzan of the Apes," he said. "Tarzan does not come to the stamping grounds of the tongani to kill. He comes as a friend."

Silence fell upon the tribe of Zugash; the silence of stunning surprise. Never before had they heard either tarmangani or gomangani speak the language of the ape-people. They had never heard of Tarzan of the Apes, whose country was far to the south; but nevertheless they were impressed by his ability to understand them and speak to them. However, he was a stranger, and so Zugash ordered him away again.

"Tarzan does not wish to remain with the tongani," replied the ape-man; "he desires only to pass them in peace."

"Go away!" growled Zugash. "I kill. I am Zugash."

Tarzan swung up the cliff quite as easily as had the baboons. It was his answer to Zugash, the king. None was there who better knew the strength, the courage, the ferocity of the tongani than he, yet he knew, too, that he might be in this country for some time and that, if he were to survive, he must establish himself definitely in the minds of all lesser creatures as one who walked without fear and whom it was well to let alone.

Barking furiously, the baboons retreated; and Tarzan gained the summit of the cliff, where he saw that the shes and balus had scattered, many of them going farther up into the hills, while the adult bulls remained to contest the way.

As Tarzan paused, just beyond the summit of the cliff, he found himself the center of a circle of snarling bulls against the combined strength and ferocity of which he would be helpless. To another than himself his position might have appeared precarious almost to the point of hopelessness; but Tarzan knew the wild peoples of his savage world too well to expect an unprovoked attack, or a killing for the love of killing such as only man, among all the creatures of the world, habitually commits. Neither was he unaware of the danger of his position should a bull, more nervous or suspicious than his fellows, mistake Tarzan's intentions or misinterpret some trivial act or gesture as a threat against the safety of the tribe.

But he knew that only an accident might precipitate a charge and that if he gave them no cause to attack him they would gladly let him proceed upon his way unmolested. However, he had hoped to achieve friendly relations with the tongani, whose knowledge of the country and its inhabitants might prove of inestimable value to him. Better, too, that the tribe of Zugash be allies than enemies. And so he assayed once more to win their confidence.

"Tell me, Zugash," he said, addressing the bristling king baboon, "if there be many tarmangani in your country. Tarzan hunts for a bad tarmangani who has many gomangani with him. They are bad men. They kill. With thunder sticks they kill. They will kill the tongani. Tarzan has come to drive them from your country."

But Zugash only growled and placed the back of his head against the ground in challenge. The other males moved restlessly sideways, their shoulders high, their tails bent in crooked curves. Now some of the younger bulls rested the backs of their heads upon the ground, imitating the challenge of their king.

Zugash, grimacing at Tarzan, raised and lowered his brows rapidly, exposing the white skin about his eyes. Thus did the savage old king seek to turn the heart of his antagonist to water by the frightfulness of his mien; but Tarzan only shrugged indifferently and moved on again as though convinced that the baboons would not accept his overtures of friendship.

Straight toward the challenging bulls that stood in his path he walked, without haste and apparently without concern; but his eyes were narrowed and watchful, his every sense on the alert. One bull, stiff legged and arrogant, moved grudgingly aside; but another stood his ground. Here, the ape-man knew the real test would come that should decide the issue.

The two were close now, face to face, when suddenly there burst from the lips of the man-beast a savage growl, and simultaneously he charged. With an answering growl and a catlike leap the baboon bounded aside; and Tarzan passed beyond the rim of the circle, victor in the game of bluff which is played by every order of living thing sufficiently advanced in the scale of intelligence to possess an imagination.

Seeing that the man-thing did not follow upward after the shes and balus, the bulls contented themselves with barking insults after him and aiming uncomplimentary gestures at his retreating figure; but such were not the acts that menaced safety, and the ape-man ignored them.

Purposely he had turned away from the shes and their young, with the intention of passing around them, rather than precipitate a genuine attack by seeming to threaten them. And thus his way took him to the edge of a shallow ravine into which, unknown either to Tarzan or the tongani, a young mother had fled with her tiny balu.

Tarzan was still in full view of the tribe of Zugash, though he alone could see into the ravine, when suddenly three things occurred that shattered the peace that seemed again descending upon the scene. A vagrant air current wafted upward from the thick verdure below him the scent of Sheeta, the panther; a baboon voiced a scream of terror; and, looking down, the ape-man saw the young she, her balu clinging to her back, fleeing upward toward him with savage Sheeta in pursuit.

As Tarzan, reacting instantly to the necessity of the moment, leaped downward with back thrown spear hand, the bulls of Zugash raced forward in answer to the note of terror in the voice of the young mother.

From his position above the actors in this sudden tragedy of the wilds the ape-man could see the panther over the head of the baboon and realizing that the beast must reach his victim before succor could arrive he hurled his spear in the forlorn hope of stopping the carnivore, if only for a moment.

The cast was one that only a practiced hand might have dared attempt, for the danger to the baboon was almost as great as that which threatened the panther should the aim of the ape-man not be perfect.

Zugash and his bulls, bounding forward at an awkward gallop, reached the edge of the ravine just in time to see the heavy spear hurtle past the head of the she by a margin of inches only and bury itself in the breast of Sheeta. Then they were down the slope, a snarling, snapping pack, and with them went an English viscount, to fall upon a surprised, pain-maddened panther.

The baboons leaped in to snap at their hereditary foe and leaped out again, and the man-beast, as quick and agile as they, leaped and struck with his hunting knife, while the frenzied cat lunged this way and that, first at one tormentor and then at another.

Twice those powerful, raking talons reached their mark and two bulls sprawled, torn and bloody, upon the ground; but the bronzed hide of the ape-man ever eluded the rage of the wounded cat.

Short was the furious battle, ferocious the growls and snarls of the combatants, prodigious the leaps and bounds of the excited shes hovering in the background; and then Sheeta, rearing high upon his hind feet, struck savagely at Tarzan and, in the same instant, plunged to earth dead, slain by the spear point puncturing his heart.

Instantly the great tarmangani, who had once been king of the great apes, leaped close and placed a foot upon the carcass of his kill. He raised his face toward Kudu, the sun; and from his lips broke the horrid challenge of the bull ape that has killed.

For a moment silence fell upon the forest, the mountain, and the jungle. Awed, the baboons ceased their restless movement and their din. Tarzan stooped and drew the spear from the quivering

Sheeta plunged to the earth dead, slain by the spear.

body of Sheeta, while the tongani watched him with a new interest.

Then Zugash approached. This time he did not rest the back of his head against the ground in challenge. "The bulls of the tribe of Zugash are the friends of Tarzan of the Apes," he said.

"Tarzan is the friend of the bulls of the tribe of Zugash," responded the ape-man.

"We have seen a tarmangani," said Zugash. "He has many gomangani. There are many thunder sticks among them. They are bad. Perhaps it is they whom Tarzan seeks."

"Perhaps," admitted the slayer of Sheeta. "Where are they?"

"They were camped where the rocks sit upon the mountain side, as here." He nodded toward the cliff.

"Where?" asked Tarzan again; and this time Zugash motioned along the foothills toward the south.

CHAPTER 9

The Great Fissure

THE MORNING SUN shone upon the bosom of Chinnereth, glancing from the breeze born ripples that moved across its surface like vast companies of soldiers passing in review with their countless spears gleaming in the sunlight—a dazzling aspect of beauty.

But to Lady Barbara Collis it connoted something quite different—a shallow splendor concealing cruel and treacherous depths, the real Chinnereth. She shuddered as she approached its shore surrounded by the apostles, preceded by Abraham, the son of Abraham, and followed by the elders and the villagers. Among them, somewhere, she knew were the six with their great net and their fibre ropes.

How alike were they all to Chinnereth, hiding their cruelty and their treachery beneath a thin veneer of godliness! But there the parallel terminated, for Chinnereth was beautiful. She glanced at the faces of the men nearest her, and again she shuddered. " 'So God created man in his own image,' " she mused. "Who, then, created these?"

During the long weeks that fate had held her in this land of Midian she had often sought an explanation of the origin of this strange race, and the deductions of her active mind had not deviated greatly from the truth. Noting the exaggerated racial characteristics of face and form that distinguished them from other peoples she had seen, recalling their common tendency to epilepsy, she had concluded that they were the inbred descendants of a common ancestor, himself a defective and an epileptic.

This theory explained much; but it failed to explain Jezebel, who insisted that she was the child of two of these creatures and that, insofar as she knew, no new strain of blood had ever been injected into the veins of the Midian by intermating with other peoples. Yet, somehow, Lady Barbara knew that such a strain must have been introduced, though she could not guess the truth nor the antiquity of the fact that lay buried in the grave of a little slave girl.

And their religion! Again she shuddered. What a hideous travesty of the teachings of Christ! It was a confused jumble of ancient Christianity and still more ancient Judaism, handed down by word of mouth through a half imbecile people who had no written language; a people who had confused Paul the Apostle with Christ the Master and lost entirely the essence of the Master's teachings, while interpolating hideous barbarisms of their own invention. Sometimes she thought she saw in this exaggerated deviation a suggestion of parallel to other so-called Christian sects of the civilized outer world.

But now her train of thoughts was interrupted by the near approach of the procession to the shore of the lake. Here was the flat-topped lava rock of grim suggestiveness and hideous memory. How long it seemed since she had watched the six hurl their screaming victim from its well worn surface, and yet it had been but yesterday. Now it was her turn. The Prophet and the Apostles were intoning their senseless gibberish, meant to impress the villagers with their erudition and cloak the real vacuity of their minds, a practice not unknown to more civilized sects.

She was halted now upon the smooth surface of the lava, polished by soft sandals and naked feet through the countless years that these cruel rites had been enacted beside the waters of Chinnereth. Again she heard the screams of yesterday's victim. But Lady Barbara Collis had not screamed, nor would she. She would rob them of that satisfaction at least.

Abraham, the son of Abraham, motioned the six to the fore; and they came, bearing their net and their cords. At their feet lay the lava fragment that would weight the net and its contents. The

Prophet raised his hands above his head and the people kneeled. In the forefront of their ranks Lady Barbara saw the golden haired Jezebel; and her heart was touched, for there were anguish in the beautiful face and tears in the lovely eyes. Here was one, at least, who could harbor love and compassion.

"I have walked with Jehovah," cried Abraham, the son of Abraham, and Lady Barbara wondered that he did not have blisters on his feet, so often he walked with Jehovah. The levity of the conceit brought an involuntary smile to her lips, a smile that the Prophet noticed. "You smile," he said, angrily. "You smile when you should scream and beg for mercy as the others do. Why do you smile?"

"Because I am not afraid," replied Lady Barbara, though she was very much afraid.

"Why art thou not afraid, woman?" demanded the old man.

"I, too, have walked with Jehovah," she replied, "and He told me to fear not, because you are a false prophet, and—"

"Silence!" thundered Abraham, the son of Abraham. "Blaspheme no more. Jehovah shall judge you in a moment." He turned to the six. "Into the net with her!"

Quickly they did his bidding; and as they commenced to swing her body to and fro, to gain momentum against the moment that they would release their holds and cast her into the deep lake, she heard The Prophet reciting her iniquities that Jehovah was about to judge in his own peculiar way. His speech was punctuated by the screams and groans of those of the company who were seized in the grip of the now familiar attacks to which Lady Barbara had become so accustomed as to be almost as callous to as the Midians themselves.

From her pocket the girl extracted the little pen knife that was her only weapon and held it firmly in one hand, the blade open and ready for the work she intended it to do. And what work was that? Surely, she could not hope to inflict instant death upon herself with that inadequate weapon! Yet, in the last stages of fear induced by utter helplessness and hopelessness one may attempt anything, even the impossible.

Now they were swinging her far out over Chinnereth. The Apostles and the elders were intoning their weird chant in voices excited to frenzy by the imminence of death, those who were not writhing upon the rocky face of the altar in the throes of seizures.

Suddenly came the word from Abraham, the son of Abraham.

Lady Barbara caught her breath in a last frightened gasp. The six released their holds. A loud scream arose from the huddled villagers—the scream of a woman—and as she plunged toward the dark waters Lady Barbara knew that it was the voice of Jezebel crying out in the anguish of sorrow. Then mysterious Chinnereth closed above her head.

At that very moment Lafayette Smith, A.M., Ph.D., Sc.D., was stumbling along a rocky mountain side that walled the great crater where lay the land of Midian and Chinnereth. He was no less aware of the tragedy being enacted upon the opposite side of that stupendous wall than of the fact that he was moving directly away from the camp he was seeking. Had there been anyone there to tell him, and had they told him, that he was hopelessly lost he would have been inclined to dispute the statement, so positive was he that he was taking a short cut to camp, which he imagined was but a little distance ahead.

Although he had been without supper and breakfast, hunger had not as yet caused him any annoyance, partially because of the fact that he had had some chocolate with him, which had materially assisted in allaying its pangs, and partially through his interest in the geologic formations that held the attention of his scholarly mind to the exclusion of such material considerations as hunger, thirst, and bodily comfort. Even the question of personal safety was relegated to the oblivion that usually engulfed all practical issues when Lafayette Smith was immersed in the pleasant waters of research.

Consequently he was unaware of the proximity of a tawny body, nor did the fixed and penetrating gaze of a pair of cruel, yellow-green eyes penetrate the armor of his preoccupation to disturb that sixth sense that is popularly supposed to warn us of unseen danger. Yet even had any premonition of threat to his life or safety disturbed him he doubtless would have ignored it, safe in the consciousness that he was adequately protected by the possession of his .32 caliber, nickel plated pistol.

Moving northward along the lower slopes of a conical mountain, the mind of the geologist became more and more deeply engrossed in the rocky story that Nature had written upon the landscape, a story so thrilling that even thoughts of camp were forgotten; and as he made his way farther and farther from camp a great lion stalked in his wake.

What hidden urge prompted Numa thus to follow the man-thing perhaps the great cat, himself, could not have guessed. He was not hungry, for he had but recently finished a kill, nor was he a man-eater, though a properly balanced combination of circumstances might easily find the scales tipped in that direction by hunger, inevitable and oft recurring. It may have been only curiosity, or, again, some motive akin to that playfulness which is inherent in all cats.

For an hour Numa followed the man—an hour of intense interest for both of them—an hour that would have been replete with far greater interest for the man, if less pleasurable, had he shared with Numa the knowledge of their propinquity. Then the man halted before a narrow vertical cleft in the rocky escarpment towering above him. Here was an interesting entry in the book of Nature! What titanic force had thus rent the solid rock of this mighty mountain? It had its own peculiar significance, but what was it? Perhaps elsewhere on the face of the mountain, that here became precipitous, there would be other evidence to point the way to a solution. Lafayette Smith looked up at the face of the cliff towering above him, he looked ahead in the direction he had been going; and then he looked back in the direction from which he had come—and saw the lion.

For a long moment the two stared at one another. Surprise and interest were the most definitely registered of the emotions that the discovery engendered in the mind of the man. Suspicion and irritability were aroused in Numa.

"Most interesting," thought Lafayette Smith. "A splendid specimen;" but his interest in lions was purely academic, and his thoughts quickly reverted to the more important phenomenon of the crack in the mountain, which now, again, claimed his undivided attention. From which it may be inferred that Lafayette Smith was either an inordinately courageous man or a fool. Neither assumption, however, would be wholly correct, especially the latter. The truth of the matter is that Lafayette Smith suffered from inexperience and impracticality. While he knew that a lion was, *per se,* a threat to longevity he saw no reason why this lion should attack him. He, Lafayette Smith, had done nothing to offend this, or any other, lion; he was attending to his own affairs and, like the gentleman he was, expected others, including lions, to be equally considerate. Furthermore, he had a childlike faith in the infallibility of his nickel plated .32 should worse develop into worst. Therefore he ignored Numa and returned to contemplation of the intriguing crack.

It was several feet wide and was apparent as far up the face of the cliff as he could see. Also there was every indication that it continued far below the present surface of the ground, but had been filled by débris brought down by erosion from above. How far into the mountain it extended he could not guess; but he hoped that it ran back, and was open, for a great distance, in which event it would offer a most unique means for studying the origin of this mountain massif.

Therefore, with this thought uppermost in his mind, and the lion already crowded into the dim background of his consciousness, he entered the narrow opening to the intriguing fissure. Here he discovered that the cleft curved gradually to the left and that it extended upward to the surface, where it was considerably wider than at the bottom, thus affording both light and air for the interior.

Thrilled with excitement and glowing with pride in his discovery, Lafayette clambered inward over the fallen rocks that littered the floor of the fissure, intent now on exploring the opening to its full extent and then working back slowly to the entrance in a more leisurely manner, at which time he would make a minute examination of whatever geological record Nature had imprinted upon the walls of this majestic corridor. Hunger, thirst, camp, and the lion were forgotten.

Numa, however, was no geologist. The great cleft aroused no palpitant enthusiasm within his broad breast. It did not cause him to forget anything, and it intrigued his interest only to the extent of causing him to speculate on why the man-thing had entered it. Having noted the indifferent attitude of the man, his lack of haste, Numa could not attribute his disappearance within the maw of the fissure to flight, of which it bore not a single earmark; and it may be recorded here that Numa was an expert on flight. All of his life things had been fleeing from him.

It had always seemed to Numa an unfair provision of Nature that things should so almost inevitably seek to escape him, especially those things he most coveted. There were, for example, Pacco, the zebra, and Wappi, the antelope, the tenderest and most delicious of his particular weaknesses, and, at the same time, the fleetest. It would have been much simpler all around had Kota the tortoise been endowed with the speed of Pacco and Pacco with the torpidity of Kota.

But in this instance there was nothing to indicate that the man-thing was fleeing him. Perhaps, then, there was treachery afoot. Numa bristled. Very cautiously he approached the fissure into which his quarry had disappeared. Numa was beginning to think of Lafayette Smith in terms of food, now, since his long stalking had commenced to arouse within his belly the first, faint suggestions of hunger. He approached the cleft and looked in. The tarmangani was not in sight. Numa was not pleased, and he evidenced his displeasure by an angry growl.

A hundred yards within the fissure Lafayette Smith heard the growl and halted abruptly. "That damn lion!" he ejaculated. "I had forgotten all about him." It now occurred to him that this might be the beast's lair—a most unhappy contretemps, if true. A realization of his predicament at last supplanted the geologic reveries that had filled his mind. But what to do? Suddenly his faith in his trusty .32 faltered. As he recalled the appearance of the great beast the weapon seemed less infallible, yet it still gave him a certain sense of assurance as his fingers caressed its grip.

He determined that it would not be wise to retrace his steps toward the entrance at this time. Of course the lion might not have entered the fissure, might not even be harboring any intention of so doing. On the other hand, he might, in which event a return toward the opening could prove embarrassing, if not disastrous. Perhaps, if he waited a while, the lion would go away; and in the meantime, he decided, it would be discreet to go still farther along the cleft, as the lion, if it entered at all, might conceivably not proceed to the uttermost depths of the corridor. Further, there was the chance that he would find some sort of sanctuary farther in—a cave, a ledge to which he could climb, a miracle. Lafayette Smith was open to anything by this time.

And so he scrambled on, tearing his clothes and his flesh as well on sharp fragments of tumbled rock, going deeper into this remarkable corridor that seemed endless. In view of what might be behind him he hoped that it was endless. He had shuddered regularly to the oft recurring expectation of running into a blank wall just beyond that portion of the gently curving fissure that lay within his view ahead. He pictured the event. With his back to the rocky end of the cul-de-sac he would face back down the corridor, his pistol ready in his hand. Presently the lion would appear and discover him.

At this point he had some difficulty in constructing the scene, because he did not know just what the lion would do. Perhaps, seeing a man, cowed by the superior gaze of the human eye, he would turn in hasty retreat. And then again, perhaps he would not. Lafayette Smith was inclined to the conclusion that he would not. But then, of course, he had not had sufficient experience of wild animals to permit him to pose as an authority on the subject. To be sure, upon another occasion, while engaged in field work, he had been chased by a cow. Yet even this experience had not been conclusive—it had not served to definitely demonstrate the cow's ultimate intent—for the very excellent reason that Lafayette had attained a fence two jumps ahead of her.

Confused as the issue now seemed to be by his total ignorance of leonine psychology, he was convinced that he must attempt to visualize the expectant scene that he might be prepared for the eventuality.

Forging grimly ahead over the roughly tumbled fragments, casting an occasional glance backward, he again pictured his last stand with his back against the corridor's rocky end. The lion was creeping slowly toward him, but Lafayette was waiting until there should be no chance of a miss. He was very cool. His hand was steady as he took careful aim.

Here regrets interrupted the even tenor of his musing—regrets that he had not practiced more assiduously with his revolver. The fact that he had never discharged it troubled him, though only vaguely, since he harbored the popular subconscious conviction that if a firearm is pointed in the general direction of an animate object it becomes a deadly weapon.

However, in this mental picture he took careful aim—the fact that he was utilizing the front sight only giving him no concern. He pulled the trigger. The lion staggered and almost fell. It required a second shot to finish him, and as he sank to the ground Lafayette Smith breathed a genuine sigh of relief. He felt himself trembling slightly to the reaction of the nervous strain he had been undergoing. He stopped, and, withdrawing a handkerchief from his pocket, mopped the perspiration from his forehead, smiling a little as he realized the pitch of excitement to which he had aroused himself. Doubtless the lion had already forgotten him and had gone on about his business, he soliloquized.

He was facing back in the direction from which he had come as this satisfying conclusion passed through his mind; and then, a hundred feet away, where the corridor passed from view around a curve, the lion appeared.

CHAPTER 10

In the Clutches of the Enemy

THE "GUNNER" WAS perturbed. It was morning, and Lafayette Smith was still missing. They had searched for him until late the previous night, and now they were setting forth again. Ogonyo, the headman, acting under instructions from the "Gunner" had divided the party into pairs and, with the exception of four men left to guard the camp, these were to search in different directions combing the country carefully for trace of the missing man.

Danny had selected Obambi as his companion, a fact which irked the black boy considerably as he had been the target for a great deal of angry vituperation ever since Danny had discovered, the afternoon before, that he had left Smith alone in the mountains.

"It don't make no difference what he told you, you punk," the "Gunner" assured him, "you didn't have no business leavin' him out there alone. Now I'm goin' to take you for a walk, and if we don't find Lafayette you aint never comin' back."

"Yes, bwana," replied Obambi, who had not even a crude idea of what the white man was talking about. One thing, however, pleased him immensely and that was that the bwana insisted on carrying his own gun, leaving nothing for Obambi to carry but a light lunch and two fifty-round drums of ammunition. Not that the nine pounds and thirteen ounces of a Thompson submachine gun would have been an exceptionally heavy burden, but that Obambi was always glad to be relieved of any burden. He would have been mildly grateful for a load reduction of even thirteen ounces.

The "Gunner," in attempting to determine the probable route that Smith would have followed in his search for camp, reasoned in accordance with what he assumed he would have done under like circumstances; and, knowing that Smith had been last seen well above the camp and a little to the north of it, he decided to search in a northerly direction along the foothills, it being obvious that a man would come down hill rather than go farther up in such an emergency.

The day was hot and by noon the "Gunner" was tired, sweating, and disgusted. He was particularly disgusted with Africa, which, he informed Obambi, was "a hell of a burgh."

"Geeze," he grumbled; "I've walked my lousy legs off, and I aint been no further than from The Loop to Cicero. I been six hours, and I could of done it in twenty minutes in a taxi. Of course they aint got no cops in Africa, but they aint got no taxis either."

"Yes, bwana," agreed Obambi.

"Shut up!" growled the "Gunner."

They were sitting beneath the shade of a tree on a hillside, resting and eating their lunch. A short distance below them the hillside dropped sheer in a fifty foot cliff, a fact that was not apparent from where they sat, any more than was the palisaded village at the cliff's base. Nor did they see the man squatting by a bush at the very brink of the cliff. His back was toward them, as, from the concealment of the bush, he gazed down upon the village below.

Here, the watcher believed, was the man he sought; but he wished to make sure, which might require days of watching. Time, however, meant little or nothing to Tarzan—no more than it did to any other jungle beast. He would come back often to this vantage spot and watch. Sooner or later he would discover the truth or falsity of his suspicion that one of the white men he saw in the village below was the slave raider for whom he had come north. And so, like a great lion, the ape-man crouched, watching his quarry.

Below him Dominic Capietro and Leon Stabutch lolled in the shade of a tree outside the hut of the raider, while a half dozen slave girls waited upon them as they leisurely ate their belated breakfast.

A couple of fiery liquid bracers had stimulated their jaded spirits, which had been at low ebb after their awakening following their debauch of the previous day, though, even so, neither could have been correctly described as being in fine fettle.

Capietro, who was even more surly and quarrelsome than usual, vented his spleen upon the hapless slaves, while Stabutch ate in morose silence, which he finally broke to revert to the subject of his mission.

"I ought to get started toward the south," he said. "From all

I can learn there's nothing to be gained looking for the ape-man in this part of the country."

"What you in such a hurry to find him for?" demanded Capietro. "Aint my company good enough for you?"

" 'Business before pleasure,' you know, comrade," Stabutch reminded the Italian in a conciliatory tone.

"I suppose so," grunted Capietro.

"I should like to visit you again after I have come back from the south," suggested Stabutch.

"You may not come back."

"I shall. Peter Zveri must be avenged. The obstacle in the path of communism must be removed."

"The monkey-man killed Zveri?"

"No, a woman killed him," replied the Russian, "but the monkey-man, as you call him, was directly responsible for the failure of all Zveri's plans and thus indirectly responsible for his death."

"You expect to fare better than Zveri, then? Good luck to you, but I don't envy you your mission. This Tarzan is like a lion with the brain of a man. He is savage. He is terrible. In his own country he is also very powerful."

"I shall get him, nevertheless," said Stabutch, confidently. "If possible I shall kill him the moment I first see him, before he has an opportunity to become suspicious; or, if I cannot do that, I shall win his confidence and his friendship and then destroy him when he least suspects his danger."

Voices carry upward to a great distance, and so, though Stabutch spoke only in normal tones, the watcher, squatting at the cliff top, smiled—just the faintest suggestion of a grim smile.

So that was why the man from "Russa," of whom Goloba the headman had told him, was inquiring as to his whereabouts? Perhaps Tarzan had suspected as much, but he was glad to have definite proof.

"I shall be glad if you do kill him," said Capietro. "He would drive me out of business if he ever learned about me. He is a scoundrel who would prevent a man from earning an honest dollar."

"You may put him from your mind, comrade," Stabutch assured the raider. "He is already as good as dead. Furnish me with men, and I shall soon be on my way toward the south."

"My villains are already saddling to go forth and find men for your safari," said Capietro, with a wave of his hand in the direction of the central compound, where a score of cutthroats were saddling their horses in preparation for a foray against a distant Galla village.

"May luck go with them," said Stabutch. "I hope—What was that?" he demanded, leaping to his feet as a sudden crash of falling rock and earth came from behind them.

Capietro was also upon his feet. "A landslide," he exclaimed. "A portion of the cliff has fallen. Look! What is that?" he pointed at an object half way up the cliff—the figure of a naked white man clinging to a tree that had found lodgment for its roots in the rocky face of the cliff. The tree, a small one, was bending beneath the weight of the man. Slowly it gave way, there was the sound of rending wood, and then the figure hurtled downward into the village where it was hidden from the sight of the two white watchers by an intervening hut.

But Stabutch had seen the giant figure of the almost naked white long enough to compare it with the description he had had of the man for whom he had come all the long way from Moscow. There could not be two such, of that he was certain. "It is the ape-man!" he cried. "Come, Capietro, he is ours!"

Instantly the Italian ordered several *shiftas* to advance and seize the ape-man.

Fortune is never necessarily with either the brave or the virtuous. She is, unfortunately, quite as likely to perch upon the banner of the poltroon or the black-guard. Today she deserted Tarzan completely. As he squatted upon the edge of the cliff, looking down upon the village of Dominic Capietro, he suddenly felt the earth giving beneath him. Catlike, he leaped to his feet, throwing his hands above his head, as one does, mechanically, to preserve his balance or seek support, but too late. With a small avalanche of earth and rock he slid over the edge of the cliff. The tree, growing part way down the face of the escarpment, broke his fall and, for a moment, gave him hope that he might escape the greater danger of the final plunge into the village, where, if the fall did not kill him it was quite evident that his enemies would. But only for a moment were his hopes aroused. With the breaking of the bending stem hope vanished as he plunged on downward.

Danny "Gunner" Patrick, having finished his lunch, lighted a cigarette and let his gaze wander out over the landscape that unfolded in a lovely panorama before him. City bred, he saw only a part of what there was to be seen and understood but little of that. What impressed him most was the loneliness of the prospect. "Geeze," he soliloquized, "what a hideout! No one wouldn't never find a guy here." His eyes suddenly focused upon an object in the foreground. "Hey, smoke," he whispered to Obambi, "what's that?" He pointed in the direction of the thing that had aroused his curiosity.

Obambi looked and, when they found it, his keen eyes recognized it for what it was. "It is a man, bwana," he said. "It is the man who killed Simba in our camp that night. It is Tarzan of the Apes."

"How t'ell do you know?" demanded the "Gunner."

"There is only one Tarzan," replied the black. "It could be no other, as no other white man in all the jungle country or the mountain country or the plains country goes thus naked."

The "Gunner" rose to his feet. He was going down to have a talk with the ape-man, who, perhaps, could help him in his search for Lafayette Smith; but as he arose he saw the man below him leap to his feet and throw his arms above his head. Then he disappeared as though swallowed up by the earth. The "Gunner" knitted his brows.

"Geeze," he remarked to Obambi, "he sure screwed, didn't he?"

"What, bwana?" asked Obambi.

"Shut up," snapped the "Gunner." "That was funny," he muttered. "Wonder what became of him. Guess I'll give him a tail. Come on, dinge," he concluded aloud to Obambi.

Having learned through experience (wholly the experience of others who had failed to do so) that attention to details is essential to the continued pursuit of life, liberty, and happiness, the "Gunner" looked carefully to his Thompson as he walked rapidly but cautiously toward the spot where Tarzan had disappeared. He saw that there was a cartridge in the chamber, that the magazine drum was properly attached and that the fire control lever was set for full automatic fire.

In the village, which he could not yet see and of the presence of which he did not dream, the *shiftas* were running toward the place where they knew the body of the fallen man must lie; and in the van were Stabutch and Capietro, when suddenly there stepped from the interior of the last hut the man they sought. They did not know that he had alighted on the thatched roof of the hut from which he had just emerged, nor that, though he had broken through it to the floor below, it had so broken his fall that he had suffered no disabling injury.

To them it seemed a miracle; and to see him thus, apparently uninjured, took the two white men so by surprise that they halted in their tracks while their followers, imitating their example, clustered about them.

Stabutch was the first to regain his presence of mind. Whipping a revolver from its holster he was about to fire point blank at the ape-man, when Capietro struck his hand up. "Wait," growled the Italian. "Do not be too fast. I am in command here."

"But it is the ape-man," cried Stabutch.

"I know that," replied Capietro, "and for that very reason I wish to take him alive. He is rich. He will bring a great ransom."

"Damn the ransom," ejaculated Stabutch. "It is his life I want."

"Wait until I have the ransom," said Capietro, "and then you can go after him."

In the meantime Tarzan stood watching the two. He saw that his situation was fraught with exceptional danger. It was to the interest of either one of these men to kill him; and while the ransom of which one spoke might deter him temporarily he knew that but little provocation would be required to induce this one to kill him rather than to take the chance that he might escape, while it was evident that the Russian already considered that he had sufficient provocation, and Tarzan did not doubt but that he would find the means to accomplish his design even in the face of the Italian's objections.

If he could but get among them, where they could not use firearms against him, because of the danger that they might kill members of their own party, he felt that, by virtue of his superior strength, speed and agility, he might fight his way to one of the palisaded walls of the village where he would have a fair chance to escape. Once there he could scale the palisade with the speed of Manu, the monkey, and with little danger other than from the revolvers of the two whites, since he held the marksmanship of the *shiftas* in contempt.

He heard Capietro call to his men to take him alive; and then, waiting not upon them, he charged straight for the two whites, while from his throat burst the savage growl of a wild beast that had, upon more than a single occasion in the past, wrought havoc with the nerves of human antagonists.

Nor did it fail in its purpose now. Shocked and unnerved for the instant, Stabutch fell back while Capietro, who had no desire to kill the ape-man unless it became necessary, leaped to one side and urged his followers to seize him.

For a moment bedlam reigned in the village of the white raider. Yelling, cursing men milled about a white giant who fought with his bare hands, seizing an antagonist and hurling him in the faces of others, or, using the body of another like a flail, sought to mow down those who opposed him.

Among the close massed fighters, excited curs ran yelping and barking, while children and women upon the outskirts of the mêlée shrieked encouragement to the men.

Slowly Tarzan was gaining ground toward one of the coveted walls of the village where, as he stepped quickly backward to avoid a blow, he stumbled over a yapping cur and went down beneath a dozen men.

From the top of the cliff "Gunner" Patrick looked down upon this scene. "That mob has sure got him on the spot," he said aloud. "He's a regular guy, too. I guess here's where I step for him."

"Yes, bwana," agreed the willing Obambi.

"Shut up," said the "Gunner," and then he raised the butt of the Thompson to his shoulder and squeezed the trigger.

Mingled with the rapid reports of the machine gun were the screams and curses of wounded and frightened men and the shrieks of terrified women and children. Like snow before a spring shower, the pack that had surrounded Tarzan melted away as men ran for the shelter of their huts or for their saddled ponies.

Capietro and Stabutch were among the latter, and even before Tarzan could realize what had happened he saw the two racing through the open gates of the village.

The "Gunner," noting the satisfactory effect of his fire, had ceased, though he stood ready again to rain a hail of death down upon the village should necessity require. He had aimed only at the outskirts of the crowd surrounding the ape-man, for fear that a bullet might strike the man he was endeavoring to succor; but he was ready to risk finer shooting should any press the naked giant too closely.

He saw Tarzan standing alone in the village street like a lion at bay, and then he saw his eyes ranging about for an explanation of the burst of fire that had liberated him.

"Up here, fellar!" shouted the "Gunner."

The ape-man raised his eyes and located Danny instantly. "Wait," he called; "I'll be up there in a moment."

CHAPTER 11

The Crucifixion

AS THE WATERS of Chinnereth closed over the head of Lady Barbara, the golden haired Jezebel sprang to her feet and ran swiftly forward among the men congregated upon the great flat lava rock from which the victim of their cruel fanaticism had been hurled to her doom. She pushed apostles roughly aside as she made her way toward the brink, tears streaming from her eyes and sobs choking her throat.

Abraham, the son of Abraham, standing directly in her path, was the first to guess her purpose to throw herself into the lake and share the fate of her loved mistress. Impelled by no humanitarian urge, but rather by a selfish determination to save the girl for another fate which he already had chosen for her, the Prophet seized her as she was about to leap into the water.

Turning upon the old man like a tigress, Jezebel scratched, bit, and kicked in an effort to free herself, which she would have succeeded in doing had not the Prophet called the six executioners to his aid. Two of them seized her; and, seeing that her efforts were futile, the girl desisted; but now she turned the flood gates of her wrath upon Abraham, the son of Abraham.

"Murderer!" she cried. "Son of Satan! May Jehovah strike thee dead for this. Curses be upon thy head and upon those of all thy kin. Damned be they and thee for the foul crime thou hast committed here this day."

"Silence, blasphemer!" screamed Abraham, the son of Abraham. "Make thy peace with Jehovah, for tonight thou shalt be judged by fire. Take her back to the village," he directed the two who held her, "and make her secure in a cave. Seest thou, too, that she escapeth not."

"Fire or water, it be all the same to me," cried the girl as they dragged her away, "just so it takes me away forever from this accursed land of Midian and the mad beast who poseth as the prophet of Jehovah."

As Jezebel moved off toward the village between her two guards the villagers fell in behind them, the women calling her foul names and otherwise reviling her, and in the rear of all came the Prophet and the Apostles, leaving a score of their fellows still lying upon the ground, where they writhed, unnoticed, in the throes of epilepsy.

The impact with the surface of the water had almost stunned Lady Barbara, but she had managed to retain her senses and control of her mental and physical powers, so that, although dazed, she was able to put into effect the plan that she had nursed from the moment that she was aware of the fate to which the Prophet had condemned her.

Being an excellent swimmer and diver the thought of being immersed below the surface of Chinnereth for a few minutes had not, in itself, caused her any great mental perturbation. Her one fear had lain in the very considerable possibility that she might be so badly injured by the impact with the water, or stunned, as to be helpless to effect her own release from the net. Her relief was great, therefore, when she discovered that she was far from helpless, nor did she delay an instant in bringing her small pocket knife to play upon the fibre strands of the net that enmeshed her.

Slashing rapidly, but yet, at the same time, in accordance with a practical plan, she severed strand after strand in a straight line, as the rock dragged her downward toward the bottom. Constantly through her mind ran a single admonition—"Keep cool! Keep cool!" Should she permit herself to give away to hysteria, even for an instant, she knew that she must be lost. The lake seemed bottomless, the strands innumerable, while the knife grew constantly duller, and her strength appeared to be rapidly ebbing.

"Keep cool! Keep cool!" Her lungs were bursting. "Just a moment more! Keep cool!" She felt unconsciousness creeping upon her. She struggled to drag herself through the opening she had made in the net—her senses reeled dizzily—she was almost unconscious as she shot rapidly toward the surface.

As her head rose above the surface those standing upon the rock above her had their attention riveted upon Jezebel who was engaged at that moment in kicking the prophet of Paul, the son of Jehovah, on the shins. Lady Barbara was ignorant of all this; but it was fortunate for her, perhaps, because it prevented any of the Midians from noticing her resurrection from the deep and permitted her to swim, unseen, beneath the shelter of the overhanging rock from which she had been precipitated into the lake.

She was very weak, and it was with a prayer of thanksgiving that she discovered a narrow ledge of beach at the water's edge beneath the great lava block that loomed above her. As she dragged herself wearily out upon it she heard the voices of those upon the rock overhead—the voice of Jezebel cursing the Prophet and the old man's threat against the girl.

A thrill of pride in the courage of Jezebel warmed the heart of Lady Barbara, as did the knowledge that she had won a friend so loyal and devoted that she would put her own life in jeopardy merely for the sake of openly accusing the murderer of her friend. How magnificent she was in the primitive savagery of her denunciation! Lady Barbara could almost see her standing there defying the greatest power that her world knew, her golden hair framing her oval face, her eyes flashing, her lips curling in scorn, her lithe young body tense with emotion.

And what she had heard, and the thought of the helplessness of the young girl against the power of the vile old man, changed Lady Barbara's plans completely. She had thought to remain in hiding until night and then seek to escape this hideous valley and its mad denizens. There would be no pursuit, for they would think her dead at the bottom of Chinnereth; and thus she might seek to find her way to the outer world with no danger of interference by the people of the land of Midian.

She and Jezebel had often speculated upon the likelihood of the existence of a possible avenue of ascent of the crater wall; and from the entrance of their cave they had chosen a spot about midway of the western face of the crater, where the rim had fallen inward, as offering the best chance of escape. Tumbled masses of rock rose here from the bottom of the valley almost to the summit of the crater, and here Lady Barbara had decided to make her first bid for freedom.

But now all was changed. She could not desert Jezebel, whose life was now definitely jeopardized because of her friendship and loyalty. But what was she to do? How could she be of assistance to the girl? She did not know. Of only one thing was she certain—she must try.

She had witnessed enough horrors in the village of the South Midians to know that whatever Abraham, the son of Abraham, planned for Jezebel would doubtless be consummated after dark, the time he chose, by preference, for all the more horrible of his so-called religious rites. Only those which took them to a distance from the village, such as immersions in the waters of Chinnereth, were performed by daylight.

With these facts in mind, Lady Barbara decided that she might, with safety, wait until after dark before approaching the village. To do so earlier might only result in her own recapture, an event that would render her helpless in effecting the succor of Jezebel, while giving the Prophet two victims instead of one.

The sound of voices above her had ceased. She had heard the vituperations of the women diminishing in the distance, and by this she had known that the party had returned to the village. It was cold beneath the shadow of the rock, with her wet clothing clinging to her tired body; and so she slipped back into the water and swam along the shore a few yards until she found a spot where she could crawl out and lie in the pleasant warmth of the sun.

Here she rested again for a few minutes, and then she cautiously ascended the bank until her eyes were on a level with the ground. At a little distance she saw a woman, lying prone, who was trying to raise herself to a sitting position. She was evidently weak and dazed, and Lady Barbara realized that she was recovering from one of those horrid seizures to which nearly all the inhabitants of the village were subject. Near her were others, some lying quietly, some struggling; and in the direction of the village she saw several who had recovered sufficiently to attempt the home-ward journey.

Lying very still, her forehead concealed behind a low shrub, Lady Barbara watched and waited for half an hour, until the last of the unfortunate band had regained consciousness and self control sufficiently to permit them to depart in the direction of their squalid habitations.

She was alone now with little or no likelihood of discovery. Her clothes were still wet and exceedingly uncomfortable; so she quickly removed them and spread them in the hot sun to dry, while she luxuriated in the soothing comfort of a sun bath, alternated with an occasional dip in the waters of the lake.

Before the sun dropped to the western rim of the crater her clothing had dried; and now she sat, fully dressed again, waiting for darkness to fall. Below her lay the waters of the lake and beyond its farther shore she could dimly see the outlines of the village of the North Midians, where dwelt the mysterious "beautiful men". of Jezebel's day dreams.

Doubtless, thought Lady Barbara, the prince charming of the golden one's imagination would prove to be a whiskered Adonis with a knotted club; but, even so, it were difficult to imagine more degraded or repulsive males than those of her own village. Almost anything—even a gorilla—might seem preferable to them.

As night approached, the girl saw little lights commence to twinkle in the northern village—the cooking fires, doubtless—and then she rose and turned her face toward the village of Abraham, the son of Abraham, of Jobab and Timothy and Jezebel, toward certain danger and possible death.

As she walked along the now familiar path toward the village, the mind of Lady Barbara Collis was vexed by the seemingly hopeless problem that confronted her, while hovering upon the verge of her consciousness was that fear of the loneliness and the darkness of an unfamiliar and inhospitable country that is inherent in most of us. Jezebel had told her that dangerous beasts were almost unknown in the land of Midian, yet her imagination conjured slinking forms in the darkness and the sound of padded feet upon the trail behind her and the breathing of savage lungs. Yet ahead of her lay a real menace more terrible, perhaps, than swiftly striking talons and powerful jaws.

She recalled that she had heard that men who had been mauled by lions, and lived to narrate their experiences, had all testified uniformly to the fact that there had been no pain and little terror during the swift moments of the experience; and she knew that there was a theory propounded by certain students of animal life that the killing of the carnivores was always swift, painless, and merciful. Why was it, she wondered, that of all created things only man was wantonly cruel and only man, and the beasts that were trained by man, killed for pleasure?

But now she was nearing the village and passing from the possibility of attack by merciful beasts to the assurance of attack by merciless men, should she be apprehended by them. To reduce this risk she skirted the village at a little distance and came to the foot of the cliff where the caves were located and where she hoped to find Jezebel and, perhaps, discover a means of liberating her.

She glanced up the face of the cliff, which seemed to be deserted, most of the villagers being congregated about a group of small cooking fires near the few huts at the foot of the cliff. They often cooked thus together gossiping and praying and narrating experiences and revelations—they all received revelations from Jehovah when they "walked" with Him, which was their explanation of their epileptic seizures.

The more imaginative members of the community were the recipients of the most remarkable revelations; but, as all of them were stupid, Jehovah had not, at least during Lady Barbara's sojourn among them, revealed anything of a particularly remarkable or inspiring nature. Their gossip, like their "experiences," was mean and narrow and sordid. Each sought constantly to discover or invent some scandal or heresy in the lives of his fellows, and if the finger pointed at one not in the good graces of the Prophet or the Apostles the victim was quite likely to make a Roman holiday.

Seeing the villagers congregated about their fires, Lady Barbara commenced the ascent of the steep path that zig-zagged up the face of the cliff. She moved slowly and cautiously, stopping often to look about her, both above and below; but, notwithstanding her fears and doubts she finally reached the mouth of the cave that she and Jezebel had occupied. If she hoped to find the golden one there she was disappointed; but at least, if Jezebel were not there, it was a relief to find that no one else was; and with a sense of greater security than she had felt since the dawn of this eventful day she crawled into the interior and threw herself down upon the straw pallet that the girls had shared.

Home! This rough lair, no better than that which housed the beasts of the wilds, was home now to Lady Barbara Collis whose life had been spent within the marble halls of the Earl of Whimsey. Permeating it were memories of the strange friendship and affection that had gradually united these two girls whose origins and backgrounds could scarcely have been more dissimilar. Here each had learned the language of the other, here they had laughed and sung together, here they had exchanged confidences, and here they had planned together a future in which they would not be separated. The cold walls seemed warmer because of the love and loyalty to which they had been silent witnesses.

But now Lady Barbara was here alone. Where was Jezebel? It was the answer to that question that the English girl must find. She recalled the Prophet's threat—"for tonight thou shalt be judged by fire." She must hasten, then, if she were to save Jezebel. But how was she to accomplish it in the face of all the seemingly insurmountable obstacles which confronted her?—her ignorance of where Jezebel was being held, the numbers of her enemies, her lack of knowledge of the country through which they would be forced to flee should she be so fortunate as to effect the girl's escape from the village.

She roused herself. Lying here upon her pallet would accomplish nothing. She rose and looked down toward the village; and instantly she was all alertness again, for there was Jezebel. She was standing between two guards, surrounded by many villagers who maintained an open space about her. Presently the spectators separated and men appeared carrying a burden. What was it? They laid it in the center of the open space, in front of Jezebel; and then Lady Barbara saw what it was—a large wooden cross.

A man was digging a hole at the center of the circular space that had been left around the prisoner; others were bringing brush and fagots. Now the men who guarded Jezebel seized her and bore her to the ground. They laid her upon the cross and stretched her arms out upon the wooden cross arm.

Lady Barbara was horror stricken. Were they going to perpetrate the horrible atrocity of nailing her to the cross? Abraham, the son of Abraham, stood at the head of the cross, his hands in the attitude of prayer, a personification of pious hypocrisy. The girl knew that no cruelty, however atrocious, was beyond him. She knew, too, that she was powerless to prevent the consummation of this foul deed, yet she cast discretion and self interest to the winds, as, with a warning cry that shattered the silence of the night, she sped swiftly down the steep pathway toward the village—a self-sacrifice offered willingly upon the altar of friendship.

Startled by her scream, every eye was turned upward toward her. In the darkness they did not recognize her, but their stupid minds were filled with questioning and with terror as they saw something speeding down the cliff face toward them. Even before she reached the circle of firelight where they stood many had collapsed in paroxysms of epilepsy induced by the nervous shock of this unexpected visitation.

When she came closer, and was recognized, others succumbed, for now indeed it appeared that a miracle had been worked and that the dead had been raised again, even as they had seen the dead girl resurrected the previous day.

Pushing aside those who did not quickly enough make way for her, Lady Barbara hastened to the center of the circle. As his eyes fell upon her, Abraham, the son of Abraham, paled and stepped back. For a moment he seemed upon the verge of a stroke.

"Who are you?" he cried. "What are you doing here?"

"You know who I am," replied Lady Barbara. "Why do you tremble if you do not know that I am the messenger of Jehovah whom you reviled and sought to destroy? I am here to save the girl Jezebel from death. Later Jehovah will send His wrath upon Abraham, the son of Abraham, and upon all the people of the land of Midian for their cruelties and their sins."

"I did not know," cried the Prophet. "Tell Jehovah that I did not know. Intercede for me, that Jehovah may forgive me; and anything within my power to grant shall be yours."

So great was her surprise at the turn events had taken that Lady Barbara, who had expected only opposition and attack, was stunned for the moment. Here was an outcome so foreign to any that she had imagined that she had no response ready. She almost laughed aloud as she recalled the fears that had constantly harassed her since she had determined to attempt Jezebel's escape. And now it was all so easy.

"Liberate the girl, Jezebel," she commanded, "and then make food ready for her and for me."

"Quick!" cried the Prophet. "Raise the girl and set her free."

"Wait!" exclaimed a thin, querulous voice behind him. "I have walked with Jehovah." All turned in the direction of the speaker. He was Jobab the apostle.

"Quick! Release her!" demanded Lady Barbara, who, in this interruption and in the manner and voice of the speaker, whom she knew as one of the most fanatically intolerant of the religious bigots of Midian, saw the first spark that might grow into a flame of resistance to the will of the Prophet; for she knew these people well enough to be sure that they would grasp at any excuse to thwart the abandonment of their cruel pleasure.

"Wait!" shrieked Jobab. "I have walked with Jehovah, and He hath spoken unto me, saying: 'Behold, Jobab the Apostle, a seeming miracle shall be wrought out of Chinnereth; but be not deceived, for I say unto ye that it shall be the work of Satan; and whosoever believeth in it shall perish.'"

"Hallelujah!" shrieked a woman, and the cry was taken up by the others. To right and left the excited villagers were being stricken by their Nemesis. A score of writhing bodies jerked and struggled upon the ground in the throes of convulsions, the horrible choking, the frothing at the mouth, adding to the horror of the scene.

For a moment, Abraham, the son of Abraham, stood silent in thought. A cunning light flickered suddenly in his crafty eyes, and then he spoke. "Amen!" he said. "Let the will of Jehovah be done as revealed to the Apostle Jobab. Let Jobab speak the word of Jehovah, and upon Jobab's head be the reward."

"Another cross," screamed Jobab; "bring another cross. Let two beacon fires light the path of Jehovah in the heavens, and if either of these be His children He will not let them be consumed," and so, as Abraham, the son of Abraham, had passed the buck to Jobab, Jobab passed it along to Jehovah, who has been the recipient of more than His share through the ages.

Futile were the threats and arguments of Lady Barbara against the blood lust of the Midians. A second cross was brought, a second hole dug, and presently both she and Jezebel were lashed to the symbols of love and raised to an upright position. The bottoms of the crosses were sunk in the holes prepared for them and earth tamped around them to hold them upright. Then willing hands brought faggots and brushwood and piled them about the bases of the two pyres.

Lady Barbara watched these preparations in silence. She looked upon the weak, degenerate faces of this degraded people; and she could not, even in the extremity of her danger, find it in her heart to condemn them too severely for doing what supposedly far more enlightened people had done, within the memory of man, in the name of religion.

She glanced at Jezebel and found the girl's eyes upon her. "You should not have come back," said the girl. "You might have escaped." Lady Barbara shook her head. "You did it for me," continued Jezebel. "May Jehovah reward you, for I may only thank you."

"You would have done the same for me at Chinnereth," replied Lady Barbara. "I heard you defy the Prophet there."

Jezebel smiled. "You are the only creature I have ever loved," she said; "the only one who I ever thought loved me. Of course I would die for you."

Abraham, the son of Abraham, was praying. Young men stood ready with flaming torches, the flickering light from which danced grotesquely upon the hideous features of the audience, upon the two great crosses, and upon the beautiful faces of the victims.

"Good bye, Jezebel," whispered Lady Barbara.
"Good bye," replied the golden one.

CHAPTER 12

Out of the Grave

NOTWITHSTANDING THE FACT that Lafayette Smith had so recently visualized this very emergency and had, as it were, rehearsed his part in it, now that he stood face to face with the lion he did none of the things exactly as he had pictured. He was not at all cool when he saw the carnivore appear at the turn in the fissure; he did not face him calmly, draw a deadly bead, and fire. Nothing was in the least as he had imagined it would be. In the first place the distance between them seemed entirely inadequate and the lion much larger than he had supposed any lion could be, while his revolver seemed to shrink to proportions that represented utter futility.

All this, however, was encompassed in a single, instantaneous and overwhelming conception. No appreciable time elapsed, therefore, between the instant that he perceived the lion and that at which he commenced to jerk the trigger of his pistol, which he accomplished, without aiming, while in the act of turning to flee.

Running headlong over the jumbled rocks Lafayette Smith fled precipitately into the unknown depths of the ancient rift, at his elbow the ghastly fear that beyond each successive turn would loom the rocky terminus of his flight, while just behind him he pictured the ravenous carnivore thirsting for his blood. The fall of swiftly moving padded feet close behind him urged him to greater speed, the hot breath of the lion surged from the savage lungs to pound upon his ears like surf upon an ocean beach.

Such is the power of imagination. It is true that Numa was bounding along the bottom of the rift, but in the opposite direction to that in which Lafayette Smith bounded. Fortunately, for Lafayette, none of his wild shots had struck the lion; but the booming reverberation of the explosions in the narrow fissure had so surprised and unnerved him that he had wheeled and fled even as the man had.

Had the pursuit been as real as Lafayette imagined it, it could have urged him to no greater speed, nor could the consequent terror have nerved him to greater endurance; but physical powers have their limits, and presently the realization that his had about reached theirs forced itself upon Lafayette's consciousness and with it realization of the futility of further flight.

It was then that he turned to make his stand. He was trembling, but with fatigue rather than fear; and inwardly he was cool as he reloaded his revolver. He was surprised to discover that the lion was not on top of him, but he expected momentarily to see him appear where the fissure turned from his sight. Seating himself on a flat rock he waited the coming of the carnivore while he rested, and as the minutes passed and no lion came his wonderment increased.

Presently his scientific eye commenced to note the structure of the fissure's walls about him, and as his interest grew in the geologic facts revealed or suggested his interest in the lion waned, until, once again, the carnivore was relegated to the background of his consciousness, while in its place returned the momentarily forgotten plan to explore the rift to its farthest extent.

Recovered from the excessive fatigue of his strenuous exertion he undertook once more the exploration so rudely interrupted. Regained was the keen pleasure of discovery; forgotten, hunger, fatigue, and personal safety as he advanced along this mysterious path of adventure.

Presently the floor of the rift dropped rapidly until it was inclined at an angle that made progress difficult; and at the same time it narrowed, giving evidence that it might be rapidly pinching out. There was now barely width for him to squeeze forward between the walls when the fissure ahead of him became suddenly shrouded in gloom. Glancing up in search of an explanation of this new phenomenon Lafayette discovered that the walls far above were converging, until directly above him there was only a small streak of sky visible while ahead the rift was evidently closed entirely at the top.

As he pushed on, the going, while still difficult because of the steepness of the floor of the fissure, was improved to some extent by the absence of jumbled rocks underfoot, the closed ceiling of the corridor having offered no crumbling rim to the raging elements of the ages; but presently another handicap made itself evident— darkness, increasing steadily with each few yards until the man was groping his way blindly, though none the less determinedly, toward the unknown that lay ahead.

That an abyss might yawn beyond his next step may have occurred to him, but so impractical was he in all worldly matters while his scientific entity was in the ascendancy that he ignored the simplest considerations of safety. However, no abyss yawned; and presently, at a turning, daylight showed ahead. It was only a small patch of daylight; and when he reached the opening through which it shone it appeared, at first, that he had achieved the end of his quest—that he could proceed no farther.

Dropping to his hands and knees he essayed the feat of worming his way through the aperture, which he then discovered was amply large to accommodate his body; and a moment later he stood erect in astonished contemplation of the scene before him.

He found himself standing near the base of a lofty escarpment overlooking a valley that his practised eye recognized immediately as the crater of a long extinct volcano. Below him spread a panorama of rolling, tree-dotted landscape, broken by occasional huge outcroppings of weathered lava rock; and in the center a blue lake danced in the rays of an afternoon sun.

Thrilling to an identical reaction such as doubtless dominated Balboa as he stood upon the heights of Darien overlooking the broad Pacific, Lafayette Smith experienced that spiritual elation that is, perhaps, the greatest reward of the explorer. Forgotten, for the moment, was the scientific interest of the geologist, submerged by intriguing speculation upon the history of this lost valley, upon which, perhaps, the eyes of no other white man had ever gazed.

Unfortunately for the permanency of this beatific state of mind two other thoughts rudely obtruded themselves, as thoughts will. One appertained to the camp, for which he was supposed to be searching, while the other involved the lion, which was supposedly searching for him. The latter reminded him that he was standing directly in front of the mouth of the fissure, at the very spot where the lion would emerge were he following; and this suggested the impracticability of the fissure as an avenue of return to the opposite side of the crater wall.

A hundred yards away Smith espied a tree, and toward this he walked as offering the nearest sanctuary in the event the lion should reappear. Here, too, he might rest while considering plans for the future; and, that he might enjoy uninterrupted peace of mind while so engaged, he climbed up into the tree, where, straddling a limb, he leaned his back against the bole.

It was a tree of meager foliage, thus affording him an almost unobstructed view of the scene before him, and as his eyes wandered across the landscape they were arrested by something at the foot of the southern wall of the crater—something that did not perfectly harmonize with its natural surroundings. Here his gaze remained fixed as he sought to identify the thing that had attracted his attention. What it looked like he was positive that it could not be, so definitely had his preconception of the inaccessibility of the valley to man impressed itself upon his mind; yet the longer he looked the more convinced he became that what he saw was a small village of thatched huts.

And what thoughts did this recognition inspire? What noble and aesthetic emotions were aroused within his breast by the sight of this lonely village in the depths of the great crater which should, by all the proofs that he had seen, have been inaccessible to man?

No, you are wrong again. What it suggested was food. For the first time since he had become lost Lafayette Smith was acutely conscious of hunger, and when he recalled that it had been more than twenty-four hours since he had eaten anything more substantial than a few chocolates his appetite waxed ravenous. Furthermore, he suddenly realized that he was actually suffering from thirst.

At a little distance lay the lake. Glancing back toward the entrance to the fissure he discovered no lion; and so he dropped to the ground and set off in the direction of the water, laying his course so that at no time was he at any great distance from a tree.

The water was cool and refreshing; and when he had drunk his fill he became acutely conscious, for the first time during the day, of an overpowering weariness. The water had temporarily relieved the pangs of hunger, and he determined to rest a few minutes before continuing on toward the distant village. Once again he assured himself that there was no pursuing lion in evidence; and then he stretched himself at full length in the deep grass that grew near the edge of the lake, and with a low tree as protection from the hot sun relaxed his tired muscles in much needed rest.

He had not intended to sleep; but his fatigue was greater than he had supposed, so that, with relaxation, unconsciousness crept upon him unawares. Insects buzzed lazily about him, a bird alighted in the tree beneath which he lay and surveyed him critically, the sun dropped lower toward the western rim, and Lafayette Smith slept on.

He dreamed that a lion was creeping toward him through high grass. He tried to rise, but he was powerless. The horror of the situation was intolerable. He tried to cry out and frighten the lion away, but no sound issued from his throat. Then he made a final supreme effort, and the shriek that resulted awakened him. He sat up, dripping with perspiration, and looked quickly and fearfully about him. There was no lion. "Whew!" he exclaimed. "What a relief."

Then he glanced at the sun and realized that he had slept away the greater part of the afternoon. Now his hunger returned and with it recollection of the distant village. Rising, he drank again at the lake, and then started on his journey toward the base of the southern rim, where he hoped he would find friendly natives and food.

The way led for the greater part around the edge of the lake; and as dusk settled and then darkness it became more and more difficult to move except at a slow and cautious pace, since the ground was often strewn with fragments of lava that were not visible in the darkness.

Night brought the cheering sight of fires in the village; and these, seeming nearer than they really were, buoyed his spirits by the assurance that his journey was nearing completion. Yet, as he stumbled onward, the conviction arose that he was pursuing a will-o'-the-wisp, as the firelight appeared to retreat as rapidly as he advanced.

At last, however, the outlines of mean huts, illumined by the fires, became distinguishable and then the figures of people clustered about them. It was not until he was almost within the village that he saw with astonishment that the people were white, and then he saw something else that brought him to a sudden halt. Upon two crosses, raised above the heads of the villagers, were two girls. The firelight played upon their faces, and he saw that both were beautiful.

What weird, unholy rite was this? What strange race inhabited this lost valley? Who were the girls? That they were not of the same race as the villagers was apparent at the first casual glance at the degraded features of the latter.

Lafayette Smith hesitated. It was evident that he was witnessing some sort of religious rite or pageant; and he assumed that to interrupt it would prove far from a satisfactory introduction to these people, whose faces, which had already repelled him, impressed him so unfavorably that he questioned the friendliness of his reception even under the most favorable auspices.

And then a movement of the crowd opened for a moment an avenue to the center of the circle where the crosses stood; and the man was horrified by what was revealed for an instant to his amazed eyes, for he saw the dry brush and the faggots piled about the bottoms of the crosses and the young men with the flaming torches ready to ignite the inflammable piles.

An old man was intoning a prayer. Here and there villagers writhed upon the ground in what Smith thought were evidences of religious ecstacy. And then the old man gave a signal, and the torch bearers applied the flames to the dry brush.

Lafayette Smith waited to see no more. Leaping forward he thrust surprised villagers from his path and sprang into the circle before the crosses. With a booted foot he kicked the already burning brush aside; and then, with his little .32 shining in his hand, he turned and faced the astonished and angry crowd.

For a moment Abraham, the son of Abraham, was paralyzed by surprise. Here was a creature beyond his experience or his ken. It might be a celestial messenger; but the old man had gone so far now, and his crazed mind was so thoroughly imbued with the lust for torture, that he might even have defied Jehovah Himself rather than forego the pleasures of the spectacle he had arranged.

At last he found his voice. "What blasphemy is this?" he screamed. "Set upon this infidel, and tear him limb from limb."

"You will have to shoot, now," said an English voice at Smith's back, "for if you don't they will kill you."

He realized that it was one of the girls upon the crosses—another astonishing mystery in this village of mysteries, that cool English voice. Then one of the torch bearers rushed him with a maniacal shriek, and Smith fired. With a scream the fellow clutched his chest and sprawled at the American's feet; and at the report of the pistol and the sudden collapse of their fellow the others, who had been moving forward upon the intruder, fell back, while upon all sides the over-excited creatures succumbed to the curse that had descended to them from Angustus the Ephesian, until the ground was strewn with contorted forms.

Realizing that the villagers were, for the moment at least, too disconcerted and overawed by the death of their fellow to press their attack, Smith turned his attention at once to the two girls. Replacing his pistol in its holster, he cut their bonds with his pocket knife before Abraham, the son of Abraham, could collect his scattered wits and attempt to urge his followers to a renewed attack.

It was more than the work of a moment to liberate the two captives as, after he had cut the bonds that held their feet Smith had been compelled to partially support each with one arm as he severed the fibres that secured their wrists to the cross arms, lest a bone be broken or a muscle wrenched as the full weight of the victim was thrown suddenly upon one wrist.

He had cut Lady Barbara down first; and she was assisting him with Jezebel, who, having been crucified for a longer time, was unable to stand alone, when Abraham, the son of Abraham, regained sufficient composure to permit him to think and act.

Both Lady Barbara and Smith were supporting Jezebel into whose numbed feet the blood was again beginning to circulate. Their backs were toward the Prophet; and, taking advantage of their preoccupation, the old man was creeping stealthily upon them from the rear. In his hand was a crude knife, but none the less formidable for its crudeness. It was the blood stained sacrificial knife of this terrible old high priest of the Midians, more terrible now because of the rage and hatred that animated the cruel, defective mind that directed the claw-like hand that wielded it.

All of his rage, all of his hatred were directed against the person of Lady Barbara, in whom he saw the author of his humiliation and his thwarted desires. Stealthily he crept upon her from behind while his followers, frozen to silence by his terrible glances, watched in breathless anticipation.

Occupied with the half-fainting Jezebel none of the three at the crosses saw the repulsive figure of the avenger as he towered suddenly behind the English girl, his right hand raised high to drive the blade deeply into her back; but they heard his sudden, choking, gasping scream and turned in time to see the knife fall from his nerveless fingers as they clutched at his throat, and to witness his collapse.

Angustus the Ephesian had reached out of a grave digged two thousand years before, to save the life of Lady Barbara Collis— though doubtless he would have turned over in that same grave had he realized the fact.

CHAPTER 13

The "Gunner" Walks

LIKE A GREAT cat, Tarzan of the Apes scaled the palisade of the raiders' village, dropped lightly to the ground upon the opposite side and ascended the cliffs a little to the south of the village where they were less precipitous. He might have taken advantage of the open gate; but the direction he chose was the shorter way; and a palisade constituted no obstacle to the foster son of Kala, the she-ape.

The "Gunner" was waiting for him upon the summit of the cliff directly behind the village, and for the second time these strangely dissimilar men met—dissimilar, and yet, in some respects, alike. Each was ordinarily quiet to taciturnity, each was self-reliant, each was a law unto himself in his own environment; but there the similarity ceased for the extremes of environment had produced psychological extremes as remotely separated as the poles.

The ape-man had been reared amidst scenes of eternal beauty and grandeur, his associates the beasts of the jungle, savage perhaps, but devoid of avarice, petty jealousy, treachery, meanness, and intentional cruelty; while the "Gunner" had known naught but the squalid aspects of scenery defiled by man, of horizons grotesque with screaming atrocities of architecture, of an earth hidden by concrete and asphaltum and littered with tin cans and garbage, his associates, in all walks of life, activated by grand and petty meannesses unknown to any but mankind.

"A machine gun has its possibilities," said the ape-man, with the flicker of a smile.

"They had you in a bad spot, mister," remarked the "Gunner."

"I think I should have gotten out all right," replied Tarzan, "but I thank you none the less. How did you happen to be here?"

"I been looking for my side-kick, and I happened to see you go over the edge here. Cotton ball here, tipped me off that you was the guy saved me from the lion,—so I was glad to step for you."

"You are looking for whom?"

"My side-kick, Smith."

"Where is he?"

"I wouldn't be lookin' for him if I knew. He's went and lost himself. Been gone since yesterday afternoon."

"Tell me the circumstances," said Tarzan, "perhaps I can help you."

"That's what I was goin' to ask you," said the "Gunner." "I know my way around south of Madison Street, but out here I'm just a punk. I aint got no idea where to look for him. Geeze, take a slant at them mountains. You might as well try to meet a guy at the corner of Oak and Polk as hunt for him there. I'll tell you how it happened," and then he briefly narrated all that was known of the disappearance of Lafayette Smith.

"Was he armed?" asked the ape-man.

"He thought he was."

"What do you mean?"

"He packed a shiny toy pistol, what if anybody ever shot me with it, and I found it out, I'd turn him over my knee and spank him."

"It might serve him in getting food," said Tarzan, "and that will be of more importance to him than anything else. He's not in much danger, except from men and starvation. Where's your camp?"

Danny nodded toward the south. "Back there about a thousand miles," he said.

"You'd better go to it and remain there where he can find you if he can make his way back to it, and where I can find you if I locate him."

"I want to help you hunt for him. He's a good guy, even if he is legitimate."

"I can move faster alone," replied the ape-man. "If you start out looking for him I'll probably have to find you, too."

The "Gunner" grinned. "I guess you aint so far off, at that," he replied. "All right, I'll beat it for camp and wait there for you. You know where our camp is at?"

"I'll find out," replied Tarzan and turned to Obambi to whom he put a few questions in the native Bantu dialect of the black. Then he turned again to the "Gunner." "I know where your camp is now. Watch out for these fellows from that village, and don't let your men wander very far from the protection of your machine gun."

"Why," demanded Danny, "what are them guys?"

"They are robbers, murderers, and slave raiders," replied Tarzan.

"Geeze," exclaimed the "Gunner," they's rackets even in Africa, aint they?"

"I do not know what a racket is," replied the ape-man, "but there is crime wherever there are men, and nowhere else." He turned then, without word of parting, and started upward toward the mountains.

"Geeze!" muttered the "Gunner." "That guy aint so crazy about men."

"What, bwana?" asked Obambi.

"Shut up," admonished Danny.

The afternoon was almost spent when the "Gunner" and Obambi approached camp. Tired and footsore as he was the white man had, none the less, pushed rapidly along the backtrail lest night descend upon them before they reached their destination, for Danny, in common with most city-bred humans, had discovered something peculiarly depressing and awe-inspiring in the mysterious sounds and silences of the nocturnal wilds. He wished the fires and companionship of men after the sun had set. And so the two covered the distance on the return in much less time than had been consumed in traversing it originally.

As he came in sight of the camp the brief twilight of the tropics had already fallen, the cooking fires were burning, and to a trained eye a change would have been apparent from the appearance of the camp when he had left it early that morning; but Danny's eyes were trained in matters of broads, bulls, and beer trucks and not in the concerns of camps and safaris; so, in the failing light of dusk, he did not notice that there were more men in camp than when he had left, nor that toward the rear of it there were horses tethered where no horses had been before.

The first intimation he had of anything unusual came from Obambi. "White men are in the camp, bwana," said the black—"and many horses. Perhaps they found the mad bwana and brought him back."

"Where do you see any white men, tar baby?" demanded the "Gunner."

"By the big fire in the center of camp, bwana," replied Obambi.

"Geeze, yes, I see 'em now," admitted Danny. "They must have found old Smithy all right; but I don't see him, do you?"

"No, bwana, but perhaps he is in his tent."

The appearance of Patrick and Obambi caused a commotion in the camp that was wholly out of proportion to its true significance. The white men leaped to their feet and drew their revolvers while strange blacks, in response to the commands of one of these, seized rifles and stood nervously alert.

"You don't have to throw no fit," called Danny, "it's only me and the smoke."

The white men were advancing to meet him now, and the two parties halted face to face near one of the fires. It was then that the eyes of one of the two strange white men alighted on the Thompson sub-machine gun. Raising his revolver he covered Danny.

"Put up your hands!" he commanded sharply.

"Wotell?" demanded the "Gunner," but he put them up as every sensible man does when thus invited at the business end of a pistol.

"Where is the ape-man?" asked the stranger.

"What ape-man? What you talkin' about? What's your racket?"

"You know who I mean—Tarzan," snapped the other.

The "Gunner" glanced quickly about the camp. He saw his own men herded under guard of villanous looking blacks in long robes that had once been white; he saw the horses tethered just beyond them; he saw nothing of Lafayette Smith. The training and the ethics of gangland controlled him on the instant. "Don't know the guy," he replied sullenly.

"You were with him today," snarled the bearded white. "You fired on my village."

"Who, me?" inquired the "Gunner" innocently. "You got me wrong, mister. I been hunting all day. I aint seen no one. I aint fired at nothing. Now it's my turn. What are you guys doin' here with this bunch of Ku Klux Klanners? If it's a stick up, hop to it; and get on your way. You got the drop on us, and they aint no one to stop you. Get it over with. I'm hungry and want to feed."

"Take the gun away from him," said Capietro, in Galla, to one of his men, "also his pistol," and there was nothing for Danny "Gunner" Patrick, with his hands above his head, to do but submit. Then they sent Obambi, under escort, to be herded with the other black prisoners and ordered the "Gunner" to accompany them to the large fire that blazed in front of Smith's tent and his own.

"Where is your companion?" demanded Capietro.

"What companion?" inquired Danny.

"The man you have been travelling with," snapped the Italian. "Who else would I mean?"

"Search me," replied the "Gunner."

"What you mean by that? You got something concealed upon your person?"

"If you mean money, I aint got none."

"You did not answer my question," continued Capietro.

"What question?"

"Where is your companion?"

"I aint got none."

"Your headman told us there were two of you. What is your name?"

"Bloom," replied Danny.

Capietro looked puzzled. "The headman said one of you was Smith and the other Patrick."

"Never heard of 'em," insisted Danny. "The smoke must of been stringin' you. I'm here alone, hunting, and my name's Bloom."

"And you didn't see Tarzan of the Apes today?"

"Never even heard of a guy with that monacker."

"Either he's lying to us," said Stabutch, "or it was the other one who fired on the village."

"Sure, it must of been two other fellows," Danny assured them. "Say, when do I eat?"

"When you tell us where Tarzan is," replied Stabutch.

"Then I guess I don't eat," remarked Danny. "Geeze, didn't I tell you I never heard of the guy? Do you think I know every monkey in Africa by his first name? Come on now, what's your racket? If we got anything you want, take it and screw. I'm sick lookin' at your mugs."

"I do not understand English so well," whispered Capietro to Stabutch. "I do not always know what he says."

"Neither do I," replied the Russian; "but I think he is lying to us. Perhaps he is trying to gain time until his companion and Tarzan arrive."

"That is possible," replied Capietro in his normal voice.

"Let's kill him and get out of here," suggested Stabutch. "We can take the prisoners and as much of the equipment as you want and be a long way from here in the morning."

"Geeze," exclaimed Danny, "this reminds me of Chi. It makes me homesick."

"How much money you pay if we don't kill you?" asked Capietro. "How much your friends pay?"

The "Gunner" laughed. "Say, mister, you're giving yourself a bum steer." He was thinking how much more one might collect for killing him, if one could make connections with certain parties on the North Side of Chicago, than for sparing his life. But here was an opportunity, perhaps, to gain time. The "Gunner" did not wish to be killed, and so he altered his technique. "My friends aint rich," he said, "but they might come across with a few grand. How much do you want?"

Capietro considered. This must be a rich American, for only rich men could afford these African big game expeditions. "One hundred thousand should not be excessive for a rich man like you," he said.

"Quit your kidding," said the "Gunner." "I ain't rich."

"What could you raise?" asked Capietro, who saw by the prisoner's expression of astonishment that the original bid was evidently out of the question.

"I might scrape up twenty grand," suggested Danny.

"What are grand?" demanded the Italian.

"Thousand—twenty thousand," explained the "Gunner."

"Poof!" cried Capietro. "That would not pay me for the trouble of keeping you until the money could be forwarded from America. Make it fifty thousand lire and it's a bargain."

"Fifty thousand lire? What's them?"

"A lire is an Italian coin worth about twenty cents in American money," explained Stabutch.

Danny achieved some rapid mental calculations before he replied; and when he had digested the result he had difficulty in repressing a smile, for he discovered that his offer of twenty thousand grand was actually twice what the Italian was now demanding. Yet he hesitated to agree too willingly. "That's ten thousand iron men," he said. "That's a lot of jack."

"Iron men? Jack? I do not understand," said Capietro.

"Smackers," explained Danny lucidly.

"Smackers? Is there such a coin in America?" asked Capietro, turning to Stabutch.

"Doubtless a vernacularism," said the Russian.

"Geeze, you wops is dumb," growled the "Gunner." "A smacker's a buck. Every one knows that."

"Perhaps if you would tell him in dollars it would be easier," suggested Stabutch. "We all understand the value of an American dollar."

"That's a lot more than some Americans understand," Danny assured him; "but it's just what I been saying right along—ten thousand dollars—and it's too damn much."

"That is for you to decide," said Capietro. "I am tired of bargaining—nobody but an American would bargain over a human life."

"What you been doing?" demanded the "Gunner." "You're the guy that started it."

Capietro shrugged. "It is not my life," he said. "You will pay me ten thousand American dollars, or you will die. Take your choice."

"Oke," said Danny. "I'll pay. Now do I eat? If you don't feed me I won't be worth nothing."

"Tie his hands," Capietro ordered one of the *shiftas,* then he fell to discussing plans with Stabutch. The Russian finally agreed with Capietro that the palisaded village of the raider would be the best place to defend themselves in the event that Tarzan enlisted aid and attacked them in force. One of their men had seen Lord Passmore's safari; and, even if their prisoner was lying to them, there was at least another white, probably well armed, who might be considered a definite menace. Ogonyo had told them that this man was alone and probably lost, but they did not know whether or not to believe the headman. If Tarzan commandeered these forces, which Capietro knew he had the influence to do, they might expect an attack upon their village.

By the light of several fires the blacks of the captured safari were compelled to break camp and, when the loads were packed, to carry them on the difficult night march toward Capietro's village. With mounted *shiftas* in advance, upon the flanks, and bringing up the rear there was no lagging and no chance to escape.

The "Gunner," plodding along at the head of his own porters, viewed the prospect of that night march with unmitigated disgust. He had traversed the route twice already since sunrise; and the thought of doing it again, in the dark, with his hands tied behind him was far from cheering. To add to his discomfort he was weak from hunger and fatigue, and now the pangs of thirst were assailing him.

"Geeze," he soliloquized, "this aint no way to treat a regular guy. When I took 'em for a ride I never made no guy walk, not even a rat. I'll get these damn wops yet, the lousy bums—a thinkin' they can put Danny Patrick on the spot, an' make him walk all the way!"

CHAPTER 14

Flight

AS THE CHOKING cry broke from the lips of Abraham, the son of Abraham, Lady Barbara and Smith wheeled to see him fall, the knife clattering to the ground from his nerveless fingers. Smith was horrified, and the girl blenched, as they realized how close death had been. She saw Jobab and the others standing there, their evil faces contorted with rage.

"We must get away from here," she said. "They will be upon us in a moment."

"I'm afraid you'll have to help me support your friend," said Smith. "She cannot walk alone."

"Put your left arm around her," directed Lady Barbara. "That will leave your right hand free for your pistol. I will support her on the other side."

"Leave me," begged Jezebel. "I will only keep you from escaping."

"Nonsense," said Smith. "Put your arm across my shoulders."

"You will soon be able to walk," Lady Barbara told her, "when the blood gets back into your feet. Come! Let's get away from here while we can."

Half carrying Jezebel, the two started to move toward the circle of menacing figures surrounding them. Jobab was the first to regain his wits since the Prophet had collapsed at the critical moment. "Stop them!" he cried, as he prepared to block their way, at the same time drawing a knife from the folds of his filthy garment.

"One side, fellow!" commanded Smith, menacing Jobab with his pistol.

"The wrath of Jehovah will be upon you," cried Lady Barbara in the Midian tongue, "as it has been upon the others who would have harmed us, if you fail to let us pass in peace."

"It is the work of Satan," shrilled Timothy. "Do not let them weaken your heart with lies, Jobab. Do not let them pass!" The elder was evidently under great mental and nervous strain. His voice shook as he spoke, and his muscles were trembling. Suddenly he, too, collapsed as had Abraham, the son of Abraham. But still Jobab stood his ground, his knife raised in a definite menace against them. All around them the circle was growing smaller and its circumference more solidly knit by the forward pressing bodies of the Midians.

"I hate to do it," said Smith, half aloud, as he raised his pistol and aimed it at Jobab. The Apostle was directly in front of Lafayette Smith and little more than a yard distant when the American, aiming point blank at his chest, jerked the trigger and fired.

An expression of surprise mingled with that of rage which had convulsed the unbecoming features of Jobab the Apostle. Lafayette Smith was also surprised and for the same reason—he had missed Jobab. It was incredible—there must be something wrong with the pistol!

But Jobab's surprise, while based upon the same miracle, was of a loftier and nobler aspect. It was clothed in the sanctity of divine revelation. It emanated from a suddenly acquired conviction that he was immune to the fire and thunder of this strange weapon that he had seen lay Lamech low but a few minutes earlier. Verily, Jehovah was his shield and his buckler!

For a moment, as the shot rang out, Jobab paused and then, clothed in the fancied immunity of this sudden revelation, he leaped upon Lafayette Smith. The sudden and unexpected impact of his body knocked the pistol from Smith's hand and simultaneously the villagers closed in upon him. A real menace now that they had witnessed the futility of the strange weapon.

Lafayette Smith was no weakling, and though his antagonist was inspired by a combination of maniacal fury and religious fanaticism the outcome of their struggle must have been a foregone conclusion had there been no outside influences to affect it. But there were. Beside the villagers, there was Lady Barbara Collis.

With consternation she had witnessed the futility of Smith's marksmanship; and when she saw him disarmed and in the grip of Jobab, with others of the villagers rushing to his undoing, she realized that now, indeed, the lives of all three of them were in direct jeopardy.

The pistol lay at her feet, but only for a second. Stooping, she seized it; and then, with the blind desperation of self-preservation, she shoved the muzzle against Jobab's side and pulled the trigger; and as he fell, a hideous shriek upon his lips, she turned the weapon upon the advancing villagers and fired again. It was enough. Screaming in terror, the Midians turned and fled. A wave of nausea swept over the girl; she swayed and might have fallen had not Smith supported her.

"I'll be all right in a moment," she said. "It was so horrible!"

"You were very brave," said Lafayette Smith.

"Not as brave as you," she replied with a weak little smile; "but a better shot."

"Oh," cried Jezebel, "I thought they would have us again. Now that they are frightened, let us go away. It will require only a word from one of the apostles to send them upon us again."

"You are right," agreed Smith. "Have you any belongings you wish to take with you?"

"Only what we wear," replied Lady Barbara.

"What is the easiest way out of the valley?" asked the man, on the chance that there might be another and nearer avenue of escape than the fissure through which he had come.

"We know of no way out," replied Jezebel.

"Then follow me," directed Smith. "I'll take you out the way I came in."

They made their way from the village and out onto the dark plain toward Chinnereth, nor did they speak again until they had gone some distance from the fires of the Midians and felt that they were safe from pursuit. It was then that Lafayette Smith asked a question prompted by natural curiosity.

"How can it be possible that you young ladies know of no way out of this valley?" he asked. "Why can't you go out the way you came in?"

"I could scarcely do that," replied Jezebel; "I was born here."

"Born here?" exclaimed Smith. "Then your parents must live in the valley. We can go to their home. Where is it?"

"We just came from it," explained Lady Barbara. "Jezebel was born in the village from which we have just escaped."

"And those beasts killed her parents?" demanded Lafayette.

"You do not understand," said Lady Barbara. "Those people are her people."

Smith was dumfounded. He almost ejaculated: "How horrible!" but stayed the impulse. "And you?" he asked presently. "Are they your people, too?" There was a note of horror in his voice.

"No," replied Lady Barbara. "I am English."

"And you don't know how you got into this valley?"

"Yes, I know—I came by parachute."

Smith halted and faced her. "You're Lady Barbara Collis!" he exclaimed.

"How did you know?" she asked. "Have you been searching for me?"

"No, but when I passed through London the papers were full of the story of your flight and your disappearance—pictures and things, you know."

"And you just stumbled onto me? What a coincidence! And how fortunate for me."

"To tell you the truth, I am lost myself," admitted Smith. "So possibly you are about as badly off as you were before."

"Scarcely," she said. "You have at least prevented my premature cremation."

"They were really going to burn you? It doesn't seem possible in this day and age of enlightenment and civilization."

"The Midians are two thousand years behind the times," she told him, "and in addition to that they are religious, as well as congenital, maniacs."

Smith glanced in the direction of Jezebel whom he could see plainly in the light of a full moon that had but just topped the eastern rim of the crater. Perhaps Lady Barbara sensed the unspoken question that disturbed him.

"Jezebel is different," she said. "I cannot explain why, but she is not at all like her people. She tells me that occasionally one such as she is born among them."

"But she speaks English," said Smith. "She cannot be of the same blood as the people I saw in the village, whose language is certainly not the same as hers, to say nothing of the dissimilarity of their physical appearance."

"I taught her English," explained Lady Barbara.

"She wants to go away and leave her parents and her people?" asked Smith.

"Of course I do," said Jezebel. "Why should I want to stay here and be murdered? My father, my mother, my brothers and sisters were in that crowd you saw about the crosses tonight. They hate me. They have hated me from the day I was born, because I am not like them. But then there is no love in the land of

Midian—only religion, which preaches love and practices hate."

Smith fell silent as the three plodded on over the rough ground down toward the shore of Chinnereth. He was considering the responsibility that Fate had loaded upon his shoulders so unexpectedly and wondering if he were equal to the emergency, who, as he was becoming to realize, could scarcely be sure of his ability to insure his own existence in this savage and unfamiliar world.

Keenly the realization smote him that in almost thirty hours that he had been thrown exclusively upon his own resources he had discovered not a single opportunity to provide food for himself, the result of which was becoming increasingly apparent in a noticeable loss of strength and endurance. What then might he hope to accomplish with two additional mouths to feed?

And what if they encountered either savage beasts or unfriendly natives? Lafayette Smith shuddered. "I hope they can run fast," he murmured.

"Who?" asked Lady Barbara. "What do you mean?"

"Oh," stammered Lafayette. "I—I did not know that I spoke aloud." How could he tell her that he had lost confidence even in his .32? He could not. Never before in his life had he felt so utterly incompetent. His futility seemed to him to border on criminality. At any rate it was dishonorable, since it was deceiving these young women who had a right to expect guidance and protection from him.

He was very bitter toward himself; but that, perhaps, was due partly to the nervous reaction following the rather horrible experience at the village and physical weakness that was bordering on exhaustion. He was excoriating himself for having dismissed Obambi, which act, he realized, was at the bottom of all his troubles; and then he recalled that had it not been for that there would have been no one to save these two girls from the horrible fate from which he had preserved them. This thought somewhat restored his self-esteem, for he could not escape the fact that he had, after all, saved them.

Jezebel, the circulation restored to her feet, had been walking without assistance for some time. The three had lapsed into a long silence, each occupied with his own thoughts, as Smith led the way in search of the opening into the fissure.

A full African moon lighted their way, its friendly beams lessening the difficulties of the night march. Chinnereth lay upon their right, a vision of loveliness in the moonlight, while all about them the grim mass of the crater walls seemed to have closed in upon them and to hang menacingly above their heads, for night and moonlight play strange tricks with perspective.

It was shortly after midnight that Smith first stumbled and fell. He arose quickly, berating his awkwardness; but as he proceeded, Jezebel, who was directly behind him, noticed that he walked unsteadily, stumbling more and more often. Presently he fell again, and this time it was apparent to both girls that it was only with considerable effort that he arose. The third time he fell they both helped him to his feet.

"I'm terribly clumsy," he said. He was swaying slightly as he stood between them.

Lady Barbara observed him closely. "You are exhausted," she said.

"Oh, no," insisted Smith. "I'm all right."

"When did you eat last?" demanded the girl.

"I had some chocolate with me," replied Smith. "I ate the last of it this afternoon sometime."

"When did you eat a meal, I mean?" persisted Lady Barbara.

"Well," he admitted, "I had a light lunch yesterday noon, or rather day before yesterday. It must be after midnight now."

"And you have been walking all the time since?"

"Oh, I ran part of the time," he replied, with a weak laugh. "That was when the lion chased me. And I slept in the afternoon before I came to the village."

"We are going to stop right here until you are rested," announced the English girl.

"Oh, no," he demurred, "we mustn't do that. I want to get you out of this valley before daylight, as they will probably pursue us as soon as the sun comes up."

"I don't think so," said Jezebel. "They are too much afraid of the North Midians to come this far from the village; and, anyway, we have such a start that we can reach the cliffs, where you say the fissure is, before they could overtake us."

"You must rest," insisted Lady Barbara.

Reluctantly Lafayette sat down. "I'm afraid I'm not going to be much help to you," he said. "You see I am not really familiar with Africa, and I fear that I am not adequately armed for your protection. I wish Danny were here."

"Who is Danny?" asked Lady Barbara.

"He's a friend who accompanied me on this trip."

"He's had African experience?"

"No," admitted Lafayette, "but one always feels safe with Danny about. He seems so familiar with firearms. You see he is a protection guy."

"What is a protection guy?" asked Lady Barbara.

"To be quite candid," replied Lafayette, "I am not at all sure that I know myself what it is. Danny is not exactly garrulous about his past; and I have hesitated to pry into his private affairs, but he did volunteer the information one day that he had been a protection guy for a big shot. It sounded reassuring."

"What is a big shot?" inquired Jezebel.

"Perhaps a big game hunter," suggested Lady Barbara.

"No," said Lafayette. "I gather from Danny's remarks that a big shot is a rich brewer or distiller who also assists in directing the affairs of a large city. It may be just another name for political boss."

"Of course," said Lady Barbara, "it would be nice if your friend were here; but he is not, so suppose you tell us something about yourself. Do you realize that we do not even know your name?"

Smith laughed. "That's about all there is to know about me," he said. "It's Lafayette Smith, and now will you introduce me to this other young lady? I already know who you are."

"Oh, this is Jezebel," said Lady Barbara.

There was a moment's silence. "Is that all?" asked Smith.

Lady Barbara laughed. "Just Jezebel," she said. "If we ever get out of here we'll have to find a surname for her. They don't use 'em in the land of Midian."

Smith lay on his back looking up at the moon. Already he was commencing to feel the beneficial effects of relaxation and rest. His thoughts were toying with the events of the past thirty hours. What an adventure for a prosaic professor of geology, he thought. He had never been particularly interested in girls, although he was far from being a misogynist, and to find himself thus thrown into the intimate relationship of protector to two beautiful young women was somewhat disconcerting. And the moon had revealed that they were beautiful. Perhaps the sun might have a different story to tell. He had heard of such things and he wondered. But sunlight could not alter the cool, crisp, well bred voice of Lady Barbara Collis. He liked to hear her talk. He had always enjoyed the accent and diction of cultured English folk.

He tried to think of something to ask her that he might listen to her voice again. That raised the question of just how he should address her. His contacts with nobility had been few—in fact almost restricted to a single Russian prince who had been a door man at a restaurant he sometimes patronized, and he had never heard him addressed otherwise than as Mike. He thought Lady Barbara would be the correct formula, though that smacked a little of familiarity. Lady Collis seemed, somehow, even less appropriate. He wished he were sure. Mike would never do. Jezebel. What an archaic name! And then he fell asleep.

Lady Barbara looked down at him and raised a warning finger to her lips lest Jezebel awaken him. Then she rose and walked away a short distance, beckoning the golden one to follow.

"He is about done up," she whispered, as they seated themselves again. "Poor chap, he has had a rough time of it. Imagine being chased by a lion with only that little pop-gun with which to defend oneself."

"Is he from your country?" asked Jezebel.

"No, he's an American. I can tell by his accent."

"He is very beautiful," said Jezebel, with a sigh.

"After looking at Abraham, the son of Abraham, and Jobab, for all these weeks I could agree with you if you insisted that St. Ghandi is an Adonis," replied Lady Barbara.

"I do not know what you mean," said Jezebel; "but do you not think him beautiful?"

"I am less interested in his pulchritude than in his marksmanship, and that is positively beastly. He's got sand though, my word! no end. He walked right into that village and took us out from under the noses of hundreds of people with nothing but his little pea-shooter for protection. That, Jezebel, was top hole."

The golden Jezebel sighed. "He is much more beautiful than the men of the land of North Midian," she said.

Lady Barbara looked at her companion for a long minute; then she sighed. "If I ever get you to civilization," she said, "I'm afraid you are going to prove something of a problem." Wherewith she stretched herself upon the ground and was soon asleep, for she, too, had a strenuous day.

CHAPTER 15

Eshbaal, the Shepherd

THE SUN SHINING on his upturned face awakened Lafayette Smith. At first he had difficulty in collecting his thoughts. The events of the previous night appeared as a dream, but when he sat up and discovered the figures of the sleeping girls a short distance from him his mind was jerked rudely back into the world of realities. His heart sank. How was he to acquit himself creditably of such a responsibility? Frankly, he did not know.

He had no doubt but that he could find the fissure and lead his charges to the outer world, but how much better off would they be then? He had no idea now, and he realized that he never had, where his camp lay. Then there was the possibility of meeting the lion again in the fissure, and if they did not there was still the question of sustenance. What were they going to use for food, and how were they going to get it?

The thought of food awoke a gnawing hunger within him. He arose and walked to the shore of the lake where he lay on his belly and filled himself with water. When he stood up the girls were sitting up looking at him.

"Good morning," he greeted them. "I was just having breakfast. Will you join me?"

They returned his salutation as they arose and came toward him. Lady Barbara was smiling. "Thank the lord, you have a sense of humor," she said. "I think we are going to need a lot of it before we get out of this."

"I would much prefer ham and eggs," he replied ruefully.

"Now I know you're an American," she said.

"I suppose you are thinking of tea and marmalade," he rejoined.

"I am trying not to think of food at all," she replied.

"Have some lake," he suggested. "You have no idea how satisfying it is if you take enough of it."

After the girls had drunk the three set off again, led by Smith, in search of the opening to the fissure. "I know just where it is," he had assured them the night before, and even now he thought that he would have little difficulty in finding it, but when they approached the base of the cliff at the point where he had expected to find it it was not there.

Along the foot of the beetling escarpment he searched, almost frantically now, but there was no sign of the opening through which he had crawled into the valley of the land of Midian. Finally, crushed, he faced Lady Barbara. "I cannot find it," he admitted, and there was a quality of hopelessness in his voice that touched her.

"Never mind," she said. "It must be somewhere. We shall just have to keep searching until we find it."

"But it's so hard on you young ladies," he said. "It must be a bitter disappointment to you. You don't know how it makes me feel to realize that, with no one to depend on but me, I have failed you so miserably."

"Don't take it that way, please," she begged. "Anyone might have lost his bearings in this hole. These cliffs scarcely change their appearance in miles."

"It's kind of you to say that, but I cannot help but feel guilty. Yet I know the opening cannot be far from here. I came in on the west side of the valley, and that is where we are now. Yes, I'm sure I must find it eventually; but there is no need for all of us to search. You and Jezebel sit down here and wait while I look for it."

"I think we should remain together," suggested Jezebel.

"By all means," agreed Lady Barbara.

"As you wish," said Smith. "We will search toward the north as far as it is possible that the opening can lie. If we don't find it we can come back here and search toward the south."

As they moved along the base of the cliff in a northerly direction Smith became more and more convinced that he was about to discover the entrance to the fissure. He thought that he discerned something familiar in the outlook across the valley from this location, but still no opening revealed itself after they had gone a considerable distance.

Presently, as they climbed the rise and gained the summit of one of the numerous low ridges that ran, buttress-like, from the face of the cliff down into the valley, he halted in discouragement.

"What is it?" asked Jezebel.

"That forest," he replied. "There was no forest in sight of the opening."

Before them spread an open forest of small trees that grew almost to the foot of the cliffs and stretched downward to the

shore of the lake, forming a landscape of exceptional beauty in
its park-like aspect. But Lafayette Smith saw no beauty there—
he saw only another proof of his inefficiency and ignorance.

"You came through no forest on your way from the cliffs to
the village?" demanded Lady Barbara.

He shook his head. "We've got to walk all the way back now,"
he said, "and search in the other direction. It is most disheartening.
I wonder if you can forgive me."

"Don't be silly," said Lady Barbara. "One might think that you
were a Cook's Tour courier who had got lost during a personally
conducted tour of the art galleries of Paris and expected to lose
his job in consequence."

"I feel worse than that," Smith admitted with a laugh, "and I
imagine that's saying a lot."

"Look!" exclaimed Lady Barbara. "There are animals of some
sort down there in the forest. Don't you see them?"

"Oh, yes," cried Jezebel, "I see them."

"What are they?" asked Smith. "They look like deer."

"They are goats," said Jezebel. "The North Midians have goats.
They roam over this end of the valley."

"They look like something to eat, to me," said Lady Barbara.
"Let's go down and get one of them."

"They will probably not let us catch them," suggested Lafayette.

"You've a pistol," the English girl reminded him.

"That's a fact," he agreed. "I can shoot one."

"Maybe," qualified Lady Barbara.

"I'd better go down alone," said Smith. "Three of us together
might frighten them."

"You'll have to be mighty careful or you'll frighten them yourself," warned Lady Barbara. "Have you ever stalked game?"

"No," admitted the American, "I never have."

Lady Barbara moistened a finger and held it up. "The wind is
right," she announced. "So all you have to do is keep out of sight
and make no noise."

"How am I going to keep out of sight?" demanded Smith.

"You'll have to crawl down to them, taking advantage of trees,
rocks and bushes—anything that will conceal you. Crawl forward
a few feet and then stop, if they show any sign of nervousness,
until they appear unconcerned again."

"That will take a long time," said Smith.

"It may be a long time before we find anything else to eat," she reminded him, "and nothing we do find is going to walk up to us and lie down and die at our feet."

"I suppose you are right," assented Smith. "Here goes! Pray for me." He dropped to his hands and knees and crawled slowly forward over the rough ground in the direction of the forest and the goats. After a few yards he turned and whispered: "This is going to be tough on the knees."

"Not half as hard as it's going to be on our stomachs if you don't succeed," replied Lady Barbara.

Smith made a wry face and resumed his crawling while the two girls, lying flat now to conceal themselves from the quarry, watched his progress.

"He's not doing half badly," commented Lady Barbara after several minutes of silent watching.

"How beautiful he is," sighed Jezebel.

"Just at present the most beautiful things in the landscape are those goats," said Lady Barbara. "If he gets close enough for a shot and misses I shall die—and I know he will miss."

"He didn't miss Lamech last night," Jezebel reminded her.

"He must have been aiming at someone else," commented Lady Barbara shortly.

Lafayette Smith crawled on apace. With numerous halts, as advised by Lady Barbara, he drew slowly nearer his unsuspecting quarry. The minutes seemed hours. Pounding constantly upon his brain was the consciousness that he must not fail, though not for the reason that one might naturally assume. The failure to procure food seemed a less dreadful consequence than the contempt of Lady Barbara Collis.

Now, at last, he was quite close to the nearest of the herd. Just a few more yards and he was positive that he could not miss. A low bush, growing just ahead of him, concealed his approach from the eyes of his victim. Lafayette Smith reached the bush and paused behind it. A little farther ahead he discovered another shrub still closer to the goat, a thin nanny with a large udder. She did not look very appetizing, but beneath that unprepossessing exterior Lafayette Smith knew there must be hidden juicy steaks and cutlets. He crawled on. His knees were raw and his neck ached from the unnatural position his unfamiliar method of locomotion had compelled it to assume.

He passed the bush behind which he had paused, failing to see the kid lying hidden upon its opposite side—hidden by a solicitous mamma while she fed. The kid saw Lafayette but it did not move. It would not move until its mother called it, unless actually touched by something, or terrified beyond the limit of its self control.

It watched Lafayette crawling toward the next bush upon his itinerary—the next and last. What it thought is unrecorded, but it is doubtful that it was impressed by Lafayette's beauty.

Now the man had reached the concealment of the last bush, unseen by any other eyes than those of the kid. He drew his pistol cautiously, lest the slightest noise alarm his potential dinner. Raising himself slightly until his eyes were above the level of the bush he took careful aim. The goat was so close that a miss appeared such a remote contingency as to be of negligible consideration.

Lafayette already felt the stirring warmth of pride with which he would toss the carcass of his kill at the feet of Lady Barbara and Jezebel. Then he jerked the trigger.

Nanny leaped straight up into the air, and when she hit the ground again she was already streaking north in company with the balance of the herd. Lafayette Smith had missed again.

He had scarcely time to realize the astounding and humiliating fact as he rose to his feet when something struck him suddenly and heavily from behind—a blow that bent his knees beneath him and brought him heavily to earth in a sitting posture. No, not to earth. He was sitting on something soft that wriggled and squirmed. His startled eyes, glancing down, saw the head of a kid protruding from between his legs—little Capra hircus had been terrified beyond the limit of his self-control.

"Missed!" cried Lady Barbara Collis. "How could he!" Tears of disappointment welled to her eyes.

Eshbaal, hunting his goats at the northern fringe of the forest cocked his ears and listened. That unfamiliar sound! And so near. From far across the valley, toward the village of the South Midians, Eshbaal had heard a similar sound, though faintly from afar, the night before. Four times it had broken the silence of the valley and no more. Eshbaal had heard it and so had his fellows in the village of Elija, the son of Noah.

Lafayette Smith seized the kid before it could wriggle free, and despite its struggles he slung it across his shoulder and started back toward the waiting girls.

"He didn't miss it!" exclaimed Jezebel. "I knew he wouldn't," and she went down to meet him, with Lady Barbara, perplexed, following in her wake.

"Splendid!" cried the English girl as they came closer. "You really did shoot one, didn't you? I was sure you missed."

"I did miss," admitted Lafayette ruefully.

"But how did you get it?"

"If I must admit it," explained the man, "I sat on it. As a matter of fact it got me."

"Well, anyway, you have it," she said.

"And it will be a whole lot better eating than the one I missed," he assured them. "That one was terribly thin and very old."

"How cute it is," said Jezebel.

"Don't," cried Lady Barbara. "We mustn't think of that. Just remember that we are starving."

"Where shall we eat it?" asked Smith.

"Right here," replied the English girl. "There is plenty of deadwood around these trees. Have you matches?"

"Yes. Now you two look the other way while I do my duty. I wish I'd hit the old one now. This is like murdering a baby."

Upon the opposite side of the forest Eshbaal was once again experiencing surprise, for suddenly the goats for which he had been searching came stampeding toward him.

"The strange noise frightened them," soliloquized Eshbaal. "Perhaps it is a miracle. The goats for which I have searched all day have been made to return unto me."

As they dashed past, the trained eye of the shepherd took note of them. There were not many goats in the bunch that had strayed, so he had no difficulty in counting them. A kid was missing. Being a shepherd there was nothing for Eshbaal to do but set forth in search of the missing one. He advanced cautiously, alert because of the noise that he had heard.

Eshbaal was a short, stocky man with blue eyes and a wealth of blond hair and beard. His features were regular and handsome in a primitive, savage way. His single garment, fashioned from a goat skin, left his right arm entirely free, nor did it impede his legs, since it fell not to his knees. He carried a club and a rude knife.

Lady Barbara took charge of the culinary activities after Lafayette had butchered the kid and admitted that, beyond hard boiling eggs, his knowledge of cooking was too sketchy to warrant serious mention. "And anyway," he said, "we haven't any eggs."

Following the directions of the English girl, Smith cut a number of chops from the carcass; and these the three grilled on pointed sticks that Lady Barbara had had him cut from a nearby tree.

"How long will it take to cook them?" demanded Smith. "I could eat mine raw. I could eat the whole kid raw, for that matter, in one sitting and have room left for the old nanny I missed."

"We'll eat only enough to keep us going," said Lady Barbara; "then we'll wrap the rest in the skin and take it with us. If we're careful, this should keep us alive for three or four days."

"Of course you're right," admitted Lafayette. "You always are."

"You can have a big meal this time," she told him, "because you've been longer without food than we."

"You have had nothing for a long time, Barbara," said Jezebel. "I am the one who needs the least."

"We all need it now," said Lafayette. "Let's have a good meal this time, get back our strength, and then ration the balance so that it will last several days. Maybe I will sit on something else before this is gone."

They all laughed; and presently the chops were done, and the three fell to upon them. "Like starving Armenians," was the simile Smith suggested.

Occupied with the delightful business of appeasing woolfish hunger, none of them saw Eshbaal halt behind a tree and observe them. Jezebel he recognized for what she was, and a sudden fire lighted his blue eyes. The others were enigmas to him—especially their strange apparel.

Of one thing Eshbaal was convinced. He had found his lost kid and there was wrath in his heart. For just a moment he watched the three; then he glided back into the forest until he was out of their sight, when he broke into a run.

The meal finished, Smith wrapped the remainder of the carcass in the skin of the kid; and the three again took up their search for the fissure.

An hour passed and then another. Still their efforts were not crowned with success. They saw no opening in the stern, forbidding face of the escarpment, nor did they see the slinking figures creeping steadily nearer and nearer—a score of stocky, yellow haired men led by Eshbaal, the Shepherd.

"We must have passed it," said Smith at last. "It just cannot be this far south," yet only a hundred yards farther on lay the illusive opening into the great fissure.

"We shall have to hunt for some other way out of the valley then," said Lady Barbara. "There is a place farther south that

Jezebel and I used to see from the mouth of our cave where the cliff looked as though it might be scaled."

"Let's have a try at it then," said Smith. "Say, look there!" he pointed toward the north.

"What is it? Where?" demanded Jezebel.

"I thought I saw a man's head behind that rock," said Smith. "Yes, there he is again. Lord, look at 'em. They're all around."

Eshbaal and his fellows, realizing that they were discovered, came into the open, advancing slowly toward the three.

"The men of North Midian!" exclaimed Jezebel. "Are they not beautiful!"

"What shall we do?" demanded Lady Barbara. "We must not let them take us."

"We'll see what they want," said Smith. "They may not be unfriendly. Anyway, we couldn't escape them by running. They would overtake us in no time. Get behind me, and if they show any signs of attacking I'll shoot a few of them."

"Perhaps you had better go out and sit on them," suggested Lady Barbara, wearily.

"I am sorry," said Smith, "that my marksmanship is so poor; but, unfortunately perhaps, it never occurred to my parents to train me in the gentle art of murder. I realize now that they erred and that my education has been sadly neglected. I am only a school teacher, and in teaching the young intellect to shoot I have failed to learn to do so myself."

"I didn't intend to be nasty," said Lady Barbara, who detected in the irony of the man's reply a suggestion of wounded pride. "Please forgive me."

The North Midians were advancing cautiously, halting occasionally for brief, whispered conferences. Presently one of them spoke, addressing the three. "Who are you?" he demanded. "What do you in the land of Midian?"

"Can you understand him?" asked Smith, over his shoulder.

"Yes," replied both girls simultaneously.

"He speaks the same language as Jezebel's people," explained Lady Barbara. "He wants to know who we are and what we are doing here."

"You talk to him, Lady Barbara," said Smith.

The English girl stepped forward. "We are strangers in Midian," she said. "We are lost. All we wish is to get out of your country."

"There is no way out of Midian," replied the man. "You have

killed a kid belonging to Eshbaal. For that you must be punished. You must come with us."

"We were starving," explained Lady Barbara. "If we could pay for the kid we would gladly do so. Let us go in peace."

The Midians held another whispered conference, after which their spokesman addressed the three again. "You must come with us," he said, "the women at least. If the man will go away we will not harm you, we do not want him; we want the women."

"What did he say?" demanded Smith, and when Lady Barbara had interpreted he shook his head. "Tell them no," he directed. "Also tell them that if they molest us I shall have to kill them."

When the girl delivered this ultimatum to the Midians they laughed. "What can one man do against twenty?" demanded their leader, then he advanced followed by his retainers. They were brandishing their clubs now, and some of them raised their voices in a savage war cry.

"You will have to shoot," said Lady Barbara. "There are at least twenty. You cannot miss them all."

"You flatter me," said Smith, as he raised his .32 and levelled it at the advancing Midians.

"Go back!" shouted Jezebel, "or you will be killed," but the attackers only came forward the faster.

Then Smith fired. At the sharp crack of the pistol the Midians halted, surprised; but no one fell. Instead, the leader hurled his club, quickly and accurately, just as Smith was about to fire again. He dodged; but the missile struck his pistol hand a glancing blow, sending the weapon flying—then the North Midians were upon them.

CHAPTER 16

Trailing

TARZAN OF THE Apes had made a kill. It was only a small rodent, but it would satisfy his hunger until the morrow. Darkness had fallen shortly after he had discovered the spoor of the missing American, and he was forced to abandon the search until daylight came again. The first sign of the spoor had been very faint—just the slightest imprint of one corner of a boot heel, but that had

Then Smith fired.

been enough for the ape-man. Clinging to a bush nearby was the scarcely perceptible scent spoor of a white man, which Tarzan might have followed even after dark; but it would have been a slow and arduous method of tracking which the ape-man did not consider the circumstances warranted. Therefore he made his kill, ate, and curled up in a patch of tall grass to sleep.

Wild beasts may not sleep with one eye open, but often it seems that they sleep with both ears cocked. The ordinary night sounds go unnoticed, while a lesser sound, portending danger or suggesting the unfamiliar, may awaken them on the instant. It was a sound falling in the latter category that awoke Tarzan shortly after midnight.

He raised his head and listened, then he lowered it and placed an ear against the ground. "Horses and men," he soliloquized as he rose to his feet. Standing erect, his great chest rising and falling to his breathing, he listened intently. His sensitive nostrils, seeking to confirm the testimony of his ears, dilated to receive and classify the messages that Usha, the wind, bore to them. They caught the scent of Tongani, the baboon, so strong as almost to negate the others. Tenuous, from a great distance came the scent spoor of Sabor, the lioness, and the sweet, heavy stench of Tantor, the elephant. One by one the ape-man read these invisible messages brought by Usha, the wind; but only those interested him that spoke of horses and men.

Why did horses and men move through the night? Who and what were the men? He scarcely needed to ask himself that latter question, and only the first one interested him.

It is the business of beasts and of men to know what their enemies do. Tarzan stretched his great muscles lazily and moved down the slope of the foot hills in the direction from which had come the evidence that his enemies were afoot.

The "Gunner" stumbled along in the darkness. Never in his twenty odd years of life had he even approximated such utter physical exhaustion. Each step he was sure must be his last. He had long since become too tired even to curse his captors as he plodded on, now almost numb to any sensation, his mind a chaos of dull misery.

But even endless journeys must ultimately end; and at last the cavalcade turned into the gateway of the village of Dominic Capietro, the raider; and the "Gunner" was escorted to a hut where he slumped to the hard earth floor after his bonds had been removed, positive that he would never rise again.

He was asleep when they brought him food; but aroused himself long enough to eat, for his hunger was fully as great as his fatigue. Then he stretched out again and slept, while a tired and disgusted *shifta* nodded drowsily on guard outside the entrance to the hut.

Tarzan had come down to the cliff above the village as the raiders were filing through the gateway. A full moon cast her revealing beams upon the scene, lighting the figures of horses and men. The ape-man recognized Capietro and Stabutch, he saw Ogonyo, the head-man of the safari of the young American geologist; and he saw the "Gunner" stumbling painfully along in bonds.

The ape-man was an interested spectator of all that transpired in the village below. He noted particularly the location of the hut into which the white prisoner had been thrust. He watched the preparation of food, and he noted the great quantities of liquor that Capietro and Stabutch consumed while waiting for the midnight supper being prepared by slaves. The more they drank the better pleased was Tarzan.

As he watched them, he wondered how supposedly rational creatures could consider the appellation *beast* a term of reproach and *man* one of glorification. The beasts, as he knew, held an opposite conception of the relative virtues of these two orders, although they were ignorant of most of man's asininities and degredations, their minds being far too pure to understand them.

Waiting with the patience of the unspoiled primitive nervous system, Tarzan watched from the cliff top until the village below seemed to have settled down for the night. He saw the sentries in the banquette inside the palisade, but he did not see the guard squatting in the shadow of the hut where the "Gunner" lay in heavy slumber.

Satisfied, the ape-man rose and moved along the cliff until he was beyond the village; and there, where the escarpment was less precipitous, he made his way to its base. Noiselessly and cautiously he crept to the palisade at a point that was hidden from the view of the sentries. The moon shone full upon him, but the opposite side of the palisade he knew must be in dense shadow. There he listened for a moment to assure himself that his approach had aroused no suspicion. He wished that he might see the sentries at the gate, for when he topped the palisade he would be in full view for an instant. When last he had seen them they had been squatting upon the banquette, their backs to the palisade, and apparently upon the verge of sleep. Would they remain thus?

Here, however, was a chance he must take, and so he gave the matter little thought and few regrets. What was, was; and if he could not change it he must ignore it; and so, leaping lightly upward, he seized the top of the palisade and drew himself up and over. Only a glance he threw in the direction of the sentries as he topped the barrier, a glance that told him they had not moved since he had last looked.

In the shadow of the palisade he paused to look about. There was nothing to cause him apprehension; and so he moved quickly, keeping ever in the shadows where he could, toward the hut where he expected to find the young white man. It was hidden from his view by another hut which he approached and had circled when he saw the figure of the guard sitting by the doorway, his rifle across his knees.

This was a contingency the ape-man had not anticipated, and it caused a change in his immediate plans. He drew back out of sight behind the hut he had been circling, lay down flat upon the ground, and then crawled forward again until his head protruded beyond the hut far enough to permit one eye to watch the unconscious guard. Here he lay waiting—a human beast watching its quarry.

For a long time he lay thus trusting to his knowledge of men that the moment for which he waited would arrive. Presently the chin of the *shifta* dropped to his chest; but immediately it snapped back again, erect. Then the fellow changed his position. He sat upon the ground, his legs stretched before him, and leaned his back against the hut. His rifle was still across his knees. It was a dangerous position for a man who would remain awake.

After a while his head rolled to one side. Tarzan watched him closely, as a cat watches a mouse. The head remained in the position to which it had rolled, the chin dropped, and the mouth gaped; the tempo of the breathing changed, denoting sleep.

Tarzan rose silently to his feet and as silently crept across the intervening space to the side of the unconscious man. There must be no outcry, no scuffle.

As strikes Histah, the snake, so struck Tarzan of the Apes. There was only the sound of parting vertebrae as the neck broke in the grip of those thews of steel.

The rifle Tarzan laid upon the ground; then he raised the corpse in his arms and bore it into the darkness of the hut's interior. Here he groped for a moment until he had located the body of the sleeping white, and knelt beside him. Cautiously he shook him, one hand ready to muffle any outcry the man might make, but the "Gunner" did not awaken. Tarzan shook him again more roughly and yet without results, then he slapped him heavily across the face.

The "Gunner" stirred. "Geeze," he muttered "can't you let a guy sleep? Didn't I tell you you'd get your ransom, you damn wop?"

Tarzan permitted a faint smile to touch his lips. "Wake up," he whispered. "Make no noise. I have come to take you away."

"Who are you?"

"Tarzan of the Apes."

"Geeze!" The "Gunner" sat up.

"Make no noise," cautioned the ape-man once more.

"Sure," whispered Danny as he raised himself stiffly to his feet.

"Follow me," said Tarzan, "and no matter what happens stay very close to me. I am going to toss you to the top of the palisade. Try not to make any noise as you climb over, and be careful when you drop to the ground on the other side to alight with your knees flexed—it is a long drop."

"You say you're going to toss me to the top of the palisade, guy?"

"Yes."

"Do you know what I weigh?"

"No, and I don't care. Keep still and follow me. Don't stumble over this body." Tarzan paused in the entrance and looked about; then he passed out, with the "Gunner" at his heels, and crossed quickly to the palisade. Even if they discovered him now he still had time to accomplish what he had set out to do, before they could interfere, unless the sentries, firing on them, chanced to make a hit; but on that score he felt little apprehension.

As they came to the palisade the "Gunner" glanced up, and his skepticism increased—a fat chance any guy would have to toss his one hundred and eighty pounds to the top of that!

The ape-man seized him by the collar and the seat of his breeches. "Catch the top!" he whispered. Then he swung the "Gunner" backward as though he had been a fifty pound sack of meal, surged forward and upward; and in the same second Danny Patrick's outstretched fingers clutched the top of the palisade.

"Geeze," he muttered, "if I'd missed I'd of gone clean over."

Catlike, the ape-man ran up the barrier and dropped to the ground on the outside almost at the instant that the "Gunner" alighted, and without a word started toward the cliff, where once again he had to assist the other to reach the summit.

Danny "Gunner" Patrick was speechless, partly from shortness of breath following his exertions, but more, by far, from astonishment. Here was a guy! In all his experience of brawny men, and it had been considerable, he had never met, nor expected to meet, such a one as this.

"I have located the spoor of your friend," said Tarzan.

"The what?" asked the "Gunner." "Is he dead?"

"His tracks," explained the ape-man, who was still leading the way up the slope toward the higher mountains.

"I gotcha," said the "Gunner." "But you aint seen him?"

"No, it was too dark to follow him when I found them. We will do so in the morning."

"If I can walk," said the "Gunner."

"What's the matter with you?" demanded Tarzan. "Injured?"

"I aint got no legs from the knees down," replied Danny. "I walked my lousy dogs off yesterday."

"I'll carry you," suggested Tarzan.

"Nix!" exclaimed Danny. "I can crawl, but I'll be damned if I'll let any guy carry me."

"It will be a hard trip if you're exhausted now," the ape-man told him. "I could leave you somewhere near here and pick you up after I find your friend."

"Nothing doing. I'm going to look for old Smithy if I wear 'em off to the hips."

"I could probably travel faster alone," suggested Tarzan.

"Go ahead," agreed the "Gunner" cheerfully. "I'll tail along behind you."

"And get lost."

"Let me come along, mister. I'm worried about that crazy nut."

"All right. It won't make much difference anyway. He may be a little hungrier when we find him, but he can't starve to death in a couple of days."

"Say," exclaimed Danny, "how come you knew them Wops had taken me for a ride?"

"I thought you walked."

"Well, what's the difference? How did you know I was in that lousy burgh of theirs?"

"I was on the cliff when they brought you in. I waited until they were asleep. I am not ready to deal with them yet."

"What you goin' to do to them?"

Tarzan shrugged but made no reply; and for a long time they walked on in silence through the night, the ape-man timing his speed to the physical condition of his companion, whose nerve he was constrained to admire, though his endurance and knowledge he viewed with contempt.

Far up in the hills, where he had bedded down earlier in the night, Tarzan halted and told the "Gunner" to get what rest he could before dawn.

"Geeze, them's the pleasantest words I've heard for years," sighed Danny, as he lay down in the high grass. "You may think you've seen a guy pound his ear, but you aint seen nothin'. Watch me," and he was asleep almost before the words had left his mouth.

Tarzan lay down at a little distance; and he, too, was soon asleep, but at the first suggestion of dawn he was up. He saw that his companion still slept, and then he slipped silently away toward a water hole he had discovered the previous day in a rocky ravine near the cliff where he had met the tribe of Zugash, the tongani.

He kept well down the slope of the foot hills, for with the coming of dawn the wind had changed, and he wished to come up wind toward the water hole. He moved as silently as the disappearing shadows of the retreating night, his nostrils quivering to catch each vagrant scent borne upon the bosom of the early morning breeze.

There was deep mud at one edge of the water hole, where the earth had been trampled by the feet of drinking beasts; and near here he found that which he sought, the sticky sweetness of whose scent had been carried to his nostrils by Usha.

Low trees grew in the bottom of the ravine and much underbrush, for here the earth held its moisture longer than on the ridges that were more exposed to Kudu's merciless rays. It was a lovely sylvan glade, nor did its beauties escape the appreciative eyes of the ape-man, though the lure of the glade lay not this morning in its aesthetic charms, but rather in the fact that it harbored Horta, the boar.

Silently to the edge of the underbrush came the ape-man as Horta came down to the pool to drink. Upon the opposite side stood Tarzan, his bow and arrows ready in his hands; but the high brush precluded a fair shot, and so the hunter stepped out in full view of the boar. So quickly he moved that his arrow sped as Horta wheeled to run, catching the boar in the side behind the left shoulder—a vital spot.

With a snort of rage Horta turned back and charged. Straight through the pool he came for Tarzan; and as he came three more arrows, shot with unbelievable accuracy and celerity, buried themselves deep in the breast of the great beast. Bloody foam flecked his jowls and his flashing tusks, fires of hate shot from his wicked little eyes as he sought to reach the author of his hurts and wreak his vengeance before he died.

Discarding his bow the ape-man met the mad charge of Horta with his spear, for there was no chance to elude the swift rush of that great body, hemmed, as he was, by the thick growth of underbrush. His feet braced, he dropped the point of his weapon the instant Horta was within its range, that he might have no opportunity to dodge it or strike it aside with his tusks. Straight through the great chest it drove, deep into the savage heart, yet the beast still strove to reach the man-thing that held it off with a strength almost equal to its own.

But already as good as dead on his feet was Horta, the boar. His brief, savage struggles ended; and he dropped in the shallow water at the edge of the pool. Then the ape-man placed a foot upon his vanquished foe and screamed forth the hideous challenge of his tribe.

The "Gunner" sat suddenly erect, awakened out of a sound sleep. "Geeze!" he exclaimed. "What was that?" Receiving no answer he looked about. "Wouldn't that eat you?" he murmured. "He's went. I wonder has he run out on me? He didn't seem like that kind of a guy. But you can't never tell—I've had pals to double-cross me before this."

In the village of Capietro a dozing sentry snapped suddenly alert, while his companion half rose to his feet. "What was that?" demanded one.

"A hairy one has made a kill," said the other.

Sheeta, the panther, down wind, stalking both the man and the boar, stopped in his tracks; then he turned aside and loped away in easy, graceful bounds; but he had not gone far before he stopped again and raised his nose up-wind. Again the scent of man; but this time a different man, nor was there any sign of the feared thunder stick that usually accompanied the scent spoor of the tarmangani. Belly low, Sheeta moved slowly up the slope toward Danny "Gunner" Patrick.

"What to do?" mused the "Gunner." "Geeze, I'm hungry! Should I wait for him or should I go on? On, where? I sure got myself in a jam all right. Where do I go? How do I eat? Hell!"

He arose and moved about, feeling out his muscles. They were lame and sore, but he realized that he was much rested. Then he scanned the distances for a sight of Tarzan and, instead, saw Sheeta, the panther, a few hundred yards away.

Danny Patrick, hoodlum, racketeer, gangster, gunman, killer, trembled in terror. Cold sweat burst from every pore, and he could feel the hair rise on his scalp. He felt a mad impulse to run; but, fortunately for Danny, his legs refused to move. He was literally, in the vernacular to which he was accustomed, scared stiff. The "Gunner," without a gun, was a very different man.

The panther had stopped and was surveying him. Caution and an hereditary fear of man gave the great cat pause; but he was angry because he had been frightened from his prey after hunting futilely all night, and he was very, very hungry. He growled, his face wrinkled in a hideous snarl; and Danny felt his knees giving beneath him.

Then, beyond the panther, he saw the high grass moving to the approach of another animal, which the "Gunner" promptly assumed was the beast's mate. There was just a single, narrow strip of this high grass; and when the animal had crossed it he, too, would see Danny, who was confident that this would spell the end. One of them might hesitate to attack a man—he didn't know—but he was sure that two would not.

He dropped to his knees and did something that he had not done for many years—he prayed. And then the grasses parted; and Tarzan of the Apes stepped into view, the carcass of a boar upon one broad shoulder. Instantly the ape-man took in the scene that his nostrils had already prepared him for.

Dropping the carcass of Horta he voiced a sudden, ferocious growl that startled Sheeta no more than it did Danny Patrick. The cat wheeled, instantly on the defensive. Tarzan charged, growls rumbling from his throat; and Sheeta did exactly what he had assumed he would do—turned and fled. Then Tarzan picked up the carcass of Horta and came up the slope to Danny, who knelt open-mouthed and petrified.

"What are you kneeling for?" asked the ape-man.

"I was just tying my boot lace," explained the "Gunner."

"Here is breakfast," said Tarzan, dropping the boar to the ground. "Help yourself."

"That sure looks good to me," said Danny. "I could eat it raw."

"That is fine," said Tarzan; and, squatting, he cut two strips from one of the hams. "Here," he said, offering one to the "Gunner."

"Quit your kidding," remonstrated the latter.

Tarzan eyed him questioningly, at the same time tearing off a mouthful of the meat with his strong teeth. "Horta is a little bit tough," he remarked, "but he is the best I could do without losing a great deal of time. Why don't you eat? I thought you were hungry."

"I got to cook mine," said the "Gunner."

"But you said you could eat it raw," the ape-man reminded him.

"That's just a saying," explained the "Gunner." "I might at that, but I aint never tried it."

"Make a fire, then; and cook yours," said Tarzan.

"Say," remarked Danny a few minutes later as he squatted before his fire grilling his meat, "did you hear that noise a little while ago?"

"What was it like?"

"I never heard nothing like it but once before—say I just took a tumble to myself! That was you killin' the pig. I heard you yell like that the night you killed the lion in our camp."

"We will be going as soon as you finish your meat," said Tarzan. He was hacking off several pieces, half of which he handed to the "Gunner" while he dropped the balance into his quiver. "Take these," he said. "You may get hungry before we can make another kill." Then he scraped a hole in the loose earth and buried the remainder of the carcass.

"What you doin' that for?" asked the "Gunner." "Afraid it will smell?"

"We may come back this way," explained Tarzan. "If we do Horta will be less tough."

The "Gunner" made no comment; but he assured himself, mentally, that he "wasn't no dog," to bury his meat and then dig it up again after it had rotted. The idea almost made him sick.

Tarzan quickly picked up the trail of Lafayette Smith and

followed it easily, though the "Gunner" saw nothing to indicate that human foot had ever trod these hills.

"I don't see nothing," he said.

"I have noticed that," returned Tarzan.

"That," thought Danny Patrick, "sounds like a dirty crack;" but he said nothing.

"A lion picked up his trail here," said the ape-man.

"You ain't spoofin' me are you?" demanded Danny. "There ain't no sign of nothin' on this ground."

"Nothing that you can see perhaps," replied Tarzan; "but then, though you may not know it, you so-called civilized men are almost blind and quite stone deaf."

Soon they came to the fissure, and here Tarzan saw that the man and the lion had both gone in, the lion following the man, and that only the lion had come out.

"That looks tough for old Smithy, doesn't it?" said the "Gunner" when Tarzan had explained the story of the spoor.

"It may," replied the ape-man. "I'll go on in and look for him. You can wait here or follow. You can't get lost if you stay inside this crack."

"Go ahead," said Danny. "I'll follow."

The fissure was much longer than Tarzan had imagined; but some distance from the entrance he discovered evidence that the lion had not attacked Smith, for he could see where Numa had turned about and that the man had continued on. Some recent scars on the sides of the fissure told him the rest of the story quite accurately.

"It's fortunate he didn't hit Numa," soliloquized the ape-man.

At the end of the fissure Tarzan had some difficulty in wriggling through the aperture that opened into the valley of the land of Midian; but once through he picked up the trail of Smith again and followed it down toward the lake, while Danny, far behind him, stumbled wearily along the rough floor of the fissure.

He walked rapidly for the spoor was plain. When he came to the shore of Chinnereth he discovered Smith's tracks intermingled with those of a woman wearing well worn European boots and another shod with sandals.

When he had first entered the valley he had seen the village of the South Midians in the distance and now he drew the false conclusion that Smith had discovered a friendly people and other whites and that he was in no danger.

His curiosity piqued by the mystery of this hidden valley, the ape-man determined to visit the village before continuing on Smith's trail. Time had never entered greatly into his calculations, trained, as he had been, by savage apes to whom time meant less than nothing; but to investigate and to know every detail of his wilderness world was as much a part of the man as is his religion to a priest.

And so he continued rapidly on toward the distant village while Danny Patrick still crawled and stumbled slowly along the rocky floor of the fissure.

Danny was tired. Momentarily he expected to meet Tarzan returning either with Smith or with word of his death; so he stopped often to rest, with the result that when he had reached the end of the fissure and crawled through to behold the mystifying sight of a strange valley spread before him, Tarzan was already out of sight.

"Geeze!" exclaimed the "Gunner." "Who would have thought that hole led into a place like this? I wonder which way that Tarzan guy went?"

This thought occupied the "Gunner" for a few minutes. He examined the ground as he had seen Tarzan do, mistook a few spots where some little rodent had scratched up the earth, or taken a dust bath, for the footprints of a man, and set forth in the wrong direction.

CHAPTER 17

She Is Mine!

THE STOCKY, BLOND warriors of Elija, the son of Noah, quickly surrounded and seized Lafayette Smith and his two companions. Elija picked up Smith's pistol and examined it with interest; then he dropped it into a goat skin pouch that was suspended from the girdle that held his single garment about him.

"This one," said Eshbaal, pointing to Jezebel, "is mine."

"Why?" asked Elija, the son of Noah.

"I saw her first," replied Eshbaal.

"Did you hear what he said?" demanded Jezebel of Lady Barbara.

The English girl nodded apathetically. Her brain was numb with the disappointment and the horror of the situation, for in some respects their fate might be worse with these men than with those of South Midian. These were lusty, primitive warriors, not half-witted creatures whose natural passions had been weakened by generations of hereditary disease of nerve and brain.

"He wants me," said Jezebel. "Is he not beautiful?"

Lady Barbara turned upon the girl almost angrily, and then suddenly she remembered that Jezebel was little more than a child in experience and that she had no conception of the fate that might await her at the hands of the North Midians.

In their narrow religious fanaticism the South Midians denied even the most obvious phases of procreation. The subject was absolutely taboo and so hideous had ages of training and custom made it appear to them that mothers often killed their first born rather than exhibit these badges of sin.

"Poor little Jezebel," said Lady Barbara.

"What do you mean, Barbara?" asked the girl. "Are you not happy that the beautiful man wants me?"

"Listen, Jezebel," said Lady Barbara. "You know I am your friend, do you not?"

"My only friend," replied the girl. "The only person I ever loved."

"Then believe me when I say that you must kill yourself, as I shall kill myself, if we are unable to escape from these creatures."

"Why?" demanded Jezebel. "Are they not more beautiful than the South Midians?"

"Forget their fatal beauty," replied Lady Barbara, "but never forget what I have told you."

"Now I am afraid," said Jezebel.

"Thank God for that," exclaimed the English girl.

The North Midians marched loosely and without discipline. They seemed a garrulous race, and their arguments and speeches were numerous and lengthy. Sometimes, so intent did they become on some point at argument, or in listening to a long winded oration by one of their fellows, that they quite forgot their prisoners, who were sometimes amongst them, sometimes in advance and once behind them.

It was what Lady Barbara had been awaiting and what she had to some extent engineered.

"Now!" she whispered. "They are not looking." She halted and turned back. They were among the trees of the forest where some concealment might be found.

Smith and Jezebel had stopped at Lady Barbara's direction; and for an instant the three paused, breathless, watching the retreating figures of their captors.

"Now run!" whispered Lady Barbara. "We'll scatter and meet again at the foot of the cliff."

Just what prompted Lady Barbara to suggest that they separate Lafayette Smith did not understand. To him it seemed a foolish and unnecessary decision; but as he had a great deal more confidence in Lady Barbara's judgment in practical matters than in his own he did not voice his doubts, though he accepted her plan with certain mental reservations, which guided his subsequent acts.

The English girl ran in a southeasterly direction, while Jezebel, obeying the commands of her friend, scurried off toward the southwest. Smith, glancing to the rear, discovered no indication that their captors had, as yet, missed them. For a moment he was hesitant as to what course to pursue. The conviction still gripped him that he was the natural protector of both girls, notwithstanding the unfortunate circumstances that had nullified his efforts to function successfully in that rôle"; but he saw that it was going to be still more difficult to protect them both now that they had elected to run in different directions.

However, his decision was soon made, difficult though it was. Jezebel was in her own world; contemplation of capture by the North Midians had, so far from alarming her, appeared rather to have met with enthusiastic anticipation on her part; she could not be worse off with them than with the only other people she knew.

Lady Barbara, on the other hand, was of another world—his own world—and he had heard her say that death would be preferable to captivity among these semi-savages. His duty, therefore, was to follow and protect Lady Barbara; and so he let Jezebel take her way unprotected back toward the cliff, while he pursued the English girl in the direction of Chinnereth.

Lady Barbara Collis ran until she was out of breath. For several minutes she had distinctly heard the sounds of pursuit behind her—the heavy footfalls of a man. Frantic from hopelessness, she drew her pocket knife from a pocket of her jacket and opened the blade as she ran.

She wondered if she could destroy herself with this inadequate weapon. She was positive that she could not inflict either fatal or disabling injuries upon her pursuer with it. Yet the thought of self-destruction revolted her. The realization was upon her that she had about reached the limit of her endurance, and that the fatal decision could not be long averted, when her heritage of English fighting blood decided the question for her. There was but one thing it would permit—she must stand and defend herself. She stopped then, suddenly, and wheeled about, the little knife clutched in her right hand—a tigress at bay.

When she saw Lafayette Smith running toward her she collapsed suddenly and sank to the ground, where she sat with her back against the bole of a tree. Lafayette Smith, breathing hard, came and sat down beside her. Neither had any breath for words.

Lady Barbara was the first to regain her power of speech. "I thought I said we would scatter," she reminded him.

"I couldn't leave you alone," he replied.

"But how about Jezebel? You left her alone."

"I couldn't go with both of you," he reminded her, "and you know Jezebel is really at home here. It means much more to you to escape than it means to her."

She shook her head. "Capture means the same thing to either of us," she said, "but of the two I am better able to take care of myself than Jezebel—she does not understand the nature of her danger."

"Nevertheless," he insisted, "you are the more important. You have relatives and friends who care for you. Poor little Jezebel has only one friend, and that is you, unless I may consider myself a friend, as I should like to do."

"I imagine we three have the unique distinction of being the closest corporation of friends in the world," she replied, with a wan smile, "and there doesn't seem to be anyone who wants to buy in."

"The Friendless Friends Corporation, Limited," he suggested.

"Perhaps we'd best hold a directors' meeting and decide what we should do next to conserve the interests of the stockholders."

"I move we move," he said.

"Seconded." The girl rose to her feet.

"You're terribly tired, aren't you?" he asked. "But I suppose the only thing we can do is to get as far away from the territory of the North Midians as possible. It's almost certain they will try to capture us again as soon as they discover we are missing."

"If we can only find a place to hide until night," she said.

"Then we can go back to the cliffs under the cover of darkness and search for Jezebel and the place that she and I thought they might be scaled."

"This forest is so open that it doesn't afford any good hiding places, but at least we can look."

"Perhaps we shall find a place near the lake," said Lady Barbara. "We ought to come to it soon."

They walked on for a considerable distance without talking, each occupied with his own thoughts; and as no sign of pursuit developed their spirits rose.

"Do you know," he said presently, "that I can't help but feel that we're going to get out of this all right in the end?"

"But what a terrible experience! It doesn't seem possible that such things could have happened to me. I can't forget Jobab." It was the first time mention had been made of the tragedy at the southern village.

"You must not give that a thought," he said. "You did the only thing possible under the circumstances. If you had not done what you did both you and Jezebel would have been recaptured, and you know what that would have meant."

"But I've killed a human being," she said. There was an awed tone in her voice.

"I killed one, too," he reminded her, "but I don't regret it in the least, notwithstanding the fact that I never killed anyone before. If I were not such a terrible marksman I should have killed another today, perhaps several. My regret is that I didn't.

"It's a strange world," he continued after a moment's reflective silence. "Now, I always considered myself rather well educated and fitted to meet the emergencies of life; and I suppose I should be, in the quiet environment of a college town; but what an awful failure I have proved to be when jolted out of my narrow little rut. I used to feel sorry for the boys who wasted their time at shooting galleries and in rabbit hunting. Men who boasted of their marksmanship merited only my contempt, yet within the last twenty-four hours I would have traded all my education along other lines for the ability to shoot straight."

"One should know something of many things to be truly educated," said the girl, "but I'm afraid you exaggerate the value of marksmanship in determining one's cultural status."

"Well, there's cooking," he admitted. "A person who cannot cook is not well educated. I had hoped one day to be an authority on geology; but with all I know of the subject, which of course isn't so much at that, I would probably starve to death in a land overrunning with game, because I can neither shoot nor cook."

Lady Barbara laughed. "Don't develop an inferiority complex at this stage," she cried. "We need every ounce of self-assurance that we can muster. I think you are top hole. You may not be much of a marksman—that I'll have to admit, and perhaps you cannot cook; but you've one thing that covers a multitude of shortcomings in a man—you are brave."

It was Lafayette Smith's turn to laugh. "That's mighty nice of you," he said. "I'd rather you thought that of me than anything else in the world; and I'd rather you thought it than any one else, because it would mean so much to me now; but it isn't true. I was scared stiff in that village last night and when those fellows came at us today, and that's the truth."

"Which only the more definitely justifies my statement," she replied.

"I don't understand."

"Cultured and intelligent people are more ready to realize and appreciate the dangers of a critical situation than are ignorant, unimaginative types. So, when such a person stands his ground determinedly in the face of danger, or voluntarily walks into a dangerous situation from a sense of duty, as you did last night, it evidences a much higher quality of courage than that possessed by the ignorant, physical lout who hasn't brains enough to visualize the contingencies that may result from his action."

"Be careful," he warned her, "or you'll make me believe all that—then I'll be unbearably egotistical. But please don't try to convince me that my inability to cook is a hallmark of virtue."

"I—listen! What was that?" she halted and turned her eyes toward the rear.

"They have found us," said Lafayette Smith. "Go on—go as fast as you can! I'll try to delay them."

"No," she replied, "there is no use. I'll remain with you, whatever happens."

"Please!" he begged. "Why should I face them if you won't take advantage of it."

"It wouldn't do any good," she said. "They'd only get me later, and your sacrifice would be useless. We might as well give ourselves up in the hope that we can persuade them to free us later, or, perhaps, find the opportunity to escape after dark."

"You had better run," he said, "because I am going to fight. I am not going to let them take you without raising a hand in your defense. If you get away now, perhaps I can get away later. We can meet at the foot of the cliffs—but don't wait for me if you can find a way out. Now, do as I tell you!" His tone was peremptory—commanding.

Obediently she continued on toward Chinnereth, but presently she stopped and turned. Three men were approaching Smith. Suddenly one of the three swung his club and hurled it at the American, at the same instant dashing forward with his fellows.

The club fell short of its mark, dropping at Smith's feet. She saw him stoop and seize it, and then she saw another detachment of the Midians coming through the woods in the wake of the first three.

Smith's antagonists were upon him as he straightened up with the club in his hand, and he swung it heavily upon the skull of the man who had hurled it at him and who had rushed forward in advance of his fellows with hands outstretched to seize the stranger.

Like a felled ox the man dropped; and then Lady Barbara saw Smith carry the unequal battle to the enemy as, swinging the club above his head, he rushed forward to meet them.

So unexpected was his attack that the men halted and turned to elude him, but one was too slow and the girl heard the fellow's skull crush beneath the heavy blow of the bludgeon.

Then the reinforcements, advancing at a run, surrounded and overwhelmed their lone antagonist, and Smith went down beneath them.

Lady Barbara could not bring herself to desert the man who had thus bravely, however hopelessly, sought to defend her; and when the North Midians had disarmed and secured Smith they saw her standing where she had stood during the brief engagement.

"I couldn't run away and leave you," she explained to Smith, as the two were being escorted toward the village of the North Midians. "I thought they were going to kill you, and I couldn't help you—Oh, it was awful. I couldn't leave you then, could I?"

He looked at her for a moment. "No," he answered. *"You* couldn't."

CHAPTER 18

A Guy and A Skirt

DANNY "GUNNER" PATRICK was tired and disgusted. He had walked for several hours imagining that he was following a spoor, but he had seen nothing of his erstwhile companion. He was thirsty, and so cast frequent glances in the direction of the lake.

"T'ell!" he muttered. "I aint goin' to tail that guy no longer till I get me a drink. My mouth feels like I'd been eating cotton for a week."

He turned away from the cliffs and started down in the direction of the lake, the inviting waters of which sparkled alluringly in the afternoon sun; but the beauties of the scene were wasted upon the "Gunner," who saw only a means of quenching his thirst.

The way led through a field of scattered boulders fallen from the towering rim above. He had to pick his way carefully among the smaller ones, and his eyes were almost constantly upon the ground. Occasionally he was compelled to skirt some of the larger masses, many of which towered above his head obstructing his view ahead.

He was damning Africa in general and this section of it in particular as he rounded the corner of an unusually large fragment of rock, when suddenly he stopped and his eyes went wide.

"Geeze!" he exclaimed aloud. "A broad!"

Before him, and coming in his direction, was a golden haired girl attired in a single, scant piece of rough material. She saw him simultaneously and halted.

"Oh," exclaimed Jezebel with a happy smile. "Who art thou?" but as she spoke in the language of the land of Midian the "Gunner" failed to understand her.

"Geeze," he said. "I knew I must of come to Africa for something, and I guess you're it. Say kid, you're about all right. I'll tell the world you *are* all right."

"Thank you," said Jezebel in English. "I am so glad that you like me."

"Geeze," said Danny. "You talk United States, don't you? Where you from?"

"Midian," replied Jezebel.

"Aint never heard of it. What you doin' here? Where're your people?"

"I am waiting for Lady Barbara," replied the girl, "and Smith," she added.

"Smith! What Smith?" he demanded.

"Oh, he is beautiful," confided Jezebel.

"Then he aint the Smith I'm lookin' for," said the "Gunner." "What's he doin' here, and who's this Lady Barbara dame?"

"Abraham, the son of Abraham, would have killed Lady Barbara and Jezebel if Smith had not come and saved us. He is very brave."

"Now I know it aint my Smith," said Danny, "though I aint sayin' he aint got guts. What I mean is he wouldn't know enough to save no one—he's a geologist."

"Who are you?" demanded Jezebel.

"Call me Danny, Kid."

"My name is not kid," she explained sweetly. "It is Jezebel."

"Jezebel! Geeze, what a monicker! You look like it ought to be Gwendolyn."

"It is Jezebel," she assured him. "Do you know who I hoped you'd be?"

"No. Now just tell me, kid, who you supposed I was. Probably President Hoover or Big Bill Thompson, eh?"

"I do not know them," said Jezebel. "I hoped that you were the 'Gunner.'"

"The 'Gunner'? What do you know about the 'Gunner,' kid?"

"My name is not kid, it is Jezebel," she corrected him, sweetly.

"Oke, Jez," conceded Danny, "but tell me who wised you up to the 'Gunner' bozo."

"My name is not Jez, it is—"

"Oh, sure kid, it's Jezebel—that's oke by me; but how about the 'Gunner'?"

"What about him?"

"I just been a-askin' you."

"But I don't understand your language," explained Jezebel. "It sounds like English, but it is not the English Lady Barbara taught me."

"It aint English," Danny assured her, seriously; "it's United States."

"It is quite like English though, isn't it?"

"Sure," said the "Gunner." "The only difference is we can

understand English but the English don't never seem to understand all of ours. I guess they're dumb."

"Oh, no, they're not dumb," Jezebel assured him. "Lady Barbara is English, and she can talk quite as well as you."

Danny scratched his head. "I didn't say they was dummies. I said they was dumb. Dummies can't talk only with their mits. If a guy's dumb, he don't know nothing."

"Oh," said Jezebel.

"But what I asked you is, who wised you up to this 'Gunner' bozo?"

"Can you say it in English, please," asked Jezebel.

"Geeze, what could be plainer? I asked who told you about the 'Gunner' and what did they tell you?" Danny was waxing impatient.

"Smith told us. He said the 'Gunner' was a friend of his; and when I saw you I thought you must be Smith's friend, hunting for him."

"Now, what do you know about that!" exclaimed Danny.

"I have just told you what I know about it," explained the girl; "but perhaps you did not understand me. Perhaps you are what you call dumb."

"Are you trying to kid me, kid?" demanded the "Gunner."

"My name is not—"

"Oh, all right, all right. I know what your name is."

"Then why do you not call me by my name? Do you not like it?"

"Sure, kid—I mean Jezebel—sure I like it. It's a swell handle when you get used to it. But tell me, where is old Smithy?"

"I do not know such a person."

"But you just told me you did."

"Oh, I see," cried Jezebel. "Smithy is the United States for Smith. But Smith is not old. He's quite young."

"Well, where is he?" demanded Danny, resignedly.

"We were captured by the beautiful men from North Midian," explained Jezebel; "but we escaped and ran away. We ran in different directions, but we are going to meet tonight farther south along the cliffs."

"Beautiful men?" demanded the "Gunner." "Did old Smithy let a bunch of fairies hoist him?"

"I do not understand," said Jezebel.

"*You* wouldn't," he assured her; "but say, kid—"

"My name—"

"Aw, forget it—you know who I mean. As I was saying, let's me and you stick together till we find old Smithy. What say?"

"That will be nice, the 'Gunner,' " she assured him.

"Say, call me Danny, k—Jezebel."

"Yes, Danny."

"Geeze, I never knew Danny was such a swell monicker till I heard you say it. What say we beat it for the big drink down there? I got me such a thirst my tongue's hanging out. Then we can come back to this here rock pile and look for old Smithy."

"That will be nice," agreed Jezebel. "I, too, am thirsty." She sighed. "You can not know how happy I am, Danny."

"Why?" he asked.

"Because you are with me."

"Geeze, k—Jezebel, but you're sure a fast worker."

"I do not know what you mean," she replied, innocently.

"Well just tell me why you're happy because I'm with you."

"It is because I feel safe with you after what Smith told us. He said he always felt safe when you were around."

"So that's it? All you want is a protection guy, eh? You don't like me for myself at all, eh?"

"Oh, of course I like you, Danny," cried the girl. "I think you are beautiful."

"Yeah? Well, listen, sister. You may be a swell kidder—I dunno—or you may be just a dumb egg—but don't call me no names. I know what my pan looks like; and it aint beautiful, and I aint never wore a béret."

Jezebel, who only caught the occasional high spots of Danny's conversation, made no reply; and they walked on in the direction of the lake, in silence, for some time. The forest was some little distance away, on their left, and they had no knowledge of what was transpiring there, nor did any sound reach their ears to acquaint them with the misfortune that was befalling Lady Barbara and Lafayette Smith.

At the lake they quenched their thirst, after which the "Gunner" announced that he was going to rest for a while before he started back toward the cliffs. "I wonder," he said, "just how far a guy can walk, because in the last two days I've walked that far and back again."

"How far is that?" inquired Jezebel.

He looked at her a moment and then shook his head. "It's

twice as far," he said, as he stretched himself at full length and closed his eyes. "Geeze, but I'm about all in," he murmured.

"In what?"

He deigned no reply, and presently the girl noted from his altered breathing that he was asleep. She sat with her eyes glued upon him, and occasionally a deep sigh broke from her lips. She was comparing Danny with Abraham, the son of Abraham, with Lafayette Smith and with the beautiful men of North Midian; and the comparison was not uncomplimentary to Danny.

The hot sun was beating down upon them, for there was no shade here; and presently its effects, combined with her fatigue, made her drowsy. She lay down near the "Gunner" and stretched luxuriously. Then she, too, fell asleep.

The "Gunner" did not sleep very long; the sun was too hot. When he awoke he raised himself on an elbow and looked around. His eyes fell on the girl and there they rested for some time, noting the graceful contours of the lithe young body, the wealth of golden hair, and the exquisite face.

"The kid's sure some looker," soliloquized Danny. "I seen a lotta broads in my day, but I aint never seen nothin' could touch her. She'd sure be a swell number dolled up in them Boul Mich rags. Geeze, wouldn't she knock their lamps out! I wonder where this Midian burgh is she says she comes from. If they's all as swell lookin' as her, that's the burgh for me."

Jezebel stirred and he reached over and shook her on the shoulder. "We'd better be beatin' it," he said. "We don't want to miss old Smithy and that dame."

Jezebel sat up and looked about her. "Oh," she exclaimed, "you frightened me. I thought something was coming."

"Why? Been dreaming?"

"No. You said we'd have to beat something."

"Aw, cheese it! I meant we'd have to be hittin' the trail for the big rocks."

Jezebel looked puzzled.

"Hike back to them cliffs where you said old Smithy and that Lady Barbara dame were going to meet you."

"Now I understand," said Jezebel. "All right, come on."

But when they reached the cliffs there was no sign of Smith or Lady Barbara, and at Jezebel's suggestion they walked slowly southward in the direction of the place where she and the English girl had hoped to make a crossing to the outer world.

"How did you get into the valley, Danny?" asked the girl.

"I come through a big crack in the mountain," he replied.

"That must be the same place Smith came through," she said. "Could you find it again?"

"Sure. That's where I'm headed for now."

It was only mid-afternoon when Danny located the opening into the fissure. They had seen nothing of Lady Barbara and Smith, and they were in a quandary as to what was best to do.

"Maybe they come along and made their getaway while we was hittin' the hay," suggested Danny.

"I don't know what you are talking about," said Jezebel, "but what I think is that they may have located the opening while we were asleep and gone out of the valley."

"Well aint that what I said?" demanded Danny.

"It didn't sound like it."

"Say, you trying to high hat me?"

"High hat?"

"Aw, what's the use?" growled the "Gunner," disgustedly. "Let's me and you beat it out of this here dump and look for old Smithy and the skirt on the other side. What say?"

"But suppose they haven't gone out?"

"Well, then we'll have to come back again; but I'm sure they must have. See this foot print?" He indicated one of his own, made earlier in the day, which pointed toward the valley. "I guess I'm getting good," he said. "Pretty soon that Tarzan guy wont have no edge on me at all."

"I'd like to see what's on the other side of the cliffs," said Jezebel. "I have always wanted to do that."

"Well, you won't see nothin' much," he assured her. "Just some more scenery. They aint even a hot dog stand or a single speakeasy."

"What are those?"

"Well, you might call 'em filling stations."

"What are filling stations?"

"Geeze, kid, what do you think I am, a college perfessor? I never saw anyone who could ask so many questions in my whole life."

"My name—"

"Yes, I know what your name is. Now come on and we'll crawl through this hole-in-the-wall. I'll go first. You follow right behind me."

The rough going along the rocky floor of the fissure taxed the

"Gunner's" endurance and his patience, but Jezebel was all excitement and anticipation. All her life she had dreamed of what might lie in the wonder-world beyond the cliffs.

Her people had told her that it was a flat expanse filled with sin, heresy, and iniquity, where, if one went too far he would surely fall over the edge and alight in the roaring flames of an eternal hades; but Jezebel had been a doubter. She had preferred to picture it as a land of flowers and trees and running water, where beautiful people laughed and sang through long, sunny days. Soon she was to see for herself, and she was much excited by the prospect.

And now at last they came to the end of the great fissure and looked out across the rolling foot hills toward a great forest in the distance.

Jezebel clasped her hands together in ecstacy. "Oh, Danny," she cried, "how beautiful it is!"

"What?" asked the "Gunner."

"Oh, everything. Don't you think it is beautiful, Danny?"

"The only beautiful thing around here, k—Jezebel, is you," said Danny.

The girl turned and looked up at him with her great blue eyes. "Do you think I am beautiful, Danny?"

"Sure I do."

"Do you think I am *too* beautiful?"

"There aint no such thing," he replied, "but if they was you're it. What made you ask?"

"Lady Barbara said I was."

The "Gunner" considered this for some moments. "I guess she's right at that kid."

"You like to call me Kid, don't you?" asked Jezebel.

"Well, it seems more friendly-like," he explained, "and it's easier to remember."

"All right, you may call me Kid if you want to, but my name is Jezebel."

"That's a bet," said Danny. "When I don't think to call you Jezebel, I'll call you kid, Sister."

The girl laughed. "You're a funny man, Danny. You like to say everything wrong. I'm not your sister, of course."

"And I'm damn glad you aint, kid."

"Why? Don't you like me?"

Danny laughed. "I never seen a kid like you before," he said.

"You sure got me guessin'. But at that," he added, a little seriously for him, "they's one thing I aint guessin' about and that's that you're a good little kid."

"I don't know what you are talking about," said Jezebel.

"And at that I'll bet you don't," he replied; "and now kid, let's sit down and rest. I'm tired."

"I'm hungry," said Jezebel.

"I aint never see a skirt that wasn't, but why did you have to bring that up? I'm so hungry I could eat hay."

"Smith killed a kid and we ate some of that," said Jezebel. "He wrapped the rest up in the skin and I suppose he lost it when the North Midians attacked us. I wish—"

"Say," exclaimed Danny, "what a dumb-bell I am!" He reached down into one of his pockets and brought out several strips of raw meat. "Here I been packin' this around all day and forgets all about it—and me starvin' to death."

"What is it?" asked Jezebel, leaning closer to inspect the unsavory morsels.

"It's pig," said Danny as he started searching for twigs and dry grass to build a fire, "and I know where they is a lot more that I thought I couldn't never eat but I know now I could—even if I had to fight with the maggots for it."

Jezebel helped him gather wood, which was extremely scarce, being limited to dead branches of a small variety of artemisia that grew on the mountain side; but at length they had collected quite a supply, and presently they were grilling pieces of the boar meat over the flames. So preoccupied were they that neither saw three horsemen draw rein at the top of a ridge a mile away and survey them.

"This is like housekeeping, aint it?" remarked the "Gunner."

"What is that?" asked Jezebel.

"That's where a guy and his girl friend get hitched and go to doin' their own cooking. Only in a way this is better—they aint goin' to be no dishes to wash."

"What is hitched, Danny?" asked Jezebel.

"Why—er," Danny flushed. He had said many things to many girls in his life, many of them things that might have brought a blush to the cheek of a wooden Indian; but this was the first time, perhaps, that Danny had felt any embarrassment.

"Why—er," he repeated, "hitched means married."

"Oh," said Jezebel. She was silent for a while, watching the pork sizzling over the little flames. Then she looked up at Danny. "I think housekeeping is fun," she said.

"So do I," agreed Danny; "with you," he added and his voice was just a trifle husky. His eyes were on her; and there was a strange light in them, that no other girl had ever seen there. "You're a funny little kid," he said presently. "I never seen one like you before," and then the neglected pork fell off the end of the sharpened twig, with which he had been holding it, and tumbled into the fire.

"Geeze!" exclaimed Danny. "Look at that!" He fished the unsavory looking morsel from the ashes and flames and surveyed it. "It don't look so good, but I'm goin' to fool it. I'm goin' to eat it anyway. I wouldn't care if a elephant had sat on it for a week—I'd eat it, and the elephant, too."

"Oh, look!" cried Jezebel. "Here come some men and they are all black. What strange beasts are they sitting on? Oh, Danny, I am afraid."

At her first exclamation the "Gunner" had turned and leaped to his feet. A single look told him who the strangers were—no strangers to him.

"Beat it, kid!" he cried. "Duck back into the crack, and hit the trail for the valley. They can't follow you on gee-gees."

The three *shiftas* were already close; and when they saw that they had been discovered they spurred forward at a gallop, and yet Jezebel stood beside the little fire, wide eyed and frightened. She had not understood the strange argot that the "Gunner" employed in lieu of English. "Beat it" and "duck" and "hit the trail" had not been included in the English idiom she had gleaned from Lady Barbara Collis. But even had she understood him it would have made no difference, for Jezebel was not of the clay that is soft in the face of danger, her little feet not of the kind that run away, leaving a companion in distress.

The "Gunner" glanced behind him and saw her. "For God's sake run, kid," he cried. "These are tough guys. I know 'em," then the *shiftas* were upon him.

To conserve ammunition, which was always scarce and difficult to obtain, they tried to ride him down, striking at him with their rifles. He dodged the leading horseman; and as the fellow reined in to wheel his mount back to the attack, the "Gunner" leaped to his side and dragged him from the saddle. The mount of a second *shifta* stumbled over the two men and fell, unhorsing its rider.

The "Gunner" seized the long rifle that had fallen from the hands of the man he had dragged down and scrambled to his feet. Jezebel watched him in wide eyed wonder and admiration. She saw him swing the rifle like a club and strike at the third horseman, and then she saw the one he had first grappled lunge forward and, seizing him around the legs, drag him down, while the second to be unhorsed ran in now and leaped upon him just as the remaining *shifta* struck him a heavy blow on the head.

As she saw him fall, the blood gushing from an ugly wound in his head, Jezebel ran forward to him; but the *shiftas* seized her. She was thrown to the back of a horse in front of one of them, the others mounted, and the three galloped away with their prisoner, leaving Danny "Gunner" Patrick lying motionless in a welter of his own blood.

CHAPTER 19

In the Village of Elija

AS TARZAN APPROACHED the village of Abraham, the son of Abraham, he was seen by a watcher who immediately warned his fellows, with the result that when the ape-man arrived the huts were deserted, the villagers having taken refuge in the caves in the face of the towering cliff.

Abraham, the son of Abraham, from the safety of the highest cave, exhorted his people to repel the advance of this strange creature, whose partial nakedness and strange armament filled him with alarm, with the result that when Tarzan came near the base of the cliff the villagers, with much shouting, rolled rocks down the steep declivity in an effort to destroy him.

The Lord of the Jungle looked up at the howling creatures above him. Whatever his emotions his face did not reveal them. Doubtless contempt was predominant, for he read in their reception of him only fear and cowardice.

As naught but curiosity had prompted his visit to this strange village, since he knew that Smith already had quitted it, he remained only long enough for a brief survey of the people and their culture, neither of which was sufficiently attractive to detain him; and then he turned and retracted his steps toward the place on the shore of Chinnereth where he had picked up the northbound spoor of Smith and Lady Barbara and Jezebel.

He made his way in a leisurely manner, stopping beside the lake to quench his thirst and eat from his small store of boar meat; and then he lay down to rest, after the manner of beasts who have fed and are not hurried.

In the village he had quitted Abraham, the son of Abraham, gave thanks to Jehovah for their deliverance from the barbarian, though reserving proper credit to himself for his masterly defense of his flock.

And how fared it with Lady Barbara and Lafayette Smith? Following their recapture they were permitted no second opportunity to escape, as, heavily guarded, they were conducted northward toward the village of Elija, the son of Noah.

The girl was much depressed; and Smith sought to reassure her, though upon what grounds he himself could scarcely explain.

"I cannot believe that they intend to harm us," he said. "We have done nothing worse than kill one of their goats and that only because we were starving. I can pay them whatever price they name for the animal, and thus they will be recompensed and have no further cause for complaint against us."

"With what will you pay them?" asked Lady Barbara.

"I have money," replied Smith.

"Of what good would it be to them?"

"Of what good would it be to them! Why they could buy another goat if they wanted to," he replied.

"These people know nothing of money," she said. "It would be worthless to them."

"I suppose you are right," he admitted. "I hadn't thought of that. Well, I could give them my pistol, then."

"They already have it."

"But it's mine," he exclaimed. "They'll have to give it back to me."

She shook her head. "You are not dealing with civilized people guided by the codes and customs of civilization or responsible to the law-enforcing agencies with which we are familiar and which, perhaps, are all that keep us civilized."

"We escaped once," he ventured; "perhaps we can escape again."

"That, I think, is our only hope."

The village of the North Midians, where they presently arrived, was more pretentious than that of the people at the southern end of the valley. While there were many crude huts there were also several of stone, while the entire appearance of the village was more cleanly and prosperous.

Several hundred villagers came to meet the party as soon as it was sighted, and the prisoners noted that there was no evidence of the degeneracy and disease which were such marked characteristics of the South Midians. On the contrary, these people appeared endowed with abundant health, they looked intelligent and, physically, they were a splendid race, many of them being handsome. All were golden haired and blue eyed. That they were descended from the same stock that had produced Abraham, the son of Abraham, and his degraded flock would have appeared impossible, yet such was the fact.

The women and children pushed and jostled one another and the men in their efforts to get close to the prisoners. They jabbered and laughed incessantly, the clothing of the prisoners seeming to arouse the greatest wonder and mirth.

Their language being practically the same as that of the South Midians Lady Barbara had no difficulty in understanding what they were saying, and from scraps of their conversation which she overheard she realized that her worst fears might be realized. However, the crowd offered them no personal injury; and it was apparent that in themselves they were not inherently a cruel people, though their religion and their customs evidently prescribed harsh treatment for enemies who fell into their hands.

Upon arrival in the village Lady Barbara and Smith were separated. She was taken to a hut and put in charge of a young woman, while Smith was confined, under guard of several men, in another.

Lady Barbara's jailer, far from being ill favored, was quite beautiful, bearing a strong resemblance to Jezebel; and she proved to be quite as loquacious as the men who had captured them.

"You are the strangest looking South Midian I ever saw," she remarked, "and the man does not look at all like one. Your hair is neither the color of those they keep nor of those they destroy— it is just between, and your garments are such as no one ever saw before."

"We are not Midians," said Lady Barbara.

"But that is impossible," cried the woman. "There are none

but Midians in the land of Midian and no way to get in or out. Some say there are people beyond the great cliffs, and some say there are only devils. If you are not a Midian perhaps you are a devil; but then, of course, you are a Midian."

"We come from a country beyond the cliffs," Lady Barbara told her, "and all we want is to go back to our own country."

"I do not think Elija will let you. He will treat you as we always treat South Midians."

"And how is that?"

"The men are put to death because of their heresy; and the women, if they are good looking, are kept as slaves. But being a slave is not bad. I am a slave. My mother was a slave. She was a South Midian who was captured by my father who owned her. She was very beautiful. After a while the South Midians would have killed her, as you do to all your beautiful women just before their first child is born.

"But we are different. We kill the bad looking ones, both boys and girls, and also any who become subject to the strange demons which afflict the South Midians. Do you have these demons?"

"I am not a Midian, I told you," said Lady Barbara.

The woman shook her head. "It is true that you do not look like them, but if Elija ever believes you are not you are lost."

"Why?" asked Lady Barbara.

"Elija is one of those who believe that the world beyond the cliffs is inhabited by demons; so, if you are not a South Midian, you must be a demon; and he would certainly destroy you as he will destroy the man; but for my part I am one of those who say they do not know. Some say that perhaps this world around Midian is inhabited by angels. Are you an angel?"

"I am not a demon," replied Lady Barbara.

"Then you must be a South Midian or an angel."

"I am no South Midian," insisted the English girl.

"Then you are an angel," reasoned the woman. "And if you are you will have no difficulty in proving it."

"How?"

"Just perform a miracle."

"Oh," said Lady Barbara.

"Is the man an angel?" demanded the woman.

"He is an American."

"I never heard of that—is it a kind of angel?"

"Europeans do not call them that."

"But really I think Elija will say he is a South Midian, and he will be destroyed."

"Why do your people hate the South Midians so?" asked Lady Barbara.

"They are heretics."

"They are very religious," said Lady Barbara; "they pray all the time to Jehovah and they never smile. Why do you think them heretics?"

"They insist that Paul's hair was black, while we know that it was yellow. They are very wicked, blasphemous people. Once, long before the memory of man, we were all one people; but there were many wicked heretics among us who had black hair and wished to kill all those with yellow hair; so those with yellow hair ran away and came to the north end of the valley. Ever since, the North Midians have killed all those with black hair and the South Midians all those with yellow hair. Do you think Paul had yellow hair?"

"Certainly I do," said Lady Barbara.

"That will be a point in your favor," said the woman.

Just then a man came to the door of the hut and summoned Lady Barbara. "Come with me," he commanded.

The English girl followed the messenger, and the woman who had been guarding her accompanied them. Before a large stone hut they found Elija surrounded by a number of the older men of the village, while the remainder of the population was grouped in a semi-circle facing them. Lafayette Smith stood before Elija, and Lady Barbara was conducted to the side of the American.

Elija, the Prophet, was a middle aged man of not unprepossessing appearance. He was short and stocky, extremely muscular in build, and his face was adorned with a wealth of blond whiskers. Like the other North Midians he was garbed in a single garment of goat skin, his only ornament being the pistol he had taken from Smith, which he wore on a leather thong that encircled his neck.

"This man," said Elija, addressing Lady Barbara, "will not talk. He makes noises, but they mean nothing. Why will he not talk?"

"He does not understand the language of the land of Midian," replied the English girl.

"He must understand it," insisted Elija; "every one understands it."

"He is not from Midian," said Lady Barbara.

"Then he must be a demon," said Elija.

"Perhaps he is an angel," suggested Lady Barbara; "he believes that Paul's hair was yellow."

This statement precipitated a wordy argument and so impressed Elija and his apostles that they withdrew into the interior of the hut for a secret conference.

"What's it all about, Lady Barbara?" asked Smith, who, of course, had understood nothing of what had been said.

"You believe Paul's hair was yellow, don't you?" she asked.

"I don't know what you are talking about."

"Well, I told them you were a firm believer in the yellowness of Paul's hair."

"Why did you tell them that?" demanded Smith.

"Because the North Midians prefer blonds," she replied.

"But who is Paul?"

"Was, you mean. He is dead."

"Of course I'm sorry to hear that, but who *was* he?" insisted the American.

"I am afraid you have neglected the scriptures." she told him.

"Oh, the apostle; but what difference does it make what color his hair was?"

"It doesn't make any difference," she explained. "What does make a difference is that you have stated, through me, that you believe he had yellow hair; and that may be the means of saving your life."

"What nonsense!"

"Of course—the other fellow's religion is always nonsense; but not to him. You are also suspected of being an angel. Can you imagine!"

"No! Who suspects me?"

"It was I; or at least I suggested it, and I am hoping Elija will now suspect it. If he does we are both safe, provided that, in your celestial capacity, you will intercede for me."

"You are as good as saved then," he said, "for inasmuch as I cannot speak their language you can put any words you wish into my mouth without fear of being called to account."

"That's a fact, isn't it?" she said, laughing. "If our emergency were not so critical I could have a lot of fun, couldn't I?"

"You seem to find fun in everything," he replied, admiringly; "even in the face of disaster."

"Perhaps I am whistling in the dark," she said.

They talked a great deal while they waited for Elija and the apostles to return, for it helped them to tide over the anxious minutes of nervous strain that slowly dragged into hours. They could hear the chatter and buzz of conversation within the hut, as Elija and his fellows debated, while, outside, the villagers kept up a constant babel of conversation.

"They like to talk," commented Smith.

"And perhaps you have noticed an idiosyncrasy of the North Midians in this respect?" she asked.

"Lots of people like to talk."

"I mean that the men gabble more than the women."

"Perhaps in self-defense."

"Here they come!" she exclaimed as Elija appeared in the doorway of the hut, fingering the pistol he wore as an ornament.

Darkness was already falling as the Prophet and the twelve apostles filed out to their places in the open. Elija raised his hands in a signal for silence and when quiet had been restored he spoke.

"With the aid of Jehovah," he said, "we have wrestled with a mighty question. There were some among us who contended that this man is a South Midian, and others that he is an angel. Mighty was the weight of the statement that he believes that Paul had yellow hair, for if such is the truth then indeed he is not a heretic; and if he is no heretic he is not a South Midian, for they, as all the world knows, are heretics. Yet again, it was brought forth that if he is a demon he might still claim that he believed in the yellowness of Paul, in order that he might deceive us.

"How were we to know? We must know lest we, through our ignorance, do sin against one of His angels and bring down the wrath of Jehovah upon our heads.

"But at last I, Elija, the son of Noah, True Prophet of Paul, the son of Jehovah, discovered the truth. The man is no angel! The revelation descended upon me in a burst of glory from Jehovah Himself—the man cannot be an angel because he has no wings!"

There was an immediate burst of "Amens" and "Hallelujahs" from the assembled villagers, while Lady Barbara went cold with dread.

"Therefore," continued Elija, "he must be either a South Midian or a demon, and in either case he must be destroyed."

Lady Barbara turned a pale face toward Lafayette Smith—pale even through its coating of tan. Her lip trembled, just a little. It was the first indication of a weaker, feminine emotion that Smith had seen this remarkable girl display.

"What is it?" he asked. "Are they going to harm you?"

"It is you, my dear friend," she replied. "You must escape."

"But how?" he asked.

"Oh, I don't know; I don't know," she cried. "There is only one way. You will have to make a break for it—now. It is dark. They will not expect it. I will do something to engage their attention, and then you make a dash for the forest."

He shook his head. "No," he said. "We shall go together, or I do not go."

"Please," she begged, "or it will be too late."

Elija had been talking to one of his apostles, and now he raised his voice again so that all might hear. "Lest we have mistaken the divine instructions of Jehovah," he said, "we shall place this man in the mercy of Jehovah and as Jehovah wills so shall it be. Make ready the grave. If he is indeed an angel he will arise unharmed."

"Oh, go; please go!" cried Lady Barbara.

"What did he say?" demanded Smith.

"They are going to bury you alive," she cried.

"And you," he asked; "what are they going to do to you?"

"I am to be held in slavery."

With sharpened sticks and instruments of bone and stone a number of men were already engaged in excavating a grave in the center of the village street before the hut of Elija, who stood waiting its completion surrounded by his apostles. The Prophet was still toying with his new found ornament, concerning the purpose and mechanism of which he was wholly ignorant.

Lady Barbara was urging Smith to attempt escape while there was yet an opportunity, and the American was considering the best plan to adopt.

"You will have to come with me," he said. "I think if we make a sudden break right back through the village toward the cliffs we shall find our best chance for success. There are fewer people congregated on that side."

From the darkness beyond the village on the forest side a pair of eyes watched the proceedings taking place before the hut of Elija. Slowly, silently the owner of the eyes crept closer until he stood in the shadow of a hut at the edge of the village.

Suddenly Smith, seizing Lady Barbara's hand, started at a run toward the north side of the village; and so unexpected was his break for liberty that, for a moment, no hand was raised to stay him; but an instant later, at a cry from Elija, the entire band leaped in pursuit, while from the shadow of the hut where he had stood concealed the watcher slipped forward into the village where he stood near the hut of Elija watching the pursuit of the escaped prisoners. He was alone, for the little central compound of the village had emptied as by magic, even the women and children having joined in the chase.

Smith ran swiftly, holding tightly to the girl's hand; and close on their heels came the leaders of the pursuit. No longer did the village fires light their way; and only darkness loomed ahead, as the moon had not yet risen.

Gradually the American bore to the left, intending to swing in a half circle toward the south. There was yet a chance that they might make good their escape if they could outdistance the nearer of their pursuers until they reached the forest, for their strait gave them both speed and endurance far above normal.

But just as success seemed near they entered a patch of broken lava rock, invisible in the darkness; and Smith stumbled and fell dragging Lady Barbara down with him. Before they could scramble to their feet the leading Midian was upon them.

The American freed himself for a moment and struggled to his feet; and again the fellow sought to seize him, but Smith swung a heavy blow to his chin and felled him.

Brief, however, was this respite, for almost immediately both the American and the English girl were overwhelmed by superior numbers and once again found themselves captives, though Smith fought until he was overpowered, knocking his antagonists to right and left.

Miserably dejected, they were dragged back to the village compound, their last hope gone; and again the Midians gathered around the open grave to witness the torture of their victim.

Smith was conducted to the edge of the excavation, where he was held by two stalwart men, while Elija raised his voice in prayer, and the remainder of the assemblage knelt, bursting forth occasionally with hallelujahs and amens.

When he had concluded his long prayer the Prophet paused. Evidently there was something on his mind which vexed him. In fact it was the pistol which dangled from the thong about his neck. He was not quite sure of its purpose, and he was about to destroy the only person who might tell him.

To Elija the pistol was quite the most remarkable possession that had ever fallen into his hands, and he was filled with a great curiosity concerning it. It might be, he argued, some magic talisman for averting evil, or, upon the other hand, it might be the charm of a demon or a sorcerer, that would work evil upon him. At that thought he quickly removed the thong from about his neck, but he still held the weapon in his hand.

"What is this?" he demanded, turning to Lady Barbara and exhibiting the pistol.

"It is a weapon," she said. "Be careful or it will kill some one."

"How does it kill?" asked Elija.

"What is he saying?" demanded Smith.

"He is asking how the pistol kills," replied the girl.

A brilliant idea occurred to the American. "Tell him to give it to me, and I will show him," he said.

But when she translated the offer to Elija he demurred. "He could then kill me with it," he said, shrewdly.

"He wont give it to you," the girl told Smith. "He is afraid you want to kill him."

"I do," replied the man.

"Tell him," said Elija, "to explain to me how I may kill some one with it."

"Repeat my instructions to him very carefully," said Smith, after Lady Barbara had translated the demand of the prophet. "Tell him how to grasp the pistol," and when Lady Barbara had done so and Elija held the weapon by the grip in his righthand, "now tell him to place his index finger through the guard, but warn him not to pull the trigger."

Elija did as he was bid. "Now," continued Smith, "explain to him that in order to see how the weapon operates he should place one eye to the muzzle and look down the barrel."

"But I can see nothing," expostulated Elija when he had done as Lady Barbara directed. "It is quite dark down the little hole."

"He says it is too dark in the barrel for him to see anything," repeated Lady Barbara to the American.

"Explain to him that if he pulls the trigger there will be a light in the barrel," said Smith.

"But that will be murder," exclaimed the girl.

"It is war," said Smith, "and in the subsequent confusion we may escape."

Lady Barbara steeled herself. "You could see nothing because you did not press the little piece of metal beneath your index finger," she explained to Elija.

"What will that do?" demanded the prophet.

"It will make a light in the little hole," said Lady Barbara.

Elija again placed his eye against the muzzle; and this time he pulled the trigger; and as the report cracked the tense silence of the watching villagers Elija, the son of Noah, pitched forward upon his face.

Instantly Lady Barbara sprang toward Smith, who simultaneously sought to break away from the grip of the men who held him; but they, although astonished at what had occurred, were not to be caught off their guard, and though he struggled desperately they held him.

For an instant there was a hushed silence; and then pandemonium broke loose as the villagers realized that their prophet was dead, slain by the wicked charm of a demon; but at the very outset of their demands for vengeance their attention was distracted by a strange and remarkable figure that sprang from the hut of Elija, stooped and picked up the pistol that had fallen from the hands of the dead man, and leaped to the side of the prisoner struggling with his guards.

This was such a man as none of them had ever seen—a giant white man with a tousled shock of black hair and with grey eyes that sent a shiver through them, so fierce and implacable were they. Naked he was but for a loin cloth of skin, and the muscles that rolled beneath his brown hide were muscles such as they never had seen before.

As the newcomer sprang toward the American one of the men guarding Smith, sensing that an attempt was being made to rescue the prisoner, swung his club in readiness to deal a blow against the strange creature advancing upon him. At the same time the other guard sought to drag Smith from the compound.

The American did not at first recognize Tarzan of the Apes, yet, though he was not aware that the stranger was bent upon his rescue, he sensed that he was an enemy of the Midians, and so struggled to prevent his guard from forcing him away.

Another Midian seized Lady Barbara with the intention of carrying her from the scene, for all the villagers believed that the strange giant was a friend of the prisoners and had come to effect their release.

Smith was successful in tearing himself free from the man who held him, and immediately sprang to the girl's assistance, felling her captor with a single blow, just as Tarzan levelled the American's pistol at the guard who was preparing to cudgel him.

The sound of this second shot and the sight of their fellow dropping to the ground, as had Elija, filled the Midians with consternation; and for a moment they fell back from the three, leaving them alone in the center of the compound.

"Quick!" called Tarzan to Smith. "You and the girl get out of here before they recover from their surprise. I will follow you. That way," he added, pointing toward the south.

As Lafayette Smith and Lady Barbara hurried from the village Tarzan backed slowly after them, keeping the little pistol in full view of the frightened villagers, who, having seen two of their number die beneath its terrifying magic, were loath to approach it too closely.

Until out of range of a thrown club Tarzan continued his slow retreat; then he wheeled and bounded off into the night in pursuit of Lafayette Smith and Lady Barbara Collis.

CHAPTER 20

The Best Three out of Five

THOUGH JEZEBEL WAS terrified by the black faces of her captors and by the strange beasts they bestrode, the like of which she had never even imagined, her fear for herself was outweighed by her sorrow. Her one thought was to escape and return to the side of the "Gunner," even though she believed him dead from the terrific blow that his assailant had struck him.

She struggled violently to free herself from the grasp of the man in front of whom she rode; but the fellow was far too powerful; and, though she was difficult to hold, at no time was there the slightest likelihood that she might escape. Her efforts, however, angered him and at last he struck her, bringing to the girl a realization of the futility of pitting her puny strength against his. She must wait, then, until she could accomplish by stealth what she could not effect by force.

The village of the raiders lay but a short distance from the point at which she had been captured, and but a few minutes had elapsed since that event when they rode up to its gates and into the central compound.

The shouts that greeted the arrival of a new and beautiful prisoner brought Capietro and Stabutch to the doorway of their hut.

"Now what have the black devils brought in?" exclaimed Capietro.

"It looks like a young woman," said Stabutch.

"It is," cried Capietro, as the *shiftas* approached the hut with their prisoner. "We shall have company, eh, Stabutch? Who have you there, my children?" he demanded of the three who were accompanying Jezebel.

"The price of a chief's ransom, perhaps," replied one of the blacks.

"Where did you find her?"

"Above the village a short distance, when we were returning from scouting. A man was with her. The man who escaped with the help of the ape-man."

"Where is he! Why did you not bring him, also?" demanded Capietro.

"He fought us, and we were forced to kill him."

"You have done well," said Capietro. "She is worth two of him—in many ways. Come girl, hold up your head, let us have a look at that pretty face. Come, you need not fear anything—if you are a good girl you will find Dommic Capietro a good fellow."

"Perhaps she does not understand Italian," suggested Stabutch.

"You are right, my friend; I shall speak to her in English."

Jezebel had looked up at Stabutch when she heard him speak a language she understood. Perhaps this man would be a friend, she thought; but when she saw his face her heart sank.

"What a beauty!" ejaculated the Russian.

"You have fallen in love with her quickly, my friend," commented Capietro. "Do you want to buy her?"

"How much do you want for her?"

"Friends should not bargain," said the Italian. "Wait, I have it! Come, girl," and he took Jezebel by the arm and led her into the hut, where Stabutch followed them.

"Why was I brought here?" asked Jezebel. "I have not harmed you. Let me go back to Danny; he is hurt."

"He is dead," said Capietro; "but don't you grieve, little one. You now have two friends in place of the one you have lost. Soon you will forget him; it is easy for a woman to forget."

"I shall never forget him," cried Jezebel. "I want to go back to him—perhaps he is not dead." Then she broke down and cried.

Stabutch stood eyeing the girl hungrily. Her youth and her beauty aroused a devil within him, and he made a mental vow that he would possess her. "Do not cry," he said, kindly. "I am your friend. Everything will be all right."

The new tone in his voice gave hope to Jezebel, and she looked up at him gratefully. "If you are my friend," she said, "take me away from here and back to Danny."

"After a while," replied Stabutch, and then to Capietro, "How much?"

"I shall not sell her to my good friend," replied the Italian. "Let us have a drink and then I shall explain my plan."

The two drank from a bottle standing on the earth floor of the hut. "Sit down," said Capietro, waving Jezebel to a seat on the dirty rug. Then he searched for a moment in his duffle bag and brought out a deck of soiled and grimy cards. "Be seated, my friend," he said to Stabutch. "Let us have another drink, and then you shall hear my plan."

Stabutch drank from the bottle and wiped his lips with the back of his hand. "Well," he said, "what is it?"

"We shall play for her," exclaimed the Italian, shuffling the deck, "and whoever wins, keeps her."

"Let us drink to that," said Stabutch. "Five games, eh, and the first to win three takes her?"

"Another drink to seal the bargain!" exclaimed the Italian. "The best three out of five!"

Stabutch won the first game, while Jezebel sat looking on in ignorance of the purpose of the bits of pasteboard, and only knowing that in some way they were to decide her fate. She hoped the younger man would win, but only because he had said that he was her friend. Perhaps she could persuade him to take her back to Danny. She wondered what kind of water was in the bottle from which they drank, for she noticed that it wrought a change in them. They talked much louder now and shouted strange words when the little cards were thrown upon the rug, and then one would appear very angry while the other always laughed immoderately. Also they swayed and lurched in a peculiar manner that she had not noticed before they had drunk so much of the water from the bottle.

Capietro won the second game and the third. Stabutch was

furious, but now he became very quiet. He exerted all his powers of concentration upon the game, and he seemed almost sober as the cards were dealt for the fourth game.

"She is as good as mine!" cried Capietro, as he looked at his hand.

"She will never be yours," growled the Russian.

"What do you mean?"

"I shall win the next two games."

The Italian laughed loudly. "That is good!" he cried. "We should drink to that." He raised the bottle to his lips and then passed it to Stabutch.

"I do not want a drink," said the Russian, in a surly tone, pushing the bottle aside.

"Ah, ha! My friend is getting nervous. He is afraid he is going to lose and so he will not drink. Sapristi! It is all the same to me. I get the brandy and the girl, too."

"Play!" snapped Stabutch.

"You are in a hurry to lose," taunted Capietro.

"To win," corrected Stabutch, and he did.

Now it was the Italian's turn to curse and rage at luck, and once again the cards were dealt and the players picked up their hands.

"It is the last game," said Stabutch.

"We have each won two," replied Capietro. "Let us drink to the winner—although I dislike proposing a toast to myself," and he laughed again, but this time there was an ugly note in his laughter.

In silence, now, they resumed their play. One by one the little pasteboards fell upon the rug. The girl looked on in wondering silence. There was a tenseness in the situation that she felt, without understanding. Poor little Jezebel, she understood so little!

Suddenly, with a triumphant oath, Capietro sprang to his feet. "I win!" he cried. "Come, friend, drink with me to my good fortune."

Sullenly the Russian drank, a very long draught this time. There was a sinister gleam in his eye as he handed the bottle back to Capietro. Leon Stabutch was a poor loser.

The Italian emptied the bottle and flung it to the ground. Then he turned toward Jezebel and stooping lifted her to her feet. "Come, my dear," he said, his coarse voice thick from drink, "Give me a kiss."

Jezebel drew back, but the Italian jerked her roughly to him and tried to draw her lips to his.

"Leave the girl alone," growled Stabutch. "Can't you see she is afraid of you?"

"What did I win her for?" demanded Capietro. "To leave her alone? Mind your own business."

"I'll make it my business," said Stabutch. "Take your hands off her." He stepped forward and laid a hand on Jezebel's arm. "She is mine by rights anyway."

"What do you mean?"

"You cheated. I caught you at it in the last game."

"You lie!" shouted Capietro and simultaneously he struck at Stabutch. The Russian dodged the blow and closed with the other.

Both were drunk and none too steady. It required much of their attention to keep from falling down. But as they wrestled about the interior of the hut a few blows were struck—enough to arouse their rage to fury and partially to sober them. Then the duel became deadly, as each sought the throat of the other.

Jezebel, wide eyed and terrified, had difficulty in keeping out of their way as they fought to and fro across the floor of the hut; and so centered was the attention of the two men upon one another that the girl might have escaped had she not been more afraid of the black men without than of the whites within.

Several times Stabutch released his hold with his right hand and sought for something beneath his coat and at last he found it—a slim dagger. Capietro did not see it.

They were standing in the center of the hut now, their arms locked about one another, and resting thus as though by mutual consent. They were panting heavily from their exertions, and neither seemed to have gained any material advantage.

Slowly the Russian's right hand crept up the back of his adversary. Jezebel saw, but only her eyes reflected her horror. Though she had seen many people killed she yet had a horror of killing. She saw the Russian feel for a spot on the other's back with the point of his thumb. Then she saw him turn his hand and place the dagger point where his thumb had been.

There was a smile upon Stabutch's face as he drove the blade home. Capietro stiffened, screamed, and died. As the body slumped to the ground and rolled over on its back the murderer stood over the corpse of his victim, a smile upon his lips, and his eyes upon the girl.

But suddenly the smile died as a new thought came to the cunning mind of the slayer and his eyes snapped from the face of Jezebel to the doorway of the hut where a filthy blanket answered the purpose of a door.

He had forgotten the horde of cut-throats who had called this thing upon the floor their chief! But now he recalled them and his soul was filled with terror. He did not need to ask himself what his fate would be when they discovered his crime.

"You have murdered him!" cried the girl suddenly, a note of horror in her voice.

"Be quiet!" snapped Stabutch. "Do you want to die? They will kill us when they discover this."

"I did not do it," protested Jezebel.

"They will kill you just the same—afterwards. They are beasts."

Suddenly he stooped, seized the corpse by the ankles and, dragging it to the far end of the hut, he covered it with rugs and clothing.

"Now keep quiet until I come back," he said to Jezebel. "If you give an alarm I'll kill you myself before they have a chance to."

He rummaged in a dark corner of the hut and brought forth a revolver with its holster and belt, which he buckled about his hips, and a rifle which he leaned beside the doorway.

"When I return be ready to come with me," he snapped, and raising the rug that covered the doorway, he stepped out into the village.

Quickly he made his way to where the ponies of the band were tethered. Here were several of the blacks loitering near the animals.

"Where is the headman?" he asked, but none of them understood English. He tried to tell them by means of signs, to saddle two horses, but they only shook their heads. If they understood him, as they doubtless did, they refused to take orders from him.

At this juncture the headman, attracted from a nearby hut, approached. He understood a little pidgin English, and Stabutch had no difficulty in making him understand that he wanted two horses saddled; but the headman wanted to know more. Did the chief want them?

"Yes, he wants them," replied Stabutch. "He sent me to get them. The chief is sick. Drink too much." Stabutch laughed and the headman seemed to understand.

"Who go with you?" asked the headman.

Stabutch hesitated. Well, he might as well tell him—everyone would see the girl ride out with him anyway. "The girl," he said.

The headman's eyes narrowed. "The Chief say?" he asked.

"Yes. The girl thinks the white man not dead. The Chief send me to look for him."

"You take men?"

"No. Man come back with us if girl say so. Be afraid of black men. No come."

The other nodded understandingly and ordered two horses saddled and bridled. "Him dead," he offered.

Stabutch shrugged. "We see," he replied, as he led the two animals toward the hut where Jezebel awaited him.

The headman accompanied him, and Stabutch was in terror. What if the man insisted on entering the hut to see his chief? Stabutch loosened the revolver in its holster. Now his greatest fear was that the shot might attract others to the hut. That would never do. He must find some other way. He stopped and the headman halted with him.

"Do not come to the hut yet," said Stabutch.

"Why?" asked the headman.

"The girl is afraid. If she sees you she will think we are deceiving her, and she may refuse to show me where the man is. We promised her that no black man would come."

The headman hesitated. Then he shrugged and turned back. "All right," he said.

"And tell them to leave the gates open till we have gone," called Stabutch.

At the hut door he called to the girl. "All ready," he said, "and hand me my rifle when you come out;" but she did not know what a rifle was and he had to step in and get it himself.

Jezebel looked at the horses with dismay.

At the thought of riding one of these strange beasts alone she was terrified. "I cannot do it," she told Stabutch.

"You will have to—or die," he whispered. "I'll lead the one you ride. Here, hurry."

He lifted her into the saddle and showed her how to use the stirrups and hold the reins. Then he put a rope about the neck of her horse; and, mounting his own, he led hers out through the village gateway while half a hundred murderers watched them depart.

As they turned upward toward the higher hills the setting sun projected their shadows far ahead, and presently night descended upon them and hid their sudden change of direction from any watchers there may have been at the village gates.

CHAPTER 21

An Awakening

DANNY "GUNNER" PATRICK opened his eyes and stared up at the blue African sky. Slowly consciousness returned and with it the realization that his head pained severely. He raised a hand and felt of it. What was that? He looked at his hand and saw that it was bloody.

"Geeze!" he muttered. "They got me!" He tried to recall how it had happened. "I knew the finger was on me, but how the hell did they get me? Where was I?" His thoughts were all back in Chicago, and he was puzzled. Vaguely he felt that he had made his get-away, and yet they had "got" him. He could not figure it out.

Then he turned his head slightly and saw lofty mountains looming near. Slowly and painfully he sat up and looked around. Memory, partial and fragmentary, returned. "I must have fell off them mountains," he mused, "while I was lookin' for camp."

Gingerly he rose to his feet and was relieved to find that he was not seriously injured—at least his arms and legs were intact. "My head never was much good. Geeze, it hurts, though."

A single urge dominated him—he must find camp. Old Smithy would be worrying about him if he did not return. Where was Obambi? "I wonder if the dinge fell off too," he muttered, looking about him. But Obambi, neither dead nor alive, was in sight; and so the "Gunner" started upon his fruitless search for camp.

At first he wandered toward the northwest, directly away from Smith's last camp. Tongani, the baboon, sitting upon his sentinel rock, saw him coming and sounded the alarm. At first Danny saw only a couple of "monkeys" coming toward him, barking and growling. He saw them stop occasionally and place the backs of their heads against the ground and he mentally classified them as "nutty monks;" but when their numbers were swollen to a hundred and he finally realized the potential danger lying in those powerful jaws and sharp fangs, he altered his course and turned toward the southwest.

For a short distance the tongani followed him, but when they saw that he intended them no harm they let him proceed and returned to their interrupted feeding, while the man, with a sigh of relief, continued on his way.

In a ravine Danny found water, and with the discovery came a realization of his thirst and his hunger. He drank at the same pool at which Tarzan had slain Horta, the boar; and he also washed the blood from his head and face as well as he could. Then he continued on his aimless wandering. This time he climbed higher up the slope toward the mountains, in a southeasterly direction, and was headed at last toward the location of the now abandoned camp. Chance and the tongani had set him upon the right trail.

In a short time he reached a spot that seemed familiar; and here he stopped and looked around in an effort to recall his wandering mental faculties, which he fully realized were not functioning properly.

"That bat on the bean sure knocked me cuckoo," he remarked, half aloud. "Geeze, what's that?" Something was moving in the tall grass through which he had just come. He watched intently and a moment later saw the head of Sheeta, the panther, parting the grasses a short distance from him. The scene was suddenly familiar.

"I gotcha Steve!" exclaimed the "Gunner." "Me and that Tarzan guy flopped here last night—now I remember."

He also remembered how Tarzan had chased the panther away by "running a bluff on him," and he wondered if he could do the same thing.

"Geeze, what a ornery lookin' pan! I'll bet you got a rotten disposition—and that Tarzan guy just growled and ran at you, and you beat it. Say, I don't believe it, if I did see it myself. Whyinell don't you go on about your business, you big stiff? You give me the heeby-jeebies." He stooped and picked up a fragment of rock. "Beat it!" he yelled, as he hurled the missile at Sheeta.

The great cat wheeled and bounded away, disappearing in the tall grass that the "Gunner" could now see waving along the path of the panther's retreat. "Well, what do you know about that?" ejaculated Danny. "I done it! Geeze, these lions aint so much."

His hunger now claimed his attention as his returning memory suggested a means of appeasing it. "I wonder could I do it?" he mused, as he hunted around on the ground until he had found a thin fragment of rock, with which he commenced to scrape away the dirt from a loose heap that rose a few inches above the contour of the surrounding ground. "I wonder could I!"

His digging soon revealed the remains of the boar Tarzan had cached against their possible return. With his pocket knife the "Gunner" hacked off several pieces, after which he scraped the dirt back over the body and busied himself in the preparation of a fire, where he grilled the meat in a sketchy fashion that produced culinary results which ordinarily would have caused him to turn up his nose in disgust. But today he was far from particular and bolted the partially cooked and partially charred morsels like a ravenous wolf.

His memory had returned now up to the point of the meal he had eaten at this same spot with Tarzan—from there on until he had regained consciousness a short time before, it was a blank. He knew now that he could find his way back to camp from the point above the raiders' village where he and Obambi had lunched, and so he turned his footsteps in that direction.

When he had found the place, he crept on down to the edge of the cliff where it overlooked the village; and here he lay down to rest and to spy upon the raiders, for he was very tired.

"The lousy bums!" he ejaculated beneath his breath, as he saw the *shiftas* moving about the village. "I wish I had my typewriter, I'd clean up that dump."

He saw Stabutch emerge from a hut and walk down to the horses. He watched him while he talked to the blacks there and to the headman. Then he saw the Russian leading two saddled horses back to the hut.

"That guy don't know it," he muttered, "but the finger is sure on him. I'll get him on the spot some day if it takes the rest of my natural life. Geeze, glom the broad!" Stabutch had summoned Jezebel from the hut. Suddenly a strange thing happened inside the head of Danny "Gunner" Patrick. It was as though someone had suddenly raised a window shade and let in a flood of light. He saw everything perfectly now in retrospection. With the sight of Jezebel his memory had returned!

It was with difficulty that he restrained an urge to call out and tell her that he was there; but caution stilled his tongue, and he lay watching while the two mounted and rode out of the gateway.

He rose to his feet and ran along the ridge toward the north, parallel to the course they were taking. It was already dusk. In a few minutes it would be dark. If he could only keep them in sight until he knew in what direction they finally went!

Exhaustion was forgotten as he ran through the approaching night. Dimly now he could see them. They rode for a short distance upward toward the cliffs; and then, just before the darkness swallowed them, he saw them turn and gallop away toward the northwest and the great forest that lay in that direction.

Reckless of life and limb, the "Gunner" half stumbled, half fell down the cliffs that here had crumbled away and spilled their fragments out upon the slope below.

"I gotta catch 'em, I gotta catch 'em," he kept repeating to himself. "The poor kid! The poor little kid! So help me God, if I catch 'em, what I won't do to that --- -- - ----- if he's hurt her?"

On through the night he stumbled, falling time and again only to pick himself up and continue his frantic and hopeless search for the little golden haired Jezebel who had come into his life for a few brief hours to leave a mark upon his heart that might never be erased.

Gradually the realization of it crept upon him as he groped blindly into the unknown, and it gave him strength to go on in the face of such physical exhaustion as he had never known before.

"Geeze," he muttered, "I sure must of fell hard for that kid."

CHAPTER 22

By a Lonely Pool

NIGHT HAD FALLEN; and Tarzan of the Apes, leading Lady Barbara Collis and Lafayette Smith from the valley of the land of Midian, did not see the spoor of Jezebel and the "Gunner."

His two charges were upon the verge of exhaustion, but the ape-man led them on through the night in accordance with a plan he had decided upon. He knew that there were two more whites missing—Jezebel and Danny Patrick—and he wanted to get Lady Barbara and Smith to a place of safety that he might be free to pursue his search for these others.

To Lady Barbara and Smith the journey seemed interminable,

yet they made no complaint, for the ape-man had explained the purpose of this forced march to them; and they were even more anxious than he concerning the fate of their friends.

Smith supported the girl as best he could; but his own strength was almost spent, and sometimes his desire to assist her tended more to impede than to aid her. Finally she stumbled and fell; and when Tarzan, striding in advance, heard and returned to them he found Smith vainly endeavoring to lift Lady Barbara.

This was the first intimation the ape-man had received that his charges were upon the verge of exhaustion, for neither had voiced a single complaint; and when he realized it he lifted Lady Barbara in his arms and carried her, while Smith, relieved at least of further anxiety concerning her, was able to keep going, though he moved like an automaton, apparently without conscious volition. Nor may his state be wondered at, when one considers what he had passed through during the preceding three days.

With Lady Barbara, he marvelled at the strength and endurance of the ape-man, which, because of his own weakened state, seemed unbelievable even as he witnessed it.

"It is not much farther," said Tarzan, guessing that the man needed encouragement.

"You are sure the hunter you told us of has not moved his camp?" asked Lady Barbara.

"He was there day before yesterday," replied the ape-man. "I think we shall find him there tonight."

"He will take us in?" asked Smith.

"Certainly, just as you would, under similar circumstances, take in anyone who needed assistance," replied the Lord of the Jungle. "He is an Englishman," he added, as though that fact in itself were a sufficient answer to their doubts.

They were in a dense forest now, following an ancient game trail; and presently they saw lights flickering ahead.

"That must be the camp," exclaimed Lady Barbara.

"Yes," replied Tarzan, and a moment later he called out in a native dialect.

Instantly came an answering voice; and a moment later Tarzan halted upon the edge of the camp, just outside the circle of beast-fires.

Several askaris were on guard, and with them Tarzan conversed for a few moments; then he advanced and lowered Lady Barbara to her feet.

"I have told them not to disturb their bwana," the ape-man explained. "There is another tent that Lady Barbara may occupy, and the headman will arrange to have a shelter thrown up for Smith. You will be perfectly safe here. The men tell me their bwana is Lord Passmore. He will doubtless arrange to get you out to rail head. In the meantime I shall try to locate your friends."

That was all—the ape-man turned and melted into the black night before they could voice any thanks.

"Why, he's gone!" exclaimed the girl. "I didn't even thank him."

"I thought he would remain here until morning," said Smith. "He must be tired."

"He seems tireless," replied Lady Barbara. "He is a super-man, if ever there was one."

"Come," said the headman, "your tent is over here. The boys are arranging a shelter for the bwana."

"Good night, Mr. Smith," said the girl. "I hope you sleep well."

"Good night, Lady Barbara," replied Smith. "I hope we wake up sometime."

And as they prepared for this welcome rest Stabutch and Jezebel were riding through the night, the man completely confused and lost.

Toward morning they drew rein at the edge of a great forest, after riding in wide circles during the greater part of the night. Stabutch was almost exhausted; and Jezebel was but little better off, but she had youth and health to give her the reserve strength that the man had undermined and wasted in dissipation.

"I've got to get some sleep," he said, dismounting.

Jezebel needed no invitation to slip from her saddle for she was stiff and sore from this unusual experience. Stabutch led the animals inside the forest and tied them to a tree. Then he threw himself upon the ground and was almost immediately asleep.

Jezebel sat in silence listening to the regular breathing of the man. "Now would be the time to escape," she thought. She rose quietly to her feet. How dark it was! Perhaps it would be better to wait until it became light enough to see. She was sure the man would sleep a long time, for it was evident that he was very tired.

She sat down again, listening to the noises of the jungle. They frightened her. Yes, she would wait until it was light; then she would untie the horses, ride one and lead the other away so that the man could not pursue her.

Slowly the minutes crept by. The sky became lighter in the east, over the distant mountains. The horses became restless. She noticed that they stood with ears pricked up and that they looked deeper into the jungle and trembled.

Suddenly there was the sound of crashing in the underbrush. The horses snorted and surged back upon their ropes, both of which broke. The noise awakened Stabutch, who sat up just as the two terrified animals wheeled and bolted. An instant later a lion leaped past the girl and the man, in pursuit of the two fleeing horses.

Stabutch sprang to his feet, his rifle in his hands. "God!" he exclaimed. "This is no place to sleep," and Jezebel's opportunity had passed.

The sun was topping the eastern mountains. The day had come. Soon the searchers would be ahorse. Now that he was afoot, Stabutch knew that he must not loiter. However, they must eat, or they would have no strength to proceed; and only by his rifle could they eat.

"Climb into that tree, little one," he said to Jezebel. "You will be safe there while I go and shoot something for our breakfast. Watch for the lion, and if you see him returning this way shout a warning. I am going farther into the forest to look for game."

Jezebel climbed into the tree, and Stabutch departed upon the hunt for breakfast. The girl watched for the lion, hoping it would return, for she had determined that she would give no warning to the man if it did.

She was afraid of the Russian because of things he had said to her during that long night ride. Much that he had said she had not understood at all, but she understood enough to know that he was a bad man. But the lion did not return, and presently Jezebel dozed and nearly fell out of the tree.

Stabutch, hunting in the forest, found a water hole not far from where he had left Jezebel; and here he hid behind bushes waiting for some animal to come down to drink. Nor had he long to wait before he saw a creature appear suddenly upon the opposite side of the pool. So quietly had it come that the Russian had not dreamed that a creature stirred within a mile of his post. The most surprising feature of the occurrence, however, was that the animal thus suddenly to step into view was a man.

Stabutch's evil eyes narrowed. It was *the* man—the man he had travelled all the way from Moscow to kill. What an opportunity! Fate was indeed kind to him. He would fulfill his mission without danger to himself, and then he would escape with the girl—that wondrous girl! Stabutch had never seen so beautiful a woman in his life, and now he was to possess her—she was to be his.

But first he must attend to the business of the moment. What a pleasant business it was, too. He raised his rifle very cautiously and aimed. Tarzan had halted and turned his head to one side. He could not see the rifle barrel of his enemy because of the bush behind which Stabutch hid and the fact that his eyes were centered on something in another direction.

The Russian realized that he was trembling, and he cursed himself under his breath. The nervous strain was too great. He tensed his muscles in an effort to hold his hands firm and the rifle steady and immovable upon the target. The front sight of the rifle was describing a tiny circle instead of remaining fixed upon that great chest which offered such a splendid target.

But he must fire! The man would not stand there thus forever. The thought hurried Stabutch, and as the sight passed again across the body of the ape-man the Russian squeezed the trigger.

At the sound of the shot Jezebel's eyes snapped open. "Perhaps the lion returned," she soliloquized, "or maybe the man has found food. If it were the lion, I hope he missed it."

Also, as the rifle spoke, the target leaped into the air, seized a low hung branch and disappeared amidst the foliage of the trees above. Stabutch had missed—he should have relaxed his muscles rather than tensed them.

The Russian was terrified. He felt as must one who stands upon the drop with the noose already about his neck. He turned and fled. His cunning mind suggested that he had better not return where the girl was. She was already lost to him, for he could not be burdened with her now in this flight, upon the success of which hung his very life. Accordingly he ran toward the south.

As he rushed headlong through the forest he was already out of breath when he felt a sudden sickening pain in his arm and at the same instant saw the feathered tip of an arrow waving beside him as he ran.

The shaft had pierced his forearm, its tip projecting from the opposite side. Sick with terror Stabutch increased his speed. Somewhere above him was his Nemesis, whom he could neither see nor hear. It was as though a ghostly assassin pursued him on silent wings.

Again an arrow struck him, sinking deep into the triceps of his other arm. With a scream of pain and horror Stabutch halted and, dropping upon his knees, raised his hands in supplication. "Spare me!" he cried. "Spare me! I have never wronged you. If you will spare—"

An arrow, speeding straight, drove through the Russian's throat. He screamed and clutched at the missile and fell forward on his face.

Jezebel, listening in the tree, heard the agonized shriek of the stricken man; and she shuddered. "The lion got him," she whispered. "He was wicked. It is the will of Jehovah!"

Tarzan of the Apes dropped lightly from a tree and warily approached the dying man. Stabutch, writhing in agony and terror, rolled over on his side. He saw the ape-man approaching, his bow and arrow ready in his hand, and, dying, reached for the revolver at his hip to complete the work that he had come so far to achieve and for which he was to give his life.

No more had his hand reached the grip of his weapon than the Lord of the Jungle loosed another shaft that drove deep through the chest of the Russian, deep through his heart. Without a sound Leon Stabutch collapsed; and a moment later there rang through the jungle the fierce, uncanny victory cry of the bull ape.

As the savage notes reverberated through the forest Jezebel slid to the ground and fled in terror. She knew not where nor to what fate her flying feet led her. She was obsessed by but a single idea— to escape from the terrors of that lonely spot.

CHAPTER 23

Captured

WITH THE COMING of day the "Gunner" found himself near a forest. He had heard no sound of horses all during the night; and now that day had come, and he could see to a distance, he scanned the landscape for some sign of Stabutch and Jezebel but without success.

"Geeze," he muttered, "there aint no use, I gotta rest. The poor little kid! If I only knew where the rat took her; but I don't, and I gotta rest." He surveyed the forest. "That looks like a swell hideout. I'll lay up there and grab off a little sleep. Geeze, I'm all in."

As he walked toward the forest his attention was attracted to something moving a couple of miles to the north of him. He stopped short, and looked more closely as two horses, racing from the forest, dashed madly toward the foothills, pursued by a lion.

"Geeze!" exclaimed the "Gunner," "those must be their horses. What if the lion got her!"

Instantly his fatigue was forgotten; and he started at a run toward the north; but he could not keep the pace up for long; and soon he was walking again, his brain a turmoil of conjecture and apprehension.

He saw the lion give up the chase and turn away almost immediately, cutting up the slope in a northeasterly direction. The "Gunner" was glad to see him go, not for his own sake so much as for Jezebel, whom, he reasoned, the lion might not have killed after all. There was a possibility, he thought, that she might have had time to climb a tree. Otherwise, he was positive, the lion must have killed her.

His knowledge of lions was slight. In common with most people, he believed that lions wandered about killing everything so unfortunate as to fall into their pathways—unless they were bluffed out as he had bluffed the panther the day before. But of course, he reasoned, Jezebel wouldn't have been able to bluff a lion.

He was walking close to the edge of the forest, making the best time that he could, when he heard a shot in the distance. It was the report of Stabutch's rifle as he fired at Tarzan. The "Gunner" tried to increase his speed. There was too much doing there, where he thought Jezebel might be, to permit of loafing; but he was too exhausted to move rapidly.

Then, a few minutes later, the Russian's scream of agony was wafted to his ears and again he was goaded on. This was followed by the uncanny cry of the ape-man, which, for some reason, Danny did not recognize, though he had heard it twice before. Perhaps the distance and the intervening trees muffled and changed it.

On he plodded, trying occasionally to run; but his overtaxed muscles had reached their limit; and he had to give up the attempt, for already he was staggering and stumbling even at a walk.

"I aint no good," he muttered; "nothing but a lousy punk. Here's a guy beatin' it with my girl, and I aint even got the guts to work my dogs. Geeze, I'm a flop."

A little farther on he entered the forest so that he could approach the spot, where he had seen the horses emerge, without being seen, if Stabutch were still there.

Suddenly he stopped. Something was crashing through the brush toward him. He recalled the lion and drew his pocket knife. Then he hid behind a bush and waited, nor did he have long to wait before the author of the disturbance broke into view.

"Jezebel!" he cried, stepping into her path. His voice trembled with emotion.

With a startled scream the girl halted, and then she recognized him. "Danny!" It was the last straw—her over-wrought nerves went to pieces; and she sank to the ground, sobbing hysterically.

The "Gunner" took a step or two toward her. He staggered, his knees gave beneath him, and he sat down heavily a few yards from her; and then a strange thing happened. Tears welled to the eyes of Danny "Gunner" Patrick; he threw himself face down on the ground; and he, too, sobbed.

For several minutes they lay there, and then Jezebel gained control of herself and sat up. "Oh, Danny," she cried. "Are you hurt? Oh, your head! Don't die, Danny."

He had quelled his emotion and was roughly wiping his eyes on his shirt sleeve. "I aint dyin'," he said; "but I oughta. Some one oughta bump me off—a great big stiff like me, cryin'!"

"It's because you've been hurt, Danny," said Jezebel.

"Naw, it aint that. I been hurt before, but I aint bawled since I was a little kid—when my mother died. It was something else, kid. I just blew up when I seen you, and knew that you was O. K. My nerves went blooey—just like that!" he snapped his fingers. "You see," he added, hesitantly, "I guess I like you an awful lot, kid."

"I like you, Danny," she told him. "You're top hole."

"I'm what? What does that mean?"

"I don't know," Jezebel admitted. "It's English, and you don't understand English, do you?"

He crawled over closer to her and took her hand in his. "Geeze," he said, "I thought I wasn't never goin' to see you again. Say," he burst out violently, "did that bum hurt you any, kid?"

"The man who took me away from the black men in the village, you mean?"

"Yes."

"No, Danny. After he killed his friend we rode all night. He was afraid the black men would catch him."

"What became of the rat? How did you make your get-away?"

She told him all that she knew, but they were unable to account for the sounds both had heard or to guess whether or not they had portended the death of Stabutch.

"I wouldn't be much good, if he showed up again," said Danny. "I gotta get my strength back some way."

"You must rest," she told him.

"I'll tell you what we'll do," he said. "We'll lay around here until we are rested up a bit; then we'll beat it back up toward the hills where I know where they's water and something to eat. It aint very good food," he added, "but it's better than none. Say, I got some of it in my pocket. We'll just have a feed now." He extracted some dirty scraps of half burned pork from one of his pockets and surveyed them ruefully.

"What is it?" asked Jezebel.

"It's pig, kid," he explained. "It don't look so hot, does it? Well, it don't taste no better than it looks; but it's food, and that's what we are needin' bad right now. Here, hop to it." He extended a handful of the scraps toward her. "Shut your eyes and hold your nose, and it aint so bad," he assured her. "Just imagine you're in the old College Inn."

Jezebel smiled and took a piece of the meat. "United States is a funny language, isn't it, Danny?"

"Why, I don't know—is it?"

"Yes, I think so. Sometimes it sounds just like English and yet I can't understand it at all."

"That's because you aint used to it," he told her; "but I'll learn you if you want me to. Do you?"

"Oke, kid," replied Jezebel.

"You're learnin' all right," said Danny, admiringly.

They lay in the growing heat of the new day and talked together of many things, as they rested. Jezebel told him the story of the land of Midian, of her childhood, of the eventful coming of Lady Barbara and its strange effect upon her life; and Danny told her of Chicago, but there were many things in his own life that he did not tell her—things that, for the first time, he was ashamed of. And he wondered why he was ashamed.

As they talked, Tarzan of the Apes quitted the forest and set out upon his search for them, going upward toward the hills, intending to start his search for their spoor at the mouth of the fissure. If he did not find it there he would know that they were still in the valley; if he did find it, he would follow it until he located them.

At break of day a hundred *shiftas* rode out of their village. They had discovered the body of Capietro, and now they knew that the Russian had tricked them and fled, after killing their chief. They wanted the girl for ransom, and they wanted the life of Stabutch.

They had not ridden far when they met two riderless horses galloping back toward the village. The *shiftas* recognized them at once, and knowing that Stabutch and the girl were now afoot they anticipated little difficulty in overhauling them.

The rolling foothills were cut by swales and canyons; so that at times the vision of the riders was limited. They had been following downward along the bottom of a shallow canyon for some time, where they could neither see to a great distance nor be seen; and then their leader turned his mount toward higher ground, and as he topped the summit of a low ridge he saw a man approaching from the direction of the forest.

Tarzan saw the *shifta* simultaneously and changed his direction obliquely to the left, breaking into a trot. He knew that if that lone rider signified a force of mounted *shiftas* he would be no match for them; and, guided by the instinct of the wild beast, he sought ground where the advantage would be with him—the rough, rocky ground leading to the cliffs, where no horse could follow him.

With a yell to his followers, the *shifta* chieftain put spurs to his horse and rode at top speed to intercept the ape-man; and close behind him came his yelling, savage horde.

Tarzan quickly saw that he could not reach the cliffs ahead of them; but he maintained his steady, tireless trot that he might be that much nearer the goal when the attack came. Perhaps he could hold them off until he reached the sanctuary of the cliffs, but certainly he had no intention of giving up without exerting every effort to escape the unequal battle that must follow if they overtook him.

With savage yells the *shiftas* approached, their loose cotton garments fluttering in the wind, their rifles waving above their heads. The chief rode in the lead; and when he was near enough, the ape-man, who had been casting occasional glances rearward across a brown shoulder, stopped, wheeled and let an arrow drive at his foe; then he was away again as the shaft sank into the breast of the *shifta* chieftain.

With a scream, the fellow rolled from his saddle; and for a moment the others drew rein, but only for a moment. Here was but a single enemy, poorly armed with primitive weapons—he was no real menace to mounted riflemen.

Shouting their anger and their treats of vengeance, they spurred forward again in pursuit; but Tarzan had gained and the rocky ground was not far away.

Spreading in a great half circle, the *shiftas* sought to surround and head off their quarry, whose strategy they had guessed the moment that they had seen the course of his flight. Now another rider ventured too near, and for a brief instant Tarzan paused to loose another arrow. As this second enemy fell, mortally wounded, the ape-man continued his flight to the accompaniment of a rattle of musketry fire; but soon he was forced to halt again as several of the horsemen passed him and cut off his line of retreat.

The hail of slugs screaming past him or kicking up the dirt around him gave him slight concern, so traditionally poor was the marksmanship of these roving bands of robbers, illy equipped with ancient firearms with which, because of habitual shortage of ammunition, they had little opportunity to practice.

Now they pressed closer, in a rough circle of which he was the center; and, firing across him from all sides, it seemed impossible that they should miss him; but miss him they did, though their bullets found targets among their own men and horses, until one, who had supplanted the slain chief, took command and ordered them to cease firing.

Turning again in the direction of his flight, Tarzan tried to shoot his way through the cordon of horsemen shutting off his retreat; but, though each arrow sped true to its mark, the yelling horde closed in upon him until, his last shaft spent, he was the center of a closely milling mass of shrieking enemies.

Shrilly above the pandemonium of battle rose the cries of the new leader. "Do not kill! Do not kill!" he screamed. "It is Tarzan of the Apes, and he is worth the ransom of a ras!"

Suddenly a giant black threw himself from his horse full upon the Lord of the Jungle, but Tarzan seized the fellow and hurled him back among the horsemen. Yet closer and closer they pressed; and now several fell upon him from their saddles, bearing him down beneath the feet of the now frantic horses.

Battling for life and liberty, the ape-man struggled against the over-powering odds that were being constantly augmented by new recruits who hurled themselves from their mounts upon the growing pile that overwhelmed him. Once he managed to struggle to his feet, shaking most of his opponents from him; but they seized him about the legs and dragged him down again; and presently succeeded in slipping nooses about his wrists and ankles, thus effectually subduing him.

Now that he was harmless many of them reviled and struck him; but there were many others who lay upon the ground, some never to rise again. The *shiftas* had captured the great Tarzan, but it had cost them dear.

Now some of them rounded up the riderless horses, while others stripped the dead of their weapons, ammunition, and any other valuables the living coveted. Tarzan was raised to an empty saddle, where he was securely bound; and four men were detailed to conduct him and the horses of the dead to the village, the wounded accompanying them, while the main body of the blacks continued the search for Stabutch and Jezebel.

CHAPTER 24

The Long Night

THE SUN WAS high in the heavens when Lady Barbara, refreshed by her long, undisturbed sleep, stepped from her tent in the camp of Lord Passmore. A smiling, handsome black boy came running toward her. "Breakfast soon be ready," he told her. "Lord Passmore very sorry. He have to go hunt."

She asked after Lafayette Smith and was told that he had just awakened, nor was it long before he joined her; and soon they were breakfasting together.

"If Jezebel and your friend were here," she said, "I should be very happy. I am praying that Tarzan finds them."

"I am sure he will," Smith assured her, "though I am only worried about Jezebel. Danny can take care of himself."

"Doesn't it seem heavenly to eat a meal again?" the girl remarked. "Do you know it has been months since I have eaten

With a scream, the fellow rolled from his saddle.

anything that even vaguely approximated a civilized meal. Lord Passmore was fortunate to get such a cook for his safari. I had no such luck."

"Have you noticed what splendid looking fellows all his men are?" asked Smith. "They would make that aggregation of mine resemble fourth rate roustabouts with hookworm and sleeping sickness."

"There is another very noticeable thing about them," said Lady Barbara.

"What is that?"

"There is not a single piece of cast off European finery among them—their garb is native, pure and simple; and, while I'll have to admit there isn't much to it, it lends a dignity to them that European clothing would change to the absurd."

"I quite agree with you," said Smith. "I wonder why I didn't get a safari like this."

"Lord Passmore is evidently an African traveller and hunter of long experience. No amateur could hope to attract such men as these."

"I shall hate to go back to my own camp, if I stay here very long," said Smith; "but I suppose I'll have to; and that suggests another unpleasant feature of the change."

"And what is that?" she asked.

"I shan't see you any more," he said with a simple directness that vouched for the sincerity of his regret.

The girl was silent for a moment, as though the suggestion had aroused a train of thought she had not before considered. "That is true, isn't it?" she remarked, presently. "We shan't see each other any more—but not for always. I'm sure you'll stop and visit me in London. Isn't it odd what old friends we seem? And yet we only met two days ago. Or, maybe, it doesn't seem that way to you. You see I was so long without seeing a human being of my own world that you were quite like a long lost brother, when you came along so unexpectedly."

"I have the same feeling," he said—"as though I had known you forever—and—," he hesitated, "—as though I could never get along without you in the future." He flushed a little as he spoke those last words.

The girl looked up at him with a quick smile—a sympathetic, understanding smile. "It was nice of you to say that," she said.

"Why it sounded almost like a declaration," she added, with a gay, friendly laugh.

He reached across the little camp table and laid a hand upon hers. "Accept it as such," he said. "I'm not very good at saying things—like that."

"Let's not be serious," she begged. "Really, we scarcely know each other, after all."

"I have known you always," he replied. "I think we were amœbas together before the first Cambrian dawn."

"Now you've compromised me," she cried, laughingly, "for I'm sure there were no chaperons way back there. I hope that you were a proper amœba. You didn't kiss me, did you?"

"Unfortunately for me amœbas have no mouths," he said, "but I've been profiting by several millions of years of evolution just to remedy that defect."

"Let's be amœbas again," she suggested.

"No," he said, "for then I couldn't tell you that I—I—" He choked and flushed.

"Please! Please, don't tell me," she cried. "We're such ripping friends—don't spoil it."

"Would it spoil it?" he asked.

"I don't know. It might. I am afraid."

"Can't I ever tell you?" he asked.

"Perhaps, some day," she said.

A sudden burst of distant rifle fire interrupted them. The blacks in the camp were instantly alert. Many of them sprang to their feet, and all were listening intently to the sounds of this mysterious engagement between armed men.

The man and the girl heard the headman speaking to his fellows in some African dialect. His manner showed no excitement, his tones were low but clear. It was evident that he was issuing instructions. The men went quickly to their shelters, and a moment later Lady Barbara saw the peaceful camp transformed. Every man was armed now. As by magic a modern rifle and a bandoleer of cartridges were in the possession of each black. White feathered headdresses were being adjusted and war paint applied to glossy hides.

Smith approached the headman. "What is the matter?" he asked. "Is something wrong?"

"I do not know, bwana," replied the black; "but we prepare."

"Is there any danger?" continued the white.

The headman straightened to his full, impressive height. "Are we not here?" he asked.

Jezebel and the "Gunner" were walking slowly in the direction of the distant water hole and the cached boar meat, following the bottom of a dip that was the mouth of a small canyon that led up into the hills.

They were stiff and lame and very tired; and the wound on the "Gunner's" head pained; but, notwithstanding, they were happy as, hand in hand, they dragged their weary feet toward water and food.

"Geeze, kid," said Danny, "it sure is a funny world. Just think, if I hadn't met old Smithy on board that ship me and you wouldn't never have met up. It all started from that," but then Danny knew nothing of Angustus the Ephesian.

"I got a few grand salted away, kid, and when we get out of this mess we'll go somewhere where nobody doesn't know me and I'll start over again. Get myself a garage or a filling station, and we'll have a little flat. Geeze, it's goin' to be great showin' you things. You don't know what you aint seen—movies and railroads and boats! Geeze! You aint seen nothin' and nobody aint go to show you nothin', only me."

"Yes, Danny," said Jezebel, "it's going to be ripping," and she squeezed his hand.

Just then they were startled by the sound of rifle fire ahead.

"What was that?" asked Jezebel.

"It sounded like the Valentine Massacre," said Danny, "but I guess it's them tough smokes from the village. We better hide, kid." He drew her toward some low bushes; and there they lay down, listening to the shouts and shots that came down to them from where Tarzan fought for his life and liberty with the odds a hundred to one against him.

After awhile the din ceased, and a little later the two heard the thudding of many galloping hoofs. The sound increased in volume as it drew nearer, and Danny and Jezebel tried to make themselves as small as possible beneath the little bush in the inadequate concealment of which they were hiding.

At a thundering gallop the *shiftas* crossed the swale just above them, and all but a few had passed when one of the stragglers discovered them. His shout, which attracted the attention of others, was carried forward until it reached the new chief, and presently the entire band had circled back to learn what their fellow had discovered.

Poor "Gunner"! Poor Jezebel! Their happiness had been short lived. Their recapture was effected with humiliating ease. Broken and dejected, they were soon on their way to the village under escort of two black ruffians.

Bound, hands and feet, they were thrown into the hut formerly occupied by Capietro and left without food or water upon the pile of dirty rugs and clothing that littered the floor.

Beside them lay the corpse of the Italian which his followers, in their haste to overtake his slayer, had not taken the time to remove. It lay upon its back, the dead eyes staring upward.

Never before in his life had the spirits of Danny Patrick sunk so low, for the very reason, perhaps, that never in his life had they risen so high as during the brief interlude of happiness he had enjoyed following his reunion with Jezebel. Now he saw no hope ahead, for, with the two white men eliminated, he feared that he might not even be able to dicker with these ignorant black men for the ransom that he would gladly pay to free Jezebel and himself.

"There goes the garage, the filling station, and the flat," he said, lugubriously.

"Where?" asked Jezebel.

"Flooie," explained Danny.

"But you are here with me," said the golden one; "so I do not care what else there is."

"That's nice, kid; but I aint much help, all tied up like a Christmas present. They sure picked out a swell bed for me— feels like I was lyin' on a piece of the kitchen stove." He rolled himself to one side and nearer Jezebel. "That's better," he said, "but I wonder what was that thing I was parked on."

"Maybe your friend will come and take us away," suggested Jezebel.

"Who, Smithy? What would he take us with—that dinky toy pistol of his?"

"I was thinking of the other that you told me about."

"Oh, that Tarzan guy! Say kid, if he knew we was here he'd walk in and push all these nutty dumps over with one mit and kick the smokes over the back fence. Geeze, you bet I wish he was here. There is one big shot, and I don't mean maybe."

In a hut on the edge of the village was the answer to the

"Gunner's" wish, bound hand and foot, as was the "Gunner," and, apparently, equally helpless. Constantly the ape-man was working on the thongs that confined his wrists—twisting, tugging, pulling.

The long day wore on and never did the giant captive cease his efforts to escape; but the thongs were heavy and securely tied, yet little by little he felt that they were loosening.

Towards evening the new chief returned with the party that had been searching for Stabutch. They had not found him; but scouts had located the camp of Lord Passmore, and now the *shiftas* were discussing plans for attacking it on the morrow.

They had not come sufficiently close to it to note the number of armed natives it contained; but they had glimpsed Smith and Lady Barbara; and, being sure that there were not more than two white men, they felt little hesitation in attempting the raid, since they were planning to start back for Abyssinia on the morrow.

"We will kill the white man we now have," said the chief, "and carry the two girls and Tarzan with us. Tarzan should bring a good ransom and the girls a good price."

"Why not keep the girls for ourselves," suggested another.

"We shall sell them," said the chief.

"Who are you, to say what we shall do?" demanded the other. "You are no chief."

"No," growled a villanous looking black squatting beside the first objector.

He who would be chief leaped, catlike, upon the first speaker, before any was aware of his purpose. A sword gleamed for an instant in the light of the new made cook fires and fell with terrific force upon the skull of the victim.

"Who am I?" repeated the killer, as he wiped the bloody blade upon the garment of the slain man. "I am chief!" He looked around upon the scowling faces about him. "Is there any who says I am not chief?" There was no demur. Ntale was chief of the *shifta* band.

Inside the dark interior of the hut where he had lain bound all day without food or water the ape-man tugged and pulled until the sweat stood in beads upon his body, but not in vain. Gradually a hand slipped through the stretched thong, and he was free. Or at least his hands were, and it took them but a moment to loosen the bonds that secured his ankles.

With a low, inaudible growl he rose to his feet and stepped to the doorway. Before him lay the village compound. He saw the *shiftas* squatting about while slaves prepared the evening meal. Nearby was the palisade. They must see him as he crossed to it, but what matter?

He would be gone before they could gather their wits. Perhaps a few stray shots would be fired; but then, had they not fired many shots at him this morning, not one of which had touched him?

He stepped out into the open, and at the same instant a burly black stepped from the next hut and saw him. With a shout of warning to his fellows the man leaped upon the escaping prisoner. Those at the fires sprang to their feet and came running toward the two.

Within their prison hut Jezebel and Danny heard the commotion and wondered.

The ape-man seized the black who would have stopped him and wheeling him about to form a shield for himself, backed quickly toward the palisade.

"Stay where you are," he called to the advancing *shiftas*, in their own dialect. "Stay where you are, or I will kill this man."

"Let him kill him then," growled Ntale. "He is not worth the ransom we are losing," and with a shout of encouragement to his followers he leaped quickly forward to intercept the ape-man.

Tarzan was already near the palisade as Ntale charged. He raised the struggling black above his head and hurled him upon the advancing chief, and as the two went down he wheeled and ran for the palisade.

Like Manu the monkey he scaled the high barrier. A few scattered shots followed him, but he dropped to the ground outside unscathed and disappeared in the growing gloom of the advancing night.

The long night of their captivity dragged on and still the "Gunner" and Jezebel lay as they had been left, without food or drink, while the silent corpse of Capietro stared at the ceiling.

"I wouldn't treat nobody like this," said the "Gunner," "not even a rat."

Jezebel raised herself to one elbow. "Why not try it?" she whispered.

"What?" demanded Danny. "I'd try anything once."

"What you said about a rat made me think of it," said Jezebel. "We have lots of rats in the land of Midian. Sometimes we catch them—they are very good to eat. We make traps, but if we do not kill the rats soon after they are caught they gnaw their way to freedom—they gnaw the cords which bind the traps together."

"Well, what of it?" demanded Danny. "We aint got no rats, and if we had—well, I wont say I wouldn't eat 'em, kid; but I don't see what it's got to do with the mess we're in."

"We're like the rats, Danny," she said. "Don't you see? We're like the rats and—we can gnaw our way to freedom!"

"Well, kid," said Danny, "if you want to gnaw your way through the side of this hut, hop to it; but if I gets a chance to duck I'm goin' through the door."

"You do not understand, Danny," insisted Jezebel. "You are an egg that cannot talk. I mean that I can gnaw the cords that fasten your wrists together."

"Geeze, kid!" exclaimed Danny. "Dumb aint no name for it, and I always thought I was the bright little boy. You sure got a bean, and I don't mean maybe."

"I wish I knew what you are talking about, Danny," said Jezebel, "and I wish you would let me try to gnaw the cords from your wrist. Can't you understand what I'm talking about?"

"Sure, kid, but I'll do the gnawing—my jaws are tougher. Roll over, and I'll get busy. When you're free you can untie me."

Jezebel rolled over on her stomach and Danny wriggled into position where he could reach the thongs at her wrists with his teeth. He fell to work with a will, but it was soon evident to him that the job was going to be much more difficult than he had anticipated.

He found, too, that he was very weak and soon tired; but though often he was forced to stop through exhaustion, he never gave up. Once, when he paused to rest, he kissed the little hands that he was trying to liberate. It was a gentle, reverent kiss, quite unlike the "Gunner"; but then love is a strange force, and when it is aroused in the breast of a man by a clean and virtuous woman it makes him always a little tenderer and a little better.

Dawn was lifting the darkness within the hut, and still the "Gunner" gnawed upon the thongs that it seemed would never part. Capietro lay staring at the ceiling, his dead eyes rolled upward, just as he had lain there staring through all the long hours of the night, unseeing.

The *shiftas* were stirring in the village, for this was to be a busy day. Slaves were preparing the loads of camp equipment and plunder that they were to carry toward the north. The fighting men were hastening their breakfasts that they might look to their weapons and their horse gear before riding out on their last raid from this village, against the camp of the English hunter.

Ntale the chief was eating beside the fire of his favorite wife. "Make haste, woman," he said. "I have work to do before we ride."

"You are chief now," she reminded him. "Let others work."

"This thing I do myself," replied the black man.

"What do you that is so important that I must hasten the preparation of the morning meal?" she demanded.

"I go to kill the white man and get the girl ready for the journey," he replied. "Have food prepared for her. She must eat or she will die."

"Let her die," replied the woman. "I do not want her around. Kill them both."

"Shut thy mouth!" snapped the man. "I am chief."

"If you do not kill her, I shall" said the woman. "I shall not cook for any white bitch."

The man rose. "I go to kill the man," he said. "Have breakfast for the girl when I return with her."

CHAPTER 25

The Waziri

"THERE!" GASPED THE "Gunner."

"I am free!" exclaimed Jezebel.

"And my jaws is wore out," said Danny.

Quickly Jezebel turned and worked upon the thongs that confined the "Gunner's" wrists before taking the time to loose her ankles. Her fingers were quite numb, for the cords had partially cut off the circulation from her hands; and she was slow and bungling at the work. It seemed to them both that she would never be done. Had they known that Ntale had already arisen from his breakfast fire with the announcement that he was going to kill the "Gunner," they would have been frantic; but they did not know it, and perhaps that were better, since to Jezebel's other handicaps was not added the nervous tension that surely would have accompanied a knowledge of the truth.

But at last the "Gunner's" hands were free; and then both fell to work upon the cords that secured their ankles, which were less tightly fastened.

At last the "Gunner" arose. "The first thing I do," he said, "is to find out what I was lyin' on yesterday. It had a familiar feel to it; and, if I'm right—boy!"

He rummaged among the filthy rags at the end of the hut, and a moment later straightened up with a Thompson submachine gun in one hand and his revolver, belt and holster in the other— a grin on his face.

"This is the first break I've had in a long time," he said. "Everything's jake now, sister."

"What are those things?" asked Jezebel.

"Them's the other half of 'Gunner' Patrick," replied Danny. "Now, bring on your tough smokes!"

As he spoke, Ntale the chief drew aside the rug at the doorway and looked in. The interior of the hut was rather dark, and at first glance he could not make out the figures of the girl and the man standing at the far side; but, silhouetted as he was against the growing morning light beyond the doorway, he was plainly visible to his intended victim; and Danny saw that the man carried a pistol ready in his hand.

The "Gunner" had already buckled his belt about him. Now he transferred the machine gun to his left hand and drew his revolver from its holster. He did these things quickly and silently. So quickly that, as he fired, Ntale had not realized that his prisoners were free of their bonds—a thing he never knew, as, doubtless, he never heard the report of the shot that killed him.

At the same instant that the "Gunner" fired, the report of his revolver was drowned by yells and a shot from a sentry at the gate, to whom the coming day had revealed a hostile force creeping upon the village.

As Danny Patrick stepped over the dead body of the chief and looked out into the village he realized something of what had occurred. He saw men running hastily toward the village gates and scrambling to the banquette. He heard a fusilade of shots that spattered against the palisade, splintering the wood and tearing through to fill the village with a screaming, terror stricken mob.

His knowledge of such things told him that only high powered rifles could send their projectiles through the heavy wood of the palisade. He saw the *shiftas* on the banquette returning the fire with their antiquated muskets. He saw the slaves and prisoners cowering in a corner of the village that was freer from the fire of the attackers than other portions.

He wondered who the enemies of the *shiftas* might be, and past experience suggested only two possibilities—either a rival "gang" or the police.

"I never thought I'd come to it, kid," he said.

"Come to what, Danny?"

"I hate to tell you what I been hopin'," he admitted.

"Tell me, Danny," she said. "I won't be angry."

"I been hopin' them guys out there was cops. Just think o' that, kid! Me, "Gunner" Patrick, a-hopin' the cops would come!"

"What are cops, Danny?"

"Laws, harness bulls—Geeze, kid, why do you ask so many questions? Cops is cops. And I'll tell you why I hope its them. If it aint cops its a rival mob, and we'd get just as tough a break with them as with these guys."

He stepped out into the village street. "Well," he said, "here goes Danny Patrick smearin' up with the police. You stay here, kid, and lie down on your bread basket, so none of them slugs'll find you, while I go out and push the smokes around."

Before the gate was a great crowd of *shiftas* firing through openings at the enemy beyond. The "Gunner" knelt and raised the machine gun to his shoulder. There was the vicious b-r-r-r as of some titanic rattle snake; and a dozen of the massed *shiftas* collapsed, dead or screaming, to the ground.

The others turned and, seeing the "Gunner," realized that they were caught between two fires, for they remembered the recent occasion upon which they had witnessed the deadly effects of this terrifying weapon.

The "Gunner" spied Ogonyo among the prisoners and slaves huddled not far from where he stood, and the sight of him suggested an idea to the white man.

"Hey! Big Smoke, you!" He waved his hand to Ogonyo. "Come here! Bring all them guys with you. Tell 'em to grab anything they can fight with if they want to make their getaway."

Whether or not Ogonyo understood even a small part of what the "Gunner" said, he seemed at least to grasp the main idea; and presently the whole mob of prisoners and slaves, except the women, had placed themselves behind Danny.

The firing from the attacking force had subsided somewhat since Danny's typewriter had spoken, as though the leader of that other party had recognized its voice and guessed that white prisoners within the village might be menaced by his rifle fire. Only an occasional shot, aimed at some specific target, was coming into the village.

The *shiftas* had regained their composure to some extent and were preparing their horses and mounting, with the evident intention of executing a sortie. They were leaderless and confused, half a dozen shouting advice and instructions at the same time.

It was at this moment that Danny advanced upon them with his motley horde armed with sticks and stones, an occasional knife and a few swords hastily stolen from the huts of their captors.

As the *shiftas* realized that they were menaced thus seriously from the rear, the "Gunner" opened fire upon them for the second time, and the confusion that followed in the village compound gave the attackers both within and without a new advantage.

The *shiftas* fought among themselves for the loose horses that were now stampeding in terror about the village; and as a number of them succeeded in mounting they rode for the village gates, overthrowing those who had remained to defend them. Some among them forced the portals open; and as the horsemen dashed out they were met by a band of black warriors, above whose heads waved white plumes, and in whose hands were modern high powered rifles.

The attacking force had been lying partially concealed behind a low ridge, and as it rose to meet the escaping *shiftas* the savage war cry of the Waziri rang above the tumult of the battle.

First to the gates was Tarzan, war chief of the Waziri, and while Muviro and a small detachment accounted for all but a few of the horsemen who had succeeded in leaving the village, the ape-man, with the remaining Waziri, charged the demoralized remnants of Capietro's band that remained within the palisade.

Surrounded by enemies, the *shiftas* threw down their rifles and begged for mercy, and soon they were herded into a corner of the village under guard of a detachment of the Waziri.

As Tarzan greeted the "Gunner" and Jezebel he expressed his relief at finding them unharmed.

"You sure come at the right time," Danny told him. "This old typewriter certainly chews up the ammunition, and that last burst just about emptied the drum; but say, who are your friends? Where did you raise this mob?"

"They are my people," replied Tarzan.

"Some gang!" ejaculated the "Gunner," admiringly; "but say, have you seen anything of old Smithy?"

"He is safe at my camp."

"And Barbara," asked Jezebel; "where is she?"

"She is with Smith," replied Tarzan. "You will see them both in a few hours. We start back as soon as I arrange for the disposal of these people." He turned away and commenced to make inquiries among the prisoners of the *shiftas*.

"Is he not beautiful!" exclaimed Jezebel.

"Hey, sister, can that 'beautiful' stuff," warned the "Gunner," "and from now on remember that I'm the only 'beautiful' guy you know, no matter what my pan looks like."

Quickly Tarzan separated the prisoners according to their tribes and villages, appointed headmen to lead them back to their homes and issued instructions to them as he explained his plans.

The weapons, ammunition, loot and belongings of the *shiftas* were divided among the prisoners, after the Waziri had been allowed to select such trifles as they desired. The captured *shiftas* were placed in charge of a large band of Gallas with orders to return them to Abyssinia and turn them over to the nearest ras.

"Why not hang them here?" asked the Galla headman. "We shall then save all the food they would eat on the long march back to our country, besides saving us much trouble and worry in guarding them—for the ras will certainly hang them."

"Take them back, as I tell you," replied Tarzan. "But if they give you trouble do with them as you see fit."

It took little more than an hour to evacuate the village. All of Smith's loads were recovered, including Danny's precious ammunition and extra drums for his beloved Thompson; and these were assigned to Smith's porters, who were once again assembled under Ogonyo.

When the village was emptied it was fired in a dozen places; and, as the black smoke curled up toward the blue heavens, the various parties took their respective ways from the scene of their captivity, but not before the several headmen had come and knelt before the Lord of the Jungle and thanked him for the deliverance of their people.

CHAPTER 26

The Last Knot Is Tied

LAFAYETTE SMITH AND Lady Barbara had been mystified witnesses to the sudden transformation of the peaceful scene in the camp of Lord Passmore. All day the warriors had remained in readiness, as though expecting a summons; and when night fell they still waited.

Evidences of restlessness were apparent; and there was no singing and little laughter in the camp, as there had been before. The last that the two whites saw, as they retired for the night, were the little groups of plumed warriors squatting about their fires, their rifles ready to their hands; and they were asleep when the summons came and the sleek, black fighting men melted silently into the dark shadows of the forest, leaving only four of their number to guard the camp and the two guests.

When Lady Barbara emerged from her tent in the morning she was astonished to find the camp all but deserted. The *boy* who acted in the capacity of personal servant and cook for her and Smith was there and three other blacks. All were constantly armed; but their attitude toward her had not changed, and she felt only curiosity relative to the other altered conditions, so obvious at first glance, rather than apprehension.

When Smith joined her a few minutes later he was equally at a loss to understand the strange metamorphosis that had transformed the laughing, joking porters and askaris into painted warriors and sent them out into the night so surreptitiously, nor could they glean the slightest information from their *boy,* who, though still courteous and smiling, seemed by some strange trick of fate suddenly to have forgotten the very fair command of English that he had exhibited with evident pride on the previous day.

The long day dragged on until mid afternoon without sign of any change. Neither Lord Passmore nor the missing blacks returned, and the enigma was as baffling as before. The two whites, however, seemed to find much pleasure in one another's company; and so, perhaps, the day passed more rapidly for them than it did for the four blacks, waiting and listening through the hot, drowsy hours.

But suddenly there was a change. Lady Barbara saw her *boy* rise and stand in an attitude of eager listening. "They come!" he said, in his own tongue, to his companions. Now they all stood and, though they may have expected only friends, their rifles were in readiness for enemies.

Gradually the sound of voices and of marching men became distinctly audible to the untrained ears of the two whites, and a little later they saw the head of a column filing through the forest toward them.

"Why there's the 'Gunner!' " exclaimed Lafayette Smith. "And Jezebel, too. How odd that they should be together."

"With Tarzan of the Apes!" cried Lady Barbara. "He has saved them both."

A slow smile touched the lips of the ape-man as he witnessed the reunion of Lady Barbara and Jezebel and that between Smith and the "Gunner"; and it broadened a little, when, after the first burst of greetings and explanations, Lady Barbara said, "It is unfortunate that our host, Lord Passmore, isn't here."

"He is," said the ape-man.

"Where?" demanded Lafayette Smith, looking about the camp.

"I am 'Lord Passmore,' " said Tarzan.

"You?" exclaimed Lady Barbara.

"Yes. I assumed this rôle when I came north to investigate the rumors I had heard concerning Capietro and his band, believing that they not only would suspect no danger, but hoping, also, that they would seek to attack and plunder my safari as they have those of others."

"Geeze," said the "Gunner." "What a jolt they would of got!"

"That is why we never saw 'Lord Passmore,' " said Lady Barbara, laughing. "I thought him a most elusive host."

"The first night I left you here," explained Tarzan, "I walked into the jungle until I was out of sight, and then I came back from another direction and entered my tent from the rear. I slept there all night. The next morning, early, I left in search of your friends—and was captured myself. But everything has worked out well, and if you have no other immediate plans I hope that you will accompany me back to my home and remain a while as my guests while you recover from the rather rough experiences Africa has afforded you. Or, perhaps," he added, "Professor Smith and his friend wish to continue their geological investigations."

"I, ah, well, you see," stammered Lafayette Smith; "I have about decided to abandon my work in Africa and devote my life to the geology of England. We, or, er—you see, Lady Barbara—"

"I am going to take him back to England and teach him to shoot before I let him return to Africa. Possibly we shall come back later, though."

"And you, Patrick," asked Tarzan, "are you remaining to hunt, perhaps?"

"Nix, mister," said Danny, emphatically. "We're goin' to California and buy a garage and filling station."

"We?" queried Lady Barbara.

"Sure," said the "Gunner"; "me and Jez."

"Really?" exclaimed Lady Barbara. "Is he in earnest, Jezebel?"

"Oke, kid—isn't it ripping?" replied the golden one.